50 GREATEST DETECTIVE STORIES

Terry O'Brien is a bestselling author of several books, an academician, a freelance media consultant and public broadcaster, a quiz enthusiast and a passionate motivational trainer. He is a man of many parts, a language expert, a versatile writer on a plethora of topics and a trainer's trainer. He has earned a distinction in history and is an expert on current affairs for news agencies.

50 GREATEST DETECTIVE STORIES

Selection and Introduction by

TERRY O'BRIEN

Published by
Rupa Publications India Pvt. Ltd 2022
161-B/4, Gulmohar House,
Yusuf Sarai Community Centre,
New Delhi 110049

Sales centres:
Bengaluru Chennai
Hyderabad Kolkata Mumbai

Edition copyright © Rupa Publications
Selection and Introduction copyright © Terry O'Brien 2022

All rights reserved.
No part of this publication may be reproduced, transmitted,
or stored in a retrieval system, in any form or by any means,
electronic, mechanical, photocopying, recording or otherwise,
without the prior permission of the publisher.

P-ISBN: 978-93-90918-63-8
E-ISBN: 978-93-90918-71-3

Tenth impression 2025

15 14 13 12 11 10

Printed in India

This book is sold subject to the condition that it shall not,
by way of trade or otherwise, be lent, resold, hired out, or otherwise
circulated, without the publisher's prior consent, in any form of
binding or cover other than that in which it is published.

CONTENTS

INTRODUCTION		IX
1.	THE INVISIBLE MAN *G.K. Chesterton*	1
2.	THE ADVENTURES OF SHAMROCK JOLNES *O. Henry*	18
3.	THE PURLOINED LETTER *Edgar Allan Poe*	24
4.	THE DETECTIVE DETECTOR *O. Henry*	43
5.	THE SOFA *Charles Dickens*	48
6.	AN UNCOMFORTABLE BED *Guy de Maupassant*	51
7.	THE CLARION CALL *O. Henry*	54
8.	THE CONFESSION *Guy de Maupassant*	62
9.	THE ADVENTURE OF THE SPECKLED BAND *Arthur Conan Doyle*	68
10.	A SCANDAL IN BOHEMIA *Arthur Conan Doyle*	94
11.	THE FIVE ORANGE PIPS *Arthur Conan Doyle*	118
12.	IN THE LIBRARY *W.W. Jacobs*	137
13.	AN IRREDUCIBLE DETECTIVE STORY *Stephen Leacock*	147

14.	THE MYSTERY OF THE RUE DE PEYCHAUD *O. Henry*	148
15.	A DEAD MAN'S REVENGE: A DETECTIVE STORY *H.P. Lovecraft*	155
16.	THE CASK OF AMONTILLADO *Edgar Allan Poe*	160
17.	MURDER IN THE MORNING *Dorothy Sayers*	167
18.	MURDER AT PENTECOST *Dorothy Sayers*	178
19.	THE FOUNTAIN PLAYS *Dorothy Sayers*	190
20.	THE MYSTERIOUS TRAVELLER *Maurice Leblanc*	204
21.	THE QUEEN'S NECKLACE *Maurice Leblanc*	219
22.	THE RETURN OF IMRAY *Rudyard Kipling*	235
23.	A MYSTERY *Anton Chekhov*	247
24.	THE ADVENTURE OF THE TWO COLLABORATORS *James M. Barrie*	252
25.	AN ARTFUL TOUCH *Charles Dickens*	256
26.	SOME SCOTLAND YARD STORIES *Sir Robert Anderson*	259
27.	THE THREE TOOLS OF DEATH *G.K. Chesterton*	267
28.	THE PAIR OF GLOVES *Charles Dickens*	281
29.	THE DEADLY TUBE *Arthur B. Reeve*	286

30.	THE SLEUTHS *O. Henry*	304
31.	THE ARREST OF ARSÈNE LUPIN *Maurice Leblanc*	311
32.	VOLPURNO—OR THE STUDENT *W.W. Collins*	324
33.	THE BLACK PEARL *Maurice Leblanc*	329
34.	HUNTED DOWN *Charles Dickens*	343
35.	THE TOXIN OF DEATH *Arthur B. Reeve*	366
36.	THE X-RAY 'MOVIES' *Arthur B. Reeve*	377
37.	THE MAN WITH THE TWISTED LIP *Arthur Conan Doyle*	389
38.	THE CABALLERO'S WAY *O. Henry*	413
39.	THE EMPTY HOUSE *Algernon Blackwood*	426
40.	THE LEOPARD MAN'S STORY *Jack London*	443
41.	THE SILENT BULLET *Arthur B. Reeve*	448
42.	INDIAN MAGIC *Edgar Wallace*	466
43.	VIOLET'S OWN *Anna Katherine Green*	479
44.	THE MAN WHO KNEW HOW *Dorothy Sayers*	494
45.	THE POISONED DOW '08 *Dorothy Sayers*	508

46.	THE STOLEN CIGAR-CASE *Bret Harte*	520
47.	THE TRAILOR MURDER MYSTERY *Abraham Lincoln*	530
48.	THE CHOPHAM AFFAIR *Edgar Wallace*	537
49.	THE SNIPER *Liam O'Flaherty*	550
50.	MARKHEIM *Robert Louis Stevenson*	555

INTRODUCTION

Detective fiction is a genre that triggers off one's intuitive nature and makes the reader's adrenalin rise and fall as the episode unfolds. Each story takes one into the labyrinth of the unfamiliar within the familiar.

There are two forms of detective fiction. First is the *whodunit* (or *whodunnit*, short for 'who done it?') and the other is *'howcatchem'*. In the *whodunit* form, the plot's aim is to conceal the identity of the criminal from the reader until the end of the book. It is only towards the end that the culprit's identity is revealed. In such stories, the plot is many layered and complex. The reader partakes in the kinetic as events unfold. The many layers of clues make one deduce the climax. The second category or the *'howcatchem'* is the inverted detective story. In this format, the crime is shown or described at the very beginning and so is the identity of the criminal. It is here that a sense of observation helps the detective unravel the mystery. The motive behind the crime slowly unfolds.

It was Edgar Allan Poe who first formulated the term 'detective'; the name of the detective Auguste Dupin in Poe etymologically comes from 'dupe' or 'deception'. Such is the response to detective fiction that Holmes' 221 b Baker's Street almost comes alive in the virtual world. Sherlock Holmes became famous for his skilful observation, deductive reasoning and forensic skills. Agatha Christie's detective characters made her the highest selling author of all times.

Now it is your turn to be the detective as you read on and decode the mystery. Do enter the labyrinth!

Happy Reading!

Terry O'Brien

1

THE INVISIBLE MAN

G.K. Chesterton

Father Brown is the prototype of the modern detective who discovers the 'unfamiliar in the familiar'. We find in him his subtle deductive powers.

In the cool blue twilight of two steep streets in Camden Town, the shop at the corner, a confectioner's, glowed like the butt of a cigar. One should rather say, perhaps, like the butt of a firework, for the light was of many colours and some complexity, broken up by many mirrors and dancing on many gilt and gaily-coloured cakes and sweetmeats. Against this one fiery glass were glued the noses of many gutter-snipes, for the chocolates were all wrapped in those red and gold and green metallic colours which are almost better than chocolate itself; and the huge white wedding-cake in the window was somehow at once remote and satisfying, just as if the whole North Pole were good to eat. Such rainbow provocations could naturally collect the youth of the neighbourhood up to the ages of ten or twelve. But this corner was also attractive to youth at a later stage; and a young man, not less than twenty-four, was staring into the same shop window. To him, also, the shop was of fiery charm, but this attraction was not wholly to be explained by chocolates; which, however, he was far from despising.

He was a tall, burly, red-haired young man, with a resolute face but a listless manner. He carried under his arm a flat, gray portfolio of black-and-white sketches, which he had sold with more or less success to publishers ever since his uncle (who was an admiral) had disinherited him for Socialism, because of a lecture which he had delivered against that economic theory. His name was John Turnbull Angus.

Entering at last, he walked through the confectioner's shop to the back room, which was a sort of pastry-cook restaurant, merely raising his hat to the young lady who was serving there. She was a dark, elegant, alert girl in black, with a high colour and very quick, dark eyes; and after the ordinary interval she followed him into the inner room to take his order.

His order was evidently a usual one. 'I want, please,' he said with precision, 'one halfpenny bun and a small cup of black coffee.' An instant before the girl could turn away he added, 'Also, I want you to marry me.'

The young lady of the shop stiffened suddenly and said, 'Those are jokes I don't allow.'

The red-haired young man lifted gray eyes of an unexpected gravity.

'Really and truly,' he said, 'it's as serious—as serious as the halfpenny bun. It is expensive, like the bun; one pays for it. It is indigestible, like the bun. It hurts.'

The dark young lady had never taken her dark eyes off him, but seemed to be studying him with almost tragic exactitude. At the end of her scrutiny she had something like the shadow of a smile, and she sat down in a chair.

'Don't you think,' observed Angus, absently, 'that it's rather cruel to eat these halfpenny buns? They might grow up into penny buns. I shall give up these brutal sports when we are married.'

The dark young lady rose from her chair and walked to the window, evidently in a state of strong but not unsympathetic cogitation. When at last she swung round again with an air of resolution she was bewildered to observe that the young man was carefully laying out on the table various objects from the shop-window. They included a pyramid of highly coloured sweets, several plates of sandwiches, and the two decanters containing that mysterious port and sherry which are peculiar to pastry-cooks. In the middle of this neat arrangement he had carefully let down the enormous load of white sugared cake which had been the huge ornament of the window.

'What on earth are you doing?' she asked.

'Duty, my dear Laura,' he began.

'Oh, for the Lord's sake, stop a minute,' she cried, 'and don't talk to me in that way. I mean, what is all that?'

'A ceremonial meal, Miss Hope.'

'And what is that?' she asked impatiently, pointing to the mountain of sugar.

'The wedding cake, Mrs Angus,' he said.

The girl marched to that article, removed it with some clatter, and put it back in the shop window; she then returned, and, putting her elegant elbows on the table, regarded the young man not unfavourably but with considerable exasperation.

'You don't give me any time to think,' she said.

'I'm not such a fool,' he answered; 'that's my Christian humility.'

She was still looking at him; but she had grown considerably graver behind the smile.

'Mr Angus,' she said steadily, 'before there is a minute more of this nonsense I must tell you something about myself as shortly as I can.'

'Delighted,' replied Angus gravely. 'You might tell me something about myself, too, while you are about it.'

'Oh, do hold your tongue and listen,' she said. 'It's nothing that I'm ashamed of, and it isn't even anything that I'm specially sorry about. But what would you say if there were something that is no business of mine and yet is my nightmare?'

'In that case,' said the man seriously, 'I should suggest that you bring back the cake.'

'Well, you must listen to the story first,' said Laura, persistently. 'To begin with, I must tell you that my father owned the inn called the "Red Fish" at Ludbury, and I used to serve people in the bar.'

'I have often wondered,' he said, 'why there was a kind of a Christian air about this one confectioner's shop.'

'Ludbury is a sleepy, grassy little hole in the Eastern Counties, and the only kind of people who ever came to the "Red Fish" were occasional commercial travellers, and for the rest, the most awful people you can see, only you've never seen them. I mean little, loungy men, who had just enough to live on and had nothing to do but lean about in bar-rooms and bet on horses, in bad clothes that were just too good for them. Even these wretched young rotters were not very common at our house; but there were two of them that were a lot too common—common in every sort of way. They both lived on money of their own, and were wearisomely idle and over-dressed. But yet I was a bit sorry for them, because I half believe they slunk into our little empty bar because each of them had a slight deformity; the sort of thing that some yokels laugh at. It wasn't exactly a deformity either; it was more an oddity. One of them was a surprisingly small man, something like a dwarf, or at least like a jockey. He was not at all jockeyish to look at, though; he had a round black head and a well-trimmed black beard, bright eyes like a bird's; he jingled money in his pockets; he jangled a great gold watch chain; and he never turned up except dressed just too much like a gentleman to be one. He was no fool though, though a futile idler; he was curiously clever at all kinds of things that couldn't be the slightest use; a sort of impromptu conjuring; making fifteen matches set fire to each other like a regular firework; or cutting a banana or some such thing into a dancing doll. His name was Isidore Smythe; and I can see him still, with his little dark face, just coming up to the counter, making a jumping kangaroo out of five cigars.

'The other fellow was more silent and more ordinary; but somehow he alarmed me much more than poor little Smythe. He was very tall and slight, and light-haired; his nose had a high bridge, and he might almost have been handsome in a spectral sort of way; but he had one of the most appalling squints I have ever seen or heard of. When he looked straight at you, you didn't know where you were yourself, let alone what he was looking at. I fancy this sort of disfigurement embittered the poor chap a little; for while Smythe was ready to show off his monkey tricks anywhere, James Welkin (that was the squinting man's name) never did anything except soak in our bar parlour, and go for great walks by himself in the flat, gray country all round. All the same, I think Smythe, too, was a little sensitive about being so small, though he carried it off more smartly. And so it was that I was really puzzled, as well as startled, and very sorry, when they both offered to marry me in the same week.

'Well, I did what I've since thought was perhaps a silly thing. But, after all, these freaks were my friends in a way; and I had a horror of their thinking I refused them for the real reason, which was that they were so impossibly ugly. So I made up some gas of another sort, about never meaning to marry anyone who hadn't carved his way in the world. I said it was a point of principle with me not to live on money that was just inherited like theirs. Two days after I had talked in this well-meaning sort of way, the whole trouble began. The first thing I heard was that both of them had gone off to seek their fortunes, as if they were in some silly fairy tale.

'Well, I've never seen either of them from that day to this. But I've had two letters from the little man called Smythe, and really they were rather exciting.'

'Ever heard of the other man?' asked Angus.

'No, he never wrote,' said the girl, after an instant's hesitation. 'Smythe's first letter was simply to say that he had started out walking with Welkin to London; but Welkin was such a good walker that the little man dropped out of it, and took a rest by the roadside. He happened to be picked up by some travelling show, and, partly because he was nearly a dwarf, and partly because he was really a clever little wretch, he got on quite well in the show business, and was soon sent up to the Aquarium, to do some tricks that I forget. That was his first letter. His second was much more of a startler, and I only got it last week.'

The man called Angus emptied his coffee-cup and regarded her with mild and patient eyes. Her own mouth took a slight twist of laughter as she resumed, 'I suppose you've seen on the hoardings all about this 'Smythe's Silent Service'? Or you must be the only person that hasn't. Oh, I don't know much about it, it's some clockwork invention for doing all the housework by machinery. You know the sort of thing: 'Press a Button—A Butler who Never Drinks.' 'Turn a Handle—Ten Housemaids who Never Flirt.' You must have seen the advertisements. Well, whatever these machines are, they are making pots of money; and they are making it all for that little imp whom I knew down in Ludbury. I can't help feeling pleased the poor little chap has fallen on his feet; but the plain fact is, I'm in terror of his turning up any minute and telling me he's carved his way in the world—as he certainly has.'

'And the other man?' repeated Angus with a sort of obstinate quietude.

Laura Hope got to her feet suddenly. 'My friend,' she said, 'I think you are a witch. Yes, you are quite right. I have not seen a line of the other man's writing; and I have no more notion than the dead of what or where he is. But it is of him that I am frightened. It is he who is all about my path. It is he who has half driven me mad. Indeed, I think he has driven me mad; for I have felt him where he could not have been, and I have heard his voice when he could not have spoken.'

'Well, my dear,' said the young man, cheerfully, 'if he were Satan himself, he is done for now you have told somebody. One goes mad all alone, old girl. But when was it you fancied you felt and heard our squinting friend?'

'I heard James Welkin laugh as plainly as I hear you speak,' said the girl, steadily. 'There was nobody there, for I stood just outside the shop at the corner, and could see down both streets at once. I had forgotten how he laughed, though his laugh was as odd as his squint. I had not thought of him for nearly a year. But it's a solemn truth that a few seconds later the first letter came from his rival.'

'Did you ever make the spectre speak or squeak, or anything?' asked Angus, with some interest.

Laura suddenly shuddered, and then said, with an unshaken voice, 'Yes. Just when I had finished reading the second letter from Isidore Smythe announcing his success. Just then, I heard Welkin say, 'He shan't have you, though.' It was quite plain, as if he were in the room. It is awful, I think I must be mad.'

'If you really were mad,' said the young man, 'you would think you must be sane. But certainly there seems to me to be something a little rum about this unseen gentleman. Two heads are better than one—I spare you allusions to any other organs and really, if you would allow me, as a sturdy, practical man, to bring back the wedding-cake out of the window—'

Even as he spoke, there was a sort of steely shriek in the street outside, and a small motor, driven at devilish speed, shot up to the door of the shop and stuck there. In the same flash of time a small man in a shiny top hat stood stamping in the outer room.

Angus, who had hitherto maintained hilarious ease from motives of mental hygiene, revealed the strain of his soul by striding abruptly out of the inner room and confronting the new-comer. A glance at him was quite sufficient to confirm the savage guesswork of a man in love. This very dapper but dwarfish figure, with the spike of black beard carried insolently forward, the clever unrestful eyes, the neat but very nervous fingers, could be none other than the man just described to him: Isidore Smythe, who made dolls out of banana skins and match-boxes. Isidore Smythe, who made millions out of undrinking butlers and unflirting housemaids of metal. For a moment the two men, instinctively understanding each other's air of possession, looked at each other with that curious cold generosity which is the soul of rivalry.

Mr Smythe, however, made no allusion to the ultimate ground of their antagonism, but said simply and explosively, 'Has Miss Hope seen that thing on the window?'

'On the window?' repeated the staring Angus.

'There's no time to explain other things,' said the small millionaire shortly. 'There's some tomfoolery going on here that has to be investigated.'

He pointed his polished walking-stick at the window, recently depleted by the bridal preparations of Mr Angus; and that gentleman was astonished to see along the front of the glass a long strip of paper pasted, which had certainly not been on the window when he looked through it sometime before. Following the energetic Smythe outside into the street, he found that some yard and a half of stamp paper had been carefully gummed along the glass outside, and on this was written in straggly characters, 'If you marry Smythe, he will die.'

'Laura,' said Angus, putting his big red head into the shop, 'you're not mad.'

'It's the writing of that fellow Welkin,' said Smythe gruffly. 'I haven't seen him for years, but he's always bothering me. Five times in the last fortnight he's had threatening letters left at my flat, and I can't even find out who leaves them, let alone if it is Welkin himself. The porter of the flats swears that no suspicious characters have been seen, and here he has pasted up a sort of dado on a public shop window, while the people in the shop—'

'Quite so,' said Angus modestly, 'while the people in the shop were having tea. Well, sir, I can assure you I appreciate your common sense in dealing so directly with the matter. We can talk about other things afterwards. The fellow cannot be very far off yet, for I swear there was no paper there when I went last to the window, ten or fifteen minutes ago. On the other hand, he's too far off to be chased, as we don't even know the direction. If you'll take my advice, Mr Smythe, you'll put this at once in the hands of some energetic inquiry man, private rather than public. I know an extremely clever fellow, who has set up in business five minutes from here in your car. His name's Flambeau, and though his youth was a bit stormy, he's a strictly honest man now, and his brains are worth money. He lives in Lucknow Mansions, Hampstead.'

'That is odd,' said the little man, arching his black eyebrows. 'I live, myself, in Himylaya Mansions, round the corner. Perhaps you might care to come with me; I can go to my rooms and sort out these queer Welkin documents, while you run round and get your friend the detective.'

'You are very good,' said Angus politely. 'Well, the sooner we act the better.'

Both men, with a queer kind of impromptu fairness, took the same sort of formal farewell of the lady, and both jumped into the brisk little car. As Smythe took the handles and they turned the great corner of the street, Angus was amused to see a gigantesque poster of "Smythe's Silent Service" with a picture of a huge headless iron doll, carrying a saucepan with the legend, "A Cook Who is Never Cross."'

'I use them in my own flat,' said the little black-bearded man, laughing, 'partly for advertisements, and partly for real convenience. Honestly, and all above board, those big clockwork dolls of mine do bring your coals or claret or a timetable quicker than any live servants

I've ever known, if you know which knob to press. But I'll never deny, between ourselves, that such servants have their disadvantages, too.'

'Indeed?' said Angus, 'is there something they can't do?'

'Yes,' replied Smythe coolly; 'they can't tell me who left those threatening letters at my flat.'

The man's motor was small and swift like himself; in fact, like his domestic service, it was of his own invention. If he was an advertising quack, he was one who believed in his own wares. The sense of something tiny and flying was accentuated as they swept up long white curves of road in the dead but open daylight of evening. Soon the white curves came sharper and dizzier; they were upon ascending spirals, as they say in the modern religions. For, indeed, they were cresting a corner of London which is almost as precipitous as Edinburgh, if not quite so picturesque. Terrace rose above terrace, and the special tower of flats they sought, rose above them all to almost Egyptian height, gilt by the level sunset. The change, as they turned the corner and entered the crescent known as Himylaya Mansions, was as abrupt as the opening of a window; for they found that pile of flats sitting above London as above a green sea of slate. Opposite to the mansions, on the other side of the gravel crescent, was a bushy enclosure more like a steep hedge or dyke than a garden, and some way below that ran a strip of artificial water, a sort of canal, like the moat of that embowered fortress. As the car swept round the crescent it passed, at one corner, the stray stall of a man selling chestnuts; and right away at the other end of the curve, Angus could see a dim blue policeman walking slowly. These were the only human shapes in that high suburban solitude; but he had an irrational sense that they expressed the speechless poetry of London. He felt as if they were figures in a story.

The little car shot up to the right house like a bullet, and shot out its owner like a bomb shell. He was immediately inquiring of a tall commissionaire in shining braid, and a short porter in shirt sleeves, whether anybody or anything had been seeking his apartments. He was assured that nobody and nothing had passed these officials since his last inquiries; whereupon he and the slightly bewildered Angus were shot up in the lift like a rocket, till they reached the top floor.

'Just come in for a minute,' said the breathless Smythe. 'I want to show you those Welkin letters. Then you might run round the corner and fetch your friend.' He pressed a button concealed in the wall, and the door opened of itself.

It opened on a long, commodious ante-room, of which the only arresting features, ordinarily speaking, were the rows of tall half-human mechanical figures that stood up on both sides like tailors' dummies. Like tailors' dummies they were headless; and like tailors' dummies they had a handsome unnecessary humpiness in the shoulders, and a pigeon-breasted protuberance of chest; but barring this, they were not much more like a human figure than any automatic machine at a station that is about the human height. They had two great hooks like arms, for carrying trays; and they were painted pea-green, or vermilion, or black for convenience of distinction; in every other way they were only automatic machines and nobody would have looked twice at them. On this occasion, at least, nobody did. For between the two rows of these domestic dummies lay something more interesting than most of the mechanics of the world. It was a white, tattered scrap of paper scrawled with red ink; and the agile inventor had snatched it up almost as soon as the door flew open. He handed it to Angus without a word. The red ink on it actually was not dry, and the message ran, 'If you have been to see her today, I shall kill you.'

There was a short silence, and then Isidore Smythe said quietly, 'Would you like a little whiskey? I rather feel as if I should.'

'Thank you; I should like a little Flambeau,' said Angus, gloomily. 'This business seems to me to be getting rather grave. I'm going round at once to fetch him.'

'Right you are,' said the other, with admirable cheerfulness. 'Bring him round here as quick as you can.'

But as Angus closed the front door behind him he saw Smythe push back a button, and one of the clockwork images glided from its place and slid along a groove in the floor carrying a tray with syphon and decanter. There did seem something a trifle weird about leaving the little man alone among those dead servants, who were coming to life as the door closed.

Six steps down from Smythe's landing the man in shirt sleeves was doing something with a pail. Angus stopped to extract a promise, fortified with a prospective bribe, that he would remain in that place until the return with the detective, and would keep count of any kind of stranger coming up those stairs. Dashing down to the front hall he then laid similar charges of vigilance on the commissionaire at the front door, from whom he learned the simplifying circumstances that there was no back door. Not content with this, he captured the floating policeman and induced him to stand opposite the entrance and watch it; and finally paused an instant for a pennyworth of chestnuts, and an inquiry as to the probable length of the merchant's stay in the neighbourhood.

The chestnut seller, turning up the collar of his coat, told him he should probably be moving shortly, as he thought it was going to snow. Indeed, the evening was growing gray and bitter, but Angus, with all his eloquence, proceeded to nail the chestnut man to his post.

'Keep yourself warm on your own chestnuts,' he said earnestly. 'Eat up your whole stock; I'll make it worth your while. I'll give you a sovereign if you'll wait here till I come back, and then tell me whether any man, woman, or child has gone into that house where the commissionaire is standing.'

He then walked away smartly, with a last look at the besieged tower.

'I've made a ring round that room, anyhow,' he said. 'They can't all four of them be Mr Welkin's accomplices.'

Lucknow Mansions were, so to speak, on a lower platform of that hill of houses, of which Himylaya Mansions might be called the peak. Mr Flambeau's semi-official flat was on the ground floor, and presented in every way a marked contrast to the American machinery and cold hotel-like luxury of the flat of the Silent Service. Flambeau, who was a friend of Angus, received him in a rococo artistic den behind his office, of which the ornaments were sabres, harquebuses, Eastern curiosities, flasks of Italian wine, savage cooking-pots, a plumy Persian cat and a small dusty-looking Roman Catholic priest, who looked particularly out of place.

'This is my friend Father Brown,' said Flambeau. 'I've often wanted you to meet him. Splendid weather, this; a little cold for Southerners like me.'

'Yes, I think it will keep clear,' said Angus, sitting down on a violet-striped Eastern ottoman.

'No,' said the priest quietly, 'it has begun to snow.'

And, indeed, as he spoke, the first few flakes, foreseen by the man of chestnuts, began to drift across the darkening windowpane.

'Well,' said Angus heavily. 'I'm afraid I've come on business, and rather jumpy business at that. The fact is, Flambeau, within a stone's throw of your house is a fellow who badly wants your help; he's perpetually being haunted and threatened by an invisible enemy—a scoundrel whom nobody has even seen.' As Angus proceeded to tell the whole tale of Smythe and Welkin, beginning with Laura's story, and going on with his own, the supernatural laugh at the corner of two empty streets, the strange distinct words spoken in an empty room, Flambeau grew more and more vividly concerned, and the little priest seemed to be left out of it, like a piece of furniture. When it came to the scribbled stamp-paper pasted on the window, Flambeau rose, seeming to fill the room with his huge shoulders.

'If you don't mind,' he said, 'I think you had better tell me the rest on the nearest road to this man's house. It strikes me, somehow, that there is no time to be lost.'

'Delighted,' said Angus, rising also, 'though he's safe enough for the present, for I've set four men to watch the only hole to his burrow.'

They turned out into the street, the small priest trundling after them with the docility of a small dog. He merely said, in a cheerful way, like one making conversation, 'How quick the snow gets thick on the ground.'

As they threaded the steep side streets already powdered with silver, Angus finished his story; and by the time they reached the crescent with the towering flats, he had leisure to turn his attention to the four sentinels. The chestnut seller, both before and after receiving a sovereign, swore stubbornly that he had watched the door and seen no visitor enter. The policeman was even more emphatic. He said he had had experience of crooks of all kinds, in top hats and in rags; he wasn't so green as to expect suspicious characters to look suspicious; he looked out for anybody, and, so help him, there had been nobody. And when all three men gathered round the gilded commissionaire, who still stood smiling astride of the porch, the verdict was more final still.

'I've got a right to ask any man, duke or dustman, what he wants in these flats,' said the genial and gold-laced giant, 'and I'll swear there's been nobody to ask since this gentleman went away.'

The unimportant Father Brown, who stood back, looking modestly at the pavement, here ventured to say meekly, 'Has nobody been up and down stairs, then, since the snow began to fall? It began while we were all round at Flambeau's.'

'Nobody's been in here, sir, you can take it from me,' said the official, with beaming authority.

'Then I wonder what that is?' said the priest, and stared at the ground blankly like a fish.

The others all looked down also; and Flambeau used a fierce exclamation and a French gesture. For it was unquestionably true that down the middle of the entrance guarded by the man in gold lace, actually between the arrogant, stretched legs of that colossus, ran a stringy pattern of gray footprints stamped upon the white snow.

'God!' cried Angus involuntarily, 'the Invisible Man!'

Without another word he turned and dashed up the stairs, with Flambeau following; but Father Brown still stood looking about him in the snow-clad street as if he had lost interest in his query.

Flambeau was plainly in a mood to break down the door with his big shoulders; but the Scotchman, with more reason, if less intuition, fumbled about on the frame of the door till he found the invisible button; and the door swung slowly open.

It showed substantially the same serried interior; the hall had grown darker, though it was still struck here and there with the last crimson shafts of sunset, and one or two of the headless machines had been moved from their places for this or that purpose, and stood here and there about the twilit place. The green and red of their coats were all darkened in the dusk; and their likeness to human shapes slightly increased by their very shapelessness. But in the middle of them all, exactly where the paper with the red ink had lain, there lay something that looked like red ink spilt out of its bottle. But it was not red ink.

With a French combination of reason and violence Flambeau simply said 'Murder!' and, plunging into the flat, had explored, every corner and cupboard of it in five minutes. But if he expected to find a corpse he found none. Isidore Smythe was not in the place, either dead or alive. After the most tearing search the two men met each other in the outer hall, with streaming faces and staring eyes. 'My friend,' said Flambeau, talking French in his excitement, 'not only is your murderer invisible, but he makes invisible also the murdered man.'

Angus looked round at the dim room full of dummies, and in some Celtic corner of his Scotch soul a shudder started. One of the life-size dolls stood immediately overshadowing the blood stain, summoned, perhaps, by the slain man an instant before he fell. One of the high-shouldered hooks that served the thing for arms, was a little lifted, and Angus had suddenly the horrid fancy that poor Smythe's own iron child had struck him down. Matter had rebelled, and these machines had killed their master. But even so, what had they done with him?

'Eaten him?' said the nightmare at his ear; and he sickened for an instant at the idea of rent, human remains absorbed and crushed into all that acephalous clockwork.

He recovered his mental health by an emphatic effort, and said to Flambeau, 'Well, there it is. The poor fellow has evaporated like a cloud and left a red streak on the floor. The tale does not belong to this world.'

'There is only one thing to be done,' said Flambeau, 'whether it belongs to this world or the other. I must go down and talk to my friend.'

They descended, passing the man with the pail, who again asseverated that he had let no intruder pass, down to the commissionaire and the hovering chestnut man, who rigidly reasserted their own watchfulness. But when Angus looked round for his fourth confirmation he could not see it, and called out with some nervousness, 'Where is the policeman?'

'I beg your pardon,' said Father Brown; 'that is my fault. I just sent him down the road to investigate something—that I just thought worth investigating.'

'Well, we want him back pretty soon,' said Angus abruptly, 'for the wretched man upstairs has not only been murdered, but wiped out.'

'How?' asked the priest.

'Father,' said Flambeau, after a pause, 'upon my soul I believe it is more in your department than mine. No friend or foe has entered the house, but Smythe is gone, as if stolen by the fairies. If that is not supernatural, I—'

As he spoke they were all checked by an unusual sight; the big blue policeman came round the corner of the crescent, running. He came straight up to Brown.

'You're right, sir,' he panted, 'they've just found poor Mr Smythe's body in the canal down below.'

Angus put his hand wildly to his head. 'Did he run down and drown himself?' he asked.

'He never came down, I'll swear,' said the constable, 'and he wasn't drowned either, for he died of a great stab over the heart.'

'And yet you saw no one enter?' said Flambeau in a grave voice.

'Let us walk down the road a little,' said the priest.

As they reached the other end of the crescent he observed abruptly, 'Stupid of me! I forgot to ask the policeman something. I wonder if they found a light brown sack.'

'Why a light brown sack?' asked Angus, astonished.

'Because if it was any other coloured sack, the case must begin over again,' said Father Brown; 'but if it was a light brown sack, why, the case is finished.'

'I am pleased to hear it,' said Angus with hearty irony. 'It hasn't begun, so far as I am concerned.'

'You must tell us all about it,' said Flambeau with a strange heavy simplicity, like a child.

Unconsciously they were walking with quickening steps down the long sweep of road on the other side of the high crescent, Father Brown leading briskly, though in silence. At last he said with an almost touching vagueness, 'Well, I'm afraid you'll think it so prosy.

We always begin at the abstract end of things, and you can't begin this story anywhere else.

'Have you ever noticed this—that people never answer what you say? They answer what you mean—or what they think you mean. Suppose one lady says to another in a country house, 'Is anybody staying with you?' the lady doesn't answer 'Yes; the butler, the three footmen, the parlourmaid, and so on,' though the parlourmaid may be in the room, or the butler behind her chair. She says 'There is nobody staying with us,' meaning nobody of the sort you mean. But suppose a doctor inquiring into an epidemic asks, 'Who is staying in the house?' then the lady will remember the butler, the parlourmaid, and the rest. All language is used like that; you never get a question answered literally, even when you get it answered truly. When those four quite honest men said that no man had gone into the Mansions, they did not really mean that no man had gone into them. They meant no man whom they could suspect of being your man. A man did go into the house, and did come out of it, but they never noticed him.'

'An invisible man?' inquired Angus, raising his red eyebrows. 'A mentally invisible man,' said Father Brown.

A minute or two after he resumed in the same unassuming voice, like a man thinking his way. 'Of course you can't think of such a man, until you do think of him. That's where his cleverness comes in. But I came to think of him through two or three little things in the tale Mr Angus told us. First, there was the fact that this Welkin went for long walks. And then there was the vast lot of stamp paper on the window. And then, most of all, there were the two things the young lady said—things that couldn't be true. Don't get annoyed,' he added hastily, noting a sudden movement of the Scotchman's head; 'she thought they were true. A person can't be quite alone in a street a second before she receives a letter. She can't be quite alone in a street when she starts reading a letter just received. There must be somebody pretty near her; he must be mentally invisible.'

'Why must there be somebody near her?' asked Angus.

'Because,' said Father Brown, 'barring carrier-pigeons, somebody must have brought her the letter.'

'Do you really mean to say,' asked Flambeau, with energy, 'that Welkin carried his rival's letters to his lady?'

'Yes,' said the priest. 'Welkin carried his rival's letters to his lady. You see, he had to.'

'Oh, I can't stand much more of this,' exploded Flambeau. 'Who is this fellow? What does he look like? What is the usual get-up of a mentally invisible man?'

'He is dressed rather handsomely in red, blue and gold,' replied the priest promptly with precision, 'and in this striking, and even showy, costume he entered Himylaya Mansions under eight human eyes; he killed Smythe in cold blood, and came down into the street again carrying the dead body in his arms—'

'Reverend sir,' cried Angus, standing still, 'are you raving mad, or am I?'

'You are not mad,' said Brown, 'only a little unobservant. You have not noticed such a man as this, for example.'

He took three quick strides forward, and put his hand on the shoulder of an ordinary passing postman who had bustled by them unnoticed under the shade of the trees.

'Nobody ever notices postmen somehow,' he said thoughtfully; 'yet they have passions like other men, and even carry large bags where a small corpse can be stowed quite easily.'

The postman, instead of turning naturally, had ducked and tumbled against the garden fence. He was a lean fair-bearded man of very ordinary appearance, but as he turned an alarmed face over his shoulder, all three men were fixed with an almost fiendish squint.

Flambeau went back to his sabres, purple rugs and Persian cat, having many things to attend to. John Turnbull Angus went back to the lady at the shop, with whom that imprudent young man contrives to be extremely comfortable. But Father Brown walked those snow-covered hills under the stars for many hours with a murderer, and what they said to each other will never be known.

2

THE ADVENTURES OF SHAMROCK JOLNES

O. Henry

Here comes a humorous parody of Arthur Conan Doyle's fictional detective Sherlock Holmes! Here we find the detective as compulsively tedious and illogical, wrongheadedly instructing sidekick.

I am so fortunate as to count Shamrock Jolnes, the great New York detective, among my muster of friends. Jolnes is what is called the 'inside man' of the city detective force. He is an expert in the use of the typewriter, and it is his duty, whenever there is a 'murder mystery' to be solved, to sit at a desk telephone at headquarters and take down the messages of 'cranks' who 'phone in their confessions' to having committed the crime.

But on certain 'off' days when confessions are coming in slowly and three or four newspapers have run to earth as many different guilty persons, Jolnes will knock about the town with me, exhibiting, to my great delight and instruction, his marvellous powers of observation and deduction.

The other day I dropped in at Headquarters and found the great detective gazing thoughtfully at a string that was tied tightly around his little finger.

'Good morning, Whatsup,' he said, without turning his head. 'I'm glad to notice that you've had your house fitted up with electric lights at last.'

'Will you please tell me,' I said, in surprise, 'how you knew that? I am sure that I never mentioned the fact to any one, and the wiring was a rush order not completed until this morning.'

'Nothing easier,' said Jolnes, genially. 'As you came in I caught the odour of the cigar you are smoking. I know an expensive cigar; and I know that not more than three men in New York can afford to smoke cigars and pay gas bills too at the present time. That was an easy one. But I am working just now on a little problem of my own.'

'Why have you that string on your finger?' I asked.

'That's the problem,' said Jolnes. 'My wife tied that on this morning to remind me of something I was to send up to the house. Sit down, Whatsup, and excuse me for a few moments.'

The distinguished detective went to a wall telephone, and stood with the receiver to his ear for probably ten minutes.

'Were you listening to a confession?' I asked, when he had returned to his chair.

'Perhaps,' said Jolnes, with a smile, 'it might be called something of the sort. To be frank with you, Whatsup, I've cut out the dope. I've been increasing the quantity for so long that morphine doesn't have much effect on me any more. I've got to have something more powerful. That telephone I just went to is connected with a room in the Waldorf where there's an author's reading in progress. Now, to get at the solution of this string.'

After five minutes of silent pondering, Jolnes looked at me, with a smile, and nodded his head.

'Wonderful man!' I exclaimed; 'already?'

'It is quite simple,' he said, holding up his finger. 'You see that knot? That is to prevent my forgetting. It is, therefore, a forget-me-knot. A forget-me-not is a flower. It was a sack of flour that I was to send home!'

'Beautiful!' I could not help crying out in admiration.

'Suppose we go out for a ramble,' suggested Jolnes.

'There is only one case of importance on hand just now. Old man McCarty, one hundred and four years old, died from eating too many bananas. The evidence points so strongly to the Mafia that the police have surrounded the Second Avenue Katzenjammer Gambrinus Club No. 2, and the capture of the assassin is only the matter of a few hours. The detective force has not yet been called on for assistance.'

Jolnes and I went out and up the street toward the corner, where we were to catch a surface car.

Half-way up the block we met Rheingelder, an acquaintance of ours, who held a City Hall position.

'Good morning, Rheingelder,' said Jolnes, halting.

'Nice breakfast that was you had this morning.' Always on the lookout for the detective's remarkable feats of deduction, I saw Jolnes's eye flash for an instant upon a long, yellow splash on the shirt bosom and a smaller one upon the chin of Rheingelder—both undoubtedly made by the yolk of an egg.

'Oh, dot is some of your detectiveness,' said Rheingelder, shaking all over with a smile. 'Vell, I pet you trinks und cigars all round dot you cannot tell vot I haf eaten for breakfast.'

'Done,' said Jolnes. 'Sausage, pumpernickel and coffee.'

Rheingelder admitted the correctness of the surmise and paid the bet. When we had proceeded on our way I said to Jolnes: 'I thought you looked at the egg spilled on his chin and shirt front.'

'I did,' said Jolnes. 'That is where I began my deduction. Rheingelder is a very economical, saving man. Yesterday eggs dropped in the market to twenty-eight cents per dozen. Today they are quoted at forty-two. Rheingelder ate eggs yesterday, and today he went back to his usual fare. A little thing like this isn't anything, Whatsup; it belongs to the primary arithmetic class.'

When we boarded the street car we found the seats all occupied—principally by ladies. Jolnes and I stood on the rear platform.

About the middle of the car there sat an elderly man with a short, gray beard, who looked to be the typical, well-dressed New Yorker. At successive corners other ladies climbed aboard, and soon three or four of them were standing over the man, clinging to straps and glaring menacingly at the man who occupied the coveted seat. But he resolutely retained his place.

'We New Yorkers,' I remarked to Jolnes, 'have about lost our manners, as far as the exercise of them in public goes.'

'Perhaps so,' said Jolnes, lightly; 'but the man you evidently refer to happens to be a very chivalrous and courteous gentleman from Old Virginia. He is spending a few days in New York with his wife and two daughters, and he leaves for the South tonight.'

'You know him, then?' I said, in amazement.

'I never saw him before we stepped on the car,' declared the detective, smilingly.

'By the gold tooth of the Witch of Endor!' I cried, 'if you can construe all that from his appearance you are dealing in nothing else than black art.'

'The habit of observation—nothing more,' said Jolnes. 'If the old gentleman gets off the car before we do, I think I can demonstrate to you the accuracy of my deduction.'

Three blocks farther along the gentleman rose to leave the car. Jolnes addressed him at the door: 'Pardon me, sir, but are you not Colonel Hunter, of Norfolk, Virginia?'

'No, suh,' was the extremely courteous answer. 'My name, suh, is Ellison—Major Winfield R. Ellison, from Fairfax County, in the same state. I know a good many people, suh, in Norfolk—the Goodriches, the Tollivers, and the Crabtrees, suh, but I never had the pleasure of meeting yo' friend, Colonel Hunter. I am happy to say, suh, that I am going back to Virginia tonight, after having spent a week in yo' city with my wife and three daughters. I shall be in Norfolk in about ten days, and if you will give me yo' name, suh, I will take pleasure in looking up Colonel Hunter and telling him that you inquired after him, suh.'

'Thank you,' said Jolnes; 'tell him that Reynolds sent his regards, if you will be so kind.'

I glanced at the great New York detective and saw that a look of intense chagrin had come upon his clear-cut features. Failure in the slightest point always galled Shamrock Jolnes.

'Did you say your three daughters?' he asked of the Virginia gentleman.

'Yes, suh, my three daughters, all as fine girls as there are in Fairfax County,' was the answer.

With that Major Ellison stopped the car and began to descend the step.

Shamrock Jolnes clutched his arm.

'One moment, sir,' he begged, in an urbane voice in which I alone detected the anxiety—'am I not right in believing that one of the young ladies is an adopted daughter?'

'You are, suh,' admitted the major, from the ground, 'but how the devil you knew it, suh, is mo' than I can tell.'

'And mo' than I can tell, too,' I said, as the car went on.

Jolnes was restored to his calm, observant serenity by having wrested victory from his apparent failure; so after we got off the car he invited me into a cafe, promising to reveal the process of his latest wonderful feat.

'In the first place,' he began after we were comfortably seated, 'I knew the gentleman was no New Yorker because he was flushed and uneasy and restless on account of the ladies that were standing, although he did not rise and give them his seat. I decided from his appearance that he was a Southerner rather than a Westerner.

'Next I began to figure out his reason for not relinquishing his seat to a lady when he evidently felt strongly, but not overpoweringly, impelled to do so. I very quickly decided upon that. I noticed that one of his eyes had received a severe jab in one corner, which was red and inflamed, and that all over his face were tiny round marks about the size of the end of an uncut lead pencil. Also upon both of his patent leather shoes were a number of deep imprints shaped like ovals cut off square at one end.

'Now, there is only one district in New York City where a man is bound to receive scars and wounds and indentations of that sort—and that is along the sidewalks of Twenty-third Street and a portion of Sixth Avenue south of there. I knew from the imprints of trampling French heels on his feet and the marks of countless jabs in the face from umbrellas and parasols carried by women in the shopping district that he had been in conflict with the Amazonian troops. And as he was a man of intelligent appearance, I knew he would not have braved such dangers unless he had been dragged thither by his own women folk. Therefore, when he got on the car, his anger at the treatment he had received was sufficient to make him keep his seat in spite of his traditions of Southern chivalry.'

'That is all very well,' I said, 'but why did you insist upon daughters—and especially two daughters? Why couldn't a wife alone have taken him shopping?'

'There had to be daughters,' said Jolnes, calmly. 'If he had only a wife, and she near his own age, he could have bluffed her into going alone. If he had a young wife she would prefer to go alone. So there you are.'

'I'll admit that,' I said; 'but, now, why two daughters? And how, in the name of all the prophets, did you guess that one was adopted when he told you he had three?'

'Don't say guess,' said Jolnes, with a touch of pride in his air; 'there is no such word in the lexicon of ratiocination. In Major Ellison's buttonhole there was a carnation and a rosebud backed by a geranium leaf. No woman ever combined a carnation and a rosebud into a boutonniere. Close your eyes, Whatsup, and give the logic of your imagination a chance. Cannot you see the lovely Adele fastening the carnation to the lapel so that papa may be gay upon the street? And then the romping Edith May dancing up with sisterly jealousy to add her rosebud to the adornment?'

'And then,' I cried, beginning to feel enthusiasm, 'when he declared that he had three daughters—'

'I could see,' said Jolnes, 'one in the background who added no flower; and I knew that she must be—'

'Adopted!' I broke in. 'I give you every credit; but how did you know he was leaving for the South tonight?'

'In his breast pocket,' said the great detective, 'something large and oval made a protuberance. Good liquor is scarce on trains, and it is a long journey from New York to Fairfax County.'

'Again, I must bow to you,' I said. 'And tell me this, so that my last shred of doubt will be cleared away; why did you decide that he was from Virginia?'

'It was very faint, I admit,' answered Shamrock Jolnes, 'but no trained observer could have failed to detect the odour of mint in the car.'

3

THE PURLOINED LETTER

Edgar Allan Poe

Nil sapientiae odiosius acumine nimio.

—Seneca

At Paris, just after dark, one gusty evening in the autumn of 18—, I was enjoying the twofold luxury of meditation and a meerschaum, in company with my friend C. Auguste Dupin, in his little back library, or book-closet, au troisieme, No. 33, Rue Dunot, Faubourg St. Germain. For one hour at least we had maintained a profound silence; while each, to any casual observer, might have seemed intently and exclusively occupied with the curling eddies of smoke that oppressed the atmosphere of the chamber. For myself, however, I was mentally discussing certain topics which had formed matter for conversation between us at an earlier period of the evening; I mean the affair of the Rue Morgue and the mystery attending the murder of Marie Roget. I looked upon it, therefore, as something of a coincidence, when the door of our apartment was thrown open and admitted our old acquaintance, Monsieur G—, the Prefect of the Parisian police.

We gave him a hearty welcome; for there was nearly half as much of the entertaining as of the contemptible about the man, and we had not seen him for several years. We had been sitting in the dark and Dupin now arose for the purpose of lighting a lamp, but sat down again, without doing so, upon G.'s saying that he had called to consult us, or rather to ask the opinion of my friend, about some official business which had occasioned a great deal of trouble.

'If it is any point requiring reflection,' observed Dupin, as he forbore to enkindle the wick, 'we shall examine it to better purpose in the dark.'

'That is another of your odd notions,' said the Prefect, who had a fashion of calling everything 'odd' that was beyond his comprehension and thus lived amid an absolute legion of 'oddities'.

'Very true,' said Dupin, as he supplied his visitor with a pipe, and rolled towards him a comfortable chair.

'And what is the difficulty now?' I asked. 'Nothing more in the assassination way, I hope?'

'Oh no; nothing of that nature. The fact is, the business is very simple indeed and I make no doubt that we can manage it sufficiently well ourselves; but then I thought Dupin would like to hear the details of it, because it is so excessively odd.'

'Simple and odd,' said Dupin.

'Why, yes; and not exactly that, either. The fact is, we have all been a good deal puzzled because the affair is so simple, and yet baffles us altogether.'

'Perhaps it is the very simplicity of the thing which puts you at fault,' said my friend.

'What nonsense you do talk!' replied the Prefect, laughing heartily.

'Perhaps the mystery is a little too plain,' said Dupin.

'Oh, good heavens! Who ever heard of such an idea?'

'A little too self-evident.'

'Ha! ha! ha! —ha! ha! ha! —ho! ho! ho!' roared our visitor, profoundly amused, 'Oh, Dupin, you will be the death of me yet!'

'And what, after all, is the matter on hand?' I asked.

'Why, I will tell you,' replied the Prefect, as he gave a long, steady, and contemplative puff, and settled himself in his chair. 'I will tell you in a few words; but, before I begin, let me caution you that this is an affair demanding the greatest secrecy, and that I should most probably lose the position I now hold, were it known that I confided it to any one.

'Proceed,' said I.

'Or not,' said Dupin.

'Well, then; I have received personal information, from a very high quarter, that a certain document of the last importance, has been purloined from the royal apartments. The individual who purloined it is known; this beyond a doubt; he was seen to take it. It is known, also, that it still remains in his possession.'

'How is this known?' asked Dupin.

'It is clearly inferred,' replied the Prefect, 'from the nature of the document, and from the nonappearance of certain results which would at once arise from its passing out of the robber's possession—that is to say, from his employing it as he must design in the end to employ it.'

'Be a little more explicit,' I said.

'Well, I may venture so far as to say that the paper gives its holder a certain power in a certain quarter where such power is immensely valuable.' The Prefect was fond of the cant of diplomacy.

'Still I do not quite understand,' said Dupin.

'No? Well, the disclosure of the document to a third person, who shall be nameless, would bring in question the honour of a personage of most exalted station; and this fact gives the holder of the document an ascendancy over the illustrious personage whose honour and peace are so jeopardized.'

'But this ascendancy,' I interposed, 'would depend upon the robber's knowledge of the loser's knowledge of the robber. Who would dare—'

'The thief,' said G., 'is the Minister D—, who dares all things, those unbecoming as well as those becoming a man. The method of the theft was not less ingenious than bold. The document in question—a letter, to be frank—had been received by the personage robbed while alone in the royal boudoir. During its perusal she was suddenly interrupted by the entrance of the other exalted personage from whom especially it was her wish to conceal it. After a hurried and vain endeavour to thrust it in a drawer, she was forced to place it, open as it was, upon a table. The address, however, was uppermost, and, the contents thus unexposed, the letter escaped notice. At this juncture enters the Minister D—. His lynx eye immediately perceives the paper, recognises the handwriting of the address, observes the confusion of the personage addressed, and fathoms her secret. After some business transactions, hurried through in his ordinary manner, he produces a letter somewhat similar to the one in question, opens it, pretends to read it, and then places it in close juxtaposition to the other. Again he converses, for some fifteen minutes, upon the public affairs. At length, in taking leave, he takes also from the table the letter to which he had no claim. Its rightful owner saw, but, of course, dared not call attention to the act, in the presence of the third personage who stood at her elbow. The minister decamped; leaving his own letter—one of no importance—upon the table.'

'Here, then,' said Dupin to me, 'you have precisely what you demand to make the ascendancy complete—the robber's knowledge of the loser's knowledge of the robber.'

'Yes,' replied the Prefect; 'and the power thus attained has, for some months past, been wielded, for political purposes, to a very dangerous extent. The personage robbed is more thoroughly convinced, every day, of the necessity of reclaiming her letter. But this, of course, cannot be done openly. In fine, driven to despair, she has committed the matter to me.'

'Than whom,' said Dupin, amid a perfect whirlwind of smoke, 'no more sagacious agent could, I suppose, be desired, or even imagined.'

'You flatter me,' replied the Prefect; 'but it is possible that some such opinion may have been entertained.'

'It is clear,' said I, 'as you observe, that the letter is still in possession of the minister; since it is this possession, and not any employment of the letter, which bestows the power. With the employment the power departs.'

'True,' said G. 'and upon this conviction I proceeded. My first care was to make thorough search of the minister's hotel; and here my chief embarrassment lay in the necessity of searching without his knowledge. Beyond all things, I have been warned of the danger which would result from giving him reason to suspect our design.'

'But,' said I, 'you are quite au fait in these investigations. The Parisian police have done this thing often before.'

'Oh yes; and for this reason I did not despair. The habits of the minister gave me, too, a great advantage. He is frequently absent from home all night. His servants are by no means numerous. They sleep at a distance from their master's apartment, and, being chiefly Neapolitans, are readily made drunk. I have keys, as you know, with which I can open any chamber or cabinet in Paris. For three months a night has not passed, during the greater part of which I have not been engaged, personally, in ransacking the D—Hotel. My honour is interested, and, to mention a great secret, the reward is enormous. So I did not abandon the search until I had become fully satisfied that the thief is a more astute man than myself. I fancy that I have investigated every nook and corner of the premises in which it is possible that the paper can be concealed.'

'But is it not possible,' I suggested, 'that although the letter may be in possession of the minister, as it unquestionably is, he may have concealed it elsewhere than upon his own premises?'

'This is barely possible,' said Dupin. 'The present peculiar condition of affairs at court, and especially of those intrigues in which D— is known to be involved, would render the instant availability of the document—its susceptibility of being produced at a moment's notice—a point of nearly equal importance with its possession.'

'Its susceptibility of being produced?' said I.

'That is to say, of being destroyed,' said Dupin.

'True,' I observed; 'the paper is clearly then upon the premises. As for its being upon the person of the minister, we may consider that as out of the question.'

'Entirely,' said the Prefect. 'He has been twice waylaid, as if by footpads, and his person rigorously searched under my own inspection.

'You might have spared yourself this trouble,' said Dupin. 'D—, I presume, is not altogether a fool, and, if not, must have anticipated these waylayings, as a matter of course.'

'Not altogether a fool,' said G., 'but then he's a poet, which I take to be only one remove from a fool.'

'True,' said Dupin, after a long and thoughtful whiff from his meerschaum, 'although I have been guilty of certain doggerel myself.'

'Suppose you detail,' said I, 'the particulars of your search.'

'Why the fact is, we took our time, and we searched everywhere. I have had long experience in these affairs. I took the entire building, room by room; devoting the nights of a whole week to each. We examined, first, the furniture of each apartment. We opened every possible drawer; and I presume you know that to a properly trained police agent, such a thing as a secret drawer is impossible. Any man is a dolt who permits a 'secret' drawer to escape him in a search of this kind. The thing is so plain. There is a certain amount of bulk—of space—to be accounted for in every cabinet. Then we have accurate rules. The fiftieth part of a line could not escape us. After the cabinets we took the chairs. The cushions we probed with the fine long needles you have seen me employ. From the tables we removed the tops.'

'Why so?'

'Sometimes the top of a table, or other similarly arranged piece of furniture, is removed by the person wishing to conceal an article; then the leg is excavated, the article deposited within the cavity and the top replaced. The bottoms and tops of bedposts are employed in the same way.'

'But could not the cavity be detected by sounding?' I asked.

'By no means, if, when the article is deposited, a sufficient wadding of cotton be placed around it. Besides, in our case, we were obliged to proceed without noise.'

'But you could not have removed—you could not have taken to pieces all articles of furniture in which it would have been possible to make a deposit in the manner you mention. A letter may be compressed into a thin spiral roll, not differing much in shape or bulk from a large knitting-needle, and in this form it might be inserted into the rung of a chair, for example. You did not take to pieces all the chairs?'

'Certainly not; but we did better—we examined the rungs of every chair in the hotel, and, indeed, the jointings of every description of furniture, by the aid of a most powerful microscope. Had there been any traces of recent disturbance we should not have failed to detect it instantly. A single grain of gimlet-dust, for example, would have been as obvious as an apple. Any disorder in the glueing—any unusual gaping in the joints—would have sufficed to insure detection.'

'I presume you looked to the mirrors, between the boards and the plates, and you probed the beds and the bed-clothes, as well as the curtains and carpets.'

'That of course; and when we had absolutely completed every particle of the furniture in this way, then we examined the house itself. We divided its entire surface into compartments, which we numbered, so that none might be missed; then we scrutinized each individual square inch throughout the premises, including the two houses immediately adjoining, with the microscope, as before.'

'The two houses adjoining!' I exclaimed; 'you must have had a great deal of trouble.'

'We had; but the reward offered is prodigious.

'You include the grounds about the houses?'

'All the grounds are paved with brick. They gave us comparatively little trouble. We examined the moss between the bricks, and found it undisturbed.'

'You looked among D—'s papers, of course, and into the books of the library?'

'Certainly; we opened every package and parcel; we not only opened every book, but we turned over every leaf in each volume, not contenting ourselves with a mere shake, according to the fashion of some of our police officers. We also measured the thickness of every book-cover, with the most accurate admeasurement and applied to each the most jealous scrutiny of the microscope. Had any of the bindings been recently meddled with, it would have been utterly impossible that the fact should have escaped observation. Some five or six volumes, just from the hands of the binder, we carefully probed, longitudinally, with the needles.'

'You explored the floors beneath the carpets?'

'Beyond doubt. We removed every carpet and examined the boards with the microscope.'

'And the paper on the walls?'

'Yes.'

'You looked into the cellars?'

'We did.'

'Then,' I said, 'you have been making a miscalculation, and the letter is not upon the premises, as you suppose.

'I fear you are right there,' said the Prefect. 'And now, Dupin, what would you advise me to do?'

'To make a thorough re-search of the premises.'

'That is absolutely needless,' replied G——. 'I am not more sure that I breathe than I am that the letter is not at the Hotel.'

'I have no better advice to give you,' said Dupin. 'You have, of course, an accurate description of the letter?'

'Oh yes!'—And here the Prefect, producing a memorandum-book, proceeded to read aloud a minute account of the internal, and especially of the external appearance of the missing document. Soon after finishing the perusal of this description, he took his departure, more entirely depressed in spirits than I had ever known the good gentleman before.

In about a month afterwards he paid us another visit, and found us occupied very nearly as before. He took a pipe and a chair and entered into some ordinary conversation. At length I said,—

'Well, but G——, what of the purloined letter? I presume you have at last made up your mind that there is no such thing as overreaching the Minister?'

'Confound him, say I—yes; I made the reexamination, however, as Dupin suggested—but it was all labour lost, as I knew it would be.'

'How much was the reward offered, did you say?' asked Dupin.

'Why, a very great deal—a very liberal reward—I don't like to say how much, precisely; but one thing I will say, that I wouldn't mind giving my individual cheque for fifty thousand francs to anyone who could obtain me that letter. The fact is, it is becoming of more and more importance every day; and the reward has been lately doubled. If it were trebled, however, I could do no more than I have done.'

'Why, yes,' said Dupin, drawlingly, between the whiffs of his meerschaum, 'I really —think, G——, you have not exerted yourself —to the utmost in this matter. You might —do a little more, I think, eh?'

'How? —In what way?'

'Why—*puff, puff*—you might—*puff, puff*—employ counsel in the matter, eh?—*puff, puff, puff*. Do you remember the story they tell of Abernethy?'

'No; hang Abernethy!'

'To be sure! Hang him and welcome. But, once upon a time, a certain rich miser conceived the design of spunging upon this Abernethy for a medical opinion. Getting up, for this purpose, an ordinary conversation in a private company, he insinuated his case to the physician, as that of an imaginary individual.

"We will suppose," said the miser, "that his symptoms are such and such; now, doctor, what would you have directed him to take?"

"Take!" said Abernethy, "why, take advice, to be sure."

'But,' said the Prefect, a little discomposed, 'I am perfectly willing to take advice and to pay for it. I would really give fifty thousand francs to any one who would aid me in the matter.'

'In that case,' replied Dupin, opening a drawer, and producing a check-book, 'you may as well fill me up a cheque for the amount mentioned. When you have signed it, I will hand you the letter.'

I was astounded. The Prefect appeared absolutely thunderstricken. For some minutes he remained speechless and motionless looking incredulously at my friend with open mouth, and eyes that seemed starting from their sockets; then, apparently in some measure, he seized a pen, and after several pauses and vacant stares, finally filled up and signed a cheque for fifty thousand francs, and handed it across the table to Dupin. The latter examined it carefully and deposited it in his pocket-book; then, unlocking an escritoire, took thence a letter and gave it to the Prefect. This functionary grasped it in a perfect agony of joy, opened it with a trembling hand, cast a rapid glance at its contents, and then, scrambling and struggling to the door, rushed at length unceremoniously from the room and from the house, without having uttered a syllable since Dupin had requested him to fill up the check.

When he had gone, my friend entered into some explanations.

'The Parisian police,' he said, 'are exceedingly able in their way. They are persevering, ingenious, cunning, and thoroughly versed in the knowledge which their duties seem chiefly to demand. Thus, when G—detailed to us his mode of searching the premises at the Hotel D—, I felt entire confidence in his having made a satisfactory investigation—so far as his labours extended.'

'So far as his labours extended?' said I.

'Yes,' said Dupin. 'The measures adopted were not only the best of their kind, but carried out to absolute perfection. Had the letter been deposited within the range of their search, these fellows would, beyond a question, have found it.'

I merely laughed—but he seemed quite serious in all that he said.

'The measures, then,' he continued, 'were good in their kind, and well executed; their defect lay in their being inapplicable to the case, and to the man. A certain set of highly ingenious resources are, with the Prefect, a sort of Procrustean bed, to which he forcibly adapts his designs. But he perpetually errs by being too deep or too shallow, for the matter in hand; and many a schoolboy is a better reasoner than he. I knew one about eight years of age, whose success at guessing in the game of 'even and odd' attracted universal admiration. This game is simple, and is played with marbles. One player holds in his hand a number of these toys, and demands of another whether that number is even or odd. If the guess is right, the guesser wins one; if wrong, he loses one. The boy to whom I allude won all the marbles of the school. Of course he had some principle of guessing; and this lay in mere observation and admeasurement of the astuteness of his opponents. For example, an arrant simpleton is his opponent, and, holding up his closed hand, asks, 'Are they even or odd?' Our schoolboy replies, 'Odd,' and loses; but upon the second trial he wins, for he then says to himself, 'the simpleton had them even upon the first trial, and his amount of cunning is just sufficient to make him have them odd upon the second; I will therefore guess odd'—he guesses odd, and wins. Now, with a simpleton a degree above the first, he would have reasoned thus: 'This fellow finds that in the first instance I guessed odd, and, in the second, he will propose to himself upon the first impulse, a simple variation from even to odd, as did the first simpleton; but then a second thought will suggest that this is too simple a variation, and finally he will decide upon putting it even as before. I will therefore guess even,' guesses even, and wins. Now this mode of reasoning in the schoolboy, whom his fellows termed 'lucky,'—what, in its last analysis, is it?'

'It is merely,' I said, 'an identification of the reasoner's intellect with that of his opponent.'

'It is,' said Dupin, 'and, upon inquiring of the boy by what means he effected the thorough identification in which his success consisted, I received answer as follows: "When I wish to find out how wise or how stupid or how good or how wicked is any one, or what are his thoughts at the moment, I fashion the expression of my face, as accurately as possible, in accordance with the expression of his, and then wait to see what thoughts or sentiments arise in my mind or heart, as if to match or correspond with the expression." This response of the schoolboy lies at the bottom of all the spurious profundity which has been attributed to Rochefoucauld, to La Bougive, to Machiavelli and to Campanella.'

'And the identification,' I said, 'of the reasoner's intellect with that of his opponent, depends, if I understand you aright upon the accuracy with which the opponent's intellect is admeasured.'

'For its practical value it depends upon this,' replied Dupin; and the Prefect and his cohort fall so frequently, first, by default of this identification, and, secondly, by ill-admeasurement, or rather through non-admeasurement, of the intellect with which they are engaged. They consider only their own ideas of ingenuity; and, in searching for anything hidden, advert only to the modes in which they would have hidden it. They are right in this much—that their own ingenuity is a faithful representative of that of the mass; but when the cunning of the individual felon is diverse in character from their own, the felon foils them, of course. This always happens when it is above their own, and very usually when it is below. They have no variation of principle in their investigations; at best, when urged by some unusual emergency—by some extraordinary reward—they extend or exaggerate their old modes of practice, without touching their principles. What, for example, in this case of D——, has been done to vary the principle of action? What is all this boring and probing, and sounding and scrutinizing with the microscope, and dividing the surface of the building into registered square inches—what is it all but an exaggeration of the application of the one principle or set of principles of search, which are based upon the one set of notions regarding human ingenuity, to which the Prefect, in the long routine of his duty, has been accustomed? Do you not see he has taken it for granted that all men proceed to conceal a letter—not exactly in a gimlet-hole bored in a chair-leg—but, at least, in some hole or corner suggested by the same tenor of thought which would urge a man to secrete a letter in a gimlet-hole bored in a chair-leg? And do you not see also, that such recherches nooks for concealment are adapted only for ordinary occasions, and would be adopted only by ordinary intellects; for, in all cases of concealment, a disposal of the article concealed—a disposal of it in this recherche manner—is, in the very first instance, presumable and presumed; and thus its discovery depends, not at all upon the acumen, but altogether upon the mere care, patience, and determination of the seekers; and where the case is of importance—or, what amounts to the same thing in the policial eyes, when the reward is of magnitude—the qualities in question have never been known to fall. You will now understand what I meant in suggesting that, had the purloined letter been hidden anywhere within the limits of the Prefect's examination—in other words, had the principle of its concealment been comprehended within the principles of the Prefect—its discovery would have been a matter altogether beyond question. This functionary, however, has been thoroughly mystified; and the remote source of his defeat lies in the supposition that the Minister is a fool, because he has acquired renown as a poet. All fools are poets, this the Prefect feels, and he is merely guilty of a non distributio medii in thence inferring that all poets are fools.'

'But is this really the poet?' I asked. 'There are two brothers, I know; and both have attained reputation in letters. The Minister I believe has written learnedly on the Differential Calculus. He is a mathematician, and no poet.'

'You are mistaken; I know him well; he is both. As poet and mathematician, he would reason well; as mere mathematician, he could not have reasoned at all, and thus would have been at the mercy of the Prefect.'

'You surprise me,' I said, 'by these opinions, which have been contradicted by the voice of the world. You do not mean to set at naught the well-digested idea of centuries. The mathematical reason has long been regarded as the reason par excellence.

'"*Il y a a parier*," replied Dupin, quoting from Chamfort, "*que toute idee publique, toute convention recue, est une sottise, car elle a convenu au plus grand nombre.*" The mathematicians, I grant you, have done their best to promulgate the popular error to which you allude, and which is none the less an error for its promulgation as truth. With an art worthy a better cause, for example, they have insinuated the term "analysis" into application to algebra. The French are the originators of this particular deception; but if a term is of any importance—if words derive any value from applicability—then "analysis" conveys "algebra" about as much as, in Latin, "ambitus" implies "ambition", "religio" religion or "homines honesti" a set of honorable men.'

'You have a quarrel on hand, I see,' said I, 'with some of the algebraists of Paris, but proceed.'

'I dispute the availability, and thus the value, of that reason which is cultivated in any especial form other than the abstractly logical. I dispute, in particular, the reason educed by mathematical study. The mathematics are the science of form and quantity; mathematical reasoning is merely logic applied to observation upon form and quantity. The great error lies in supposing that even the truths of what is called pure algebra, are abstract or general truths. And this error is so egregious that I am confounded at the universality with which it has been received. Mathematical axioms are not axioms of general truth. What is true of relation—of form and quantity—is often grossly false in regard to morals, for example. In this latter science it is very usually untrue that the aggregated parts are equal to the whole. In chemistry also the axiom fails. In the consideration of motive it fails; for two motives, each of a given value, have not, necessarily, a value when united, equal to the sum of their values apart. There are numerous other mathematical truths which are only truths within the limits of relation. But the mathematician argues, from his finite truths, through habit, as if they were of an absolutely general applicability—as the world indeed imagines them to be. Bryant, in his very learned *Mythology* mentions an analogous source of error, when he says that "although the

Pagan fables are not believed, yet we forget ourselves continually, and make inferences from them as existing realities." With the algebraists, however, who are Pagans themselves, the "Pagan fables" are believed, and the inferences are made, not so much through lapse of memory, as through an unaccountable addling of the brains. In short, I never yet encountered the mere mathematician who could be trusted out of equal roots, or one who did not clandestinely hold it as a point of his faith that x squared $+ px$ was absolutely and unconditionally equal to q. Say to one of these gentlemen, by way of experiment, if you please, that you believe occasions may occur where x squared $+ px$ is not altogether equal to q, and, having made him understand what you mean, get out of his reach as speedily as convenient, for, beyond doubt, he will endeavour to knock you down.

'I mean to say,' continued Dupin, while I merely laughed at his last observations, 'that if the Minister had been no more than a mathematician, the Prefect would have been under no necessity of giving me this check. I knew him, however, as both mathematician and poet, and my measures were adapted to his capacity, with reference to the circumstances by which he was surrounded. I knew him as a courtier, too, and as a bold intriguant. Such a man, I considered, could not fail to be aware of the ordinary policial modes of action. He could not have failed to anticipate—and events have proved that he did not fail to anticipate—the waylayings to which he was subjected. He must have foreseen, I reflected, the secret investigations of his premises. His frequent absences from home at night, which were hailed by the Prefect as certain aids to his success, I regarded only as ruses, to afford opportunity for thorough search to the police, and thus the sooner to impress them with the conviction to which G—, in fact, did finally arrive—the conviction that the letter was not upon the premises. I felt, also, that the whole train of thought, which I was at some pains in detailing to you just now, concerning the invariable principle of policial action in searches for articles concealed—I felt that this whole train of thought would necessarily pass through the mind of the Minister. It would imperatively lead him to despise all the ordinary nooks of concealment. He could not, I reflected, be so weak as not to see that the most intricate and remote recess of his hotel would be as open as his commonest closets to the eyes, to the probes, to the gimlets, and to the microscopes of the Prefect. I saw, in fine, that he would be driven, as a matter of course, to simplicity, if not deliberately induced to it as a matter of choice. You will remember, perhaps, how desperately the Prefect laughed when I suggested, upon our first interview, that it was just possible this mystery troubled him so much on account of its being so very self-evident.'

'Yes,' said I, 'I remember his merriment well. I really thought he would have fallen into convulsions.'

'The material world,' continued Dupin, 'abounds with very strict analogies to the immaterial; and thus some colour of truth has been given to the rhetorical dogma, that metaphor, or simile, may be made to strengthen an argument, as well as to embellish a description. The principle of the vis inertiae, for example, seems to be identical in physics and metaphysics. It is not more true in the former, that a large body is with more difficulty set in motion than a smaller one, and that its subsequent momentum is commensurate with this difficulty, than it is, in the latter, that intellects of the vaster capacity, while more forcible, more constant, and more eventful in their movements than those of inferior grade, are yet the less readily moved, and more embarrassed and full of hesitation in the first few steps of their progress. Again: have you ever noticed which of the street signs, over the shop doors, are the most attractive of attention?'

'I have never given the matter a thought,' I said.

'There is a game of puzzles,' he resumed, 'which is played upon a map. One party playing requires another to find a given word—the name of town, river, state or empire—any word, in short, upon the motley and perplexed surface of the chart. A novice in the game generally seeks to embarrass his opponents by giving them the most minutely lettered names; but the adept selects such words as stretch, in large characters, from one end of the chart to the other. These, like the over-largely lettered signs and placards of the street, escape observation by dint of being excessively obvious; and here the physical oversight is precisely analogous with the moral inapprehension by which the intellect suffers to pass unnoticed those considerations which are too obtrusively and too palpably self-evident. But this is a point, it appears, somewhat above or beneath the understanding of the Prefect. He never once thought it probable, or possible, that the Minister had deposited the letter immediately beneath the nose of the whole world, by way of best preventing any portion of that world from perceiving it.

'But the more I reflected upon the daring, dashing, and discriminating ingenuity of D——; upon the fact that the document must always have been at hand, if he intended to use it to good purpose; and upon the decisive evidence, obtained by the Prefect, that it was not hidden within the limits of that dignitary's ordinary search—the more satisfied I became that, to conceal this letter, the Minister had resorted to the comprehensive and sagacious expedient of not attempting to conceal it at all.

'Full of these ideas, I prepared myself with a pair of green spectacles, and called one fine morning, quite by accident, at the Ministerial hotel. I found D——at home, yawning, lounging, and dawdling, as usual, and pretending to be in the last extremity of ennui. He is, perhaps, the most really energetic human being now alive—but that is only when nobody sees him.

'To be even with him, I complained of my weak eyes, and lamented the necessity of the spectacles, under cover of which I cautiously and thoroughly surveyed the apartment, while seemingly intent only upon the conversation of my host.

'I paid special attention to a large writing-table near which he sat, and upon which lay confusedly, some miscellaneous letters and other papers, with one or two musical instruments and a few books. Here, however, after a long and very deliberate scrutiny, I saw nothing to excite particular suspicion.

'At length my eyes, in going the circuit of the room, fell upon a trumpery filigree card-rack of pasteboard, that hung dangling by a dirty blue ribbon, from a little brass knob just beneath the middle of the mantelpiece. In this rack, which had three or four compartments, were five or six visiting cards and a solitary letter. This last was much soiled and crumpled. It was torn nearly in two, across the middle—as if a design, in the first instance, to tear it entirely up as worthless, had been altered, or stayed, in the second. It had a large black seal, bearing the D—cipher very conspicuously, and was addressed, in a diminutive female hand, to D—, the minister, himself. It was thrust carelessly, and even, as it seemed, contemptuously, into one of the upper divisions of the rack.

'No sooner had I glanced at this letter, than I concluded it to be that of which I was in search. To be sure, it was, to all appearance, radically different from the one of which the Prefect had read us so minute a description. Here the seal was large and black, with the D—cipher; there it was small and red, with the ducal arms of the S—family. Here, the address, to the Minister, was diminutive and feminine; there the superscription, to a certain royal personage, was markedly bold and decided; the size alone formed a point of correspondence. But, then, the radicalness of these differences, which was excessive; the dirt; the soiled and torn condition of the paper, so inconsistent with the true methodical habits of D—, and so suggestive of a design to delude the beholder into an idea of the worthlessness of the document; these things, together with the hyperobtrusive situation of this document, full in the view of every visitor, and thus exactly in accordance with the conclusions to which I had previously arrived; these things, I say, were strongly corroborative of suspicion, in one who came with the intention to suspect.

'I protracted my visit as long as possible, and, while I maintained a most animated discussion with the Minister, on a topic which I knew well had never failed to interest and excite him, I kept my attention really riveted upon the letter. In this examination, I committed to memory its external appearance and arrangement in the rack; and also fell, at length, upon a discovery which set at rest whatever trivial doubt I might have entertained. In scrutinizing the edges of the paper, I observed them to be more chafed than seemed necessary. They presented the broken appearance which is manifested when a stiff paper, having been once folded and pressed with a folder, is refolded in a reversed direction, in the same creases or edges which had formed the original fold. This discovery was sufficient. It was clear to me that the letter had been turned, as a glove, inside out, re-directed, and re-sealed. I bade the Minister good morning, and took my departure at once, leaving a gold snuff-box upon the table.

'The next morning I called for the snuff-box, when we resumed, quite eagerly, the conversation of the preceding day. While thus engaged, however, a loud report, as if of a pistol, was heard immediately beneath the windows of the hotel, and was succeeded by a series of fearful screams, and the shoutings of a mob. D—rushed to a casement, threw it open, and looked out. In the meantime, I stepped to the card-rack, took the letter, put it in my pocket, and replaced it by a facsimile, (so far as regards externals,) which I had carefully prepared at my lodgings; imitating the D—cipher, very readily, by means of a seal formed of bread.

'The disturbance in the street had been occasioned by the frantic behaviour of a man with a musket. He had fired it among a crowd of women and children. It proved, however, to have been without ball, and the fellow was suffered to go his way as a lunatic or a drunkard. When he had gone, D-came from the window, whither I had followed him immediately upon securing the object in view. Soon afterwards I bade him farewell. The pretended lunatic was a man in my own pay.

'But what purpose had you,' I asked, in replacing the letter by a facsimile? Would it not have been better, at the first visit, to have seized it openly, and departed?'

'D—,' replied Dupin, 'is a desperate man, and a man of nerve. His hotel, too, is not without attendants devoted to his interests. Had I made the wild attempt you suggest, I might never have left the Ministerial presence alive. The good people of Paris might have heard of me no more. But I had an object apart from these considerations. You know my political prepossessions. In this matter, I act as a partisan of the lady concerned. For eighteen months the Minister has had her in his power. She has now him in hers; since, being unaware that the letter is not in his possession, he will proceed with his exactions as if it was. Thus will he inevitably commit himself, at once, to his political destruction. His downfall, too, will not be more precipitate than awkward. It is all very well to talk about the *facilis descensus*

Averni; but in all kinds of climbing, as Catalani said of singing, it is far more easy to get up than to come down. In the present instance I have no sympathy—at least no pity—for him who descends. He is the monstrum horrendum, an unprincipled man of genius. I confess, however, that I should like very well to know the precise character of his thoughts, when, being defied by her whom the Prefect terms "a certain personage" he is reduced to opening the letter which I left for him in the card-rack.'

'How? Did you put any thing particular in it?'

'Why—it did not seem altogether right to leave the interior blank—that would have been insulting. D—, at Vienna once, did me an evil turn, which I told him, quite good-humouredly, that I should remember. So, as I knew he would feel some curiosity in regard to the identity of the person who had outwitted him, I thought it a pity not to give him a clue. He is well acquainted with my MS., and I just copied into the middle of the blank sheet the words—*Un dessein si funeste, S'il n'est digne d'Atrée, est digne de Thyeste.*

They are to be found in Crebillon's *Atrée*.'

4

THE DETECTIVE DETECTOR

O. Henry

Another delightful Sherlock Holmes parody featuring Shamrock Jolnes.

I was walking in Central Park with Avery Knight, the great New York burglar, highwayman and murderer.

'But, my dear Knight,' said I, 'it sounds incredible. You have undoubtedly performed some of the most wonderful feats in your profession known to modern crime. You have committed some marvellous deeds under the very noses of the police—you have boldly entered the homes of millionaires and held them up with an empty gun while you made free with their silver and jewels; you have sandbagged citizens in the glare of Broadway's electric lights; you have killed and robbed with superb openness and absolute impunity—but when you boast that within forty-eight hours after committing a murder you can run down and actually bring me face to face with the detective assigned to apprehend you, I must beg leave to express my doubts—remember, you are in New York.'

Avery Knight smiled indulgently.

'You pique my professional pride, doctor,' he said in a nettled tone. 'I will convince you.'

About twelve yards in advance of us a prosperous-looking citizen was rounding a clump of bushes where the walk curved. Knight suddenly drew a revolver and shot the man in the back. His victim fell and lay without moving.

The great murderer went up to him leisurely and took from his clothes his money, watch, and a valuable ring and cravat pin. He then rejoined me smiling calmly, and we continued our walk.

Ten steps and we met a policeman running toward the spot where the shot had been fired. Avery Knight stopped him.

'I have just killed a man,' he announced, seriously, 'and robbed him of his possessions.'

'G'wan,' said the policeman, angrily, 'or I'll run yez in! Want yer name in the papers, don't yez? I never knew the cranks to come around so quick after a shootin' before. Out of th' park, now, for yours, or I'll fan yez.'

'What you have done,' I said, argumentatively, as Knight and I walked on, 'was easy. But when you come to the task of hunting down the detective that they send upon your trail you will find that you have undertaken a difficult feat.'

'Perhaps so,' said Knight, lightly. 'I will admit that my success depends in a degree upon the sort of man they start after me. If it should be an ordinary plain-clothes man I might fail to gain a sight of him. If they honour me by giving the case to someone of their celebrated sleuths I do not fear to match my cunning and powers of induction against his.'

On the next afternoon Knight entered my office with a satisfied look on his keen countenance.

'How goes the mysterious murder?' I asked.

'As usual,' said Knight, smilingly. 'I have put in the morning at the police station and at the inquest. It seems that a card case of mine containing cards with my name and address was found near the body. They have three witnesses who saw the shooting and gave a description of me. The case has been placed in the hands of Shamrock Jolnes, the famous detective. He left Headquarters at 11:30 on the assignment. I waited at my address until two, thinking he might call there.'

I laughed, tauntingly.

'You will never see Jolnes,' I continued, 'until this murder has been forgotten, two or three weeks from now. I had a better opinion of your shrewdness, Knight. During the three hours and a half that you waited he has got out of your ken. He is after you on true induction theories now, and no wrongdoer has yet been known to come upon him while thus engaged. I advise you to give it up.'

'Doctor,' said Knight, with a sudden glint in his keen gray eye and a squaring of his chin, 'in spite of the record your city holds of something like a dozen homicides without a subsequent meeting of the perpetrator, and the sleuth in charge of the case, I will undertake to break that record. Tomorrow I will take you to Shamrock Jolnes—I will unmask him before you and prove to you that it is not an impossibility for an officer of the law and a manslayer to stand face to face in your city.'

'Do it,' said I, 'and you'll have the sincere thanks of the Police Department.'

On the next day Knight called for me in a cab.

'I've been on one or two false scents, doctor,' he admitted. 'I know something of detectives' methods, and I followed out a few of them, expecting to find Jolnes at the other end. The pistol being a .45-caliber, I thought surely I would find him at work on the clue in Forty-fifth Street. Then, again, I looked for the detective at the Columbia University, as the man's being shot in the back naturally suggested hazing. But I could not find a trace of him.'

'—Nor will you,' I said, emphatically.

'Not by ordinary methods,' said Knight. 'I might walk up and down Broadway for a month without success. But you have aroused my pride, doctor; and if I fail to show you Shamrock Jolnes this day, I promise you I will never kill or rob in your city again.'

'Nonsense, man,' I replied. 'When our burglars walk into our houses and politely demand, thousands of dollars' worth of jewels, and then dine and bang the piano an hour or two before leaving, how do you, a mere murderer, expect to come in contact with the detective that is looking for you?'

Avery Knight, sat lost in thought for a while. At length he looked up brightly.

'Doc,' said he, 'I have it. Put on your hat and come with me. In half an hour I guarantee that you shall stand in the presence of Shamrock Jolnes.'

I entered a cab with Avery Knight. I did not hear his instructions to the driver, but the vehicle set out at a smart pace up Broadway, turning presently into Fifth Avenue, and proceeding northward again. It was with a rapidly beating heart that I accompanied this wonderful and gifted assassin, whose analytical genius and superb self-confidence had prompted him to make me the tremendous promise of bringing me into the presence of a murderer and the New York detective in pursuit of him simultaneously. Even yet I could not believe it possible.

'Are you sure that you are not being led into some trap?' I asked. 'Suppose that your clue, whatever it is, should bring us only into the presence of the Commissioner of Police and a couple of dozen cops!'

'My dear doctor,' said Knight, a little stiffly. 'I would remind you that I am no gambler.'

'I beg your pardon,' said I. 'But I do not think you will find Jolnes.'

The cab stopped before one of the handsomest residences on the avenue. Walking up and down in front of the house was a man with long red whiskers, with a detective's badge showing on the lapel of his coat. Now and then the man would remove his whiskers to wipe his face, and then I would recognize at once the well-known features of the great New York detective. Jolnes was keeping a sharp watch upon the doors and windows of the house.

'Well, doctor,' said Knight, unable to repress a note of triumph in his voice, 'have you seen?'

'It is wonderful—wonderful!' I could not help exclaiming as our cab started on its return trip. 'But how did you do it? By what process of induction—'

'My dear doctor,' interrupted the great murderer, 'the inductive theory is what the detectives use. My process is more modern. I call it the saltatorial theory. Without bothering with the tedious mental phenomena necessary to the solution of a mystery from slight clues, I jump at once to a conclusion. I will explain to you the method I employed in this case.

'In the first place, I argued that as the crime was committed in New York City in broad daylight, in a public place and under peculiarly atrocious circumstances, and that as the most skilful sleuth available was let loose upon the case, the perpetrator would never be discovered. Do you not think my postulation justified by precedent?'

'Perhaps so,' I replied, doggedly. 'But if Big Bill Dev—'

'Stop that,' interrupted Knight, with a smile, 'I've heard that several times. It's too late now. I will proceed.

'If homicides in New York went undiscovered, I reasoned, although the best detective talent was employed to ferret them out, it must be true that the detectives went about their work in the wrong way. And not only in the wrong way, but exactly opposite from the right way. That was my clue.

'I slew the man in Central Park. Now, let me describe myself to you.

'I am tall, with a black beard, and I hate publicity. I have no money to speak of; I do not like oatmeal, and it is the one ambition of my life to die rich. I am of a cold and heartless disposition. I do not care for my fellowmen and I never give a cent to beggars or charity.

'Now, my dear doctor, that is the true description of myself, the man whom that shrewd detective was to hunt down. You who are familiar with the history of crime in New York of late should be able to foretell the result. When I promised you to exhibit to your incredulous gaze the sleuth who was set upon me, you laughed at me because you said that detectives and murderers never met in New York. I have demonstrated to you that the theory is possible.'

'But how did you do it?' I asked again.

'It was very simple,' replied the distinguished murderer. 'I assumed that the detective would go exactly opposite to the clues he had. I have given you a description of myself. Therefore, he must necessarily set to work and trail a short man with a white beard who likes to be in the papers, who is very wealthy, is fond 'of oatmeal, wants to die poor and is of an extremely generous and philanthropic disposition. When thus far is reached the mind hesitates no longer. I conveyed you at once to the spot where Shamrock Jolnes was piping off Andrew Carnegie's residence.'

'Knight,' said I, 'you're a wonder. If there was no danger of your reforming, what a rounds man you'd make for the Nineteenth Precinct!'

5

THE SOFA

Charles Dickens

...Lets find out... can a bad case simply end with a bad end...

'What young men will do, sometimes, to ruin themselves and break their friends' hearts,' said Sergeant Dornton, 'it's surprising! I had a case at Saint Blank's Hospital which was of this sort. A bad case, indeed, with a bad end!

'The Secretary, and the House-Surgeon, and the Treasurer, of Saint Blank's Hospital, came to Scotland Yard to give information of numerous robberies having been committed on the students. The students could leave nothing in the pockets of their great-coats, while the great-coats were hanging at the hospital, but it was almost certain to be stolen. Property of various descriptions was constantly being lost; and the gentlemen were naturally uneasy about it, and anxious, for the credit of the institution, that the thief or thieves should be discovered. The case was entrusted to me, and I went to the hospital.

'"Now, gentlemen," said I, after we had talked it over; "I understand this property is usually lost from one room."

'Yes, they said. It was.

"I should wish, if you please," said I, "to see the room."

'It was a good-sized bare room down-stairs, with a few tables and forms in it, and a row of pegs, all round, for hats and coats.

'"Next, gentlemen," said I, "do you suspect anybody?"

'Yes, they said. They did suspect somebody. They were sorry to say, they suspected one of the porters.

'"I should like," said I, "to have that man pointed out to me, and to have a little time to look after him."

'He was pointed out, and I looked after him, and then I went back to the hospital, and said, "Now, gentlemen, it's not the porter. He's, unfortunately for himself, a little too fond of drink, but he's nothing worse. My suspicion is, that these robberies are committed by one of the students; and if you'll put me a sofa into that room where the pegs are—as there's no closet—I think I shall be able to detect the thief. I wish the sofa, if you please, to be covered with chintz, or something of that sort, so that I may lie on my chest, underneath it, without being seen."

'The sofa was provided, and next day at eleven o'clock, before any of the students came, I went there, with those gentlemen, to get underneath it. It turned out to be one of those old-fashioned sofas with a great cross-beam at the bottom, that would have broken my back in no time if I could ever have got below it. We had quite a job to break all this away in the time; however, I fell to work, and they fell to work, and we broke it out, and made a clear place for me. I got under the sofa, lay down on my chest, took out my knife, and made a convenient hole in the chintz to look through. It was then settled between me and the gentlemen that when the students were all up in the wards, one of the gentlemen should come in, and hang up a great-coat on one of the pegs. And that that great-coat should have, in one of the pockets, a pocket-book containing marked money.

'After I had been there some time, the students began to drop into the room, by ones, and twos, and threes, and to talk about all sorts of things, little thinking there was anybody under the sofa—and then to go up-stairs. At last there came in one who remained until he was alone in the room by himself. A tallish, good-looking young man of one or two and twenty, with a light whisker. He went to a particular hat-peg, took off a good hat that was hanging there, tried it on, hung his own hat in its place, and hung that hat on another peg, nearly opposite to me. I then felt quite certain that he was the thief, and would come back by-and-by.

'When they were all up-stairs, the gentleman came in with the great-coat. I showed him where to hang it, so that I might have a good view of it; and he went away; and I lay under the sofa on my chest, for a couple of hours or so, waiting.

'At last, the same young man came down. He walked across the room, whistling—stopped and listened—took another walk and whistled—stopped again, and listened—then began to go regularly round the pegs, feeling in the pockets of all the coats. When he came to the great-coat, and felt the pocket-book, he was so eager and so hurried that he broke the strap in tearing it open. As he began to put the money in his pocket, I crawled out from under the sofa, and his eyes met mine.

'My face, as you may perceive, is brown now, but it was pale at that time, my health not being good; and looked as long as a horse's. Besides which, there was a great draught of air from the door, underneath the sofa, and I had tied a handkerchief round my head; so what I looked like, altogether, I don't know. He turned blue—literally blue—when he saw me crawling out, and I couldn't feel surprised at it.

'"I am an officer of the Detective Police," said I, "and have been lying here, since you first came in this morning. I regret, for the sake of yourself and your friends, that you should have done what you have; but this case is complete. You have the pocket-book in your hand and the money upon you; and I must take you into custody!"

'It was impossible to make out any case in his behalf, and on his trial he pleaded guilty. How or when he got the means I don't know; but while he was awaiting his sentence, he poisoned himself in Newgate.'

We inquired of this officer, on the conclusion of the foregoing anecdote, whether the time appeared long, or short, when he lay in that constrained position under the sofa?

'Why, you see, sir,' he replied, 'if he hadn't come in, the first time, and I had not been quite sure he was the thief, and would return, the time would have seemed long. But, as it was, I being dead certain of my man, the time seemed pretty short.'

6

AN UNCOMFORTABLE BED

Guy de Maupassant

... Everyone seemed to me an object of suspicion, and I even looked distrustfully at the faces of the servants...

One autumn I went to stay for the hunting season with some friends in a chateau in Picardy. My friends were fond of practical joking, as all my friends are. I do not care to know any other sort of people.

When I arrived, they gave me a princely reception, which at once aroused distrust in my breast. We had some capital shooting. They embraced me, they cajoled me, as if they expected to have great fun at my expense. I said to myself: 'Look out, old ferret! They have something in preparation for you.'

During the dinner, the mirth was excessive, far too great, in fact. I thought: 'Here are people who take a double share of amusement, and apparently without reason. They must be looking out in their own minds for some good bit of fun. Assuredly I am to be the victim of the joke. Attention!'

During the entire evening, everyone laughed in an exaggerated fashion. I smelled a practical joke in the air, as a dog smells game. But what was it? I was watchful, restless. I did not let a word or a meaning or a gesture escape me. Everyone seemed to me an object of suspicion, and I even looked distrustfully at the faces of the servants.

The hour rang for going to bed, and the whole household came to escort me to my room. Why? They called to me: 'Good night.' I entered the apartment, shut the door and remained standing, without moving a single step, holding the wax candle in my hand.

I heard laughter and whispering in the corridor. Without doubt they were spying on me. I cast a glance around the walls, the furniture, the ceiling, the hangings, the floor. I saw nothing to justify suspicion. I heard persons moving about outside my door. I had no doubt they were looking through the keyhole.

An idea came into my head: 'My candle may suddenly go out, and leave me in darkness.'

Then I went across to the mantelpiece, and lighted all the wax candles that were on it. After that, I cast another glance around me without discovering anything. I advanced with short steps, carefully examining the apartment. Nothing. I inspected every article one after the other. Still nothing. I went over to the window. The shutters, large wooden shutters, were open. I shut them with great care, and then drew the curtains, enormous velvet curtains, and I placed a chair in front of them, so as to have nothing to fear from without.

Then I cautiously sat down. The armchair was solid. I did not venture to get into the bed. However, time was flying; and I ended by coming to the conclusion that I was ridiculous. If they were spying on me, as I supposed, they must, while waiting for the success of the joke they had been preparing for me, have been laughing enormously at my terror. So I made up my mind to go to bed. But the bed was particularly suspicious-looking. I pulled at the curtains. They seemed to be secure. All the same, there was danger. I was going perhaps to receive a cold shower-bath from overhead, or perhaps, the moment I stretched myself out, to find myself sinking under the floor with my mattress. I searched in my memory for all the practical jokes of which I ever had experience. And I did not want to be caught. Ah! Certainly not! Certainly not! Then I suddenly bethought myself of a precaution which I consider one of extreme efficacy: I caught hold of the side of the mattress gingerly, and very slowly drew it toward me. It came away, followed by the sheet and the rest of the bedclothes. I dragged all these objects into the very middle of the room, facing the entrance door. I made my bed over again as best I could at some distance from the suspected bedstead and the corner which had filled me with such anxiety. Then, I extinguished all the candles, and, groping my way, slipped under the bedclothes.

For at least another hour, I remained awake, starting at the slightest sound. Everything seemed quiet in the chateau. I fell asleep. I must have been in a deep sleep for a long time, but all of a sudden, I was awakened with a start by the fall of a heavy body tumbling right on top of my own body, and, at the same time, I received on my face, on my neck and on my chest a burning liquid which made me utter a howl of pain. And a dreadful noise, as if a sideboard laden with plates and dishes had fallen down, penetrated my ears.

I felt myself suffocating under the weight that was crushing me and preventing me from moving. I stretched out my hand to find out what was the nature of this object. I felt a face, a nose, and whiskers. Then with all my strength I launched out a blow over this face. But I immediately received a hail of cuffings which made me jump straight out of the soaked sheets, and rush in my nightshirt into the corridor, the door of which I found open.

O stupor! It was broad daylight. The noise brought my friends hurrying into the apartment, and we found, sprawling over my improvised bed, the dismayed valet, who, while bringing me my morning cup of tea, had tripped over this obstacle in the middle of the floor, and fallen on his stomach, spilling, in spite of himself, my breakfast over my face.

The precautions I had taken in closing the shutters and going to sleep in the middle of the room had only brought about the interlude I had been striving to avoid.

Ah! how they all laughed that day!

7

THE CLARION CALL

O. Henry

...It takes nine tailors to make a man, but one can do a man up...

Half of this story can be found in the records of the Police Department; the other half belong behind the business counter of a newspaper office.

One afternoon, two weeks after Millionaire Norcross was found in his apartment murdered by a burglar, the murderer, while strolling serenely down Broadway ran plump against Detective Barney Woods.

'Is that you, Johnny Kernan?' asked Woods, who had been near-sighted in public for five years.

'No less,' cried Kernan, heartily. 'If it isn't Barney Woods, late and early of old Saint Jo! You'll have to show me! What are you doing East? Do the green-goods circulars get out that far?' said Woods.

'I've been in New York some years, I'm on the city detective force.'

'Well, well!' said Kernan, breathing smiling joy and patting the detective's arm.

'Come into Muller's,' said Woods, 'and let's hunt a quiet table. I'd like to talk to you awhile.'

It lacked a few minutes to the hour of four. The tides of trade were not yet loosed, and they found a quiet corner of the cafe. Kernan, well dressed, slightly swaggering, self-confident, seated himself opposite the little detective, with his pale, sandy mustache, squinting eyes and ready-made cheviot suit.

'What business are you in now?' asked Woods. 'You know you left Saint Jo a year before I did.'

'I'm selling shares in a copper mine,' said Kernan. 'I may establish an office here. Well, well! and so old Barney is a New York detective. You always had a turn that way. You were on the police in Saint Jo after I left there, weren't you?'

'Six months,' said Woods. 'And now there's one more question, Johnny. I've followed your record pretty close ever since you did that hotel job in Saratoga, and I never knew you to use your gun before. Why did you kill Norcross?'

Kernan stared for a few moments with concentrated attention at the slice of lemon in his high-ball; and then he looked at the detective with a sudden, crooked, brilliant smile.

'How did you guess it, Barney?' he asked, admiringly. 'I swear I thought the job was as clean and as smooth as a peeled onion. Did I leave a string hanging out anywhere? '

Woods laid upon the table a small gold pencil intended for a watch charm.

'It's the one I gave you the last Christmas we were in Saint Jo. I've got your shaving mug yet. I found this under a corner of the rug in Norcross's room. I warn you to be careful what you say. I've got it put on to you, Johnny. We were old friends once, but I must do my duty. You'll have to go to the chair for Norcross.'

Kernan laughed. 'My luck stays with me,' said he. 'Who'd have thought old Barney was on my trail!' He slipped one hand inside his coat. In an instant Woods had a revolver against his side.

'Put it away,' said Kernan, wrinkling his nose. 'I'm only investigating. Aha! It takes nine tailors to make a man, but one can do a man up. There's a hole in that vest pocket. I took that pencil off my chain and slipped it in there in case of a scrap. Put up your gun, Barney, and I'll tell you why I had to shoot Norcross. The old fool started down the hall after me, popping at the buttons on the back of my coat with a peevish little .22 and I had to stop him. The old lady was a darling. She just lay in bed and saw her $12,000 diamond necklace go without a chirp, while she begged like a panhandler to have back a little thin gold ring with a garnet worth about $3. 1 guess she married old Norcross for his money, all right. Don't they hang on to the little trinkets from the Man Who Lost Out, though? There were six rings, two brooches and a chatelaine watch. Fifteen thousand would cover the lot.'

'I warned you not to talk,' said Woods.

'Oh, that's all right,' said Kernan. 'The stuff is in my suit case at the hotel. And now I'll tell you why I'm talking. Because it's safe. I'm talking to a man I know. You owe me a thousand dollars, Barney Woods, and even if you wanted to arrest me your hand wouldn't make the move.'

'I haven't forgotten,' said Woods. 'You counted out twenty fifties without a word. I'll pay it back some day. That thousand saved me and—well, they were piling my furniture out on the sidewalk when I got back to the house.'

'And so,' continued Kernan, 'you being Barney Woods, born as true as steel, and bound to play a white man's game, can't lift a finger to arrest the man you're indebted to. Oh, I have to study men as well as Yale locks and window fastenings in my business. Now, keep quiet while I ring for the waiter. I've had a thirst for a year or two that worries me a little. If I'm ever caught the lucky sleuth will have to divide honours with old boy Booze. But I never drink during business hours. After a job I can crook elbows with my old friend Barney with a clear conscience. What are you taking?'

The waiter came with the little decanters and the siphon and left them alone again.

'You've called the turn,' said Woods, as he rolled the little gold pencil about with a thoughtful forefinger. 'I've got to pass you up. I can't lay a hand on you. If I'd a-paid that money back—but I didn't, and that settles it. It's a bad break I'm making, Johnny, but I can't dodge it. You helped me once, and it calls for the same.'

'I knew it,' said Kernan, raising his glass, with a flushed smile of self-appreciation. 'I can judge men. Here's to Barney, for—"he's a jolly good fellow."'

'I don't believe,' went on Woods quietly, as if he were thinking aloud, 'that if accounts had been square between you and me, all the money in all the banks in New York could have bought you out of my hands tonight.'

'I know it couldn't,' said Kernan. 'That's why I knew I was safe with you.'

'Most people,' continued the detective, 'look sideways at my business. They don't class it among the fine arts and the professions. But I've always taken a kind of fool pride in it. And here is where I go "busted". I guess I'm a man first and a detective afterward. I've got to let you go, and then I've got to resign from the force. I guess I can drive an express wagon. Your thousand dollars is further off than ever, Johnny.'

'Oh, you're welcome to it,' said Kernan, with a lordly air. 'I'd be willing to call the debt off, but I know you wouldn't have it. It was a lucky day for me when you borrowed it. And now, let's drop the subject. I'm off to the West on a morning train. I know a place out there where I can negotiate the Norcross sparks. Drink up, Barney, and forget your troubles. We'll have a jolly time while the police are knocking their heads together over the case. I've got one of my Sahara thirsts on tonight. But I'm in the bands—the unofficial bands—of my old friend Barney, and I won't even dream of a cop.'

And then, as Kernan's ready finger kept the button and the waiter working, his weak point—a tremendous vanity and arrogant egotism, began to show itself. He recounted story after story of his successful plunderings, ingenious plots and infamous transgressions until Woods, with all his familiarity with evil-doers, felt growing within him a cold abhorrence toward the utterly vicious man who had once been his benefactor.

'I'm disposed of, of course,' said Woods, at length. 'But I advise you to keep under cover for a spell. The newspapers may take up this Norcross affair. There has been an epidemic of burglaries and manslaughter in town this summer.'

The word sent Kernan into a high glow of sullen and vindictive rage.

'To hell with the newspapers,' he growled. 'What do they spell but brag and blow and boodle in box-car letters? Suppose they do take up a case, what does it amount to? The police are easy enough to fool; but what do the newspapers do? They send a lot of pin-head reporters around to the scene; and they make for the nearest saloon and have beer while they take photos of the bartender's oldest daughter in evening dress, to print as the fiancée of the young man in the tenth story, who thought he heard a noise below on the night of the murder. That's about as near as the newspapers ever come to running down Mr Burglar.'

'Well, I don't know,' said Woods, reflecting. 'Some of the papers have done good work in that line. There's the Morning Mars, for instance. It warmed up two or three trails, and got the man after the police had let 'em get cold.'

'I'll show you,' said Tiernan, rising, and expanding his chest. 'I'll show you what I think of newspapers in general, and your Morning Mars in particular.'

Three feet from their table was the telephone booth. Kernan went inside and sat at the instrument, leaving the door open. He found a number in the book, took down the receiver and made his demand upon Central. Woods sat still, looking at the sneering, cold, vigilant face waiting close to the transmitter, and listened to the words that came from the thin, truculent lips curved into a contemptuous smile.

'That the Morning Mars? ... I want to speak to the managing editor ... Why, tell him it's someone who wants to talk to him about the Norcross murder.

'You the editor? ... All right... I am the man who killed old Norcross ...Wait! Hold the wire; I'm not the usual crank ... oh, there isn't the slightest danger. I've just been discussing it with a detective friend of mine. I killed the old man at 2:30 a.m. two weeks ago tomorrow... Have a drink with you? Now, hadn't you better leave that kind of talk to your funny man? Can't you tell whether a man's guying you or whether you're being offered the biggest scoop your dull dishrag of a paper ever had? ... Well, that's so; it's a bobtail scoop—but you can hardly expect me to 'phone in my name and address.

'... Why? Oh, because I beard you make a specialty of solving mysterious crimes that stump the police... No, that's not all. I want to tell you that your rotten, lying, penny sheet is of no more use in tracking an intelligent murderer or highwayman than a blind poodle would be... What? ... Oh, no, this isn't a rival newspaper office; you're getting it straight. I did the Norcross job, and I've got the jewels in my suit case at—"the name of the hotel could not be learned"—you recognize that phrase, don't you? I thought so. You've used it often enough. Kind of rattles you, doesn't it, to have the mysterious villain call up your great, big, all-powerful organ of right and justice and good government and tell you what a helpless old gas-bag you are? ... Cut that out; you're not that big a fool—no, you don't think I'm a fraud. I can tell it by your voice... Now, listen, and I'll give you a pointer that will prove it to you. Of course you've had this murder case worked over by your staff of bright young blockheads. Half of the second button on old Mrs Norcross's nightgown is broken off. I saw it when I took the garnet ring off her finger. I thought it was a ruby...—Stop that! it won't work.'

Kernan turned to Woods with a diabolic smile.

'I've got him going. He believes me now. He didn't quite cover the transmitter with his hand when he told somebody to call up Central on another 'phone and get our number. I'll give him just one more dig, and then we'll make a get-away.'

'Hello! ... Yes. I'm here yet. You didn't think—I'd run from such a little subsidized, turncoat rag of a newspaper, did you? ... Have me inside of forty-eight hours? Say, will you quit being funny? Now, you let grown men alone and attend to your business of hunting up divorce cases and street-car accidents and printing the filth and scandal that you make your living by. Goodbye, old boy—sorry I haven't time to call on you. I'd feel perfectly safe in your sanctum asinorum. Tra-la!'

'He's as mad as a cat that's lost a mouse,' said Kernan, hanging up the receiver and coming out.

'And now, Barney, my boy, we'll go to a show and enjoy ourselves until a reasonable bedtime. Four hours' sleep for me, and then the west-bound.'

The two dined in a Broadway restaurant. Kernan was pleased with himself. He spent money like a prince of fiction. And then a weird and gorgeous musical comedy engaged their attention. Afterward there was a late supper in a grillroom, with champagne, and Kernan at the height of his complacency.

Half-past three in the morning found them in a corner of an all-night cafe, Kernan still boasting in a vapid and rambling way, Woods thinking moodily over the end that had come to his usefulness as an upholder of the law.

But, as he pondered, his eye brightened with a speculative light.

'I wonder if it's possible,' be said to himself, 'I won-der if it's pos-si-ble!

And then outside the cafe the comparative stillness of the early morning was punctured by faint, uncertain cries that seemed mere fireflies of sound, some growing louder, some fainter, waxing and waning amid the rumble of milk wagons and infrequent cars. Shrill cries they were when near—well-known cries that conveyed many meanings to the ears of those of the slumbering millions of the great city who waked to hear them. Cries that bore upon their significant, small volume the weight of a world's woe and laughter and delight and stress. To some, cowering beneath the protection of a night's ephemeral cover, they brought news of the hideous, bright day; to others, wrapped in happy sleep, they announced a morning that would dawn blacker than sable night. To many of the rich they brought a besom to sweep away what had been theirs while the stars shone; to the poor they brought—another day.

All over the city the cries were starting up, keen and sonorous, heralding the chances that the slipping of one cogwheel in the machinery of time had made; apportioning to the sleepers while they lay at the mercy of fate, the vengeance, profit, grief, reward and doom that the new figure in the calendar had brought them. Shrill and yet plaintive were the cries, as if the young voices grieved that so much evil and so little good was in their irresponsible hands. Thus echoed in the streets of the helpless city the transmission of the latest decrees of the gods, the cries of the newsboys—the Clarion Call of the Press.

Woods flipped a dime to the waiter, and said: 'Get me a Morning Mars.'

When the paper came he glanced at its first page, and then tore a leaf out of his memorandum book and began to write on it with the little old pencil.

'What's the news?' yawned Kernan.

Woods flipped over to him the piece of writing:

'*The New York Morning Mars*: "Please pay to the order of John Kernan the one thousand dollars reward coming to me for his arrest and conviction.

"BARNARD WOODS."

'I kind of thought they would do that,' said Woods, 'when you were jollying them so hard. Now, Johnny, you'll come to the police station with me.

8

THE CONFESSION

Guy de Maupassant

…The apartment had that sinister aspect, that air of hopeless farewells, which belongs to the chambers of the dying…

Marguerite de Thérelles was dying. Although but fifty-six, she seemed like seventy-five at least. She panted, paler than the sheets, shaken by dreadful shiverings, her face convulsed, her eyes haggard, as if she had seen some horrible thing.

Her eldest sister, Suzanne, six years older, sobbed on her knees beside the bed. A little table drawn close to the couch of the dying woman, and covered with a napkin, bore two lighted candles, the priest being momentarily expected to give extreme unction and the communion, which should be the last.

The apartment had that sinister aspect, that air of hopeless farewells, which belongs to the chambers of the dying. Medicine bottles stood about on the furniture, linen lay in the corners, pushed aside by foot or broom. The disordered chairs themselves seemed affrighted, as if they had run, in all the senses of the word. Death, the formidable, was there, hidden, waiting.

The story of the two sisters was very touching. It was quoted far and wide; it had made many eyes weep.

Suzanne, the elder, had once been madly in love with a young man, who had also been in love with her. They were engaged, and were only waiting the day fixed for the contract, when Henry de Lampierre suddenly died.

The despair of the young girl was dreadful, and she vowed that she would never marry. She kept her word. She put on widow's weeds, which she never took off.

Then her sister, her little sister Marguérite, who was only twelve years old, came one morning to throw herself into the arms of the elder, and said: 'Big Sister, I do not want thee to be unhappy. I do not want thee to cry all thy life. I will never leave thee, never, never! I—I, too, shall never marry. I shall stay with thee always, always, always!'

Suzanne, touched by the devotion of the child, kissed her, but did not believe.

Yet the little one, also, kept her word, and despite the entreaties of her parents, despite the supplications of the elder, she never married. She was pretty, very pretty; she refused many a young man who seemed to love her truly; and she never left her sister more.

They lived together all the days of their life, without ever being separated a single time. They went side by side, inseparably united. But Marguérite seemed always sad, oppressed, more melancholy than the elder, as though perhaps her sublime sacrifice had broken her spirit. She aged more quickly, had white hair from the age of thirty, and often suffering, seemed afflicted by some secret, gnawing trouble.

Now she was to be the first to die.

Since yesterday she was no longer able to speak. She had only said, at the first glimmers of day-dawn: 'Go fetch Monsieur le Curé, the moment has come.'

And she had remained since then upon her back, shaken with spasms, her lips agitated as though dreadful words were mounting from her heart without power of issue, her look mad with fear, terrible to see.

Her sister, torn by sorrow, wept wildly, her forehead resting on the edge of the bed, and kept repeating: 'Margot, my poor Margot, my little one!'

She had always called her, 'Little One,' just as the younger had always called her 'Big Sister.'

Steps were heard on the stairs. The door opened. A choir boy appeared, followed by an old priest in a surplice. As soon as she perceived him, the dying woman, with one shudder, sat up, opened her lips, stammered two or three words, and began to scratch the sheets with her nails as if she had wished to make a hole.

The Abbé Simon approached, took her hand, kissed her brow, and with a soft voice: 'God pardon thee, my child; have courage, the moment is now come, speak.'

Then Marguérite, shivering from head to foot, shaking her whole couch with nervous movements, stammered: 'Sit down, Big Sister... listen.'

The priest bent down toward Suzanne, who was still flung upon the bed's foot. He raised her, placed her in an armchair, and taking a hand of each of the sisters in one of his own, he pronounced: 'Lord, my God! Endue them with strength, cast Thy mercy upon them.'

And Marguérite began to speak. The words issued from her throat one by one, raucous, with sharp pauses, as though very feeble.

◆

'Pardon, pardon, Big Sister; oh, forgive! If thou knewest how I have had fear of this moment all my life...'

Suzanne stammered through her tears: 'Forgive thee what, Little One? Thou hast given all to me, sacrificed everything; thou art an angel...'

But Marguérite interrupted her: 'Hush, hush! Let me speak... do not stop me. It is dreadful... let me tell all... to the very end, without flinching. Listen. Thou rememberest... thou rememberest... Henry...'

Suzanne trembled and looked at her sister. The younger continued: 'Thou must hear all, to understand. I was twelve years old, only twelve years old; thou rememberest well, is it not so? And I was spoiled, I did everything that I liked! Thou rememberest, surely, how they spoiled me? Listen. The first time that he came he had varnished boots. He got down from his horse at the great steps, and he begged pardon for his costume, but he came to bring some news to papa. Thou rememberest, is it not so? Don't speak—listen. When I saw him I was completely carried away, I found him so very beautiful; and I remained standing in a corner of the *salon* all the time that he was talking. Children are strange... and terrible. Oh yes... I have dreamed of all that.

'He came back again... several times... I looked at him with all my eyes, with all my soul... I was large of my age... and very much more knowing than anyone thought. He came back often... I thought only of him. I said, very low:

"Henry... Henry de Lampierre!"

'Then they said that he was going to marry thee. It was a sorrow; oh, Big Sister, a sorrow... a sorrow! I cried for three nights without sleeping. He came back every day, in the afternoon, after his lunch... thou rememberest, is it not so? Say nothing... listen. Thou madest him cakes which he liked... with meal, with butter and milk. Oh, I know well how. I could make them yet if it were needed. He ate them at one mouthful, and... and then he drank a glass of wine, and then he said, "It is delicious." Thou rememberest how he would say that?

'I was jealous, jealous! The moment of thy marriage approached. There were only two weeks more. I became crazy. I said to myself: "He shall not marry Suzanne, no, I will not have it! It is I whom he will marry when I am grown up. I shall never find anyone whom I love so much." But one night, ten days before the contract, thou tookest a walk with him in front of the chateau by moonlight... and there... under the fir, under the great fir... he kissed thee... kissed... holding thee in his two arms... so long. Thou rememberest, is it not so? It was probably the first time... yes... Thou wast so pale when thou earnest back to the salon.

'I had seen you two; I was there, in the shrubbery. I was angry! If I could I should have killed you both!

'I said to myself: "He shall not marry Suzanne, never! He shall marry no one. I should be too unhappy." And all of a sudden I began to hate him dreadfully.

'Then, dost thou know what I did? Listen. I had seen the gardener making little balls to kill strange dogs. He pounded up a bottle with a stone and put the powdered glass in a little ball of meat.

'I took a little medicine bottle that mamma had; I broke it small with a hammer, and I hid the glass in my pocket. It was a shining powder... The next day, as soon as you had made the little cakes... I split them with a knife and I put in the glass... He ate three of them... I too, I ate one... I threw the other six into the pond. The two swans died three days after... Dost thou remember? Oh, say nothing... listen, listen. I, I alone did not die... but I have always been sick. Listen... He died—thou knowest well... listen... that, that is nothing. It is afterwards, later... always... the worst... listen.

'My life, all my life... what torture! I said to myself: "I will never leave my sister. And at the hour of death I will tell her all..." There! And ever since, I have always thought of that moment when I should tell thee all. Now it is come. It is terrible. Oh... Big Sister!

'I have always thought, morning and evening, by night and by day, "Some time I must tell her that..." I waited... What agony!... It is done. Say nothing. Now I am afraid... am afraid... oh, I am afraid. If I am going to see him again, soon, when I am dead. See him again... think of it! The first! Before thou! I shall not dare. I must... I am going to die... I want you to forgive me. I want it... I cannot go off to meet him without that. Oh, tell her to forgive me, Monsieur le Curé, tell her... I implore you to do it. I cannot die without that...'

◆

She was silent, and remained panting, always scratching the sheet with her withered nails.

Suzanne had hidden her face in her hands, and did not move. She was thinking of him whom she might have loved so long! What a good life they should have lived together! She saw him once again in that vanished bygone time, in that old past which was put out forever. The beloved dead—how they tear your hearts! Oh, that kiss, his only kiss! She had hidden it in her soul. And after it nothing, nothing more her whole life long!

All of a sudden the priest stood straight, and, with a strong vibrant voice, he cried:

'Mademoiselle Suzanne, your sister is dying!'

Then Suzanne, opening her hands, showed her face soaked with tears, and throwing herself upon her sister, she kissed her with all her might, stammering:

'I forgive thee, I forgive thee, Little One.'

9

THE ADVENTURE OF THE SPECKLED BAND

Arthur Conan Doyle

...It seems to me to be a most dark and sinister business...

On glancing over my notes of the seventy odd cases in which I have during the last eight years studied the methods of my friend Sherlock Holmes, I find many tragic, some comic, a large number merely strange, but none commonplace; for, working as he did rather for the love of his art than for the acquirement of wealth, he refused to associate himself with any investigation which did not tend towards the unusual, and even the fantastic. Of all these varied cases, however, I cannot recall any which presented more singular features than that which was associated with the well-known Surrey family of the Roylotts of Stoke Moran. The events in question occurred in the early days of my association with Holmes, when we were sharing rooms as bachelors in Baker Street. It is possible that I might have placed them upon record before, but a promise of secrecy was made at the time, from which I have only been freed during the last month by the untimely death of the lady to whom the pledge was given. It is perhaps as well that the facts should now come to light, for I have reasons to know that there are widespread rumours as to the death of Dr Grimesby Roylott which tend to make the matter even more terrible than the truth.

It was early in April in the year '83 that I woke one morning to find Sherlock Holmes standing, fully dressed, by the side of my bed. He was a late riser, as a rule, and as the clock on the mantelpiece showed me that it was only a quarter-past seven, I blinked up at him in some surprise, and perhaps just a little resentment, for I was myself regular in my habits.

'Very sorry to knock you up, Watson,' said he, 'but it's the common lot this morning. Mrs Hudson has been knocked up, she retorted upon me, and I on you.'

'What is it, then—a fire?'

'No; a client. It seems that a young lady has arrived in a considerable state of excitement, who insists upon seeing me. She is waiting now in the sitting-room. Now, when young ladies wander about the metropolis at this hour of the morning, and knock sleepy people up out of their beds, I presume that it is something very pressing which they have to communicate. Should it prove to be an interesting case, you would, I am sure, wish to follow it from the outset. I thought, at any rate, that I should call you and give you the chance.'

'My dear fellow, I would not miss it for anything.'

I had no keener pleasure than in following Holmes in his professional investigations, and in admiring the rapid deductions, as swift as intuitions, and yet always founded on a logical basis with which he unravelled the problems which were submitted to him. I rapidly threw on my clothes and was ready in a few minutes to accompany my friend down to the sitting-room. A lady dressed in black and heavily veiled, who had been sitting in the window, rose as we entered.

'Good-morning, madam,' said Holmes cheerily. 'My name is Sherlock Holmes. This is my intimate friend and associate, Dr Watson, before whom you can speak as freely as before myself. Ha! I am glad to see that Mrs Hudson has had the good sense to light the fire. Pray draw up to it, and I shall order you a cup of hot coffee, for I observe that you are shivering.'

'It is not cold which makes me shiver,' said the woman in a low voice, changing her seat as requested.

'What, then?'

'It is fear, Mr Holmes. It is terror.' She raised her veil as she spoke, and we could see that she was indeed in a pitiable state of agitation, her face all drawn and grey, with restless frightened eyes, like those of some hunted animal. Her features and figure were those of a woman of thirty, but her hair was shot with premature grey, and her expression was weary and haggard. Sherlock Holmes ran her over with one of his quick, all-comprehensive glances.

'You must not fear,' said he soothingly, bending forward and patting her forearm. 'We shall soon set matters right, I have no doubt. You have come in by train this morning, I see.'

'You know me, then?'

'No, but I observe the second half of a return ticket in the palm of your left glove. You must have started early, and yet you had a good drive in a dog-cart, along heavy roads, before you reached the station.'

The lady gave a violent start and stared in bewilderment at my companion.

'There is no mystery, my dear madam,' said he, smiling. 'The left arm of your jacket is spattered with mud in no less than seven places. The marks are perfectly fresh. There is no vehicle save a dog-cart which throws up mud in that way, and then only when you sit on the left-hand side of the driver.'

'Whatever your reasons may be, you are perfectly correct,' said she. 'I started from home before six, reached Leatherhead at twenty past, and came in by the first train to Waterloo. Sir, I can stand this strain no longer; I shall go mad if it continues. I have no one to turn to—none, save only one, who cares for me, and he, poor fellow, can be of little aid. I have heard of you, Mr Holmes; I have heard of you from Mrs Farintosh, whom you helped in the hour of her sore need. It was from her that I had your address. Oh, sir, do you not think that you could help me, too, and at least throw a little light through the dense darkness which surrounds me? At present it is out of my power to reward you for your services, but in a month or six weeks I shall be married, with the control of my own income, and then at least you shall not find me ungrateful.'

Holmes turned to his desk and, unlocking it, drew out a small case-book, which he consulted.

'Farintosh,' said he. 'Ah yes, I recall the case; it was concerned with an opal tiara. I think it was before your time, Watson. I can only say, madam, that I shall be happy to devote the same care to your case as I did to that of your friend. As to reward, my profession is its own reward; but you are at liberty to defray whatever expenses

I may be put to, at the time which suits you best. And now I beg that you will lay before us everything that may help us in forming an opinion upon the matter.'

'Alas!' replied our visitor, 'the very horror of my situation lies in the fact that my fears are so vague, and my suspicions depend so entirely upon small points, which might seem trivial to another, that even he to whom of all others I have a right to look for help and advice looks upon all that I tell him about it as the fancies of a nervous woman. He does not say so, but I can read it from his soothing answers and averted eyes. But I have heard, Mr Holmes, that you can see deeply into the manifold wickedness of the human heart. You may advise me how to walk amid the dangers which encompass me.'

'I am all attention, madam.'

'My name is Helen Stoner, and I am living with my stepfather, who is the last survivor of one of the oldest Saxon families in England, the Roylotts of Stoke Moran, on the western border of Surrey.'

Holmes nodded his head. 'The name is familiar to me,' said he.

'The family was at one time among the richest in England, and the estates extended over the borders into Berkshire in the north, and Hampshire in the west. In the last century, however, four successive heirs were of a dissolute and wasteful disposition, and the family ruin was eventually completed by a gambler in the days of the Regency. Nothing was left save a few acres of ground, and the two-hundred-year-old house, which is itself crushed under a heavy mortgage. The last squire dragged out his existence there, living the horrible life of an aristocratic pauper; but his only son, my stepfather, seeing that he must adapt himself to the new conditions, obtained an advance from a relative, which enabled him to take a medical degree and went out to Calcutta, where, by his professional skill and his force of character, he established a large practice. In a fit of anger, however, caused by some robberies which had been perpetrated in the house, he beat his native butler to death and narrowly escaped a capital sentence. As it was, he suffered a long term of imprisonment and afterwards returned to England a morose and disappointed man.

'When Dr Roylott was in India he married my mother, Mrs Stoner, the young widow of Major-General Stoner, of the Bengal Artillery. My sister Julia and I were twins, and we were only two years old at the time of my mother's re-marriage. She had a considerable sum of money—not less than £ 1000 a year—and this she bequeathed to Dr Roylott entirely while we resided with him, with a provision that a certain annual sum should be allowed to each of us in the event of our marriage. Shortly after our return to England my mother died— she was killed eight years ago in a railway accident near Crewe. Dr Roylott then abandoned his attempts to establish himself in practice in London and took us to live with him in the old ancestral house at Stoke Moran. The money which my mother had left was enough for all our wants, and there seemed to be no obstacle to our happiness.

'But a terrible change came over our stepfather about this time. Instead of making friends and exchanging visits with our neighbours, who had at first been overjoyed to see a Roylott of Stoke Moran back in the old family seat, he shut himself up in his house and seldom came out save to indulge in ferocious quarrels with whoever might cross his path. Violence of temper approaching to mania has been hereditary in the men of the family, and in my stepfather's case it had, I believe, been intensified by his long residence in the tropics. A series of disgraceful brawls took place, two of which ended in the police-court, until at last he became the terror of the village, and the folks would fly at his approach, for he is a man of immense strength, and absolutely uncontrollable in his anger.

'Last week he hurled the local blacksmith over a parapet into a stream, and it was only by paying over all the money which I could gather together that I was able to avert another public exposure. He had no friends at all save the wandering gipsies, and he would give these vagabonds leave to encamp upon the few acres of bramble-covered land which represent the family estate, and would accept in return the hospitality of their tents, wandering away with them sometimes for weeks on end. He has a passion also for Indian animals, which are sent over to him by a correspondent, and he has at this moment a cheetah and a baboon, which wander freely over his grounds and are feared by the villagers almost as much as their master.

'You can imagine from what I say that my poor sister Julia and I had no great pleasure in our lives. No servant would stay with us, and for a long time we did all the work of the house. She was but thirty at the time of her death, and yet her hair had already begun to whiten, even as mine has.'

'Your sister is dead, then?'

'She died just two years ago, and it is of her death that I wish to speak to you. You can understand that, living the life which I have described, we were little likely to see anyone of our own age and position. We had, however, an aunt, my mother's maiden sister, Miss Honoria Westphail, who lives near Harrow, and we were occasionally allowed to pay short visits at this lady's house. Julia went there at Christmas two years ago, and met there a half-pay major of marines, to whom she became engaged. My stepfather learned of the engagement when my sister returned and offered no objection to the marriage; but within a fortnight of the day which had been fixed for the wedding, the terrible event occurred which has deprived me of my only companion.'

Sherlock Holmes had been leaning back in his chair with his eyes closed and his head sunk in a cushion, but he half opened his lids now and glanced across at his visitor.

'Pray be precise as to details,' said he.

'It is easy for me to be so, for every event of that dreadful time is seared into my memory. The manor-house is, as I have already said, very old, and only one wing is now inhabited. The bedrooms in this wing are on the ground floor, the sitting-rooms being in the central block of the buildings. Of these bedrooms the first is Dr Roylott's, the second my sister's, and the third my own. There is no communication between them, but they all open out into the same corridor. Do I make myself plain?'

'Perfectly so.'

'The windows of the three rooms open out upon the lawn. That fatal night Dr Roylott had gone to his room early, though we knew that he had not retired to rest, for my sister was troubled by the smell of the strong Indian cigars which it was his custom to smoke. She left her room, therefore, and came into mine, where she sat for some time, chatting about her approaching wedding. At eleven o'clock she rose to leave me, but she paused at the door and looked back.

'"Tell me, Helen," said she, "have you ever heard anyone whistle in the dead of the night?"

'"Never," said I.

'"I suppose that you could not possibly whistle, yourself, in your sleep?"

'"Certainly not. But why?"

'"Because during the last few nights I have always, about three in the morning, heard a low, clear whistle. I am a light sleeper, and it has awakened me. I cannot tell where it came from—perhaps from the next room, perhaps from the lawn. I thought that I would just ask you whether you had heard it."

'"No, I have not. It must be those wretched gipsies in the plantation."

'"Very likely. And yet if it were on the lawn, I wonder that you did not hear it also."

'"Ah, but I sleep more heavily than you."

'"Well, it is of no great consequence, at any rate." She smiled back at me, closed my door, and a few moments later I heard her key turn in the lock.'

'Indeed,' said Holmes. 'Was it your custom always to lock yourselves in at night?'

'Always.'

'And why?'

'I think that I mentioned to you that the Doctor kept a cheetah and a baboon. We had no feeling of security unless our doors were locked.'

'Quite so. Pray proceed with your statement.'

'I could not sleep that night. A vague feeling of impending misfortune impressed me. My sister and I, you will recollect, were twins, and you know how subtle are the links which bind two souls which are so closely allied. It was a wild night. The wind was howling outside, and the rain was beating and splashing against the windows. Suddenly, amid all the hubbub of the gale, there burst forth the wild scream of a terrified woman. I knew that it was my sister's voice. I sprang from my bed, wrapped a shawl round me, and rushed into the corridor. As I opened my door I seemed to hear a low whistle, such as my sister described, and a few moments later a clanging sound, as if a mass of metal had fallen. As I ran down the passage, my sister's door was unlocked, and revolved slowly upon its hinges. I stared at it horror-stricken, not knowing what was about to issue from it. By the light of the corridor-lamp I saw my sister appear at the opening, her face blanched with terror, her hands groping for help, her whole figure swaying to and fro like that of a drunkard. I ran to her and threw my arms round her, but at that moment her knees seemed to give way and she fell to the ground. She writhed as one who is in terrible pain, and her limbs were dreadfully convulsed. At first I thought that she had not recognized me, but as I bent over her she suddenly shrieked out in a voice which I shall never forget, 'Oh, my God! Helen! It was the band! The speckled band!' There was something else which she would fain have said, and she stabbed with her finger into the air in the direction of the Doctor's room, but a fresh convulsion seized her and choked her words. I rushed out, calling loudly for my stepfather, and I met him hastening from his room in his dressing-gown. When he reached my sister's side she was unconscious, and though he poured brandy down her throat and sent for medical aid from the village, all efforts were in vain, for she slowly sank and died without having recovered her consciousness. Such was the dreadful end of my beloved sister.'

'One moment,' said Holmes, 'are you sure about this whistle and metallic sound? Could you swear to it?'

'That was what the county coroner asked me at the inquiry. It is my strong impression that I heard it, and yet, among the crash of the gale and the creaking of an old house, I may possibly have been deceived.'

'Was your sister dressed?'

'No, she was in her night-dress. In her right hand was found the charred stump of a match, and in her left a match-box.'

'Showing that she had struck a light and looked about her when the alarm took place. That is important. And what conclusions did the coroner come to?'

'He investigated the case with great care, for Dr Roylott's conduct had long been notorious in the county, but he was unable to find any satisfactory cause of death. My evidence showed that the door had been fastened upon the inner side, and the windows were blocked by old-fashioned shutters with broad iron bars, which were secured every night. The walls were carefully sounded, and were shown to be quite solid all round, and the flooring was also thoroughly examined, with the same result. The chimney is wide, but is barred up by four large staples. It is certain, therefore, that my sister was quite alone when she met her end. Besides, there were no marks of any violence upon her.'

'How about poison?'

'The doctors examined her for it, but without success.'

'What do you think that this unfortunate lady died of, then?'

'It is my belief that she died of pure fear and nervous shock, though what it was that frightened her I cannot imagine.'

'Were there gypsies in the plantation at the time?'

'Yes, there are nearly always some there.'

'Ah, and what did you gather from this allusion to a band—a speckled band?'

'Sometimes I have thought that it was merely the wild talk of delirium, sometimes that it may have referred to some band of people, perhaps to these very gipsies in the plantation. I do not know whether the spotted handkerchiefs which so many of them wear over their heads might have suggested the strange adjective which she used.'

Holmes shook his head like a man who is far from being satisfied.

'These are very deep waters,' said he; 'pray go on with your narrative.'

'Two years have passed since then, and my life has been until lately lonelier than ever. A month ago, however, a dear friend, whom I have known for many years, has done me the honour to ask my hand in marriage. His name is Armitage—Percy Armitage—the second son of Mr Armitage, of Crane Water, near Reading. My stepfather has offered no opposition to the match, and we are to be married in the course of the spring. Two days ago some repairs were started in the west wing of the building, and my bedroom wall has been pierced, so that I have had to move into the chamber in which my sister died, and to sleep in the very bed in which she slept. Imagine, then, my thrill of terror when last night, as I lay awake, thinking over her terrible fate, I suddenly heard in the silence of the night the low whistle which had been the herald of her own death. I sprang up and lit the lamp, but nothing was to be seen in the room. I was too shaken to go to bed again, however, so I dressed, and as soon as it was daylight I slipped down, got a dog-cart at the Crown Inn, which is opposite, and drove to Leatherhead, from whence I have come on this morning with the one object of seeing you and asking your advice.'

'You have done wisely,' said my friend. 'But have you told me all?'

'Yes, all.'

'Miss Roylott, you have not. You are screening your stepfather.'

'Why, what do you mean?'

For answer Holmes pushed back the frill of black lace which fringed the hand that lay upon our visitor's knee. Five little livid spots, the marks of four fingers and a thumb, were printed upon the white wrist.

'You have been cruelly used,' said Holmes.

The lady coloured deeply and covered over her injured wrist. 'He is a hard man,' she said, 'and perhaps he hardly knows his own strength.'

There was a long silence, during which Holmes leaned his chin upon his hands and stared into the crackling fire.

'This is a very deep business,' he said at last. 'There are a thousand details which I should desire to know before I decide upon our course of action. Yet we have not a moment to lose. If we were to come to Stoke Moran to-day, would it be possible for us to see over these rooms without the knowledge of your stepfather?'

'As it happens, he spoke of coming into town to-day upon some most important business. It is probable that he will be away all day, and that there would be nothing to disturb you. We have a housekeeper now, but she is old and foolish, and I could easily get her out of the way.'

'Excellent. You are not averse to this trip, Watson?'

'By no means.'

'Then we shall both come. What are you going to do yourself?'

'I have one or two things which I would wish to do now that I am in town. But I shall return by the twelve o'clock train, so as to be there in time for your coming.'

'And you may expect us early in the afternoon. I have myself some small business matters to attend to. Will you not wait and breakfast?'

'No, I must go. My heart is lightened already since I have confided my trouble to you. I shall look forward to seeing you again this afternoon.' She dropped her thick black veil over her face and glided from the room.

'And what do you think of it all, Watson?' asked Sherlock Holmes, leaning back in his chair.

'It seems to me to be a most dark and sinister business.'

'Dark enough and sinister enough.'

'Yet if the lady is correct in saying that the flooring and walls are sound, and that the door, window, and chimney are impassable, then her sister must have been undoubtedly alone when she met her mysterious end.'

'What becomes, then, of these nocturnal whistles, and what of the very peculiar words of the dying woman?'

'I cannot think.'

'When you combine the ideas of whistles at night, the presence of a band of gipsies who are on intimate terms with this old doctor, the fact that we have every reason to believe that the doctor has an interest in preventing his stepdaughter's marriage, the dying allusion to a band, and, finally, the fact that Miss Helen Stoner heard a metallic clang, which might have been caused by one of those metal bars that secured the shutters falling back into its place, I think that there is good ground to think that the mystery may be cleared along those lines.'

'But what, then, did the gipsies do?'

'I cannot imagine.'

'I see many objections to any such theory.'

'And so do I. It is precisely for that reason that we are going to Stoke Moran this day. I want to see whether the objections are fatal, or if they may be explained away. But what in the name of the devil!'

The ejaculation had been drawn from my companion by the fact that our door had been suddenly dashed open, and that a huge man had framed himself in the aperture. His costume was a peculiar mixture of the professional and of the agricultural, having a black top-hat, a long frock-coat, and a pair of high gaiters, with a hunting-crop swinging in his hand. So tall was he that his hat actually brushed the cross bar of the doorway, and his breadth seemed to span it across from side to side. A large face, seared with a thousand wrinkles, burned yellow with the sun, and marked with every evil passion, was turned from one to the other of us, while his deep-set, bile-shot eyes, and his high, thin, fleshless nose, gave him somewhat the resemblance to a fierce old bird of prey.

'Which of you is Holmes?' asked this apparition.

'My name, sir; but you have the advantage of me,' said my companion quietly.

'I am Dr Grimesby Roylott, of Stoke Moran.'

'Indeed, Doctor,' said Holmes blandly. 'Pray take a seat.'

'I will do nothing of the kind. My stepdaughter has been here. I have traced her. What has she been saying to you?'

'It is a little cold for the time of the year,' said Holmes.

'What has she been saying to you?' screamed the old man furiously.

'But I have heard that the crocuses promise well,' continued my companion imperturbably.

'Ha! You put me off, do you?' said our new visitor, taking a step forward and shaking his hunting-crop. 'I know you, you scoundrel! I have heard of you before. You are Holmes, the meddler.'

My friend smiled.

'Holmes, the busybody!'

His smile broadened.

'Holmes, the Scotland Yard Jack-in-office!'

Holmes chuckled heartily. 'Your conversation is most entertaining,' said he. 'When you go out close the door, for there is a decided draught.'

'I will go when I have had my say. Don't you dare to meddle with my affairs. I know that Miss Stoner has been here. I traced her! I am a dangerous man to fall foul of! See here.' He stepped swiftly forward, seized the poker, and bent it into a curve with his huge brown hands.

'See that you keep yourself out of my grip,' he snarled, and hurling the twisted poker into the fireplace he strode out of the room.

'He seems a very amiable person,' said Holmes, laughing. 'I am not quite so bulky, but if he had remained I might have shown him that my grip was not much more feeble than his own.' As he spoke he picked up the steel poker and, with a sudden effort, straightened it out again.

'Fancy his having the insolence to confound me with the official detective force! This incident gives zest to our investigation, however, and I only trust that our little friend will not suffer from her imprudence in allowing this brute to trace her. And now, Watson, we shall order breakfast, and afterwards I shall walk down to Doctors' Commons, where I hope to get some data which may help us in this matter.'

It was nearly one o'clock when Sherlock Holmes returned from his excursion. He held in his hand a sheet of blue paper, scrawled over with notes and figures.

'I have seen the will of the deceased wife,' said he. 'To determine its exact meaning I have been obliged to work out the present prices of the investments with which it is concerned. The total income, which at the time of the wife's death was little short of £ 1,100, is now, through the fall in agricultural prices, not more than £ 750. Each daughter can claim an income of £ 250, in case of marriage. It is evident, therefore, that if both girls had married, this beauty would have had a mere pittance, while even one of them would cripple him to a very serious extent. My morning's work has not been wasted, since it has proved that he has the very strongest motives for standing in the way of anything of the sort. And now, Watson, this is too serious for dawdling, especially as the old man is aware that we are interesting ourselves in his affairs; so if you are ready, we shall call a cab and drive to Waterloo. I should be very much obliged if you would slip your revolver into your pocket. An Eley's No. 2 is an excellent argument with gentlemen who can twist steel pokers into knots. That and a tooth-brush are, I think, all that we need.'

At Waterloo we were fortunate in catching a train for Leatherhead, where we hired a trap at the station inn and drove for four or five miles through the lovely Surrey lanes. It was a perfect day, with a bright sun and a few fleecy clouds in the heavens. The trees and wayside hedges were just throwing out their first green shoots, and the air was full of the pleasant smell of the moist earth. To me at least there was a strange contrast between the sweet promise of the spring and this sinister quest upon which we were engaged. My companion sat in the front of the trap, his arms folded, his hat pulled down over his eyes, and his chin sunk upon his breast, buried in the deepest thought. Suddenly, however, he started, tapped me on the shoulder, and pointed over the meadows.

'Look there!' said he.

A heavily timbered park stretched up in a gentle slope, thickening into a grove at the highest point. From amid the branches there jutted out the grey gables and high roof-tree of a very old mansion.

'Stoke Moran?' said he.

'Yes, sir, that be the house of Dr Grimesby Roylott,' remarked the driver.

'There is some building going on there,' said Holmes; 'that is where we are going.'

'There's the village,' said the driver, pointing to a cluster of roofs some distance to the left; 'but if you want to get to the house, you'll find it shorter to get over this stile, and so by the footpath over the fields. There it is, where the lady is walking.'

'And the lady, I fancy, is Miss Stoner,' observed Holmes, shading his eyes. 'Yes, I think we had better do as you suggest.'

We got off, paid our fare, and the trap rattled back on its way to Leatherhead.

'I thought it as well,' said Holmes as we climbed the stile, 'that this fellow should think we had come here as architects, or on some definite business. It may stop his gossip. Good-afternoon, Miss Stoner. You see that we have been as good as our word.'

Our client of the morning had hurried forward to meet us with a face which spoke her joy. 'I have been waiting so eagerly for you,' she cried, shaking hands with us warmly. 'All has turned out splendidly.

Dr Roylott has gone to town, and it is unlikely that he will be back before evening.'

'We have had the pleasure of making the Doctor's acquaintance,' said Holmes, and in a few words he sketched out what had occurred. Miss Stoner turned white to the lips as she listened.

'Good heavens!' she cried, 'he has followed me, then.'

'So it appears.'

'He is so cunning that I never know when I am safe from him. What will he say when he returns?'

'He must guard himself, for he may find that there is someone more cunning than himself upon his track. You must lock yourself up from him to-night. If he is violent, we shall take you away to your aunt's at Harrow. Now, we must make the best use of our time, so kindly take us at once to the rooms which we are to examine.'

The building was of grey, lichen-blotched stone, with a high central portion and two curving wings, like the claws of a crab, thrown out on each side. In one of these wings the windows were broken and blocked with wooden boards, while the roof was partly caved in, a picture of ruin. The central portion was in little better repair, but the right-hand block was comparatively modern, and the blinds in the windows, with the blue smoke curling up from the chimneys, showed that this was where the family resided. Some scaffolding had been erected against the end wall, and the stone-work had been broken into, but there were no signs of any workmen at the moment of our visit. Holmes walked slowly up and down the ill-trimmed lawn and examined with deep attention the outsides of the windows.

'This, I take it, belongs to the room in which you used to sleep, the centre one to your sister's, and the one next to the main building to Dr Roylott's chamber?'

'Exactly so. But I am now sleeping in the middle one.'

'Pending the alterations, as I understand. By the way, there does not seem to be any very pressing need for repairs at that end wall.'

'There were none. I believe that it was an excuse to move me from my room.'

'Ah! that is suggestive. Now, on the other side of this narrow wing runs the corridor from which these three rooms open. There are windows in it, of course?'

'Yes, but very small ones. Too narrow for anyone to pass through.'

'As you both locked your doors at night, your rooms were unapproachable from that side. Now, would you have the kindness to go into your room and bar your shutters?'

Miss Stoner did so, and Holmes, after a careful examination through the open window, endeavoured in every way to force the shutter open, but without success. There was no slit through which a knife could be passed to raise the bar. Then with his lens he tested the hinges, but they were of solid iron, built firmly into the massive masonry. 'Hum!' said he, scratching his chin in some perplexity, 'my theory certainly presents some difficulties. No one could pass these shutters if they were bolted. Well, we shall see if the inside throws any light upon the matter.'

A small side door led into the whitewashed corridor from which the three bedrooms opened. Holmes refused to examine the third chamber, so we passed at once to the second, that in which Miss Stoner was now sleeping, and in which her sister had met with her fate. It was a homely little room, with a low ceiling and a gaping fireplace, after the fashion of old country-houses. A brown chest of drawers stood in one corner, a narrow white-counterpaned bed in another, and a dressing-table on the left-hand side of the window. These articles, with two small wicker-work chairs, made up all the furniture in the room save for a square of Wilton carpet in the centre. The boards round and the panelling of the walls were of brown, worm-eaten oak, so old and discoloured that it may have dated from the original building of the house. Holmes drew one of the chairs into a corner and sat silent, while his eyes travelled round and round and up and down, taking in every detail of the apartment.

'Where does that bell communicate with?' he asked at last pointing to a thick bell-rope which hung down beside the bed, the tassel actually lying upon the pillow.

'It goes to the housekeeper's room.'

'It looks newer than the other things?'

'Yes, it was only put there a couple of years ago.'

'Your sister asked for it, I suppose?'

'No, I never heard of her using it. We used always to get what we wanted for ourselves.'

'Indeed, it seemed unnecessary to put so nice a bell-pull there. You will excuse me for a few minutes while I satisfy myself as to this floor.' He threw himself down upon his face with his lens in his hand and crawled swiftly backward and forward, examining minutely the cracks between the boards. Then he did the same with the wood-work with which the chamber was panelled. Finally he walked over to the bed and spent some time in staring at it and in running his eye up and down the wall. Finally he took the bell-rope in his hand and gave it a brisk tug.

'Why, it's a dummy,' said he.

'Won't it ring?'

'No, it is not even attached to a wire. This is very interesting. You can see now that it is fastened to a hook just above where the little opening for the ventilator is.'

'How very absurd! I never noticed that before.'

'Very strange!' muttered Holmes, pulling at the rope. 'There are one or two very singular points about this room. For example, what a fool a builder must be to open a ventilator into another room, when, with the same trouble, he might have communicated with the outside air!'

'That is also quite modern,' said the lady.

'Done about the same time as the bell-rope?' remarked Holmes.

'Yes, there were several little changes carried out about that time.'

'They seem to have been of a most interesting character—dummy bell-ropes, and ventilators which do not ventilate. With your permission, Miss Stoner, we shall now carry our researches into the inner apartment.'

Dr Grimesby Roylott's chamber was larger than that of his stepdaughter, but was as plainly furnished. A camp-bed, a small wooden shelf full of books, mostly of a technical character, an armchair beside the bed, a plain wooden chair against the wall, a round table, and a large iron safe were the principal things which met the eye. Holmes walked slowly round and examined each and all of them with the keenest interest.

'What's in here?' he asked, tapping the safe.

'My stepfather's business papers.'

'Oh! you have seen inside, then?'

'Only once, some years ago. I remember that it was full of papers.'

'There isn't a cat in it, for example?'

'No. What a strange idea!'

'Well, look at this!' He took up a small saucer of milk which stood on the top of it.

'No; we don't keep a cat. But there is a cheetah and a baboon.'

'Ah, yes, of course! Well, a cheetah is just a big cat, and yet a saucer of milk does not go very far in satisfying its wants, I daresay. There is one point which I should wish to determine.' He squatted down in front of the wooden chair and examined the seat of it with the greatest attention.

'Thank you. That is quite settled,' said he, rising and putting his lens in his pocket. 'Hullo! Here is something interesting!'

The object which had caught his eye was a small dog lash hung on one corner of the bed. The lash, however, was curled upon itself and tied so as to make a loop of whipcord.

'What do you make of that, Watson?'

'It's a common enough lash. But I don't know why it should be tied.'

'That is not quite so common, is it? Ah, me! it's a wicked world, and when a clever man turns his brains to crime it is the worst of all. I think that I have seen enough now, Miss Stoner, and with your permission we shall walk out upon the lawn.'

I had never seen my friend's face so grim or his brow so dark as it was when we turned from the scene of this investigation. We had walked several times up and down the lawn, neither Miss Stoner nor myself liking to break in upon his thoughts before he roused himself from his reverie.

'It is very essential, Miss Stoner,' said he, 'that you should absolutely follow my advice in every respect.'

'I shall most certainly do so.'

'The matter is too serious for any hesitation. Your life may depend upon your compliance.'

'I assure you that I am in your hands.'

'In the first place, both my friend and I must spend the night in your room.'

Both Miss Stoner and I gazed at him in astonishment.

'Yes, it must be so. Let me explain. I believe that that is the village inn over there?'

'Yes, that is the Crown.'

'Very good. Your windows would be visible from there?'

'Certainly.'

'You must confine yourself to your room, on pretence of a headache, when your stepfather comes back. Then when you hear him retire for the night, you must open the shutters of your window, undo the hasp, put your lamp there as a signal to us, and then withdraw quietly with everything which you are likely to want into the room which you used to occupy. I have no doubt that, in spite of the repairs, you could manage there for one night.'

'Oh, yes, easily.'

'The rest you will leave in our hands.'

'But what will you do?'

'We shall spend the night in your room, and we shall investigate the cause of this noise which has disturbed you.'

'I believe, Mr Holmes, that you have already made up your mind,' said Miss Stoner, laying her hand upon my companion's sleeve.

'Perhaps I have.'

'Then, for pity's sake, tell me what was the cause of my sister's death.'

'I should prefer to have clearer proofs before I speak.'

'You can at least tell me whether my own thought is correct, and if she died from some sudden fright.'

'No, I do not think so. I think that there was probably some more tangible cause. And now, Miss Stoner, we must leave you for if Dr Roylott returned and saw us our journey would be in vain. Good-bye, and be brave, for if you will do what I have told you, you may rest assured that we shall soon drive away the dangers that threaten you.'

Sherlock Holmes and I had no difficulty in engaging a bedroom and sitting-room at the Crown Inn. They were on the upper floor, and from our window we could command a view of the avenue gate, and of the inhabited wing of Stoke Moran Manor House. At dusk we saw Dr Grimesby Roylott drive past, his huge form looming up beside the little figure of the lad who drove him. The boy had some slight difficulty in undoing the heavy iron gates, and we heard the hoarse roar of the Doctor's voice and saw the fury with which he shook his clinched fists at him. The trap drove on, and a few minutes later we saw a sudden light spring up among the trees as the lamp was lit in one of the sitting-rooms.

'Do you know, Watson,' said Holmes as we sat together in the gathering darkness, 'I have really some scruples as to taking you to-night. There is a distinct element of danger.'

'Can I be of assistance?'

'Your presence might be invaluable.'

'Then I shall certainly come.'

'It is very kind of you.'

'You speak of danger. You have evidently seen more in these rooms than was visible to me.'

'No, but I fancy that I may have deduced a little more. I imagine that you saw all that I did.'

'I saw nothing remarkable save the bell-rope, and what purpose that could answer I confess is more than I can imagine.'

'You saw the ventilator, too?'

'Yes, but I do not think that it is such a very unusual thing to have a small opening between two rooms. It was so small that a rat could hardly pass through.'

'I knew that we should find a ventilator before ever we came to Stoke Moran.'

'My dear Holmes!'

'Oh, yes, I did. You remember in her statement she said that her sister could smell Dr Roylott's cigar. Now, of course that suggested at once that there must be a communication between the two rooms. It could only be a small one, or it would have been remarked upon at the coroner's inquiry. I deduced a ventilator.'

'But what harm can there be in that?'

'Well, there is at least a curious coincidence of dates. A ventilator is made, a cord is hung, and a lady who sleeps in the bed dies. Does not that strike you?'

'I cannot as yet see any connection.'

'Did you observe anything very peculiar about that bed?'

'No.'

'It was clamped to the floor. Did you ever see a bed fastened like that before?'

'I cannot say that I have.'

'The lady could not move her bed. It must always be in the same relative position to the ventilator and to the rope—or so we may call it, since it was clearly never meant for a bell-pull.'

'Holmes,' I cried, 'I seem to see dimly what you are hinting at. We are only just in time to prevent some subtle and horrible crime.'

'Subtle enough and horrible enough. When a doctor does go wrong he is the first of criminals. He has nerve and he has knowledge. Palmer and Pritchard were among the heads of their profession. This man strikes even deeper, but I think, Watson, that we shall be able to strike deeper still. But we shall have horrors enough before the night is over; for goodness' sake let us have a quiet pipe and turn our minds for a few hours to something more cheerful.'

About nine o'clock the light among the trees was extinguished, and all was dark in the direction of the Manor House. Two hours passed slowly away, and then, suddenly, just at the stroke of eleven, a single bright light shone out right in front of us.

'That is our signal,' said Holmes, springing to his feet; 'it comes from the middle window.'

As we passed out he exchanged a few words with the landlord, explaining that we were going on a late visit to an acquaintance, and that it was possible that we might spend the night there. A moment later we were out on the dark road, a chill wind blowing in our faces, and one yellow light twinkling in front of us through the gloom to guide us on our sombre errand.

There was little difficulty in entering the grounds, for unrepaired breaches gaped in the old park wall. Making our way among the trees, we reached the lawn, crossed it, and were about to enter through the window when out from a clump of laurel bushes there darted what seemed to be a hideous and distorted child, who threw itself upon the grass with writhing limbs and then ran swiftly across the lawn into the darkness.

'My God!' I whispered; 'did you see it?'

Holmes was for the moment as startled as I. His hand closed like a vice upon my wrist in his agitation. Then he broke into a low laugh and put his lips to my ear.

'It is a nice household,' he murmured. 'That is the baboon.'

I had forgotten the strange pets which the Doctor affected. There was a cheetah, too; perhaps we might find it upon our shoulders at any moment. I confess that I felt easier in my mind when, after following Holmes' example and slipping off my shoes, I found myself inside the bedroom. My companion noiselessly closed the shutters, moved the lamp onto the table, and cast his eyes round the room. All was as we had seen it in the daytime. Then creeping up to me and making a trumpet of his hand, he whispered into my ear again so gently that it was all that I could do to distinguish the words:

'The least sound would be fatal to our plans.'

I nodded to show that I had heard.

'We must sit without light. He would see it through the ventilator.'

I nodded again.

'Do not go asleep; your very life may depend upon it. Have your pistol ready in case we should need it. I will sit on the side of the bed, and you in that chair.'

I took out my revolver and laid it on the corner of the table.

Holmes had brought up a long thin cane, and this he placed upon the bed beside him. By it he laid the box of matches and the stump of a candle. Then he turned down the lamp, and we were left in darkness.

How shall I ever forget that dreadful vigil? I could not hear a sound, not even the drawing of a breath, and yet I knew that my companion sat open-eyed, within a few feet of me, in the same state of nervous tension in which I was myself. The shutters cut off the least ray of light, and we waited in absolute darkness.

From outside came the occasional cry of a night-bird, and once at our very window a long drawn catlike whine, which told us that the cheetah was indeed at liberty. Far away we could hear the deep tones of the parish clock, which boomed out every quarter of an hour. How long they seemed, those quarters! Twelve struck, and one and two and three, and still we sat waiting silently for whatever might befall.

Suddenly there was the momentary gleam of a light up in the direction of the ventilator, which vanished immediately, but was succeeded by a strong smell of burning oil and heated metal. Someone in the next room had lit a dark-lantern. I heard a gentle sound of movement, and then all was silent once more, though the smell grew stronger. For half an hour I sat with straining ears. Then suddenly another sound became audible—a very gentle, soothing sound, like that of a small jet of steam escaping continually from a kettle. The instant that we heard it, Holmes sprang from the bed, struck a match, and lashed furiously with his cane at the bell-pull.

'You see it, Watson?' he yelled. 'You see it?'

But I saw nothing. At the moment when Holmes struck the light I heard a low, clear whistle, but the sudden glare flashing into my weary eyes made it impossible for me to tell what it was at which my friend lashed so savagely. I could, however, see that his face was deadly pale and filled with horror and loathing. He had ceased to strike and was gazing up at the ventilator when suddenly there broke from the silence of the night the most horrible cry to which I have ever listened. It swelled up louder and louder, a hoarse yell of pain and fear and anger all mingled in the one dreadful shriek. They say that away down in the village, and even in the distant parsonage, that cry raised the sleepers from their beds. It struck cold to our hearts, and I stood gazing at Holmes, and he at me, until the last echoes of it had died away into the silence from which it rose.

'What can it mean?' I gasped.

'It means that it is all over,' Holmes answered. 'And perhaps, after all, it is for the best. Take your pistol, and we will enter Dr Roylott's room.'

With a grave face he lit the lamp and led the way down the corridor. Twice he struck at the chamber door without any reply from within. Then he turned the handle and entered, I at his heels, with the cocked pistol in my hand.

It was a singular sight which met our eyes. On the table stood a dark-lantern with the shutter half open, throwing a brilliant beam of light upon the iron safe, the door of which was ajar. Beside this table, on the wooden chair, sat Dr Grimesby Roylott clad in a long grey dressing-gown, his bare ankles protruding beneath, and his feet thrust into red heelless Turkish slippers. Across his lap lay the short stock with the long lash which we had noticed during the day. His chin was cocked upward and his eyes were fixed in a dreadful, rigid stare at the corner of the ceiling. Round his brow he had a peculiar yellow band, with brownish speckles, which seemed to be bound tightly round his head. As we entered he made neither sound nor motion.

'The band! the speckled band!' whispered Holmes.

I took a step forward. In an instant his strange headgear began to move, and there reared itself from among his hair the squat diamond-shaped head and puffed neck of a loathsome serpent.

'It is a swamp adder!' cried Holmes; 'the deadliest snake in India. He has died within ten seconds of being bitten. Violence does, in truth, recoil upon the violent, and the schemer falls into the pit which he digs for another. Let us thrust this creature back into its den, and we can then remove Miss Stoner to some place of shelter and let the county police know what has happened.'

As he spoke he drew the dog-whip swiftly from the dead man's lap, and throwing the noose round the reptile's neck he drew it from its horrid perch and, carrying it at arm's length, threw it into the iron safe, which he closed upon it.

Such are the true facts of the death of Dr Grimesby Roylott, of Stoke Moran. It is not necessary that I should prolong a narrative which has already run to too great a length by telling how we broke the sad news to the terrified girl, how we conveyed her by the morning train to the care of her good aunt at Harrow, of how the slow process of official inquiry came to the conclusion that the doctor met his fate while indiscreetly playing with a dangerous pet. The little which I had yet to learn of the case was told me by Sherlock Holmes as we travelled back next day.

'I had,' said he, 'come to an entirely erroneous conclusion which shows, my dear Watson, how dangerous it always is to reason from insufficient data. The presence of the gipsies, and the use of the word 'band,' which was used by the poor girl, no doubt, to explain the appearance which she had caught a hurried glimpse of by the light of her match, were sufficient to put me upon an entirely wrong scent. I can only claim the merit that I instantly reconsidered my position when, however, it became clear to me that whatever danger threatened an occupant of the room could not come either from the window or the door. My attention was speedily drawn, as I have already remarked to you, to this ventilator, and to the bell-rope which hung down to the bed. The discovery that this was a dummy, and that the bed was clamped to the floor, instantly gave rise to the suspicion that the rope was there as a bridge for something passing through the hole and coming to the bed. The idea of a snake instantly occurred to me, and when I coupled it with my knowledge that the doctor was furnished with a supply of creatures from India, I felt that I was probably on the right track. The idea of using a form of poison which could not possibly be discovered by any chemical test was just such a one as would occur to a clever and ruthless man who had had an Eastern training. The rapidity with which such a poison would take effect would also, from his point of view, be an advantage. It would be a sharp-eyed coroner, indeed, who could distinguish the two little dark punctures which would show where the poison fangs had done their work. Then I thought of the whistle. Of course he must recall the snake before the morning light revealed it to the victim. He had trained it, probably by the use of the milk which we saw, to return to him when summoned. He would put it through this ventilator at the hour that he thought best, with the certainty that it would crawl down the rope and land on the bed. It might or might not bite the occupant, perhaps she might escape every night for a week, but sooner or later she must fall a victim.

'I had come to these conclusions before ever I had entered his room. An inspection of his chair showed me that he had been in the habit of standing on it, which of course would be necessary in order that he should reach the ventilator. The sight of the safe, the saucer of milk, and the loop of whipcord were enough to finally dispel any doubts which may have remained. The metallic clang heard by Miss Stoner was obviously caused by her stepfather hastily closing the door of his safe upon its terrible occupant. Having once made up my mind, you know the steps which I took in order to put the matter to the proof. I heard the creature hiss as I have no doubt that you did also, and I instantly lit the light and attacked it.'

'With the result of driving it through the ventilator.'

'And also with the result of causing it to turn upon its master at the other side. Some of the blows of my cane came home and roused its snakish temper, so that it flew upon the first person it saw. In this way I am no doubt indirectly responsible for Dr Grimesby Roylott's death, and I cannot say that it is likely to weigh very heavily upon my conscience.'

10

A SCANDAL IN BOHEMIA
Arthur Conan Doyle

…Sherlock Holmes never loved women. But after their meeting he never forgot her…

I

To Sherlock Holmes she is always *the* woman. I have seldom heard him mention her under any other name. In his eyes she eclipses and predominates the whole of her sex. It was not that he felt any emotion akin to love for Irene Adler. All emotions, and that one particularly, were abhorrent to his cold, precise, but admirably balanced mind. He was, I take it, the most perfect reasoning and observing machine that the world has seen; but, as a lover, he would have placed himself in a false position. He never spoke of the softer passions, save with a gibe and a sneer. They were admirable things for the observer—excellent for drawing the veil from men's motives and actions. But for the trained reasoner to admit such intrusions into his own delicate and finely adjusted temperament was to introduce a distracting factor which might throw a doubt upon all his mental results. Grit in a sensitive instrument, or a crack in one of his own high-power lenses, would not be more disturbing than a strong emotion in a nature such as his. And yet there was but one woman to him, and that woman was the late Irene Adler, of dubious and questionable memory.

I had seen little of Holmes lately. My marriage had drifted us away from each other. My own complete happiness, and the home-centred interests which rise up around the man who first finds himself master of his own establishment, were sufficient to absorb all my attention; while

Holmes, loathed every form of society with his whole Bohemian soul, remained our lodgings in Baker Street, buried among his old books, and alternating from week to week between cocaine and ambition, the drowsiness of the drug, and the fierce energy of his own keen nature. He was still, as ever, deeply attracted by the study of crime, and occupied his immense faculties and extraordinary powers of observation in following out those clues, and clearing up those mysteries, which had been abandoned as hopeless by the official police. From time to time I heard some vague account of his doings: of his summons to Odessa in the case of the Trepoff murder, of his clearing up of the singular tragedy of the Atkinson brothers at Trincomalee, and finally of the mission which he had accomplished so delicately and successfully for the reigning family of Holland. Beyond these signs of his activity, however, which I merely shared with all the readers of the daily press, I knew little of my former friend and companion.

One night—it was on the 20th of March, 1888—I was returning from a journey to a patient (for I had now returned to civil practice), when my way led me through Baker Street. As I passed the well-remembered door, which must always be associated in my mind with my wooing, and with the dark incidents of the Study in Scarlet, I was seized with a keen desire to see Holmes again, and to know how he was employing his extraordinary powers. His rooms were brilliantly lit, and, even as I looked up, I saw his tall, spare figure pass twice in a dark silhouette against the blind. He was pacing the room swiftly, eagerly, with his head sunk upon his chest and his hands clasped behind him. To me, who knew his every mood and habit, his attitude and manner told their own story. He was at work again. He had arisen out of his drug-created dreams, and was hot upon the scent of some new problem. I rang the bell, and was shown up to the chamber which had formerly been in part my own.

His manner was not effusive. It seldom was; but he was glad, I think, to see me. With hardly a word spoken, but with a kindly eye, he waved me to an arm-chair, threw across his case of cigars, and indicated a spirit case and a gasogene in the corner. Then he stood before the fire, and looked me over in his singular introspective fashion.

'Wedlock suits you,' he remarked. 'I think, Watson, that you have put on seven and a half pounds since I saw you.'

'Seven!' I answered.

'Indeed, I should have thought a little more. Just a trifle more, I fancy, Watson. And in practice again, I observe. You did not tell me that you intended to go into harness.'

'Then, how do you know?'

'I see it, I deduce it. How do I know that you have been getting yourself very wet lately, and that you have a most clumsy and careless servant girl?'

'My dear Holmes,' said I, 'this is too much. You would certainly have been burned, had you lived a few centuries ago. It is true that I had a country walk on Thursday and came home in a dreadful mess; but, as I have changed my clothes, I can't imagine how you deduce it. As to Mary Jane, she is incorrigible, and my wife has given her notice; but there, again, I fail to see how you work it out.'

He chuckled to himself and rubbed his long, nervous hands together.

'It is simplicity itself,' said he; 'my eyes tell me that on the inside of your left shoe, just where the firelight strikes it, the leather is scored by six almost parallel cuts. Obviously they have been caused by someone who has very carelessly scraped round the edges of the sole in order to remove crusted mud from it. Hence, you see, my double deduction that you had been out in vile weather, and that you had a particularly malignant boot-slitting specimen of the London slavey. As to your practice, if a gentleman walks into my rooms smelling of iodoform, with a black mark of nitrate of silver upon his right forefinger, and a bulge on the side of his top-hat to show where he has secreted his stethoscope, I must be dull, indeed, if I do not pronounce him to be an active member of the medical profession.'

I could not help laughing at the ease with which he explained his process of deduction. 'When I hear you give your reasons,' I remarked, 'the thing always appears to me to be so ridiculously simple that I could easily do it myself, though at each successive instance of your reasoning I am baffled, until you explain your process. And yet I believe that my eyes are as good as yours.'

'Quite so,' he answered, lighting a cigarette, and throwing himself down into an arm-chair. 'You see, but you do not observe. The distinction is clear. For example, you have frequently seen the steps which lead up from the hall to this room.'

'Frequently.'

'How often?'

'Well, some hundreds of times.'

'Then how many are there?'

'How many? I don't know.'

'Quite so! You have not observed. And yet you have seen. That is just my point. Now, I know that there are seventeen steps, because I have both seen and observed. By-the-way, since you are interested in these little problems, and since you are good enough to chronicle one or two of my trifling experiences, you may be interested in this.' He threw over a sheet of thick, pink-tinted note-paper which had been lying open upon the table. 'It came by the last post,' said he. 'Read it aloud.'

The note was undated, and without either signature or address.

'There will call upon you tonight, at a quarter to eight o'clock,' it said, 'a gentleman who desires to consult you upon a matter of the very deepest moment. Your recent services to one of the royal houses of Europe have shown that you are one who may safely be trusted with matters which are of an importance which can hardly be exaggerated. This account of you we have from all quarters received. Be in your chamber then at that hour, and do not take it amiss if your visitor wear a mask.'

'This is indeed a mystery,' I remarked. 'What do you imagine that it means?'

'I have no data yet. It is a capital mistake to theorize before one has data. Insensibly one begins to twist facts to suit theories, instead of theories to suit facts. But the note itself. What do you deduce from it?'

I carefully examined the writing, and the paper upon which it was written.

'The man who wrote it was presumably well to do,' I remarked, endeavouring to imitate my companion's processes. 'Such paper could not be bought under half a crown a packet. It is peculiarly strong and stiff.'

'Peculiar—that is the very word,' said Holmes. 'It is not an English paper at all. Hold it up to the light.'

I did so, and saw a large *E* with a small *g*, a *P*, and a large *G* with a small *t* woven into the texture of the paper.

'What do you make of that?' asked Holmes.

'The name of the maker, no doubt; or his monogram, rather.'

'Not at all. The *G* with the small *t* stands for "Gesellschaft" which is the German for "Company". It is a customary contraction like our 'Co.' *P*, of course, stands for 'Papier.' Now for the *Eg*. Let us glance at our *Continental Gazetteer*.' He took down a heavy brown volume from his shelves. 'Eglow, Eglonitz—here we are, Egria. It is in a German-speaking country—in Bohemia, not far from Carlsbad. 'Remarkable as being the scene of the death of Wallenstein, and for its numerous glass-factories and paper-mills.' Ha, ha, my boy, what do you make of that?' His eyes sparkled, and he sent up a great blue triumphant cloud from his cigarette.

'The paper was made in Bohemia,' I said.

'Precisely. And the man who wrote the note is a German. Do you note the peculiar construction of the sentence—'This account of you we have from all quarters received.' A Frenchman or Russian could not have written that. It is the German who is so uncourteous to his verbs. It only remains, therefore, to discover what is wanted by this German who writes upon Bohemian paper, and prefers wearing a mask to showing his face. And here he comes, if I am not mistaken, to resolve all our doubts.'

As he spoke there was the sharp sound of horses' hoofs and grating wheels against the curb, followed by a sharp pull at the bell. Holmes whistled.

'A pair, by the sound,' said he. 'Yes,' he continued, glancing out of the window. 'A nice little brougham and a pair of beauties. A hundred and fifty guineas apiece. There's money in this case, Watson, if there is nothing else.'

'I think that I had better go, Holmes.'

'Not a bit, doctor. Stay where you are. I am lost without my

Boswell. And this promises to be interesting. It would be a pity to miss it.'

'But your client—'

'Never mind him. I may want your help, and so may he. Here he comes. Sit down in that arm-chair, doctor, and give us your best attention.'

A slow and heavy step, which had been heard upon the stairs and in the passage, paused immediately outside the door. Then there was a loud and authoritative tap.

'Come in!' said Holmes.

A man entered who could hardly have been less than six feet six inches in height, with the chest and limbs of a Hercules. His dress was rich with a richness which would, in England, be looked upon as akin to bad taste. Heavy bands of Astrakhan were slashed across the sleeves and fronts of his double-breasted coat, while the deep blue cloak which was thrown over his shoulders was lined with flame-coloured silk, and secured at the neck with a brooch which consisted of a single flaming beryl. Boots which extended half-way up his calves, and which were trimmed at the tops with rich brown fur, completed the impression of barbaric opulence which was suggested by his whole appearance. He carried a broad-brimmed hat in his hand, while he wore across the upper part of his face, extending down past the cheek-bones, a black vizard mask, which he had apparently adjusted that very moment, for his hand was still raised to it as he entered. From the lower part of the face he appeared to be a man of strong character, with a thick, hanging lip, and a long, straight chin, suggestive of resolution pushed to the length of obstinacy.

'You had my note?' he asked, with a deep harsh voice and a strongly marked German accent. 'I told you that I would call.' He looked from one to the other of us, as if uncertain which to address.

'Pray take a seat,' said Holmes. 'This is my friend and colleague. Dr Watson, who is occasionally good enough to help me in my cases. Whom have I the honour to address?'

'You may address me as the Count Von Kramm, a Bohemian nobleman. I understand that this gentleman, your friend, is a man of honour and discretion, whom I may trust with a matter of the most extreme importance. If not, I should much prefer to communicate with you alone.'

I rose to go, but Holmes caught me by the wrist and pushed me back into my chair. 'It is both, or none,' said he. 'You may say before this gentleman anything which you may say to me.'

The count shrugged his broad shoulders. 'Then I must begin,' said he, 'by binding you both to absolute secrecy for two years, at the end of that time the matter will be of no importance. At present it is not too much to say that it is of such weight it may have an influence upon European history.'

'I promise,' said Holmes.

'And I.'

'You will excuse this mask,' continued our strange visitor. 'The august person who employs me wishes his agent to be unknown to you, and I may confess at once that the title by which I have just called myself is not exactly my own.'

'I was aware of it,' said Holmes, dryly.

'The circumstances are of great delicacy, and every precaution has to be taken to quench what might grow to be an immense scandal and seriously compromise one of the reigning families of Europe. To speak plainly, the matter implicates the great House of Ormstein, hereditary kings of Bohemia.'

'I was also aware of that,' murmured Holmes, settling himself down in his arm-chair and closing his eyes.

Our visitor glanced with some apparent surprise at the languid, lounging figure of the man who had been no doubt depicted to him as the most incisive reasoner and most energetic agent in Europe. Holmes slowly reopened his eyes and looked impatiently at his gigantic client.

'If your Majesty would condescend to state your case,' he remarked, 'I should be better able to advise you.'

The man sprang from his chair and paced up and down the room in uncontrollable agitation. Then, with a gesture of desperation, he tore the mask from his face and hurled it upon the ground. 'You are right,' he cried; 'I am the King. Why should I attempt to conceal it?'

'Why, indeed?' murmured Holmes. 'Your Majesty had not spoken before I was aware that I was addressing Wilhelm Gottsreich Sigismond von Ormstein, Grand Duke of Cassel-Felstein, and hereditary King of Bohemia.'

'But you can understand,' said our strange visitor, sitting down once more and passing his hand over his high, white forehead, 'you can understand that I am not accustomed to doing such business in my own person. Yet the matter was so delicate that I could not confide it to an agent without putting myself in his power. I have come *incognito* from Prague for the purpose of consulting you.'

'Then, pray consult,' said Holmes, shutting his eyes once more.

'The facts are briefly these: Some five years ago, during a lengthy visit to Warsaw, I made the acquaintance of the well-known adventuress, Irene Adler. The name is no doubt familiar to you.'

'Kindly look her up in my index, doctor,' murmured Holmes, without opening his eyes. For many years he had adopted a system of docketing all paragraphs concerning men and things, so that it was difficult to name a subject or a person on which he could not at once furnish information. In this case I found her biography sandwiched in between that of a Hebrew Rabbi and that of a staff-commander who had written a monograph upon the deep-sea fishes.

'Let me see!' said Holmes. 'Hum! Born in New Jersey in the year 1858. Contralto—hum! La Scala, hum! Prima donna Imperial Opera of Warsaw—Yes! Retired from operatic stage—ha! Living in London—quite so! Your Majesty, as I understand, became entangled with this young person, wrote her some compromising letters, and is now desirous of getting those letters back.'

'Precisely so. But how—'

'Was there a secret marriage?'

'None.'

'No legal papers or certificates?'

'None.'

'Then I fail to follow your Majesty. If this young person should produce her letters for blackmailing or other purposes, how is she to prove their authenticity?'

'There is the writing.'

'Pooh, pooh! Forgery.'

'My private note-paper.'

'Stolen.'

'My own seal.'

'Imitated.'

'My photograph.'

'Bought.'

'We were both in the photograph.'

'Oh dear! That is very bad! Your Majesty has indeed committed an indiscretion.'

'I was mad—insane.'

'You have compromised yourself seriously.'

'I was only Crown Prince then. I was young. I am but thirty now.'

'It must be recovered.'

'We have tried and failed.'

'Your Majesty must pay. It must be bought.'

'She will not sell.'

'Stolen, then.'

'Five attempts have been made. Twice burglars in my pay ransacked her house. Once we diverted her luggage when she travelled. Twice she has been waylaid. There has been no result.'

'No sign of it?'

'Absolutely none.'

Holmes laughed. 'It is quite a pretty little problem,' said he.

'But a very serious one to me,' returned the King, reproachfully.

'Very, indeed. And what does she propose to do with the photograph?'

'To ruin me.'

'But how?'

'I am about to be married.'

'So I have heard.'

'To Clotilde Lothman von Saxe-Meningen, second daughter of the King of Scandinavia. You may know the strict principles of her family. She is herself the very soul of delicacy. A shadow of a doubt as to my conduct would bring the matter to an end.'

'And Irene Adler?'

'Threatens to send them the photograph. And she will do it. I know that she will do it. You do not know her, but she has a soul of steel. She has the face of the most beautiful of women, and the mind of the most resolute of men. Rather than I should marry another woman, there are no lengths to which she would not go—none.'

'You are sure that she has not sent it yet?'

'I am sure.'

'And why?'

'Because she has said that she would send it on the day when the betrothal was publicly proclaimed. That will be next Monday.'

'Oh, then, we have three days yet,' said Holmes, with a yawn. 'That is very fortunate, as I have one or two matters of importance to look into just at present. Your Majesty will, of course, stay in London for the present?'

'Certainly. You will find me at the Langham, under the name of the Count Von Kramm.'

'Then I shall drop you a line to let you know how we progress.'

'Pray do so. I shall be all anxiety.'

'Then, as to money?'

'You have *carte blanche*.'

'Absolutely?'

'I tell you that I would give one of the provinces of my kingdom to have that photograph.'

'And for present expenses?'

The king took a heavy chamois leather bag from under his cloak and laid it on the table.

'There are three hundred pounds in gold and seven hundred in notes,' he said.

Holmes scribbled a receipt upon a sheet of his note-book and handed it to him.

'And mademoiselle's address?' he asked.

'Is Briony Lodge, Serpentine Avenue, St. John's Wood.'

Holmes took a note of it. 'One other question,' said he. 'Was the photograph a cabinet?'

'It was.'

'Then, goodnight, your Majesty, and I trust that we shall soon have some good news for you. And goodnight, Watson,' he added, as the wheels of the royal brougham rolled down the street. 'If you will be good enough to call tomorrow afternoon, at three o'clock, I should like to chat this little matter over with you.'

II

At three o'clock precisely I was at Baker Street, but Holmes had not yet returned. The landlady informed me that he had left the house shortly after eight o'clock in the morning. I sat down beside the fire, however, with the intention of awaiting him, however long he might be. I was already deeply interested in his inquiry, for, though it was surrounded by none of the grim and strange features which were associated with the two crimes which I have already recorded, still, the nature of the case and the exalted station of his client gave it a character of its own. Indeed, apart from the nature of the investigation which my friend had on hand, there was something in his masterly grasp of a situation, and his keen, incisive reasoning, which made it a pleasure to me to study his system of work, and to follow the quick, subtle methods by which he disentangled the most inextricable mysteries. So accustomed was I to his invariable success that the very possibility of his failing had ceased to enter into my head.

It was close upon four before the door opened, and a drunken-looking groom, ill-kempt and side-whiskered, with an inflamed face and disreputable clothes, walked into the room. Accustomed as I was to my friend's amazing powers in the use of disguises, I had to look three times before I was certain that it was indeed he. With a nod he vanished into the bedroom, whence he emerged in five minutes tweed-suited and respectable, as of old. Putting his hands into his pockets, he stretched out his legs in front of the fire, and laughed heartily for some minutes.

'Well, really!' he cried, and then he choked; and laughed again until he was obliged to lie back, limp and helpless, in the chair.

'What is it?'

'It's quite too funny. I am sure you could never guess how I employed my morning, or what I ended by doing.'

'I can't imagine. I suppose that you have been watching the habits, and perhaps the house, of Miss Irene Adler.'

'Quite so; but the sequel was rather unusual. I will tell you, however. I left the house a little after eight o'clock this morning, in the character of a groom out of work. There is a wonderful sympathy and freemasonry among horsey men. Be one of them, and you will know all that there is to know. I soon found Briony Lodge. It is a *bijou* villa, with a garden at the back, but built out in front right up to the road, two stories. Chubb lock to the door. Large sitting-room on the right side, well furnished, with long windows almost to the floor, and those preposterous English window fasteners which a child could open. Behind there was nothing remarkable, save that the passage window could be reached from the top of the coach-house. I walked round it and examined it closely from every point of view, but without noting anything else of interest.

'I then lounged down the street, and found, as I expected, that there was a mews in a lane which runs down by one wall of the garden. I lent the ostlers a hand in rubbing down their horses, and I received in exchange twopence, a glass of half-and-half, two fills of shag tobacco, and as much information as I could desire about Miss Adler, to say nothing of half a dozen other people in the neighbourhood in whom I was not in the least interested, but whose biographies I was compelled to listen to.'

'And what of Irene Adler?' I asked.

'Oh, she has turned all the men's heads down in that part. She is the daintiest thing under a bonnet on this planet. So say the Serpentine-mews, to a man. She lives quietly, sings at concerts, drives out at five every day, and returns at seven sharp for dinner. Seldom goes out at other times, except when she sings. Has only one male visitor, but a good deal of him. He is dark, handsome, and dashing, never calls less than once a day, and often twice. He is a Mr Godfrey Norton, of the Inner Temple. See the advantages of a cabman as a confidant. They had driven him home a dozen times from Serpentine-mews, and knew all about him. When I had listened to all that they had to tell, I began to walk up and down near Briony Lodge once more, and to think over my plan of campaign.

'This Godfrey Norton was evidently an important factor in the matter. He was a lawyer. That sounded ominous. What was the relation between them, and what the object of his repeated visits? Was she his client, his friend, or his mistress? If the former, she had probably transferred the photograph to his keeping. If the latter, it was less likely. On the issue of this question depended whether I should continue my work at Briony Lodge, or turn my attention to the gentleman's chambers in the Temple. It was a delicate point, and it widened the field of my inquiry. I fear that I bore you with these details, but I have to let you see my little difficulties, if you are to understand the situation.'

'I am following you closely,' I answered.

'I was still balancing the matter in my mind, when a hansom cab drove up to Briony Lodge, and a gentleman sprang out. He was a remarkably handsome man, dark, aquiline, and mustached—evidently the man of whom I had heard. He appeared to be in a great hurry, shouted to the cabman to wait, and brushed past the maid who opened the door with the air of a man who was thoroughly at home.

'He was in the house about half an hour, and I could catch glimpses of him in the windows of the sitting-room, pacing up and down, talking excitedly, and waving his arms. Of her I could see nothing. Presently he emerged, looking even more flurried than before. As he stepped up to the cab, he pulled a gold watch from his pocket and looked at it earnestly. 'Drive like the devil,' he shouted, 'first to Gross & Hankey's in Regent Street, and then to the church of St. Monica in the Edgware Road. Half a guinea if you do it in twenty minutes!'

'Away they went, and I was just wondering whether I should not do well to follow them, when up the lane came a neat little landau, the coachman with his coat only half-buttoned, and his tie under his ear, while all the tags of his harness were sticking out of the buckles.

It hadn't pulled up before she shot out of the hall door and into it. I only caught a glimpse of her at the moment, but she was a lovely woman, with a face that a man might die for.

"The Church of St. Monica, John," she cried, "and half a sovereign if you reach it in twenty minutes."

'This was quite too good to lose, Watson. I was just balancing whether I should run for it, or whether I should perch behind her landau, when a cab came through the street. The driver looked twice at such a shabby fare; but I jumped in before he could object. "The Church of St. Monica," said I, "and half a sovereign if you reach it in twenty minutes." It was twenty-five minutes to twelve, and of course it was clear enough what was in the wind.

'My cabby drove fast. I don't think I ever drove faster, but the others were there before us. The cab and the landau with their steaming horses were in front of the door when I arrived. I paid the man and hurried into the church. There was not a soul there save the two whom I had followed and a surpliced clergyman, who seemed to be expostulating with them. They were all three standing in a knot in front of the altar. I lounged up the side aisle like any other idler who has dropped into a church. Suddenly, to my surprise, the three at the altar faced round to me, and Godfrey Norton came running as hard as he could towards me.'

'Thank God!' he cried. 'You'll do. Come! Come!'

'What then?' I asked.

'Come, man, come, only three minutes, or it won't be legal.'

I was half-dragged up to the altar, and, before I knew where I was, I found myself mumbling responses which were whispered in my ear, and vouching for things of which I knew nothing, and generally assisting in the secure tying up of Irene Adler, spinster, to Godfrey Norton, bachelor. It was all done in an instant, and there was the gentleman thanking me on the one side and the lady on the other, while the clergyman beamed on me in front. It was the most preposterous position in which I ever found myself in my life, and it was the thought of it that started me laughing just now. It seems that there had been some informality about their license, that the clergyman absolutely refused to marry them without a witness of some sort, and that my lucky appearance saved the bridegroom from having to sally out into the streets in search of a best man. The bride gave me a sovereign, and I mean to wear it on my watch-chain in memory of the occasion.'

'This is a very unexpected turn of affairs,' said I; 'and what then?'

'Well, I found my plans very seriously menaced. It looked as if the pair might take an immediate departure, and so necessitate very prompt and energetic measures on my part. At the church door, however, they separated, he driving back to the Temple, and she to her own house. "I shall drive out in the park at five as usual," she said, as she left him. I heard no more. They drove away in different directions, and I went off to make my own arrangements.'

'Which are?'

'Some cold beef and a glass of beer,' he answered, ringing the bell. 'I have been too busy to think of food, and I am likely to be busier still this evening. By the way, doctor, I shall want your co-operation.'

'I shall be delighted.'

'You don't mind breaking the law?'

'Not in the least.'

'Nor running a chance of arrest?'

'Not in a good cause.'

'Oh, the cause is excellent!'

'Then I am your man.'

'I was sure that I might rely on you.'

'But what is it you wish?'

'When Mrs Turner has brought in the tray I will make it clear to you. Now,' he said, as he turned hungrily on the simple fare that our landlady had provided, 'I must discuss it while I eat, for I have not much time. It is nearly five now. In two hours we must be on the scene of action. Miss Irene, or Madame, rather, returns from her drive at seven. We must be at Briony Lodge to meet her.'

'And what then?'

'You must leave that to me. I have already arranged what is to occur. There is only one point on which I must insist. You must not interfere, come what may. You understand?'

'I am to be neutral?'

'To do nothing whatever. There will probably be some small unpleasantness. Do not join in it. It will end in my being conveyed into the house. Four or five minutes afterwards the sitting-room window will open. You are to station yourself close to that open window.'

'Yes.'

'You are to watch me, for I will be visible to you.'

'Yes.'

'And when I raise my hand—so—you will throw into the room what I give you to throw, and will, at the same time, raise the cry of fire. You quite follow me?'

'Entirely.'

'It is nothing very formidable,' he said, taking a long cigar-shaped roll from his pocket. 'It is an ordinary plumber's smoke-rocket, fitted with a cap at either end to make it self-lighting. Your task is confined to that. When you raise your cry of fire, it will be taken up by quite a number of people. You may then walk to the end of the street, and I will rejoin you in ten minutes. I hope that I have made myself clear?'

'I am to remain neutral, to get near the window, to watch you, and, at the signal, to throw in this object, then to raise the cry of fire, and to wait you at the corner of the street.'

'Precisely.'

'Then you may entirely rely on me.'

'That is excellent. I think, perhaps, it is almost time that I prepare for the new role I have to play.'

He disappeared into his bedroom, and returned in a few minutes in the character of an amiable and simple-minded Nonconformist clergyman. His broad black hat, his baggy trousers, his white tie, his sympathetic smile, and general look of peering and benevolent curiosity were such as Mr John Hare alone could have equalled. It was not merely that Holmes changed his costume. His expression, his manner, his very soul seemed to vary with every fresh part that he assumed. The stage lost a fine actor, even as science lost an acute reasoner, when he became a specialist in crime.

It was a quarter past six when we left Baker Street, and it still wanted ten minutes to the hour when we found ourselves in Serpentine Avenue. It was already dusk, and the lamps were just being lighted as we paced up and down in front of Briony Lodge, waiting for the coming of its occupant. The house was just such as I had pictured it from Sherlock Holmes' succinct description, but the locality appeared to be less private that I expected. On the contrary, for a small street in a quiet neighbourhood, it was remarkably animated. There was a group of shabbily-dressed men smoking and laughing in a corner, a scissors-grinder with his wheel, two guardsmen who were flirting with a nurse-girl, and several well-dressed young men who were lounging up and down with cigars in their mouths.

'You see,' remarked Holmes, as we paced to and fro in front of the house, 'this marriage rather simplifies matters. The photograph becomes a double-edged weapon now. The chances are that she would be as averse to its being seen by Mr Godfrey Norton, as our client is to its coming to the eyes of his princess. Now the question is, where are we to find the photograph?'

'Where, indeed?'

'It is most unlikely that she carries it about with her. It is cabinet size. Too large for easy concealment about a woman's dress. She knows that the King is capable of having her waylaid and searched. Two attempts of the sort have already been made. We may take it, then, that she does not carry it about with her.'

'Where, then?'

'Her banker or her lawyer. There is that double possibility. But I am inclined to think neither. Women are naturally secretive, and they like to do their own secreting. Why should she hand it over to any one else? She could trust her own guardianship, but she could not tell what indirect or political influence might be brought to bear upon a business man. Besides, remember that she had resolved to use it within a few days. It must be where she can lay her hands upon it. It must be in her own house.'

'But it has twice been burgled.'

'Pshaw! They did not know how to look.'

'But how will you look?'

'I will not look.'

'What then?'

'I will get her to show me.'

'But she will refuse.'

'She will not be able to. But I hear the rumble of wheels. It is her carriage. Now carry out my orders to the letter.'

As he spoke the gleam of the side-lights of a carriage came round the curve of the avenue. It was a smart little landau which rattled up to the door of Briony Lodge. As it pulled up, one of the loafing men at the comer dashed forward to open the door in the hope of earning a copper, but was elbowed away by another loafer, who had rushed up with the same intention. A fierce quarrel broke out, which was increased by the two guardsmen, who took sides with one of the loungers, and by the scissors-grinder, who was equally hot upon the other side. A blow was struck, and in an instant the lady, who had stepped from her carriage, was the centre of a little knot of flushed and struggling men, who struck savagely at each other with their fists and sticks. Holmes dashed into the crowd to protect the lady; but just as he reached her he gave a cry and dropped to the ground, with the blood running freely down his face. At his fall the guardsmen took to their heels in one direction and the loungers in the other, while a number of better dressed people, who had watched the scuffle without taking part in it, crowded in to help the lady and to attend to the injured man. Irene Adler, as I will still call her, had hurried up the steps; but she stood at the top with her superb figure outlined against the lights of the hall, looking back into the street.

'Is the poor gentleman much hurt?' she asked.

'He is dead,' cried several voices.

'No, no, there's life in him!' shouted another. 'But he'll be gone before you can get him to hospital.'

'He's a brave fellow,' said a woman. 'They would have had the lady's purse and watch if it hadn't been for him. They were a gang, and a rough one, too. Ah, he's breathing now.'

'He can't lie in the street. May we bring him in, marm?'

'Surely. Bring him into the sitting-room. There is a comfortable sofa. This way, please!'

Slowly and solemnly he was borne into Briony Lodge and laid out in the principal room, while I still observed the proceedings from my post by the window. The lamps had been lit, but the blinds had not been drawn, so that I could see Holmes as he lay upon the couch. I do not know whether he was seized with compunction at that moment for the part he was playing, but I know that I never felt more heartily ashamed of myself in my life than when I saw the beautiful creature against whom I was conspiring, or the grace and kindliness with which she waited upon the injured man. And yet it would be the blackest treachery to Holmes to draw back now from the part which he had intrusted to me. I hardened my heart, and took the smoke-rocket from under my ulster. After all, I thought, we are not injuring her. We are but preventing her from injuring another.

Holmes had sat up upon the couch, and I saw him motion like a man who is in need of air. A maid rushed across and threw open the window. At the same instant I saw him raise his hand, and at the signal I tossed my rocket into the room with a cry of 'Fire!' The word was no sooner out of my mouth than the whole crowd of spectators, well dressed and ill—gentlemen, ostlers, and servant-maids—joined in a general shriek of 'Fire!' Thick clouds of smoke curled through the room and out at the open window. I caught a glimpse of rushing figures, and a moment later the voice of Holmes from within assuring them that it was a false alarm. Slipping through the shouting crowd I made my way to the corner of the street, and in ten minutes was rejoiced to find my friend's arm in mine, and to get away from the scene of uproar. He walked swiftly and in silence for some few minutes, until we had turned down one of the quiet streets which lead towards the Edgware Road.

'You did it very nicely, doctor,' he remarked. 'Nothing could have been better. It is all right.'

'You have the photograph?'

'I know where it is.'

'And how did you find out?'

'She showed me, as I told you that she would.'

'I am still in the dark.'

'I do not wish to make a mystery,' said he, laughing. 'The matter was perfectly simple. You, of course, saw that every one in the street was an accomplice. They were all engaged for the evening.'

'I guessed as much.'

'Then, when the row broke out, I had a little moist red paint in the palm of my hand. I rushed forward, fell down, clapped my hand to my face, and became a piteous spectacle. It is an old trick.'

'That also I could fathom.'

'Then they carried me in. She was bound to have me in. What else could she do? And into her sitting-room, which was the very room which I suspected. It lay between that and her bedroom, and I was determined to see which. They laid me on a couch, I motioned for air, they were compelled to open the window, and you had your chance.'

'How did that help you?'

'It was all-important. When a woman thinks that her house is on fire, her instinct is at once to rush to the thing which she values most. It is a perfectly overpowering impulse, and I have more than once taken advantage of it. In the case of the Darlington Substitution Scandal it was of use to me, and also in the Arnsworth Castle business. A married woman grabs at her baby; an unmarried one reaches for her jewel-box. Now it was clear to me that our lady of today had nothing in the house more precious to her than what we are in quest of. She would rush to secure it. The alarm of fire was admirably done. The smoke and shouting were enough to shake nerves of steel. She responded beautifully. The photograph is in a recess behind a sliding panel just above the right bell-pull. She was there in an instant, and I caught a glimpse of it as she half-drew it out. When I cried out that it was a false alarm, she replaced it, glanced at the rocket, rushed from the room, and I have not seen her since. I rose, and, making my excuses, escaped from the house. I hesitated whether to attempt to secure the photograph at once; but the coachman had come in, and as he was watching me narrowly, it seemed safer to wait. A little over-precipitance may ruin all.'

'And now?' I asked.

'Our quest is practically finished. I shall call with the King tomorrow, and with you, if you care to come with us. We will be shown into the sitting-room to wait for the lady, but it is probable that when she comes she may find neither us nor the photograph. It might be a satisfaction to His Majesty to regain it with his own hands.'

'And when will you call?'

'At eight in the morning. She will not be up, so that we shall have a clear field. Besides, we must be prompt, for this marriage may mean a complete change in her life and habits. I must wire to the King without delay.'

We had reached Baker Street, and had stopped at the door. He was searching his pockets for the key, when someone passing said:

'Goodnight, Mister Sherlock Holmes.'

There were several people on the pavement at the time, but the greeting appeared to come from a slim youth in an ulster who had hurried by.

'I've heard that voice before,' said Holmes, staring down the dimly-lit street. 'Now, I wonder who the deuce that could have been.'

III

I SLEPT at Baker Street that night, and we were engaged upon our toast and coffee in the morning when the King of Bohemia rushed into the room.

'You have really got it!' he cried, grasping Sherlock Holmes by either shoulder, and looking eagerly into his face.

'Not yet.'

'But you have hopes?'

'I have hopes.'

'Then, come. I am all impatience to be gone.'

'We must have a cab.'

'No, my brougham is waiting.'

'Then that will simplify matters.' We descended, and started off once more for Briony Lodge.

'Irene Adler is married,' remarked Holmes.

'Married! When?'

'Yesterday.'

'But to whom?'

'To an English lawyer named Norton.'

'But she could not love him?'

'I am in hopes that she does.'

'And why in hopes?'

'Because it would spare your Majesty all fear of future annoyance. If the lady loves her husband, she does not love your Majesty. If she does not love your Majesty, there is no reason why she should interfere with your Majesty's plan.'

'It is true. And yet—Well! I wish she had been of my own station! What a queen she would have made!' He relapsed into a moody silence, which was not broken until we drew up in Serpentine Avenue.

The door of Briony Lodge was open, and an elderly woman stood upon the steps. She watched us with a sardonic eye as we stepped from the brougham.

'Mr Sherlock Holmes, I believe?' said she.

'I am Mr Holmes,' answered my companion, looking at her with a questioning and rather startled gaze.

'Indeed! My mistress told me that you were likely to call. She left this morning with her husband by the 5.15 train from Charing Cross for the Continent.'

'What!' Sherlock Holmes staggered back, white with chagrin and surprise. 'Do you mean that she has left England?'

'Never to return.'

'And the papers?' asked the King, hoarsely. 'All is lost.'

'We shall see.' He pushed past the servant and rushed into the drawing-room, followed by the King and myself. The furniture was scattered about in every direction, with dismantled shelves and open drawers, as if the lady had hurriedly ransacked them before her flight. Holmes rushed at the bell-pull, tore back a small sliding shutter, and, plunging in his hand, pulled out a photograph and a letter. The photograph was of Irene Adler herself in evening dress, the letter was superscribed to 'Sherlock Holmes, Esq. To be left till called for.' My friend tore it open, and we all three read it together. It was dated at midnight of the preceding night, and ran in this way:

'My Dear Mr Sherlock Holmes—You really did it very well. You took me in completely. Until after the alarm of fire, I had not a suspicion. But then, when I found how I had betrayed myself, I began to think. I had been warned against you months ago. I had been told that, if the King employed an agent, it would certainly be you. And your address had been given me. Yet, with all this, you made me reveal what you wanted to know. Even after I became suspicious, I found it hard to think evil of such a dear, kind old clergyman. But, you know, I have been trained as an actress myself. Male costume is nothing new to me. I often take advantage of the freedom which it gives. I sent John, the coachman, to watch you, ran up-stairs, got into my walking-clothes, as I call them, and came down just as you departed.

'Well, I followed you to your door, and so made sure that I was really an object of interest to the celebrated Mr Sherlock Holmes. Then I, rather imprudently, wished you goodnight, and started for the Temple to see my husband.

'We both thought the best resource was flight, when pursued by so formidable an antagonist; so you will find the nest empty when you call tomorrow. As to the photograph, your client may rest in peace. I love and am loved by a better man than he. The King may do what he will without hinderance from one whom he has cruelly wronged. I keep it only to safeguard myself, and to preserve a weapon which will always secure me from any steps which he might take in the future. I leave a photograph which he might care to possess; and I remain, dear Mr Sherlock Holmes, very truly yours,

Irene Norton, *née* Adler.'

'What a woman—oh, what a woman!' cried the King of Bohemia, when we had all three read this epistle. 'Did I not tell you how quick and resolute she was? Would she not have made an admirable queen? Is it not a pity that she was not on my level?'

'From what I have seen of the lady she seems indeed to be on a very different level to your Majesty,' said Holmes, coldly. 'I am sorry that I have not been able to bring your Majesty's business to a more successful conclusion.'

'On the contrary, my dear sir,' cried the King; 'nothing could be more successful. I know that her word is inviolate. The photograph is now as safe as if it were in the fire.'

'I am glad to hear your Majesty say so.'

'I am immensely indebted to you. Pray tell me in what way I can reward you. This ring—' He slipped an emerald snake ring from his finger and held it out upon the palm of his hand.

'Your Majesty has something which I should value even more highly,' said Holmes.

'You have but to name it.'

'This photograph!'

The King stared at him in amazement.

'Irene's photograph!' he cried. 'Certainly, if you wish it.'

'I thank your Majesty. Then there is no more to be done in the matter. I have the honour to wish you a very good-morning.' He bowed, and, turning away without observing the hand which the King had stretched out to him, he set off in my company for his chambers.

And that was how a great scandal threatened to affect the kingdom of Bohemia, and how the best plans of Mr Sherlock Holmes were beaten by a woman's wit. He used to make merry over the cleverness of women, but I have not heard him do it of late. And when he speaks of Irene Adler, or when he refers to her photograph, it is always under the honorable title of *the* woman.

11

THE FIVE ORANGE PIPS

Arthur Conan Doyle

...I've heard of you, Mr Holmes. People say you know everything. I don't know what to do...

When I glance over my notes and records of the Sherlock Holmes cases between the years '82 and '90, I am faced by so many which present strange and interesting features that it is no easy matter to know which to choose and which to leave. Some, however, have already gained publicity through the papers, and others have not offered a field for those peculiar qualities which my friend possessed in so high a degree, and which it is the object of these papers to illustrate. Some, too, have baffled his analytical skill, and would be, as narratives, beginnings without an ending, while others have been but partially cleared up, and have their explanations founded rather upon conjecture and surmise than on that absolute logical proof which was so dear to him. There is, however, one of these last which was so remarkable in its details and so startling in its results that I am tempted to give some account of it in spite of the fact that there are points in connection with it which never have been, and probably never will be, entirely cleared up.

The year '87 furnished us with a long series of cases of greater or less interest, of which I retain the records. Among my headings under this one twelve months I find an account of the adventure of the Paradol Chamber, of the Amateur Mendicant Society, who held a luxurious club in the lower vault of a furniture warehouse, of the facts connected with the loss of the British barque *Sophy Anderson*, of the singular adventures of the Grice Patersons in the island of Uffa, and finally of the Camberwell poisoning case. In the latter, as may be remembered, Sherlock Holmes was able, by winding up the dead man's watch, to prove that it had been wound up two hours before, and that therefore the deceased had gone to bed within that time—a deduction which was of the greatest importance in clearing up the case. All these I may sketch out at some future date, but none of them present such singular features as the strange train of circumstances which I have now taken up my pen to describe.

It was in the latter days of September, and the equinoctial gales had set in with exceptional violence. All day the wind had screamed and the rain had beaten against the windows, so that even here in the heart of great, hand-made London we were forced to raise our minds for the instant from the routine of life and to recognize the presence of those great elemental forces which shriek at mankind through the bars of his civilization, like untamed beasts in a cage. As evening drew in, the storm grew higher and louder, and the wind cried and sobbed like a child in the chimney. Sherlock Holmes sat moodily at one side of the fireplace cross-indexing his records of crime, while I at the other was deep in one of Clark Russell's fine sea-stories until the howl of the gale from without seemed to blend with the text, and the splash of the rain to lengthen out into the long swash of the sea waves. My wife was on a visit to her mother's, and for a few days I was a dweller once more in my old quarters at Baker Street.

'Why,' said I, glancing up at my companion, 'that was surely the bell. Who could come tonight? Some friend of yours, perhaps?'

'Except yourself I have none,' he answered. 'I do not encourage visitors.'

'A client, then?'

'If so, it is a serious case. Nothing less would bring a man out on such a day and at such an hour. But I take it that it is more likely to be some crony of the landlady's.'

Sherlock Holmes was wrong in his conjecture, however, for there came a step in the passage and a tapping at the door. He stretched out his long arm to turn the lamp away from himself and towards the vacant chair upon which a newcomer must sit.

'Come in!' said he.

The man who entered was young, some two-and-twenty at the outside, well-groomed and trimly clad, with something of refinement and delicacy in his bearing. The streaming umbrella which he held in his hand, and his long shining waterproof told of the fierce weather through which he had come. He looked about him anxiously in the glare of the lamp, and I could see that his face was pale and his eyes heavy, like those of a man who is weighed down with some great anxiety.

'I owe you an apology,' he said, raising his golden *pince-nez* to his eyes. 'I trust that I am not intruding. I fear that I have brought some traces of the storm and rain into your snug chamber.'

'Give me your coat and umbrella,' said Holmes. 'They may rest here on the hook and will be dry presently. You have come up from the south-west, I see.'

'Yes, from Horsham.'

'That clay and chalk mixture which I see upon your toe caps is quite distinctive.'

'I have come for advice.'

'That is easily got.'

'And help.'

'That is not always so easy.'

'I have heard of you, Mr Holmes. I heard from Major Prendergast how you saved him in the Tankerville Club scandal.'

'Ah, of course. He was wrongfully accused of cheating at cards.'

'He said that you could solve anything.'

'He said too much.'

'That you are never beaten.'

'I have been beaten four times—three times by men, and once by a woman.'

'But what is that compared with the number of your successes?'

'It is true that I have been generally successful.'

'Then you may be so with me.'

'I beg that you will draw your chair up to the fire and favour me with some details as to your case.'

'It is no ordinary one.'

'None of those which come to me are. I am the last court of appeal.'

'And yet I question, sir, whether, in all your experience, you have ever listened to a more mysterious and inexplicable chain of events than those which have happened in my own family.'

'You fill me with interest,' said Holmes. 'Pray give us the essential facts from the commencement, and I can afterwards question you as to those details which seem to me to be most important.'

The young man pulled his chair up and pushed his wet feet out towards the blaze.

'My name,' said he, 'is John Openshaw, but my own affairs have, as far as I can understand, little to do with this awful business. It is a hereditary matter; so in order to give you an idea of the facts, I must go back to the commencement of the affair.

'You must know that my grandfather had two sons—my uncle Elias and my father Joseph. My father had a small factory at Coventry, which he enlarged at the time of the invention of bicycling. He was a patentee of the Openshaw unbreakable tire, and his business met with such success that he was able to sell it and to retire upon a handsome competence.

'My uncle Elias emigrated to America when he was a young man and became a planter in Florida, where he was reported to have done very well. At the time of the war he fought in Jackson's army, and afterwards under Hood, where he rose to be a colonel. When Lee laid down his arms my uncle returned to his plantation, where he remained for three or four years. About 1869 or 1870 he came back to Europe and took a small estate in Sussex, near Horsham. He had made a very considerable fortune in the States, and his reason for leaving them was his aversion to the negroes, and his dislike of the Republican policy in extending the franchise to them. He was a singular man, fierce and quick-tempered, very foul-mouthed when he was angry, and of a most retiring disposition. During all the years that he lived at Horsham, I doubt if ever he set foot in the town. He had a garden and two or three fields round his house, and there he would take his exercise, though very often for weeks on end he would never leave his room. He drank a great deal of brandy and smoked very heavily, but he would see no society and did not want any friends, not even his own brother.

'He didn't mind me; in fact, he took a fancy to me, for at the time when he saw me first I was a youngster of twelve or so. This would be in the year 1878, after he had been eight or nine years in England. He begged my father to let me live with him and he was very kind to me in his way. When he was sober he used to be fond of playing backgammon and draughts with me, and he would make me his representative both with the servants and with the tradespeople, so that by the time that I was sixteen I was quite master of the house. I kept all the keys and could go where I liked and do what I liked, so long as I did not disturb him in his privacy. There was one singular exception, however, for he had a single room, a lumber-room up among the attics, which was invariably locked, and which he would never permit either me or anyone else to enter. With a boy's curiosity I have peeped through the keyhole, but I was never able to see more than such a collection of old trunks and bundles as would be expected in such a room.

'One day—it was in March, 1883—a letter with a foreign stamp lay upon the table in front of the colonel's plate. It was not a common thing for him to receive letters, for his bills were all paid in ready money, and he had no friends of any sort. "From India!" said he as he took it up, "Pondicherry postmark! What can this be?" Opening it hurriedly, out there jumped five little dried orange pips, which pattered down upon his plate. I began to laugh at this, but the laugh was struck from my lips at the sight of his face. His lip had fallen, his eyes were protruding, his skin the colour of putty, and he glared at the envelope which he still held in his trembling hand, "K.K.K.!" he shrieked, and then, "My God, my God, my sins have overtaken me!"

'What is it, uncle?' I cried.

"Death," said he, and rising from the table he retired to his room, leaving me palpitating with horror. I took up the envelope and saw scrawled in red ink upon the inner flap, just above the gum, the letter K three times repeated. There was nothing else save the five dried pips. What could be the reason of his over-powering terror? I left the breakfast-table, and as I ascended the stair I met him coming down with an old rusty key, which must have belonged to the attic, in one hand, and a small brass box, like a cashbox, in the other.

"They may do what they like, but I'll checkmate them still," said he with an oath. "Tell Mary that I shall want a fire in my room today, and send down to Fordham, the Horsham lawyer."

'I did as he ordered, and when the lawyer arrived I was asked to step up to the room. The fire was burning brightly, and in the grate there was a mass of black, fluffy ashes, as of burned paper, while the brass box stood open and empty beside it. As I glanced at the box I noticed, with a start, that upon the lid was printed the treble K which I had read in the morning upon the envelope.

"I wish you, John," said my uncle, "to witness my will. I leave my estate, with all its advantages and all its disadvantages, to my brother, your father, whence it will, no doubt, descend to you. If you can enjoy it in peace, well and good! If you find you cannot, take my advice, my boy, and leave it to your deadliest enemy. I am sorry to give you such a two-edged thing, but I can't say what turn things are going to take. Kindly sign the paper where Mr Fordham shows you."

'I signed the paper as directed, and the lawyer took it away with him. The singular incident made, as you may think, the deepest impression upon me, and I pondered over it and turned it every way in my mind without being able to make anything of it. Yet I could not shake off the vague feeling of dread which it left behind, though the sensation grew less keen as the weeks passed and nothing happened to disturb the usual routine of our lives. I could see a change in my uncle, however. He drank more than ever, and he was less inclined for any sort of society. Most of his time he would spend in his room, with the door locked upon the inside, but sometimes he would emerge in a sort of drunken frenzy and would burst out of the house and tear about the garden with a revolver in his hand, screaming out that he was afraid of no man, and that he was not to be cooped up, like a sheep in a pen, by man or devil. When these hot fits were over however, he would rush tumultuously in at the door and lock and bar it behind him, like a man who can brazen it out no longer against the terror which lies at the roots of his soul. At such times I have seen his face, even on a cold day, glisten with moisture, as though it were new raised from a basin.

'Well, to come to an end of the matter, Mr Holmes, and not to abuse your patience, there came a night when he made one of those drunken sallies from which he never came back. We found him, when we went to search for him, face downward in a little green-scummed pool, which lay at the foot of the garden. There was no sign of any violence, and the water was but two feet deep, so that the jury, having regard to his known eccentricity, brought in a verdict of "suicide". But I, who knew how he winced from the very thought of death, had much ado to persuade myself that he had gone out of his way to meet it. The matter passed, however, and my father entered into possession of the estate, and of some 14,000 pounds, which lay to his credit at the bank.'

'One moment,' Holmes interposed, 'your statement is, I foresee, one of the most remarkable to which I have ever listened. Let me have the date of the reception by your uncle of the letter, and the date of his supposed suicide.'

'The letter arrived on March 10, 1883. His death was seven weeks later, upon the night of May 2nd.'

'Thank you. Pray proceed.'

'When my father took over the Horsham property, he, at my request, made a careful examination of the attic, which had been always locked up. We found the brass box there, although its contents had been destroyed. On the inside of the cover was a paper label, with the initials of K.K.K. repeated upon it, and "Letters, memoranda, receipts, and a register" written beneath. These, we presume, indicated the nature of the papers which had been destroyed by Colonel Openshaw. For the rest, there was nothing of much importance in the attic save a great many scattered papers and note-books bearing upon my uncle's life in America. Some of them were of the war time and showed that he had done his duty well and had borne the repute of a brave soldier. Others were of a date during the reconstruction of the Southern states, and were mostly concerned with politics, for he had evidently taken a strong part in opposing the carpet-bag politicians who had been sent down from the North.

'Well, it was the beginning of '84 when my father came to live at

Horsham, and all went as well as possible with us until the January of '85. On the fourth day after the new year I heard my father give a sharp cry of surprise as we sat together at the breakfast-table. There he was, sitting with a newly opened envelope in one hand and five dried orange pips in the outstretched palm of the other one. He had always laughed at what he called my cock-and-bull story about the colonel, but he looked very scared and puzzled now that the same thing had come upon himself.

"Why, what on earth does this mean, John?" he stammered.

"My heart had turned to lead. It is K.K.K.," said I.

'He looked inside the envelope. "So it is," he cried. "Here are the very letters. But what is this written above them?"

"Put the papers on the sundial," I read, peeping over his shoulder.

"What papers? What sundial?" he asked.

"The sundial in the garden. There is no other," said I; "but the papers must be those that are destroyed."

"Pooh!" said he, gripping hard at his courage. "We are in a civilized land here, and we can't have tomfoolery of this kind. Where does the thing come from?"

"From Dundee," I answered, glancing at the postmark.

"Some preposterous practical joke," said he. "What have I to do with sundials and papers? I shall take no notice of such nonsense."

"I should certainly speak to the police," I said.

"And be laughed at for my pains. Nothing of the sort."

"Then let me do so?"

"No, I forbid you. I won't have a fuss made about such nonsense."

'It was in vain to argue with him, for he was a very obstinate man. I went about, however, with a heart which was full of forebodings.

'On the third day after the coming of the letter my father went from home to visit an old friend of his, Major Freebody, who is in command of one of the forts upon Portsdown Hill. I was glad that he should go, for it seemed to me that he was farther from danger when he was away from home. In that, however, I was in error. Upon the second day of his absence I received a telegram from the major, imploring me to come at once. My father had fallen over one of the deep chalk-pits which abound in the neighbourhood, and was lying senseless, with a shattered skull. I hurried to him, but he passed away without having ever recovered his consciousness. He had, as it appears, been returning from Fareham in the twilight, and as the country was unknown to him, and the chalk-pit unfenced, the jury had no hesitation in bringing in a verdict of "death from accidental causes". Carefully as I examined every fact connected with his death, I was unable to find anything which could suggest the idea of murder. There were no signs of violence, no footmarks, no robbery, no record of strangers having been seen upon the roads. And yet I need not tell you that my mind was far from at ease, and that I was well-nigh certain that some foul plot had been woven round him.

'In this sinister way I came into my inheritance. You will ask me why I did not dispose of it? I answer, because I was well convinced that our troubles were in some way dependent upon an incident in my uncle's life, and that the danger would be as pressing in one house as in another.

'It was in January, '85, that my poor father met his end, and two years and eight months have elapsed since then. During that time I have lived happily at Horsham, and I had begun to hope that this curse had passed way from the family, and that it had ended with the last generation. I had begun to take comfort too soon, however; yesterday morning the blow fell in the very shape in which it had come upon my father.'

The young man took from his waistcoat a crumpled envelope, and turning to the table he shook out upon it five little dried orange pips.

'This is the envelope,' he continued. 'The postmark is London—eastern division. Within are the very words which were upon my father's last message: "K.K.K."; and then "Put the papers on the sundial."'

'What have you done?' asked Holmes.

'Nothing.'

'Nothing?'

'To tell the truth'—he sank his face into his thin, white hands—'I have felt helpless. I have felt like one of those poor rabbits when the snake is writhing towards it. I seem to be in the grasp of some resistless, inexorable evil, which no foresight and no precautions can guard against.'

'Tut! tut!' cried Sherlock Holmes. 'You must act, man, or you are lost. Nothing but energy can save you. This is no time for despair.'

'I have seen the police.'

'Ah!'

'But they listened to my story with a smile. I am convinced that the inspector has formed the opinion that the letters are all practical jokes, and that the deaths of my relations were really accidents, as the jury stated, and were not to be connected with the warnings.'

Holmes shook his clenched hands in the air. 'Incredible imbecility!' he cried.

'They have, however, allowed me a policeman, who may remain in the house with me.'

'Has he come with you tonight?'

'No. His orders were to stay in the house.'

Again Holmes raved in the air.

'Why did you not come to me,' he cried, 'and, above all, why did you not come at once?'

'I did not know. It was only today that I spoke to Major Prendergast about my troubles and was advised by him to come to you.'

'It is really two days since you had the letter. We should have acted before this. You have no further evidence, I suppose, than that which you have placed before us—no suggestive detail which might help us?'

'There is one thing,' said John Openshaw. He rummaged in his coat pocket, and, drawing out a piece of discoloured, blue-tinted paper, he laid it out upon the table. 'I have some remembrance,' said he, 'that on the day when my uncle burned the papers I observed that the small, unburned margins which lay amid the ashes were of this particular colour. I found this single sheet upon the floor of his room, and I am inclined to think that it may be one of the papers which has, perhaps, fluttered out from among the others, and in that way has escaped destruction. Beyond the mention of pips, I do not see that it helps us much. I think myself that it is a page from some private diary. The writing is undoubtedly my uncle's.'

Holmes moved the lamp, and we both bent over the sheet of paper, which showed by its ragged edge that it had indeed been torn from a book. It was headed, 'March, 1869,' and beneath were the following enigmatical notices:

4th. Hudson came. Same old platform.

7th. Set the pips on McCauley, Paramore, and John Swain, of St. Augustine.

9th. McCauley cleared.

10th. John Swain cleared.

12th. Visited Paramore. All well.

'Thank you!' said Holmes, folding up the paper and returning it to our visitor. 'And now you must on no account lose another instant. We cannot spare time even to discuss what you have told me. You must get home instantly and act.'

'What shall I do?'

'There is but one thing to do. It must be done at once. You must put this piece of paper which you have shown us into the brass box which you have described. You must also put in a note to say that all the other papers were burned by your uncle, and that this is the only one which remains. You must assert that in such words as will carry conviction with them. Having done this, you must at once put the box out upon the sundial, as directed. Do you understand?'

'Entirely.'

'Do not think of revenge, or anything of the sort, at present. I think that we may gain that by means of the law; but we have our web to weave, while theirs is already woven. The first consideration is to remove the pressing danger which threatens you. The second is to clear up the mystery and to punish the guilty parties.'

'I thank you,' said the young man, rising and pulling on his overcoat. 'You have given me fresh life and hope. I shall certainly do as you advise.'

'Do not lose an instant. And, above all, take care of yourself in the meanwhile, for I do not think that there can be a doubt that you are threatened by a very real and imminent danger. How do you go back?'

'By train from Waterloo.'

'It is not yet nine. The streets will be crowded, so I trust that you may be in safety. And yet you cannot guard yourself too closely.'

'I am armed.'

'That is well. Tomorrow I shall set to work upon your case.'

'I shall see you at Horsham, then?'

'No, your secret lies in London. It is there that I shall seek it.'

'Then I shall call upon you in a day, or in two days, with news as to the box and the papers. I shall take your advice in every particular.' He shook hands with us and took his leave. Outside the wind still screamed and the rain splashed and pattered against the windows. This strange, wild story seemed to have come to us from amid the mad elements—blown in upon us like a sheet of sea-weed in a gale—and now to have been reabsorbed by them once more.

Sherlock Holmes sat for some time in silence, with his head sunk forward and his eyes bent upon the red glow of the fire. Then he lit his pipe, and leaning back in his chair he watched the blue smoke-rings as they chased each other up to the ceiling.

'I think, Watson,' he remarked at last, 'that of all our cases we have had none more fantastic than this.'

'Save, perhaps, the Sign of Four.'

'Well, yes. Save, perhaps, that. And yet this John Openshaw seems to me to be walking amid even greater perils than did the Sholtos.'

'But have you,' I asked, 'formed any definite conception as to what these perils are?'

'There can be no question as to their nature,' he answered.

'Then what are they? Who is this K.K.K., and why does he pursue this unhappy family?'

Sherlock Holmes closed his eyes and placed his elbows upon the arms of his chair, with his finger-tips together. 'The ideal reasoner,' he remarked, 'would, when he had once been shown a single fact in all its bearings, deduce from it not only all the chain of events which led up to it but also all the results which would follow from it. As Cuvier could correctly describe a whole animal by the contemplation of a single bone, so the observer who has thoroughly understood one link in a series of incidents should be able to accurately state all the other ones, both before and after. We have not yet grasped the results which the reason alone can attain to. Problems may be solved in the study which have baffled all those who have sought a solution by the aid of their senses. To carry the art, however, to its highest pitch, it is necessary that the reasoner should be able to utilize all the facts which have come to his knowledge; and this in itself implies, as you will readily see, a possession of all knowledge, which, even in these days of free education and encyclopaedias, is a somewhat rare accomplishment. It is not so impossible, however, that a man should possess all knowledge which is likely to be useful to him in his work, and this I have endeavoured in my case to do. If I remember rightly, you on one occasion, in the early days of our friendship, defined my limits in a very precise fashion.'

'Yes,' I answered, laughing. 'It was a singular document. Philosophy, astronomy, and politics were marked at zero, I remember. Botany variable, geology profound as regards the mud-stains from any region within fifty miles of town, chemistry eccentric, anatomy unsystematic, sensational literature and crime records unique, violin-player, boxer, swordsman, lawyer, and self-poisoner by cocaine and tobacco. Those, I think, were the main points of my analysis.'

Holmes grinned at the last item. 'Well,' he said, 'I say now, as I said then, that a man should keep his little brain-attic stocked with all the furniture that he is likely to use, and the rest he can put away in the lumber-room of his library, where he can get it if he wants it. Now, for such a case as the one which has been submitted to us tonight, we need certainly to muster all our resources. Kindly hand me down the letter K of the American Encyclopaedia which stands upon the shelf beside you. Thank you. Now let us consider the situation and see what may be deduced from it. In the first place, we may start with a strong presumption that Colonel Openshaw had some very strong reason for leaving America. Men at his time of life do not change all their habits and exchange willingly the charming climate of Florida for the lonely life of an English provincial town. His extreme love of solitude in England suggests the idea that he was in fear of someone or something, so we may assume as a working hypothesis that it was fear of someone or something which drove him from America. As to what it was he feared, we can only deduce that by considering the formidable letters which were received by himself and his successors. Did you remark the postmarks of those letters?'

'The first was from Pondicherry, the second from Dundee, and the third from London.'

'From East London. What do you deduce from that?'

'They are all seaports. That the writer was on board of a ship.'

'Excellent. We have already a clue. There can be no doubt that the probability—the strong probability—is that the writer was on board of a ship. And now let us consider another point. In the case of Pondicherry, seven weeks elapsed between the threat and its fulfilment, in Dundee it was only some three or four days. Does that suggest anything?'

'A greater distance to travel.'

'But the letter had also a greater distance to come.'

'Then I do not see the point.'

'There is at least a presumption that the vessel in which the man or men are is a sailing-ship. It looks as if they always sent their singular warning or token before them when starting upon their mission. You see how quickly the deed followed the sign when it came from Dundee. If they had come from Pondicherry in a steamer they would have arrived almost as soon as their letter. But, as a matter of fact, seven weeks elapsed. I think that those seven weeks represented the difference between the mail-boat which brought the letter and the sailing vessel which brought the writer.'

'It is possible.'

'More than that. It is probable. And now you see the deadly urgency of this new case, and why I urged young Openshaw to caution. The blow has always fallen at the end of the time which it would take the senders to travel the distance. But this one comes from London, and therefore we cannot count upon delay.'

'Good God!' I cried. 'What can it mean, this relentless persecution?'

'The papers which Openshaw carried are obviously of vital importance to the person or persons in the sailing-ship. I think that it is quite clear that there must be more than one of them. A single man could not have carried out two deaths in such a way as to deceive a coroner's jury. There must have been several in it, and they must have been men of resource and determination. Their papers they mean to have, be the holder of them who it may. In this way you see K.K.K. ceases to be the initials of an individual and becomes the badge of a society.'

'But of what society?'

'Have you never—' said Sherlock Holmes, bending forward and sinking his voice—'have you never heard of the Ku Klux Klan?'

'I never have.'

Holmes turned over the leaves of the book upon his knee. 'Here it is,' said he presently:

'Ku Klux Klan. A name derived from the fanciful resemblance to the sound produced by cocking a rifle. This terrible secret society was formed by some ex-Confederate soldiers in the Southern states after the Civil War, and it rapidly formed local branches in different parts of the country, notably in Tennessee, Louisiana, the Carolinas, Georgia, and Florida. Its power was used for political purposes, principally for the terrorizing of the negro voters and the murdering and driving from the country of those who were opposed to its views. Its outrages were usually preceded by a warning sent to the marked man in some fantastic but generally recognized shape—a sprig of oak-leaves in some parts, melon seeds or orange pips in others. On receiving this the victim might either openly abjure his former ways, or might fly from the country. If he braved the matter out, death would unfailingly come upon him, and usually in some strange and unforeseen manner. So perfect was the organization of the society, and so systematic its methods, that there is hardly a case upon record where any man succeeded in braving it with impunity, or in which any of its outrages were traced home to the perpetrators. For some years the organization flourished in spite of the efforts of the United States government and of the better classes of the community in the South. Eventually, in the year 1869, the movement rather suddenly collapsed, although there have been sporadic outbreaks of the same sort since that date.

'You will observe,' said Holmes, laying down the volume, 'that the sudden breaking up of the society was coincident with the disappearance of Openshaw from America with their papers. It may well have been cause and effect. It is no wonder that he and his family have some of the more implacable spirits upon their track. You can understand that this register and diary may implicate some of the first men in the South, and that there may be many who will not sleep easy at night until it is recovered.'

'Then the page we have seen—'

'Is such as we might expect. It ran, if I remember right, "sent the pips to A, B, and C"—that is, sent the society's warning to them. Then there are successive entries that A and B cleared, or left the country, and finally that C was visited, with, I fear, a sinister result for C. Well, I think, Doctor, that we may let some light into this dark place, and I believe that the only chance young Openshaw has in the meantime is to do what I have told him. There is nothing more to be said or to be done tonight, so hand me over my violin and let us try to forget for half an hour the miserable weather and the still more miserable ways of our fellowmen.'

It had cleared in the morning, and the sun was shining with a subdued brightness through the dim veil which hangs over the great city. Sherlock Holmes was already at breakfast when I came down.

'You will excuse me for not waiting for you,' said he; 'I have, I foresee, a very busy day before me in looking into this case of young Openshaw's.'

'What steps will you take?' I asked.

'It will very much depend upon the results of my first inquiries. I may have to go down to Horsham, after all.'

'You will not go there first?'

'No, I shall commence with the City. Just ring the bell and the maid will bring up your coffee.'

As I waited, I lifted the unopened newspaper from the table and glanced my eye over it. It rested upon a heading which sent a chill to my heart.

'Holmes,' I cried, 'you are too late.'

'Ah!' said he, laying down his cup, 'I feared as much. How was it done?' He spoke calmly, but I could see that he was deeply moved.

'My eye caught the name of Openshaw, and the heading "Tragedy

Near Waterloo Bridge". Here is the account:

"Between nine and ten last night Police-Constable Cook, of the H Division, on duty near Waterloo Bridge, heard a cry for help and a splash in the water. The night, however, was extremely dark and stormy, so that, in spite of the help of several passers-by, it was quite impossible to effect a rescue. The alarm, however, was given, and, by the aid of the water-police, the body was eventually recovered. It proved to be that of a young gentleman whose name, as it appears from an envelope which was found in his pocket, was John Openshaw, and whose residence is near Horsham. It is conjectured that he may have been hurrying down to catch the last train from Waterloo Station, and that in his haste and the extreme darkness he missed his path and walked over the edge of one of the small landing-places for river steamboats. The body exhibited no traces of violence, and there can be no doubt that the deceased had been the victim of an unfortunate accident, which should have the effect of calling the attention of the authorities to the condition of the riverside landing-stages."

We sat in silence for some minutes, Holmes more depressed and shaken than I had ever seen him.

'That hurts my pride, Watson,' he said at last. 'It is a petty feeling, no doubt, but it hurts my pride. It becomes a personal matter with me now, and, if God sends me health, I shall set my hand upon this gang. That he should come to me for help, and that I should send him away to his death—!' He sprang from his chair and paced about the room in uncontrollable agitation, with a flush upon his sallow cheeks and a nervous clasping and unclasping of his long thin hands.

'They must be cunning devils,' he exclaimed at last. 'How could they have decoyed him down there? The Embankment is not on the direct line to the station. The bridge, no doubt, was too crowded, even on such a night, for their purpose. Well, Watson, we shall see who will win in the long run. I am going out now!'

'To the police?'

'No; I shall be my own police. When I have spun the web they may take the flies, but not before.'

All day I was engaged in my professional work, and it was late in the evening before I returned to Baker Street. Sherlock Holmes had not come back yet. It was nearly ten o'clock before he entered, looking pale and worn. He walked up to the sideboard, and tearing a piece from the loaf he devoured it voraciously, washing it down with a long draught of water.

'You are hungry,' I remarked.

'Starving. It had escaped my memory. I have had nothing since breakfast.'

'Nothing?'

'Not a bite. I had no time to think of it.'

'And how have you succeeded?'

'Well.'

'You have a clue?'

'I have them in the hollow of my hand. Young Openshaw shall not long remain unavenged. Why, Watson, let us put their own devilish trade-mark upon them. It is well thought of!'

'What do you mean?'

He took an orange from the cupboard, and tearing it to pieces he squeezed out the pips upon the table. Of these he took five and thrust them into an envelope. On the inside of the flap he wrote 'S. H. for J. O.' Then he sealed it and addressed it to 'Captain James Calhoun, Barque *Lone Star*, Savannah, Georgia.'

'That will await him when he enters port,' said he, chuckling. 'It may give him a sleepless night. He will find it as sure a precursor of his fate as Openshaw did before him.'

'And who is this Captain Calhoun?'

'The leader of the gang. I shall have the others, but he first.'

'How did you trace it, then?'

He took a large sheet of paper from his pocket, all covered with dates and names.

'I have spent the whole day,' said he, 'over Lloyd's registers and files of the old papers, following the future career of every vessel which touched at Pondicherry in January and February in '83. There were thirty-six ships of fair tonnage which were reported there during those months. Of these, one, the *Lone Star*, instantly attracted my attention, since, although it was reported as having cleared from London, the name is that which is given to one of the states of the Union.'

'Texas, I think.'

'I was not and am not sure which; but I knew that the ship must have an American origin.'

'What then?'

'I searched the Dundee records, and when I found that the barque *Lone Star* was there in January, '85, my suspicion became a certainty. I then inquired as to the vessels which lay at present in the port of London.'

'Yes?'

'The *Lone Star* had arrived here last week. I went down to the Albert Dock and found that she had been taken down the river by the early tide this morning, homeward bound to Savannah. I wired to Gravesend and learned that she had passed some time ago, and as the wind is easterly I have no doubt that she is now past the Goodwins and not very far from the Isle of Wight.'

'What will you do, then?'

'Oh, I have my hand upon him. He and the two mates, are as I learn, the only native-born Americans in the ship. The others are Finns and Germans. I know, also, that they were all three away from the ship last night. I had it from the stevedore who has been loading their cargo. By the time that their sailing-ship reaches Savannah the mail-boat will have carried this letter, and the cable will have informed the police of Savannah that these three gentlemen are badly wanted here upon a charge of murder.'

There is ever a flaw, however, in the best laid of human plans, and the murderers of John Openshaw were never to receive the orange pips which would show them that another, as cunning and as resolute as themselves, was upon their track. Very long and very severe were the equinoctial gales that year. We waited long for news of the *Lone Star* of Savannah, but none ever reached us. We did at last hear that somewhere far out in the Atlantic a shattered stern-post of the boat was seen swinging in the trough of a wave, with the letters 'L. S.' carved upon it, and that is all which we shall ever know of the fate of the *Lone* Star.

12

IN THE LIBRARY

W.W. Jacobs

... The first horror had now to some extent passed, and was succeeded by the fear of death...

The fire had burnt low in the library, for the night was wet and warm. It was now little more than a gray shell, and looked desolate. Trayton Burleigh, still hot, rose from his armchair, and turning out one of the gas-jets, took a cigar from a box on a side-table and resumed his seat again.

The apartment, which was on the third floor at the back of the house, was a combination of library, study, and smoke-room, and was the daily despair of the old housekeeper who, with the assistance of one servant, managed the house. It was a bachelor establishment, and had been left to Trayton Burleigh and James Fletcher by a distant connection of both men some ten years before.

Trayton Burleigh sat back in his chair watching the smoke of his cigar through half-closed eyes. Occasionally he opened them a little wider and glanced round the comfortable, well-furnished room, or stared with a cold gleam of hatred at Fletcher as he sat sucking stolidly at his brier pipe. It was a comfortable room and a valuable house, half of which belonged to Trayton Burleigh; and yet he was to leave it in the morning and become a rogue and a wanderer over the face of the earth. James Fletcher had said so. James Fletcher, with the pipe still between his teeth and speaking from one corner of his mouth only, had pronounced his sentence.

'It hasn't occurred to you, I suppose,' said Burleigh, speaking suddenly, 'that I might refuse your terms.'

'No,' said Fletcher, simply.

Burleigh took a great mouthful of smoke and let it roll slowly out.

'I am to go out and leave you in possession?' he continued. 'You will stay here sole proprietor of the house; you will stay at the office sole owner and representative of the firm? You are a good hand at a deal, James Fletcher.'

'I am an honest man,' said Fletcher, 'and to raise sufficient money to make your defalcations good will not by any means leave me the gainer, as you very well know.'

'There is no necessity to borrow,' began Burleigh, eagerly. 'We can pay the interest easily, and in course of time make the principal good without a soul being the wiser.'

'That you suggested before,' said Fletcher, 'and my answer is the same. I will be no man's confederate in dishonesty; I will raise every penny at all costs, and save the name of the firm—and yours with it—but I will never have you darken the office again, or sit in this house after tonight.'

'You won't,' cried Burleigh, starting up in a frenzy of rage.

'I won't,' said Fletcher. 'You can choose the alternative: disgrace and penal servitude. Don't stand over me; you won't frighten me, I can assure you. Sit down.'

'You have arranged so many things in your kindness,' said Burleigh, slowly, resuming his seat again, 'have you arranged how I am to live?'

'You have two strong hands, and health,' replied Fletcher. 'I will give you the two hundred pounds I mentioned, and after that you must look out for yourself. You can take it now.'

He took a leather case from his breast pocket, and drew out a roll of notes. Burleigh, watching him calmly, stretched out his hand and took them from the table. Then he gave way to a sudden access of rage, and crumpling them in his hand, threw them into a corner of the room. Fletcher smoked on.

'Mrs Marl is out?' said Burleigh, suddenly.

Fletcher nodded.

'She will be away the night,' he said, slowly; 'and Jane too; they have gone together somewhere, but they will be back at half-past eight in the morning.'

'You are going to let me have one more breakfast in the old place, then,' said Burleigh. 'Half-past eight, half-past—'

He rose from his chair again. This time Fletcher took his pipe from his mouth and watched him closely. Burleigh stooped, and picking up the notes, placed them in his pocket.

'If I am to be turned adrift, it shall not be to leave you here,' he said, in a thick voice.

He crossed over and shut the door; as he turned back Fletcher rose from his chair and stood confronting him. Burleigh put his hand to the wall, and drawing a small Japanese sword from its sheath of carved ivory, stepped slowly toward him.

'I give you one chance, Fletcher,' he said, grimly. 'You are a man of your word. Hush this up and let things be as they were before, and you are safe.'

'Put that down,' said Fletcher, sharply.

'By—, I mean what I say!' cried the other.

'I mean what I said!' answered Fletcher.

He looked round at the last moment for a weapon, then he turned suddenly at a sharp sudden pain, and saw Burleigh's clenched fist nearly touching his breast-bone. The hand came away from his breast again, and something with it. It went a long way off. Trayton Burleigh suddenly went to a great distance and the room darkened. It got quite dark, and Fletcher, with an attempt to raise his hands, let them fall to his side instead, and fell in a heap to the floor.

He was so still that Burleigh could hardly realize that it was all over, and stood stupidly waiting for him to rise again. Then he took out his handkerchief as though to wipe the sword, and thinking better of it, put it back into his pocket again, and threw the weapon on to the floor.

The body of Fletcher lay where it had fallen, the white face turned up to the gas. In life he had been a commonplace-looking man, not to say vulgar; now Burleigh, with a feeling of nausea, drew back toward the door, until the body was hidden by the table, and relieved from the sight, he could think more clearly. He looked down carefully and examined his clothes and his boots. Then he crossed the room again, and with his face averted, turned out the gas. Something seemed to stir in the darkness, and with a faint cry he blundered toward the door before he had realized that it was the clock. It struck twelve.

He stood at the head of the stairs trying to recover himself; trying to think. The gas on the landing below, the stairs and the furniture, all looked so prosaic and familiar that he could not realize what had occurred. He walked slowly down and turned the light out. The darkness of the upper part of the house was now almost appalling, and in a sudden panic he ran down stairs into the lighted hall, and snatching a hat from the stand, went to the door and walked down to the gate.

Except for one window the neighbouring houses were in darkness, and the lamps shone tip a silent street. There was a little rain in the air, and the muddy road was full of pebbles. He stood at the gate trying to screw up his courage to enter the house again. Then he noticed a figure coming slowly up the road and keeping close to the palings.

The full realization of what he had done broke in upon him when he found himself turning to fly from the approach of the constable. The wet cape glistening in the lamplight, the slow, heavy step, made him tremble. Suppose the thing upstairs was not quite dead and should cry out? Suppose the constable should think it strange for him to be standing there and follow him in? He assumed a careless attitude, which did not feel careless, and as the man passed bade him goodnight, and made a remark as to the weather.

Ere the sound of the other's footsteps had gone quite out of hearing, he turned and entered the house again before the sense of companionship should have quite departed. The first flight of stairs was lighted by the gas in the hall, and he went up slowly. Then he struck a match and went up steadily, past the library door, and with firm fingers turned on the gas in his bedroom and lit it. He opened the window a little way, and sitting down on his bed, tried to think.

He had got eight hours. Eight hours and two hundred pounds in small notes. He opened his safe and took out all the loose cash it contained, and walking about the room, gathered up and placed in his pockets such articles of jewellery as he possessed.

The first horror had now to some extent passed, and was succeeded by the fear of death.

With this fear on him he sat down again and tried to think out the first moves in that game of skill of which his life was the stake. He had often read of people of hasty temper, evading the police for a time, and eventually falling into their hands for lack of the most elementary common sense. He had heard it said that they always made some stupid blunder, left behind them some damning clue. He took his revolver from a drawer and saw that it was loaded. If the worst came to the worst, he would die quickly.

Eight hours' start; two hundred odd pounds. He would take lodgings at first in some populous district, and let the hair on his face grow. When the hue-and-cry had ceased, he would go abroad and start life again. He would go out of a night and post letters to himself, or better still, postcards, which his landlady would read. Postcards from cheery friends, from a sister, from a brother. During the day he would stay in and write, as became a man who described himself as a journalist.

Or suppose he went to the sea? Who would look for him in flannels, bathing and boating with ordinary happy mortals? He sat and pondered. One might mean life, and the other death. Which?

His face burned as he thought of the responsibility of the choice. So many people went to the sea at that time of year that he would surely pass unnoticed. But at the sea one might meet acquaintances. He got up and nervously paced the room again. It was not so simple, now that it meant so much, as he had thought.

The sharp little clock on the mantel-piece rang out 'one,' followed immediately by the deeper note of that in the library. He thought of the clock, it seemed the only live thing in that room, and shuddered. He wondered whether the thing lying by the far side of the table heard it. He wondered—

He started and held his breath with fear. Somewhere down stairs a board creaked loudly, then another. He went to the door, and opening it a little way, but without looking out, listened. The house was so still that he could hear the ticking of the old clock in the kitchen below. He opened the door a little wider and peeped out. As he did so there was a sudden sharp outcry on the stairs, and he drew back into the room and stood trembling before he had quite realized that the noise had been made by the cat. The cry was unmistakable; but what had disturbed it?

There was silence again, and he drew near the door once more. He became certain that something was moving stealthily on the stairs. He heard the boards creak again, and once the rails of the balustrade rattled. The silence and suspense were frightful. Suppose that the something which had been Fletcher waited for him in the darkness outside?

He fought his fears down, and opening the door, determined to see what was beyond. The light from his room streamed out on to the landing, and he peered about fearfully. Was it fancy, or did the door of Fletcher's room opposite close as he looked? Was it fancy, or did the handle of the door really turn?

In perfect silence, and watching the door as he moved, to see that nothing came out and followed him, he proceeded slowly down the dark stairs. Then his jaw fell, and he turned sick and faint again. The library door, which he distinctly remembered closing, and which, moreover, he had seen was closed when he went upstairs to his room, now stood open some four or five inches. He fancied that there was a rustling inside, but his brain refused to be certain. Then plainly and unmistakably he heard a chair pushed against the wall.

He crept to the door, hoping to pass it before the thing inside became aware of his presence. Something crept stealthily about the room. With a sudden impulse he caught the handle of the door, and, closing it violently, turned the key in the lock, and ran madly down the stairs.

A fearful cry sounded from the room, and a heavy hand beat upon the panels of the door. The house rang with the blows, but above them sounded the loud hoarse cries of human fear. Burleigh, half-way down to the hall, stopped with his hand on the balustrade and listened. The beating ceased, and a man's voice cried out loudly for God's sake to let him out.

At once Burleigh saw what had happened and what it might mean for him. He had left the hall door open after his visit to the front, and some wandering bird of the night had entered the house. No need for him to go now. No need to hide either from the hangman's rope or the felon's cell. The fool above had saved him. He turned and ran upstairs again just as the prisoner in his furious efforts to escape wrenched the handle from the door.

'Who's there?' he cried, loudly.

'Let me out!' cried a frantic voice. 'For God's sake, open the door! There's something here.'

'Stay where you are!' shouted Burleigh, sternly. 'Stay where you are! If you come out, I'll shoot you like a dog!'

The only response was a smashing blow on the lock of the door. Burleigh raised his pistol, and aiming at the height of a man's chest, fired through the panel.

The report and the crashing of the wood made one noise, succeeded by an unearthly stillness, then the noise of a window hastily opened. Burleigh fled hastily down the stairs, and flinging wide the hall door, shouted loudly for assistance.

It happened that a sergeant and the constable on the beat had just met in the road. They came toward the house at a run. Burleigh, with incoherent explanations, ran upstairs before them, and halted outside the library door. The prisoner was still inside, still trying to demolish the lock of the sturdy oaken door. Burleigh tried to turn the key, but the lock was too damaged to admit of its moving. The sergeant drew back, and, shoulder foremost, hurled himself at the door and burst it open.

He stumbled into the room, followed by the constable, and two shafts of light from the lanterns at their belts danced round the room. A man lurking behind the door made a dash for it, and the next instant the three men were locked together.

Burleigh, standing in the doorway, looked on coldly, reserving himself for the scene which was to follow. Except for the stumbling of the men and the sharp catch of the prisoner's breath, there was no noise. A helmet fell off and bounced and rolled along the floor. The men fell; there was a sobbing snarl and a sharp click. A tall figure rose from the floor; the other, on his knees, still held the man down. The standing figure felt in his pocket, and, striking a match, lit the gas.

The light fell on the flushed face and fair beard of the sergeant. He was bare-headed, and his hair dishevelled. Burleigh entered the room and gazed eagerly at the half-insensible man on the floor-a short, thick-set fellow with a white, dirty face and a black moustache. His lip was cut and bled down his neck. Burleigh glanced furtively at the table. The cloth had come off in the struggle, and was now in the place where he had left Fletcher.

'Hot work, sir,' said the sergeant, with a smile. 'It's fortunate we were handy.'

The prisoner raised a heavy head and looked up with unmistakable terror in his eyes.

'All right, sir,' he said, trembling, as the constable increased the pressure of his knee. 'I 'ain't been in the house ten minutes altogether. By—, I've not.'

The sergeant regarded him curiously.

'It don't signify,' he said, slowly; 'ten minutes or ten seconds won't make any difference.'

The man shook and began to whimper.

'It was 'ere when I come,' he said, eagerly; 'take that down, sir. I've only just come, and it was 'ere when I come. I tried to get away then, but I was locked in.'

'What was?' demanded the sergeant.

'That,' he said, desperately.

The sergeant, following the direction of the terror-stricken black eyes, stooped by the table. Then, with a sharp exclamation, he dragged away the cloth. Burleigh, with a sharp cry of horror, reeled back against the wall.

'All right, sir,' said the sergeant, catching him; 'all right. Turn your head away.'

He pushed him into a chair, and crossing the room, poured out a glass of whiskey and brought it to him. The glass rattled against his teeth, but he drank it greedily, and then groaned faintly. The sergeant waited patiently. There was no hurry.

'Who is it, sir?' he asked at length.

'My friend—Fletcher,' said Burleigh, with an effort. 'We lived together.' He turned to the prisoner.

'You damned villain!'

'He was dead when I come in the room, gentlemen,' said the prisoner, strenuously. 'He was on the floor dead, and when I see 'im, I tried to get out. S' 'elp me he was. You heard me call out, sir. I shouldn't ha' called out if I'd killed him.'

'All right,' said the sergeant, gruffly; 'you'd better hold your tongue, you know.'

'You keep quiet,' urged the constable.

The sergeant knelt down and raised the dead man's head.

'I 'ad nothing to do with it,' repeated the man on the floor. 'I 'ad nothing to do with it. I never thought of such a thing. I've only been in the place ten minutes; put that down, sir.'

The sergeant groped with his left hand, and picking up the Japanese sword, held it at him.

'I've never seen it before,' said the prisoner, struggling.

'It used to hang on the wall,' said Burleigh. 'He must have snatched it down. It was on the wall when I left Fletcher a little while ago.'

'How long?' inquired the sergeant.

'Perhaps an hour, perhaps half an hour,' was the reply. 'I went to my bedroom.'

The man on the floor twisted his head and regarded him narrowly.

'You done it!' he cried, fiercely. 'You done it, and you want me to swing for it.'

'That'll do,' said the indignant constable.

The sergeant let his burden gently to the floor again.

'You hold your tongue, you devil!' he said, menacingly.

He crossed to the table and poured a little spirit into a glass and took it in his hand. Then he put it down again and crossed to Burleigh.

'Feeling better, sir?' he asked.

The other nodded faintly.

'You won't want this thing any more,' said the sergeant.

He pointed to the pistol which the other still held, and taking it from him gently, put it into his pocket.

'You've hurt your wrist, sir,' he said, anxiously.

Burleigh raised one hand sharply, and then the other.

'This one, I think,' said the sergeant. 'I saw it just now.'

He took the other's wrists in his hand, and suddenly holding them in the grip of a vice, whipped out something from his pocket—something hard and cold, which snapped suddenly on Burleigh's wrists, and held them fast.

'That's right,' said the sergeant; 'keep quiet.'

The constable turned round in amaze; Burleigh sprang toward him furiously.

'Take these things off!' he choked. 'Have you gone mad? Take them off!'

'All in good time,' said the sergeant.

'Take them off!' cried Burleigh again.

For answer the sergeant took him in a powerful grip, and staring steadily at his white face and gleaming eyes, forced him to the other end of the room and pushed him into a chair.

'Collins,' he said, sharply.

'Sir?' said the astonished subordinate.

'Run to the doctor at the corner hard as you can run!' said the other. 'This man is not dead!'

As the man left the room the sergeant took up the glass of spirits he had poured out, and kneeling down by Fletcher again, raised his head and tried to pour a little down his throat. Burleigh, sitting in his corner, watched like one in a trance. He saw the constable return with the breathless surgeon, saw the three men bending over Fletcher, and then saw the eyes of the dying man open and the lips of the dying man move. He was conscious that the sergeant made some notes in a pocket-book, and that all three men eyed him closely. The sergeant stepped toward him and placed his hand on his shoulder, and obedient to the touch, he arose and went with him out into the night.

13

AN IRREDUCIBLE DETECTIVE STORY

Stephen Leacock

...Hanged by a hair or a murder mystery minimized...

The mystery had now reached its climax. First, the man had been undoubtedly murdered. Secondly, it was as absolutely certain that no conceivable person had done it. It was therefore time to call in the great detective. He gave one searching glance at the corpse. In a moment he whipped out a microscope. 'Ha! Ha!' he said, as he picked a hair off the lapel of the dead man's coat. 'The mystery is solved.' He held up the hair. 'Listen,' he said, 'we have only to find the man who lost the hair and the criminal is in our hands.' The inexorable chain of logic was complete. The detective set himself to search. For four days and nights he moved, unobserved, through the streets of New York scanning closely every face he passed, looking for a man who had lost a hair. On the fifth day he discovered a man, disguised as a tourist, his head enveloped in a steamer cap that reached below his ears. The man was about to go on board the Gloritania. The detective followed him on board. 'Arrest him!' he said, and then drawing himself to his full height, he brandished aloft the hair. 'This is his,' said the great detective. 'It proves his guilt.' 'Remove his hat,' said the ship's captain sternly. They did so. The man was entirely bald. 'Ha!' said the great detective without a moment of hesitation. 'He has committed not one murder but about a million.'

14

THE MYSTERY OF THE RUE DE PEYCHAUD
O. Henry

...It is the hour when crime and vice and wickedness reign...

'Tis midnight in Paris. A myriad of lamps that line the Champs Élysées and the Rouge et Noir, cast their reflection in the dark waters of the Seine as it flows gloomily past the Place Vendôme and the black walls of the Convent Notadam. The great French capital is astir.

It is the hour when crime and vice and wickedness reign. Hundreds of fiacres drive madly through the streets conveying women, flashing with jewels and as beautiful as dreams, from opera and concert, and the little bijou supper rooms of the Café Tout le Temps are filled with laughing groups, while bon mots, persiflage and repartee fly upon the air—the jewels of thought and conversation.

Luxury and poverty brush each other in the streets. The homeless gamin, begging a sou with which to purchase a bed, and the spendthrift roué, scattering golden louis d'or, tread the same pavement.

When other cities sleep, Paris has just begun her wild revelry.

The first scene of our story is a cellar beneath the Rue de Peychaud.

The room is filled with smoke of pipes, and is stifling with the reeking breath of its inmates. A single flaring gas jet dimly lights the scene, which is one Rembrandt or Moreland and Keisel would have loved to paint.

A garçon is selling absinthe to such of the motley crowd as have a few sous, dealing it out in niggardly portions in broken teacups. Leaning against the bar is Carnaignole Cusheau—generally known as the Gray Wolf. He is the worst man in Paris.

He is more than four feet ten in height, and his sharp, ferocious looking face and the mass of long, tangled 'gray hair that covers his face and head, have earned for him the name he bears.

His striped blouse is wide open at the neck and falls outside of his dingy leather trousers. The handle of a deadly looking knife protrudes from his belt. One stroke of its blade would open a box of the finest French sardines.

'Voilà, Gray Wolf,' cries Couteau, the bartender. 'How many victims today? There is no blood upon your hands. Has the Gray Wolf forgotten how to bite?'

'Sacrè Bleu, Mille Tonnerre, by George,' hisses the Gray Wolf. 'Monsieur Couteau, you are bold indeed to speak to me thus.

'By Ventre St. Gris! I have not even dined today. Spoils indeed. There is no living in Paris now. But one rich American have I garrotted in a fortnight.

'Bah! Those Democrats. They have ruined the country. With their income tax and their free trade, they have destroyed the millionaire business. Carrambo! Diable! D—n it!'

'Hist!' suddenly says Chamounix the rag-picker, who is worth 20,000,000 francs, 'someone comes!'

The cellar door opened and a man crept softly down the rickety steps. The crowd watches him with silent awe.

He went to the bar, laid his card on the counter, bought a drink of absinthe, and then drawing from his pocket a little mirror, set it up on the counter and proceeded to don a false beard and hair and paint his face into wrinkles, until he closely resembled an old man seventy-one years of age.

He then went into a dark corner and watched the crowd of people with sharp, ferret-like eyes. Gray Wolf slipped cautiously to the bar and examined the card left by the newcomer.

'Holy Saint Bridget!' he exclaims. 'It is Tictocq, the detective.'

Ten minutes later a beautiful woman enters the cellar. Tenderly nurtured, and accustomed to every luxury that money could procure, she had, when a young vivandière at the Convent of Saint Susan de la Montarde, run away with the Gray Wolf, fascinated by his many crimes and the knowledge that his business never allowed him to scrape his feet in the hall or snore.

'Parbleu, Marie,' snarls the Gray Wolf. 'Que voulez vous? Avez-vous le beau cheval de mon frère, oule joli chien de votre père?'

'No, no, Gray Wolf,' shouts the motley group of assassins, rogues and pickpockets, even their hardened hearts appalled at his fearful words. 'Mon Dieu! You cannot be so cruel!'

'Tiens!' shouts the Gray Wolf, now maddened to desperation, and drawing his gleaming knife. 'Voilà! Canaille! Tout le monde, carte blanche enbonpoint sauve que peut entre nous revenez nous a nous moutons!'

The horrified sans-culottes shrink back in terror as the Gray Wolf seizes Maria by the hair and cuts her into twenty-nine pieces, each exactly the same size.

As he stands with reeking hands above the corpse, amid a deep silence, the old, gray-bearded man who has been watching the scene springs forward, tears off his false beard and locks, and Tictocq, the famous French detective, stands before them.

Spellbound and immovable, the denizens of the cellar gaze at the greatest modern detective as he goes about the customary duties of his office.

He first measures the distance from the murdered woman to a point on the wall, then he takes down the name of the bartender and the day of the month and the year. Then drawing from his pocket a powerful microscope, he examines a little of the blood that stands upon the floor in little pools.

'Mon Dieu!' he mutters, 'it is as I feared—human blood.'

He then enters rapidly in a memorandum book the result of his investigations, and leaves the cellar.

Tictocq bends his rapid steps in the direction of the headquarters of the Paris gendarmerie, but suddenly pausing, he strikes his hand upon his brow with a gesture of impatience.

'Mille tonnerre,' he mutters. 'I should have asked the name of that man with the knife in his hand.'

It is reception night at the palace of the Duchess Valerie du Bellairs.

The apartments are flooded with a mellow light from paraffine candles in solid silver candelabra.

The company is the most aristocratic and wealthy in Paris.

Three or four brass bands are playing behind a portière between the coal shed, and also behind time. Footmen in gay-laced livery bring in beer noiselessly and carry out apple-peelings dropped by the guests.

Valerie, seventh Duchess du Bellairs, leans back on a solid gold ottoman on eiderdown cushions, surrounded by the wittiest, the bravest, and the handsomest courtiers in the capital.

'Ah, madame,' said the Prince Champvilliers, of Palais Royale, corner of Seventy-third Street, 'as Montesquiaux says, "Rien de plus bon tutti frutti"—Youth seems your inheritance. You are tonight the most beautiful, the wittiest in your own salon. I can scarce believe my own senses, when I remember that thirty-one years ago you—'

'Saw it off!' says the Duchess peremptorily.

The Prince bows low, and drawing a jewelled dagger, stabs himself to the heart.

'The displeasure of your grace is worse than death,' he says, as he takes his overcoat and hat from a corner of the mantelpiece and leaves the room.

'Voilà,' says Bèebè Francillon, fanning herself languidly. 'That is the way with men. Flatter them, and they kiss your hand. Loose but a moment the silken leash that holds them captive through their vanity and self-opinionativeness, and the son-of-a-gun gets on his ear at once. The devil go with him, I say.'

'Ah, mon Princesse,' sighs the Count Pumpernickel, stooping and whispering with eloquent eyes into her ear. 'You are too hard upon us. Balzac says, "All women are not to themselves what no one else is to another." Do you not agree with him?'

'Cheese it!' says the Princess. 'Philosophy palls upon me. I'll shake you.'

'Hosses?' says the Count.

Arm and arm they go out to the salon au Beurre.

Armande de Fleury, the young pianissimo danseuse from the Folies Bergère is about to sing.

She slightly clears her throat and lays a voluptuous cud of chewing gum upon the piano as the first notes of the accompaniment ring through the salon.

As she prepares to sing, the Duchess du Bellairs grasps the arm of her ottoman in a vice-like grip, and she watches with an expression of almost anguished suspense.

She scarcely breathes.

Then, as Armande de Fleury, before uttering a note, reels, wavers, turns white as snow and falls dead upon the floor, the Duchess breathes a sigh of relief.

The Duchess had poisoned her. Then the guests crowd about the piano, gazing with bated breath, and shuddering as they look upon the music rack and observe that the song that Armande came so near singing is 'Sweet Marie.'

Twenty minutes later a dark and muffled figure was seen to emerge from a recess in the mullioned wall of the Arc de Triomphe and pass rapidly northward. It was no other than Tictocq, the detective.

The network of evidence was fast being drawn about the murderer of Marie Cusheau.

It is midnight on the steeple of the Cathedral of Notadam. It is also the same time at other given points in the vicinity.

The spire of the Cathedral is 20,000 feet above the pavement, and a casual observer, by making a rapid mathematical calculation, would have readily perceived that this Cathedral is, at least, double the height of others that measure only 10,000 feet.

At the summit of the spire there is a little wooden platform on which there is room for but one man to stand.

Crouching on this precarious footing, which swayed, dizzily with every breeze that blew, was a man closely muffled, and disguised as a wholesale grocer.

Old François Beongfallong, the great astronomer, who is studying the sidereal spheres from his attic window in the Rue de Bologny, shudders as he turns his telescope upon the solitary figure upon the spire.

'Sacrè Bleu!' he hisses between his new celluloid teeth. 'It is Tictocq, the detective. I wonder whom he is following now?'

While Tictocq is watching with lynx-like eyes the hill of Montmartre, he suddenly hears a heavy breathing beside him, and turning, gazes into the ferocious eyes of the Gray Wolf.

Carnaignole Cusheau had put on his W.U. Tel. Co. climbers and climbed the steeple.

'Parbleu, monsieur,' says Tictocq. 'To whom am I indebted for the honour of this visit?'

The Gray Wolf smiled softly and depreciatingly.

'You are Tictocq, the detective?' he said.

'I am.'

'Then listen. I am the murderer of Marie Cusheau. She was my wife and she had cold feet and ate onions. What was I to do? Yet life is sweet to me. I do not wish to be guillotined. I have heard that you are on my track. Is it true that the case is in your hands?'

'It is.'

'Thank le bon Dieu, then, I am saved.'

The Gray Wolf carefully adjusts the climbers on his feet and descends the spire.

Tictocq takes out his notebook and writes in it.

'At last,' he says, 'I have a clue.'

Monsieur le Compte Carnaignole Cusheau, once known as the Gray Wolf, stands in the magnificent drawing-room of his palace on East 47th Street.

Three days after his confession to Tictocq, he happened to look in the pockets of a discarded pair of pants and found twenty million francs in gold.

Suddenly the door opens and Tictocq, the detective, with a dozen gensd'arme, enters the room.

'You are my prisoner,' says the detective.

'On what charge?'

'The murder of Marie Cusheau on the night of August 17th.'

'Your proofs?'

'I saw you do it, and your own confession on the spire of Notadam.'

The Count laughed and took a paper from his pocket. 'Read this,' he said, 'here is proof that Marie Cusheau died of heart failure.'

Tictocq looked at the paper.

It was a cheque for 100,000 francs.

Tictocq dismissed the gensd'arme with a wave of his hand.

'We have made a mistake, monsieurs,' he said, but as he turns to leave the room, Count Carnaignole stops him.

'One moment, monsieur.'

The Count Carnaignole tears from his own face a false beard and reveals the flashing eyes and well-known features of Tictocq, the detective.

Then, springing forward, he snatches a wig and false eyebrows from his visitor, and the Gray Wolf, grinding his teeth in rage, stands before him.

The murderer of Marie Cusheau was never discovered.

15

A DEAD MAN'S REVENGE: A DETECTIVE STORY
H.P. Lovecraft[1]

… Before you put my body in the tomb, drop this ball onto the floor, at a spot marked 'A'…

I
The Burns's Tomb.

It was noon in the Little village of Mainville, and a sorrowful group of people were standing around the Burns's Tomb. Joseph Burns was dead. (when dying, he had given the following strange orders: 'Before you put my body in the tomb, drop this ball onto the floor, at a spot marked "A".' he then handed a small golden ball to the rector.) The people greatly regretted his death. After The funeral services were finished, Mr Dobson (the rector) said, 'My friends, I will now gratify the last wishes of the deceased. So saying, he descended into the tomb. (to lay the ball on the spot marked 'A') Soon the funeral party Began to be impatient, and after a time Mr Cha's. Greene (the Lawyer) descended to make a search. Soon he came up with a frightened face, and said, 'Mr Dobson is not there'!

II
Mysterious Mr Bell

It was 3.10 o'clock in ye afternoone whenne The door bell of the Dobson mansion rang loudly, and the servant on going to the door, found an elderly man, with black hair, and side whiskers. He asked to see Miss Dobson. Upon arriving in her presence he said, 'Miss

---

[1] The story was written in 1898, making Lovecraft only 8 or 9 at the time.

Dobson, I know where your father is, and for £10,000 I will restore him. My name is Mr Bell.' 'Mr Bell,' said Miss Dobson, 'will you excuse me from the room a moment?' 'Certainly'. replied Mr Bell. In a short time she returned, and said, 'Mr Bell, I understand you. You have abducted my father, and hold him for a ransom'

III
At The Police Station

It was 3.20 o'clock in the afternoon when the telephone bell at the North End Police Station rang furiously, and Gibson, (the telephone Man) Inquired what was the matter,

'Have found out about fathers dissapearance'! a womans voice said. 'Im Miss Dobson, and father has been abducted, 'Send King John'! King John was a famous western detective. Just then a man rushed in, and shouted, 'Oh! Terrors! Come To the Graveyard!'

IV
The West Window

Now let us return to the Dobson Mansion. Mr Bell was rather taken aback by Miss Dobson's plain speaking, but when he recovered his speech he said, 'Don't put it quite so plain, Miss Dobson, for I—' He was interrupted by the entrance of King John, who with a brace of revolvers in his hands, barred all egress by the doorway. But quicker than thought Bell sprang to a west window—and jumped.

V
The Secret of The Grave

Now let us return to the station house. After the exited visitor had calmed somewhat, he could tell his story straighter. He had seen three men in the graveyard shouting 'Bell! Bell! where are you old man!?' and acting very suspiciously. He then followed them, and they entered The Burns's Tomb! He then followed them in and they touched a spring at a point marked "A" and then Dissapeared'. 'I wish king John were here', Said Gibson, 'What's your name,'? 'John Spratt'. replied the visitor.

VI
The Chase for Bell

Now let us return To the Dobson Mansion again: King John was utterly confounded at the Sudden movement of Bell, but when he recovered from his surprise, his first thought was of chase. Accordingly, he started in pursuit of the abductor. He tracked him down to the R. R. Station and found to his dismay that he had taken the train for Kent, a large city toward the south, and between which and Mainville there existed no telegraph or telephone. The train had Just Started!

VII
The Negro Hackman

The Kent train started at 10.35, and about 10.36 an exited, dusty, and tired man1 rushed into the Mainville hack. office and said to a negro hackman who was standing by the door—'If you can take me to Kent in 15 minutes I will give you a dollar'. 'I doan' see how I'm ter git there', said the negro 'I hab'n't got a decent pair of hosses an' I hab—' 'Two Dollars'! Shouted The Traveller, 'all right' said the Hackman. It was King John.

VIII
Bell's Surprise

It was 11 o'clock at Kent, all of the stores were closed but one, a dingy, dirty, little shop, down at the west end. It lay between Kent Harbour, & the Kent & Mainville R.R. In the Front room a shabbily dressed person of doubtful age was conversing with a middle aged woman with gray haire, 'I have agreed to do the job, Lindy,' he said, 'Bell will arrive at 11.30 and the carraige is ready to take him down to the wharf, where a ship for Africa sails tonighte'.

'But If King John were to come?' queried 'Lindy'.

'Then we'd get nabbed, an' Bell would be hung' Replied The man.

Just then a rap sounded at the door 'Are you Bell'? inquired Lindy 'Yes' was the response, 'And I caught the 10.35 and King John got Left, so we are all right'. At 11.40 the party reached The Landing, and saw a ship Loom up in the darkness. 'The Kehdive' 'of Africa' was painted on the hull, and Just as they were to step on board, a man stepped forward in the darkness and said 'John Bell, I arrest you in the Queen's name'!

It was King John.

IX
The Trial

The daye of The Trial had arrived, and a crowd of people had gathered around the Little grove, (which served for a court house in summer) To hear the trial of John Bell on the charge of kidnapping. 'Mr Bell,' said the judge 'what is the secret of the Burns's tomb'

'I well tell you this much' said Bell, 'If you go into the tomb and touch a certain spot marked "A" you will find out'

'Now where is Mr Dobson'? queried the judge, 'Here'! said a voice behind them, and The figure of Mr Dobson HIMSELF loomed up in the doorway.

'How did you get here'! was chorused. 'Tis a long story,' said Dobson.

X
Dobson's Story

'When I went down into the tomb,' Said Dobson, 'Everything was darkness, I could see nothing. but Finally I discerned the letter "A" printed in white on the onyx floor, I dropped the ball on the Letter, and immediately a trap-door opened and a man sprang up. It was this man, here,' he said (pointing at Bell, who stood Trembling on the prisoner's docke) 'and he pulled me down into a brilliantly lighted, and palatial apartment where I have Lived until today. One day a young man rushed in and exclaimed "The secret Is revealed!" and was gone. He did not see me. Once Bell left his key behind, and I took the impression in wax, and the next day was spent in filing keys to fit the Lock. The next day my key fitted and the next day (which is today) I escaped.'

XI
The Mystery Unveiled

'Why did the late J. Burns, ask you to put the ball there'? (at 'A'?) queried the Judge? 'To get me into trouble' replied Dobson 'He, and Francis Burns, (his brother) have plotted against me for years, and I knew not, in what way they would harm me'. 'Sieze Francis Burns'! yelled the Judge.

XII
Conclusion

Francis Burns, and John Bell, were sent to prison for life. Mr Dobson was cordially welcomed by his daughter, who, by the way had become Mrs King John. 'Lindy' and her accomplice were sent to Newgate for 30 days as aidors and abbettors of a criminal escape.

16

THE CASK OF AMONTILLADO
Edgar Allan Poe

... walls of piled skeletons, with casks and puncheons intermingling, into the inmost recesses of the catacombs...

The thousand injuries of Fortunato I had borne as I best could, but when he ventured upon insult I vowed revenge. You, who so well know the nature of my soul, will not suppose, however, that gave utterance to a threat. At length I would be avenged; this was a point definitely, settled—but the very definitiveness with which it was resolved precluded the idea of risk. I must not only punish but punish with impunity. A wrong is unredressed when retribution overtakes its redresser. It is equally unredressed when the avenger fails to make himself felt as such to him who has done the wrong. It must be understood that neither by word nor deed had I given Fortunato cause to doubt my good will. I continued to smile in his face, and he did not perceive that my smile now was at the thought of his immolation.

He had a weak point—this Fortunato—although in other regards he was a man to be respected and even feared. He prided himself on his connoisseurship in wine. Few Italians have the true virtuoso spirit. For the most part their enthusiasm is adopted to suit the time and opportunity, to practise imposture upon the British and Austrian millionaires. In painting and gemmary, Fortunato, like his countrymen, was a quack, but in the matter of old wines he was sincere. In this respect I did not differ from him materially—I was skilful in the Italian vintages myself, and bought largely whenever I could. It was about dusk, one evening during the supreme madness of the carnival season, that I encountered my friend. He accosted me with excessive warmth, for he had been drinking much. The man wore motley. He had on a tight-fitting parti-striped dress, and his head was surmounted by the conical cap and bells. I was so pleased to see him that I thought I should never have done wringing his hand. I said to him—'My dear Fortunato, you are luckily met. How remarkably well you are looking today. But I have received a pipe of what passes for Amontillado, and I have my doubts.'

'How?' said he. 'Amontillado, a pipe? Impossible! And in the middle of the carnival!'

'I have my doubts,' I replied; 'and I was silly enough to pay the full Amontillado price without consulting you in the matter. You were not to be found, and I was fearful of losing a bargain.'

'Amontillado!'

'I have my doubts.'

'Amontillado!'

'And I must satisfy them.'

'Amontillado!'

'As you are engaged, I am on my way to Luchresi. If anyone has a critical turn it is he. He will tell me—'

'Luchresi cannot tell Amontillado from Sherry.'

'And yet some fools will have it that his taste is a match for your own.

'Come, let us go.'

'Whither?'

'To your vaults.'

'My friend, no; I will not impose upon your good nature. I perceive you have an engagement. Luchresi—'

'I have no engagement;—come.'

'My friend, no. It is not the engagement, but the severe cold with which I perceive you are afflicted. The vaults are insufferably damp. They are encrusted with nitre.'

'Let us go, nevertheless. The cold is merely nothing. Amontillado! You have been imposed upon. And as for Luchresi, he cannot distinguish Sherry from Amontillado.'

Thus speaking, Fortunato possessed himself of my arm; and putting on a mask of black silk and drawing a roquelaire closely about my person, I suffered him to hurry me to my palazzo.

There were no attendants at home; they had absconded to make merry in honour of the time. I had told them that I should not return until the morning, and had given them explicit orders not to stir from the house. These orders were sufficient. I well knew, to insure their immediate disappearance, one and all, as soon as my back was turned. I took from their sconces two flambeaux, and giving one to Fortunato, bowed him through several suites of rooms to the archway that led into the vaults. I passed down a long and winding staircase, requesting him to be cautious as he followed. We came at length to the foot of the descent, and stood together upon the damp ground of the catacombs of the Montresors.

The gait of my friend was unsteady, and the bells upon his cap jingled as he strode.

'The pipe,' he said.

'It is farther on,' said I; 'but observe the white web-work which gleams from these cavern walls.'

He turned towards me, and looked into my eyes with two filmy orbs that distilled the rheum of intoxication.

'Nitre?' he asked, at length.

'Nitre,' I replied.

'How long have you had that cough?'

'Ugh! ugh! ugh!—ugh! ugh! ugh!—ugh! ugh! ugh!—ugh! ugh! ugh!—ugh! ugh! ugh!'

My poor friend found it impossible to reply for many minutes.

'It is nothing,' he said, at last.

'Come,' I said, with decision, 'we will go back; your health is precious. You are rich, respected, admired, beloved; you are happy, as once I was. You are a man to be missed. For me it is no matter. We will go back; you will be ill, and I cannot be responsible. Besides, there is Luchresi—'

'Enough,' he said; 'the cough's a mere nothing; it will not kill me. I shall not die of a cough.'

'True—true,' I replied; 'and, indeed, I had no intention of alarming you unnecessarily—but you should use all proper caution. A draught of this Medoc will defend us from the damps.

Here I knocked off the neck of a bottle which I drew from a long row of its fellows that lay upon the mould.

'Drink,' I said, presenting him the wine.

He raised it to his lips with a leer. He paused and nodded to me familiarly, while his bells jingled.

'I drink,' he said, 'to the buried that repose around us.'

'And I to your long life.'

He again took my arm, and we proceeded.

'These vaults,' he said, 'are extensive.'

'The Montresors,' I replied, 'were a great and numerous family.'

'I forget your arms.'

'A huge human foot d'or, in a field azure; the foot crushes a serpent rampant whose fangs are imbedded in the heel.'

'And the motto?'

'Nemo me impune lacessit.'

'Good!' he said.

The wine sparkled in his eyes and the bells jingled. My own fancy grew warm with the Medoc. We had passed through long walls of piled skeletons, with casks and puncheons intermingling, into the inmost recesses of the catacombs. I paused again, and this time I made bold to seize Fortunato by an arm above the elbow.

'The nitre!' I said; 'see, it increases. It hangs like moss upon the vaults. We are below the river's bed. The drops of moisture trickle among the bones. Come, we will go back ere it is too late. Your cough—'

'It is nothing,' he said; 'let us go on. But first, another draught of the Medoc.'

I broke and reached him a flagon of De Grave. He emptied it at a breath. His eyes flashed with a fierce light. He laughed and threw the bottle upwards with a gesticulation I did not understand.

I looked at him in surprise. He repeated the movement—a grotesque one.

'You do not comprehend?' he said.

'Not I,' I replied.

'Then you are not of the brotherhood.'
'How?'
'You are not of the masons.'
'Yes, yes,' I said; 'yes, yes.'
'You? Impossible! A mason?'
'A mason,' I replied.
'A sign,' he said, 'a sign.'
'It is this,' I answered, producing from beneath the folds of my roquelaire a trowel.

'You jest,' he exclaimed, recoiling a few paces. 'But let us proceed to the Amontillado.'

'Be it so,' I said, replacing the tool beneath the cloak and again offering him my arm. He leaned upon it heavily. We continued our route in search of the Amontillado. We passed through a range of low arches, descended, passed on, and descending again, arrived at a deep crypt, in which the foulness of the air caused our flambeaux rather to glow than flame.

At the most remote end of the crypt there appeared another less spacious. Its walls had been lined with human remains, piled to the vault overhead, in the fashion of the great catacombs of Paris. Three sides of this interior crypt were still ornamented in this manner. From the fourth side the bones had been thrown down, and lay promiscuously upon the earth, forming at one point a mound of some size. Within the wall thus exposed by the displacing of the bones, we perceived a still interior crypt or recess, in depth about four feet, in width three, in height six or seven. It seemed to have been constructed for no especial use within itself, but formed merely the interval between two of the colossal supports of the roof of the catacombs, and was backed by one of their circumscribing walls of solid granite.

It was in vain that Fortunato, uplifting his dull torch, endeavoured to pry into the depth of the recess. Its termination the feeble light did not enable us to see.

'Proceed,' I said; 'herein is the Amontillado. As for Luchresi—'
'He is an ignoramus,' interrupted my friend, as he stepped unsteadily forward, while I followed immediately at his heels. In

niche, and finding an instant he had reached the extremity of the niche, and finding his progress arrested by the rock, stood stupidly bewildered. A moment more and I had fettered him to the granite. In its surface were two iron staples, distant from each other about two feet, horizontally. From one of these depended a short chain, from the other a padlock. Throwing the links about his waist, it was but the work of a few seconds to secure it. He was too much astounded to resist. Withdrawing the key I stepped back from the recess.

'Pass your hand,' I said, 'over the wall; you cannot help feeling the nitre. Indeed, it is very damp. Once more let me implore you to return. No? Then I must positively leave you. But I must first render you all the little attentions in my power.'

'The Amontillado!' ejaculated my friend, not yet recovered from his astonishment.

'True,' I replied; 'the Amontillado.'

As I said these words I busied myself among the pile of bones of which I have before spoken. Throwing them aside, I soon uncovered a quantity of building stone and mortar. With these materials and with the aid of my trowel, I began vigorously to wall up the entrance of the niche. I had scarcely laid the first tier of the masonry when I discovered that the intoxication of Fortunato had in a great measure worn off. The earliest indication I had of this was a low moaning cry from the depth of the recess. It was not the cry of a drunken man. There was then a long and obstinate silence. I laid the second tier, and the third, and the fourth; and then I heard the furious vibrations of the chain. The noise lasted for several minutes, during which, that I might hearken to it with the more satisfaction, I ceased my labours and sat down upon the bones. When at last the clanking subsided, I resumed the trowel, and finished without interruption the fifth, the sixth, and the seventh tier. The wall was now nearly upon a level with my breast. I again paused, and holding the flambeaux over the mason-work, threw a few feeble rays upon the figure within.

A succession of loud and shrill screams, bursting suddenly from the throat of the chained form, seemed to thrust me violently back. For a brief moment I hesitated, I trembled. Unsheathing my rapier,

I began to grope with it about the recess; but the thought of an instant reassured me. I placed my hand upon the solid fabric of the catacombs, and felt satisfied. I reapproached the wall; I replied to the yells of him who clamoured. I re-echoed, I aided, I surpassed them in volume and in strength. I did this, and the clamourer grew still.

It was now midnight, and my task was drawing to a close. I had completed the eighth, the ninth and the tenth tier. I had finished a portion of the last and the eleventh; there remained but a single stone to be fitted and plastered in. I struggled with its weight; I placed it partially in its destined position. But now there came from out the niche a low laugh that erected the hairs upon my head. It was succeeded by a sad voice, which I had difficulty in recognizing as that of the noble Fortunato.

The voice said—'Ha! ha! ha!—he! he! he!—a very good joke, indeed—an excellent jest. We will have many a rich laugh about it at the palazzo—he! he! he!—over our wine—he! he! he!'

'The Amontillado!' I said.

'He! he! he!—he! he! he!—yes, the Amontillado. But is it not getting late? Will not they be awaiting us at the palazzo, the Lady Fortunato and the rest? Let us be gone.'

'Yes,' I said, 'let us be gone.'

'For the love of God, Montresor!'

'Yes,' I said, 'for the love of God!'

But to these words I hearkened in vain for a reply. I grew impatient. I called aloud—'Fortunato!'

No answer. I called again—'Fortunato!'

No answer still. I thrust a torch through the remaining aperture and let it fall within. There came forth in return only a jingling of the bells. My heart grew sick; it was the dampness of the catacombs that made it so. I hastened to make an end of my labour. I forced the last stone into its position; I plastered it up. Against the new masonry I re-erected the old rampart of bones. For the half of a century no mortal has disturbed them. *In pace requiescat!*

17

MURDER IN THE MORNING

Dorothy Sayers

...What he saw made him whistle softly...

'Half a mile along the main road to Ditchley, and then turn off to the left at the sign-post,' said the Traveller in Mangles; 'but I think you'll be wasting your time.'

'Oh, well,' said Mr Montague Egg cheerfully, 'I'll have a shot at the old bird. As the *Salesman's Handbook* says: "Don't let the smallest chance slip by; you never know until you try." After all, he's supposed to be rich, isn't he?'

'Mattresses stuffed with gold sovereigns, or so the neighbours say,' acknowledged the Traveller in Mangles with a grin. 'But they'd say anything.'

'Thought you said there weren't any neighbours.'

'No more they are. Manner of speaking. Well, good luck to it!'

Mr Egg acknowledged the courtesy with a wave of his smart trilby, and let his clutch in with quiet determination.

The main road was thronged with the usual traffic of a Saturday morning in June—worthy holiday-makers bound for Melbury Woods or for the seashore about Beachampton—but as soon as he turned into the little narrow lane by the sign-post which said 'Hatchford Mill 2 Miles', he was plunged into a profound solitude and silence, broken only by the scurry of an occasional rabbit from the hedgerow and the chug of his own Morris. Whatever else the mysterious Mr Pinchbeck might be, he certainly was a solitary soul, and when, about a mile and a half down the lane, Monty caught sight of the tiny cottage, set far back in the middle of a neglected-looking field, he began to think that the Traveller in Mangles had been right. Rich though he might be, Mr Pinchbeck was probably not a very likely customer for the wines and spirits supplied by Messrs. Plummet & Rose of Piccadilly. But, remembering Maxim Five of the *Salesman's Handbook*, 'If you're a salesman worth the name at all, you can sell razors to a billiard-ball,' Mr Egg stopped his car at the entrance to the field, lifted the sagging gate and dragged it open, creaking in every rotten rail, and drove forward over the rough track, scarred with the ruts left by wet-weather traffic.

The cottage door was shut. Monty beat a cheerful tattoo upon its blistered surface, and was not very much surprised to get no answer. He knocked again, and then, unwilling to abandon his quest now he had come so far, walked round to the back. Here again he got no answer. Was Mr Pinchbeck out? It was said that he never went out. Being by nature persistent and inquisitive, Mr Egg stepped up to the window and looked in. What he saw made him whistle softly. He returned to the back door, pushed it open and entered.

When you arrive at a person's house with no intention beyond selling him a case of whisky or a dozen or so of port, it is disconcerting to find him stretched on his own kitchen floor, with his head battered to pulp. Mr Egg had served two years on the Western Front, but he did not like what he saw. He put the table-cloth over it. Then, being a methodical sort of person, he looked at his watch, which marked 10.25. After a minute's pause for consideration, he made a rapid tour of the premises, then set off, driving as fast as he could, to fetch the police.

The inquest upon Mr Humphrey Pinchbeck took place the following day, and resulted in a verdict of wilful murder against some person or persons unknown. During the next fortnight, Mr Montague Egg, with some uneasiness, watched the newspapers. The police were following up a clue. A man was requested to communicate with the police. The man was described—a striking-looking person with a red beard and a check suit, driving a sports car with the registered number WOE 1313. The man was found. The man was charged, and Mr Montague Egg, three hundred miles away, was informed, to his disgust, that he would be required to give evidence before the magistrates at Beachampton.

The accused, who gave his name as Theodore Barton, age forty-two, profession poet (at which Monty stared very hard, never having seen a poet at such close quarters), was a tall, powerfully built man, dressed in flamboyant tweeds, and having a certain air of rather disreputable magnificence about him. One would expect, thought Monty, to find him hanging about bars in the East Central district of London. His eyes were bold, and the upper part of his face handsome in its way; the mouth was hidden by the abundance of his tawny beard. He appeared to be perfectly at his ease, and was represented by a solicitor.

Montague Egg was called at an early stage to give evidence of the finding of the body. He mentioned that the time was 10.25 a.m. on Saturday, June 18th, and that the body was still quite warm when he saw it. The front door was locked; the back door shut, but not locked. The kitchen was greatly disordered, as though there had been a violent struggle, and a blood-stained poker lay beside the dead man. He had made a rapid search before sending for the police. In a bedroom upstairs he had seen a heavy iron box standing open and empty, with the keys hanging from the lock. There was no other person in the cottage, nor yet concealed about the little yard, but there were marks as though a large car had recently stood in a shed at the back of the house. In the sitting-room were the remains of breakfast for two persons. He (Mr Egg) had passed down the lane from the high-road in his car, and had met nobody at all on the way. He had spent perhaps five or ten minutes in searching the place, and had then driven back by the way he came.

At this point Detective-Inspector Ramage explained that the lane leading to the cottage ran on for half a mile or so to pass Hatchford Mill, and then bent back to enter the main Beachampton road again at a point three miles nearer Ditchley.

The next witness was a baker named Bowles. He gave evidence that he had called at the cottage with his van at 10.15, to deliver two loaves of bread. He had gone to the back door, which had been opened by Mr Pinchbeck in person. The old gentleman had appeared to be in perfect health, but a little flurried and irritable. He had not seen any other person in the kitchen, but had an impression that before he knocked he had heard two men's voices talking loudly and excitedly. The lad who had accompanied Bowles on his round confirmed this, adding that he fancied he had seen the outline of a man move across the kitchen window.

Mrs Chapman, from Hatchford Mill, then came forward to say that she was accustomed to go in every week-day to Mr Pinchbeck's cottage to do a bit of cleaning. She arrived at 7.30 and left at 9 o'clock. On Saturday 18th she had come as usual, to find that a visitor had arrived unexpectedly the night before. She identified the accused, Theodore Barton, as that visitor. He had apparently slept on the couch in the sitting-room, and was departing again that morning. She saw his car in the shed; it was a little sports one, and she had particularly noticed the number, WOE 1313, thinking that there was an unlucky number and no mistake. The interior of the shed was not visible from the back door. She had set breakfast for the two of them. The milkman and the postman had called before she left, and the grocer's van must have come soon after, for it was down at the Mill by 9.30. Nobody else ever called at the cottage, so far as she knew. Mr Pinchbeck was a vegetarian and grew his own garden-stuff. She had never known him have a visitor before. She had heard nothing in the nature of 'words' between Mr Pinchbeck and the accused, but had thought the old man was not in the best of spirits. 'He seemed a bit put out, like.'

Then came another witness from the Mill, who had heard a car with a powerful engine drive very rapidly past the Mill a little before half-past ten. He had run out to look, fast cars being a rarity in the lane, but had seen nothing, on account of the trees which bordered the road at the corner just beyond the Mill.

At this point the police put in a statement made by the accused on his arrest. He said that he was the nephew of the deceased, and frankly admitted that he had spent the night at the cottage. Deceased had seemed pleased to see him, as they had not met for some time. On hearing that his nephew was 'rather hard up,' deceased had remonstrated with him about following so ill paid a profession as poetry, but had kindly offered him a small loan, which he, the accused, had gratefully accepted. Mr Pinchbeck had then opened the box in his bedroom and brought out a number of banknotes, of which he had handed over 'ten fivers,' accompanying the gift by a little sermon on hard work and thrift. This had happened at about 9.45 or a little earlier—at any rate, after Mrs Chapman was safely off the premises. The box had appeared to be full of banknotes and securities, and Mr Pinchbeck had expressed distrust both of Mrs Chapman and of the tradesmen in general. (Here Mrs Chapman voiced an indignant protest, and had to be soothed by the Bench.) The statement went on to say that the accused had had no sort of quarrel with his uncle, and had left the cottage at, he thought, 10 o'clock or thereabouts, and driven on through Ditchley and Frogthorpe to Beachampton. There he had left his car with a friend, to whom it belonged, and had hired a motor-boat and gone over to spend a fortnight in Brittany. Here he had heard nothing about his uncle's death till the arrival of Detective-Inspector Ramage had informed him of the suspicion against him. He had, of course, hastened back immediately to establish his innocence.

The police theory was that, as soon as the last tradesman had left the house, Barton had killed the old man, taken his keys, stolen the money, and escaped, supposing that the body would not be found till Mrs Chapman arrived on the Monday morning.

While Theodore Barton's solicitor was extracting from Inspector Ramage the admission that the only money found on the accused at the time of his arrest was six Bank of England five-pound notes and a few shillings' worth of French money, Mr Egg became aware that somebody was breathing very hard and excitedly down the back of his neck, and, on turning round, found himself face to face with an elderly woman, whose rather prominent eyes seemed ready to pop out of her head with agitation.

'Oh!' said the woman, bouncing in her seat. 'Oh, dear!'

'I beg your pardon,' said Mr Egg, ever courteous. 'Am I in your way, or anything?'

'Oh! oh, thank you! Oh, do tell me what I ought to do. There's something I ought to tell them. Poor man. He isn't guilty at all. I *know* he isn't. Oh, please do tell me what I ought to do. Do I have to go to the police? Oh, dear, oh, dear! I thought—I didn't know—I've never been in a place like this before! Oh, I know they'll bring him in guilty. Please, *please* stop them!'

'They can't bring him in guilty in this court,' said Monty soothingly. 'They can send him up for trial—'

'Oh, but they mustn't! He didn't do it. He wasn't there. Oh, please do something about it.'

She appeared so earnest that Mr Egg, slightly clearing his throat and settling his tie, rose boldly to his feet and exclaimed in stentorian accents: 'Your Worship!'

The bench stared. The solicitor stared. The accused stared. Everybody stared.

'There is a lady here,' said Monty, feeling that he must go through with it, 'who tells me she has important evidence to give on behalf of the accused.'

The staring eyes became focused upon the lady, who instantly started up, dropping her handbag, and crying: 'Oh, dear! I'm so sorry! I'm afraid I ought to have gone to the police.'

The solicitor, in whose face surprise, annoyance and anticipation struggled curiously together, at once came forward. The lady was extricated and a short whispered consultation followed, after which the solicitor said:

'Your worship, my client's instructions were to reserve his defence, but, since the lady, whom I have never seen until this moment, has so generously come forward with her statement, which appears to be a complete answer to the charge, perhaps your worship would prefer to hear her at this stage.'

After a little discussion, the Bench decided that they would like to hear the evidence, if the accused was agreeable. Accordingly, the lady was put in the box, and sworn, in the name of Millicent Adela Queek.

'I am a spinster, and employed as art mistress at Woodbury High School for Girls. Saturday 18th was a holiday, of course, and I thought I would have a little picnic, all by my lonesome, in Melbury Woods.

I started off in my own little car just about 9.30. It would take me about half an hour to get to Ditchley—I never drive very fast, and there was a lot of traffic on the road—most dangerous. When I got to Ditchley, I turned to the right, along the main road to Beachampton. After a little time I began to wonder whether I had put in quite enough petrol. My gauge isn't very reliable, you know, so I thought I'd better stop and make *quite* certain. So I pulled up at a roadside garage. I don't know *exactly* where it was, but it was quite a little way beyond Ditchley—between that and Helpington. It was one of those *dreadfully* ugly places, made of corrugated iron painted bright red. I don't think they should allow them to put up things like that. I asked the man there—a most obliging young man—to fill my tank, and while I was there I saw this gentleman—yes, I mean Mr Barton, the accused—drive up in his car. He was coming from the Ditchley direction and driving rather fast. He pulled up on the left-hand side of the road. The garage is on the right, but I saw him very distinctly. I couldn't mistake him—his beard, you know, and the clothes he was wearing—so distinctive. It was the same suit he is wearing now. Besides, I noticed the number of his car. Such a curious one, is it not? WOE 1313. Yes. Well, he opened the bonnet and did something to his plugs, I think, and then he drove on.'

'What time was this?'

'I was just going to tell you. When I came to look at my watch I found it had stopped. Most vexatious. I think it was due to the vibration of the steering-wheel. But I looked up at the garage clock—there was one just over the door—and it said 10.20. So I set my watch by that. Then I went on to Melbury Woods and had my little picnic. So fortunate, wasn't it? that I looked at the clock then. Because my watch stopped again later on. But I do *know* that it was 10.20 when this gentleman stopped at the garage, so I don't see how he could have been doing a murder at that poor man's cottage between 10.15 and 10.25, because it must be well over twenty miles away—more, I should think.'

Miss Queek ended her statement with a little gasp, and looked round triumphantly.

Detective-Inspector Ramage's face was a study. Miss Queek went on to explain why she had not come forward earlier with her story.

'When I read the description in the papers I thought it *must* be the same car I had seen, because of the number—but of course I couldn't be sure it was the same man, could I? Descriptions are *so* misleading. And naturally I didn't want to be mixed up with a police case. The school, you know—parents don't like it. But I thought, if I came and saw this gentleman for myself, then I should be quite certain. And Miss Wagstaffe—our head-mistress—so kindly gave me leave to come, though today is very inconvenient, being my busiest afternoon. But I said it might be a matter of life and death, and so it is, isn't it?'

The magistrate thanked Miss Queek for her public-spirited intervention, and then, at the urgent request of both parties, adjourned the court for further inquiry into the new evidence.

Since it was extremely important that Miss Queek should identify the garage in question as soon as possible, it was arranged that she should set out at once in search of it, accompanied by Inspector Ramage and his sergeant, Mr Barton's solicitor going with them to see fair play for his client. A slight difficulty arose, however. It appeared that the police car was not quite big enough to take the whole party comfortably, and Mr Montague Egg, climbing into his own Morris, found himself hailed by the inspector with the request for a lift.

'By all means,' said Monty; 'a pleasure. Besides, you'll be able to keep your eye on me. Because, if that chap didn't do it, it looks to me as though I must be the guilty party.'

'I wouldn't say that, sir,' said the inspector, obviously taken aback by this bit of thought-reading.

'I couldn't blame you if you did,' said Monty. He smiled, remembering his favourite motto for salesmen: 'A cheerful voice and cheerful look put orders in the order-book,' and buzzed merrily away in the wake of the police car along the road from Beachampton to Ditchley.

'We ought to be getting near it now,' remarked Ramage when they had left Helpington behind them. 'We're ten miles from Ditchley and about twenty-five from Pinchbeck's cottage. Let's see—it'll be the left-hand side of the road, going in this direction. Hullo! this looks rather like it,' he added presently. 'They're pulling up.'

The police car had stopped before an ugly corrugated-iron structure, standing rather isolated on the near side of the road, and adorned with a miscellaneous collection of enamelled advertisement-boards and a lot of petrol pumps. Mr Egg brought the Morris alongside.

'Is this the place, Miss Queek?'

'Well, I don't know. It was like this, and it was about here. But I can't be sure. All these dreadful little places are so much alike, but—Well, there! how stupid of me! Of course this isn't it. There's no clock. There ought to be a clock just over the door. *So* sorry to have made such a silly mistake. We must go on a little farther. It must be quite near here.'

The little procession moved forward again, and five miles farther on came once more to a halt. This time there could surely be no mistake. Another hideous red corrugated garage, more boards, more petrol-pumps, and a clock, whose hands pointed (correctly, as the inspector ascertained by reference to his watch) to 7.15.

'I'm sure this must be it,' said Miss Queek. 'Yes—I recognise the man,' she added, as the garage proprietor came out to see what was wanted.

The proprietor, when questioned, was not able to swear with any certainty to having filled Miss Queek's tank on June 18th. He had filled so many tanks before and since. But in the matter of the clock he was definite. It kept, and always had kept, perfect time, and it had never stopped or been out of order since it was first installed. If his clock had pointed to 10.20, then 10.20 was the time, and he would testify as much in any court in the kingdom. He could not remember having seen the car with the registered number WOE 1313, but there was no reason why he should, since it had not come in for attention. Motorists who wanted to do a spot of inspection often pulled up near his garage, in case they should find some trouble that needed expert assistance, but such incidents were so usual that he would pay no heed to them, especially on a busy morning.

Miss Queek, however, felt quite certain. She recognised the man, the garage and the clock. As a further precaution, the party went on as far as Ditchley, but, though the roadside was peppered the whole way with garages, there was no other exactly corresponding to the description. Either they were the wrong colour, or built of the wrong materials, or they had no clock.

'Well,' said the inspector, rather ruefully, 'unless we can prove collusion (which doesn't seem likely, seeing the kind of woman she is), that washes that out. That garage where she saw Barton is eighteen miles from Pinchbeck's cottage, and since we know the old man was alive at 10.15, Barton can't have killed him—not unless he was averaging 200 miles an hour or so, which can't be done yet awhile. Well, we've got to start all over again.'

'It looks a bit awkward for me,' said Monty pleasantly.

'I don't know about that. There's the voices that baker fellow heard in the kitchen. I know that couldn't have been you, because I've checked up your times.' Mr Ramage grinned. 'Perhaps the rest of the money may turn up somewhere. It's all in the day's work. We'd better be getting back again.'

Monty drove the first eighteen miles in thoughtful silence. They had just passed the garage with the clock (at which the inspector shook a mortified fist in passing), when Mr Egg uttered an exclamation and pulled up.

'Hullo!' said the inspector.

'I've got an idea,' said Monty. He pulled out a pocket-diary and consulted it. 'Yes—I thought so. I've discovered a coincidence. Let's check up on it. Do you mind? "Don't trust to luck, but be exact and verify the smallest fact."' He replaced the diary and drove on, overhauling the police car. In process of time they came to the garage which had first attracted their attention—the one which conformed to specification, except in the particular that it displayed no clock. Here he stopped, and the police car, following in their tracks, stopped also.

The proprietor emerged expectantly, and the first thing that struck one about him was his resemblance to the man they had interviewed at the other garage. Monty commented politely on the fact.

'Quite right,' said the man. 'He's my brother.'

'Your garages are alike, too,' said Monty.

'Bought off the same firm,' said the man. 'Supplied in parts. Mass-production. Readily erected overnight by any handy man.'

'That's the stuff,' said Mr Egg approvingly. 'Standardisation means immense saving in labour, time, expense. You haven't got a clock, though.'

'Not yet. I've got one on order.'

'Never had one?'

'Never.'

'Ever seen this lady before?'

The man looked Miss Queek carefully over from head to foot.

'Yes, I fancy I have. Came in one morning for petrol, didn't you, miss? Saturday fortnight or thereabouts. I've a good memory for faces.'

'What time would that be?'

'Ten to eleven, or a few minutes after. I remember I was just boiling up a kettle for my elevenses. I generally take a cup of tea about then.'

'Ten-fifty,' said the inspector eagerly. 'And this is—' he made a rapid calculation—'just on twenty-two miles from the cottage. Say half an hour from the time of the murder. Forty-four miles an hour—he could do that on his head in a fast sports car.'

'Yes, but—' interrupted the solicitor.

'Just a minute,' said Monty. 'Didn't you,' he went on, addressing the proprietor, 'once have one of those clock-faces with movable hands to show lighting-up time?'

'Yes, I did. I've still got it, as a matter of fact. It used to hang over the door. But I took it down last Sunday. People found it rather a nuisance; they were always mistaking it for a real clock.'

'And lighting-up time on June 18th,' said Monty softly, 'was 10.20, according to my diary.'

'Well, there,' said Inspector Ramage, smiting his thigh. 'Now, that's really clever of you, Mr Egg.'

'A brain-wave, a brain-wave,' admitted Monty. '"The salesman who will use his brains will spare himself a world of pains"—or so the *Handbook* says.'

18

MURDER AT PENTECOST

Dorothy Sayers

…Some public benefactor has just murdered the Master…

'Buzz off, Flathers,' said the young man in flannels. 'We're thrilled by your news, but we don't want your religious opinions. And, for the Lord's sake, stop talking about "undergrads", like a ruddy commercial traveller. Hop it!'

The person addressed, a pimply youth in a commoner's gown, bleated a little, but withdrew from the table, intimidated.

'Appalling little tick,' commented the young man in flannels to his companion. 'He's on my staircase, too. Thank Heaven, I move out next term. I suppose it's true about the Master? Poor old blighter—I'm quite sorry I cut his lecture. Have some more coffee?'

'No, thanks, Radcott. I must be pushing off in a minute. It's getting too near lunch-time.'

Mr Montague Egg, seated at the next small table, had pricked up his ears. He now turned, with an apologetic cough, to the young man called Radcott.

'Excuse me, sir,' he said, with some diffidence. 'I didn't intend to overhear what you gentlemen were saying, but might I ask a question?' Emboldened by Radcott's expression, which, though surprised, was frank and friendly, he went on: 'I happen to be a commercial traveller—Egg is my name, Montague Egg, representing Plummet & Rose, wines and spirits, Piccadilly. Might I ask what is wrong with saying "undergrads"? Is the expression offensive in any way?'

Mr Radcott blushed a fiery red to the roots of his flaxen hair.

'I'm frightfully sorry,' he said ingenuously, and suddenly looking extremely young. 'Damn stupid thing of me to say. Beastly brick.'

'Don't mention it, I'm sure,' said Monty.

'Didn't mean anything personal. Only, that chap Flathers gets my goat. He ought to know that nobody says "undergrads" except townees and journalists and people outside the university.'

'What ought we to say? "Undergraduates"?'

'"Undergraduates" is correct.'

'I'm very much obliged,' said Monty. 'Always willing to learn. It's easy to make a mistake in a thing like that, and, of course, it prejudices the customer against one. The *Salesman's Handbook* doesn't give any guidance about it; I shall have to make a memo for myself. Let me see. How would this do? "To call an Oxford gent an—"'

'I think I should say "Oxford man"—it's the more technical form of expression.'

'Oh, yes. "To call an Oxford man an undergrad proclaims you an outsider and a cad." That's very easy to remember.'

'You seem to have a turn for this kind of thing,' said Radcott, amused.

'Well, I think perhaps I have,' admitted Monty, with a touch of pride. 'Would the same thing apply at Cambridge?'

'Certainly,' replied Radcott's companion. 'And you might add that "To call the university the 'varsity is out of date, if not precisely narsity." I apologise for the rhyme. 'Varsity has somehow a flavour of the 'nineties.'

'So has the port I'm recommending,' said Mr Egg brightly. 'Still, one's sales-talk must be up to date, naturally; and smart, though not vulgar. In the wine and spirit trade we make refinement our aim. I am really much obliged to you, gentlemen, for your help. This is my first visit to Oxford. Could you tell me where to find Pentecost College? I have a letter of introduction to a gentleman there.'

'Pentecost?' said Radcott. 'I don't think I'd start there, if I were you.'

'No?' said Mr Egg, suspecting some obscure point of university etiquette. 'Why not?'

'Because,' replied Radcott surprisingly, 'I understand from the regrettable Flathers that some public benefactor has just murdered the Master, and in the circumstances I doubt whether the Bursar will be able to give proper attention to the merits of rival vintages.'

'Murdered the Master?' echoed Mr Egg.

'Socked him one—literally, I am told, with a brickbat enclosed in a Woolworth sock—as he was returning to his house from delivering his too-well-known lecture on Plato's use of the Enclitics. The whole school of *Literæ Humaniores* will naturally be under suspicion, but, personally, I believe Flathers did it himself. You may have heard him informing us that judgment overtakes the evil-doer, and inviting us to a meeting for prayer and repentance in the South Lecture-Room. Such men are dangerous.'

'Was the Master of Pentecost an evil-doer?'

'He has written several learned works disproving the existence of Providence, and I must say that I, in common with the whole Pentecostal community, have always looked on him as one of Nature's worst mistakes. Still, to slay him more or less on his own doorstep seems to me to be in poor taste. It will upset the examination candidates, who face their ordeal next week. And it will mean cancelling the Commem. Ball. Besides, the police have been called in, and are certain to annoy the Senior Common Room by walking on the grass in the quad. However, what's done can't be undone. Let us pass to a pleasanter subject. I understand that you have some port to dispose of. I, on the other hand, have recently suffered bereavement at the hands of a bunch of rowing hearties, who invaded my rooms the other night and poured my last dozen of Cockburn '04 down their leathery and undiscriminating throttles. If you care to stroll round with me to Pentecost, Mr Egg, bringing your literature with you, we might be able to do business.'

Mr Egg expressed himself as delighted to accept Radcott's invitation, and was soon trotting along the Cornmarket at his conductor's athletic heels. At the corner of Broad Street the second undergraduate left them, while they turned on, past Balliol and Trinity, asleep in the June sunshine, and presently reached the main entrance of Pentecost.

Just as they did so, a small, elderly man, wearing a light overcoat and carrying an M.A. gown over his arm, came ambling short-sightedly across the street from the direction of the Bodleian Library. A passing car just missed whirling him into eternity, as Radcott stretched out a long arm and raked him into safety on the pavement.

'Look out, Mr Temple,' said Radcott. 'We shall be having you murdered next.'

'Murdered?' queried Mr Temple, blinking. 'Oh, you refer to the motor-car. But I saw it coming. I saw it quite distinctly. Yes, yes. But why "next"? Has anybody else been murdered?'

'Only the Master of Pentecost,' said Radcott, pinching Mr Egg's arm.

'The Master? Dr Greeby? You don't say so! Murdered? Dear me! Poor Greeby! This will upset my whole day's work.' His pale-blue eyes shifted, and a curious, wavering look came into them. 'Justice is slow but sure. Yes, yes. The sword of the Lord and of Gideon. But the blood—that is always so disconcerting, is it not? And yet, I washed my hands, you know.' He stretched out both hands and looked at them in a puzzled way. 'Ah, yes—poor Greeby has paid the price of his sins. Excuse my running away from you—I have urgent business at the police-station.'

'If,' said Mr Radcott, again pinching Monty's arm, 'you want to give yourself up for the murder, Mr Temple, you had better come along with us. The police are bound to be about the place somewhere.'

'Oh, yes, of course, so they are. Yes. Very thoughtful of you. That will save me a great deal of time, and I have an important chapter to finish. A beautiful day, is it not, Mr—I fear I do not know your name. Or do I? I am growing sadly forgetful.'

Radcott mentioned his name, and the oddly assorted trio turned together towards the main entrance to the college. The great gate was shut; at the postern stood the porter, and at his side a massive figure in blue, who demanded their names.

Radcott, having been duly identified by the porter, produced Monty and his credentials.

'And this,' he went on, 'is, of course, Mr Temple. You know him. He is looking for your Superintendent.'

'Right you are, sir,' replied the policeman. 'You'll find him in the cloisters ... At his old game, I suppose?' he added, as the small figure of Mr Temple shuffled away across the sun-baked expanse of the quad.

'Oh, yes,' said Radcott. 'He was on to it like a shot. Must be quite exciting for the old bird to have a murder so near home. Where was his last?'

'Lincoln, sir; last Tuesday. Young fellow shot his young woman in the Cathedral. Mr Temple was down at the station the next day, just before lunch, explaining that he'd done it because the poor girl was the Scarlet Woman.'

'Mr Temple,' said Radcott, 'has a mission in life. He is the sword of the Lord and of Gideon. Every time a murder is committed in this country, Mr Temple lays claim to it. It is true that his body can always be shown to have been quietly in bed or at the Bodleian while the dirty work was afoot, but to an idealistic philosopher that need present no difficulty. But what *is* all this about the Master, actually?'

'Well, sir, you know that little entry between the cloisters and the Master's residence? At twenty minutes past ten this morning, Dr Greeby was found lying dead there, with his lecture-notes scattered all round him and a brickbat in a woollen sock lying beside his head. He'd been lecturing in a room in the Main Quadrangle at nine o'clock, and was, as far as we can tell, the last to leave the lecture-room. A party of American ladies and gentlemen passed through the cloisters a little after 10 o'clock, and they have been found, and say there was nobody about there then, so far as they could see—but, of course, sir, the murderer might have been hanging about the entry, because, naturally, they wouldn't go that way but through Boniface Passage to the Inner Quad and the chapel. One of the young gentlemen says he saw the Master cross the Main Quad on his way to the cloisters at 10.5, so he'd reach the entry in about two minutes after that. The Regius Professor of Morphology came along at 10.20, and found the body, and when the doctor arrived, five minutes later, he said Dr Greeby must have been dead about a quarter of an hour. So that puts it somewhere round about 10.10, you see, sir.'

'When did these Americans leave the chapel?'

'Ah, there you are, sir!' replied the constable. He seemed very ready to talk, thought Mr Egg, and deduced, rightly, that Mr Radcott was well and favourably known to the Oxford branch of the Force. 'If that there party had come back through the cloisters, they might have been able to tell us something. But they didn't. They went on through the Inner Quad into the garden, and the verger didn't leave the chapel, on account of a lady who had just arrived and wanted to look at the carving on the reredos.'

'And did the lady also come through the cloisters?'

'She did, sir, and she's the person we want to find, because it seems as though she must have passed through the cloisters very close to the time of the murder. She came into the chapel just on 10.15, because the verger recollected of the clock chiming a few minutes after she came in and her mentioning how sweet the notes was. You see the lady come in, didn't you, Mr Dabbs?'

'I saw *a* lady,' replied the porter, 'but then I see a lot of ladies one way and another. This one came across from the Bodleian round about 10 o'clock. Elderly lady, she was, dressed kind of old-fashioned, with her skirts round her heels and one of them hats like a rook's nest and a bit of elastic round the back. Looked like she might be a female don—leastways, the way female dons used to look. And she had the twitches—you know—jerked her head a bit. You get hundreds like 'em. They goes to sit in the cloisters and listen to the fountain and the little birds. But as to noticing a corpse or a murderer, it's my belief they wouldn't know such a thing if they saw it. I didn't see the lady again, so she must have gone out through the garden.'

'Very likely,' said Radcott. 'May Mr Egg and I go in through the cloisters, officer? Because it's the only way to my rooms, unless we go round by St. Scholastica's Gate.'

'All the other gates are locked, sir. You go on and speak to the Super; he'll let you through. You'll find him in the cloisters with Professor Staines and Dr Moyle.'

'Bodley's Librarian? What's he got to do with it?'

'They think he may know the lady, sir, if she's a Bodley reader.'

'Oh, I see. Come along, Mr Egg.'

Radcott led the way across the Main Quadrangle and through a dark little passage at one corner, into the cool shade of the cloisters. Framed by the arcades of ancient stone, the green lawn drowsed tranquilly in the noonday heat. There was no sound but the echo of their own footsteps, the plash and tinkle of the little fountain and the subdued chirping of chaffinches, as they paced the alternate sunshine and shadow of the pavement. About midway along the north side of the cloisters they came upon another dim little covered passageway, at the entrance to which a police-sergeant was kneeling, examining the ground with the aid of an electric torch.

'Hullo, sergeant!' said Radcott. 'Doing the Sherlock Holmes stunt? Show us the bloodstained footprints.'

'No blood, sir, unfortunately. Might make our job easier if there were. And no footprints neither. The poor gentleman was sandbagged, and we think the murderer must have climbed up here to do it, for the deceased was a tall gentleman and he was hit right on the top of the head, sir.' The sergeant indicated a little niche, like a blocked-up window, about four feet from the ground. 'Looks as if he'd waited up here, sir, for Dr Greeby to go by.'

'He must have been well acquainted with his victim's habits,' suggested Mr Egg.

'Not a bit of it,' retorted Radcott. 'He'd only to look at the lecture-list to know the time and place. This passage leads to the Master's House and the Fellows' Garden and nowhere else, and it's the way Dr Greeby would naturally go after his lecture, unless he was lecturing elsewhere, which he wasn't. Fairly able-bodied, your murderer, sergeant, to get up here. At least—I don't know.'

Before the policeman could stop him, he had placed one hand on the side of the niche and a foot on a projecting band of masonry below it, and swung himself up.

'Hi, sir! Come down, please. The Super won't like that.'

'Why? Oh, gosh! Fingerprints, I suppose. I forgot. Never mind; you can take mine if you want them, for comparison. Give you practice. Anyhow, a baby in arms could get up here. Come on, Mr Egg; we'd better beat it before I'm arrested for obstruction.'

But at this moment Radcott was hailed by a worried-looking

don, who came through the passage from the far side, accompanied by three or four other people.

'Oh, Mr Radcott! One moment, Superintendent, this gentleman will be able to tell you what you want to know; he was at Dr Greeby's lecture. That is so, is it not, Mr Radcott?'

'Well, no, not exactly, sir,' replied Radcott, with some embarrassment. 'I should have been, but, by a regrettable accident, I cut—that is to say, I was on the river, sir, and didn't get back in time.'

'Very vexatious,' said Professor Staines, while the Superintendent merely observed:

'Any witness to your being on the river, sir?'

'None,' replied Radcott. 'I was alone in a canoe, up a backwater—earnestly studying Aristotle. But I really didn't murder the Master. His lectures were—if I may say so—dull, but not to that point exasperating.'

'That is a very impudent observation, Mr Radcott,' said the Professor severely, 'and in execrable taste.'

The Superintendent, murmuring something about routine, took down in a note-book the alleged times of Mr Radcott's departure and return, and then said:

'I don't think I need detain any of you gentlemen further. If we want to see you again, Mr Temple, we will let you know.'

'Certainly, certainly. I shall just have a sandwich at the café and return to the Bodleian. As for the lady, I can only repeat that she sat at my table from about half-past nine till just before ten, and returned again at ten-thirty. Very restless and disturbing. I do wish, Dr Moyle, that some arrangement could be made to give me that table to myself, or that I could be given a place apart in the library. Ladies are always restless and disturbing. She was still there when I left, but I very much hope she has now gone for good. You are sure you don't want to lock me up now? I am quite at your service.'

'Not just yet, sir. You will hear from us presently.'

'Thank you, thank you. I should like to finish my chapter. For the present, then, I will wish you good-day.'

The little bent figure wandered away, and the Superintendent touched his head significantly.

'Poor gentleman! Quite harmless, of course, I needn't ask you, Dr Moyle, where *he* was at the time?'

'Oh, he was in his usual corner of Duke Humphrey's Library. He admits it, you see, when he is asked. In any case, I know definitely that he was there this morning, because he took out a Phi book, and of course had to apply personally to me for it. He asked for it at 9.30 and returned it at 12.15. As regards the lady, I think I have seen her before. One of the older school of learned ladies, I fancy. If she is an outside reader, I must have her name and address somewhere, but she may, of course, be a member of the University. I fear I could not undertake to know them all by sight. But I will inquire. It is, in fact, quite possible that she is still in the library, and, if not, Franklin may know when she went and who she is. I will look into the matter immediately. I need not say, professor, how deeply I deplore this lamentable affair. Poor dear Greeby! Such a loss to classical scholarship!'

At this point, Radcott gently drew Mr Egg away. A few yards farther down the cloisters, they turned into another and rather wider passage, which brought them out into the Inner Quadrangle, one side of which was occupied by the chapel. Mounting three dark flights of stone steps on the opposite side, they reached Radcott's rooms, where the undergraduate thrust his new acquaintance into an armchair, and, producing some bottles of beer from beneath the window-seat, besought him to make himself at home.

'Well,' he observed presently, 'you've had a fairly lively introduction to Oxford life—one murder and one madman. Poor old Temple. Quite one of our prize exhibits. Used to be a Fellow here, donkey's years ago. There was some fuss, and he disappeared for a time. Then he turned up again, ten years since, perfectly potty; took lodgings in Holywell, and has haunted the Bodder and the police-station alternately ever since. Fine Greek scholar he is, too. Quite reasonable, except on the one point. I hope old Moyle finds his mysterious lady, though it's nonsense to pretend that they keep tabs on all the people who use the library. You've only got to walk in firmly, as if the place belonged to you, and, if you're challenged, say in a loud, injured tone that you've been a reader for years. If you borrow a gown, they won't even challenge you.'

'Is that so, really?' said Mr Egg.

'Prove it, if you like. Take my gown, toddle across to the Bodder, march straight in past the showcases and through the little wicket marked "Readers Only", into Duke Humphrey's Library; do what you like, short of stealing the books or setting fire to the place—and if anybody says anything to you, I'll order six dozen of anything you like. That's fair, isn't it?'

Mr Egg accepted this offer with alacrity, and in a few moments, arrayed in a scholar's gown, was climbing the stair that leads to England's most famous library. With a slight tremor, he pushed open the swinging glass door and plunged into the hallowed atmosphere of mouldering leather that distinguishes such temples of learning.

Just inside, he came upon Dr Moyle in conversation with the door-keeper. Mr Egg, bending nonchalantly to examine an illegible manuscript in a showcase, had little difficulty in hearing what they said, since, like all official attendants upon reading-rooms, they took no trouble to lower their voices.

'I know the lady, Dr Moyle. That is to say, she has been here several times lately. She usually wears an M.A. gown. I saw her here this morning, but I didn't notice when she left. I don't think I ever heard her name, but seeing that she was a senior member of the University—'

Mr Egg waited to hear no more. An idea was burgeoning in his mind. He walked away, courageously pushed open the Readers' Wicket, and stalked down the solemn mediæval length of Duke Humphrey's Library. In the remotest and darkest bay, he observed Mr Temple, who, having apparently had his sandwich and forgotten about the murder, sat alone, writing busily, amid a pile of repellent volumes, with a large attaché-case full of papers open before him.

Leaning over the table, Mr Egg addressed him in an urgent whisper:

'Excuse me, sir. The police Superintendent asked me to say that they think they have found the lady, and would be glad if you would kindly step down at once and identify her.'

'The lady?' Mr Temple looked up vaguely. 'Oh, yes—the lady. To be sure. Immediately? That is not very convenient. Is it so very urgent?'

'They said particularly to lose no time, sir,' said Mr Egg.

Mr Temple muttered something, rose, seemed to hesitate whether to clear up his papers or not, and finally shovelled them all into the bulging attaché-case, which he locked upon them.

'Let me carry this for you, sir,' said Monty, seizing it promptly and shepherding Mr Temple briskly out. 'They're still in the cloisters, I think, but the Super said, would you kindly wait a few moments for him in the porter's lodge. Here we are.'

He handed Mr Temple and his attaché-case over to the care of the porter, who looked a little surprised at seeing Mr Egg in academic dress, but, on hearing the Superintendent's name, said nothing. Mr Egg hastened through quad and cloisters and mounted Mr Radcott's staircase at a run.

'Excuse me, sir,' he demanded breathlessly of that young gentleman, 'but what is a Phi book?'

'A Phi book,' replied Radcott, in some surprise, 'is a book deemed by Bodley's Librarian to be of an indelicate nature, and catalogued accordingly, by some dead-and-gone humourist, under the Greek letter *phi*. Why the question?'

'Well,' said Mr Egg, 'it just occurred to me how simple it would be for anybody to walk into the Bodleian, disguise himself in a retired corner—say in Duke Humphrey's Library—walk out, commit a murder, return, change back to his own clothes and walk out. Nobody would stop a person from coming in again, if he—or she—had previously been seen to go out—especially if the disguise had been used in the library before. Just a change of clothes and an M.A. gown would be enough.'

'What in the world are you getting at?'

'This lady, who was in the cloisters at the time of the murder. Mr Temple says she was sitting at his table. But isn't it funny that Mr Temple should have drawn special attention to himself by asking for a Phi book, today of all days? If he was once a Fellow of this college, he'd know which way Dr Greeby would go after his lecture; and he may have had a grudge against him on account of that old trouble, whatever it was. He'd know about the niche in the wall, too. And he's got an attaché-case with him that might easily hold a lady's hat and a skirt long enough to hide his trousers. And why is he wearing a top-coat on such a hot day, if not to conceal the upper portion of his garments? Not that it's any business of mine—but—well, I just took the liberty of asking myself. And I've got him out there, with his case, and the porter keeping an eye on him.'

Thus Mr Egg, rather breathlessly. Radcott gaped at him.

'Temple? My dear man, you're as potty as he is. Why, he's always confessing—he confessed to this—you can't possibly suppose—'

'I daresay I'm wrong,' said Mr Egg. 'But isn't there a fable about the man who cried "Wolf!" so often that nobody would believe him when the wolf really came? There's a motto in the *Salesman's Handbook* that I always admire very much. It says: "Discretion plays a major part in making up the salesman's art, for truths that no one can believe are calculated to deceive." I think that's rather subtle, don't you?'

19

THE FOUNTAIN PLAYS

Dorothy Sayers

...I turn the fountain off at night, for instance, to save leakage and waste...

'Yes,' said Mr Spiller, in a satisfied tone, 'I must say I like a bit of ornamental water. Gives a finish to the place.'

'The Versailles touch,' agreed Ronald Proudfoot.

Mr Spiller glanced sharply at him, as though suspecting sarcasm, but his lean face expressed nothing whatever. Mr Spiller was never quite at his ease in the company of his daughter's fiancé, though he was proud of the girl's achievement. With all his (to Mr Spiller) unamiable qualities, Ronald Proudfoot was a perfect gentleman, and Betty was completely wrapped up in him.

'The only thing it wants,' continued Mr Spiller, 'to *my* mind, that is, is Opening Up. To make a Vista, so to say. You don't get the Effect with these bushes on all four sides.'

'Oh, I don't know, Mr Spiller,' objected Mrs Digby in her mild voice. 'Don't you think it makes rather a fascinating surprise? You come along the path, never dreaming there's anything behind those lilacs, and then you turn the corner and come suddenly upon it. I'm sure, when you brought me down to see it this afternoon, it quite took my breath away.'

'There's that, of course,' admitted Mr Spiller. It occurred to him not for the first time, that there was something very attractive about Mrs Digby's silvery personality. She had distinction, too. A widow and widower of the sensible time of life, with a bit of money on both sides, might do worse than settle down comfortably in a pleasant house with half an acre of garden and a bit of ornamental water.

'And it's so pretty and secluded,' went on Mrs Digby, 'with these glorious rhododendrons. Look how pretty they are, all sprayed with the water—like fairy jewels—and the rustic seat against those dark cypresses at the back. Really Italian. And the scent of the lilac is so marvellous!'

Mr Spiller knew that the cypresses were, in fact, yews, but he did not correct her. A little ignorance was becoming in a woman. He glanced from the cotoneasters at one side of the fountain to the rhododendrons on the other, their rainbow flower-trusses sparkling with diamond drops.

'I wasn't thinking of touching the rhododendrons or the cotoneasters,' he said. 'I only thought of cutting through that great hedge of lilac, so as to make a vista from the house. But the ladies must always have the last word, mustn't they—er—Ronald?' (He never could bring out Proudfoot's Christian name naturally.) 'If you like it as it is, Mrs Digby, that settles it. The lilacs shall stay.'

'It's too flattering of you,' said Mrs Digby, 'but you mustn't think of altering your plans for me. I haven't any right to interfere with your beautiful garden.'

'Indeed you have,' said Mr Spiller. 'I defer to your taste entirely. You have spoken for the lilacs, and henceforward they are sacred.'

'I shall be afraid to give an opinion on anything, after that,' said Mrs Digby, shaking her head. 'But whatever you decide to do, I'm sure it will be lovely. It was a marvellous idea to think of putting the fountain there. It makes all the difference to the garden.'

Mr Spiller thought she was quite right. And indeed, though the fountain was rather flattered by the name of 'ornamental water,' consisting as it did of a marble basin set in the centre of a pool about four feet square, it made a brave show, with its plume of dancing water, fifteen feet high, towering over the smaller shrubs and almost overtopping the tall lilacs. And its cooling splash and tinkle soothed the ear on this pleasant day of early summer.

'Costs a bit to run, doesn't it?' demanded Mr Gooch. He had been silent up till now, and Mrs Digby felt that his remark betrayed a rather sordid outlook on life. Indeed, from the first moment of meeting Mr Gooch, she had pronounced him decidedly common, and wondered that he should be on such intimate terms with her host.

'No, no,' replied Mr Spiller. 'No, it's not expensive. You see, it uses the same water over and over again. Most ingenious. The fountains in Trafalgar Square work on the same principle, I believe. Of course, I had to pay a bit to have it put in, but I think it's worth the money.'

'Yes, indeed,' said Mrs Digby.

'I always said you were a warm man, Spiller,' said Mr Gooch, with his vulgar laugh. 'Wish I was in your shoes. A snug spot, that's what I call this place. Snug.'

'I'm not a millionaire,' answered Mr Spiller, rather shortly. 'But things might be worse in these times. Of course,' he added, more cheerfully, 'one has to be careful. I turn the fountain off at night, for instance, to save leakage and waste.'

'I'll swear you do, you damned old miser,' said Mr Gooch, offensively.

Mr Spiller was saved replying by the sounding of a gong in the distance.

'Ah! there's dinner,' he announced, with a certain relief in his tone. The party wound their way out between the lilacs, and paced gently up the long crazy pavement, past the herbaceous borders and the two long beds of raw little ticketed roses, to the glorified villa which Mr Spiller had christened 'The Pleasaunce'.

It seemed to Mrs Digby that there was a slightly strained atmosphere about dinner, though Betty, pretty as a picture and very much in love with Ronald Proudfoot, made a perfectly charming little hostess. The jarring note was sounded by Mr Gooch. He ate too noisily, drank far too freely, got on Proudfoot's nerves and behaved to Mr Spiller with a kind of veiled insolence which was embarrassing and disagreeable to listen to. She wondered again where he had come from, and why Mr Spiller put up with him. She knew little about him, except that from time to time he turned up on a visit to 'The Pleasaunce', usually staying there about a month and being, apparently, well supplied with cash. She had an idea that he was some kind of commission agent, though she could not recall any distinct statement on this point. Mr Spiller had settled down in the village about three years previously, and she had always liked him. Though not, in any sense of the word, a cultivated man, he was kind, generous and unassuming, and his devotion to Betty had something very lovable about it. Mr Gooch had started coming about a year later. Mrs Digby said to herself that if ever she was in a position to lay down the law at 'The Pleasaunce'—and she had begun to think matters were tending that way—her influence would be directed to getting rid of Mr Gooch.

'How about a spot of bridge?' suggested Ronald Proudfoot, when coffee had been served. It was nice, reflected Mrs Digby, to have coffee brought in by the manservant. Masters was really a very well-trained butler, though he did combine the office with that of chauffeur. One would be comfortable at 'The Pleasaunce.' From the dining-room window she could see the neat garage housing the Wolseley saloon on the ground floor, with a room for the chauffeur above it, and topped off by a handsome gilded weather-vane a-glitter in the last rays of the sun. A good cook, a smart parlourmaid and everything done exactly as one could wish—if she were to marry Mr Spiller she would be able, for the first time in her life, to afford a personal maid as well. There would be plenty of room in the house, and of course, when Betty was married—

Betty, she thought, was not over-pleased that Ronald had suggested bridge. Bridge is not a game that lends itself to the expression of tender feeling, and it would perhaps have looked better if Ronald had enticed Betty out to sit in the lilac-scented dusk under the yew-hedge by the fountain. Mrs Digby was sometimes afraid that Betty was the more in love of the two. But if Ronald wanted anything he had to have it, of course, and personally, Mrs Digby enjoyed nothing better than a quiet rubber. Besides, the arrangement had the advantage that it got rid of Mr Gooch. 'Don't play bridge,' Mr Gooch was wont to say. 'Never had time to learn. We didn't play bridge where I was brought up.' He repeated the remark now, and followed it up with a contemptuous snort directed at Mr Spiller.

'Never too late to begin,' said the latter pacifically.

'Not me!' retorted Mr Gooch. 'I'm going to have a turn in the garden. Where's that fellow Masters? Tell him to take the whisky and soda down to the fountain. The decanter, mind—one drink's no good to yours truly.' He plunged a thick hand into the box of Coronas on the side-table, took out a handful of cigars and passed out through the French window of the library on to the terrace. Mr Spiller rang the bell and gave the order without comment, and presently they saw Masters pad down the long crazy path between the rose-beds and the herbaceous borders, bearing the whisky and soda on a tray.

The other four played on till 10.30, when, a rubber coming to an end, Mrs Digby rose and said it was time she went home. Her host gallantly offered to accompany her. 'These two young people can look after themselves for a moment,' he added, with a conspiratorial smile.

'The young can look after themselves better than the old, these days.' She laughed a little shyly, and raised no objection when Mr Spiller drew her hand into his arm as they walked the couple of hundred yards to her cottage. She hesitated a moment whether to ask him in, but decided that a sweet decorum suited her style best. She stretched out a soft, beringed hand to him over the top of the little white gate. His pressure lingered—he would have kissed the hand, so insidious was the scent of the red and white hawthorns in her trim garden, but before he had summoned up courage, she had withdrawn it from his clasp and was gone.

Mr Spiller, opening his own front door in an agreeable dream, encountered Masters.

'Where is everybody, Masters?'

'Mr Proudfoot left five or ten minutes since, sir, and Miss Elizabeth has retired.'

'Oh!' Mr Spiller was a little startled. The new generation, he thought sadly, did not make love like the old. He hoped there was nothing wrong. Another irritating thought presented itself.

'Has Mr Gooch come in?'

'I could not say, sir. Shall I go and see?'

'No, never mind.' If Gooch had been sozzling himself up with whisky since dinner-time, it was just as well Masters should keep away from him. You never knew. Masters was one of these soft-spoken beggars, but he might take advantage. Better not to trust servants, anyhow.

'You can cut along to bed. I'll lock up.'

'Very good, sir.'

'Oh, by the way, is the fountain turned off?'

'Yes, sir. I turned it off myself, sir, at half-past ten, seeing that you were engaged, sir.'

'Quite right. Goodnight, Masters.'

'Goodnight, sir.'

He heard the man go out by the back and cross the paved court to the garage. Thoughtfully he bolted both entrances, and returned to the library. The whisky decanter was not in its usual place—no doubt it was still with Gooch in the garden—but he mixed himself a small brandy and soda, and drank it. He supposed he must now face the tiresome business of getting Gooch up to bed. Then, suddenly, he realised that the encounter would take place here and not in the garden. Gooch was coming in through the French window. He was drunk, but not, Mr Spiller observed with relief, incapably so.

'Well?' said Gooch.

'Well?' retorted Mr Spiller.

'Had a good time with the accommodating widow, eh? Enjoyed yourself? Lucky old hound, aren't you? Fallen soft in your old age, eh?'

'There, that'll do,' said Mr Spiller.

'Oh, will it? That's good. That's rich. That'll do, eh? Think I'm Masters, talking to me like that?' Mr Gooch gave a thick chuckle. 'Well, I'm not Masters, I'm master here. Get that into your head. I'm master and you damn well know it.'

'All right,' replied Mr Spiller meekly, 'but buzz off to bed now, there's a good fellow. It's getting late and I'm tired.'

'You'll be tireder before I've done with you.' Mr Gooch thrust both hands into his pockets and stood—a bulky and threatening figure—swaying rather dangerously. 'I'm short of cash,' he added. 'Had a bad week—cleaned me out. Time you stumped up a bit more.'

'Nonsense,' said Mr Spiller, with some spirit. 'I pay you your allowance as we agreed, and let you come and stay here whenever you like, and that's all you get from me.'

'Oh, is it? Getting a bit above yourself, aren't you, Number Bleeding 4132?'

'Hush!' said Mr Spiller, glancing hastily round as though the furniture had ears and tongues.

'Hush! hush!' repeated Mr Gooch mockingly. 'You're in a good position to dictate terms, aren't you, 4132? Hush! The servants might hear! Betty might hear! Betty's young man might hear. Hah! Betty's young man—he'd be particularly pleased to know her father was an escaped jail-bird, wouldn't he? Liable at any moment to be hauled back to work out his ten years' hard for forgery? And when I think,' added Mr Gooch, 'that a man like me, that was only in for a short stretch and worked it out good and proper, is dependent on the charity—ha, ha! —of my dear friend 4132, while he's rolling in wealth—'

'I'm not rolling in wealth, Sam,' said Mr Spiller, 'and you know darn well I'm not. But I don't want any trouble. I'll do what I can, if you'll promise faithfully this time that you won't ask for any more of these big sums, because my income won't stand it.'

'Oh, I'll promise that all right,' agreed Mr Gooch cheerfully. 'You give me five thousand down—'

Mr Spiller uttered a strangled exclamation.

'Five thousand? How do you suppose I'm to lay hands on five thousand all at once? Don't be an idiot, Sam. I'll give you a cheque for five hundred—'

'Five thousand,' insisted Mr Gooch, 'or up goes the monkey.'

'But I haven't got it,' objected Mr Spiller.

'Then you'd bloody well better find it,' returned Mr Gooch.

'How do you expect me to find all that?'

'That's your look-out. You oughtn't to be so damned extravagant. Spending good money, that you ought to be giving *me*, on fountains and stuff. Now, it's no good kicking, Mr Respectable 4132—I'm the man on top and you're for it, my lad, if you don't look after me properly. See?'

Mr Spiller saw only too clearly. He saw, as he had seen indeed for some time, that his friend Gooch had him by the short hairs. He expostulated again feebly, and Gooch replied with a laugh and an offensive reference to Mrs Digby.

Mr Spiller did not realise that he had struck very hard. He hardly realised that he had struck at all. He thought he had aimed a blow, and that Gooch had dodged it and tripped over the leg of the occasional table. But he was not very clear in his mind, except on one point. Gooch was dead.

He had not fainted; he was not stunned. He was dead. He must have caught the brass curb of the fender as he fell. There was no blood, but Mr Spiller, exploring the inert head with anxious fingers, found a spot above the temple where the bone yielded to pressure like a cracked egg-shell. The noise of the fall had been thunderous. Kneeling on the library floor, Mr Spiller waited for the inevitable cry and footsteps from upstairs.

Nothing happened. He remembered—with difficulty, for his mind seemed to be working slowly and stiffly—that above the library there was only the long drawing-room, and over that the spare-room and bathrooms. No inhabited bedroom looked out on that side of the house.

A slow, grinding, grating noise startled him. He whisked round hastily. The old-fashioned grandfather clock, wheezing as the hammer rose into action, struck eleven. He wiped the sweat from his forehead, got up and poured himself out another, and a stiffer, brandy.

The drink did him good. It seemed to take the brake off his mind, and the wheels span energetically. An extraordinary clarity took the place of his previous confusion.

He had murdered Gooch. He had not exactly intended to do so, but he had done it. It had not felt to him like murder, but there was not the slightest doubt what the police would think about it. And once he was in the hands of the police—Mr Spiller shuddered. They would almost certainly want to take his fingerprints, and would be surprised to recognise a bunch of old friends.

Masters had heard him say that he would wait up for Gooch. Masters knew that everybody else had gone to bed. Masters would undoubtedly guess something. But stop!

Could Masters prove that he himself had gone to bed? Yes, probably he could. Somebody would have heard him cross the court and seen the light go up over the garage. One could not hope to throw suspicion on Masters—besides, the man hardly deserved that. But the mere idea had started Mr Spiller's brain on a new and attractive line of thought.

What he really wanted was an alibi. If he could only confuse the police as to the time at which Gooch had died. If Gooch could be made to seem alive after he was dead... somehow...

He cast his thoughts back over stories he had read on holiday, dealing with this very matter. You dressed up as the dead man and impersonated him. You telephoned in his name. In the hearing of the butler, you spoke to the dead as though he were alive. You made a gramophone record of his voice and played it. You hid the body, and thereafter sent a forged letter from some distant place—

He paused for a moment. Forgery—but he did not want to start that old game over again. And all these things were too elaborate, or else impracticable at that time of night.

And then it came to him suddenly that he was a fool. Gooch must not be made to live later, but to die earlier. He should die before 10.30, at the time when Mr Spiller, under the eyes of three observers, had been playing bridge.

So far, the idea was sound and even, in its broad outline, obvious. But now one had to come down to detail. How could he establish the time? Was there anything that had happened at 10.30?

He helped himself to another drink, and then, quite suddenly, as though lit by a floodlight, he saw his whole plan, picked out vividly complete, with every join and angle clear-cut.

He glanced at his watch; the hands stood at twenty minutes past eleven. He had the night before him.

He fetched an electric torch from the hall and stepped boldly out of the French window. Close beside it, against the wall of the house, were two taps, one ending in a nozzle for the garden hose, the other controlling the fountain at the bottom of the garden. This latter he turned on, and then, without troubling to muffle his footsteps, followed the crazy-paved path down to the lilac hedge, and round by the bed of cotoneasters. The sky, despite the beauty of the early evening, had now turned very dark, and he could scarcely see the tall column of pale water above the dark shrubbery, but he heard its comforting splash and ripple, and as he stepped upon the surrounding grass, he felt the blown spray upon his face. The beam of the torch showed him the garden seat beneath the yews, and the tray, as he had expected, standing upon it. The whisky decanter was about half full. He emptied the greater part of its contents into the basin, wrapping the neck of the decanter in his handkerchief, so as to leave no fingerprints. Then, returning to the other side of the lilacs, he satisfied himself that the spray of the fountain was invisible from house or garden.

The next part of the performance he did not care about. It was risky; it might be heard; in fact, he wanted it to be heard if necessary—but it was a risk. He licked his dry lips and called the dead man by name:

'Gooch! Gooch!'

No answer, except the splash of the fountain, sounding to his anxious ear abnormally loud in the stillness. He glanced round, almost as though he expected the corpse to stalk awfully out upon him from the darkness, its head hanging and its dark mouth dropping open to show the pale gleam of its dentures. Then, pulling himself together, he walked briskly back up the path and, when he reached the house again, listened. There was no movement, no sound but the ticking of the clocks. He shut the library door gently. From now on there must be no noise.

There was a pair of galoshes in the cloak-room near the pantry. He put them on and slipped like a shadow through the French window again; then round the house into the courtyard. He glanced up at the garage; there was no light in the upper story and he breathed a sigh of relief, for Masters was apt sometimes to be wakeful. Groping his way to an outhouse, he switched the torch on. His wife had been an invalid for some years before her death, and he had brought her wheeled chair with him to 'The Pleasaunce', having a dim, sentimental reluctance to sell the thing. He was thankful for that, now; thankful, too, that he had purchased it from a good maker and that it ran so lightly and silently on its pneumatic tyres. He found the bicycle pump and blew the tyres up hard and, for further precaution, administered a drop of oil here and there. Then, with infinite precaution, he wheeled the chair round to the library window. How fortunate that he had put down stone flags and crazy paving everywhere, so that no wheel-tracks could show.

The job of getting the body through the window and into the chair took it out of him. Gooch had been a heavy man, and he himself was not in good training. But it was done at last. Resisting the impulse to run, he pushed his burden gently and steadily along the narrow strip of paving. He could not see very well, and he was afraid to flash his torch too often. A slip off the path into the herbaceous border would be fatal; he set his teeth and kept his gaze fixed steadily ahead of him. He felt as though, if he looked back at the house, he would see the upper windows thronged with staring white faces. The impulse to turn his head was almost irresistible, but he determined that he would not turn it.

At length he was round the edge of the lilacs and hidden from the house. The sweat was running down his face and the most ticklish part of his task was still to do. If he broke his heart in the effort, he must carry the body over the plot of lawn. No wheel-marks or heel-marks or signs of dragging must be left for the police to see. He braced himself for the effort.

It was done. The corpse of Gooch lay there by the fountain, the bruise upon the temple carefully adjusted upon the sharp stone edge of the pool, one hand dragging in the water, the limbs disposed as naturally as possible, to look as though the man had stumbled and fallen. Over it, from head to foot, the water of the fountain sprayed, swaying and bending in the night wind. Mr Spiller looked upon his work and saw that it was good. The journey back with the lightened chair was easy. When he had returned the vehicle to the outhouse and passed for the last time through the library window, he felt as though the burden of years had been rolled from his back.

His back! He had remembered to take off his dinner-jacket while stooping in the spray of the fountain, and only his shirt was drenched. That he could dispose of in the linen-basket, but the seat of his trousers gave him some uneasiness. He mopped at himself as best he could with his handkerchief. Then he made his calculations. If he left the fountain to play for an hour or so it would, he thought, produce the desired effect. Controlling his devouring impatience, he sat down and mixed himself a final brandy.

At one o'clock he rose, turned off the fountain, shut the library window with no more and no less than the usual noise and force, and went with firm footsteps up to bed.

Inspector Frampton was, to Mr Spiller's delight, a highly intelligent officer. He picked up the clues thrown to him with the eagerness of a trained terrier. The dead man was last seen alive by Masters after dinner—8.30—just so. After which, the rest of the party had played bridge together till 10.30. Mr Spiller had then gone out with Mrs Digby. Just after he left, Masters had turned off the fountain. Mr Proudfoot had left at 10.40 and Miss Spiller and the maids had then retired. Mr Spiller had come in again at 10.45 or 10.50, and inquired for Mr Gooch. After this, Masters had gone across to the garage, leaving Mr Spiller to lock up. Later on, Mr Spiller had gone down the garden to look for Mr Gooch. He had gone no farther than the lilac hedge, and there calling to him and getting no answer, had concluded that his guest had already come in and gone to bed. The housemaid fancied she had heard him calling Mr Gooch. She placed this episode at about half-past eleven—certainly not later. Mr Spiller had subsequently sat up reading in the library till one o'clock, when he had shut the window and gone to bed also.

The body, when found by the gardener at 6.30 a.m., was still wet with the spray from the fountain, which had also soaked the grass beneath it. Since the fountain had been turned off at 10.30, this meant that Gooch must have lain there for an appreciable period before that. In view of the large quantity of whisky that he had drunk, it seemed probable that he had had a heart-attack, or had drunkenly stumbled, and, in falling, had struck his head on the edge of the pool. All these considerations fixed the time of death at from 9.30 to 10 o'clock—an opinion with which the doctor, though declining to commit himself within an hour or so, concurred, and the coroner entered a verdict of accidental death.

Only the man who has been for years the helpless victim of blackmail could fully enter into Mr Spiller's feelings. Compunction played no part in them—the relief was far too great. To be rid of the daily irritation of Gooch's presence, of his insatiable demands for money, of the perpetual menace of his drunken malice—these boons were well worth a murder. And, Mr Spiller insisted to himself, as he sat musing on the rustic seat by the fountain, it had not really been murder. He determined to call on Mrs Digby that afternoon. He could ask her to marry him now without haunting fear for the future. The scent of the lilac was intoxicating.

'Excuse me, sir,' said Masters.

Mr Spiller, withdrawing his meditative gaze from the spouting water, looked inquiringly at the manservant, who stood in a respectful attitude beside him.

'If it is convenient to you, sir, I should wish to have my bedroom changed. I should wish to sleep indoors.'

'Oh?' said Mr Spiller. 'Why that, Masters?'

'I am subject to be a light sleeper, sir, ever since the war, and I find the creaking of the weather-vane very disturbing.'

'It creaks, does it?'

'Yes, sir. On the night that Mr Gooch sustained his unfortunate accident, sir, the wind changed at a quarter-past eleven. The creaking woke me out of my first sleep, sir, and disturbed me very much.'

A coldness gripped Mr Spiller at the pit of the stomach. The servant's eyes, in that moment, reminded him curiously of Gooch. He had never noticed any resemblance before.

'It's a curious thing, sir, if I may say so, that, with the wind shifting as it did at 11.15, Mr Gooch's body should have become sprayed by the fountain. Up till 11.15, the spray was falling on the other side, sir. The appearance presented was as though the body had been placed in position subsequently to 11.15, sir, and the fountain turned on again.'

'Very strange,' said Mr Spiller. On the other side of the lilac hedge, he heard the voices of Betty and Ronald Proudfoot, chattering as they paced to and fro between the herbaceous borders. They seemed to be happy together. The whole house seemed happier, now that Gooch was gone.

'Very strange indeed, sir. I may add that, after hearing the inspector's observations, I took the precaution to dry your dress-trousers in the linen-cupboard in the bathroom.'

'Oh, yes,' said Mr Spiller.

'I shall not, of course, mention the change of wind to the authorities, sir, and now that the inquest is over, it is not likely to occur to anybody, unless their attention should be drawn to it. I think, sir, all things being taken into consideration, you might find it worth your while to retain me permanently in your service at—shall we say double my present wage to begin with?'

Mr Spiller opened his mouth to say, 'Go to Hell,' but his voice failed him. He bowed his head.

'I am much obliged to you, sir,' said Masters, and withdrew on silent feet.

Mr Spiller looked at the fountain, with its tall water wavering and bending in the wind.

'Ingenious,' he muttered automatically, 'and it really costs nothing to run. It uses the same water over and over again.'

20

THE MYSTERIOUS TRAVELLER

Maurice Leblanc

...But, where the devil had I seen that face before? Because, beyond all possible doubt, I had seen it...

The evening before, I had sent my automobile to Rouen by the highway. I was to travel to Rouen by rail, on my way to visit some friends that live on the banks of the Seine.

At Paris, a few minutes before the train started, seven gentlemen entered my compartment; five of them were smoking. No matter that the journey was a short one, the thought of traveling with such a company was not agreeable to me, especially as the car was built on the old model, without a corridor. I picked up my overcoat, my newspapers and my time-table, and sought refuge in a neighbouring compartment.

It was occupied by a lady, who, at sight of me, made a gesture of annoyance that did not escape my notice, and she leaned toward a gentleman who was standing on the step and was, no doubt, her husband. The gentleman scrutinized me closely, and, apparently, my appearance did not displease him, for he smiled as he spoke to his wife with the air of one who reassures a frightened child. She smiled also, and gave me a friendly glance as if she now understood that I was one of those gallant men with whom a woman can remain shut up for two hours in a little box, six feet square, and have nothing to fear.

Her husband said to her: 'I have an important appointment, my dear, and cannot wait any longer. Adieu.'

He kissed her affectionately and went away. His wife threw him a few kisses and waved her handkerchief. The whistle sounded, and the train started.

At that precise moment, and despite the protests of the guards, the door was opened, and a man rushed into our compartment. My companion, who was standing and arranging her luggage, uttered a cry of terror and fell upon the seat. I am not a coward—far from it—but I confess that such intrusions at the last minute are always disconcerting. They have a suspicious, unnatural aspect.

However, the appearance of the new arrival greatly modified the unfavourable impression produced by his precipitant action. He was correctly and elegantly dressed, wore a tasteful cravat, correct gloves, and his face was refined and intelligent. But, where the devil had I seen that face before? Because, beyond all possible doubt, I had seen it. And yet the memory of it was so vague and indistinct that I felt it would be useless to try to recall it at that time.

Then, directing my attention to the lady, I was amazed at the pallor and anxiety I saw in her face. She was looking at her neighbour—they occupied seats on the same side of the compartment—with an expression of intense alarm, and I perceived that one of her trembling hands was slowly gliding toward a little traveling bag that was lying on the seat about twenty inches from her. She finished by seizing it and nervously drawing it to her. Our eyes met, and I read in hers so much anxiety and fear that I could not refrain from speaking to her:

'Are you ill, madame? Shall I open the window?'

Her only reply was a gesture indicating that she was afraid of our companion. I smiled, as her husband had done, shrugged my shoulders, and explained to her, in pantomime, that she had nothing to fear, that I was there, and, besides, the gentleman appeared to be a very harmless individual. At that moment, he turned toward us, scrutinized both of us from head to foot, then settled down in his corner and paid us no more attention.

After a short silence, the lady, as if she had mustered all her energy to perform a desperate act, said to me, in an almost inaudible voice:

'Do you know who is on our train?'

'Who?'

'He...he...I assure you...'

'Who is he?'

'Arsene Lupin!'

She had not taken her eyes off our companion, and it was to him rather than to me that she uttered the syllables of that disquieting name. He drew his hat over his face. Was that to conceal his agitation or, simply, to arrange himself for sleep? Then I said to her:

'Yesterday, through contumacy, Arsene Lupin was sentenced to twenty years' imprisonment at hard labour. Therefore it is improbable that he would be so imprudent, today, as to show himself in public. Moreover, the newspapers have announced his appearance in Turkey since his escape from the Sante.'

'But he is on this train at the present moment,' the lady proclaimed, with the obvious intention of being heard by our companion; 'my husband is one of the directors in the penitentiary service, and it was the stationmaster himself who told us that a search was being made for Arsene Lupin.'

'They may have been mistaken—'

'No; he was seen in the waiting-room. He bought a first-class ticket for Rouen.'

'He has disappeared. The guard at the waiting-room door did not see him pass, and it is supposed that he had got into the express that leaves ten minutes after us.'

'In that case, they will be sure to catch him.'

'Unless, at the last moment, he leaped from that train to come here, into our train...which is quite probable...which is almost certain.'

'If so, he will be arrested just the same; for the employees and guards would no doubt observe his passage from one train to the other, and, when we arrive at Rouen, they will arrest him there.'

'Him—never! He will find some means of escape.'

'In that case, I wish him "bon voyage."'

'But, in the meantime, think what he may do!'

'What?'

'I don't know. He may do anything.'

She was greatly agitated, and, truly, the situation justified, to some extent, her nervous excitement. I was impelled to say to her:

'Of course, there are many strange coincidences, but you need have no fear. Admitting that Arsene Lupin is on this train, he will not commit any indiscretion; he will be only too happy to escape the peril that already threatens him.'

My words did not reassure her, but she remained silent for a time. I unfolded my newspapers and read reports of Arsene Lupin's trial, but, as they contained nothing that was new to me, I was not greatly interested. Moreover, I was tired and sleepy. I felt my eyelids close and my head drop.

'But, monsieur, you are not going to sleep!'

She seized my newspaper, and looked at me with indignation.

'Certainly not,' I said.

'That would be very imprudent.'

'Of course,' I assented.

I struggled to keep awake. I looked through the window at the landscape and the fleeting clouds, but in a short time all that became confused and indistinct; the image of the nervous lady and the drowsy gentleman were effaced from my memory, and I was buried in the soothing depths of a profound sleep. The tranquillity of my response was soon disturbed by disquieting dreams, wherein a creature that had played the part and bore the name of Arsene Lupin held an important place. He appeared to me with his black laden with articles of value; he leaped over walls, and plundered castles. But the outlines of that creature, who was no longer Arsene Lupin, assumed a more definite form. He came toward me, growing larger and larger, leaped into the compartment with incredible agility, and landed squarely on my chest. With a cry of fright and pain, I awoke. The man, the traveller, our companion, with his knee on my breast, held me by the throat.

My sight was very indistinct, for my eyes were suffused with blood. I could see the lady, in a corner of the compartment, convulsed with fright. I tried even not to resist. Besides, I did not have the strength. My temples throbbed; I was almost strangled. One minute more, and I would have breathed my last. The man must have realized it, for he relaxed his grip, but did not remove his hand. Then he took a cord, in which he had prepared a slip-knot, and tied my wrists together. In an instant, I was bound, gagged and helpless.

Certainly, he accomplished the trick with an ease and skill that revealed the hand of a master; he was, no doubt, a professional thief. Not a word, not a nervous movement; only coolness and audacity. And I was there, lying on the bench, bound like a mummy, I—Arsene Lupin!

It was anything but a laughing matter, and yet, despite the gravity of the situation, I keenly appreciated the humour and irony that it involved. Arsene Lupin seized and bound like a novice! Robbed as if I were an unsophisticated rustic—for, you must understand, the scoundrel had deprived me of my purse and wallet! Arsene Lupin, a victim, duped, vanquished...What an adventure!

The lady did not move. He did not even notice her. He contented himself with picking up her traveling-bag that had fallen to the floor and taking from it the jewels, purse, and gold and silver trinkets that it contained. The lady opened her eyes, trembled with fear, drew the rings from her fingers and handed them to the man as if she wished to spare him unnecessary trouble. He took the rings and looked at her. She swooned.

Then, quite unruffled, he resumed his seat, lighted a cigarette, and proceeded to examine the treasure that he had acquired. The examination appeared to give him perfect satisfaction.

But I was not so well satisfied. I do not speak of the twelve thousand francs of which I had been unduly deprived: that was only a temporary loss, because I was certain that I would recover possession of that money after a very brief delay, together with the important papers contained in my wallet: plans, specifications, addresses, lists of correspondents, and compromising letters. But, for the moment, a more immediate and more serious question troubled me: How would this affair end? What would be the outcome of this adventure?

As you can imagine, the disturbance created by my passage through the Saint-Lazare station has not escaped my notice. Going to visit friends who knew me under the name of Guillaume Berlat, and amongst whom my resemblance to Arsene Lupin was a subject of many innocent jests, I could not assume a disguise, and my presence had been remarked. So, beyond question, the commissary of police at Rouen, notified by telegraph, and assisted by numerous agents, would be awaiting the train, would question all suspicious passengers, and proceed to search the cars.

Of course, I had foreseen all that, but it had not disturbed me, as I was certain that the police of Rouen would not be any shrewder than the police of Paris and that I could escape recognition; would it not be sufficient for me to carelessly display my card as 'depute,' thanks to which I had inspired complete confidence in the gate-keeper at Saint-Lazare?—But the situation was greatly changed. I was no longer free. It was impossible to attempt one of my usual tricks. In one of the compartments, the commissary of police would find Mon. Arsene Lupin, bound hand and foot, as docile as a lamb, packed up, all ready to be dumped into a prison-van. He would have simply to accept delivery of the parcel, the same as if it were so much merchandise or a basket of fruit and vegetables. Yet, to avoid that shameful denouement, what could I do?—bound and gagged, as I was? And the train was rushing on toward Rouen, the next and only station.

Another problem was presented, in which I was less interested, but the solution of which aroused my professional curiosity. What were the intentions of my rascally companion? Of course, if I had been alone, he could, on our arrival at Rouen, leave the car slowly and fearlessly. But the lady? As soon as the door of the compartment should be opened, the lady, now so quiet and humble, would scream and call for help. That was the dilemma that perplexed me! Why had he not reduced her to a helpless condition similar to mine? That would have given him ample time to disappear before his double crime was discovered.

He was still smoking, with his eyes fixed upon the window that was now being streaked with drops of rain. Once he turned, picked up my time-table, and consulted it.

The lady had to feign a continued lack of consciousness in order to deceive the enemy. But fits of coughing, provoked by the smoke, exposed her true condition. As to me, I was very uncomfortable, and very tired. And I meditated; I plotted.

The train was rushing on, joyously, intoxicated with its own speed.

Saint Etienne!...At that moment, the man arose and took two steps toward us, which caused the lady to utter a cry of alarm and fall into a genuine swoon. What was the man about to do? He lowered the window on our side. A heavy rain was now falling, and, by a gesture, the man expressed his annoyance at his not having an umbrella or an overcoat. He glanced at the rack. The lady's umbrella was there. He took it. He also took my overcoat and put it on.

We were now crossing the Seine. He turned up the bottoms of his trousers, then leaned over and raised the exterior latch of the door. Was he going to throw himself upon the track? At that speed, it would have been instant death. We now entered a tunnel. The man opened the door half-way and stood on the upper step. What folly! The darkness, the smoke, the noise, all gave a fantastic appearance to his actions. But suddenly, the train diminished its speed. A moment later it increased its speed, then slowed up again. Probably, some repairs were being made in that part of the tunnel which obliged the trains to diminish their speed, and the man was aware of the fact. He immediately stepped down to the lower step, closed the door behind him, and leaped to the ground. He was gone.

The lady immediately recovered her wits, and her first act was to lament the loss of her jewels. I gave her an imploring look. She understood, and quickly removed the gag that stifled me. She wished to untie the cords that bound me, but I prevented her.

'No, no, the police must see everything exactly as it stands. I want them to see what the rascal did to us.'

'Suppose I pull the alarm-bell?'

'Too late. You should have done that when he made the attack on me.'

'But he would have killed me. Ah! monsieur, didn't I tell you that he was on this train. I recognized him from his portrait. And now he has gone off with my jewels.'

'Don't worry. The police will catch him.'

'Catch Arsene Lupin! Never.'

'That depends on you, madame. Listen. When we arrive at Rouen, be at the door and call. Make a noise. The police and the railway employees will come. Tell what you have seen: the assault made on me and the flight of Arsene Lupin. Give a description of him—soft hat, umbrella—yours—gray overcoat...'

'Yours,' said she.

'What! mine? Not at all. It was his. I didn't have any.'

'It seems to me he didn't have one when he came in.'

'Yes, yes...unless the coat was one that someone had forgotten and left in the rack. At all events, he had it when he went away, and that is the essential point. A gray overcoat—remember!...Ah! I forgot. You must tell your name, first thing you do. Your husband's official position will stimulate the zeal of the police.'

We arrived at the station. I gave her some further instructions in a rather imperious tone: 'Tell them my name—Guillaume Berlat. If necessary, say that you know me. That will save time. We must expedite the preliminary investigation. The important thing is the pursuit of Arsene Lupin. Your jewels, remember! Let there be no mistake. Guillaume Berlat, a friend of your husband.'

'I understand...Guillaume Berlat.'

She was already calling and gesticulating. As soon as the train stopped, several men entered the compartment. The critical moment had come.

Panting for breath, the lady exclaimed: 'Arsene Lupin...he attacked us...he stole my jewels...I am Madame Renaud...my husband is a director of the penitentiary service...Ah! here is my brother, Georges Ardelle, director of the Credit Rouennais...you must know...'

She embraced a young man who had just joined us, and whom the commissary saluted. Then she continued, weeping: 'Yes, Arsene Lupin...while monsieur was sleeping, he seized him by the throat... Mon. Berlat, a friend of my husband.'

The commissary asked: 'But where is Arsene Lupin?'

'He leaped from the train, when passing through the tunnel.'

'Are you sure that it was he?'

'Am I sure! I recognized him perfectly. Besides, he was seen at the Saint-Lazare station. He wore a soft hat—'

'No, a hard felt, like that,' said the commissary, pointing to my hat.

'He had a soft hat, I am sure,' repeated Madame Renaud, 'and a gray overcoat.'

'Yes, that is right,' replied the commissary, 'the telegram says he wore a gray overcoat with a black velvet collar.'

'Exactly, a black velvet collar,' exclaimed Madame Renaud, triumphantly.

I breathed freely. Ah! the excellent friend I had in that little woman.

The police agents had now released me. I bit my lips until they ran blood. Stooping over, with my handkerchief over my mouth, an attitude quite natural in a person who has remained for a long time in an uncomfortable position, and whose mouth shows the bloody marks of the gag, I addressed the commissary, in a weak voice:

'Monsieur, it was Arsene Lupin. There is no doubt about that. If we make haste, he can be caught yet. I think I may be of some service to you.'

The railway car, in which the crime occurred, was detached from the train to serve as a mute witness at the official investigation. The train continued on its way to Havre. We were then conducted to the station-master's office through a crowd of curious spectators.

Then, I had a sudden access of doubt and discretion. Under some pretext or other, I must gain my automobile, and escape. To remain there was dangerous. Something might happen; for instance, a telegram from Paris, and I would be lost.

Yes, but what about my thief? Abandoned to my own resources, in an unfamiliar country, I could not hope to catch him.

'Bah! I must make the attempt,' I said to myself. 'It may be a difficult game, but an amusing one, and the stake is well worth the trouble.'

And when the commissary asked us to repeat the story of the robbery, I exclaimed: 'Monsieur, really, Arsene Lupin is getting the start of us. My automobile is waiting in the courtyard. If you will be so kind as to use it, we can try...'

The commissary smiled, and replied: 'The idea is a good one; so good, indeed, that it is already being carried out. Two of my men have set out on bicycles. They have been gone for some time.'

'Where did they go?'

'To the entrance of the tunnel. There, they will gather evidence, secure witnesses, and follow on the track of Arsene Lupin.'

I could not refrain from shrugging my shoulders, as I replied: 'Your men will not secure any evidence or any witnesses.'

'Really!'

'Arsene Lupin will not allow anyone to see him emerge from the tunnel. He will take the first road—'

'To Rouen, where we will arrest him.'

'He will not go to Rouen.'

'Then he will remain in the vicinity, where his capture will be even more certain.'

'He will not remain in the vicinity.'

'Oh! oh! And where will he hide?'

I looked at my watch, and said: 'At the present moment, Arsene Lupin is prowling around the station at Darnetal. At ten fifty, that is, in twenty-two minutes from now, he will take the train that goes from Rouen to Amiens.'

'Do you think so? How do you know it?'

'Oh! it is quite simple. While we were in the car, Arsene Lupin consulted my railway guide. Why did he do it? Was there, not far from the spot where he disappeared, another line of railway, a station upon that line, and a train stopping at that station? On consulting my railway guide, I found such to be the case.'

'Really, monsieur,' said the commissary, 'that is a marvelous deduction. I congratulate you on your skill.'

I was now convinced that I had made a mistake in displaying so much cleverness. The commissary regarded me with astonishment, and I though a slight suspicion entered his official mind...Oh! scarcely that, for the photographs distributed broadcast by the police department were too imperfect; they presented an Arsene Lupin so different from the one he had before him, that he could not possibly recognize me by it. But, all the same, he was troubled, confused and ill-at-ease.

'Mon Dieu! nothing stimulates the comprehension so much as the loss of a pocketbook and the desire to recover it. And it seems to me that if you will give me two of your men, we may be able...'

'Oh! I beg of you, monsieur le commissaire,' cried Madame Renaud, 'listen to Mon. Berlat.'

The intervention of my excellent friend was decisive. Pronounced by her, the wife of an influential official, the name of Berlat became really my own, and gave me an identity that no mere suspicion could affect. The commissary arose, and said: 'Believe me, Monsieur Berlat, I shall be delighted to see you succeed. I am as much interested as you are in the arrest of Arsene Lupin.'

He accompanied me to the automobile, and introduced two of his men, Honore Massol and Gaston Delivet, who were assigned to assist me. My chauffer cranked up the car and I took my place at the wheel. A few seconds later, we left the station. I was saved.

Ah! I must confess that in rolling over the boulevards that surrounded the old Norman city, in my swift thirty-five horse-power Moreau-Lepton, I experienced a deep feeling of pride, and the motor responded, sympathetically to my desires. At right and left, the trees flew past us with startling rapidity, and I, free, out of danger, had simply to arrange my little personal affairs with the two honest representatives of the Rouen police who were sitting behind me. Arsene Lupin was going in search of Arsene Lupin!

Modest guardians of social order—Gaston Delivet and Honore Massol—how valuable was your assistance! What would I have done without you? Without you, many times, at the cross-roads, I might have taken the wrong route! Without you, Arsene Lupin would have made a mistake, and the other would have escaped!

But the end was not yet. Far from it. I had yet to capture the thief and recover the stolen papers. Under no circumstances must my two acolytes be permitted to see those papers, much less to seize them. That was a point that might give me some difficulty.

We arrived at Darnetal three minutes after the departure of the train. True, I had the consolation of learning that a man wearing a gray overcoat with a black velvet collar had taken the train at the station. He had bought a second-class ticket for Amiens. Certainly, my debut as detective was a promising one.

Delivet said to me: 'The train is express, and the next stop is Monterolier-Buchy in nineteen minutes. If we do not reach there before Arsene Lupin, he can proceed to Amiens, or change for the train going to Cleres, and, from that point, reach Dieppe or Paris.'

'How far to Monterolier?'

'Twenty-three kilometres.'

'Twenty-three kilometres in nineteen minutes...We will be there ahead of him.'

We were off again! Never had my faithful Moreau-Repton responded to my impatience with such ardour and regularity. It participated in my anxiety. It indorsed my determination. It comprehended my animosity against that rascally Arsene Lupin. The knave! The traitor!

'Turn to the right,' cried Delivet, 'then to the left.'

We fairly flew, scarcely touching the ground. The milestones looked like little timid beasts that vanished at our approach. Suddenly, at a turn of the road, we saw a vortex of smoke. It was the Northern Express. For a kilometre, it was a struggle, side by side, but an unequal struggle in which the issue was certain. We won the race by twenty lengths.

In three seconds we were on the platform standing before the second-class carriages. The doors were opened, and some passengers alighted, but not my thief. We made a search through the compartments. No sign of Arsene Lupin.

'Sapristi!' I cried, 'he must have recognized me in the automobile as we were racing, side by side, and he leaped from the train.'

'Ah! There he is now! Crossing the track.'

I started in pursuit of the man, followed by my two acolytes, or rather followed by one of them, for the other, Massol, proved himself to be a runner of exceptional speed and endurance. In a few moments, he had made an appreciable gain upon the fugitive. The man noticed it, leaped over a hedge, scampered across a meadow, and entered a thick grove. When we reached this grove, Massol was waiting for us. He went no farther, for fear of losing us.

'Quite right, my dear friend,' I said. 'After such a run, our victim must be out of wind. We will catch him now.'

I examined the surroundings with the idea of proceeding alone in the arrest of the fugitive, in order to recover my papers, concerning which the authorities would doubtless ask many disagreeable questions. Then I returned to my companions, and said: 'It is all quite easy. You,

Massol, take your place at the left; you, Delivet, at the right. From there, you can observe the entire posterior line of the bush, and he cannot escape without you seeing him, except by that ravine, and I shall watch it. If he does not come out voluntarily, I will enter and drive him out toward one or the other of you. You have simply to wait. Ah! I forgot: in case I need you, a pistol shot.'

Massol and Delivet walked away to their respective posts. As soon as they had disappeared, I entered the grove with the greatest precaution so as to be neither seen nor heard. I encountered dense thickets, through which narrow paths had been cut, but the overhanging boughs compelled me to adopt a stooping posture. One of these paths led to a clearing in which I found footsteps upon the wet grass. I followed them; they led me to the foot of a mound which was surmounted by a deserted, dilapidated hovel.

'He must be there,' I said to myself. 'It is a well-chosen retreat.'

I crept cautiously to the side of the building. A slight noise informed me that he was there; and, then, through an opening, I saw him. His back was turned toward me. In two bounds, I was upon him. He tried to fire a revolver that he held in his hand. But he had no time. I threw him to the ground, in such a manner that his arms were beneath him, twisted and helpless, whilst I held him down with my knee on his breast.

'Listen, my boy,' I whispered in his ear. 'I am Arsene Lupin. You are to deliver over to me, immediately and gracefully, my pocketbook and the lady's jewels, and, in return therefore, I will save you from the police and enrol you amongst my friends. One word: yes or no?'

'Yes,' he murmured.

'Very good. Your escape, this morning, was well planned. I congratulate you.'

I arose. He fumbled in his pocket, drew out a large knife and tried to strike me with it.

'Imbecile!' I exclaimed.

With one hand, I parried the attack; with the other, I gave him a sharp blow on the carotid artery. He fell—stunned!

In my pocketbook, I recovered my papers and bank-notes. Out of curiosity, I took his. Upon an envelope, addressed to him, I read his name: Pierre Onfrey. It startled me. Pierre Onfrey, the assassin of the rue Lafontaine at Auteuil! Pierre Onfrey, he who had cut the throats of Madame Delbois and her two daughters. I leaned over him. Yes, those were the features which, in the compartment, had evoked in me the memory of a face I could not then recall.

But time was passing. I placed in an envelope two bank-notes of one hundred francs each, with a card bearing these words: 'Arsene Lupin to his worthy colleagues Honore Massol and Gaston Delivet, as a slight token of his gratitude.' I placed it in a prominent spot in the room, where they would be sure to find it. Beside it, I placed Madame Renaud's handbag. Why could I not return it to the lady who had befriended me? I must confess that I had taken from it everything that possessed any interest or value, leaving there only a shell comb, a stick of rouge Dorin for the lips, and an empty purse. But, you know, business is business. And then, really, her husband is engaged in such a dishonourable vocation!

The man was becoming conscious. What was I to do? I was unable to save him or condemn him. So I took his revolver and fired a shot in the air.

'My two acolytes will come and attend to his case,' I said to myself, as I hastened away by the road through the ravine. Twenty minutes later, I was seated in my automobile.

At four o'clock, I telegraphed to my friends at Rouen that an unexpected event would prevent me from making my promised visit. Between ourselves, considering what my friends must now know, my visit is postponed indefinitely. A cruel disillusion for them!

At six o'clock I was in Paris. The evening newspapers informed me that Pierre Onfrey had been captured at last.

Next day—let us not despise the advantages of judicious advertising—the *Echo de France* published this sensational item:

'Yesterday, near Buchy, after numerous exciting incidents, Arsene Lupin effected the arrest of Pierre Onfrey. The assassin of the rue Lafontaine had robbed Madame Renaud, wife of the director in the penitentiary service, in a railway carriage on the Paris-Havre line. Arsene

Lupin restored to Madame Renaud the hand-bag that contained her jewels, and gave a generous recompense to the two detectives who had assisted him in making that dramatic arrest.'

21

THE QUEEN'S NECKLACE

Maurice Leblanc

...the lady had to feign a continued lack of consciousness in order to deceive the enemy...

Two or three times each year, on occasions of unusual importance, such as the balls at the Austrian Embassy or the soirées of Lady Billingstone, the Countess de Dreux-Soubise wore upon her white shoulders 'The Queen's Necklace'.

It was, indeed, the famous necklace, the legendary necklace that Boehmer and Bassenge, court jewellers, had made for Madame Du Barry; the veritable necklace that the Cardinal de Rohan-Soubise intended to give to Marie-Antoinette, Queen of France; and the same that the adventuress Jeanne de Valois, Countess de la Motte, had pulled to pieces one evening in February, 1785, with the aid of her husband and their accomplice, Rétaux de Villette.

To tell the truth, the mounting alone was genuine. Rétaux de Villette had kept it, whilst the Count de la Motte and his wife scattered to the four winds of heaven the beautiful stones so carefully chosen by Bohmer. Later, he sold the mounting to Gaston de Dreux-Soubise, nephew and heir of the Cardinal, who re-purchased the few diamonds that remained in the possession of the English jeweller, Jeffreys; supplemented them with other stones of the same size but of much inferior quality, and thus restored the marvelous necklace to the form in which it had come from the hands of Bohmer and Bassenge.

For nearly a century, the house of Dreux-Soubise had prided itself upon the possession of this historic jewel. Although adverse circumstances had greatly reduced their fortune, they preferred to curtail their household expenses rather than part with this relic of royalty. More particularly, the present count clung to it as a man clings to the home of his ancestors. As a matter of prudence, he had rented a safety-deposit box at the Crédit Lyonnais in which to keep it. He went for it himself on the afternoon of the day on which his wife wished to wear it, and he, himself, carried it back next morning.

On this particular evening, at the reception given at the Palais de Castille, the Countess achieved a remarkable success; and King Christian, in whose honour the fête was given, commented on her grace and beauty. The thousand facets of the diamond sparkled and shone like flames of fire about her shapely neck and shoulders, and it is safe to say that none but she could have borne the weight of such an ornament with so much ease and grace.

This was a double triumph, and the Count de Dreux was highly elated when they returned to their chamber in the old house of the faubourg Saint-Germain. He was proud of his wife, and quite as proud, perhaps, of the necklace that had conferred added lustre to his noble house for generations. His wife, also, regarded the necklace with an almost childish vanity, and it was not without regret that she removed it from her shoulders and handed it to her husband who admired it as passionately as if he had never seen it before. Then, having placed it in its case of red leather, stamped with the Cardinal's arms, he passed into an adjoining room which was simply an alcove or cabinet that had been cut off from their chamber, and which could be entered only by means of a door at the foot of their bed. As he had done on previous occasions, he hid it on a high shelf amongst hat-boxes and piles of linen. He closed the door, and retired.

Next morning, he arose about nine o'clock, intending to go to the Crédit Lyonnais before breakfast. He dressed, drank a cup of coffee, and went to the stables to give his orders. The condition of one of the horses worried him. He caused it to be exercised in his presence. Then he returned to his wife, who had not yet left the chamber. Her maid was dressing her hair. When her husband entered, she asked:

'Are you going out?'

'Yes, as far as the bank.'

'Of course. That is wise.'

He entered the cabinet; but, after a few seconds, and without any sign of astonishment, he asked:

'Did you take it, my dear?'

'What?... No, I have not taken anything.'

'You must have moved it.'

'Not at all. I have not even opened that door.'

He appeared at the door, disconcerted, and stammered, in a scarcely intelligible voice:

'You haven't... It wasn't you?... Then...'

She hastened to his assistance, and, together, they made a thorough search, throwing the boxes to the floor and overturning the piles of linen. Then the count said, quite discouraged:

'It is useless to look any more. I put it here, on this shelf.'

'You must be mistaken.'

'No, no, it was on this shelf—nowhere else.'

They lighted a candle, as the room was quite dark, and then carried out all the linen and other articles that the room contained. And, when the room was emptied, they confessed, in despair, that the famous necklace had disappeared. Without losing time in vain lamentations, the countess notified the commissary of police, Mon. Valorbe, who came at once, and, after hearing their story, inquired of the count:

'Are you sure that no one passed through your chamber during the night?'

'Absolutely sure, as I am a very light sleeper. Besides, the chamber door was bolted, and I remember unbolting it this morning when my wife rang for her maid.'

'And there is no other entrance to the cabinet?'

'None.'

'No windows?'

'Yes, but it is closed up.'

'I will look at it.'

Candles were lighted, and Mon. Valorbe observed at once that the lower half of the window was covered by a large press which was, however, so narrow that it did not touch the casement on either side.

'On what does this window open?'

'A small inner court.'

'And you have a floor above this?'

'Two; but, on a level with the servant's floor, there is a close grating over the court. That is why this room is so dark.'

When the press was moved, they found that the window was fastened, which would not have been the case if anyone had entered that way.

'Unless,' said the count, 'they went out through our chamber.'

'In that case, you would have found the door unbolted.'

The commissary considered the situation for a moment, then asked the countess:

'Did any of your servants know that you wore the necklace last evening?'

'Certainly; I didn't conceal the fact. But nobody knew that it was hidden in that cabinet.'

'No one?'

'No one... unless...'

'Be quite sure, madam, as it is a very important point.'

She turned to her husband, and said:

'I was thinking of Henriette.'

'Henriette? She didn't know where we kept it.'

'Are you sure?'

'Who is this woman Henriette?' asked Mon. Valorbe.

'A school-mate, who was disowned by her family for marrying beneath her. After her husband's death, I furnished an apartment in this house for her and her son. She is clever with her needle and has done some work for me.'

'What floor is she on?'

'Same as ours...at the end of the corridor...and I think...the window of her kitchen...'

'Opens on this little court, does it not?'

'Yes, just opposite ours.'

Mon. Valorbe then asked to see Henriette. They went to her apartment; she was sewing, whilst her son Raoul, about six years old, was sitting beside her, reading. The commissary was surprised to see the wretched apartment that had been provided for the woman. It consisted of one room without a fireplace, and a very small room that served as a kitchen. The commissary proceeded to question her. She appeared to be overwhelmed on learning of the theft. Last evening she had herself dressed the countess and placed the necklace upon her shoulders.

'Good God!' she exclaimed, 'it can't be possible!'

'And you have no idea? Not the least suspicion? Is it possible that the thief may have passed through your room?'

She laughed heartily, never supposing that she could be an object of suspicion.

'But I have not left my room. I never go out. And, perhaps, you have not seen?'

She opened the kitchen window, and said:

'See, it is at least three metres to the ledge of the opposite window.'

'Who told you that we supposed the theft might have been committed in that way?'

'But...the necklace was in the cabinet, wasn't it?'

'How do you know that?'

'Why, I have always known that it was kept there at night. It had been mentioned in my presence.'

Her face, though still young, bore unmistakable traces of sorrow and resignation. And it now assumed an expression of anxiety as if some danger threatened her. She drew her son toward her. The child took her hand, and kissed it affectionately.

When they were alone again, the count said to the commissary:

'I do not suppose you suspect Henriette. I can answer for her. She is honesty itself.'

'I quite agree with you,' replied Mon. Valorbe. 'At most, I thought there might have been an unconscious complicity. But I confess that even that theory must be abandoned, as it does not help solve the problem now before us.'

The commissary of police abandoned the investigation, which was now taken up and completed by the examining judge. He questioned the servants, examined the condition of the bolt, experimented with the opening and closing of the cabinet window, and explored the little court from top to bottom. All was in vain. The bolt was intact. The window could not be opened or closed from the outside.

The inquiries especially concerned Henriette, for, in spite of everything, they always turned in her direction. They made a thorough investigation of her past life, and ascertained that, during the last three years, she had left the house only four times, and her business, on those occasions, was satisfactorily explained. As a matter of fact, she acted as chambermaid and seamstress to the countess, who treated her with great strictness and even severity.

At the end of a week, the examining judge had secured no more definite information than the commissary of police. The judge said:

'Admitting that we know the guilty party, which we do not, we are confronted by the fact that we do not know how the theft was committed. We are brought face to face with two obstacles: a door and a window—both closed and fastened. It is thus a double mystery. How could anyone enter, and, moreover, how could any one escape, leaving behind him a bolted door and a fastened window?'

At the end of four months, the secret opinion of the judge was that the count and countess, being hard pressed for money, which was their normal condition, had sold the Queen's Necklace. He closed the investigation.

The loss of the famous jewel was a severe blow to the Dreux-Soubise. Their credit being no longer propped up by the reserve fund that such a treasure constituted, they found themselves confronted by more exacting creditors and money-lenders. They were obliged to cut down to the quick, to sell or mortgage every article that possessed any commercial value. In brief, it would have been their ruin, if two large legacies from some distant relatives had not saved them.

Their pride also suffered a downfall, as if they had lost a quartering from their escutcheon. And, strange to relate, it was upon her former schoolmate, Henriette, that the countess vented her spleen. Toward her, the countess displayed the most spiteful feelings, and even openly accused her. First, Henriette was relegated to the servants' quarters, and, next day, discharged.

For some time, the count and countess passed an uneventful life. They travelled a great deal. Only one incident of record occurred during that period. Some months after the departure of Henriette, the countess was surprised when she received and read the following letter, signed by Henriette:

'Madame,'

'I do not know how to thank you; for it was you, was it not, who sent me that? It could not have been anyone else. No one but you knows where I live. If I am wrong, excuse me, and accept my sincere thanks for your past favours...'

What did the letter mean? The present or past favours of the countess consisted principally of injustice and neglect. Why, then, this letter of thanks?

When asked for an explanation, Henriette replied that she had received a letter, through the mails, enclosing two bank-notes of one thousand francs each. The envelope, which she enclosed with her reply, bore the Paris post-mark, and was addressed in a handwriting that was obviously disguised. Now, whence came those two thousand francs? Who had sent them? And why had they sent them?

Henriette received a similar letter and a like sum of money twelve months later. And a third time; and a fourth; and each year for a period of six years, with this difference, that in the fifth and sixth years the sum was doubled. There was another difference: the post-office authorities having seized one of the letters under the pretext that it was not registered, the last two letters were duly sent according to the postal regulations, the first dated from Saint-Germain, the other from Suresnes. The writer signed the first one, 'Anquety'; and the other, 'Péchard.' The addresses that he gave were false.

At the end of six years, Henriette died, and the mystery remained unsolved.

All these events are known to the public. The case was one of those which excite public interest, and it was a strange coincidence that this necklace, which had caused such a great commotion in France at the close of the eighteenth century, should create a similar commotion a century later. But what I am about to relate is known only to the parties directly interested and a few others from whom the count exacted a promise of secrecy. As it is probable that some day or other that promise will be broken, I have no hesitation in rending the veil and thus disclosing the key to the mystery, the explanation of the letter published in the morning papers two days ago; an extraordinary letter which increased, if possible, the mists and shadows that envelope this inscrutable drama.

Five days ago, a number of guests were dining with the Count de Dreux-Soubise. There were several ladies present, including his two nieces and his cousin, and the following gentlemen: the president of Essaville, the deputy Bochas, the chevalier Floriani, whom the count had known in Sicily, and General Marquis de Rouzières, an old club friend.

After the repast, coffee was served by the ladies, who gave the gentlemen permission to smoke their cigarettes, provided they would not desert the salon. The conversation was general, and finally one of the guests chanced to speak of celebrated crimes. And that gave the Marquis de Rouzières, who delighted to tease the count, an opportunity to mention the affair of the Queen's Necklace, a subject that the count detested.

Each one expressed his own opinion of the affair; and, of course, their various theories were not only contradictory but impossible.

'And you, monsieur,' said the countess to the chevalier Floriani, 'what is your opinion?'

'Oh! I—I have no opinion, madame.'

All the guests protested; for the chevalier had just related in an entertaining manner various adventures in which he had participated with his father, a magistrate at Palermo, and which established his judgment and taste in such manners.

'I confess,' said he, 'I have sometimes succeeded in unravelling mysteries that the cleverest detectives have renounced; yet I do not claim to be Sherlock Holmes. Moreover, I know very little about the affair of the Queen's Necklace.'

Everybody now turned to the count, who was thus obliged, quite unwillingly, to narrate all the circumstances connected with the theft.

The chevalier listened, reflected, asked a few questions, and said:

'It is very strange... At first sight, the problem appears to be a very simple one.'

The count shrugged his shoulders. The others drew closer to the chevalier, who continued, in a dogmatic tone:

'As a general rule, in order to find the author of a crime or a theft, it is necessary to determine how that crime or theft was committed, or, at least, how it could have been committed. In the present case, nothing is more simple, because we are face to face, not with several theories, but with one positive fact, that is to say: the thief could only enter by the chamber door or the window of the cabinet. Now, a person cannot open a bolted door from the outside. Therefore, he must have entered through the window.'

'But it was closed and fastened, and we found it fastened afterward,' declared the count.

'In order to do that,' continued Floriani, without heeding the interruption, 'he had simply to construct a bridge, a plank or a ladder, between the balcony of the kitchen and the ledge of the window, and as the jewel-case—'

'But I repeat that the window was fastened,' exclaimed the count, impatiently.

This time, Floriani was obliged to reply. He did so with the greatest tranquillity, as if the objection was the most insignificant affair in the world.

'I will admit that it was; but is there not a transom in the upper part of the window?'

'How do you know that?'

'In the first place, that was customary in houses of that date; and, in the second place, without such a transom, the theft cannot be explained.'

'Yes, there is one, but it was closed, the same as the window. Consequently, we did not pay attention to it.'

'That was a mistake; for, if you had examined it, you would have found that it had been opened.'

'But how?'

'I presume that, like all others, it opens by means of a wire with a ring on the lower end.'

'Yes, but I do not see—'

'Now, through a hole in the window, a person could, by the aid of some instrument, let us say a poker with a hook at the end, grip the ring, pull down, and open the transom.'

The count laughed and said:

'Excellent! excellent! Your scheme is very cleverly constructed, but you overlook one thing, monsieur, there is no hole in the window.'

'There was a hole.'

'Nonsense, we would have seen it.'

'In order to see it, you must look for it, and no one has looked. The hole is there; it must be there, at the side of the window, in the putty. In a vertical direction, of course.'

The count arose. He was greatly excited. He paced up and down the room, two or three times, in a nervous manner; then, approaching Floriani, said:

'Nobody has been in that room since; nothing has been changed.'

'Very well, monsieur, you can easily satisfy yourself that my explanation is correct.'

'It does not agree with the facts established by the examining judge. You have seen nothing, and yet you contradict all that we have seen and all that we know.'

Floriani paid no attention to the count's petulance. He simply smiled and said:

'Mon Dieu, monsieur, I submit my theory; that is all. If I am mistaken, you can easily prove it.'

'I will do so at once... I confess that your assurance—'

The count muttered a few more words; then suddenly rushed to the door and passed out. Not a word was uttered in his absence; and this profound silence gave the situation an air of almost tragic importance. Finally, the count returned. He was pale and nervous. He said to his friends, in a trembling voice:

'I beg your pardon...the revelations of the chevalier were so unexpected... I should never have thought...'

His wife questioned him, eagerly:

'Speak...what is it?'

He stammered: 'The hole is there, at the very spot, at the side of the window—'

He seized the chevalier's arm, and said to him in an imperious tone:

'Now, monsieur, proceed. I admit that you are right so far, but now...that is not all... go on...tell us the rest of it.

Floriani disengaged his arm gently, and, after a moment, continued:

'Well, in my opinion, this is what happened. The thief, knowing that the countess was going to wear the necklace that evening, had prepared his gangway or bridge during your absence. He watched you through the window and saw you hide the necklace. Afterward, he cut the glass and pulled the ring.'

'Ah! but the distance was so great that it would be impossible for him to reach the window-fastening through the transom.'

'Well, then, if he could not open the window by reaching through the transom, he must have crawled through the transom.'

'Impossible; it is too small. No man could crawl through it.'

'Then it was not a man,' declared Floriani.

'What!'

'If the transom is too small to admit a man, it must have been a child.'

'A child!'

'Did you not say that your friend Henriette had a son?'

'Yes; a son named Raoul.'

'Then, in all probability, it was Raoul who committed the theft.'

'What proof have you of that?'

'What proof! Plenty of it... For instance—'

He stopped, and reflected for a moment, then continued:

'For instance, that gangway or bridge. It is improbable that the child could have brought it in from outside the house and carried it away again without being observed. He must have used something close at hand. In the little room used by Henriette as a kitchen, were there not some shelves against the wall on which she placed her pans and dishes?'

'Two shelves, to the best of my memory.'

'Are you sure that those shelves are really fastened to the wooden brackets that support them? For, if they are not, we could be justified in presuming that the child removed them, fastened them together, and thus formed his bridge. Perhaps, also, since there was a stove, we might find the bent poker that he used to open the transom.'

Without saying a word, the count left the room; and, this time, those present did not feel the nervous anxiety they had experienced the first time. They were confident that Floriani was right, and no one was surprised when the count returned and declared:

'It was the child. Everything proves it.'

'You have seen the shelves and the poker?'

'Yes. The shelves have been unnailed, and the poker is there yet.'

But the countess exclaimed:

'You had better say it was his mother. Henriette is the guilty party. She must have compelled her son—'

'No,' declared the chevalier, 'the mother had nothing to do with it.'

'Nonsense! they occupied the same room. The child could not have done it without the mother's knowledge.'

'True, they lived in the same room, but all this happened in the adjoining room, during the night, while the mother was asleep.'

'And the necklace?' said the count. 'It would have been found amongst the child's things.'

'Pardon me! He had been out. That morning, on which you found him reading, he had just come from school, and perhaps the commissary of police, instead of wasting his time on the innocent mother, would have been better employed in searching the child's desk amongst his school-books.'

'But how do you explain those two thousand francs that Henriette received each year? Are they not evidence of her complicity?'

'If she had been an accomplice, would she have thanked you for that money? And then, was she not closely watched? But the child, being free, could easily go to a neighbouring city, negotiate with some dealer and sell him one diamond or two diamonds, as he might wish, upon condition that the money should be sent from Paris, and that proceeding could be repeated from year to year.'

An indescribable anxiety oppressed the Dreux-Soubise and their guests. There was something in the tone and attitude of Floriani—something more than the chevalier's assurance which, from the beginning, had so annoyed the count. There was a touch of irony, that seemed rather hostile than sympathetic. But the count affected to laugh, as he said:

'All that is very ingenious and interesting, and I congratulate you upon your vivid imagination.'

'No, not at all,' replied Floriani, with the utmost gravity, 'I imagine nothing. I simply describe the events as they must have occurred.'

'But what do you know about them?'

'What you yourself have told me. I picture to myself the life of the mother and child down there in the country; the illness of the mother, the schemes of and inventions of the child to sell the precious stones in order to save his mother's life, or, at least, soothe her dying moments. Her illness overcomes her. She dies. Years roll on. The child becomes a man; and then—and now I will give my imagination a free rein—let us suppose that the man feels a desire to return to the home of his childhood, that he does so, and that he meets there certain people who suspect and accuse his mother... do you realize the sorrow and anguish of such an interview in the very house wherein the original drama was played?'

His words seemed to echo for a few seconds in the ensuing silence, and one could read upon the faces of the Count and Countess de Dreux a bewildered effort to comprehend his meaning and, at the same time, the fear and anguish of such a comprehension. The count spoke at last, and said:

'Who are you, monsieur?'

'I? The chevalier Floriani, whom you met at Palermo, and whom you have been gracious enough to invite to your house on several occasions.'

'Then what does this story mean?'

'Oh! nothing at all! It is simply a pastime, so far as I am concerned. I endeavour to depict the pleasure that Henriette's son, if he still lives, would have in telling you that he was the guilty party, and that he did it because his mother was unhappy, as she was on the point of losing the place of a...servant, by which she lived, and because the child suffered at sight of his mother's sorrow.'

He spoke with suppressed emotion, rose partially and inclined toward the countess. There could be no doubt that the chevalier Floriani was Henriette's son. His attitude and words proclaimed it. Besides, was it not his obvious intention and desire to be recognized as such?

The count hesitated. What action would he take against the audacious guest? Ring? Provoke a scandal? Unmask the man who had once robbed him? But that was a long time ago! And who would believe that absurd story about the guilty child? No; better far to accept the situation, and pretend not to comprehend the true meaning of it. So the count, turning to Floriani, exclaimed:

'Your story is very curious, very entertaining; I enjoyed it much. But what do you think has become of this young man, this model son? I hope he has not abandoned the career in which he made such a brilliant début.'

'Oh! Certainly not.'

'After such a début! To steal the Queen's Necklace at six years of age; the celebrated necklace that was coveted by Marie-Antoinette!'

'And to steal it,' remarked Floriani, falling in with the count's mood, 'without costing him the slightest trouble, without anyone thinking to examine the condition of the window, or to observe that the window-sill was too clean—that window-sill which he had wiped in order to efface the marks he had made in the thick dust. We must admit that it was sufficient to turn the head of a boy at that age. It was all so easy. He had simply to desire the thing, and reach out his hand to get it.'

'And he reached out his hand.'

'Both hands,' replied the chevalier, laughing.

His companions received a shock. What mystery surrounded the life of the so-called Floriani? How wonderful must have been the life of that adventurer, a thief at six years of age, and who, today, in search of excitement or, at most, to gratify a feeling of resentment, had come to brave his victim in her own house, audaciously, foolishly, and yet with all the grace and delicacy of a courteous guest!

He arose and approached the countess to bid her adieu. She recoiled, unconsciously. He smiled.

'Oh! Madame, you are afraid of me! Did I pursue my role of parlour-magician a step too far?'

She controlled herself, and replied, with her accustomed ease:

'Not at all, monsieur. The legend of that dutiful son interested me very much, and I am pleased to know that my necklace had such a brilliant destiny. But do you not think that the son of that woman, that Henriette, was the victim of hereditary influence in the choice of his vocation?'

He shuddered, feeling the point, and replied:

'I am sure of it; and, moreover, his natural tendency to crime must have been very strong or he would have been discouraged.'

'Why so?'

'Because, as you must know, the majority of the diamonds were false. The only genuine stones were the few purchased from the English jeweller, the others having been sold, one by one, to meet the cruel necessities of life.'

'It was still the Queen's Necklace, monsieur,' replied the countess, haughtily, 'and that is something that he, Henriette's son, could not appreciate.'

'He was able to appreciate, madame, that, whether true or false, the necklace was nothing more that an object of parade, an emblem of senseless pride.'

The count made a threatening gesture, but his wife stopped him.

'Monsieur,' she said, 'if the man to whom you allude has the slightest sense of honour—'

She stopped, intimidated by Floriani's cool manner.

'If that man has the slightest sense of honour,' he repeated.

She felt that she would not gain anything by speaking to him in that manner, and in spite of her anger and indignation, trembling as she was from humiliated pride, she said to him, almost politely:

'Monsieur, the legend says that Rétaux de Villette, when in

possession of the Queen's Necklace, did not disfigure the mounting. He understood that the diamonds were simply the ornament, the accessory, and that the mounting was the essential work, the creation of the artist, and he respected it accordingly. Do you think that this man had the same feeling?'

'I have no doubt that the mounting still exists. The child respected it.'

'Well, monsieur, if you should happen to meet him, will you tell him that he unjustly keeps possession of a relic that is the property and pride of a certain family, and that, although the stones have been removed, the Queen's necklace still belongs to the house of Dreux-Soubise. It belongs to us as much as our name or our honour.'

The chevalier replied, simply:

'I shall tell him, madame.'

He bowed to her, saluted the count and the other guests, and departed.

Four days later, the countess de Dreux found upon the table in her chamber a red leather case bearing the cardinal's arms. She opened it, and found the Queen's Necklace.

But as all things must, in the life of a man who strives for unity and logic, converge toward the same goal—and as a little advertising never does any harm—on the following day, the *Echo de France* published these sensational lines:

'The Queen's Necklace, the famous historical jewellery stolen from the family of Dreux-Soubise, has been recovered by Arsène Lupin, who hastened to restore it to its rightful owner. We cannot too highly commend such a delicate and chivalrous act.'

22

THE RETURN OF IMRAY

Rudyard Kipling

...Imray from being a man became a mystery...

Imray achieved the impossible. Without warning, for no conceivable motive, in his youth, at the threshold of his career he chose to disappear from the world—which is to say, the little Indian station where he lived.

Upon a day he was alive, well, happy, and in great evidence among the billiard-tables at his Club. Upon a morning, he was not, and no manner of search could make sure where he might be. He had stepped out of his place; he had not appeared at his office at the proper time, and his dogcart was not upon the public roads. For these reasons, and because he was hampering, in a microscopical degree, the administration of the Indian Empire, that Empire paused for one microscopical moment to make inquiry into the fate of Imray. Ponds were dragged, wells were plumbed, telegrams were despatched down the lines of railways and to the nearest seaport town-twelve hundred miles away; but Imray was not at the end of the drag-ropes nor the telegraph wires. He was gone, and his place knew him no more.

Then the work of the great Indian Empire swept forward, because it could not be delayed, and Imray from being a man became a mystery—such a thing as men talk over at their tables in the Club for a month, and then forget utterly. His guns, horses, and carts were sold to the highest bidder. His superior officer wrote an altogether absurd letter to his mother, saying that Imray had unaccountably disappeared, and his bungalow stood empty.

After three or four months of the scorching hot weather had gone by, my friend Strickland, of the Police, saw fit to rent the bungalow from the native landlord. This was before he was engaged to Miss Youghal—an affair which has been described in another place—and while he was pursuing his investigations into native life. His own life was sufficiently peculiar, and men complained of his manners and customs. There was always food in his house, but there were no regular times for meals. He ate, standing up and walking about, whatever he might find at the sideboard, and this is not good for human beings. His domestic equipment was limited to six rifles, three shot-guns, five saddles, and a collection of stiff-jointed mahseer-rods, bigger and stronger than the largest salmon-rods. These occupied one-half of his bungalow, and the other half was given up to Strickland and his dog Tietjens—an enormous Rampur slut who devoured daily the rations of two men. She spoke to Strickland in a language of her own; and whenever, walking abroad, she saw things calculated to destroy the peace of Her Majesty the Queen-Empress, she returned to her master and laid information. Strickland would take steps at once, and the end of his labours was trouble and fine and imprisonment for other people. The natives believed that Tietjens was a familiar spirit, and treated her with the great reverence that is born of hate and fear. One room in the bungalow was set apart for her special use. She owned a bedstead, a blanket, and a drinking-trough, and if any one came into Strickland's room at night her custom was to knock down the invader and give tongue till someone came with a light. Strickland owed his life to her, when he was on the Frontier, in search of a local murderer, who came in the gray dawn to send Strickland much farther than the Andaman Islands. Tietjens caught the man as he was crawling into Strickland's tent with a dagger between his teeth; and after his record of iniquity was established in the eyes of the law he was hanged. From that date Tietjens wore a collar of rough silver, and employed a monogram on her night-blanket; and the blanket was of double woven Kashmir cloth, for she was a delicate dog.

Under no circumstances would she be separated from Strickland; and once, when he was ill with fever, made great trouble for the doctors, because she did not know how to help her master and would not allow another creature to attempt aid. Macarnaght, of the Indian Medical Service, beat her over her head with a gun-butt before she could understand that she must give room for those who could give quinine.

A short time after Strickland had taken Imray's bungalow, my business took me through that Station, and naturally, the Club quarters being full, I quartered myself upon Strickland. It was a desirable bungalow, eight-roomed and heavily thatched against any chance of leakage from rain. Under the pitch of the roof ran a ceiling-cloth which looked just as neat as a white-washed ceiling. The landlord had repainted it when Strickland took the bungalow. Unless you knew how Indian bungalows were built you would never have suspected that above the cloth lay the dark three-cornered cavern of the roof, where the beams and the underside of the thatch harboured all manner of rats, bats, ants, and foul things.

Tietjens met me in the verandah with a bay like the boom of the bell of St. Paul's, putting her paws on my shoulder to show she was glad to see me. Strickland had contrived to claw together a sort of meal which he called lunch, and immediately after it was finished went out about his business. I was left alone with Tietjens and my own affairs. The heat of the summer had broken up and turned to the warm damp of the rains. There was no motion in the heated air, but the rain fell like ramrods on the earth, and flung up a blue mist when it splashed back. The bamboos, and the custard-apples, the poinsettias, and the mango-trees in the garden stood still while the warm water lashed through them, and the frogs began to sing among the aloe hedges. A little before the light failed, and when the rain was at its worst, I sat in the back verandah and heard the water roar from the eaves, and scratched myself because I was covered with the thing called prickly-heat. Tietjens came out with me and put her head in my lap and was very sorrowful; so I gave her biscuits when tea was ready, and I took tea in the back verandah on account of the little coolness found there. The rooms of the house were dark behind me. I could smell Strickland's saddlery and the oil on his guns, and I had no desire to sit among these things. My own servant came to me in the twilight, the muslin of his clothes clinging tightly to his drenched body, and told me that a gentleman had called and wished to see someone. Very much against my will, but only because of the darkness of the rooms, I went into the naked drawing-room, telling my man to bring the lights. There might or might not have been a caller waiting—it seemed to me that I saw a figure by one of the windows—but when the lights came there was nothing save the spikes of the rain without, and the smell of the drinking earth in my nostrils. I explained to my servant that he was no wiser than he ought to be, and went back to the verandah to talk to Tietjens. She had gone out into the wet, and I could hardly coax her back to me; even with biscuits with sugar tops. Strickland came home, dripping wet, just before dinner, and the first thing he said was.

'Has any one called?'

I explained, with apologies, that my servant had summoned me into the drawing-room on a false alarm; or that some loafer had tried to call on Strickland, and thinking better of it had fled after giving his name. Strickland ordered dinner, without comment, and since it was a real dinner with a white tablecloth attached, we sat down.

At nine o'clock Strickland wanted to go to bed, and I was tired too. Tietjens, who had been lying underneath the table, rose up, and swung into the least exposed verandah as soon as her master moved to his own room, which was next to the stately chamber set apart for Tietjens. If a mere wife had wished to sleep out of doors in that pelting rain it would not have mattered; but Tietjens was a dog, and therefore the better animal. I looked at Strickland, expecting to see him flay her with a whip. He smiled queerly, as a man would smile after telling some unpleasant domestic tragedy. 'She has done this ever since I moved in here,' said he. 'Let her go.'

The dog was Strickland's dog, so I said nothing, but I felt all that Strickland felt in being thus made light of. Tietjens encamped outside my bedroom window, and storm after storm came up, thundered on the thatch, and died away. The lightning spattered the sky as a thrown egg spatters a barn-door, but the light was pale blue, not yellow; and, looking through my split bamboo blinds, I could see the great dog standing, not sleeping, in the verandah, the hackles alift on her back and her feet anchored as tensely as the drawn wire-rope of a suspension bridge. In the very short pauses of the thunder I tried to sleep, but it seemed that someone wanted me very urgently. He, whoever he was, was trying to call me by name, but his voice was no more than a husky whisper. The thunder ceased, and Tietjens went into the garden and howled at the low moon. Somebody tried to open my door, walked about and about through the house and stood breathing heavily in the verandahs, and just when I was falling asleep I fancied that I heard a wild hammering and clamouring above my head or on the door.

I ran into Strickland's room and asked him whether he was ill, and had been calling for me. He was lying on his bed half dressed, a pipe in his mouth. 'I thought you'd come,' he said. 'Have I been walking round the house recently?'

I explained that he had been tramping in the dining-room and the smoking-room and two or three other places, and he laughed and told me to go back to bed. I went back to bed and slept till the morning, but through all my mixed dreams I was sure I was doing someone an injustice in not attending to his wants. What those wants were I could not tell; but a fluttering, whispering, bolt-fumbling, lurking, loitering Someone was reproaching me for my slackness, and, half awake, I heard the howling of Tietjens in the garden and the threshing of the rain.

I lived in that house for two days. Strickland went to his office daily, leaving me alone for eight or ten hours with Tietjens for my only companion. As long as the full light lasted I was comfortable, and so was Tietjens; but in the twilight she and I moved into the back verandah and cuddled each other for company. We were alone in the house, but none the less it was much too fully occupied by a tenant with whom I did not wish to interfere. I never saw him, but I could see the curtains between the rooms quivering where he had just passed through; I could hear the chairs creaking as the bamboos sprung under a weight that had just quitted them; and I could feel when I went to get a book from the dining-room that somebody was waiting in the shadows of the front verandah till I should have gone away. Tietjens made the twilight more interesting by glaring into the darkened rooms with every hair erect, and following the motions of something that I could not see. She never entered the rooms, but her eyes moved interestedly: that was quite sufficient. Only when my servant came to trim the lamps and make all light and habitable she would come in with me and spend her time sitting on her haunches, watching an invisible extra man as he moved about behind my shoulder. Dogs are cheerful companions.

I explained to Strickland, gently as might be, that I would go over to the Club and find for myself quarters there. I admired his hospitality, was pleased with his guns and rods, but I did not much care for his house and its atmosphere. He heard me out to the end, and then smiled very wearily, but without contempt, for he is a man who understands things. 'Stay on,' he said, 'and see what this thing means. All you have talked about I have known since I took the bungalow. Stay on and wait. Tietjens has left me. Are you going too?'

I had seen him through one little affair, connected with a heathen idol, that had brought me to the doors of a lunatic asylum, and I had no desire to help him through further experiences. He was a man to whom unpleasantnesses arrived as do dinners to ordinary people.

Therefore, I explained more clearly than ever that I liked him immensely, and would be happy to see him in the daytime; but that I did not care to sleep under his roof. This was after dinner, when Tietjens had gone out to lie in the verandah.

"Pon my soul, I don't wonder,' said Strickland, with his eyes on the ceiling-cloth. 'Look at that!'

The tails of two brown snakes were hanging between the cloth and the cornice of the wall. They threw long shadows in the lamplight.

'If you are afraid of snakes of course—' said Strickland.

I hate and fear snakes, because if you look into the eyes of any snake you will see that it knows all and more of the mystery of man's fall, and that it feels all the contempt that the Devil felt when Adam was evicted from Eden. Besides which its bite is generally fatal, and it twists up trouser legs.

'You ought to get your thatch overhauled,' I said.

'Give me a mahseer-rod, and we'll poke 'em down.'

'They'll hide among the roof-beams,' said Strickland. 'I can't stand snakes overhead. I'm going up into the roof. If I shake 'em down, stand by with a cleaning-rod and break their backs.'

I was not anxious to assist Strickland in his work, but I took the cleaning-rod and waited in the dining-room, while Strickland brought a gardener's ladder from the verandah, and set it against the side of the room.

The snake-tails drew themselves up and disappeared. We could hear the dry rushing scuttle of long bodies running over the baggy ceiling-cloth. Strickland took a lamp with him, while I tried to make clear to him the danger of hunting roof-snakes between a ceiling-cloth and a thatch, apart from the deterioration of property caused by ripping out ceiling-cloths.

'Nonsense!' said Strickland. 'They're sure to hide near the walls by the cloth. The bricks are too cold for 'em, and the heat of the room is just what they like.' He put his hand to the corner of the stuff and ripped it from the cornice. It gave with a great sound of tearing, and Strickland put his head through the opening into the dark of the angle of the roof-beams. I set my teeth and lifted the rod, for I had not the least knowledge of what might descend.

'H'm!' said Strickland, and his voice rolled and rumbled in the roof. 'There's room for another set of rooms up here, and, by Jove, someone is occupying 'em!'

'Snakes?' I said from below.

'No. It's a buffalo. Hand me up the two last joints of a mahseer-rod, and I'll prod it. It's lying on the main roof-beam.'

I handed up the rod.

'What a nest for owls and serpents! No wonder the snakes live here,' said Strickland, climbing farther into the roof. I could see his elbow thrusting with the rod. 'Come out of that, whoever you are! Heads below there! It's falling.'

I saw the ceiling-cloth nearly in the centre of the room bag with a shape that was pressing it downwards and downwards towards the lighted lamp on the table. I snatched the lamp out of danger and stood back. Then the cloth ripped out from the walls, tore, split, swayed, and shot down upon the table something that I dared not look at, till Strickland had slid down the ladder and was standing by my side.

He did not say much, being a man of few words; but he picked up the loose end of the tablecloth and threw it over the remnants on the table.

'It strikes me,' said he, putting down the lamp, 'our friend Imray has come back. Oh! you would, would you?'

There was a movement under the cloth, and a little snake wriggled out, to be back-broken by the butt of the mahseer-rod. I was sufficiently sick to make no remarks worth recording.

Strickland meditated, and helped himself to drinks. The arrangement under the cloth made no more signs of life.

'Is it Imray?' I said.

Strickland turned back the cloth for a moment, and looked.

'It is Imray,' he said; 'and his throat is cut from ear to ear.'

Then we spoke, both together and to ourselves: 'That's why he whispered about the house.'

Tietjens, in the garden, began to bay furiously. A little later her great nose heaved open the dining-room door.

She sniffed and was still. The tattered ceiling-cloth hung down almost to the level of the table, and there was hardly room to move away from the discovery.

Tietjens came in and sat down; her teeth bared under her lip and her forepaws planted. She looked at Strickland.

'It's a bad business, old lady,' said he. 'Men don't climb up into the roofs of their bungalows to die, and they don't fasten up the ceiling cloth behind 'em. Let's think it out.'

'Let's think it out somewhere else,' I said.

'Excellent idea! Turn the lamps out. We'll get into my room.'

I did not turn the lamps out. I went into Strickland's room first, and allowed him to make the darkness. Then he followed me, and we lit tobacco and thought. Strickland thought. I smoked furiously, because I was afraid.

'Imray is back,' said Strickland. 'The question is—who killed Imray? Don't talk, I've a notion of my own. When I took this bungalow I took over most of Imray's servants. Imray was guileless and inoffensive, wasn't he?'

I agreed; though the heap under the cloth had looked neither one thing nor the other.

'If I call in all the servants they will stand fast in a crowd and lie like Aryans. What do you suggest?'

'Call 'em in one by one,' I said.

'They'll run away and give the news to all their fellows,' said Strickland. 'We must segregate 'em. Do you suppose your servant knows anything about it?'

'He may, for aught I know; but I don't think it's likely. He has only been here two or three days,' I answered. 'What's your notion?'

'I can't quite tell. How the dickens did the man get the wrong side of the ceiling-cloth?'

There was a heavy coughing outside Strickland's bedroom door. This showed that Bahadur Khan, his body-servant, had waked from sleep and wished to put Strickland to bed.

'Come in,' said Strickland. 'It's a very warm night, isn't it?'

Bahadur Khan, a great, green-turbaned, six-foot Mahomedan, said that it was a very warm night; but that there was more rain pending, which, by his Honour's favour, would bring relief to the country.

'It will be so, if God pleases,' said Strickland, tugging off his boots. 'It is in my mind, Bahadur Khan, that I have worked thee remorselessly for many days—ever since that time when thou first earnest into my service. What time was that?'

'Has the Heaven-born forgotten? It was when Imray Sahib went secretly to Europe without warning given; and I-even I-came into the honoured service of the protector of the poor.'

'And Imray Sahib went to Europe?'

'It is so said among those who were his servants.'

'And thou wilt take service with him when he returns?'

'Assuredly, Sahib. He was a good master, and cherished his dependants.'

'That is true. I am very tired, but I go buck-shooting tomorrow. Give me the little sharp rifle that I use for black-buck; it is in the case yonder.'

The man stooped over the case; handed barrels, stock, and fore-end to Strickland, who fitted all together, yawning dolefully. Then he reached down to the gun-case, took a solid-drawn cartridge, and slipped it into the breech of the '360 Express.

'And Imray Sahib has gone to Europe secretly! That is very strange, Bahadur Khan, is it not?'

'What do I know of the ways of the white man. Heaven-born?'

'Very little, truly. But thou shalt know more anon. It has reached me that Imray Sahib has returned from his so long journeyings, and that even now he lies in the next room, waiting his servant.'

'Sahib!'

The lamplight slid along the barrels of the rifle as they levelled themselves at Bahadur Khan's broad breast.

'Go and look!' said Strickland. 'Take a lamp. Thy master is tired, and he waits thee. Go!'

The man picked up a lamp, and went into the dining-room, Strickland following, and almost pushing him with the muzzle of the rifle. He looked for a moment at the black depths behind the ceiling-cloth; at the writhing snake under foot; and last, a gray glaze settling on his face, at the thing under the tablecloth.

'Hast thou seen?' said Strickland after a pause.

'I have seen. I am clay in the white man's hands. What does the Presence do?'

'Hang thee within the month. What else?'

'For killing him? Nay, Sahib, consider. Walking among us, his servants, he cast his eyes upon my child, who was four years old. Him he bewitched, and in ten days he died of the fever—my child!'

'What said Imray Sahib?'

'He said he was a handsome child, and patted him on the head; wherefore my child died. Wherefore I killed Imray Sahib in the twilight, when he had come back from office, and was sleeping. Wherefore I dragged him up into the roof-beams and made all fast behind him. The Heaven-born knows all things. I am the servant of the Heaven-born.'

Strickland looked at me above the rifle, and said, in the vernacular, 'Thou art witness to this saying? He has killed.'

Bahadur Khan stood ashen gray in the light of the one lamp. The need for justification came upon him very swiftly. 'I am trapped,' he said, 'but the offence was that man's. He cast an evil eye upon my child, and I killed and hid him. Only such as are served by devils,' he glared at Tietjens, couched stolidly before him, 'only such could know what I did.'

'It was clever. But thou shouldst have lashed him to the beam with a rope. Now, thou thyself wilt hang by a rope. Orderly!'

A drowsy policeman answered Strickland's call. He was followed by another, and Tietjens sat wondrous still.

'Take him to the police-station,' said Strickland. 'There is a case toward.'

'Do I hang, then?' said Bahadur Khan, making no attempt to escape, and keeping his eyes on the ground.

'If the sun shines or the water runs—yes!' said Strickland.

Bahadur Khan stepped back one long pace, quivered, and stood still. The two policemen waited further orders.

'Go!' said Strickland.

'Nay; but I go very swiftly,' said Bahadur Khan. 'Look! I am even now a dead man.'

He lifted his foot, and to the little toe there clung the head of the half-killed snake, firm fixed in the agony of death.

'I come of land-holding stock,' said Bahadur Khan, rocking where he stood. 'It were a disgrace to me to go to the public scaffold: therefore I take this way. Be it remembered that the Sahib's shirts are correctly enumerated, and that there is an extra piece of soap in his washbasin. My child was bewitched, and I slew the wizard. Why should you seek to slay me with the rope? My honour is saved, and—and—I die.'

At the end of an hour he died, as they die who are bitten by the little brown karait, and the policemen bore him and the thing under the tablecloth to their appointed places. All were needed to make clear the disappearance of Imray.

'This,' said Strickland, very calmly, as he climbed into bed, 'is called the nineteenth century. Did you hear what that man said?'

'I heard,' I answered. 'Imray made a mistake.'

'Simply and solely through not knowing the nature of the Oriental, and the coincidence of a little seasonal fever. Bahadur Khan had been with him for four years.'

I shuddered. My own servant had been with me for exactly that length of time. When I went over to my own room I found my man waiting, impassive as the copper head on a penny, to pull off my boots.

'What has befallen Bahadur Khan?' said I.

'He was bitten by a snake and died. The rest the Sahib knows,' was the answer.

'And how much of this matter hast thou known?'

'As much as might be gathered from One coming in in the twilight to seek satisfaction. Gently, Sahib. Let me pull off those boots.'

I had just settled to the sleep of exhaustion when I heard Strickland shouting from his side of the house —

'Tietjens has come back to her place!'

And so she had. The great deerhound was couched statelily on her own bedstead on her own blanket, while, in the next room, the idle, empty, ceiling-cloth waggled as it trailed on the table.

23

A MYSTERY

Anton Chekhov

...It's devilish queer! But I will find out who he is...Who the devil this Fedyukov was...

On the evening of Easter Sunday the actual Civil Councillor, Navagin, on his return from paying calls, picked up the sheet of paper on which visitors had inscribed their names in the hall, and went with it into his study. After taking off his outer garments and drinking some seltzer water, he settled himself comfortably on a couch and began reading the signatures in the list. When his eyes reached the middle of the long list of signatures, he started, gave an ejaculation of astonishment and snapped his fingers, while his face expressed the utmost perplexity.

'Again!' he said, slapping his knee. 'It's extraordinary! Again! Again there is the signature of that fellow, goodness knows who he is! Fedyukov! Again!'

Among the numerous signatures on the paper was the signature of a certain Fedyukov. Who the devil this Fedyukov was, Navagin had not a notion. He went over in his memory all his acquaintances, relations and subordinates in the service, recalled his remote past but could recollect no name like Fedyukov. What was so strange was that this incognito, Fedyukov, had signed his name regularly every Christmas and Easter for the last thirteen years. Neither Navagin, his wife, nor his house porter knew who he was, where he came from or what he was like.

'It's extraordinary!' Navagin thought in perplexity, as he paced about the study. 'It's strange and incomprehensible! It's like sorcery!'

'Call the porter here!' he shouted.

'It's devilish queer! But I will find out who he is!'

'I say, Grigory,' he said, addressing the porter as he entered, 'that Fedyukov has signed his name again! Did you see him?'

'No, your Excellency.'

'Upon my word, but he has signed his name! So he must have been in the hall. Has he been?'

'No, he hasn't, your Excellency.'

'How could he have signed his name without being there?'

'I can't tell.'

'Who is to tell, then? You sit gaping there in the hall. Try and remember, perhaps someone you didn't know came in? Think a minute!'

'No, your Excellency, there has been no one I didn't know. Our clerks have been, the baroness came to see her Excellency, the priests have been with the Cross, and there has been no one else...'

'Why, he was invisible when he signed his name, then, was he?'

'I can't say: but there has been no Fedyukov here. That I will swear before the holy image...'

'It's queer! It's incomprehensible! It's extraordinary!' mused Navagin. 'It's positively ludicrous. A man has been signing his name here for thirteen years and you can't find out who he is. Perhaps it's a joke? Perhaps some clerk writes that name as well as his own for fun.'

And Navagin began examining Fedyukov's signature.

The bold, florid signature in the old-fashioned style with twirls and flourishes was utterly unlike the handwriting of the other signatures. It was next below the signature of Shtutchkin, the provincial secretary, a scared, timorous little man who would certainly have died of fright if he had ventured upon such an impudent joke.

'The mysterious Fedyukov has signed his name again!' said Navagin, going in to see his wife. 'Again I fail to find out who he is.'

Madame Navagin was a spiritualist, and so for all phenomena in nature, comprehensible or incomprehensible, she had a very simple explanation.

'There's nothing extraordinary about it,' she said. 'You don't believe it, of course, but I have said it already and I say it again: there is a great deal in the world that is supernatural, which our feeble intellect can never grasp. I am convinced that this Fedyukov is a spirit who has a sympathy for you... If I were you, I would call him up and ask him what he wants.'

'Nonsense, nonsense!'

Navagin was free from superstitions, but the phenomenon which interested him was so mysterious that all sorts of uncanny devilry intruded into his mind against his will. All the evening he was imagining that the incognito Fedyukov was the spirit of some long-dead clerk, who had been discharged from the service by Navagin's ancestors and was now revenging himself on their descendant; or perhaps it was the kinsman of some petty official dismissed by Navagin himself, or of a girl seduced by him...

All night Navagin dreamed of a gaunt old clerk in a shabby uniform, with a face as yellow as a lemon, hair that stood up like a brush, and pewtery eyes; the clerk said something in a sepulchral voice and shook a bony finger at him. And Navagin almost had an attack of inflammation of the brain.

For a fortnight he was silent and gloomy and kept walking up and down and thinking. In the end he overcame his sceptical vanity, and going into his wife's room he said in a hollow voice:

'Zina, call up Fedyukov!'

The spiritualistic lady was delighted; she sent for a sheet of cardboard and a saucer, made her husband sit down beside her, and began upon the magic rites.

Fedyukov did not keep them waiting long...

'What do you want?' asked Navagin.

'Repent,' answered the saucer.

'What were you on earth?'

'A sinner...'

'There, you see!' whispered his wife, 'and you did not believe!'

Navagin conversed for a long time with Fedyukov, and then called up Napoleon, Hannibal, Askotchensky, his aunt Klavdya Zaharovna, and they all gave him brief but correct answers full of deep significance. He was busy with the saucer for four hours, and fell asleep soothed and happy that he had become acquainted with a mysterious world that was new to him. After that he studied spiritualism every day, and at the office, informed the clerks that there was a great deal in nature that was supernatural and marvellous to which our men of science ought to have turned their attention long ago.

Hypnotism, mediumism, bishopism, spiritualism, the fourth dimension, and other misty notions took complete possession of him, so that for whole days at a time, to the great delight of his wife, he read books on spiritualism or devoted himself to the saucer, table-turning, and discussions of supernatural phenomena. At his instigation all his clerks took up spiritualism, too, and with such ardour that the old managing clerk went out of his mind and one day sent a telegram: 'Hell. Government House. I feel that I am turning into an evil spirit. What's to be done? Reply paid. Vassily Krinolinsky.'

After reading several hundreds of treatises on spiritualism Navagin had a strong desire to write something himself. For five months he sat composing, and in the end had written a huge monograph, entitled: My Opinion. When he had finished this essay he determined to send it to a spiritualist journal.

The day on which it was intended to despatch it to the journal was a very memorable one for him. Navagin remembers that on that never-to-be-forgotten day the secretary who had made a fair copy of his article and the sacristan of the parish who had been sent for on business were in his study. Navagin's face was beaming. He looked lovingly at his creation, felt between his fingers how thick it was, and with a happy smile said to the secretary:

'I propose, Filipp Sergeyitch, to send it registered. It will be safer...' And raising his eyes to the sacristan, he said: 'I have sent for you on business, my good man. I am putting my youngest son to the high school and I must have a certificate of baptism; only could you let me have it quickly?'

'Very good, your Excellency!' said the sacristan, bowing. 'Very good, I understand...'

'Can you let me have it by tomorrow?'

'Very well, your Excellency, set your mind at rest! Tomorrow it shall be ready! Will you send someone to the church tomorrow before evening service? I shall be there. Bid him ask for Fedyukov. I am always there...'

'What!' cried the general, turning pale.

'Fedyukov.'

'You, ... you are Fedyukov?' asked Navagin, looking at him with wide-open eyes.

'Just so, Fedyukov.'

'You... you signed your name in my hall?'

'Yes ...' the sacristan admitted, and was overcome with confusion. 'When we come with the Cross, your Excellency, to grand gentlemen's houses I always sign my name... I like doing it... Excuse me, but when I see the list of names in the hall I feel an impulse to sign mine...'

In dumb stupefaction, understanding nothing, hearing nothing, Navagin paced about his study. He touched the curtain over the door, three times waved his hands like a jeune premier in a ballet when he sees her, gave a whistle and a meaningless smile, and pointed with his finger into space.

'So I will send off the article at once, your Excellency,' said the secretary.

These words roused Navagin from his stupour. He looked blankly at the secretary and the sacristan, remembered, and stamping, his foot irritably, screamed in a high, breaking tenor: 'Leave me in peace! Lea-eave me in peace, I tell you! What you want of me I don't understand.'

The secretary and the sacristan went out of the study and reached the street while he was still stamping and shouting:

'Leave me in peace! What you want of me I don't understand. Lea-eave me in peace!'

24

THE ADVENTURE OF THE TWO COLLABORATORS

James M. Barrie

...two collaborators in comic opera...

In bringing to a close the adventures of my friend Sherlock Holmes I am perforce reminded that he never, save on the occasion which, as you will now hear, brought his singular career to an end, consented to act in any mystery which was concerned with persons who made a livelihood by their pen. 'I am not particular about the people I mix among for business purposes,' he would say, 'but at literary characters I draw the line.'

We were in our rooms in Baker Street one evening. I was (I remember) by the centre table writing out *The Adventure of the Man without a Cork Leg* (which had so puzzled the Royal Society and all the other scientific bodies of Europe), and Holmes was amusing himself with a little revolver practice. It was his custom of a summer evening to fire round my head, just shaving my face, until he had made a photograph of me on the opposite wall, and it is a slight proof of his skill that many of these portraits in pistol shots are considered admirable likenesses.

I happened to look out of the window, and perceiving two gentlemen advancing rapidly along Baker Street asked him who they were. He immediately lit his pipe, and, twisting himself on a chair into the figure 8, replied:

'They are two collaborators in comic opera, and their play has not been a triumph.'

THE ADVENTURE OF THE TWO COLLABORATORS

I sprang from my chair to the ceiling in amazement, and he then explained:

'My dear Watson, they are obviously men who follow some low calling. That much even you should be able to read in their faces. Those little pieces of blue paper which they fling angrily from them are Durrant's Press Notices. Of these they have obviously hundreds about their person (see how their pockets bulge). They would not dance on them if they were pleasant reading.'

I again sprang to the ceiling (which is much dented), and shouted: 'Amazing! But they may be mere authors.'

'No,' said Holmes, 'for mere authors only get one press notice a week. Only criminals, dramatists and actors get them by the hundred.'

'Then they may be actors.'

'No, actors would come in a carriage.'

'Can you tell me anything else about them?'

'A great deal. From the mud on the boots of the tall one I perceive that he comes from South Norwood. The other is as obviously a Scotch author.'

'How can you tell that?'

'He is carrying in his pocket a book called (I clearly see) Auld Licht Something. Would anyone but the author be likely to carry about a book with such a title?'

I had to confess that this was improbable. It was now evident that the two men (if such they can be called) were seeking our lodgings. I have said (often) that my friend Holmes seldom gave way to emotion of any kind, but he now turned livid with passion. Presently this gave place to a strange look of triumph.

'Watson,' he said, 'that big fellow has for years taken the credit for my most remarkable doings, but at last I have him—at last'

Up I went to the ceiling, and when I returned the strangers were in the room.

'I perceive, gentlemen,' said Mr Sherlock Holmes, 'that you are at present afflicted by an extraordinary novelty.'

The handsomer of our visitors asked in amazement how he knew this, but the big one only scowled.

'You forget that you wear a ring on your fourth finger,' replied Mr Holmes calmly.

I was about to jump to the ceiling when the big brute interposed.

'That tommy-rot is all very well for the public, Holmes,' said he, 'but you can drop it before me. And, Watson, if you go up to the ceiling again I shall make you stay there.'

Here I observed a curious phenomenon. My friend Sherlock Holmes shrank. He became small before our eyes. I looked longingly at the ceiling, but dared not.

'Let us cut the first four pages,' said big man, 'and proceed to business. I want to know why—'

'Allow me,' said Mr Holmes, with some of his old courage. 'You want to know why the public does not go to your opera.'

'Exactly,' said the other ironically, 'as you perceive by my shirt stud.' He added more gravely, 'And as you can only find out in one way I must insist on your witnessing an entire performance of the piece.'

It was an anxious moment for me. I shuddered, for I knew that if Holmes went I should have to go with him. But my friend had a heart of gold.

'Never,' he cried fiercely, 'I will do anything for you save that.'

'Your continued existence depends on it,' said the big man menacingly.

'I would rather melt into air,' replied Holmes, proudly taking another chair. 'But I can tell you why the public don't go to your piece without sitting the thing out myself.'

'Why?'

'Because,' replied Holmes calmly, 'they prefer to stay away.'

A dead silence followed that extraordinary remark. For a moment the two intruders gazed with awe upon the man who had unravelled their mystery so wonderfully. Then drawing their knives—Holmes grew less and less, until nothing was left save a ring of smoke which slowly circled to the ceiling.

The last words of great men are often noteworthy. These were the last words of Sherlock Holmes: 'Fool, fool! I have kept you in luxury for years. By my help you have ridden extensively in cabs, where no author was ever seen before. Henceforth you will ride in buses,'

The brute sunk into a chair aghast. The other author did not turn a hair.

To A. Conan Doyle, from his friend J. M. Barrie

25

AN ARTFUL TOUCH
Charles Dickens

...artful touch transported him...

'One of the most beautiful things that ever was done, perhaps,' said Inspector Wield, emphasising the adjective, as preparing us to expect dexterity or ingenuity rather than strong interest, 'was a move of Sergeant Witchem's. It was a lovely idea!

'Witchem and me were down at Epsom one Derby Day, waiting at the station for the Swell Mob. As I mentioned, when we were talking about these things before, we are ready at the station when there's races, or an Agricultural Show, or a Chancellor sworn in for an university, or Jenny Lind, or any thing of that sort; and as the Swell Mob come down, we send 'em back again by the next train. But se of the Swell Mob, on the occasion of this Derby that I refer to, so far kiddied us as to hire a horse and shay; start away from London by Whitechapel, and miles round; come into Epsom from the opposite direction; and go to work, right and left, on the course, while we were waiting for 'em at the Rail. That, however, ain't the point of what I'm going to tell you.

'While Witchem and me were waiting at the station, there comes up one Mr Tatt; a gentleman formerly in the public line, quite an amateur Detective in his way, and very much respected. "Halloa, Charley Wield," he says. "What are you doing here? On the look out for some of your old friends?" Yes, the old move, Mr Tatt. "Come along," he says, "you and Witchem, and have a glass of sherry." 'We can't stir from the place,' says I, 'till the next train comes in; but after that, we will with pleasure.' Mr Tatt waits, and the train comes in, and then Witchem and me go off with him to the Hotel. Mr Tatt he's got up quite regardless of expense, for the occasion; and in his shin-front there's a beautiful diamond prop, cost him fifteen or twenty pounds—a very handsome pin indeed. We drink our sherry at the bar, and have our three or four glasses, when Witchem cries suddenly, 'Look out, Mr Wield! Stand fast!' and a dash is made into the place by the swell mob—four of 'em—that have come down as I tell you, and in a moment Mr Tatt's prop is gone! Witchem, he cuts 'em off at the door, I lay about me as hard as I can, Mr Tatt shows fight like a good 'un, and there we are, all down together, heads and heels, knocking about on the floor of the bar—perhaps you never see such a scene of confusion! However, we stick to our men (Mr Tatt being as good as any officer), and we take 'em all, and carry 'em off to the station. The station's full of people, who have been took on the course; and it's a precious piece of work to get 'em secured. However, we do it at last, and we search 'em; but nothing's found upon 'em, and they're locked up; and a pretty state of heat we are in by that time, I assure you!

'I was very blank over it myself, to think that the prop had been passed away; and I said to Witchem, when we had set 'em to rights, and were cooling ourselves along with Mr Tatt, "We don't take much by this move, anyway, for nothing's found upon 'em, and it's only the braggadocio after all." "What do you mean, Mr Wield," says Witchem. "Here's the diamond pin!" and in the palm of his hand there it was, safe and sound! 'Why, in the name of wonder,' says me and Mr Tatt, in astonishment, 'how did you come by that?' "I'll tell you how I come by it," says he. "I saw which of 'em took it; and when we were all down on the floor together, knocking about, I just gave him a little touch on the back of his hand, as I knew his pal would; and he thought it was his pal; and gave it me!" It was beautiful, beau-ti-ful!

'Even that was hardly the best of the case, for that chap was tried at the Quarter Sessions at Guildford. You know what Quarter Sessions are, sir. Well, if you'll believe me, while them slow justices were looking over the Acts of Parliament to see what they could do to him, I'm blowed if he didn't cut out of the dock before their faces! He cut out of the dock, sir, then and there; swam across a river; and got up into a tree to dry himself. In the tree he was took—an old woman having seen him climb up—and Witchem's artful touch transported him!'

26

SOME SCOTLAND YARD STORIES

Sir Robert Anderson

… one of my principal subordinates was trying to impose on me as though I were an ignoramus…

When I took charge of the Criminal Investigation Department I was no novice in matters relating to criminals and crime. In addition to experience gained at the Bar and on the Prison Commission, secret-service work had kept me in close touch with 'Scotland Yard' for twenty years, and during all that time I had the confidence, not only of the chiefs, but of the principal officers of the detective force. I thus entered on my duties with very exceptional advantages.

I was not a little surprised, therefore, to find occasion to suspect that one of my principal subordinates was trying to impose on me as though I were an ignoramus. For when any important crime of a certain kind occurred, and I set myself to investigate it—à la—Sherlock Holmes, he used to listen to me in the way that so many people listen to sermons in church; and when I was done he would stolidly announce that the crime was the work of A, B, C, or D, naming some of his stock heroes. Though a keen and shrewd police officer, the man was unimaginative, and I thus accounted for the fact that his list was always brief, and that the same names came up repeatedly. It was 'Old Carr,' or 'Wirth,' or 'Sausage,' or 'Shrimps,' or 'Quiet Joe,' or 'Red Bob,' etc., etc., one name or another being put forward according to the kind of crime I was investigating.

It was easy to test my prosaic subordinate's statements by methods with which I was familiar in secret-service work; and I soon found that he was generally right. Great crimes are the work of great criminals, and great criminals are very few. And by 'great crimes' I mean, not crimes that loom large in the public view because of their moral heinousness, but crimes that are the work of skilled and resourceful criminals. The problem in such cases is not to find the offender in a population of many millions, but to pick him out from among a few definitely known 'specialists' in the particular sort of crime under investigation.

A volume might be filled with cases to illustrate my meaning; but a very few must here suffice. It fell upon a day, for example, that a 'ladder larceny' was committed at a country house in Cheshire. It was the usual story. While the family were at dinner, the house was entered by means of a ladder placed against a bedroom window, all outer doors and ground-floor windows having been fastened from outside by screws or wire or rope; and wires were stretched across the lawn to baffle pursuit in case the thieves were discovered. The next day the Chief Constable of the county called on me; for, as he said, such a crime was beyond the capacity of provincial practitioners, and he expected us to find the delinquents among our pets at Scotland Yard. He gave me a vague description of two strangers who had been seen near the house the day before, and in return I gave him three photographs. Two of these were promptly identified as the men who had come under observation. Arrest and conviction followed, and the criminals received 'a punishment suited to their sin.' One of them was 'Quiet Joe'; the other, his special 'pal.'

Their sentences expired about the time of my retirement from office, and thus my official acquaintance with them came to an end. But in the newspaper reports of a similar case the year after I left office, I recognized my old friends. Rascals of this type are worth watching, and the police had noticed that they were meeting at the Lambeth Free Library, where their special study was provincial directories and books of reference. They were tracked to a bookshop where they bought a map of Bristol, and to other shops where they procured the plant for a 'ladder larceny.' They then booked for Bristol and there took observations of the suburban house they had fixed upon. At this stage the local detectives, to whom of course the metropolitan officers were bound to give the case, declared themselves and seized the criminals; and the case was disposed of by a nine months' sentence on a minor issue.

Most people can be wise after the event, but even that sort of belated wisdom seems lacking to the legislature and the law. If on the occasion of their previous conviction, these men had been asked what they would do on the termination of their sentence, they would have answered, 'Why, go back to business, of course; what else?' And at Bristol they would have replied with equal frankness. On that occasion they openly expressed their gratification that the officers did not wait to 'catch them fair on the job, as another long stretch would about finish them'—a playful allusion to the fact that, as they were both in their seventh decade, another penal servitude sentence would have seen the end of them; whereas their return to the practice of their calling was only deferred for a few months. Meanwhile they would live without expense, and a paternal government would take care that the money found in their pockets on their arrest would be restored to them on their release, to enable them to buy more jimmies and wire and screws, so that no time would be lost in getting to work. Such is our 'punishment-of-crime' system!

'Quiet Joe' made a good income by the practice of his profession; but he was a thriftless fellow who spent his earnings freely, and never paid income tax. 'Old Carr' was of a different type. The man never did an honest day's work in his life. He was a thief, a financier and trainer of thieves, and a notorious receiver of stolen property. But though his wealth was ill-gotten, he knew how to hoard it. Upon his last conviction I was appointed statutory 'administrator' of his estate. I soon discovered that he owned a good deal of valuable house property. But this I declined to deal with, and took charge only of his portable securities for money. The value of this part of his estate may be estimated by the fact that on his discharge he brought an action against me for mal-administration of it, claiming £5000 damages, and submitting detailed accounts in support of his claim. Mr Augustine Birrell was my leading counsel in the suit; and I may add that though the old rascal carried his case to the Court of Appeal he did not get his £5000.

The man lived in crime and by crime; and old though he was (he was born in 1828), and 'rolling in wealth,' he at once 'resumed the practice of his profession.' He was arrested abroad this year during a trip taken to dispose of some stolen notes, the proceeds of a Liverpool crime, and his evil life came to an end in a foreign prison.

When I refused to deal with Carr's house property I allowed him to nominate a friend to take charge of it, and he nominated a brother professional, a man of the same kidney as himself, known in police circles as 'Sausage.' A couple of years later, however, I learned from the tenants that the agent had disappeared, and that their cheques for rent had been returned to them. I knew what that meant, and at once instituted inquiries to find the man, first in the metropolis and then throughout the provinces; but my inquiries were fruitless. I learned, however, that, when last at Scotland Yard, the man had said with emphasis that 'he would never again do anything at home.' This was in answer to a warning and an appeal; a warning that he would get no mercy if again brought to justice, and an appeal to change his ways, as he had made his pile and could afford to live in luxurious idleness. With this clue to guide me, I soon learned that the man's insatiable zest for crime had led him to cross the Channel in hope of finding a safer sphere of work, and that he was serving a sentence in a French prison.

No words, surely, can be needed to point the moral of cases such as these. The criminals who keep society in a state of siege are as strong as they are clever. If the risk of a few years' penal servitude on conviction gave place to the certainty of final loss of liberty, these professionals would put up with the tedium of an honest life. Lombroso theories have no application to such men. Benson, of the famous 'Benson and Kerr frauds,' was the son of an English clergyman. He was a man of real ability, of rare charms of manner and address, and an accomplished linguist. Upon the occasion of one of Madame Patti's visits to America he ingratiated himself with the customs officers at New York, and thus got on board the liner before the arrival of the 'Reception Committee.' He was of course a stranger to the great singer, but she was naturally charmed by his appearance and bearing, and the perfection of his Italian, and she had no reason to doubt that he had been commissioned for the part he played so acceptably. And when the Reception Committee arrived they assumed that he was a friend of Madame Patti's. Upon his arm it was, therefore, that she leaned when disembarking. All this was done with a view to carry out a huge fraud, the detection of which eventually brought him to ruin. The man was capable of filling any position; but the life of adventure and ease which a criminal career provided had a fascination for him.

Facts like these failed to convince Dr. Max Nordau when he called upon me years ago. At his last visit I put his 'type' theory to a test. I had two photographs so covered that nothing showed but the face, and telling him that the one was an eminent public man and the other a notorious criminal, I challenged him to say which was the 'type.' He shirked my challenge. For as a matter of fact the criminal's face looked more benevolent than the other, and it was certainly as 'strong.' The one was Raymond—alias—Wirth—the most eminent of the criminal fraternity of my time—and the other was Archbishop Temple. Need I add that my story is intended to discredit—not His Grace of Canterbury, but—the Lombroso 'type' theory.

Raymond, like Benson, had a respectable parentage. In early manhood he was sentenced to a long term of imprisonment for a big crime committed in New York. But he escaped and came to England. His schemes were Napoleonic. His most famous—coup—was a great diamond robbery. His cupidity was excited by the accounts of the Kimberley mines. He sailed for South Africa, visited the mines, accompanied a convoy of diamonds to the coast, and investigated the whole problem on the spot. Dick Turpin would have recruited a body of bushrangers and seized one of the convoys. But the methods of the sportsmanlike criminal of our day are very different. The arrival of the diamonds at the coast was timed to catch the mail steamer for England; and if a convoy were accidentally delayed—en route, the treasure had to lie in the post office till the next mail left. Raymond's plan of campaign was soon settled. He was a man who could make his way in any company, and he had no difficulty in obtaining wax impressions of the postmaster's keys. The postmaster, indeed, was one of a group of admiring friends whom he entertained at dinner the evening before he sailed for England.

Some months later he returned to South Africa under a clever disguise and an assumed name, and made his way up country to a place at which the diamond convoys had to cross a river ferry on their way to the coast. Unshipping the chain of the ferry, he let the boat drift down stream, and the next convoy missed the mail steamer. £90,000 worth of diamonds had to be deposited in the strong room of the post office; and those diamonds ultimately reached England in Raymond's possession. He afterward boasted that he sold them to their lawful owners in Hatton Garden.

If I had ever possessed £90,000 worth of anything, the government would have had to find someone else to look after Fenians and burglars. But Raymond loved his work for its own sake; and though he lived in luxury and style, he kept to it to the last, organizing and financing many an important crime.

A friend of mine who has a large medical practice in one of the London suburbs told me once of an extraordinary patient of his. The man was a Dives and lived sumptuously, but he was extremely hypochondriacal. Every now and then an urgent summons would bring the doctor to the house, to find the patient in bed, though with nothing whatever the matter with him. But the man always insisted on having a prescription, which was promptly sent to the chemist. My friend's last summons had been exceptionally urgent; and on his entering the room with unusual abruptness, the man sprang up in bed and covered him with a revolver! I might have relieved his curiosity by explaining that this eccentric patient was a prince among criminals. Raymond knew that his movements were matter of interest to the police; and if he had reason to fear that he had been seen in dangerous company, he bolted home and 'shammed sick.' And the doctor's evidence, confirmed by the chemist's books, would prove that he was ill in bed till after the hour at which the police supposed they had seen him miles away.

Raymond it was who stole the famous Gainsborough picture for which Mr Agnew had recently paid the record price of £10,000. I may here say that the owner acted very well in this matter. Though the picture was offered him more than once on tempting terms he refused to treat for it, save with the sanction of the police. And it was not until I intimated to him that he might deal with the thieves that he took steps for its recovery.

The story of another crime will explain my action in this case. The Channel gang of thieves mentioned on a previous page sometimes went for larger game than purses and pocket-books. They occasionally robbed the treasure chest of the mail steamer when a parcel of valuable securities was passing from London to Paris. Tidings reached me that they were planning a coup of this kind upon a certain night, and I ascertained by inquiry that a city insurance company meant to send a large consignment of bonds to Paris on the night in question. How the thieves got the information is a mystery; their organization must have been admirable. But Scotland Yard was a match for them. I sent officers to Dover and Calais to deal with the case, and the men were arrested on landing at Calais. But they were taken empty-handed. A capricious order of the railway company's marine superintendent at Dover had changed the steamer that night an hour before the time of sailing; and while upon the thieves was found a key for the treasure chest of the advertised boat, they had none for the boat in which they had actually crossed. But, *mirabile dictu*, during the passage they had managed to get a wax impression of it! We also got hold of a cloak-room ticket for a portmanteau which was found to contain some £2000 worth of coupons stolen by the gang on a former trip. The men included in the 'bag' were 'Shrimps,' 'Red Bob,' and an old sinner named Powell. But the criminal law is skilfully framed in the interest of criminals, and it was impossible to make a case against them. I succeeded, however, by dint of urgent appeals to the French authorities, in having them kept in gaol for three months.

And now for the point of my story. Powell had left a blank cheque with his 'wife,' to be used in case he came to grief; and on his return to England he found she had been false to him. She had drawn out all his money, and gone off with another man; and the poor old rascal died of want in the streets of Southampton. It was him who was Raymond's accomplice in stealing Mr Agnew's picture, and with his death all hope of a prosecution came to an end.

If my purpose here were to amuse, I might fill many a page with narratives of this kind. But my object is to expose the error and folly of our present system of dealing with crime. When a criminal court claims to anticipate the judgment of the Great Assize in the case of a hooligan convicted of some vulgar act of violence, the silliness and profanity of the claim may pass unnoticed. But when the 'punishment-of-crime' system is applied to criminals of the type here described, the imbecility of it must be apparent to all. With such men crime is 'the business of their lives.' They delight in it. Their zest for it never flags, even in old age. What leads men like Raymond or Carr to risk a sentence of penal servitude is not a sense of want—that is a forgotten memory. Nor is it even a craving for filthy lucre. The controlling impulse is a love of sport, for every great criminal is a thorough sportsman. And in the case of a man who is free from the weakness of having a conscience, it is not easy to estimate the fascination of a life of crime. Fancy the long-sustained excitement of planning and executing crimes like Raymond's. In comparison with such sport, hunting wild game is work for savages; salmon-fishing and grouse-shooting, for lunatics and idiots! The theft of the Gold Cup at Ascot illustrates what I am saying here. The thieves arrived in motor cars; they were, we are told, 'of gentlemanly appearance, and immaculately dressed,' and they paid their way into the grand stand. The list of criminals of that type is a short one; and no one need suppose that such men would risk penal servitude for the paltry sum the cup would fetch. A crime involving far less risk would bring them ten times as much booty. For no winner of the cup ever derived more pleasure from the possession of it than the thieves must have experienced as they drove to London with the treasure under the seat of their motor car. For it was not the lust of filthy lucre, but the love of sport that incited them to the venture. There are hundreds of our undergraduates who would eagerly emulate the feat, were they not deterred by its dangers. And a rule of three sum may explain my proposal to put an end to such crimes. Let the consequences to the professional criminal be made equal to what imprisonment would mean to a 'Varsity' man, and the thing is done.

27

THE THREE TOOLS OF DEATH

G.K. Chesterton

...The inquiry is just going to begin...

Both by calling and conviction Father Brown knew better than most of us, that every man is dignified when he is dead. But even he felt a pang of incongruity when he was knocked up at daybreak and told that Sir Aaron Armstrong had been murdered. There was something absurd and unseemly about secret violence in connection with so entirely entertaining and popular a figure. For Sir Aaron Armstrong was entertaining to the point of being comic; and popular in such a manner as to be almost legendary. It was like hearing that Sunny Jim had hanged himself; or that Mr Pickwick had died in Hanwell. For though Sir Aaron was a philanthropist, and thus dealt with the darker side of our society, he prided himself on dealing with it in the brightest possible style. His political and social speeches were cataracts of anecdotes and 'loud laughter'; his bodily health was of a bursting sort; his ethics were all optimism; and he dealt with the Drink problem (his favourite topic) with that immortal or even monotonous gaiety which is so often a mark of the prosperous total abstainer.

The established story of his conversion was familiar on the more puritanic platforms and pulpits, how he had been, when only a boy, drawn away from Scotch theology to Scotch whisky, and how he had risen out of both and become (as he modestly put it) what he was. Yet his wide white beard, cherubic face, and sparkling spectacles, at the numberless dinners and congresses where they appeared, made it hard to believe, somehow, that he had ever been anything so morbid as either a dram-drinker or a Calvinist. He was, one felt, the most seriously merry of all the sons of men.

He had lived on the rural skirt of Hampstead in a handsome house, high but not broad, a modern and prosaic tower. The narrowest of its narrow sides overhung the steep green bank of a railway, and was shaken by passing trains. Sir Aaron Armstrong, as he boisterously explained, had no nerves. But if the train had often given a shock to the house, that morning the tables were turned, and it was the house that gave a shock to the train.

The engine slowed down and stopped just beyond that point where an angle of the house impinged upon the sharp slope of turf. The arrest of most mechanical things must be slow; but the living cause of this had been very rapid. A man clad completely in black, even (it was remembered) to the dreadful detail of black gloves, appeared on the ridge above the engine, and waved his black hands like some sable windmill. This in itself would hardly have stopped even a lingering train. But there came out of him a cry which was talked of afterwards as something utterly unnatural and new. It was one of those shouts that are horridly distinct even when we cannot hear what is shouted. The word in this case was 'Murder!'

But the engine-driver swears he would have pulled up just the same if he had heard only the dreadful and definite accent and not the word.

The train once arrested, the most superficial stare could take in many features of the tragedy. The man in black on the green bank was Sir Aaron Armstrong's man-servant Magnus. The baronet in his optimism had often laughed at the black gloves of this dismal attendant; but no one was likely to laugh at him just now.

So soon as an inquirer or two had stepped off the line and across the smoky hedge, they saw, rolled down almost to the bottom of the bank, the body of an old man in a yellow dressing-gown with a very vivid scarlet lining. A scrap of rope seemed caught about his leg, entangled presumably in a struggle. There was a smear or so of blood, though very little; but the body was bent or broken into a posture impossible to any living thing. It was Sir Aaron Armstrong. A few more bewildered moments brought out a big fair-bearded man, whom some travellers could salute as the dead man's secretary, Patrick Royce, once well known in Bohemian society and even famous in the Bohemian arts. In a manner more vague, but even more convincing, he echoed the agony of the servant. By the time the third figure of that household, Alice Armstrong, daughter of the dead man, had come already tottering and waving into the garden, the engine-driver had put a stop to his stoppage. The whistle had blown and the train had panted on to get help from the next station.

Father Brown had been thus rapidly summoned at the request of Patrick Royce, the big ex-Bohemian secretary. Royce was an Irishman by birth; and that casual kind of Catholic that never remembers his religion until he is really in a hole. But Royce's request might have been less promptly complied with if one of the official detectives had not been a friend and admirer of the unofficial Flambeau; and it was impossible to be a friend of Flambeau without hearing numberless stories about Father Brown. Hence, while the young detective (whose name was Merton) led the little priest across the fields to the railway, their talk was more confidential than could be expected between two total strangers.

'As far as I can see,' said Mr Merton candidly, 'there is no sense to be made of it at all. There is nobody one can suspect. Magnus is a solemn old fool; far too much of a fool to be an assassin. Royce has been the baronet's best friend for years; and his daughter undoubtedly adored him. Besides, it's all too absurd. Who would kill such a cheery old chap as Armstrong? Who could dip his hands in the gore of an after-dinner speaker? It would be like killing Father Christmas.'

'Yes, it was a cheery house,' assented Father Brown. 'It was a cheery house while he was alive. Do you think it will be cheery now he is dead?'

Merton started a little and regarded his companion with an enlivened eye. 'Now he is dead?' he repeated.

'Yes,' continued the priest stolidly, 'he was cheerful. But did he communicate his cheerfulness? Frankly, was anyone else in the house cheerful but he?'

A window in Merton's mind let in that strange light of surprise in which we see for the first time things we have known all along. He had often been to the Armstrongs', on little police jobs of the philanthropist; and, now he came to think of it, it was in itself a depressing house. The rooms were very high and very cold; the decoration mean and provincial; the draughty corridors were lit by electricity that was bleaker than moonlight. And though the old man's scarlet face and silver beard had blazed like a bonfire in each room or passage in turn, it did not leave any warmth behind it. Doubtless this spectral discomfort in the place was partly due to the very vitality and exuberance of its owner; he needed no stoves or lamps, he would say, but carried his own warmth with him. But when Merton recalled the other inmates, he was compelled to confess that they also were as shadows of their lord. The moody man-servant, with his monstrous black gloves, was almost a nightmare; Royce, the secretary, was solid enough, a big bull of a man, in tweeds, with a short beard; but the straw-coloured beard was startlingly salted with gray like the tweeds, and the broad forehead was barred with premature wrinkles. He was good-natured enough also, but it was a sad sort of good-nature, almost a heart-broken sort—he had the general air of being some sort of failure in life. As for Armstrong's daughter, it was almost incredible that she was his daughter; she was so pallid in colour and sensitive in outline. She was graceful, but there was a quiver in the very shape of her that was like the lines of an aspen. Merton had sometimes wondered if she had learnt to quail at the crash of the passing trains.

'You see,' said Father Brown, blinking modestly, 'I'm not sure that the Armstrong cheerfulness is so very cheerful—for other people. You say that nobody could kill such a happy old man, but I'm not sure; ne nos inducas in tentationem. If ever I murdered somebody,' he added quite simply, 'I dare say it might be an Optimist.'

'Why?' cried Merton amused. 'Do you think people dislike cheerfulness?'

'People like frequent laughter,' answered Father Brown, 'but I don't think they like a permanent smile. Cheerfulness without humour is a very trying thing.'

They walked some way in silence along the windy grassy bank by the rail, and just as they came under the far-flung shadow of the tall Armstrong house, Father Brown said suddenly, like a man throwing away a troublesome thought rather than offering it seriously: 'Of course, drink is neither good nor bad in itself. But I can't help sometimes feeling that men like Armstrong want an occasional glass of wine to sadden them.'

Merton's official superior, a grizzled and capable detective named Gilder, was standing on the green bank waiting for the coroner, talking to Patrick Royce, whose big shoulders and bristly beard and hair towered above him. This was the more noticeable because Royce walked always with a sort of powerful stoop, and seemed to be going about his small clerical and domestic duties in a heavy and humbled style, like a buffalo drawing a go-cart.

He raised his head with unusual pleasure at the sight of the priest, and took him a few paces apart. Meanwhile Merton was addressing the older detective respectfully indeed, but not without a certain boyish impatience.

'Well, Mr Gilder, have you got much farther with the mystery?'

'There is no mystery,' replied Gilder, as he looked under dreamy eyelids at the rooks.

'Well, there is for me, at any rate,' said Merton, smiling.

'It is simple enough, my boy,' observed the senior investigator, stroking his gray, pointed beard. 'Three minutes after you'd gone for Mr Royce's parson the whole thing came out. You know that pasty-faced servant in the black gloves who stopped the train?'

'I should know him anywhere. Somehow he rather gave me the creeps.'

'Well,' drawled Gilder, 'when the train had gone on again, that man had gone too. Rather a cool criminal, don't you think, to escape by the very train that went off for the police?'

'You're pretty sure, I suppose,' remarked the young man, 'that he really did kill his master?'

'Yes, my son, I'm pretty sure,' replied Gilder drily, 'for the trifling reason that he has gone off with twenty thousand pounds in papers that were in his master's desk. No, the only thing worth calling a difficulty is how he killed him. The skull seems broken as with some big weapon, but there's no weapon at all lying about, and the murderer would have found it awkward to carry it away, unless the weapon was too small to be noticed.'

'Perhaps the weapon was too big to be noticed,' said the priest, with an odd little giggle.

Gilder looked round at this wild remark, and rather sternly asked Brown what he meant.

'Silly way of putting it, I know,' said Father Brown apologetically. 'Sounds like a fairy tale. But poor Armstrong was killed with a giant's club, a great green club, too big to be seen, and which we call the earth. He was broken against this green bank we are standing on.'

'How do you mean?' asked the detective quickly.

Father Brown turned his moon face up to the narrow facade of the house and blinked hopelessly up. Following his eyes, they saw that right at the top of this otherwise blind back quarter of the building, an attic window stood open.

'Don't you see,' he explained, pointing a little awkwardly like a child, 'he was thrown down from there?'

Gilder frowningly scrutinised the window, and then said: 'Well, it is certainly possible. But I don't see why you are so sure about it.'

Brown opened his gray eyes wide. 'Why,' he said, 'there's a bit of rope round the dead man's leg. Don't you see that other bit of rope up there caught at the corner of the window?'

At that height the thing looked like the faintest particle of dust or hair, but the shrewd old investigator was satisfied. 'You're quite right, sir,' he said to Father Brown; 'that is certainly one to you.'

Almost as he spoke a special train with one carriage took the curve of the line on their left, and, stopping, disgorged another group of policemen, in whose midst was the hangdog visage of Magnus, the absconded servant.

'By Jove! They've got him,' cried Gilder, and stepped forward with quite a new alertness.

'Have you got the money!' he cried to the first policeman.

The man looked him in the face with a rather curious expression and said: 'No.' Then he added: 'At least, not here.'

'Which is the inspector, please?' asked the man called Magnus.

When he spoke everyone instantly understood how this voice had stopped a train. He was a dull-looking man with flat black hair, a colourless face, and a faint suggestion of the East in the level slits in his eyes and mouth. His blood and name, indeed, had remained dubious, ever since Sir Aaron had 'rescued' him from a waitership in a London restaurant, and (as some said) from more infamous things. But his voice was as vivid as his face was dead. Whether through exactitude in a foreign language, or in deference to his master (who had been somewhat deaf), Magnus's tones had a peculiarly ringing and piercing quality, and the whole group quite jumped when he spoke.

'I always knew this would happen,' he said aloud with brazen blandness. 'My poor old master made game of me for wearing black; but I always said I should be ready for his funeral.'

And he made a momentary movement with his two dark-gloved hands.

'Sergeant,' said Inspector Gilder, eyeing the black hands with wrath, 'aren't you putting the bracelets on this fellow; he looks pretty dangerous.'

'Well, sir,' said the sergeant, with the same odd look of wonder, 'I don't know that we can.'

'What do you mean?' asked the other sharply. 'Haven't you arrested him?'

A faint scorn widened the slit-like mouth, and the whistle of an approaching train seemed oddly to echo the mockery.

'We arrested him,' replied the sergeant gravely, 'just as he was coming out of the police station at Highgate, where he had deposited all his master's money in the care of Inspector Robinson.'

Gilder looked at the man-servant in utter amazement. 'Why on earth did you do that?' he asked of Magnus.

'To keep it safe from the criminal, of course,' replied that person placidly.

'Surely,' said Gilder, 'Sir Aaron's money might have been safely left with Sir Aaron's family.'

The tail of his sentence was drowned in the roar of the train as it went rocking and clanking; but through all the hell of noises to which that unhappy house was periodically subject, they could hear the syllables of Magnus's answer, in all their bell-like distinctness: 'I have no reason to feel confidence in Sir Aaron's family.'

All the motionless men had the ghostly sensation of the presence of some new person; and Merton was scarcely surprised when he looked up and saw the pale face of Armstrong's daughter over Father Brown's shoulder. She was still young and beautiful in a silvery style, but her hair was of so dusty and hueless a brown that in some shadows it seemed to have turned totally gray.

'Be careful what you say,' said Royce gruffly, 'you'll frighten Miss Armstrong.'

'I hope so,' said the man with the clear voice.

As the woman winced and everyone else wondered, he went on: 'I am somewhat used to Miss Armstrong's tremors. I have seen her trembling off and on for years. And some said she was shaking with cold and some she was shaking with fear, but I know she was shaking with hate and wicked anger—fiends that have had their feast this morning. She would have been away by now with her lover and all the money but for me. Ever since my poor old master prevented her from marrying that tipsy blackguard—'

'Stop,' said Gilder very sternly. 'We have nothing to do with your family fancies or suspicions. Unless you have some practical evidence, your mere opinions—'

'Oh! I'll give you practical evidence,' cut in Magnus, in his hacking accent. 'You'll have to subpoena me, Mr Inspector, and I shall have to tell the truth. And the truth is this: An instant after the old man was pitched bleeding out of the window, I ran into the attic, and found his daughter swooning on the floor with a red dagger still in her hand. Allow me to hand that also to the proper authorities.' He took from his tail-pocket a long horn-hilted knife with a red smear on it, and handed it politely to the sergeant. Then he stood back again, and his slits of eyes almost faded from his face in one fat Chinese sneer.

Merton felt an almost bodily sickness at the sight of him; and he muttered to Gilder: 'Surely you would take Miss Armstrong's word against his?'

Father Brown suddenly lifted a face so absurdly fresh that it looked somehow as if he had just washed it. 'Yes,' he said, radiating innocence, 'but is Miss Armstrong's word against his?'

The girl uttered a startled, singular little cry; everyone looked at her. Her figure was rigid as if paralysed; only her face within its frame of faint brown hair was alive with an appalling surprise. She stood like one of a sudden lassooed and throttled.

'This man,' said Mr Gilder gravely, 'actually says that you were found grasping a knife, insensible, after the murder.'

'He says the truth,' answered Alice.

The next fact of which they were conscious was that Patrick Royce strode with his great stooping head into their ring and uttered the singular words: 'Well, if I've got to go, I'll have a bit of pleasure first.'

His huge shoulder heaved and he sent an iron fist smash into Magnus's bland Mongolian visage, laying him on the lawn as flat as a starfish. Two or three of the police instantly put their hands on Royce; but to the rest it seemed as if all reason had broken up and the universe were turning into a brainless harlequinade.

'None of that, Mr Royce,' Gilder had called out authoritatively. 'I shall arrest you for assault.'

'No, you won't,' answered the secretary in a voice like an iron gong, 'you will arrest me for murder.'

Gilder threw an alarmed glance at the man knocked down; but since that outraged person was already sitting up and wiping a little blood off a substantially uninjured face, he only said shortly: 'What do you mean?'

'It is quite true, as this fellow says,' explained Royce, 'that Miss Armstrong fainted with a knife in her hand. But she had not snatched the knife to attack her father, but to defend him.'

'To defend him,' repeated Gilder gravely. 'Against whom?'

'Against me,' answered the secretary.

Alice looked at him with a complex and baffling face; then she said in a low voice: 'After it all, I am still glad you are brave.'

'Come upstairs,' said Patrick Royce heavily, 'and I will show you the whole cursed thing.'

The attic, which was the secretary's private place (and rather a small cell for so large a hermit), had indeed all the vestiges of a violent drama. Near the centre of the floor lay a large revolver as if flung away; nearer to the left was rolled a whisky bottle, open but not quite empty. The cloth of the little table lay dragged and trampled, and a length of cord, like that found on the corpse, was cast wildly across the windowsill. Two vases were smashed on the mantelpiece and one on the carpet.

'I was drunk,' said Royce; and this simplicity in the prematurely battered man somehow had the pathos of the first sin of a baby.

'You all know about me,' he continued huskily; 'everybody knows how my story began, and it may as well end like that too. I was called a clever man once, and might have been a happy one; Armstrong saved the remains of a brain and body from the taverns, and was always kind to me in his own way, poor fellow! Only he wouldn't let me marry Alice here; and it will always be said that he was right enough. Well, you can form your own conclusions, and you won't want me to go into details. That is my whisky bottle half emptied in the corner; that is my revolver quite emptied on the carpet. It was the rope from my box that was found on the corpse, and it was from my window the corpse was thrown. You need not set detectives to grub up my tragedy; it is a common enough weed in this world. I give myself to the gallows; and, by God, that is enough!'

At a sufficiently delicate sign, the police gathered round the large man to lead him away; but their unobtrusiveness was somewhat staggered by the remarkable appearance of Father Brown, who was on his hands and knees on the carpet in the doorway, as if engaged in some kind of undignified prayers. Being a person utterly insensible to the social figure he cut, he remained in this posture, but turned a bright round face up at the company, presenting the appearance of a quadruped with a very comic human head.

'I say,' he said good-naturedly, 'this really won't do at all, you know. At the beginning you said we'd found no weapon. But now we're finding too many; there's the knife to stab, and the rope to strangle, and the pistol to shoot; and after all he broke his neck by falling out of a window! It won't do. It's not economical.' And he shook his head at the ground as a horse does grazing.

Inspector Gilder had opened his mouth with serious intentions, but before he could speak the grotesque figure on the floor had gone on quite volubly.

'And now three quite impossible things. First, these holes in the carpet, where the six bullets have gone in. Why on earth should anybody fire at the carpet? A drunken man lets fly at his enemy's head, the thing that's grinning at him. He doesn't pick a quarrel with his feet, or lay siege to his slippers. And then there's the rope'—and having done with the carpet the speaker lifted his hands and put them in his pocket, but continued unaffectedly on his knees—'in what conceivable intoxication would anybody try to put a rope round a man's neck and finally put it round his leg? Royce, anyhow, was not so drunk as that, or he would be sleeping like a log by now. And, plainest of all, the whisky bottle. You suggest a dipsomaniac fought for the whisky bottle, and then having won, rolled it away in a corner, spilling one half and leaving the other. That is the very last thing a dipsomaniac would do.'

He scrambled awkwardly to his feet, and said to the self-accused murderer in tones of limpid penitence: 'I'm awfully sorry, my dear sir, but your tale is really rubbish.'

'Sir,' said Alice Armstrong in a low tone to the priest, 'can I speak to you alone for a moment?'

This request forced the communicative cleric out of the gangway, and before he could speak in the next room, the girl was talking with strange incisiveness.

'You are a clever man,' she said, 'and you are trying to save Patrick, I know. But it's no use. The core of all this is black, and the more things you find out the more there will be against the miserable man I love.'

'Why?' asked Brown, looking at her steadily.

'Because,' she answered equally steadily, 'I saw him commit the crime myself.'

'Ah!' said the unmoved Brown, 'and what did he do?'

'I was in this room next to them,' she explained; 'both doors were closed, but I suddenly heard a voice, such as I had never heard on earth, roaring 'Hell, hell, hell,' again and again, and then the two doors shook with the first explosion of the revolver. Thrice again the thing banged before I got the two doors open and found the room full of smoke; but the pistol was smoking in my poor, mad Patrick's hand; and I saw him fire the last murderous volley with my own eyes. Then he leapt on my father, who was clinging in terror to the window-sill, and, grappling, tried to strangle him with the rope, which he threw over his head, but which slipped over his struggling shoulders to his feet. Then it tightened round one leg and Patrick dragged him along like a maniac. I snatched a knife from the mat, and, rushing between them, managed to cut the rope before I fainted.'

'I see,' said Father Brown, with the same wooden civility. 'Thank you.'

As the girl collapsed under her memories, the priest passed stiffly into the next room, where he found Gilder and Merton alone with Patrick Royce, who sat in a chair, handcuffed. There he said to the Inspector submissively:

'Might I say a word to the prisoner in your presence; and might he take off those funny cuffs for a minute?'

'He is a very powerful man,' said Merton in an undertone. 'Why do you want them taken off?'

'Why, I thought,' replied the priest humbly, 'that perhaps I might have the very great honour of shaking hands with him.'

Both detectives stared, and Father Brown added: 'Won't you tell them about it, sir?'

The man on the chair shook his tousled head, and the priest turned impatiently.

'Then I will,' he said. 'Private lives are more important than public reputations. I am going to save the living, and let the dead bury their dead.'

He went to the fatal window, and blinked out of it as he went on talking.

'I told you that in this case there were too many weapons and only one death. I tell you now that they were not weapons, and were not used to cause death. All those grisly tools, the noose, the bloody knife, the exploding pistol, were instruments of a curious mercy. They were not used to kill Sir Aaron, but to save him.'

'To save him!' repeated Gilder. 'And from what?'

'From himself,' said Father Brown. 'He was a suicidal maniac.'

'What?' cried Merton in an incredulous tone. 'And the Religion of Cheerfulness—'

'It is a cruel religion,' said the priest, looking out of the window. 'Why couldn't they let him weep a little, like his fathers before him? His plans stiffened, his views grew cold; behind that merry mask was the empty mind of the atheist. At last, to keep up his hilarious public level, he fell back on that dram-drinking he had abandoned long ago. But there is this horror about alcoholism in a sincere teetotaller: that he pictures and expects that psychological inferno from which he has warned others. It leapt upon poor Armstrong prematurely, and by this morning he was in such a case that he sat here and cried he was in hell, in so crazy a voice that his daughter did not know it. He was mad for death, and with the monkey tricks of the mad he had scattered round him death in many shapes—a running noose and his friend's revolver and a knife. Royce entered accidentally and acted in a flash. He flung the knife on the mat behind him, snatched up the revolver, and having no time to unload it, emptied it shot after shot all over the floor. The suicide saw a fourth shape of death, and made a dash for the window. The rescuer did the only thing he could—ran after him with the rope and tried to tie him hand and foot. Then it was that the unlucky girl ran in, and misunderstanding the struggle, strove to slash her father free. At first she only slashed poor Royce's knuckles, from which has come all the little blood in this affair. But, of course, you noticed that he left blood, but no wound, on that servant's face? Only before the poor woman swooned, she did hack her father loose, so that he went crashing through that window into eternity.'

There was a long stillness slowly broken by the metallic noises of Gilder unlocking the handcuffs of Patrick Royce, to whom he said:

'I think I should have told the truth, sir. You and the young lady are worth more than Armstrong's obituary notices.'

'Confound Armstrong's notices,' cried Royce roughly. 'Don't you see it was because she mustn't know?'

'Mustn't know what?' asked Merton.

'Why, that she killed her father, you fool!' roared the other. 'He'd have been alive now but for her. It might craze her to know that.'

'No, I don't think it would,' remarked Father Brown, as he picked up his hat. 'I rather think I should tell her. Even the most murderous blunders don't poison life like sins; anyhow, I think you may both be the happier now. I've got to go back to the Deaf School.'

As he went out on to the gusty grass an acquaintance from Highgate stopped him and said:

'The Coroner has arrived. The inquiry is just going to begin.'

'I've got to get back to the Deaf School,' said Father Brown. 'I'm sorry I can't stop for the inquiry.'

28

THE PAIR OF GLOVES

Charles Dickens

...To see a woman lying dead with her throat cut... Can make a man low in his spirits...

'It's a singler story, sir,' said Inspector Wield, of the Detective Police, who, in company with Sergeants Dornton and Mith, paid us another twilight visit, one July evening; 'and I've been thinking you might like to know it.

'It's concerning the murder of the young woman, Eliza Grimwood, some years ago, over in the Waterloo Road. She was commonly called The Countess, because of her handsome appearance and her proud way of carrying of herself; and when I saw the poor Countess (I had known her well to speak to), lying dead, with her throat cut, on the floor of her bedroom, you'll believe me that a variety of reflections calculated to make a man rather low in his spirits, came into my head.

'That's neither here nor there. I went to the house the morning after the murder, and examined the body, and made a general observation of the bedroom where it was. Turning down the pillow of the bed with my hand, I found, underneath it, a pair of gloves. A pair of gentleman's dress gloves, very dirty; and inside the lining, the letters TR, and a cross.

'Well, sir, I took them gloves away, and I showed 'em to the magistrate, over at Union Hall, before whom the case was. He says, "Wield," he says, "there's no doubt this is a discovery that may lead to something very important; and what you have got to do, Wield, is, to find out the owner of these gloves."

'I was of the same opinion, of course, and I went at it immediately.

I looked at the gloves pretty narrowly, and it was my opinion that they had been cleaned. There was a smell of sulphur and rosin about 'em, you know, which cleaned gloves usually have, more or less. I took 'em over to a friend of mine at Kennington, who was in that line, and I put it to him. 'What do you say now? Have these gloves been cleaned?' 'These gloves have been cleaned,' says he. 'Have you any idea who cleaned them?' says I. 'Not at all,' says he; 'I've a very distinct idea who DIDN'T clean 'em, and that's myself. But I'll tell you what, Wield, there ain't above eight or nine reg'lar glove-cleaners in London,'—there were not, at that time, it seems—'and I think I can give you their addresses, and you may find out, by that means, who did clean 'em.' Accordingly, he gave me the directions, and I went here, and I went there, and I looked up this man, and I looked up that man; but, though they all agreed that the gloves had been cleaned, I couldn't find the man, woman, or child, that had cleaned that aforesaid pair of gloves.

'What with this person not being at home, and that person being expected home in the afternoon, and so forth, the inquiry took me three days. On the evening of the third day, coming over Waterloo Bridge from the Surrey side of the river, quite beat, and very much vexed and disappointed, I thought I'd have a shilling's worth of entertainment at the Lyceum Theatre to freshen myself up. So I went into the Pit, at half-price, and I sat myself down next to a very quiet, modest sort of young man. Seeing I was a stranger (which I thought it just as well to appear to be) he told me the names of the actors on the stage, and we got into conversation. When the play was over, we came out together, and I said, "We've been very companionable and agreeable, and perhaps you wouldn't object to a drain?" "Well, you're very good," says he; "I SHOULDN'T object to a drain." Accordingly, we went to a public house, near the Theatre, sat ourselves down in a quiet room upstairs on the first floor, and called for a pint of half-and-half, apiece, and a pipe.

'Well, sir, we put our pipes aboard, and we drank our half-and-half, and sat a-talking, very sociably, when the young man says, "You must excuse me stopping very long," he says, "because I'm forced to go home in good time. I must be at work all night." "At work all night?" says I. "You ain't a baker?" "No," he says, laughing, "I ain't a baker." "I thought not," says I, "you haven't the looks of a baker." "No," says he, "I'm a glove-cleaner."

'I never was more astonished in my life, than when I heard them words come out of his lips. "You're a glove-cleaner, are you?" says I. "Yes," he says, "I am." "Then, perhaps," says I, taking the gloves out of my pocket, "you can tell me who cleaned this pair of gloves? It's a rum story," I says. "I was dining over at Lambeth, the other day, at a free-and-easy—quite promiscuous—with a public company—when some gentleman, he left these gloves behind him! Another gentleman and me, you see, we laid a wager of a sovereign, that I wouldn't find out who they belonged to. I've spent as much as seven shillings already, in trying to discover; but, if you could help me, I'd stand another seven and welcome. You see there's TR and a cross, inside." "I see," he says. "Bless you, I know these gloves very well! I've seen dozens of pairs belonging to the same party." "No?" says I. "Yes," says he. "Then you know who cleaned 'em?" says I. "Rather so," says he. "My father cleaned 'em."

'"Where does your father live?" says I. "Just round the corner," says the young man, "near Exeter Street, here. He'll tell you who they belong to, directly." "Would you come round with me now?" says I. "Certainly," says he, "but you needn't tell my father that you found me at the play, you know, because he mightn't like it." "All right!" We went round to the place, and there we found an old man in a white apron, with two or three daughters, all rubbing and cleaning away at lots of gloves, in a front parlour. "Oh, Father!" says the young man, "here's a person been and made a bet about the ownership of a pair of gloves, and I've told him you can settle it." "Good evening, sir," says I to the old gentleman. "Here's the gloves your son speaks of. Letters TR, you see, and a cross." "Oh yes," he says, "I know these gloves very well; I've cleaned dozens of pairs of 'em. They belong to Mr Trinkle, the great upholsterer in Cheapside." "Did you get 'em from Mr Trinkle, direct," says I, "if you'll excuse my asking the question?" "No," says he; "Mr Trinkle always sends 'em to Mr Phibbs's, the haberdasher's, opposite his shop, and the haberdasher sends 'em to me." "Perhaps YOU wouldn't object to a drain?" says I. "Not in the least!" says he. So I took the old gentleman out, and had a little more talk with him and his son, over a glass, and we parted excellent friends.

'This was late on a Saturday night. First thing on the Monday morning, I went to the haberdasher's shop, opposite Mr Trinkle's, the great upholsterer's in Cheapside. "Mr Phibbs in the way?" "My name is Phibbs." "Oh! I believe you sent this pair of gloves to be cleaned?" "Yes, I did, for young Mr Trinkle over the way. There he is in the shop!" "Oh! that's him in the shop, is it? Him in the green coat?" "The same individual." "Well, Mr Phibbs, this is an unpleasant affair; but the fact is, I am Inspector Wield of the Detective Police, and I found these gloves under the pillow of the young woman that was murdered the other day, over in the Waterloo Road!" "Good Heaven!" says he. "He's a most respectable young man, and if his father was to hear of it, it would be the ruin of him!" "I'm very sorry for it," says I, "but I must take him into custody." "Good Heaven!" says Mr Phibbs, again; "can nothing be done?" "Nothing," says I. "Will you allow me to call him over here," says he, "that his father may not see it done?" "I don't object to that," says I; "but unfortunately, Mr Phibbs, I can't allow of any communication between you. If any was attempted, I should have to interfere directly. Perhaps you'll beckon him over here?" Mr Phibbs went to the door and beckoned, and the young fellow came across the street directly; a smart, brisk young fellow.

'"Good morning, sir," says I. "Good morning, sir," says he. "Would you allow me to inquire, sir," says I, "if you ever had any acquaintance with a party of the name of Grimwood?" "Grimwood! Grimwood!" says he. "No!" "You know the Waterloo Road?" "Oh! of course I know the Waterloo Road!" "Happen to have heard of a young woman being murdered there?" "Yes, I read it in the paper, and very sorry I was to read it." "Here's a pair of gloves belonging to you, that I found under her pillow the morning afterwards!"

'He was in a dreadful state, sir; a dreadful state. "Mr Wield," he says, "upon my solemn oath I never was there. I never so much as saw her, to my knowledge, in my life!" "I am very sorry," says I. "To tell you the truth; I don't think you ARE the murderer, but I must take you to Union Hall in a cab. However, I think it's a case of that sort, that, at present, at all events, the magistrate will hear it in private."

'A private examination took place, and then it came out that this young man was acquainted with a cousin of the unfortunate Eliza Grimwood, and that, calling to see this cousin a day or two before the murder, he left these gloves upon the table. Who should come in, shortly afterwards, but Eliza Grimwood! "Whose gloves are these?" she says, taking 'em up. "Those are Mr Trinkle's gloves," says her cousin. "Oh!" says she, "they are very dirty, and of no use to him, I am sure. I shall take 'em away for my girl to clean the stoves with." And she put 'em in her pocket. The girl had used 'em to clean the stoves, and, I have no doubt, had left 'em lying on the bedroom mantelpiece, or on the drawers, or somewhere; and her mistress, looking round to see that the room was tidy, had caught 'em up and put 'em under the pillow where I found 'em.

That's the story, sir.'

29

THE DEADLY TUBE

Arthur B. Reeve

Arthur Reeve with his mind boggling mysteries makes him America's Arthur Conan Doyle!

'For Heaven's sake, Gregory, what is the matter?' asked Craig Kennedy as a tall, nervous man stalked into our apartment one evening. 'Jameson, shake hands with Dr Gregory. What's the matter, Doctor? Surely your X-ray work hasn't knocked you out like this?'

The doctor shook hands with me mechanically. His hand was icy. 'The blow has fallen,' he exclaimed, as he sank limply into a chair and tossed an evening paper over to Kennedy.

In red ink on the first page, in the little square headed 'Latest News,' Kennedy read the caption, 'Society Woman Crippled for Life by X-Ray Treatment.'

'A terrible tragedy was revealed in the suit begun today,' continued the article, 'by Mrs Huntington Close against Dr James Gregory, an X-ray specialist with offices at Madison Avenue, to recover damages for injuries which Mrs Close alleges she received while under his care. Several months ago she began a course of X-ray treatment to remove a birthmark on her neck. In her complaint Mrs Close alleges that Dr Gregory has carelessly caused X-ray dermatitis, a skin disease of cancerous nature, and that she has also been rendered a nervous wreck through the effects of the rays. Simultaneously with filing the suit she left home and entered a private hospital. Mrs Close is one of the most popular hostesses in the smart set, and her loss will be keenly felt.'

'What am I to do, Kennedy?' asked the doctor imploringly. 'You remember I told you the other day about this case—that there was something queer about it, that after a few treatments I was afraid to carry on any more and refused to do so? She really has dermatitis and nervous prostration, exactly as she alleges in her complaint. But, before Heaven, Kennedy, I can't see how she could possibly have been so affected by the few treatments I gave her. And tonight, just as I was leaving the office, I received a telephone call from her husband's attorney, Lawrence, very kindly informing me that the case would be pushed to the limit. I tell you, it looks black for me.'

'What can they do?'

'Do? Do you suppose any jury is going to take enough expert testimony to outweigh the tragedy of a beautiful woman? Do? Why, they can ruin me, even if I get a verdict of acquittal. They can leave me with a reputation for carelessness that no mere court decision can ever overcome.'

'Gregory, you can rely on me,' said Kennedy. 'Anything I can do to help you I will gladly do. Jameson and I were on the point of going out to dinner. Join us, and after that we will go down to your office and talk things over.'

'You are really too kind,' murmured the doctor. The air of relief that was written on his face was pathetically eloquent.

'Now not a word about the case till we have had dinner,' commanded Craig. 'I see very plainly that you have been worrying about the blow for a long time. Well, it has fallen. The neat thing to do is to look over the situation and see where we stand.'

Dinner over, we rode down-town in the subway, and Gregory ushered us into an office-building on Madison Avenue, where he had a very handsome suite of several rooms. We sat own in his waiting-room to discuss the affair.

'It is indeed a very tragic case,' began Kennedy, 'almost more tragic than if the victim had been killed outright. Mrs Huntington Close is—or rather I suppose I should say was—one of the famous beauties of the city. From what the paper says, her beauty has been hopelessly ruined by this dermatitis, which, I understand, Doctor, is practically incurable.'

Dr Gregory nodded, and I could not help following his eyes as he looked at his own rough and scarred hands.

'Also,' continued Craig, with his eyes half closed and his finger-tips together, as if, he were taking a mental inventory of the facts in the case, 'her nerves are so shattered that she will be years in recovering, if she ever recovers.'

'Yes,' said the doctor simply. 'I myself, for instance, am subject to the most unexpected attacks of neuritis. But, of course, I am under the influence of the rays fifty or sixty times a day, while she had only a few treatments at intervals of many days.'

'Now, on the other hand,' resumed Craig, 'I know you, Gregory, very well. Only the other day, before any of this came out, you told me the whole story with your fears as to the outcome. I know that that lawyer of Close's has been keeping this thing hanging over your head for a long time. And I also know that you are one of the most careful X-ray operators in the city. If this suit goes against you, one of the most brilliant men of science in America will be ruined. Now, having said this much, let me ask you to describe just exactly what treatments you gave Mrs Close.'

The doctor led us into his X-ray room adjoining. A number of X-ray tubes were neatly put away in a great glass case, and at one end of the room was an operating-table with an X-ray apparatus suspended over it. A glance at the room showed that Kennedy's praise was not exaggerated. 'How many treatments did you give Mrs Close?' asked Kennedy.

'Not over a dozen, I should say;' replied Gregory. 'I have a record of them and the dates, which I will give you presently. Certainly they were not numerous enough or frequent enough to have caused a dermatitis such as she has. Besides, look here. I have an apparatus which, for safety to the patient, has few equals in the country. This big lead-glass bowl, which is placed over my X-ray tube when in use, cuts off the rays at every point except exactly where they are needed.'

He switched on the electric current, and the apparatus began to sputter. The pungent odour of ozone from the electric discharge filled the room. Through the lead-glass bowl I could see the X-ray tube inside suffused with its peculiar, yellowish-green light, divided into two hemispheres of different shades. That, I knew, was the cathode ray, not the X-ray, for the X-ray itself, which streams outside the tube, is invisible to the human eye. The doctor placed in our hands a couple of fluoroscopes, an apparatus by which X-rays can be detected. It consists simply of a closed box with an opening to which the eyes are placed. The opposite end of the box is a piece of board coated with a salt such as platino-barium cyanide. When the X-ray strikes this salt it makes it glow, or fluoresce, and objects held between the X-ray tube and the fluoroscope cast shadows according to the density of the parts which the X-rays penetrate.

With the lead-glass bowl removed, the X-ray tube sent forth its wonderful invisible radiation and made the back of the fluoroscope glow with light. I could see the bones of my fingers as I held them up between the X-ray tube and the fluoroscope. But with the lead-glass bowl in position over the tube, the fluoroscope was simply a black box into which I looked and saw nothing. So very little of the radiation escaped from the bowl that it was negligible—except at one point where there was an opening in the bottom of the bowl to allow the rays to pass freely through exactly on the spot on the patient where they were to be used.

'The dermatitis, they say, has appeared all over her body, particularly on her head and shoulders,' added Dr Gregory. 'Now I have shown you my apparatus to impress on you how really impossible it would have been for her to contract it from her treatments here. I've made thousands of exposures with never an X-ray burn before—except to myself. As for myself, I'm as careful as I can be, but you can see I am under the rays very often, while the patient is only under them once in a while.'

To illustrate his care he pointed out to us a cabinet directly back of the operating-table, lined with thick sheets of lead. From this cabinet he conducted most of his treatments as far as possible. A little peep-hole enabled him to see the patient and the X-ray apparatus, while an arrangement of mirrors and a fluorescent screen enabled him to see exactly what the X-rays were disclosing, without his leaving the lead-lined cabinet.

'I can think of no more perfect protection for either patient or operator,' said Kennedy admiringly. 'By the way, did Mrs Close come alone?'

'No, the first time Mr Close came with her. After that, she came with her French maid.'

The next day we paid a visit to Mrs Close herself at the private hospital. Kennedy had been casting about in his mind for an excuse to see her, and I had suggested that we go as reporters from the Star. Fortunately after sending up my card on which I had written Craig's name we were at length allowed to go up to her room.

We found the patient reclining in an easy chair, swathed in bandages, a wreck of her former self. I felt the tragedy keenly. All that social position and beauty had meant to her had been suddenly blasted.

'You will pardon my presumption,' began Craig, 'but, Mrs Close, I assure you that I am actuated by the best of motives. We represent the New York Star—' v 'Isn't it terrible enough that I should suffer so,' she interrupted, 'but must the newspapers hound me, too?'

'I beg your pardon, Mrs Close,' said Craig, 'but you must be aware that the news of your suit of Dr Gregory has now become public property. I couldn't stop the Star, much less the other papers, from talking about it. But I can and will do this, Mrs Close. I will see that justice is done to you and all others concerned. Believe me, I am not here as a yellow journalist to make newspaper copy out of your misfortune. I am here to get at the truth sympathetically. Incidentally, I may be able to render you a service, too.'

'You can render me no service except to expedite the suit against that careless doctor—I hate him.'

'Perhaps,' said Craig. 'But suppose someone else should be proved to have been really responsible? Would you still want to press the suit and let the guilty person escape?'

She bit her lip. 'What is it you want of me?' she asked.

'I merely want permission to visit your rooms at your home and to talk with your maid. I do not mean to spy on you, far from it; but consider, Mrs Close, if I should be able to get at the bottom of this thing, find out the real cause of your misfortune, perhaps show that you are the victim of a cruel wrong rather than of carelessness, would you not be willing to let me go ahead? I am frank to tell you that I suspect there is more to this affair than you yourself have any idea of.'

'No, you are mistaken, Mr Kennedy. I know the cause of it. It was my love of beauty. I couldn't resist the temptation to get rid of even a slight defect. If I had left well enough alone I should not be here now. A friend recommended Dr Gregory to my husband, who took me there. My husband wishes me to remain at home, but I tell him I feel more comfortable here in the hospital. I shall never go to that house again—the memory of the torture of sleepless nights in my room there when I felt my good looks going, going'—she shuddered—'is such that I can never forget it. He says I would be better off there, but no, I cannot go. Still,' she continued wearily, 'there can be no harm in your talking to my maid.'

Kennedy noted attentively what she was saying. 'I thank you, Mrs Close,' he replied. 'I am sure you will not regret your permission. Would you be so kind as to give me a note to her?'

She rang, dictated a short note to a nurse, signed it, and languidly dismissed us.

I don't know that I ever felt as depressed as I did after that interview with one who had entered a living death to ambition, for while Craig had done all the talking I had absorbed nothing but depression. I vowed that if Gregory or anybody else was responsible I would do my share toward bringing on him retribution.

The Closes lived in a splendid big house in the Murray Hill section. The presentation of the note quickly brought Mrs Close's maid down to us. She had not gone to the hospital because Mrs Close had considered the services of the trained nurses quite sufficient.

Yes, the maid had noticed how her mistress had been failing, had noticed it long ago, in fact almost at the time when she had begun the X-ray treatment. She had seemed to improve once when she went away for a few days, but that was at the start, and directly after her return she grew worse again, until she was no longer herself.

'Did Dr Gregory, the X-ray specialist, ever attend Mrs Close at her home, in her room?' asked Craig.

'Yes, once, twice, he call, but he do no good,' she said with her French accent.

'Did Mrs Close have other callers?'

'But, m'sieur, everyone in society has many. What does m'sieur mean?'

'Frequent callers—a Mr Lawrence, for instance?'

'Oh, yes, Mr Lawrence frequently.'

'When Mr Close was at home?'

'Yes, on business and on business, too, when he was not at home. He is the attorney, m'sieur.' v 'How did Mrs Close receive him?'

'He is the attorney, m'sieur,' Marie repeated persistently.

'And he, did he always call on business?'

'Oh, yes, always on business, but well, madame, she was a very beautiful woman. Perhaps he like beautiful women—eh bien? That was before the Doctor Gregory treated madame. After the doctor treated madame M'sieur Lawrence do not call so often. That's all.'

'Are you thoroughly devoted to Mrs Close? Would you do a favour for her?' asked Craig point-blank.

'Sir, I would give my life, almost, for madame. She was always so good to me.' 'I don't ask you to give your life for her, Marie,' said Craig, 'but you can do her a great service, a very great service.' 'I will do it.'

'Tonight,' said Craig, 'I want you to sleep in Mrs Close's room. You can do so, for I know that Mr Close is living at the St. Francis Club until his wife returns from the sanitarium. Tomorrow morning come to my laboratory'—Craig handed her his card—'and I will tell you what to do next. By the way, don't say anything to anyone in the house about it, and keep a sharp watch on the actions of any of the servants who may go into Mrs Close's room.' 'Well,' said Craig, 'there is nothing more to be done immediately.' We had once more regained the street and were walking up-town. We walked in silence for several blocks.

'Yes,' mused Craig, 'there is something you can do, after all, Walter. I would like you to look up Gregory and Close and Lawrence. I already know something about them. But you can find out a good deal with your newspaper connections. I would like to have every bit of scandal that has ever been connected with them, or with Mrs Close, or,' he added significantly, 'with any other woman. It isn't necessary to say that not a breath of it must be published—yet.'

I found a good deal of gossip, but very little of it, indeed, seemed to me at the time to be of importance. Dropping in at the St. Francis Club, where I had some friends, I casually mentioned the troubles of the Huntington Closes. I was surprised to learn that Close spent little of his time at the Club, none at home, and only dropped into the hospital to make formal inquiries as to his wife's condition. It then occurred to me to drop into the office of Society Squibs, whose editor I had long known. The editor told me, with that nameless look of the cynical scandalmonger, that if I wanted to learn anything about Huntington Close I had best watch Mrs Frances Tulkington, a very wealthy Western divorcee about whom the smart set were much excited, particularly those whose wealth made it difficult to stand the pace of society as it was going at present.

'And before the tragedy,' said the editor with another nameless look, as if he were imparting a most valuable piece of gossip, 'it was the talk of the town, the attention that Close's lawyer was paying to Mrs Close. But to her credit let me say that she never gave us a chance to hint at anything, and—well, you know us; we don't need much to make snappy society news.'

The editor then waged even more confidential, for if I am anything at all, I am a good listener, and I have found that often by sitting tight and listening I can get more than if I were a too-eager questioner.

'It really was a shame—the way that man Lawrence played his game,' he went on. 'I understand that it was he who introduced Close to Mrs T. They were both his clients. Lawrence had fought her case in the courts when she sued old Tulkington for divorce, and a handsome settlement he got for her, too. They say his fee ran up into the hundred thousands—contingent, you know. I don't know what his game was'—here he lowered his voice to a whisper 'but they say Close owes him a good deal of money. You can figure it out for yourself as you like. Now, I've told you all I know. Come in again,

Jameson, when you want some more scandal, and remember me to the boys down on the Star.'

The following day the maid visited Kennedy at his laboratory while I was reporting to him on the result of my investigations.

She looked worn and haggard. She had spent a sleepless night and begged that Kennedy would not ask her to repeat the experiment.

'I can promise you, Marie,' he said, 'that you will rest better tonight. But you must spend one more night in Mrs Close's room. By the way, can you arrange for me to go through the room this morning when you go back?'

Marie said she could, and an hour or so later Craig and I quietly slipped into the Close residence under her guidance. He was carrying something that looked like a miniature barrel, and I had another package which he had given me, both carefully wrapped up. The butler eyed us suspiciously, but Marie spoke a few words to him and I think showed him Mrs Close's note. Anyhow he said nothing.

Within the room that the unfortunate woman had occupied Kennedy took the coverings off the packages. It was nothing but a portable electric vacuum cleaner, which he quickly attached and set running. Up and down the floor, around and under the bed he pushed the cleaner. He used the various attachments to clean the curtains, the walls, and even the furniture. Particularly did he pay attention to the base board on the wall back of the bed. Then he carefully removed the dust from the cleaner and sealed it up in a leaden box.

He was about to detach and pack up the cleaner when another idea seemed to occur to him. 'Might as well make a thorough job of it, Walter,' he said, adjusting the apparatus again. 'I've cleaned everything but the mattress and the brass bars behind the mattress on the bed. Now I'll tackle them. I think we ought to go into the suction-cleaning business—more money in it than in being a detective, I'll bet.'

The cleaner was run over and under the mattress and along every crack and cranny of the brass bed. This done and this dust also carefully stowed away, we departed, very much to the mystification of Marie and, I could not help feeling, of other eyes that peered in through keyholes or cracks in doors.

'At any rate,' said Kennedy exultingly, 'I think we have stolen a march on them. I don't believe they were prepared for this, not at least at this stage in the game. Don't ask me any questions, Walter. Then you will have no secrets to keep if anyone should try to pry them loose. Only remember that this man Lawrence is a shrewd character.'

The next day Marie came, looking even more careworn than before.

'What's the matter, mademoiselle?' asked Craig. 'Didn't you pass a better night?'

'Oh, mon Dieu, I rest well, yes. But this morning, while I am at breakfast, Mr Close send for me. He say that I am discharged. Some servant tell of your visit and he verry angr-ry. And now what is to become of me—will madame his wife give a recommendation now?'

'Walter, we have been discovered,' exclaimed Craig with considerable vexation. Then he remembered the poor girl who had been an involuntary sacrifice to our investigation. Turning to her he said: 'Marie, I know several very good families, and I am sure you will not suffer for what you have done by being faithful to your mistress. Only be patient a few days. Go live with some of your folks. I will see that you are placed again.'

The girl was profuse in her thanks as she dried her tears and departed.

'I hadn't anticipated having my hand forced so soon,' said Craig after she had gone, leaving her address. 'However, we are on the right track. What was it that you were going to tell me when Marie came in?'

'Something that may be very important, Craig,' I said, 'though I don't understand it myself. Pressure is being brought to bear on the Star to keep this thing out of the papers, or at least to minimise it.'

'I'm not surprised,' commented Craig. 'What do you mean by pressure being brought?'

'Why, Close's lawyer, Lawrence, called up the editor this morning—I don't suppose that you know, but he has some connection with the interests which control the Star—and said that the activity of one of the reporters from the Star, Jameson by name, was very distasteful to Mr Close and that this reporter was employing a man named Kennedy to assist him.

'I don't understand it, Craig;' I confessed, 'but here one day they give the news to the papers, and two days later they almost threaten us with suit if we don't stop publishing it.'

'It is perplexing,' said Craig, with the air of one who was not a bit perplexed, but rather enlightened.

He pulled down the district telegraph messenger lever three times, and we sat in silence for a while.

'However,' he resumed, 'I shall be ready for them tonight.'

I said nothing. Several minutes elapsed. Then the messenger rapped on the door.

'I want these two notes delivered right away,' said Craig to the boy; 'here's a quarter for you. Now mind you don't get interested in a detective story and forget the notes. If you are back here quickly with the receipts I'll give you another quarter. Now scurry along.'

Then, after the boy had gone, he said casually to me: 'Two notes to Close and Gregory, asking them to be present with their attorneys tonight. Close will bring Lawrence, and Gregory will bring a young lawyer named Asche, a very clever fellow. The notes are so worded that they can hardly refuse the invitation.'

Meanwhile I carried out an assignment for the Star, and telephoned my story in so as to be sure of being with Craig at the crucial moment. For I was thoroughly curious about his next move in the game. I found him still in his laboratory attaching two coils of thin wire to the connections on the outside of a queer-looking little black box.

'What's that?' I asked, eyeing the sinister looking little box suspiciously. 'An infernal machine? You're not going to blow the culprit into eternity, I hope.'

'Never mind what it is, Walter. You'll find that out in due time. It may or it may not be an infernal machine of a different sort than any you have probably ever heard of. The less you know now the less likely you are to give anything away by a look or an act. Come now, make yourself useful as well as ornamental. Take these wires and lay them in the cracks of the floor, and be careful not to let them show. A little dust over them will conceal them beautifully.'

Craig now placed the black box back of one of the chairs well down toward the floor, where it could hardly have been perceived unless one were suspecting something of the sort. While he was doing so I ran the wires across the floor, and around the edge of the room to the door.

'There,' he said, taking the wires from me. 'Now I'll complete the job by carrying them into the next room. And while I'm doing it, go over the wires again and make sure they are absolutely concealed.'

That night six men gathered in Kennedy's laboratory. In my utter ignorance of what was about to happen I was perfectly calm, and so were all the rest, except Gregory. He was easily the most nervous of us all, though his lawyer Asche tried repeatedly to reassure him.

'Mr Close,' began Kennedy, 'if you and Mr Lawrence will sit over here on this side of the room while Dr Gregory and Mr Asche sit on the opposite side with Mr Jameson in the middle, I think both of you opposing parties will be better suited. For I apprehend that at various stages in what I am about to say both you, Mr Close, and you, Dr Gregory, will want to consult your attorneys. That, of course, would be embarrassing, if not impossible, should you be sitting near each other. Now, if we are ready, I shall begin.'

Kennedy placed a small leaden casket on the table of his lecture hall. 'In this casket,' he commenced solemnly, 'there is a certain substance which I have recovered from the dust swept up by a vacuum cleaner in the room of Mrs Close.'

One could feel the very air of the room surcharged with excitement. Craig drew on a pair of gloves and carefully opened the casket. With his thumb and forefinger he lifted out a glass tube and held it gingerly at arm's length. My eyes were riveted on it, for the bottom of the tube glowed with a dazzling point of light.

Both Gregory and his attorney and Close and Lawrence whispered to each other when the tube was displayed, as indeed they did throughout the whole exhibition of Kennedy's evidence.

'No infernal machine was ever more subtle,' said Craig, 'than the tube which I hold in my hand. The imagination of the most sensational writer of fiction might well be thrilled with the mysteries of this fatal tube and its power to work fearful deeds. A larger quantity of this substance in the tube would produce on me, as I now hold it, incurable burns, just as it did on its discoverer before his death. A smaller amount, of course, would not act so quickly. The amount in this tube, if distributed about, would produce the burns inevitably, providing I remained near enough for a long-enough time.'

Craig paused a moment to emphasise his remarks.

'Here in my hand, gentlemen, I hold the price of a woman's beauty.'

He stopped again for several moments, then resumed.

'And now, having shown it to you, for my own safety I will place it back in its leaden casket.'

Drawing off his gloves, he proceeded.

'I have found out by a cablegram today that seven weeks ago an order for one hundred milligrams of radium bromide at thirty-five dollars a milligram from a certain person in America was filled by a corporation dealing in this substance.'

Kennedy said this with measured words, and I felt a thrill run through me as he developed his case.

'At that same time, Mrs Close began a series of treatments with an X-ray specialist in New York,' pursued Kennedy. 'Now, it is not generally known outside scientific circles, but the fact is that in their physiological effects the X-ray and radium are quite one and the same. Radium possesses this advantage, however, that no elaborate apparatus is necessary for its use. And, in addition, the emanation from radium is steady and constant, whereas the X-ray at best varies slightly with changing conditions of the current and vacuum in the X-ray tube. Still, the effects on the body are much the same.

'A few days before this order was placed I recall the following despatch which appeared in the New York papers. I will read it.

'"Liege, Belgium, Oct.—, 1910. What is believed to be the first criminal case in which radium figures as a death-dealing agent is engaging public attention at this university town. A wealthy old bachelor, Pailin by name, was found dead in his flat. A stroke of apoplexy was at first believed to have caused his death, but a close examination revealed a curious discolouration of his skin. A specialist called in to view the body gave as his opinion that the old man had been exposed for a long time to the emanations of X-ray or radium. The police theory is that M. Pailin was done to death by a systematic application of either X-rays or radium by a student in the university who roomed next to him. The student has disappeared."

'Now here, I believe, was the suggestion which this American criminal followed, for I cut it out of the paper rather expecting sooner or later that some clever person would act on it. I have thoroughly examined the room of Mrs Close. She herself told me she never wanted to return to it, that her memory of sleepless nights in it was too vivid. That served to fix the impression that I had already formed from reading this clipping. Either the X-ray or radium had caused her dermatitis and nervousness. Which was it? I wished to be sure that I would make no mistake. Of course I knew it was useless to look for an X-ray machine in or near Mrs Close's room. Such a thing could never have been concealed. The alternative? Radium! Ah! that was different. I determined on an experiment. Mrs Close's maid was prevailed on to sleep in her mistress's room. Of course radiations of brief duration would do her no permanent harm, although they would produce their effect, nevertheless. In one night the maid became extremely nervous. If she had stayed under them several nights no doubt the beginning of a dermatitis would have affected her, if not more serious trouble. A systematic application, covering weeks and months, might in the end even have led to death.

'The next day I managed, as I have said, to go over the room thoroughly with a vacuum cleaner—a new one of my own which I had bought myself. But tests of the dust which I got from the floors, curtains, and furniture showed nothing at all. As a last thought I had, however, cleaned the mattress of the bed and the cracks and crevices in the brass bars. Tests of that dust showed it to be extremely radioactive. I had the dust dissolved, by a chemist who understands that sort of thing, recrystallised, and the radium salts were extracted from the refuse. Thus I found that I had recovered all but a very few milligrams of the radium that had been originally purchased in London. Here it is in this deadly tube in the leaden casket.

'It is needless to add that the night after I had cleaned out this deadly element the maid slept the sleep of the just—and would have been all right when next I saw her but for the interference of the unjust on whom I had stolen a march.'

Craig paused while the lawyers whispered again to their clients. Then he Continued: 'Now three persons in this room had an opportunity to secrete the contents of this deadly tube in the crevices of the metal work of Mrs Close's bed. One of these persons must have placed an order through a confidential agent in London to purchase the radium from the English Radium Corporation. One of these persons had a compelling motive, something to gain by using this deadly element. The radium in this tube in the casket was secreted, as I have said, in the metal work of Mrs Close's bed, not in large enough quantities to be immediately fatal, but mixed with dust so as to produce the result more slowly but no less surely, and thus avoid suspicion. At the same time Mrs Close was persuaded—I will not say by whom—through her natural pride, to take a course of X-ray treatment for a slight defect. That would further serve to divert suspicion. The fact is that a more horrible plot could hardly have been planned or executed. This person sought to ruin her beauty to gain a most selfish and despicable end.'

Again Craig paused to let his words sink into our minds.

'Now I wish to state that anything you gentlemen may say will be used against you. That is why I have asked you to bring your attorneys. You may consult with them, of course, while I am getting ready my next disclosure.'

As Kennedy had developed his points in the case I had been more and more amazed. But I had not failed to notice how keenly Lawrence was following him.

With half a sneer on his astute face, Lawrence drawled: 'I cannot see that you have accomplished anything by this rather extraordinary summoning of us to your laboratory. The evidence is just as black against Dr Gregory as before. You may think you're clever, Kennedy, but on the very statement of facts as you have brought them out there is plenty of circumstantial evidence against Gregory—more than there was before. As for anyone else in the room, I can't see that you have anything on us—unless perhaps this new evidence you speak of may implicate Asche, or Jameson,' he added, including me in a wave of his hand, as if he were already addressing a jury. 'It's my opinion that twelve of our peers would be quite as likely to bring in a verdict of guilty against them as against anyone else even remotely connected with this case, except Gregory. No, you'll have to do better than this in your next case, if you expect to maintain that so-called reputation of yours for being a professor of criminal science.'

As for Close, taking his cue from his attorney, he scornfully added: 'I came to find out some new evidence against the wretch who wrecked the beauty of my wife. All I've got is a tiresome lecture on X-rays and radium. I suppose what you say is true. Well, it only bears out what I thought before. Gregory treated my wife at home, after he saw the damage his office treatments had done. I guess he was capable of making a complete job out of it—covering up his carelessness by getting rid of the woman who was such a damning piece of evidence against his professional skill.'

Never a shade passed Craig's face as he listened to this tirade. 'Excuse me a moment,' was all he said, opening the door to leave the room. 'I have just one more fact to disclose. I will be back directly.'

Kennedy was gone several minutes, during which Close and Lawrence fell to whispering behind their hands, with the assurance of those who believed that this was only Kennedy's method of admitting a defeat. Gregory and Asche exchanged a few words similarly, and it was plain that Asche was endeavouring to put a better interpretation on something than Gregory himself dared hope.

As Kennedy re-entered, Close was buttoning up his coat preparatory to leaving, and Lawrence was lighting a fresh cigar.

In his hand Kennedy held a notebook. 'My stenographer writes a very legible shorthand; at least I find it so—from long practice, I suppose. As I glance over her notes I find many facts which will interest you later—at the trial. But—ah, here at the end—let me read:

"'Well, he's very clever, but he has nothing against me, has he?"

"'No, not unless he can produce the agent who bought the radium for you."

"'But he can't do that. No one could ever have recognised you on your flying trip to London disguised as a diamond merchant who had just learned that he could make his faulty diamonds good by applications of radium and who wanted a good stock of the stuff."

"'Still, we'll have to drop the suit against Gregory after all, in spite of what I said. That part is hopelessly spoiled.'

"'Yes, I suppose so. Oh, well, I'm free now. She can hardly help but consent to a divorce now, and a quiet settlement. She brought it on herself—we tried every other way to do it, but she—she was too good to fall into it. She forced us to it.'

"'Yes, you'll get a good divorce now. But can't we shut up this man Kennedy? Even if he can't prove anything against us, the mere rumour of such a thing coming to the ears of Mrs Tulkington would be unpleasant.'

"'Go as far as you like, Lawrence. You know what the marriage will mean to me. It will settle my debts to you and all the rest.'

"'I'll see what I can do, Close. He'll be back in a moment.'"

Close's face was livid. 'It's a pack of lies!' he shouted, advancing toward Kennedy, 'a pack of lies! You are a fakir and a blackmailer. I'll have you in jail for this, by God—and you too, Gregory.'

'One moment, please,' said Kennedy calmly. 'Mr Lawrence, will you be so kind as to reach behind your chair? What do you find?'

Lawrence lifted up the plain black box and with it he pulled up the wires which I had so carefully concealed in the cracks of the floor.

'That,' said Kennedy, 'is a little instrument called the microphone. Its chief merit lies in the fact that it will magnify a sound sixteen hundred times, and carry it to any given point where you wish to place the receiver. Originally this device was invented for the aid of the deaf, but I see no reason why it should not be used to aid the law. One needn't eavesdrop at the keyhole with this little instrument about. Inside that box there is nothing but a series of plugs from which wires, much finer than a thread, are stretched taut. Yet a fly walking near it will make a noise as loud as a draft-horse. If the microphone is placed in any part of the room, especially if near the persons talking—even if they are talking in a whisper—a whisper such as occurred several times during the evening and particularly while I was in the next room getting the notes made by my stenographer—a whisper, I say, is like shouting your guilt from the housetops.

'You two men, Close and Lawrence, may consider yourselves under arrest for conspiracy and whatever other indictments will lie against such creatures as you. The police will be here in a moment. No, Close, violence won't do now. The doors are locked—and see, we are four to two.'

30

THE SLEUTHS

O. Henry

...a man will disappear with the suddenness and completeness of a flame of candle...

In The Big City a man will disappear with the suddenness and completeness of the flame of a candle that is blown out. All the agencies of inquisition—the hounds of the trail, the sleuths of the city's labyrinths, the closet detectives of theory and induction—will be invoked to the search. Most often the man's face will be seen no more. Sometimes he will reappear in Sheboygan or in the wilds of Terre Haute, calling himself one of the synonyms of 'Smith,' and without memory of events up to a certain time, including his grocer's bill. Sometimes it will be found, after dragging the rivers, and polling the restaurants to see if he may be waiting for a well-done sirloin, that he has moved next door.

This snuffing out of a human being like the erasure of a chalk man from a blackboard is one of the most impressive themes in dramaturgy.

The case of Mary Snyder, in point, should not be without interest.

A man of middle age, of the name of Meeks, came from the West to New York to find his sister, Mrs Mary Snyder, a widow, aged fifty-two, who had been living for a year in a tenement house in a crowded neighbourhood.

At her address he was told that Mary Snyder had moved away longer than a month before. No one could tell him her new address.

On coming out Mr Meeks addressed a policeman who was standing on the corner, and explained his dilemma.

'My sister is very poor,' he said, 'and I am anxious to find her. I have recently made quite a lot of money in a lead mine, and I want her to share my prosperity. There is no use in advertising her, because she cannot read.'

The policeman pulled his moustache and looked so thoughtful and mighty that Meeks could almost feel the joyful tears of his sister Mary dropping upon his bright blue tie.

'You go down in the Canal Street neighbourhood,' said the policeman, 'and get a job drivin' the biggest dray you can find. There's old women always gettin' knocked over by drays down there. You might see 'er among 'em. If you don't want to do that you better go 'round to headquarters and get 'em to put a fly cop onto the dame.'

At police headquarters, Meeks received ready assistance. A general alarm was sent out, and copies of a photograph of Mary Snyder that her brother had were distributed among the stations. In Mulberry Street the chief assigned Detective Mullins to the case.

The detective took Meeks aside and said:

'This is not a very difficult case to unravel. Shave off your whiskers, fill your pockets with good cigars, and meet me in the cafe of the Waldorf at three o'clock this afternoon.'

Meeks obeyed. He found Mullins there. They had a bottle of wine, while the detective asked questions concerning the missing woman.

'Now,' said Mullins, 'New York is a big city, but we've got the detective business systematized. There are two ways we can go about finding your sister. We will try one of 'em first. You say she's fifty-two?'

'A little past,' said Meeks.

The detective conducted the Westerner to a branch advertising office of one of the largest dailies. There he wrote the following 'ad' and submitted it to Meeks:

'Wanted, at once—one hundred attractive chorus girls for a new musical comedy. Apply all day at No. —Broadway.'

Meeks was indignant.

'My sister,' said he, 'is a poor, hard-working, elderly woman. I do not see what aid an advertisement of this kind would be toward finding her.'

'All right,' said the detective. 'I guess you don't know New York.

But if you've got a grouch against this scheme we'll try the other one. It's a sure thing. But it'll cost you more.'

'Never mind the expense,' said Meeks; 'we'll try it.'

The sleuth led him back to the Waldorf. 'Engage a couple of bedrooms and a parlour,' he advised, 'and let's go up.'

This was done, and the two were shown to a superb suite on the fourth floor. Meeks looked puzzled. The detective sank into a velvet armchair, and pulled out his cigar case.

'I forgot to suggest, old man,' he said, 'that you should have taken the rooms by the month. They wouldn't have stuck you so much for 'em'.

'By the month!' exclaimed Meeks. 'What do you mean?'

'Oh, it'll take time to work the game this way. I told you it would cost you more. We'll have to wait till spring. There'll be a new city directory out then. Very likely your sister's name and address will be in it.'

Meeks rid himself of the city detective at once. On the next day someone advised him to consult Shamrock Jolnes, New York's famous private detective, who demanded fabulous fees, but performed miracles in the way of solving mysteries and crimes.

After waiting for two hours in the anteroom of the great detective's apartment, Meeks was shown into his presence. Jolnes sat in a purple dressing-gown at an inlaid ivory chess table, with a magazine before him, trying to solve the mystery of 'They'. The famous sleuth's thin, intellectual face, piercing eyes, and rate per word are too well known to need description.

Meeks set forth his errand. 'My fee, if successful, will be $500,' said Shamrock Jolnes.

Meeks bowed his agreement to the price.

'I will undertake your case, Mr Meeks,' said Jolnes, finally. 'The disappearance of people in this city has always been an interesting problem to me. I remember a case that I brought to a successful outcome a year ago. A family bearing the name of Clark disappeared suddenly from a small flat in which they were living. I watched the flat building for two months for a clue. One day it struck me that a certain milkman and a grocer's boy always walked backward when they carried their wares upstairs. Following out by induction the idea that this observation gave me, I at once located the missing family. They had moved into the flat across the hall and changed their name to Kralc.'

Shamrock Jolnes and his client went to the tenement house where Mary Snyder had lived, and the detective demanded to be shown the room in which she had lived. It had been occupied by no tenant since her disappearance.

The room was small, dingy, and poorly furnished. Meeks seated himself dejectedly on a broken chair, while the great detective searched the walls and floor and the few sticks of old, rickety furniture for a clue.

At the end of half an hour Jolnes had collected a few seemingly unintelligible articles—a cheap black hat pin, a piece torn off a theatre programme, and the end of a small torn card on which was the word 'left' and the characters 'C 12.'

Shamrock Jolnes leaned against the mantel for ten minutes, with his head resting upon his hand, and an absorbed look upon his intellectual face. At the end of that time he exclaimed, with animation:

'Come, Mr Meeks; the problem is solved. I can take you directly to the house where your sister is living. And you may have no fears concerning her welfare, for she is amply provided with funds—for the present at least.'

Meeks felt joy and wonder in equal proportions.

'How did you manage it?' he asked, with admiration in his tones.

Perhaps Jolnes's only weakness was a professional pride in his wonderful achievements in induction. He was ever ready to astound and charm his listeners by describing his methods.

'By elimination,' said Jolnes, spreading his clues upon a little table, 'I got rid of certain parts of the city to which Mrs Snyder might have removed. You see this hatpin? That eliminates Brooklyn. No woman attempts to board a car at the Brooklyn Bridge without being sure that she carries a hatpin with which to fight her way into a seat. And now I will demonstrate to you that she could not have gone to Harlem. Behind this door are two hooks in the wall. Upon one of these Mrs

Snyder has hung her bonnet, and upon the other her shawl. You will observe that the bottom of the hanging shawl has gradually made a soiled streak against the plastered wall. The mark is clean-cut, proving that there is no fringe on the shawl. Now, was there ever a case where a middle-aged woman, wearing a shawl, boarded a Harlem train without there being a fringe on the shawl to catch in the gate and delay the passengers behind her? So we eliminate Harlem.

'Therefore I conclude that Mrs Snyder has not moved very far away. On this torn piece of card you see the word "Left", the letter "C", and the number "12". Now, I happen to know that No. 12 Avenue C is a first-class boarding house, far beyond your sister's means—as we suppose. But then I find this piece of a theatre programme, crumpled into an odd shape. What meaning does it convey. None to you, very likely, Mr Meeks; but it is eloquent to one whose habits and training take cognizance of the smallest things.

'You have told me that your sister was a scrub woman. She scrubbed the floors of offices and hallways. Let us assume that she procured such work to perform in a theatre. Where is valuable jewellery lost the oftenest, Mr Meeks? In the theatres, of course. Look at that piece of programme, Mr Meeks. Observe the round impression in it. It has been wrapped around a ring—perhaps a ring of great value. Mrs Snyder found the ring while at work in the theatre. She hastily tore off a piece of a programme, wrapped the ring carefully, and thrust it into her bosom. The next day she disposed of it, and, with her increased means, looked about her for a more comfortable place in which to live. When I reach thus far in the chain I see nothing impossible about No. 12 Avenue C. It is there we will find your sister, Mr Meeks.'

Shamrock Jolnes concluded his convincing speech with the smile of a successful artist. Meeks's admiration was too great for words. Together they went to No. 12 Avenue C. It was an old-fashioned brownstone house in a prosperous and respectable neighbourhood.

They rang the bell, and on inquiring were told that no Mrs Snyder was known there, and that not within six months had a new occupant come to the house.

When they reached the sidewalk again, Meeks examined the clues which he had brought away from his sister's old room.

'I am no detective,' he remarked to Jolnes as he raised the piece of theatre programme to his nose, 'but it seems to me that instead of a ring having been wrapped in this paper it was one of those round peppermint drops. And this piece with the address on it looks to me like the end of a seat coupon—No. 12, row C, left aisle.'

Shamrock Jolnes had a far-away look in his eyes.

'I think you would do well to consult Juggins,' said he.

'Who is Juggins?' asked Meeks.

'He is the leader,' said Jolnes, 'of a new modern school of detectives. Their methods are different from ours, but it is said that Juggins has solved some extremely puzzling cases. I will take you to him.'

They found the greater Juggins in his office. He was a small man with light hair, deeply absorbed in reading one of the bourgeois works of Nathaniel Hawthorne.

The two great detectives of different schools shook hands with ceremony, and Meeks was introduced.

'State the facts,' said Juggins, going on with his reading.

When Meeks ceased, the greater one closed his book and said:

'Do I understand that your sister is fifty-two years of age, with a large mole on the side of her nose, and that she is a very poor widow, making a scanty living by scrubbing, and with a very homely face and figure?'

'That describes her exactly,' admitted Meeks. Juggins rose and put on his hat.

'In fifteen minutes,' he said, 'I will return, bringing you her present address.'

Shamrock Jolnes turned pale, but forced a smile.

Within the specified time Juggins returned and consulted a little slip of paper held in his hand.

'Your sister, Mary Snyder,' he announced calmly, 'will be found at No. 162 Chilton street. She is living in the back hall bedroom, five flights up. The house is only four blocks from here,' he continued, addressing Meeks. 'Suppose you go and verify the statement and then return here. Mr Jolnes will await you, I dare say.'

Meeks hurried away. In twenty minutes he was back again, with a beaming face.

'She is there and well!' he cried. 'Name your fee!'

'Two dollars,' said Juggins.

When Meeks had settled his bill and departed, Shamrock Jolnes stood with his hat in his hand before Juggins.

'If it would not be asking too much,' he stammered—'if you would favour me so far—would you object to—'

'Certainly not,' said Juggins pleasantly. 'I will tell you how I did it. You remember the description of Mrs Snyder? Did you ever know a woman like that who wasn't paying weekly instalments on an enlarged crayon portrait of herself? The biggest factory of that kind in the country is just around the corner. I went there and got her address off the books. That's all.'

31

THE ARREST OF ARSÈNE LUPIN

Maurice Leblanc

... Arsène Lupin, the man of a thousand disguises: in turn a chauffer, detective, bookmaker, Russian physician, Spanish bull-fighter, commercial traveler, robust youth, or decrepit old man...

It was a strange ending to a voyage that had commenced in a most auspicious manner. The transatlantic steamship 'La Provence' was a swift and comfortable vessel, under the command of a most affable man. The passengers constituted a select and delightful society. The charm of new acquaintances and improvised amusements served to make the time pass agreeably. We enjoyed the pleasant sensation of being separated from the world, living, as it were, upon an unknown island, and consequently obliged to be sociable with each other.

Have you ever stopped to consider how much originality and spontaneity emanate from these various individuals who, on the preceding evening, did not even know each other, and who are now, for several days, condemned to lead a life of extreme intimacy, jointly defying the anger of the ocean, the terrible onslaught of the waves, the violence of the tempest and the agonizing monotony of the calm and sleepy water? Such a life becomes a sort of tragic existence, with its storms and its grandeurs, its monotony and its diversity; and that is why, perhaps, we embark upon that short voyage with mingled feelings of pleasure and fear.

But, during the past few years, a new sensation had been added to the life of the transatlantic traveler. The little floating island is now attached to the world from which it was once quite free. A bond united them, even in the very heart of the watery wastes of the Atlantic. That bond is the wireless telegraph, by means of which we receive news in the most mysterious manner. We know full well that the message is not transported by the medium of a hollow wire. No, the mystery is even more inexplicable, more romantic, and we must have recourse to the wings of the air in order to explain this new miracle. During the first day of the voyage, we felt that we were being followed, escorted, preceded even, by that distant voice, which, from time to time, whispered to one of us a few words from the receding world. Two friends spoke to me. Ten, twenty others sent gay or somber words of parting to other passengers.

On the second day, at a distance of five hundred miles from the French coast, in the midst of a violent storm, we received the following message by means of the wireless telegraph:

'Arsène Lupin is on your vessel, first cabin, blonde hair, wound right fore-arm, traveling alone under name of R...'

At that moment, a terrible flash of lightning rent the stormy skies. The electric waves were interrupted. The remainder of the dispatch never reached us. Of the name under which Arsène Lupin was concealing himself, we knew only the initial.

If the news had been of some other character, I have no doubt that the secret would have been carefully guarded by the telegraphic operator as well as by the officers of the vessel. But it was one of those events calculated to escape from the most rigorous discretion. The same day, no one knew how, the incident became a matter of current gossip and every passenger was aware that the famous Arsène Lupin was hiding in our midst.

Arsène Lupin in our midst! The irresponsible burglar whose exploits had been narrated in all the newspapers during the past few months! The mysterious individual with whom Ganimard, our shrewdest detective, had been engaged in an implacable conflict amidst interesting and picturesque surroundings. Arsène Lupin, the eccentric gentleman who operates only in the châteaux and salons, and who, one night, entered the residence of Baron Schormann, but emerged empty-handed, leaving, however, his card on which he had scribbled these words: 'Arsène Lupin, gentleman-burglar, will return when the furniture is genuine.' Arsène Lupin, the man of a thousand disguises: in turn a chauffer, detective, bookmaker, Russian physician, Spanish bull-fighter, commercial traveler, robust youth, or decrepit old man.

Then consider this startling situation: Arsène Lupin was wandering about within the limited bounds of a transatlantic steamer; in that very small corner of the world, in that dining saloon, in that smoking room, in that music room! Arsène Lupin was, perhaps, this gentleman… or that one… my neighbor at the table… the sharer of my stateroom…

'And this condition of affairs will last for five days!' exclaimed Miss Nelly Underdown, next morning. 'It is unbearable! I hope he will be arrested.'

Then, addressing me, she added:

'And you, Monsieur d'Andrézy, you are on intimate terms with the captain; surely you know something?'

I should have been delighted had I possessed any information that would interest Miss Nelly. She was one of those magnificent creatures who inevitably attract attention in every assembly. Wealth and beauty form an irresistible combination, and Nelly possessed both.

Educated in Paris under the care of a French mother, she was now going to visit her father, the millionaire Underdown of Chicago. She was accompanied by one of her friends, Lady Jerland.

At first, I had decided to open a flirtation with her; but, in the rapidly growing intimacy of the voyage, I was soon impressed by her charming manner and my feelings became too deep and reverential for a mere flirtation. Moreover, she accepted my attentions with a certain degree of favor. She condescended to laugh at my witticisms and display an interest in my stories. Yet I felt that I had a rival in the person of a young man with quiet and refined tastes; and it struck me, at times, that she preferred his taciturn humor to my Parisian frivolity. He formed one in the circle of admirers that surrounded Miss Nelly at the time she addressed to me the foregoing question. We were all comfortably seated in our deck-chairs. The storm of the preceding evening had cleared the sky. The weather was now delightful.

'I have no definite knowledge, mademoiselle,' I replied, 'but can not we, ourselves, investigate the mystery quite as well as the detective Ganimard, the personal enemy of Arsène Lupin?'

'Oh! oh! You are progressing very fast, monsieur.'

'Not at all, mademoiselle. In the first place, let me ask, do you find the problem a complicated one?'

'Very complicated.'

'Have you forgotten the key we hold for the solution to the problem?'

'What key?'

'In the first place, Lupin calls himself Monsieur R———.'

'Rather vague information,' she replied.

'Secondly, he is traveling alone.'

'Does that help you?' she asked.

'Thirdly, he is blonde.'

'Well?'

'Then we have only to peruse the passenger-list, and proceed by process of elimination.'

I had that list in my pocket. I took it out and glanced through it. Then I remarked:

'I find that there are only thirteen men on the passenger-list whose names begin with the letter R.'

'Only thirteen?'

'Yes, in the first cabin. And of those thirteen, I find that nine of them are accompanied by women, children or servants. That leaves only four who are traveling alone. First, the Marquis de Raverdan——'

'Secretary to the American Ambassador,' interrupted Miss Nelly. 'I know him.'

'Major Rawson,' I continued.

'He is my uncle,' some one said.

'Mon. Rivolta.'

'Here!' exclaimed an Italian, whose face was concealed beneath a heavy black beard.

Miss Nelly burst into laughter, and exclaimed: 'That gentleman can scarcely be called a blonde.'

'Very well, then,' I said, 'we are forced to the conclusion that the guilty party is the last one on the list.'

'What is his name?'

'Mon. Rozaine. Does anyone know him?'

No one answered. But Miss Nelly turned to the taciturn young man, whose attentions to her had annoyed me, and said:

'Well, Monsieur Rozaine, why do you not answer?'

All eyes were now turned upon him. He was a blonde. I must confess that I myself felt a shock of surprise, and the profound silence that followed her question indicated that the others present also viewed the situation with a feeling of sudden alarm. However, the idea was an absurd one, because the gentleman in question presented an air of the most perfect innocence.

'Why do I not answer?' he said. 'Because, considering my name, my position as a solitary traveler and the color of my hair, I have already reached the same conclusion, and now think that I should be arrested.'

He presented a strange appearance as he uttered these words. His thin lips were drawn closer than usual and his face was ghastly pale, whilst his eyes were streaked with blood. Of course, he was joking, yet his appearance and attitude impressed us strangely.

'But you have not the wound?' said Miss Nelly, naively.

'That is true,' he replied, 'I lack the wound.'

Then he pulled up his sleeve, removing his cuff, and showed us his arm. But that action did not deceive me. He had shown us his left arm, and I was on the point of calling his attention to the fact, when another incident diverted our attention. Lady Jerland, Miss Nelly's friend, came running towards us in a state of great excitement, exclaiming:

'My jewels, my pearls! Someone has stolen them all!'

No, they were not all gone, as we soon found out. The thief had taken only part of them; a very curious thing. Of the diamond sunbursts, jeweled pendants, bracelets and necklaces, the thief had taken, not the largest but the finest and most valuable stones. The mountings were lying upon the table. I saw them there, despoiled of their jewels, like flowers from which the beautiful colored petals had been ruthlessly plucked. And this theft must have been committed at the time Lady Jerland was taking her tea; in broad daylight, in a stateroom opening on a much frequented corridor; moreover, the thief had been obliged to force open the door of the stateroom, search for the jewel-case, which was hidden at the bottom of a hat-box, open it, select his booty and remove it from the mountings.

Of course, all the passengers instantly reached the same conclusion; it was the work of Arsène Lupin.

That day, at the dinner table, the seats to the right and left of Rozaine remained vacant; and, during the evening, it was rumored that the captain had placed him under arrest, which information produced a feeling of safety and relief. We breathed once more. That evening, we resumed our games and dances. Miss Nelly, especially, displayed a spirit of thoughtless gayety which convinced me that if Rozaine's attentions had been agreeable to her in the beginning, she had already forgotten them. Her charm and good humor completed my conquest. At midnight, under a bright moon, I declared my devotion with an ardor that did not seem to displease her.

But, next day, to our general amazement, Rozaine was at liberty. We learned that the evidence against him was not sufficient. He had produced documents that were perfectly regular, which showed that he was the son of a wealthy merchant of Bordeaux. Besides, his arms did not bear the slightest trace of a wound.

'Documents! Certificates of birth!' exclaimed the enemies of Rozaine, 'of course, Arsène Lupin will furnish you as many as you desire. And as to the wound, he never had it, or he has removed it.'

Then it was proven that, at the time of the theft, Rozaine was promenading on the deck. To which fact, his enemies replied that a man like Arsène Lupin could commit a crime without being actually present. And then, apart from all other circumstances, there remained one point which even the most skeptical could not answer: Who except Rozaine, was traveling alone, was a blonde, and bore a name beginning with R? To whom did the telegram point, if it were not Rozaine?

And when Rozaine, a few minutes before breakfast, came boldly toward our group, Miss Nelly and Lady Jerland arose and walked away.

An hour later, a manuscript circular was passed from hand to hand amongst the sailors, the stewards, and the passengers of all classes. It announced that Mon. Louis Rozaine offered a reward of ten thousand francs for the discovery of Arsène Lupin or other person in possession of the stolen jewels.

'And if no one assists me, I will unmask the scoundrel myself,' declared Rozaine.

Rozaine against Arsène Lupin, or rather, according to current opinion, Arsène Lupin himself against Arsène Lupin; the contest promised to be interesting.

Nothing developed during the next two days. We saw Rozaine wandering about, day and night, searching, questioning, investigating. The captain, also, displayed commendable activity. He caused the vessel to be searched from stem to stern; ransacked every stateroom under the plausible theory that the jewels might be concealed anywhere, except in the thief's own room.

'I suppose they will find out something soon,' remarked Miss Nelly to me. 'He may be a wizard, but he cannot make diamonds and pearls become invisible.'

'Certainly not,' I replied, 'but he should examine the lining of our hats and vests and everything we carry with us.'

Then, exhibiting my Kodak, a 9x12 with which I had been photographing her in various poses, I added: 'In an apparatus no larger than that, a person could hide all of Lady Jerland's jewels. He could pretend to take pictures and no one would suspect the game.'

'But I have heard it said that every thief leaves some clue behind him.'

'That may be generally true,' I replied, 'but there is one exception: Arsène Lupin.'

'Why?'

'Because he concentrates his thoughts not only on the theft, but on all the circumstances connected with it that could serve as a clue to his identity.'

'A few days ago, you were more confident.'

'Yes, but since then I have seen him at work.'

'And what do you think about it now?' she asked.

'Well, in my opinion, we are wasting our time.'

And, as a matter of fact, the investigation had produced no result. But, in the meantime, the captain's watch had been stolen. He was furious. He quickened his efforts and watched Rozaine more closely than before. But, on the following day, the watch was found in the second officer's collar box.

This incident caused considerable astonishment, and displayed the humorous side of Arsène Lupin, burglar though he was, but dilettante as well. He combined business with pleasure. He reminded us of the author who almost died in a fit of laughter provoked by his own play. Certainly, he was an artist in his particular line of work, and whenever I saw Rozaine, gloomy and reserved, and thought of the double role that he was playing, I accorded him a certain measure of admiration.

On the following evening, the officer on deck duty heard groans emanating from the darkest corner of the ship. He approached and found a man lying there, his head enveloped in a thick gray scarf and his hands tied together with a heavy cord. It was Rozaine. He had been assaulted, thrown down and robbed. A card, pinned to his coat, bore these words: 'Arsène Lupin accepts with pleasure the ten thousand francs offered by Mon. Rozaine.' As a matter of fact, the stolen pocket-book contained twenty thousand francs.

Of course, some accused the unfortunate man of having simulated this attack on himself. But, apart from the fact that he could not have bound himself in that manner, it was established that the writing on the card was entirely different from that of Rozaine, but, on the contrary, resembled the handwriting of Arsène Lupin as it was reproduced in an old newspaper found on board.

Thus it appeared that Rozaine was not Arsène Lupin; but was Rozaine, the son of a Bordeaux merchant. And the presence of Arsène Lupin was once more affirmed, and that in a most alarming manner.

Such was the state of terror amongst the passengers that none would remain alone in a stateroom or wander singly in unfrequented parts of the vessel. We clung together as a matter of safety. And yet the most intimate acquaintances were estranged by a mutual feeling of distrust. Arsène Lupin was, now, anybody and everybody. Our excited imaginations attributed to him miraculous and unlimited power. We supposed him capable of assuming the most unexpected disguises; of being, by turns, the highly respectable Major Rawson or the noble Marquis de Raverdan, or even—for we no longer stopped with the accusing letter of R—or even such or such a person well known to all of us, and having wife, children and servants.

The first wireless dispatches from America brought no news; at least, the captain did not communicate any to us. The silence was not reassuring.

Our last day on the steamer seemed interminable. We lived in constant fear of some disaster. This time, it would not be a simple theft or a comparatively harmless assault; it would be a crime, a murder. No one imagined that Arsène Lupin would confine himself to those two trifling offenses. Absolute master of the ship, the authorities powerless, he could do whatever he pleased; our property and lives were at his mercy.

Yet those were delightful hours for me, since they secured to me the confidence of Miss Nelly. Deeply moved by those startling events and being of a highly nervous nature, she spontaneously sought at my side a protection and security that I was pleased to give her. Inwardly, I blessed Arsène Lupin. Had he not been the means of bringing me and Miss Nelly closer to each other? Thanks to him, I could now indulge in delicious dreams of love and happiness—dreams that, I felt, were not unwelcome to Miss Nelly. Her smiling eyes authorized me to make them; the softness of her voice bade me hope.

As we approached the American shore, the active search for the thief was apparently abandoned, and we were anxiously awaiting the supreme moment in which the mysterious enigma would be explained. Who was Arsène Lupin? Under what name, under what disguise was the famous Arsène Lupin concealing himself? And, at last, that supreme moment arrived. If I live one hundred years, I shall not forget the slightest details of it.

'How pale you are, Miss Nelly,' I said to my companion, as she leaned upon my arm, almost fainting.

'And you!' she replied, 'ah! you are so changed.'

'Just think! This is a most exciting moment, and I am delighted to spend it with you, Miss Nelly. I hope that your memory will sometimes revert—'

But she was not listening. She was nervous and excited. The gangway was placed in position, but, before we could use it, the uniformed customs officers came on board. Miss Nelly murmured:

'I shouldn't be surprised to hear that Arsène Lupin escaped from the vessel during the voyage.'

'Perhaps he preferred death to dishonor, and plunged into the Atlantic rather than be arrested.'

'Oh, do not laugh,' she said.

Suddenly I started, and, in answer to her question, I said:

'Do you see that little old man standing at the bottom of the gangway?'

'With an umbrella and an olive-green coat?'

'It is Ganimard.'

'Ganimard?'

'Yes, the celebrated detective who has sworn to capture Arsène Lupin. Ah! I can understand now why we did not receive any news from this side of the Atlantic. Ganimard was here! And he always keeps his business secret.'

'Then you think he will arrest Arsène Lupin?'

'Who can tell? The unexpected always happens when Arsène Lupin is concerned in the affair.'

'Oh!' she exclaimed, with that morbid curiosity peculiar to women, 'I should like to see him arrested.'

'You will have to be patient. No doubt, Arsène Lupin has already seen his enemy and will not be in a hurry to leave the steamer.'

The passengers were now leaving the steamer. Leaning on his umbrella, with an air of careless indifference, Ganimard appeared to be paying no attention to the crowd that was hurrying down the gangway. The Marquis de Raverdan, Major Rawson, the Italian Rivolta, and many others had already left the vessel before Rozaine appeared.

Poor Rozaine!

'Perhaps it is he, after all,' said Miss Nelly to me. 'What do you think?'

'I think it would be very interesting to have Ganimard and Rozaine in the same picture. You take the camera. I am loaded down.'

I gave her the camera, but too late for her to use it. Rozaine was already passing the detective. An American officer, standing behind Ganimard, leaned forward and whispered in his ear. The French detective shrugged his shoulders and Rozaine passed on. Then, my God, who was Arsène Lupin?

'Yes,' said Miss Nelly, aloud, 'who can it be?'

Not more than twenty people now remained on board. She scrutinized them one by one, fearful that Arsène Lupin was not amongst them.

'We cannot wait much longer,' I said to her.

She started toward the gangway. I followed. But we had not taken ten steps when Ganimard barred our passage.

'Well, what is it?' I exclaimed.

'One moment, monsieur. What's your hurry?'

'I am escorting mademoiselle.'

'One moment,' he repeated, in a tone of authority. Then, gazing into my eyes, he said:

'Arsène Lupin, is it not?'

I laughed, and replied: 'No, simply Bernard d'Andrézy.'

'Bernard d'Andrézy died in Macedonia three years ago.'

'If Bernard d'Andrézy were dead, I should not be here. But you are mistaken. Here are my papers.'

'They are his; and I can tell you exactly how they came into your possession.'

'You are a fool!' I exclaimed. 'Arsène Lupin sailed under the name of R—'

'Yes, another of your tricks; a false scent that deceived them at Havre. You play a good game, my boy, but this time luck is against you.'

I hesitated a moment. Then he hit me a sharp blow on the right arm, which caused me to utter a cry of pain. He had struck the wound, yet unhealed, referred to in the telegram.

I was obliged to surrender. There was no alternative. I turned to Miss Nelly, who had heard everything. Our eyes met; then she glanced at the Kodak I had placed in her hands, and made a gesture that conveyed to me the impression that she understood everything. Yes, there, between the narrow folds of black leather, in the hollow centre of the small object that I had taken the precaution to place in her hands before Ganimard arrested me, it was there I had deposited Rozaine's twenty thousand francs and Lady Jerland's pearls and diamonds.

Oh! I pledge my oath that, at that solemn moment, when I was in the grasp of Ganimard and his two assistants, I was perfectly indifferent to everything, to my arrest, the hostility of the people, everything except this one question: what will Miss Nelly do with the things I had confided to her?

In the absence of that material and conclusive proof, I had nothing to fear; but would Miss Nelly decide to furnish that proof? Would she betray me? Would she act the part of an enemy who cannot forgive, or that of a woman whose scorn is softened by feelings of indulgence and involuntary sympathy?

She passed in front of me. I said nothing, but bowed very low. Mingled with the other passengers, she advanced to the gangway with my Kodak in her hand. It occurred to me that she would not dare to expose me publicly, but she might do so when she reached a more private place. However, when she had passed only a few feet down the gangway, with a movement of simulated awkwardness, she let the camera fall into the water between the vessel and the pier. Then she walked down the gangway, and was quickly lost to sight in the crowd. She had passed out of my life forever.

For a moment, I stood motionless. Then, to Ganimard's great astonishment, I muttered:

'What a pity that I am not an honest man!'

Such was the story of his arrest as narrated to me by Arsène Lupin himself. The various incidents, which I shall record in writing at a later day, have established between us certain ties... shall I say of friendship? Yes, I venture to believe that Arsène Lupin honors me with his friendship, and that it is through friendship that he occasionally calls on me, and brings, into the silence of my library, his youthful exuberance of spirits, the contagion of his enthusiasm, and the mirth of a man for whom destiny has naught but favors and smiles.

His portrait? How can I describe him? I have seen him twenty times and each time he was a different person; even he himself said to me on one occasion: 'I no longer know who I am. I cannot recognize myself in the mirror.' Certainly, he was a great actor, and possessed a marvelous faculty for disguising himself. Without the slightest effort, he could adopt the voice, gestures and mannerisms of another person.

'Why,' said he, 'why should I retain a definite form and feature? Why not avoid the danger of a personality that is ever the same? My actions will serve to identify me.'

Then he added, with a touch of pride:

'So much the better if no one can ever say with absolute certainty: There is Arsène Lupin! The essential point is that the public may be able to refer to my work and say, without fear of mistake: Arsène Lupin did that!'

32

VOLPURNO—OR THE STUDENT
W.W. Collins

'—Memory, like a drop that, night and day,
Falls cold and ceaseless, wore her heart away.'

—Lalla Rookh

Perfectly overcome by the heat of an Italian evening at Venice, I quitted the bustling gaiety of St Mark's Place for the quiet of a gondola, and directing the man to shape his course for the island of Lido, (a narrow strip of land dividing the 'lagunes,' or shallows beyond the city, from the open sea,) I seated myself on the prow of the vessel, with a firm determination to make the most of the flimsy wafts of air that every now and then ruffled the surface of the still, dark waters.

Nothing intercepted my view of the distant city, whose mighty buildings glowed beneath the long, red rays of the setting sun, save occasionally, when a market boat on its return floated lazily past us, or the hull of some tall merchantman shut out for an instant the dome of a magnificent church or the deep red brickwork of the Ducal Palace. Inexpressibly beautiful was the glimmering of the far off lights in the houses, as, one after another, they seemed to start out of the bosom of the deep; and at that quiet hour the repose—the peculiar repose of Venice—seemed mellowed into perfect harmony with the delicious languor of the atmosphere. The sounds of laughter, or snatches of rude songs that now and then came over the waves, instead of interupting [sic], invested with fresh charms the luxurious silence of the moment. We touched the narrow strip of sand that forms the beach of the little island, and stepping ashore, I enjoyed the only particle of green sward in all Venice.

I walked backward and forward for some time, thinking of England and English friends, (for at such hours the mind wanders to distant scenes and old customs,) without interruption, until a slight rustling among the bushes of the island reminded me that I was not the only tenant of the garden of the Lido, and looking through the fast gathering darkness, I discovered an aged female pacing the smooth walk near, apparently lost in contemplation.

My curiosity was rather excited by the presence of a lone old woman in such an unfrequented place; but the haze of the evening prevented my observing her with any degree of accuracy, and as I feared to disturb her by advancing too near, I could only guess at her features. At last the dwarf trees in the island 'began to glitter with the climbing moon,' and I saw that she was weeping bitterly. Her thick gray tresses were braided over a face that had evidently once been beautiful, and there was a dignity and propriety in her demeanour, and a native nobleness of expression in her countenance, which told me that I looked on no common person. She continued her solitary walk for some time, occasionally pausing to look up to the stars that now gemmed the clear glowing firmament, or to pluck a few dead leaves from a little rose bush that grew in an obscure corner of the garden, until a thought seemed suddenly to strike her, and hastening to the shore she stepped into a small gondola that was in waiting and rapidly disappeared.

On my return to Venice, I mentioned the circumstance to my cicerone, or guide, a remarkably intelligent fellow; and much to my astonishment, he solved the mystery of the lonely lady to me immediately. As her history is one of great devotion and misfortune, it may perhaps merit repetition.

It appeared, then, from the statement of the cicerone, that the elderly lady was an English woman who had once been the beauty of the gay circles of Venice. She had there met with a student in astronomy; and whether it was his lonely mystic life, the charm of his conversation and person, or his scientific attainments, that won her, I know not, but he gained her affections, and it is still remembered by those acquainted with her at the time, that her attachment to him so intensely passive in its devotion as to seem almost unearthly, and that very Lido, now the scene of her affliction, was once the favourite spot for their early love greetings.

He was a strange, wild creature, that student—his family were natives of a distant land, and he had travelled to Italy to devote himself, body and mind, to his favourite pursuit. From the after testimony of one of his friends, it appeared that in childhood he had been attacked with fits of temporary derangement, and his extraordinary application to the mysterious, exciting study of astronomy had increased this infirmity in a most extraordinary and terrible manner. At times he was haunted by a vision of a woman of disgusting ugliness who seemed to pursue and torment him wherever he went. In a few hours, delirium, and sometimes raging madness, would ensue from this hallucination, and though he regularly recovered free from the terrible creation of his mind, it was with a constitution more and more decayed by each successive ravage of his disorder. As he advanced, however, to manhood, these violent and destructive fits became less and less frequent and at the time that he met with the beautiful English lady, though his conscience seemed to tell him that he was no companion for a delicate woman, he tried to persuade himself that his constitution had at last mastered his imagination and that he was as fit for society as his less excitable fellow men. And he thought there was much excuse for him, for who could withstand the quiet yet intense affection of the English woman? Who could resist the temptation of listening to her sweet musical voice, of watching her sad soft blue eyes, or of hearing her fascinating conversation? She was so devoted, so gentle, so enthusiastic on his favourite subject, so patient of his little fits of peevishness, and melancholy, so considerate of his enjoyments, so comforting in his afflictions, he must surely have been without heart or feeling to have been coldly calculating on possibilities at such a time. He schooled himself to think that it was his solitary life that had so affected his faculties, and that a companion—and such a companion as his betrothed—would drive out all remains of his disorder, even supposing it to be still existing. In short, the eloquent pleading of the heart prevailed over the still small whisper of conscience; the wedding day was fixed, and it was remarked with surprise that the nearer it approached, the more melancholy did Volpurno become. However, the ceremony was performed with great splendour, and the bridal party set out to spend the day on the mainland, where the friends of the bride were to say farewell before she proceeded with her husband on the wedding tour. They were chatting merrily in the little hotel at Mestri, on the mainland, when they were horrified by suddenly hearing sounds of frantic laughter, followed by wild shrieks of agony, and the student rushed into the room, his frame convulsed with horror, with a drawn sword in his hand, as if pursuing something a few yards before him, with an expression of mingled fury and despair. Before the horrified guests could interfere, he had jumped from the window, and with the same shrieks of laughter, sped across the country in pursuit of his phantom enemy.

Assistance was at hand; he was instantly followed; but with supernatural strength he held on his course for hours. He was occasionally seen, as he paused for an instant to strike furiously in the air, and his cries of anguish were sometimes borne by the wind to the ears of his pursuers; but they never gained on him, and unless he neared a village, and was stopped by the inhabitants, his capture seemed impracticable. At last, as night grew on, he sunk exhausted at a lone hovel by the way side, and the bride and her party came up with the maniac bridegroom. But the stern fit was past and gone, and he was lifted insensible upon a coarse pallet in the hut. The Englishwoman sat by his side and bathed his temples, and watched his deep, long slumber, from the rise of the moon to the bright advent of day. And thus passed the bridal night of the heiress and the beauty.

Towards the going down of the sun, Volpurno became conscious, and though the fit had left him, the agony of his situation allowed no repose to his jarred, disordered nerves. His remorse was terrible to behold: over and over again did he heap curses on his selfishness in drawing an innocent. Trusting woman into such a labyrinth of suffering. All her repeated assurances of her forgiveness, of her happiness at his recovery, of her hopes for the future, failed to quiet him; and so, between soothing his anguish and administering his remedies, three days passed, and on the third a material changed took place. The dim eye of the student brightened, and his wan cheek flushed with the hue of health. He commanded all to leave the room but his bride, and to her he made full confession of his terrible infirmity, and of its seizing him with tenfold violence at the inn at Mestri, and of the frightful forebodings he had felt as their wedding approached. And then he grew calmer, and the smile again came forth upon his lip, and the melody returned to his voice, and at his favourite hour of midnight—in a peaceful quietude that had been unknown to him in his life—Volpurno died.

The corpse was carried to Venice and interred by the Englishwoman by her former trysting-place on the Lido. People wondered at her calmness under such an affliction, for she lived on, but little changed—save that she was paler and thinner—from the quiet creature that had won the fatal affection of Volpurno.

By degrees her more immediate friends died, or were called into other countries, and she was left alone in Venice: and then her solitary pilgrimages to the Lido became more and more frequent. As years grew on, and the finger of time imprinted the first furrows on the fair, delicate cheek, and planted the gray among the rich beauties of her hair, these visits increased. While, from day to day, the powers of her body became older, the faculties of her heart grew greener and younger. Years dulled not the pristine delicacy of her feelings, and age seemed in her to nourish instead of impairing the silent growth of memory.

◆

A few months afterwards I again visited the Lido at the same hour, but the Englishwoman did not appear. I walked towards the rose bush which I conjectured grew over the grave of Volpurno; its withered leaves were untrimmed, and the earth around it was newly heaped up. I asked no more questions; the freshness of the mould, and the neglect of the rose tree, were eloquent informers.

33

THE BLACK PEARL

Maurice Leblanc

… what had happened in the dread silence of the night?…

A violent ringing of the bell awakened the concierge of number nine, avenue Hoche. She pulled the doorstring, grumbling:

'I thought everybody was in. It must be three o'clock!'

'Perhaps it is someone for the doctor,' muttered her husband.

At that moment, a voice inquired:

'Doctor Harel … what floor?'

'Third floor, left. But the doctor won't go out at night.'

'He must go to-night.'

The visitor entered the vestibule, ascended to the first floor, the second, the third, and, without stopping at the doctor's door, he continued to the fifth floor. There, he tried two keys. One of them fitted the lock.

'Ah! good!' he murmured, 'that simplifies the business wonderfully. But before I commence work I had better arrange for my retreat. Let me see… have I had sufficient time to rouse the doctor and be dismissed by him? Not yet… a few minutes more.'

At the end of ten minutes, he descended the stairs, grumbling noisily about the doctor. The concierge opened the door for him and heard it click behind him. But the door did not lock, as the man had quickly inserted a piece of iron in the lock in such a manner that the bolt could not enter. Then, quietly, he entered the house again, unknown to the concierge. In case of alarm, his retreat was assured. Noiselessly, he ascended to the fifth floor once more. In the antechamber, by the light of his electric lantern, he placed his hat and overcoat on one of the chairs, took a seat on another, and covered his heavy shoes with felt slippers.

'Ouf! Here I am—and how simple it was! I wonder why more people do not adopt the profitable and pleasant occupation of burglar. With a little care and reflection, it becomes a most delightful profession. Not too quiet and monotonous, of course, as it would then become wearisome.'

He unfolded a detailed plan of the apartment.

'Let me commence by locating myself. Here, I see the vestibule in which I am sitting. On the street front, the drawing-room, the boudoir and dining-room. Useless to waste any time there, as it appears that the countess has a deplorable taste... not a bibelot of any value!...Now, let's get down to business!... Ah! here is a corridor; it must lead to the bed chambers. At a distance of three metres, I should come to the door of the wardrobe-closet which connects with the chamber of the countess.' He folded his plan, extinguished his lantern, and proceeded down the corridor, counting his distance, thus:

'One metre... two metres... three metres...Here is the door... Mon Dieu, how easy it is! Only a small, simple bolt now separates me from the chamber, and I know that the bolt is located exactly one metre, forty-three centimeters, from the floor. So that, thanks to a small incision I am about to make, I can soon get rid of the bolt.'

He drew from his pocket the necessary instruments. Then the following idea occurred to him:

'Suppose, by chance, the door is not bolted. I will try it first.'

He turned the knob, and the door opened.

'My brave Lupin, surely fortune favors you...What's to be done now? You know the situation of the rooms; you know the place in which the countess hides the black pearl. Therefore, in order to secure the black pearl, you have simply to be more silent than silence, more invisible than darkness itself.'

Arsène Lupin was employed fully a half-hour in opening the second door—a glass door that led to the countess' bedchamber. But he accomplished it with so much skill and precaution, that even had the countess been awake, she would not have heard the slightest sound.

According to the plan of the rooms, that he holds, he has merely to pass around a reclining chair and, beyond that, a small table close to the bed. On the table, there was a box of letter-paper, and the black pearl was concealed in that box. He stooped and crept cautiously over the carpet, following the outlines of the reclining-chair. When he reached the extremity of it, he stopped in order to repress the throbbing of his heart. Although he was not moved by any sense of fear, he found it impossible to overcome the nervous anxiety that one usually feels in the midst of profound silence. That circumstance astonished him, because he had passed through many more solemn moments without the slightest trace of emotion. No danger threatened him. Then why did his heart throb like an alarm-bell? Was it that sleeping woman who affected him? Was it the proximity of another pulsating heart?

He listened, and thought he could discern the rhythmical breathing of a person asleep. It gave him confidence, like the presence of a friend. He sought and found the armchair; then, by slow, cautious movements, advanced toward the table, feeling ahead of him with outstretched arm. His right had touched one of the feet of the table. Ah! now, he had simply to rise, take the pearl, and escape. That was fortunate, as his heart was leaping in his breast like a wild beast, and made so much noise that he feared it would waken the countess. By a powerful effort of the will, he subdued the wild throbbing of his heart, and was about to rise from the floor when his left hand encountered, lying on the floor, an object which he recognized as a candlestick—an overturned candlestick. A moment later, his hand encountered another object: a clock—one of those small traveling clocks, covered with leather.

Well! What had happened? He could not understand. That candlestick, that clock; why were those articles not in their accustomed places? Ah! what had happened in the dread silence of the night?

Suddenly a cry escaped him. He had touched—oh! some strange, unutterable thing! 'No! no!' he thought, 'it cannot be. It is some fantasy of my excited brain.' For twenty seconds, thirty seconds, he remained motionless, terrified, his forehead bathed with perspiration, and his fingers still retained the sensation of that dreadful contact.

Making a desperate effort, he ventured to extend his arm again.

Once more, his hand encountered that strange, unutterable thing. He felt it. He must feel it and find out what it is. He found that it was hair, human hair, and a human face; and that face was cold, almost icy.

However frightful the circumstances may be, a man like Arsène Lupin controls himself and commands the situation as soon as he learns what it is. So, Arsène Lupin quickly brought his lantern into use. A woman was lying before him, covered with blood. Her neck and shoulders were covered with gaping wounds. He leaned over her and made a closer examination. She was dead.

'Dead! Dead!' he repeated, with a bewildered air.

He stared at those fixed eyes, that grim mouth, that livid flesh, and that blood—all that blood which had flowed over the carpet and congealed there in thick, black spots. He arose and turned on the electric lights. Then he beheld all the marks of a desperate struggle. The bed was in a state of great disorder. On the floor, the candlestick, and the clock, with the hands pointing to twenty minutes after eleven; then, further away, an overturned chair; and, everywhere, there was blood, spots of blood and pools of blood.

'And the black pearl?' he murmured.

The box of letter-paper was in its place. He opened it, eagerly. The jewel-case was there, but it was empty.

'Fichtre!' he muttered. 'You boasted of your good fortune much too soon, my friend Lupin. With the countess lying cold and dead, and the black pearl vanished, the situation is anything but pleasant. Get out of here as soon as you can, or you may get into serious trouble.'

Yet, he did not move.

'Get out of here? Yes, of course. Any person would, except Arsène Lupin. He has something better to do. Now, to proceed in an orderly way. At all events, you have a clear conscience. Let us suppose that you are the commissary of police and that you are proceeding to make an inquiry concerning this affair—Yes, but in order to do that, I require a clearer brain. Mine is muddled like a ragout.'

He tumbled into an armchair, with his clenched hands pressed against his burning forehead.

◆

The murder of the avenue Hoche is one of those which have recently surprised and puzzled the Parisian public, and, certainly, I should never have mentioned the affair if the veil of mystery had not been removed by Arsène Lupin himself. No one knew the exact truth of the case.

Who did not know—from having met her in the Bois—the fair Léotine Zalti, the once-famous cantatrice, wife and widow of the Count d'Andillot; the Zalti, whose luxury dazzled all Paris some twenty years ago; the Zalti who acquired an European reputation for the magnificence of her diamonds and pearls? It was said that she wore upon her shoulders the capital of several banking houses and the gold mines of numerous Australian companies. Skilful jewelers worked for Zalti as they had formerly wrought for kings and queens. And who does not remember the catastrophe in which all that wealth was swallowed up? Of all that marvelous collection, nothing remained except the famous black pearl. The black pearl! That is to say a fortune, if she had wished to part with it.

But she preferred to keep it, to live in a commonplace apartment with her companion, her cook, and a man-servant, rather than sell that inestimable jewel. There was a reason for it; a reason she was not afraid to disclose: the black pearl was the gift of an emperor! Almost ruined, and reduced to the most mediocre existence, she remained faithful to the companion of her happy and brilliant youth. The black pearl never left her possession. She wore it during the day, and, at night, concealed it in a place known to her alone.

All these facts, being republished in the columns of the public press, served to stimulate curiosity; and, strange to say, but quite obvious to those who have the key to the mystery, the arrest of the presumed assassin only complicated the question and prolonged the excitement. Two days later, the newspapers published the following item:

'Information has reached us of the arrest of Victor Danègre, the servant of the Countess d'Andillot. The evidence against him is clear and convincing. On the silken sleeve of his liveried waistcoat, which chief detective Dudouis found in his garret between the mattresses of his bed, several spots of blood were discovered. In addition, a cloth-covered button was missing from that garment, and this button was found beneath the bed of the victim.

'It is supposed that, after dinner, in place of going to his own room, Danègre slipped into the wardrobe-closet, and, through the glass door, had seen the countess hide the precious black pearl. This is simply a theory, as yet unverified by any evidence. There is, also, another obscure point. At seven o'clock in the morning, Danègre went to the tobacco-shop on the Boulevard de Courcelles; the concierge and the shop-keeper both affirm this fact. On the other hand, the countess' companion and cook, who sleep at the end of the hall, both declare that, when they arose at eight o'clock, the door of the antechamber and the door of the kitchen were locked. These two persons have been in the service of the countess for twenty years, and are above suspicion. The question is: How did Danègre leave the apartment? Did he have another key? These are matters that the police will investigate.'

As a matter of fact, the police investigation threw no light on the mystery. It was learned that Victor Danègre was a dangerous criminal, a drunkard and a debauchee. But, as they proceeded with the investigation, the mystery deepened and new complications arose. In the first place, a young woman, Mlle. De Sinclèves, the cousin and sole heiress of the countess, declared that the countess, a month before her death, had written a letter to her and in it described the manner in which the black pearl was concealed. The letter disappeared the day after she received it. Who had stolen it?

Again, the concierge related how she had opened the door for a person who had inquired for Doctor Harel. On being questioned, the doctor testified that no one had rung his bell. Then who was that person? An accomplice?

The theory of an accomplice was thereupon adopted by the press and public, and also by Ganimard, the famous detective.

'Lupin is at the bottom of this affair,' he said to the judge.

'Bah!' exclaimed the judge, 'you have Lupin on the brain. You see him everywhere.'

'I see him everywhere, because he is everywhere.'

'Say rather that you see him every time you encounter something you cannot explain. Besides, you overlook the fact that the crime was committed at twenty minutes past eleven in the evening, as is shown by the clock, while the nocturnal visit, mentioned by the concierge, occurred at three o'clock in the morning.'

Officers of the law frequently form a hasty conviction as to the guilt of a suspected person, and then distort all subsequent discoveries to conform to their established theory. The deplorable antecedents of Victor Danègre, habitual criminal, drunkard and rake, influenced the judge, and despite the fact that nothing new was discovered in corroboration of the early clues, his official opinion remained firm and unshaken. He closed his investigation, and, a few weeks later, the trial commenced. It proved to be slow and tedious. The judge was listless, and the public prosecutor presented the case in a careless manner. Under those circumstances, Danègre's counsel had an easy task. He pointed out the defects and inconsistencies of the case for the prosecution, and argued that the evidence was quite insufficient to convict the accused. Who had made the key, the indispensable key without which Danègre, on leaving the apartment, could not have locked the door behind him? Who had ever seen such a key, and what had become of it? Who had seen the assassin's knife, and where is it now?

'In any event,' argued the prisoner's counsel, 'the prosecution must prove, beyond any reasonable doubt, that the prisoner committed the murder. The prosecution must show that the mysterious individual who entered the house at three o'clock in the morning is not the guilty party. To be sure, the clock indicated eleven o'clock. But what of that? I contend, that proves nothing. The assassin could turn the hands of the clock to any hour he pleased, and thus deceive us in regard to the exact hour of the crime.'

Victor Danègre was acquitted.

He left the prison on Friday about dusk in the evening, weak and depressed by his six months' imprisonment. The inquisition, the solitude, the trial, the deliberations of the jury, combined to fill him with a nervous fear. At night, he had been afflicted with terrible nightmares and haunted by weird visions of the scaffold. He was a mental and physical wreck.

Under the assumed name of Anatole Dufour, he rented a small room on the heights of Montmartre, and lived by doing odd jobs wherever he could find them. He led a pitiful existence. Three times, he obtained regular employment, only to be recognized and then discharged. Sometimes, he had an idea that men were following him—detectives, no doubt, who were seeking to trap and denounce him. He could almost feel the strong hand of the law clutching him by the collar.

One evening, as he was eating his dinner at a neighboring restaurant, a man entered and took a seat at the same table. He was a person about forty years of age, and wore a frock-coat of doubtful cleanliness. He ordered soup, vegetables, and a bottle of wine. After he had finished his soup, he turned his eyes on Danègre, and gazed at him intently. Danègre winced. He was certain that this was one of the men who had been following him for several weeks. What did he want? Danègre tried to rise, but failed. His limbs refused to support him. The man poured himself a glass of wine, and then filled Danègre's glass. The man raised his glass, and said:

'To your health, Victor Danègre.'

Victor started in alarm, and stammered:

'I!...I!... no, no...I swear to you...'

'You will swear what? That you are not yourself? The servant of the countess?'

'What servant? My name is Dufour. Ask the proprietor.'

'Yes, Anatole Dufour to the proprietor of this restaurant, but Victor Danègre to the officers of the law.'

'That's not true! Someone has lied to you.'

The new-comer took a card from his pocket and handed it to Victor, who read on it: 'Grimaudan, ex-inspector of the detective force. Private business transacted.' Victor shuddered as he said:

'You are connected with the police?'

'No, not now, but I have a liking for the business and I continue to work at it in a manner more—profitable. From time to time I strike upon a golden opportunity—such as your case presents.'

'My case?'

'Yes, yours. I assure you it is a most promising affair, provided you are inclined to be reasonable.'

'But if I am not reasonable?'

'Oh! my good fellow, you are not in a position to refuse me anything I may ask.'

'What is it... you want?' stammered Victor, fearfully.

'Well, I will inform you in a few words. I am sent by Mademoiselle de Sinclèves, the heiress of the Countess d'Andillot.'

'What for?'

'To recover the black pearl.'

'Black pearl?'

'That you stole.'

'But I haven't got it.'

'You have it.'

'If I had, then I would be the assassin.'

'You are the assassin.'

Danègre showed a forced smile.

'Fortunately for me, monsieur, the Assizecourt was not of your opinion. The jury returned an unanimous verdict of acquittal. And when a man has a clear conscience and twelve good men in his favor—'

The ex-inspector seized him by the arm and said:

'No fine phrases, my boy. Now, listen to me and weigh my words carefully. You will find they are worthy of your consideration. Now, Danègre, three weeks before the murder, you abstracted the cook's key to the servants' door, and had a duplicate key made by a locksmith named Outard, 244 rue Oberkampf.'

'It's a lie—it's a lie!' growled Victor. 'No person has seen that key. There is no such key.'

'Here it is.'

After a silence, Grimaudan continued:

'You killed the countess with a knife purchased by you at the Bazar de la Republique on the same day as you ordered the duplicate key. It has a triangular blade with a groove running from end to end.'

'That is all nonsense. You are simply guessing at something you don't know. No one ever saw the knife.'

'Here it is.'

Victor Danègre recoiled. The ex-inspector continued:

'There are some spots of rust upon it. Shall I tell you how they came there?'

'Well!... you have a key and a knife. Who can prove that they belong to me?'

'The locksmith, and the clerk from whom you bought the knife. I have already refreshed their memories, and, when you confront them, they cannot fail to recognize you.'

His speech was dry and hard, with a tone of firmness and precision. Danègre was trembling with fear, and yet he struggled desperately to maintain an air of indifference.

'Is that all the evidence you have?'

'Oh! no, not at all. I have plenty more. For instance, after the crime, you went out the same way you had entered. But, in the centre of the wardrobe-room, being seized by some sudden fear, you leaned against the wall for support.'

'How do you know that? No one could know such a thing,' argued the desperate man.

'The police know nothing about it, of course. They never think of lighting a candle and examining the walls. But if they had done so, they would have found on the white plaster a faint red spot, quite distinct, however, to trace in it the imprint of your thumb which you had pressed against the wall while it was wet with blood. Now, as you are well aware, under the Bertillon system, thumb-marks are one of the principal means of identification.'

Victor Danègre was livid; great drops of perspiration rolled down his face and fell upon the table. He gazed, with a wild look, at the strange man who had narrated the story of his crime as faithfully as if he had been an invisible witness to it. Overcome and powerless, Victor bowed his head. He felt that it was useless to struggle against this marvelous man. So he said:

'How much will you give me, if I give you the pearl?'

'Nothing.'

'Oh! you are joking! Or do you mean that I should give you an article worth thousands and hundreds of thousands and get nothing in return?'

'You will get your life. Is that nothing?'

The unfortunate man shuddered. Then Grimaudan added, in a milder tone:

'Come, Danègre, that pearl has no value in your hands. It is quite impossible for you to sell it; so what is the use of your keeping it?'

'There are pawnbrokers… and, some day, I will be able to get something for it.'

'But that day may be too late.'

'Why?'

'Because by that time you may be in the hands of the police, and, with the evidence that I can furnish—the knife, the key, the thumb-mark—what will become of you?'

Victor rested his head on his hands and reflected. He felt that he was lost, irremediably lost, and, at the same time, a sense of weariness and depression overcame him. He murmured, faintly:

'When must I give it to you?'

'To-night—within an hour.'

'If I refuse?'

'If you refuse, I shall post this letter to the Procureur of the Republic; in which letter Mademoiselle de Sinclèves denounces you as the assassin.'

Danègre poured out two glasses of wine which he drank in rapid succession, then, rising, said:

'Pay the bill, and let us go. I have had enough of the cursed affair.'

Night had fallen. The two men walked down the rue Lepic and followed the exterior boulevards in the direction of the Place de l'Etoile. They pursued their way in silence; Victor had a stooping carriage and a dejected face. When they reached the Parc Monceau, he said:

'We are near the house.'

'Parbleu! You only left the house once, before your arrest, and that was to go to the tobacco-shop.'

'Here it is,' said Danègre, in a dull voice.

They passed along the garden wall of the countess' house, and crossed a street on a corner of which stood the tobacco-shop. A few steps further on, Danègre stopped; his limbs shook beneath him, and he sank to a bench.

'Well! what now?' demanded his companion.

'It is there.'

'Where? Come, now, no nonsense!'

'There—in front of us.'

'Where?'

'Between two paving-stones.'

'Which?'

'Look for it.'

'Which stones?'

Victor made no reply.

'Ah; I see!' exclaimed Grimaudan, 'you want me to pay for the information.'

'No... but...I am afraid I will starve to death.'

'So! that is why you hesitate. Well, I'll not be hard on you. How much do you want?'

'Enough to buy a steerage pass to America.'

'All right.'

'And a hundred francs to keep me until I get work there.'

'You shall have two hundred. Now, speak.'

'Count the paving-stones to the right from the sewer-hole. The pearl is between the twelfth and thirteenth.'

'In the gutter?'

'Yes, close to the sidewalk.'

Grimaudan glanced around to see if anyone were looking. Some tram-cars and pedestrians were passing. But, bah, they will not suspect anything. He opened his pocketknife and thrust it between the twelfth and thirteenth stones.

'And if it is not there?' he said to Victor.

'It must be there, unless someone saw me stoop down and hide it.'

Could it be possible that the black pearl had been cast into the mud and filth of the gutter to be picked up by the first comer? The black pearl—a fortune!

'How far down?' he asked.

'About ten centimetres.'

He dug up the wet earth. The point of his knife struck something. He enlarged the hole with his finger. Then he abstracted the black pearl from its filthy hiding place.

'Good! Here are your two hundred francs. I will send you the ticket for America.'

On the following day, this article was published in the 'Echo de France,' and was copied by the leading newspapers throughout the world:

'Yesterday, the famous black pearl came into the possession of Arsène Lupin, who recovered it from the murderer of the Countess d'Andillot. In a short time, fac-similes of that precious jewel will be exhibited in London, St. Petersburg, Calcutta, Buenos Ayres and New York.

'Arsène Lupin will be pleased to consider all propositions submitted to him through his agents.'

◆

'And that is how crime is always punished and virtue rewarded,' said Arsène Lupin, after he had told me the foregoing history of the black pearl.

'And that is how you, under the assumed name of Grimaudan, ex-inspector of detectives, were chosen by fate to deprive the criminal of the benefit of his crime.'

'Exactly. And I confess that the affair gives me infinite satisfaction and pride. The forty minutes that I passed in the apartment of the Countess d'Andillot, after learning of her death, were the most thrilling and absorbing moments of my life. In those forty minutes, involved as I was in a most dangerous plight, I calmly studied the scene of the murder and reached the conclusion that the crime must have been committed by one of the house servants. I also decided that, in order to get the pearl, that servant must be arrested, and so I left the wainscoat button; it was necessary, also, for me to hold some convincing evidence of his guilt, so I carried away the knife which I found upon the floor, and the key which I found in the lock. I closed and locked the door, and erased the finger-marks from the plaster in the wardrobe-closet. In my opinion, that was one of those flashes—'

'Of genius,' I said, interrupting.

'Of genius, if you wish. But, I flatter myself, it would not have occurred to the average mortal. To frame, instantly, the two elements of the problem—an arrest and an acquittal; to make use of the formidable machinery of the law to crush and humble my victim, and reduce him to a condition in which, when free, he would be certain to fall into the trap I was laying for him!'

'Poor devil—'

'Poor devil, do you say? Victor Danègre, the assassin! He might have descended to the lowest depths of vice and crime, if he had retained the black pearl. Now, he lives! Think of that: Victor Danègre is alive!'

'And you have the black pearl.'

He took it out of one of the secret pockets of his wallet, examined it, gazed at it tenderly, and caressed it with loving fingers, and sighed, as he said:

'What cold Russian prince, what vain and foolish rajah may some day possess this priceless treasure! Or, perhaps, some American millionaire is destined to become the owner of this morsel of exquisite beauty that once adorned the fair bosom of Leontine Zalti, the Countess d'Andillot.'

34

HUNTED DOWN

Charles Dickens

...A hair or two will show where a lion is hidden. A very little key will open a very heavy door...

I

Most of us see some romances in life. In my capacity as Chief Manager of a Life Assurance Office, I think I have within the last thirty years seen more romances than the generality of men, however unpromising the opportunity may, at first sight, seem.

As I have retired, and live at my ease, I possess the means that I used to want, of considering what I have seen, at leisure. My experiences have a more remarkable aspect, so reviewed, than they had when they were in progress. I have come home from the Play now, and can recall the scenes of the Drama upon which the curtain has fallen, free from the glare, bewilderment, and bustle of the Theatre.

Let me recall one of these Romances of the real world.

There is nothing truer than physiognomy, taken in connection with manner. The art of reading that book of which Eternal Wisdom obliges every human creature to present his or her own page with the individual character written on it, is a difficult one, perhaps, and is little studied. It may require some natural aptitude, and it must require (for everything does) some patience and some pains. That these are not usually given to it,—that numbers of people accept a few stock commonplace expressions of the face as the whole list of characteristics, and neither seek nor know the refinements that are truest,—that You, for instance, give a great deal of time and attention to the reading of music, Greek, Latin, French, Italian, Hebrew, if you please, and do not qualify yourself to read the face of the master or mistress looking over your shoulder teaching it to you,—I assume to be five hundred times more probable than improbable. Perhaps a little self-sufficiency may be at the bottom of this; facial expression requires no study from you, you think; it comes by nature to you to know enough about it, and you are not to be taken in.

I confess, for my part, that I *have* been taken in, over and over again. I have been taken in by acquaintances, and I have been taken in (of course) by friends; far oftener by friends than by any other class of persons. How came I to be so deceived? Had I quite misread their faces?

No. Believe me, my first impression of those people, founded on face and manner alone, was invariably true. My mistake was in suffering them to come nearer to me and explain themselves away.

II

The partition which separated my own office from our general outer office in the City was of thick plate-glass. I could see through it what passed in the outer office, without hearing a word. I had it put up in place of a wall that had been there for years,—ever since the house was built. It is no matter whether I did or did not make the change in order that I might derive my first impression of strangers, who came to us on business, from their faces alone, without being influenced by anything they said. Enough to mention that I turned my glass partition to that account, and that a Life Assurance Office is at all times exposed to be practised upon by the most crafty and cruel of the human race.

It was through my glass partition that I first saw the gentleman whose story I am going to tell.

He had come in without my observing it, and had put his hat and umbrella on the broad counter, and was bending over it to take some papers from one of the clerks. He was about forty or so, dark, exceedingly well dressed in black,—being in mourning,—and the hand he extended with a polite air, had a particularly well-fitting black-kid glove upon it. His hair, which was elaborately brushed and oiled, was parted straight up the middle; and he presented this parting to the clerk, exactly (to my thinking) as if he had said, in so many words: 'You must take me, if you please, my friend, just as I show myself. Come straight up here, follow the gravel path, keep off the grass, I allow no trespassing.'

I conceived a very great aversion to that man the moment I thus saw him.

He had asked for some of our printed forms, and the clerk was giving them to him and explaining them. An obliged and agreeable smile was on his face, and his eyes met those of the clerk with a sprightly look. (I have known a vast quantity of nonsense talked about bad men not looking you in the face. Don't trust that conventional idea. Dishonesty will stare honesty out of countenance, any day in the week, if there is anything to be got by it.)

I saw, in the corner of his eyelash, that he became aware of my looking at him. Immediately he turned the parting in his hair toward the glass partition, as if he said to me with a sweet smile, 'Straight up here, if you please. Off the grass!'

In a few moments he had put on his hat and taken up his umbrella, and was gone.

I beckoned the clerk into my room, and asked, 'Who was that?'

He had the gentleman's card in his hand. 'Mr Julius Slinkton, Middle Temple.'

'A barrister, Mr Adams?'

'I think not, sir.'

'I should have thought him a clergyman, but for his having no Reverend here,' said I.

'Probably, from his appearance,' Mr Adams replied, 'he is reading for orders.'

I should mention that he wore a dainty white cravat, and dainty linen altogether.

'What did he want, Mr Adams?'

'Merely a form of proposal, sir, and form of reference.'

'Recommended here? Did he say?'

'Yes, he said he was recommended here by a friend of yours. He noticed you, but said that as he had not the pleasure of your personal acquaintance he would not trouble you.'

'Did he know my name?'

'O yes, sir! He said, "There *is* Mr Sampson, I see!"'

'A well-spoken gentleman, apparently?'

'Remarkably so, sir.'

'Insinuating manners, apparently?'

'Very much so, indeed, sir.'

'Hah!' said I. 'I want nothing at present, Mr Adams.'

Within a fortnight of that day I went to dine with a friend of mine, a merchant, a man of taste, who buys pictures and books, and the first man I saw among the company was Mr Julius Slinkton. There he was, standing before the fire, with good large eyes and an open expression of face; but still (I thought) requiring everybody to come at him by the prepared way he offered, and by no other.

I noticed him ask my friend to introduce him to Mr Sampson, and my friend did so. Mr Slinkton was very happy to see me. Not too happy; there was no over-doing of the matter; happy in a thoroughly well-bred, perfectly unmeaning way.

'I thought you had met,' our host observed.

'No,' said Mr Slinkton. 'I did look in at Mr Sampson's office, on your recommendation; but I really did not feel justified in troubling Mr Sampson himself, on a point in the everyday routine of an ordinary clerk.'

I said I should have been glad to show him any attention on our friend's introduction.

'I am sure of that,' said he, 'and am much obliged. At another time, perhaps, I may be less delicate. Only, however, if I have real business; for I know, Mr Sampson, how precious business time is, and what a vast number of impertinent people there are in the world.'

I acknowledged his consideration with a slight bow. 'You were thinking,' said I, 'of effecting a policy on your life.'

'O dear no! I am afraid I am not so prudent as you pay me the compliment of supposing me to be, Mr Sampson. I merely inquired for a friend. But you know what friends are in such matters. Nothing may ever come of it. I have the greatest reluctance to trouble men of business with inquiries for friends, knowing the probabilities to be a thousand to one that the friends will never follow them up. People are so fickle, so selfish, so inconsiderate. Don't you, in your business, find them so every day, Mr Sampson?'

I was going to give a qualified answer; but he turned his smooth, white parting on me with its 'Straight up here, if you please!' and I answered 'Yes.'

'I hear, Mr Sampson,' he resumed presently, for our friend had a new cook, and dinner was not so punctual as usual, 'that your profession has recently suffered a great loss.'

'In money?' said I.

He laughed at my ready association of loss with money, and replied, 'No, in talent and vigour.'

Not at once following out his allusion, I considered for a moment. '*Has* it sustained a loss of that kind?' said I. 'I was not aware of it.'

'Understand me, Mr Sampson. I don't imagine that you have retired. It is not so bad as that. But Mr Meltham—'

'O, to be sure!' said I. 'Yes! Mr Meltham, the young actuary of the "Inestimable."'

'Just so,' he returned in a consoling way.

'He is a great loss. He was at once the most profound, the most original, and the most energetic man I have ever known connected with Life Assurance.'

I spoke strongly; for I had a high esteem and admiration for Meltham; and my gentleman had indefinitely conveyed to me some suspicion that he wanted to sneer at him. He recalled me to my guard by presenting that trim pathway up his head, with its internal 'Not on the grass, if you please—the gravel.'

'You knew him, Mr Slinkton.'

'Only by reputation. To have known him as an acquaintance or as a friend, is an honour I should have sought if he had remained in society, though I might never have had the good fortune to attain it, being a man of far inferior mark. He was scarcely above thirty, I suppose?'

'About thirty.'

'Ah!' he sighed in his former consoling way. 'What creatures we are! To break up, Mr Sampson, and become incapable of business at that time of life!—Any reason assigned for the melancholy fact?'

('Humph!' thought I, as I looked at him. 'But I WON'T go up the track, and I WILL go on the grass.')

'What reason have you heard assigned, Mr Slinkton?' I asked, point-blank.

'Most likely a false one. You know what Rumour is, Mr Sampson. I never repeat what I hear; it is the only way of paring the nails and shaving the head of Rumour. But when *you* ask me what reason I have heard assigned for Mr Meltham's passing away from among men, it is another thing. I am not gratifying idle gossip then. I was told, Mr Sampson, that Mr Meltham had relinquished all his avocations and all his prospects, because he was, in fact, broken-hearted. A disappointed attachment I heard,—though it hardly seems probable, in the case of a man so distinguished and so attractive.'

'Attractions and distinctions are no armour against death,' said I.

'O, she died? Pray pardon me. I did not hear that. That, indeed, makes it very, very sad. Poor Mr Meltham! She died? Ah, dear me! Lamentable, lamentable!'

I still thought his pity was not quite genuine, and I still suspected an unaccountable sneer under all this, until he said, as we were parted, like the other knots of talkers, by the announcement of dinner:

'Mr Sampson, you are surprised to see me so moved on behalf of a man whom I have never known. I am not so disinterested as you may suppose. I have suffered, and recently too, from death myself. I have lost one of two charming nieces, who were my constant companions. She died young—barely three-and-twenty; and even her remaining sister is far from strong. The world is a grave!'

He said this with deep feeling, and I felt reproached for the coldness of my manner. Coldness and distrust had been engendered in me, I knew, by my bad experiences; they were not natural to me; and I often thought how much I had lost in life, losing trustfulness, and how little I had gained, gaining hard caution. This state of mind being habitual to me, I troubled myself more about this conversation than I might have troubled myself about a greater matter. I listened to his talk at dinner, and observed how readily other men responded to it, and with what a graceful instinct he adapted his subjects to the knowledge and habits of those he talked with. As, in talking with me, he had easily started the subject I might be supposed to understand best, and to be the most interested in, so, in talking with others, he guided himself by the same rule. The company was of a varied character; but he was not at fault, that I could discover, with any member of it. He knew just as much of each man's pursuit as made him agreeable to that man in reference to it, and just as little as made it natural in him to seek modestly for information when the theme was broached.

As he talked and talked—but really not too much, for the rest of us seemed to force it upon him—I became quite angry with myself. I took his face to pieces in my mind, like a watch, and examined it in detail. I could not say much against any of his features separately; I could say even less against them when they were put together. 'Then is it not monstrous,' I asked myself, 'that because a man happens to part his hair straight up the middle of his head, I should permit myself to suspect, and even to detest him?'

(I may stop to remark that this was no proof of my sense. An observer of men who finds himself steadily repelled by some apparently trifling thing in a stranger is right to give it great weight. It may be the clue to the whole mystery. A hair or two will show where a lion is hidden. A very little key will open a very heavy door.)

I took my part in the conversation with him after a time, and we got on remarkably well. In the drawing-room I asked the host how long he had known Mr Slinkton. He answered, not many months; he had met him at the house of a celebrated painter then present, who had known him well when he was travelling with his nieces in Italy for their health. His plans in life being broken by the death of one of them, he was reading with the intention of going back to college as a matter of form, taking his degree, and going into orders. I could not but argue with myself that here was the true explanation of his interest in poor Meltham, and that I had been almost brutal in my distrust on that simple head.

III

On the very next day but one I was sitting behind my glass partition, as before, when he came into the outer office, as before. The moment I saw him again without hearing him, I hated him worse than ever.

It was only for a moment that I had this opportunity; for he waved his tight-fitting black glove the instant I looked at him, and came straight in.

'Mr Sampson, good-day! I presume, you see, upon your kind permission to intrude upon you. I don't keep my word in being justified by business, for my business here—if I may so abuse the word—is of the slightest nature.'

I asked, was it anything I could assist him in?

'I thank you, no. I merely called to inquire outside whether my dilatory friend had been so false to himself as to be practical and sensible. But, of course, he has done nothing. I gave him your papers with my own hand, and he was hot upon the intention, but of course he has done nothing. Apart from the general human disinclination to do anything that ought to be done, I dare say there is a specialty about assuring one's life. You find it like will-making. People are so superstitious, and take it for granted they will die soon afterwards.'

'Up here, if you please; straight up here, Mr Sampson. Neither to the right nor to the left.' I almost fancied I could hear him breathe the words as he sat smiling at me, with that intolerable parting exactly opposite the bridge of my nose.

'There is such a feeling sometimes, no doubt,' I replied; 'but I don't think it obtains to any great extent.'

'Well,' said he, with a shrug and a smile, 'I wish some good angel would influence my friend in the right direction. I rashly promised his mother and sister in Norfolk to see it done, and he promised them that he would do it. But I suppose he never will.'

He spoke for a minute or two on indifferent topics, and went away.

I had scarcely unlocked the drawers of my writing-table next morning, when he reappeared. I noticed that he came straight to the door in the glass partition, and did not pause a single moment outside.

'Can you spare me two minutes, my dear Mr Sampson?'

'By all means.'

'Much obliged,' laying his hat and umbrella on the table; 'I came early, not to interrupt you. The fact is, I am taken by surprise in reference to this proposal my friend has made.'

'Has he made one?' said I.

'Ye-es,' he answered, deliberately looking at me; and then a bright idea seemed to strike him—'or he only tells me he has. Perhaps that may be a new way of evading the matter. By Jupiter, I never thought of that!'

Mr Adams was opening the morning's letters in the outer office. 'What is the name, Mr Slinkton?' I asked.

'Beckwith.'

I looked out at the door and requested Mr Adams, if there were a proposal in that name, to bring it in. He had already laid it out of his hand on the counter. It was easily selected from the rest, and he gave it me. Alfred Beckwith. Proposal to effect a policy with us for two thousand pounds. Dated yesterday.

'From the Middle Temple, I see, Mr Slinkton.'

'Yes. He lives on the same staircase with me; his door is opposite. I never thought he would make me his reference though.'

'It seems natural enough that he should.'

'Quite so, Mr Sampson; but I never thought of it. Let me see.' He took the printed paper from his pocket. 'How am I to answer all these questions?'

'According to the truth, of course,' said I.

'O, of course!' he answered, looking up from the paper with a smile; 'I meant they were so many. But you do right to be particular. It stands to reason that you must be particular. Will you allow me to use your pen and ink?'

'Certainly.'

'And your desk?'

'Certainly.'

He had been hovering about between his hat and his umbrella for a place to write on. He now sat down in my chair, at my blotting-paper and inkstand, with the long walk up his head in accurate perspective before me, as I stood with my back to the fire.

Before answering each question he ran over it aloud, and discussed it. How long had he known Mr Alfred Beckwith? That he had to calculate by years upon his fingers. What were his habits? No difficulty about them; temperate in the last degree, and took a little too much exercise, if anything. All the answers were satisfactory. When he had written them all, he looked them over, and finally signed them in a very pretty hand. He supposed he had now done with the business. I told him he was not likely to be troubled any farther. Should he leave the papers there? If he pleased. Much obliged. Good-morning.

I had had one other visitor before him; not at the office, but at my own house. That visitor had come to my bedside when it was not yet daylight, and had been seen by no one else but by my faithful confidential servant.

A second reference paper (for we required always two) was sent down into Norfolk, and was duly received back by post. This, likewise, was satisfactorily answered in every respect. Our forms were all complied with; we accepted the proposal, and the premium for one year was paid.

IV

For six or seven months I saw no more of Mr Slinkton. He called once at my house, but I was not at home; and he once asked me to dine with him in the Temple, but I was engaged. His friend's assurance was effected in March. Late in September or early in October I was down at Scarborough for a breath of sea-air, where I met him on the beach. It was a hot evening; he came toward me with his hat in his hand; and there was the walk I had felt so strongly disinclined to take in perfect order again, exactly in front of the bridge of my nose.

He was not alone, but had a young lady on his arm.

She was dressed in mourning, and I looked at her with great interest. She had the appearance of being extremely delicate, and her face was remarkably pale and melancholy; but she was very pretty. He introduced her as his niece, Miss Niner.

'Are you strolling, Mr Sampson? Is it possible you can be idle?'

It *was* possible, and I *was* strolling.

'Shall we stroll together?'

'With pleasure.'

The young lady walked between us, and we walked on the cool sea sand, in the direction of Filey.

'There have been wheels here,' said Mr Slinkton. 'And now I look again, the wheels of a hand-carriage! Margaret, my love, your shadow without doubt!'

'Miss Niner's shadow?' I repeated, looking down at it on the sand.

'Not that one,' Mr Slinkton returned, laughing. 'Margaret, my dear, tell Mr Sampson.'

'Indeed,' said the young lady, turning to me, 'there is nothing to tell—except that I constantly see the same invalid old gentleman at all times, wherever I go. I have mentioned it to my uncle, and he calls the gentleman my shadow.'

'Does he live in Scarborough?' I asked.

'He is staying here.'

'Do you live in Scarborough?'

'No, I am staying here. My uncle has placed me with a family here, for my health.'

'And your shadow?' said I, smiling.

'My shadow,' she answered, smiling too, 'is—like myself—not very robust, I fear; for I lose my shadow sometimes, as my shadow loses me at other times. We both seem liable to confinement to the house. I have not seen my shadow for days and days; but it does oddly happen, occasionally, that wherever I go, for many days together, this gentleman goes. We have come together in the most unfrequented nooks on this shore.'

'Is this he?' said I, pointing before us.

The wheels had swept down to the water's edge, and described a great loop on the sand in turning. Bringing the loop back towards us, and spinning it out as it came, was a hand-carriage, drawn by a man.

'Yes,' said Miss Niner, 'this really is my shadow, uncle.'

As the carriage approached us and we approached the carriage, I saw within it an old man, whose head was sunk on his breast, and who was enveloped in a variety of wrappers. He was drawn by a very quiet but very keen-looking man, with iron-gray hair, who was slightly lame. They had passed us, when the carriage stopped, and the old gentleman within, putting out his arm, called to me by my name. I went back, and was absent from Mr Slinkton and his niece for about five minutes.

When I rejoined them, Mr Slinkton was the first to speak. Indeed, he said to me in a raised voice before I came up with him:

'It is well you have not been longer, or my niece might have died of curiosity to know who her shadow is, Mr Sampson.'

'An old East India Director,' said I. 'An intimate friend of our friend's, at whose house I first had the pleasure of meeting you. A certain Major Banks. You have heard of him?'

'Never.'

'Very rich, Miss Niner; but very old, and very crippled. An amiable man, sensible—much interested in you. He has just been expatiating on the affection that he has observed to exist between you and your uncle.'

Mr Slinkton was holding his hat again, and he passed his hand up the straight walk, as if he himself went up it serenely, after me.

'Mr Sampson,' he said, tenderly pressing his niece's arm in his, 'our affection was always a strong one, for we have had but few near ties. We have still fewer now. We have associations to bring us together, that are not of this world, Margaret.'

'Dear uncle!' murmured the young lady, and turned her face aside to hide her tears.

'My niece and I have such remembrances and regrets in common, Mr Sampson,' he feelingly pursued, 'that it would be strange indeed if the relations between us were cold or indifferent. If I remember a conversation we once had together, you will understand the reference I make. Cheer up, dear Margaret. Don't droop, don't droop. My Margaret! I cannot bear to see you droop!'

The poor young lady was very much affected, but controlled herself.

His feelings, too, were very acute. In a word, he found himself under such great need of a restorative, that he presently went away, to take a bath of sea-water, leaving the young lady and me sitting by a point of rock, and probably presuming—but that you will say was a pardonable indulgence in a luxury—that she would praise him with all her heart.

She did, poor thing! With all her confiding heart, she praised him to me, for his care of her dead sister, and for his untiring devotion in her last illness. The sister had wasted away very slowly, and wild and terrible fantasies had come over her toward the end, but he had never been impatient with her, or at a loss; had always been gentle, watchful, and self-possessed. The sister had known him, as she had known him, to be the best of men, the kindest of men, and yet a man of such admirable strength of character, as to be a very tower for the support of their weak natures while their poor lives endured.

'I shall leave him, Mr Sampson, very soon,' said the young lady; 'I know my life is drawing to an end; and when I am gone, I hope he will marry and be happy. I am sure he has lived single so long, only for my sake, and for my poor, poor sister's.'

The little hand-carriage had made another great loop on the damp sand, and was coming back again, gradually spinning out a slim figure of eight, half a mile long.

'Young lady,' said I, looking around, laying my hand upon her arm, and speaking in a low voice, 'time presses. You hear the gentle murmur of that sea?'

She looked at me with the utmost wonder and alarm, saying, 'Yes!'

'And you know what a voice is in it when the storm comes?'

'Yes!'

'You see how quiet and peaceful it lies before us, and you know what an awful sight of power without pity it might be, this very night!'

'Yes!'

'But if you had never heard or seen it, or heard of it in its cruelty, could you believe that it beats every inanimate thing in its way to pieces, without mercy, and destroys life without remorse?'

'You terrify me, sir, by these questions!'

'To save you, young lady, to save you! For God's sake, collect your strength and collect your firmness! If you were here alone, and hemmed in by the rising tide on the flow to fifty feet above your head, you could not be in greater danger than the danger you are now to be saved from.'

The figure on the sand was spun out, and straggled off into a crooked little jerk that ended at the cliff very near us.

'As I am, before Heaven and the Judge of all mankind, your friend, and your dead sister's friend, I solemnly entreat you, Miss Niner, without one moment's loss of time, to come to this gentleman with me!'

If the little carriage had been less near to us, I doubt if I could have got her away; but it was so near that we were there before she had recovered the hurry of being urged from the rock. I did not remain there with her two minutes. Certainly within five, I had the inexpressible satisfaction of seeing her—from the point we had sat on, and to which I had returned—half supported and half carried up some rude steps notched in the cliff, by the figure of an active man. With that figure beside her, I knew she was safe anywhere.

I sat alone on the rock, awaiting Mr Slinkton's return. The twilight was deepening and the shadows were heavy, when he came round the point, with his hat hanging at his button-hole, smoothing his wet hair with one of his hands, and picking out the old path with the other and a pocket-comb.

'My niece not here, Mr Sampson?' he said, looking about.

'Miss Niner seemed to feel a chill in the air after the sun was down, and has gone home.'

He looked surprised, as though she were not accustomed to do anything without him; even to originate so slight a proceeding.

'I persuaded Miss Niner,' I explained.

'Ah!' said he. 'She is easily persuaded—for her good. Thank you, Mr Sampson; she is better within doors. The bathing-place was farther than I thought, to say the truth.'

'Miss Niner is very delicate,' I observed.

He shook his head and drew a deep sigh. 'Very, very, very. You may recollect my saying so. The time that has since intervened has not strengthened her. The gloomy shadow that fell upon her sister so early in life seems, in my anxious eyes, to gather over her, ever darker, ever darker. Dear Margaret, dear Margaret! But we must hope.'

The hand-carriage was spinning away before us at a most indecorous pace for an invalid vehicle, and was making most irregular curves upon the sand. Mr Slinkton, noticing it after he had put his handkerchief to his eyes, said:

'If I may judge from appearances, your friend will be upset, Mr Sampson.'

'It looks probable, certainly,' said I.

'The servant must be drunk.'

'The servants of old gentlemen will get drunk sometimes,' said I.

'The major draws very light, Mr Sampson.'

'The major does draw light,' said I.

By this time the carriage, much to my relief, was lost in the darkness. We walked on for a little, side by side over the sand, in silence. After a short while he said, in a voice still affected by the emotion that his niece's state of health had awakened in him,

'Do you stay here long, Mr Sampson?'

'Why, no. I am going away to-night.'

'So soon? But business always holds you in request. Men like Mr Sampson are too important to others, to be spared to their own need of relaxation and enjoyment.'

'I don't know about that,' said I. 'However, I am going back.'

'To London?'

'To London.'

'I shall be there too, soon after you.'

I knew that as well as he did. But I did not tell him so. Any more than I told him what defensive weapon my right hand rested on in my pocket, as I walked by his side. Any more than I told him why I did not walk on the sea side of him with the night closing in.

We left the beach, and our ways diverged. We exchanged good-night, and had parted indeed, when he said, returning,

'Mr Sampson, *may* I ask? Poor Meltham, whom we spoke of,—dead yet?'

'Not when I last heard of him; but too broken a man to live long, and hopelessly lost to his old calling.'

'Dear, dear, dear!' said he, with great feeling. 'Sad, sad, sad! The world is a grave!' And so went his way.

It was not his fault if the world were not a grave; but I did not call that observation after him, any more than I had mentioned those other things just now enumerated. He went his way, and I went mine with all expedition. This happened, as I have said, either at the end of September or beginning of October. The next time I saw him, and the last time, was late in November.

V

I had a very particular engagement to breakfast in the Temple. It was a bitter north-easterly morning, and the sleet and slush lay inches deep in the streets. I could get no conveyance, and was soon wet to the knees; but I should have been true to that appointment, though I had to wade to it up to my neck in the same impediments.

The appointment took me to some chambers in the Temple. They were at the top of a lonely corner house overlooking the river. The name, Mr Alfred Beckwith, was painted on the outer door. On the door opposite, on the same landing, the name Mr Julius Slinkton. The doors of both sets of chambers stood open, so that anything said aloud in one set could be heard in the other.

I had never been in those chambers before. They were dismal, close, unwholesome, and oppressive; the furniture, originally good, and not yet old, was faded and dirty,—the rooms were in great disorder; there was a strong prevailing smell of opium, brandy, and tobacco; the grate and fire-irons were splashed all over with unsightly blotches of rust; and on a sofa by the fire, in the room where breakfast had been prepared, lay the host, Mr Beckwith, a man with all the appearances of the worst kind of drunkard, very far advanced upon his shameful way to death.

'Slinkton is not come yet,' said this creature, staggering up when I went in; 'I'll call him.—Halloa! Julius Cæsar! Come and drink!' As he hoarsely roared this out, he beat the poker and tongs together in a mad way, as if that were his usual manner of summoning his associate.

The voice of Mr Slinkton was heard through the clatter from the opposite side of the staircase, and he came in. He had not expected the pleasure of meeting me. I have seen several artful men brought to a stand, but I never saw a man so aghast as he was when his eyes rested on mine.

'Julius Cæsar,' cried Beckwith, staggering between us, 'Mist' Sampson! Mist' Sampson, Julius Cæsar! Julius, Mist' Sampson, is the friend of my soul. Julius keeps me plied with liquor, morning, noon, and night. Julius is a real benefactor. Julius threw the tea and coffee out of window when I used to have any. Julius empties all the water-jugs of their contents, and fills 'em with spirits. Julius winds me up and keeps me going.—Boil the brandy, Julius!'

There was a rusty and furred saucepan in the ashes,—the ashes looked like the accumulation of weeks,—and Beckwith, rolling and staggering between us as if he were going to plunge headlong into the fire, got the saucepan out, and tried to force it into Slinkton's hand.

'Boil the brandy, Julius Cæsar! Come! Do your usual office. Boil the brandy!'

He became so fierce in his gesticulations with the saucepan, that I expected to see him lay open Slinkton's head with it. I therefore put out my hand to check him. He reeled back to the sofa, and sat there panting, shaking, and red-eyed, in his rags of dressing-gown, looking at us both. I noticed then that there was nothing to drink on the table but brandy, and nothing to eat but salted herrings, and a hot, sickly, highly-peppered stew.

'At all events, Mr Sampson,' said Slinkton, offering me the smooth gravel path for the last time, 'I thank you for interfering between me and this unfortunate man's violence. However you came here, Mr Sampson, or with whatever motive you came here, at least I thank you for that.'

'Boil the brandy,' muttered Beckwith.

Without gratifying his desire to know how I came there, I said, quietly, 'How is your niece, Mr Slinkton?'

He looked hard at me, and I looked hard at him.

'I am sorry to say, Mr Sampson, that my niece has proved

treacherous and ungrateful to her best friend. She left me without a word of notice or explanation. She was misled, no doubt, by some designing rascal. Perhaps you may have heard of it.'

'I did hear that she was misled by a designing rascal. In fact, I have proof of it.'

'Are you sure of that?' said he.

'Quite.'

'Boil the brandy,' muttered Beckwith. 'Company to breakfast, Julius Cæsar. Do your usual office,—provide the usual breakfast, dinner, tea, and supper. Boil the brandy!'

The eyes of Slinkton looked from him to me, and he said, after a moment's consideration,

'Mr Sampson, you are a man of the world, and so am I. I will be plain with you.'

'O no, you won't,' said I, shaking my head.

'I tell you, sir, I will be plain with you.'

'And I tell you you will not,' said I. 'I know all about you. *You* plain with any one? Nonsense, nonsense!'

'I plainly tell you, Mr Sampson,' he went on, with a manner almost composed, 'that I understand your object. You want to save your funds, and escape from your liabilities; these are old tricks of trade with you Office-gentlemen. But you will not do it, sir; you will not succeed. You have not an easy adversary to play against, when you play against me. We shall have to inquire, in due time, when and how Mr Beckwith fell into his present habits. With that remark, sir, I put this poor creature, and his incoherent wanderings of speech, aside, and wish you a good morning and a better case next time.'

While he was saying this, Beckwith had filled a half-pint glass with brandy. At this moment, he threw the brandy at his face, and threw the glass after it. Slinkton put his hands up, half blinded with the spirit, and cut with the glass across the forehead. At the sound of the breakage, a fourth person came into the room, closed the door, and stood at it; he was a very quiet but very keen-looking man, with iron-gray hair, and slightly lame.

Slinkton pulled out his handkerchief, assuaged the pain in his smarting eyes, and dabbled the blood on his forehead. He was a long time about it, and I saw that in the doing of it, a tremendous change came over him, occasioned by the change in Beckwith,—who ceased to pant and tremble, sat upright, and never took his eyes off him. I never in my life saw a face in which abhorrence and determination were so forcibly painted as in Beckwith's then.

'Look at me, you villain,' said Beckwith, 'and see me as I really am. I took these rooms, to make them a trap for you. I came into them as a drunkard, to bait the trap for you. You fell into the trap, and you will never leave it alive. On the morning when you last went to Mr Sampson's office, I had seen him first. Your plot has been known to both of us, all along, and you have been counter-plotted all along. What? Having been cajoled into putting that prize of two thousand pounds in your power, I was to be done to death with brandy, and, brandy not proving quick enough, with something quicker? Have I never seen you, when you thought my senses gone, pouring from your little bottle into my glass? Why, you Murderer and Forger, alone here with you in the dead of night, as I have so often been, I have had my hand upon the trigger of a pistol, twenty times, to blow your brains out!'

This sudden starting up of the thing that he had supposed to be his imbecile victim into a determined man, with a settled resolution to hunt him down and be the death of him, mercilessly expressed from head to foot, was, in the first shock, too much for him. Without any figure of speech, he staggered under it. But there is no greater mistake than to suppose that a man who is a calculating criminal, is, in any phase of his guilt, otherwise than true to himself, and perfectly consistent with his whole character. Such a man commits murder, and murder is the natural culmination of his course; such a man has to outface murder, and will do it with hardihood and effrontery. It is a sort of fashion to express surprise that any notorious criminal, having such crime upon his conscience, can so brave it out. Do you think that if he had it on his conscience at all, or had a conscience to have it upon, he would ever have committed the crime?

Perfectly consistent with himself, as I believe all such monsters to be, this Slinkton recovered himself, and showed a defiance that was sufficiently cold and quiet. He was white, he was haggard, he was changed; but only as a sharper who had played for a great stake and had been outwitted and had lost the game.

'Listen to me, you villain,' said Beckwith, 'and let every word you hear me say be a stab in your wicked heart. When I took these rooms, to throw myself in your way and lead you on to the scheme that I knew my appearance and supposed character and habits would suggest to such a devil, how did I know that? Because you were no stranger to me. I knew you well. And I knew you to be the cruel wretch who, for so much money, had killed one innocent girl while she trusted him implicitly, and who was by inches killing another.'

Slinkton took out a snuff-box, took a pinch of snuff, and laughed.

'But see here,' said Beckwith, never looking away, never raising his voice, never relaxing his face, never unclenching his hand. 'See what a dull wolf you have been, after all! The infatuated drunkard who never drank a fiftieth part of the liquor you plied him with, but poured it away, here, there, everywhere—almost before your eyes; who bought over the fellow you set to watch him and to ply him, by outbidding you in his bribe, before he had been at his work three days—with whom you have observed no caution, yet who was so bent on ridding the earth of you as a wild beast, that he would have defeated you if you had been ever so prudent—that drunkard whom you have, many a time, left on the floor of this room, and who has even let you go out of it, alive and undeceived, when you have turned him over with your foot—has, almost as often, on the same night, within an hour, within a few minutes, watched you awake, had his hand at your pillow when you were asleep, turned over your papers, taken samples from your bottles and packets of powder, changed their contents, rifled every secret of your life!'

He had had another pinch of snuff in his hand, but had gradually let it drop from between his fingers to the floor; where he now smoothed it out with his foot, looking down at it the while.

'That drunkard,' said Beckwith, 'who had free access to your rooms at all times, that he might drink the strong drinks that you left in his way and be the sooner ended, holding no more terms with you than he would hold with a tiger, has had his master-key for all your locks, his test for all your poisons, his clue to your cipher-writing. He can tell you, as well as you can tell him, how long it took to complete that deed, what doses there were, what intervals, what signs of gradual decay upon mind and body; what distempered fancies were produced, what observable changes, what physical pain. He can tell you, as well as you can tell him, that all this was recorded day by day, as a lesson of experience for future service. He can tell you, better than you can tell him, where that journal is at this moment.'

Slinkton stopped the action of his foot, and looked at Beckwith.

'No,' said the latter, as if answering a question from him. 'Not in the drawer of the writing-desk that opens with a spring; it is not there, and it never will be there again.'

'Then you are a thief!' said Slinkton.

Without any change whatever in the inflexible purpose, which it was quite terrific even to me to contemplate, and from the power of which I had always felt convinced it was impossible for this wretch to escape, Beckwith returned,

'And I am your niece's shadow, too.'

With an imprecation Slinkton put his hand to his head, tore out some hair, and flung it to the ground. It was the end of the smooth walk; he destroyed it in the action, and it will soon be seen that his use for it was past.

Beckwith went on: 'Whenever you left here, I left here. Although I understood that you found it necessary to pause in the completion of that purpose, to avert suspicion, still I watched you close, with the poor confiding girl. When I had the diary, and could read it word by word,—it was only about the night before your last visit to Scarborough,—you remember the night? you slept with a small flat vial tied to your wrist,—I sent to Mr Sampson, who was kept out of view. This is Mr Sampson's trusty servant standing by the door. We three saved your niece among us.'

Slinkton looked at us all, took an uncertain step or two from the place where he had stood, returned to it, and glanced about him in a very curious way,—as one of the meaner reptiles might, looking for a hole to hide in. I noticed at the same time, that a singular change took place in the figure of the man,—as if it collapsed within his clothes, and they consequently became ill-shapen and ill-fitting.

'You shall know,' said Beckwith, 'for I hope the knowledge will be bitter and terrible to you, why you have been pursued by one man, and why, when the whole interest that Mr Sampson represents would have expended any money in hunting you down, you have been tracked to death at a single individual's charge. I hear you have had the name of Meltham on your lips sometimes?'

I saw, in addition to those other changes, a sudden stoppage come upon his breathing.

'When you sent the sweet girl whom you murdered (you know with what artfully made-out surroundings and probabilities you sent her) to Meltham's office, before taking her abroad to originate the transaction that doomed her to the grave, it fell to Meltham's lot to see her and to speak with her. It did not fall to his lot to save her, though I know he would freely give his own life to have done it. He admired her;—I would say he loved her deeply, if I thought it possible that you could understand the word. When she was sacrificed, he was thoroughly assured of your guilt. Having lost her, he had but one object left in life, and that was to avenge her and destroy you.'

I saw the villain's nostrils rise and fall convulsively; but I saw no moving at his mouth.

'That man Meltham,' Beckwith steadily pursued, 'was as absolutely certain that you could never elude him in this world, if he devoted himself to your destruction with his utmost fidelity and earnestness, and if he divided the sacred duty with no other duty in life, as he was certain that in achieving it he would be a poor instrument in the hands of Providence, and would do well before Heaven in striking you out from among living men. I am that man, and I thank God that I have done my work!'

If Slinkton had been running for his life from swift-footed savages, a dozen miles, he could not have shown more emphatic signs of being oppressed at heart and labouring for breath, than he showed now, when he looked at the pursuer who had so relentlessly hunted him down.

'You never saw me under my right name before; you see me under my right name now. You shall see me once again in the body, when you are tried for your life. You shall see me once again in the spirit, when the cord is round your neck, and the crowd are crying against you!'

When Meltham had spoken these last words, the miscreant suddenly turned away his face, and seemed to strike his mouth with his open hand. At the same instant, the room was filled with a new and powerful odour, and, almost at the same instant, he broke into a crooked run, leap, start,—I have no name for the spasm,—and fell, with a dull weight that shook the heavy old doors and windows in their frames.

That was the fitting end of him.

When we saw that he was dead, we drew away from the room, and Meltham, giving me his hand, said, with a weary air,

'I have no more work on earth, my friend. But I shall see her again elsewhere.'

It was in vain that I tried to rally him. He might have saved her, he said; he had not saved her, and he reproached himself; he had lost her, and he was broken-hearted.

'The purpose that sustained me is over, Sampson, and there is nothing now to hold me to life. I am not fit for life; I am weak and spiritless; I have no hope and no object; my day is done.'

In truth, I could hardly have believed that the broken man who then spoke to me was the man who had so strongly and so differently impressed me when his purpose was before him. I used such entreaties with him, as I could; but he still said, and always said, in a patient, undemonstrative way,—nothing could avail him,—he was broken-hearted.

He died early in the next spring. He was buried by the side of the poor young lady for whom he had cherished those tender and unhappy regrets; and he left all he had to her sister. She lived to be a happy wife and mother; she married my sister's son, who succeeded poor Meltham; she is living now, and her children ride about the garden on my walking-stick when I go to see her.

35

THE TOXIN OF DEATH

Arthur B. Reeve

…Was she telling the truth? Would she stop at anything to avoid the scandal and disgrace of the charge of bigamy?…

The note of appeal in her tone was powerful, but I could not so readily shake off my first suspicions of the woman. Whether or not she convinced Kennedy, he did not show.

'I was only a young girl when I met Mr Thornton,' she raced on. 'I was not yet eighteen when we were married. Too late, I found out the curse of his life—and of mine. He was a drug fiend. From the very first life with him was insupportable. I stood it as long as I could, but when he beat me because he had no money to buy drugs, I left him. I gave myself up to my career on the stage. Later I heard that he was dead—a suicide. I worked, day and night, slaved, and rose in the profession—until, at last, I met Mr Pitts.'

She paused, and it was evident that it was with a struggle that she could talk so.

'Three months after I was married to him, Thornton suddenly reappeared, from the dead it seemed to me. He did not want me back. No, indeed. All he wanted was money. I gave him money, my own. money, for I made a great deal in my stage days. But his demands increased. To silence him I have paid him thousands. He squandered them faster than ever. And finally, when it became unbearable, I appealed to a friend. That friend has now succeeded in placing this man quietly in a sanitarium for the insane.'

'And the murder of the chef?' shot out Kennedy.

She looked from one to the other of us in alarm. 'Before God, I know no more of that than does Mr Pitts.'

Was she telling the truth? Would she stop at anything to avoid the scandal and disgrace of the charge of bigamy? Was there not something still that she was concealing? She took refuge in the last resort—tears.

Encouraging as it was to have made such progress, it did not seem to me that we were much nearer, after all, to the solution of the mystery. Kennedy, as usual, had nothing to say until he was absolutely sure of his ground. He spent the greater part of the next day hard at work over the minute investigations of his laboratory, leaving me to arrange the details of a meeting he planned for that night.

There were present Mr and Mrs Pitts, the former in charge of Dr Lord. The valet, Edward, was also there, and in a neighbouring room was Thornton in charge of two nurses from the sanitarium. Thornton was a sad wreck of a man now, whatever he might have been when his blackmail furnished him with an unlimited supply of his favourite drugs.

'Let us go back to the very start of the case,' began Kennedy when we had all assembled, 'the murder of the chef, Sam.'

It seemed that the mere sound of his voice electrified his little audience. I fancied a shudder passed over the slight form of Mrs Pitts, as she must have realised that this was the point where Kennedy had left off, in his questioning her the night before.

'There is,' he went on slowly, 'a blood test so delicate that one might almost say that he could identify a criminal by his very blood-crystals—the fingerprints, so to speak, of his blood. It was by means of these "haemoglobin clues" if I may call them so, that I was able to get on the right trail. For the fact is that a man's blood is not like that of any other living creature. Blood of different men, of men and women differ. I believe that in time we shall be able to refine this test to tell the exact individual, too.

'What is this principle? It is that the haemoglobin or red colouring-matter of the blood forms crystals. That has long been known, but working on this fact Dr Reichert and Professor Brown of the University of Pennsylvania have made some wonderful discoveries.

'We could distinguish human from animal blood before, it is true.

But the discovery of these two scientists takes us much further. By means of blood-crystals we can distinguish the blood of man from that of the animals and in addition that of white men from that of negroes and other races. It is often the only way of differentiating between various kinds of blood.

'The variations in crystals in the blood are in part of form and in part of molecular structure, the latter being discovered only by means of the polarising microscope. A blood-crystal is only one two-thousand-two-hundred-and-fiftieth of an inch in length and one nine-thousandth of an inch in breadth. And yet minute as these crystals are, this discovery is of immense medico-legal importance. Crime may now be traced by blood-crystals.'

He displayed on his table a number of enlarged micro-photographs. Some were labelled, 'Characteristic crystals of white man's blood'; others 'Crystallisation of negro blood'; still others, 'Blood-crystals of the cat'.

'I have here,' he resumed, after we had all examined the photographs and had seen that there was indeed a vast amount of difference, 'three characteristic kinds of crystals, all of which I found in the various spots in the kitchen of Mr Pitts. There were three kinds of blood, by the infallible Reichert test.'

I had been prepared for his discovery of two kinds, but three heightened the mystery still more.

'There was only a very little of the blood which was that of the poor, faithful, unfortunate Sam, the negro chef,' Kennedy went on. 'A little more, found far from his body, is that of a white person. But most of it is not human blood at all. It was the blood of a cat.'

The revelation was startling. Before any of us could ask, he hastened to explain.

'It was placed there by someone who wished to exaggerate the struggle in order to divert suspicion. That person had indeed been wounded slightly, but wished it to appear that the wounds were very serious. The fact of the matter is that the carving-knife is spotted deeply with blood, but it is not human blood. It is the blood of a cat. A few years ago even a scientific detective would have concluded that a fierce hand-to-hand struggle had been waged and that the murderer was, perhaps, fatally wounded. Now, another conclusion stands, proved infallibly by this Reichert test. The murderer was wounded, but not badly. That person even went out of the room and returned later, probably with a can of animal blood, sprinkled it about to give the appearance of a struggle, perhaps thought of preparing in this way a plea of self-defence. If that latter was the case, this Reichert test completely destroys it, clever though it was.' No one spoke, but the same thought was openly in all our minds. Who was this wounded criminal?

I asked myself the usual query of the lawyers and the detectives—Who would benefit most by the death of Pitts? There was but one answer, apparently, to that. It was Minna Pitts. Yet it was difficult for me to believe that a woman of her ordinary gentleness could be here tonight, faced even by so great exposure, yet be so solicitous for him as she had been and then at the same time be plotting against him. I gave it up, determining to let Kennedy unravel it in his own way.

Craig evidently had the same thought in his mind, however, for he continued: 'Was it a woman who killed the chef? No, for the third specimen of blood, that of the white person, was the blood of a man; not of a woman.'

Pitts had been following closely, his unnatural eyes now gleaming. 'You said he was wounded, you remember,' he interrupted, as if casting about in his mind to recall someone who bore a recent wound. 'Perhaps it was not a bad wound, but it was a wound nevertheless, and someone must have seen it, must know about it. It is not three days.'

Kennedy shook his head. It was a point that had bothered him a great deal.

'As to the wounds,' he added in a measured tone 'although this occurred scarcely three days ago, there is no person even remotely suspected of the crime who can be said to bear on his hands or face others than old scars of wounds.'

He paused. Then he shot out in quick staccato, 'Did you ever hear of Dr Carrel's most recent discovery of accelerating the healing of wounds so that those which under ordinary circumstances might take ten days to heal might be healed in twenty-four hours?'

Rapidly, now, he sketched the theory. 'If the factors that bring about the multiplication of cells and the growth of tissues were discovered, Dr Carrel said to himself, it would perhaps become possible to hasten artificially the process of repair of the body. Aseptic wounds could probably be made to cicatrise more rapidly. If the rate of reparation of tissue were hastened only ten times, a skin wound would heal in less than twenty-four hours and a fracture of the leg in four or five days.

'For five years Dr Carrel has been studying the subject, applying various extracts to wounded tissues. All of them increased the growth of connective tissue, but the degree of acceleration varied greatly. In some cases it was as high, as forty times the normal. Dr Carrel's dream of ten times the normal was exceeded by himself.'

Astounded as we were by this revelation, Kennedy did not seem to consider it as important as one that he was now hastening to show us. He took a few cubic centimetres of some culture which he had been preparing, placed it in a tube, and poured in eight or ten drops of sulphuric acid. He shook it.

'I have here a culture from some of the food that I found was being or had been prepared for Mr Pitts. It was in the icebox.'

Then he took another tube. 'This,' he remarked, 'is a one-to-one-thousand solution of sodium nitrite.'

He held it up carefully and poured three or four cubic centimetres of it into the first tube so that it ran carefully down the side in a manner such as to form a sharp line of contact between the heavier culture with the acid and the lighter nitrite solution.

'You see,' he said, 'the reaction is very clear cut if you do it this way. The ordinary method in the laboratory and the text-books is crude and uncertain.'

'What is it?' asked Pitts eagerly, leaning forward with unwonted strength and noting the pink colour that appeared at the junction of the two liquids, contrasting sharply with the portions above and below.

'The ring or contact test for indol,' Kennedy replied, with evident satisfaction. 'When the acid and the nitrites are mixed the colour reaction is unsatisfactory. The natural yellow tint masks that pink tint, or sometimes causes it to disappear, if the tube is shaken. But this is simple, clear, delicate—unescapable. There was indol in that food of yours, Mr Pitts.'

'Indol?' repeated Pitts.

'Is,' explained Kennedy, 'a chemical compound—one of the toxins secreted by intestinal bacteria and responsible for many of the symptoms of senility. It used to be thought that large doses of indol might be consumed with little or no effect on normal man, but now we know that headache, insomnia, confusion, irritability, decreased activity of the cells, and intoxication are possible from it. Comparatively small doses over a long time produce changes in organs that lead to serious results.

'It is,' went on Kennedy, as the full horror of the thing sank into our minds, 'the indol-and phenol-producing bacteria which are the undesirable citizens of the body, while the lactic-acid producing germs check the production of indol and phenol. In my tests here today, I injected four one-hundredths of a grain of indol into a guinea-pig. The animal had sclerosis or hardening of the aorta. The liver, kidneys, and supra-renals were affected, and there was a hardening of the brain. In short, there were all the symptoms of old age.'

We sat aghast. Indol! What black magic was this? Who put it in the food?

'It is present,' continued Craig, 'in much larger quantities than all the Metchnikoff germs could neutralise. What the chef was ordered to put into the food to benefit you, Mr Pitts, was rendered valueless, and a deadly poison was added by what another—'

Minna Pitts had been clutching for support at the arms of her chair as Kennedy proceeded. She now threw herself at the feet of Emery Pitts,

'Forgive me,' she sobbed. 'I can stand it no longer. I had tried to keep this thing about Thornton from you. I have tried to make you happy and well—oh—tried so hard, so faithfully. Yet that old skeleton of my past which I thought was buried would not stay buried. I have bought Thornton off again and again, with money—my money—only to find him threatening again. But about this other thing, this poison, I am as innocent, and I believe Thornton is as—'

Craig laid a gentle hand on her lips. She rose wildly and faced him in passionate appeal.

'Who—who is this Thornton?' demanded Emery Pitts.

Quickly, delicately, sparing her as much as he could, Craig hurried over our experiences.

'He is in the next room,' Craig went on, then facing Pitts added: 'With you alive, Emery Pitts, this blackmail of your wife might have gone on, although there was always the danger that you might hear of it—and do as I see you have already done—forgive, and plan to right the unfortunate mistake. But with you dead, this Thornton, or rather someone using him, might take away from Minna Pitts her whole interest in your estate, at a word. The law, or your heirs at law, would never forgive as you would.'

Pitts, long poisoned by the subtle microbic poison, stared at Kennedy as if dazed.

'Who was caught in your kitchen, Mr Pitts, and, to escape detection, killed your faithful chef and covered his own traces so cleverly?' rapped out Kennedy. 'Who would have known the new process of healing wounds? Who knew about the fatal properties of indol? Who was willing to forego a one-hundred-thousand-dollar prize in order to gain a fortune of many hundreds of thousands?'

Kennedy paused, then finished with irresistibly dramatic logic;

'Who else but the man who held the secret of Minna Pitts's past and power over her future so long as he could keep alive the unfortunate Thornton—the up-to-date doctor who substituted an elixir of death at night for the elixir of life prescribed for you by him in the daytime—Dr Lord.'

Kennedy had moved quietly toward the door. It was unnecessary. Dr Lord was cornered and knew it. He made no fight. In fact, instantly his keen mind was busy outlining his battle in court, relying on the conflicting testimony of hired experts.

'Minna,' murmured Pitts, falling back, exhausted by the excitement, on his pillows, 'Minna—forgive? What is there to forgive? The only thing to do is to correct. I shall be well—soon now—my dear. Then all will be straightened out.'

'Walter,' whispered Kennedy to me, 'while we are waiting, you can arrange to have Thornton cared for at Dr Hodge's Sanitarium.'

He handed me a card with the directions where to take the unfortunate man. When at last I had Thornton placed where no one else could do any harm through him, I hastened back to the laboratory.

Craig was still there, waiting alone.

'That Dr Lord will be a tough customer,' he remarked. 'Of course you're not interested in what happens in a case after we have caught the criminal. But that often is really only the beginning of the fight. We've got him safely lodged in the Tombs now, however.'

'I wish there was some elixir for fatigue,' I remarked, as we closed the laboratory that night.

'There is,' he replied. 'A homeopathic remedy—more fatigue.'

We started on our usual brisk roundabout walk to the apartment. But instead of going to bed, Kennedy drew a book from the bookcase.

'I shall read myself to sleep tonight,' he explained, settling deeply in his chair.

As for me, I went directly to my room, planning that tomorrow I would take several hours off and catch up in my notes.

That morning Kennedy was summoned downtown and had to interrupt more important duties in order to appear before Dr Leslie in the coroner's inquest over the death of the chef. Dr Lord was held for the Grand Jury, but it was not until nearly noon that Craig returned.

We were just about to go out to luncheon, when the door buzzer sounded.

'A note for Mr Kennedy,' announced a man in a police uniform, with a blue anchor edged with white on his coat sleeve.

Craig tore open the envelope quickly with his forefinger. Headed 'Harbour Police, Station No. 3, Staten Island,' was an urgent message from our old friend Deputy Commissioner O'Connor.

'I have taken personal charge of a case here that is sufficiently out of the ordinary to interest you,' I read when Kennedy tossed the note over to me and nodded to the man from the harbour squad to wait for us. 'The Curtis family wish to retain a private detective to work in conjunction with the police in investigating the death of Bertha Curtis, whose body was found this morning in the waters of Kill van Kull.'

Kennedy and I lost no time in starting downtown with the policeman who had brought the note.

The Curtises, as we knew, were among the prominent families of Manhattan and I recalled having heard that at one time Bertha Curtis had been an actress, in spite of the means and social position of her family, from whom she had become estranged as a result.

At the station of the harbour police, O'Connor and another man, who was in a state of extreme excitement, greeted us almost before we had landed.

'There have been some queer doings about here,' exclaimed the deputy as he grasped Kennedy's hand, 'but first of all let me introduce Mr Walker Curtis.'

In a lower tone as we walked up the dock O'Connor continued, 'He is the brother of the girl whose body the men in the launch at the station found in the Kill this morning. They thought at first that the girl had committed suicide, making it doubly sure by jumping into the water, but he will not believe it and—well, if you'll just come over with us to the local undertaking establishment, I'd like to have you take a look at the body and see if your opinion coincides with mine.

'Ordinarily,' pursued O'Connor, 'there isn't much romance in harbour police work nowadays, but in this case some other elements seem to be present which are not usually associated with violent deaths in the waters of the bay, and I have, as you will see, thought it necessary to take personal charge of the investigation.

'Now, to shorten the story as much as possible, Kennedy, you know of course that the legislature at the last session enacted laws prohibiting the sale of such drugs as opium, morphine, cocaine, chloral and others, under much heavier penalties than before. The Health authorities not long ago reported to us that dope was being sold almost openly, without orders from physicians, at several scores of places and we have begun a crusade for the enforcement of the law. Of course you know how prohibition works in many places and how the law is beaten. The dope fiends seem to be doing the same thing with this law.

'Of course nowadays everybody talks about a 'system' controlling everything, so I suppose people would say that there is a 'dope trust.' At any rate we have run up against at least a number of places that seem to be banded together in some way, from the lowest down in Chinatown to one very swell joint uptown around what the newspapers are calling 'Crime Square.' It is not that this place is pandering to criminals or the women of the Tenderloin that interests us so much as that its patrons are men and women of fashionable society whose jangled nerves seem to demand a strong narcotic.

'This particular place seems to be a headquarters for obtaining them, especially opium and its derivatives.

'One of the frequenters of the place was this unfortunate girl, Bertha Curtis. I have watched her go in and out myself, wild-eyed, nervous, mentally and physically wrecked for life. Perhaps twenty-five or thirty persons visit the place each day. It is run by a man known as 'Big Jack' Clendenin who was once an actor and, I believe, met and fascinated Miss Curtis during her brief career on the stage. He has an attendant there, a Jap, named Nichi Moto, who is a perfect enigma. I can't understand him on any reasonable theory. A long time ago we raided the place and packed up a lot of opium, pipes, material and other stuff. We found Clendenin there, this girl, several others, and the Jap. I never understood just how it was but somehow Clendenin got off with a nominal fine and a few days later opened up again. We were watching the place, getting ready to raid it again and present such evidence that Clendenin couldn't possibly beat it, when all of a sudden along came this—this tragedy.'

We had at last arrived at the private establishment which was doing duty as a morgue. The bedraggled form that had been bandied about by the tides all night lay covered up in the cold damp basement. Bertha Curtis had been a girl of striking beauty once. For a long time I gazed at the swollen features before I realised what it was that fascinated and puzzled me about her. Kennedy, however, after a casual glance had arrived at at least a part of her story.

'That girl,' he whispered to me so that her brother could not hear, 'has led a pretty fast life. Look at those nails, yellow and dark. It isn't a weak face, either. I wouldn't be surprised if the whole thing, the

Oriental glamour and all that, fascinated her as much as the drug.'

So far the case with its heartrending tragedy had all the earmarks of suicide.

36

THE X-RAY 'MOVIES'

Arthur B. Reeve

...another case before even this one is fairly cleaned up?...

Still holding Dana Phelps between us, we hurried toward the tomb and entered. While our attention had been diverted in the direction of the swamp, the body of Montague Phelps had been stolen.

Dana Phelps was still deliberately brushing off his clothes. Had he been in league with them, executing a flank movement to divert our attention? Or had it all been pure chance?

'Well?' demanded Andrews.

'Well?' replied Dana.

Kennedy said nothing, and I felt that, with our capture, the mystery seemed to have deepened rather than cleared.

As Andrews and Phelps faced each other, I noticed that the latter was now and then endeavouring to cover his wrist, where the dog had torn his coat sleeve.

'Are you hurt badly?' inquired Kennedy.

Dana said nothing, but backed away. Kennedy advanced, insisting on looking at the wounds. As he looked he disclosed a semicircle of marks.

'Not a dog bite,' he whispered, turning to me and fumbling in his pocket. 'Besides, those marks are a couple of days old. They have scabs on them.'

He had pulled out a pencil and a piece of paper, and, unknown to Phelps, was writing in the darkness. I leaned over. Near the point, in the tube through which the point for writing was, protruded a small accumulator and tiny electric lamp which threw a little disc of light, so small that it could be hidden by the hand, yet quite sufficient to guide Craig in moving the point of his pencil for the proper formation of whatever he was recording on the surface of the paper.

'An electric-light pencil,' he remarked laconically, in an undertone.

'Who were the others?' demanded Andrews of Dana.

There was a pause as though he were debating whether or not to answer at all. 'I don't know,' he said at length. 'I wish I did.'

'You don't know?' queried Andrews, with incredulity.

'No, I say I wish I did know. You and your dog interrupted me just as I was about to find out, too.'

We looked at each other in amazement. Andrews was frankly sceptical of the coolness of the young man. Kennedy said nothing for some moments.

'I see you don't want to talk,' he put in shortly. v 'Nothing to talk about,' grunted Dana, in disgust.

'Then why are you here?'

'Nothing but conjecture. No facts, only suspicions,' said Dana, half to himself.

'You expect us to believe that?' insinuated Andrews.

'I can't help what you believe. That is the fact.'

'And you were not with them?'

'No.'

'You'll be within call, if we let you go now, any time that we want you?' interrupted Kennedy, much to the surprise of Andrews.

'I shall stay in Woodbine as long as there is any hope of clearing up this case. If you want me, I suppose I shall have to stay anyhow, even if there is a clue somewhere else.'

'I'll take your word for it,' offered Kennedy.

'I'll give it.'

I must say that I rather liked the young chap, although I could make nothing out of him.

As Dana Phelps disappeared down the road, Andrews turned to Kennedy. 'What did you do that for?' he asked, half critically.

'Because we can watch him, anyway,' answered Craig, with a significant glance at the now empty casket. 'Have him shadowed,

Andrews. It may lead to something and it may not. But in any case don't let him get out of reach.'

'Here we are in a worse mystery than ever,' grumbled Andrews. 'We have caught a prisoner, but the body is gone, and we can't even show that he was an accomplice.'

'What were you writing?' I asked Craig, endeavouring to change the subject to one more promising.

'Just copying the peculiar shape of those marks on Phelps' arm. Perhaps we can improve on the finger-print method of identification. Those were the marks of human teeth.'

He was glancing casually at his sketch as he displayed it to us. I wondered whether he really expected to obtain proof of the identity of at least one of the ghouls by the tooth-marks.

'It shows eight teeth, one of them decayed,' he remarked. 'By the way, there's no use watching here any longer. I have some more work to do in the laboratory which will keep me another day. Tomorrow night I shall be ready. Andrews, in the mean time I leave the shadowing of Dana to you, and with the help of Jameson I want you to arrange to have all those connected with the case at my laboratory tomorrow night without fail.'

Andrews and I had to do some clever scheming to bring pressure to bear on the various persons interested to insure their attendance, now that Craig was ready to act. Of course there was no difficulty in getting Dana Phelps. Andrews's shadows reported nothing in his actions of the following day that indicated anything. Mrs Phelps came down to town by train and Doctor Forden motored in. Andrews even took the precaution to secure Shaughnessy and the trained nurse, Miss Tracy, who had been with Montague Phelps during his illness but had not contributed anything toward untangling the case. Andrews and myself completed the little audience.

We found Kennedy heating a large mass of some composition such as dentists use in taking impressions of the teeth.

'I shall be ready in a moment,' he excused himself, still bending over his Bunsen flame. 'By the way, Mr Phelps, if you will permit me.'

He had detached a wad of the softened material. Phelps, taken by surprise, allowed him to make an impression of his teeth, almost before he realised what Kennedy was doing. The precedent set, so to speak, Kennedy approached Doctor Forden. He demurred, but finally consented. Mrs Phelps followed, then the nurse, and even Shaughnessy.

With a quick glance at each impression, Kennedy laid them aside to harden.

'I am ready to begin,' he remarked at length, turning to a peculiar looking instrument, something like three telescopes pointing at a centre in which was a series of glass prisms.

'These five senses of ours are pretty dull detectives sometimes,' Kennedy began. 'But I find that when we are able to call in outside aid we usually find that there are no more mysteries.'

He placed something in a test-tube in line before one of the barrels of the telescopes, near a brilliant electric light.

'What do you see, Walter?' he asked, indicating an eyepiece.

I looked. 'A series of lines,' I replied. 'What is it?'

'That,' he explained, 'is a spectroscope, and those are the lines of the absorption spectrum. Each of those lines, by its presence, denotes a different substance. Now, on the pavement of the Phelps mausoleum I found, you will recall, some roundish spots. I have made a very diluted solution of them which is placed in this tube.

'The applicability of the spectroscope to the differentiation of various substances is too well known to need explanation. Its value lies in the exact nature of the evidence furnished. Even the very dilute solution which I have been able to make of the material scraped from these spots gives characteristic absorption bands between the D and E lines, as they are called. Their wave-lengths are between 5774 and 5390. It is such a distinct absorption spectrum that it is possible to determine with certainty that the fluid actually contains a certain substance, even though the microscope might fail to give sure proof. Blood—human blood—that was what those stains were.'

He paused. 'The spectra of the blood pigments,' he added, 'of the extremely minute quantities of blood and the decomposition products of haemoglobin in the blood are here infallibly shown, varying very distinctly with the chemical changes which the pigments may undergo.'

Whose blood was it? I asked myself. Was it of someone who had visited the tomb, who was surprised there or surprised someone else there? I was hardly ready for Kennedy's quick remark.

'There were two kinds of blood there. One was contained in the spots on the floor all about the mausoleum. There are marks on the arm of Dana Phelps which he probably might say were made by the teeth of my police-dog, Schaef. They are human tooth-marks, however. He was bitten by someone in a struggle. It was his blood on the floor of the mausoleum. Whose were the teeth?'

Kennedy fingered the now set impressions, then resumed: 'Before I answer that question, what else does the spectroscope show? I found some spots near the coffin, which has been broken open by a heavy object. It had slipped and had injured the body of Montague Phelps. From the injury some drops had oozed. My spectroscope tells me that that, too, is blood. The blood and other muscular and nervous fluids of the body had remained in an aqueous condition instead of becoming pectous. That is a remarkable circumstance.'

It flashed over me what Kennedy had been driving at in his inquiry regarding embalming. If the poisons of the embalming fluid had not been injected, he had now clear proof regarding anything his spectroscope discovered.

'I had expected to find a poison, perhaps an alkaloid,' he continued slowly, as he outlined his discoveries by the use of one of the most fascinating branches of modern science, spectroscopy. 'In cases of poisoning by these substances, the spectroscope often has obvious advantages over chemical methods, for minute amounts will produce a well-defined spectrum. The spectroscope 'spots' the substance, to use a police idiom, the moment the case is turned over to it. There was no poison there.' He had raised his voice to emphasise the startling revelation. 'Instead, I found an extraordinary amount of the substance and products of glycogen. The liver, where this substance is stored, is literally surcharged in the body of Phelps.'

He had started his moving-picture machine.

'Here I have one of the latest developments in the moving-picture art,' he resumed, 'an X-ray moving picture, a feat which was until recently visionary, a science now in its infancy, bearing the formidable names of biorontgenography, or kinematoradiography.'

Kennedy was holding his little audience breathless as he proceeded. I fancied I could see Anginette Phelps give a little shudder at the prospect of looking into the very interior of a human body. But she was pale with the fascination of it. Neither Forden nor the nurse looked to the right or to the left. Dana Phelps was open-eyed with wonder.

'In one X-ray photograph, or even in several,' continued Kennedy, 'it is difficult to discover slight motions. Not so in a moving picture. For instance, here I have a picture which will show you a living body in all its moving details.'

On the screen before us was projected a huge shadowgraph of a chest and abdomen. We could see the vertebrae of the spinal column, the ribs, and the various organs.

'It is difficult to get a series of photographs directly from a fluorescent screen,' Kennedy went on. 'I overcome the difficulty by having lenses of sufficient rapidity to photograph even faint images on that screen. It is better than the so-called serial method, by which a number of separate X-ray pictures are taken and then pieced together and rephotographed to make the film. I can focus the X-rays first on the screen by means of a special quartz objective which I have devised. Then I take the pictures.

'Here, you see, are the lungs in slow or rapid respiration. There is the rhythmically beating heart, distinctly pulsating in perfect outline. There is the liver, moving up and down with the diaphragm, the intestines, and the stomach. You can see the bones moving with the limbs, as well as the inner visceral life. All that is hidden to the eye by the flesh is now made visible in striking manner.'

Never have I seen an audience at the 'movies' so thrilled as we were now, as Kennedy swayed our interest at his will. I had been dividing my attention between Kennedy and the extraordinary beauty of the famous Russian dancer. I forgot Anginette Phelps entirely.

Kennedy placed another film in the holder.

'You are now looking into the body of Montague Phelps,' he announced suddenly.

We leaned forward eagerly. Mrs Phelps gave a half-suppressed gasp. What was the secret hidden in it?

There was the stomach, a curved sack something like a bagpipe or a badly made boot, with a tiny canal at the toe connecting it with the small intestine. There were the heart and lungs.

'I have rendered the stomach visible,' resumed Kennedy, 'made it 'metallic,' so to speak, by injecting a solution of bismuth in buttermilk, the usual method, by which it becomes more impervious to the X-rays and hence darker in the skiagraph. I took these pictures not at the rate of fourteen or so a second, like the others, but at intervals of a few seconds. I did that so that, when I run them off, I get a sort of compressed moving picture. What you see in a short space of time actually took much longer to occur. I could have either kind of picture, but I prefer the latter.

'For, you will take notice that there is movement here—of the heart, of the lungs, of the stomach—faint, imperceptible under ordinary circumstances, but nevertheless, movement.'

He was pointing at the lungs. 'A single peristaltic contraction takes place normally in a very few seconds. Here it takes minutes. And the stomach. Notice what the bismuth mixture shows. There is a very slow series of regular wave-contractions from the fundus to the pylorus. Ordinarily one wave takes ten seconds to traverse it; here it is so slow as almost to be unnoticed.'

What was the implication of his startling, almost gruesome, discovery? I saw it clearly, yet hung on his words, afraid to admit even to myself the logical interpretation of what I saw.

'Reconstruct the case,' continued Craig excitedly. 'Mr Phelps, always a bon vivant and now so situated by marriage that he must be so, comes back to America to find his personal fortune—gone.

'What was left? He did as many have done. He took out a new large policy on his life. How was he to profit by it? Others have committed suicide, have died to win. Cases are common now where men have ended their lives under such circumstances by swallowing bichloride-of-mercury tablets, a favourite method, it seems, lately.

'But Phelps did not want to die to win. Life was too sweet to him. He had another scheme.' Kennedy dropped his voice.

'One of the most fascinating problems in speculation as to the future of the race under the influence of science is that of suspended animation. The usual attitude is one of reserve or scepticism. There is no necessity for it. Records exist of cases where vital functions have been practically suspended, with no food and little air. Every day science is getting closer to the control of metabolism. In the trance the body functions are so slowed as to simulate death. You have heard of the Indian fakirs who bury themselves alive and are dug up days later? You have doubted it. But there is nothing improbable in it.

'Experiments have been made with toads which have been imprisoned in porous rock where they could get the necessary air. They have lived for months in a stupor. In impervious rock they have died. Frozen fish can revive; bears and other animals hibernate. There are all gradations from ordinary sleep to the torpor of death. Science can slow down almost to a standstill the vital processes so that excretions disappear and respiration and heart-beat are almost nil.

'What the Indian fakir does in a cataleptic condition may be duplicated. It is not incredible that they may possess some vegetable extract by which they perform their as yet unexplained feats of prolonged living burial. For, if an animal free from disease is subjected to the action of some chemical and physical agencies which have the property of reducing to the extreme limit the motor forces and nervous stimulus, the body of even a warm-blooded animal may be brought down to a condition so closely resembling death that the most careful examination may fail to detect any signs of life. The heart will continue working regularly at low tension, supplying muscles and other parts with sufficient blood to sustain molecular life, and the stomach would naturally react to artificial stimulus. At any time before decomposition of tissue has set in, the heart might be made to resume its work and life come back.

'Phelps had travelled extensively. In Siberia he must undoubtedly have heard of the Buriats, a tribe of natives who hibernate, almost like the animals, during the winters, succumbing to a long sleep known as the "leshka". He must have heard of the experiments of Professor

Bakhmetieff, who studied the Buriats and found that they subsisted on foods rich in glycogen, a substance in the liver which science has discovered makes possible life during suspended animation. He must have heard of "anabiose" as the famous Russian calls it, by which consciousness can be totally removed and respiration and digestion cease almost completely.'

'But—the body—is gone!' someone interrupted. I turned. It was Dana Phelps, now leaning forward in wide-eyed excitement.

'Yes,' exclaimed Craig. 'Time was passing rapidly. The insurance had not been paid. He had expected to be revived and to disappear with Anginette Phelps long before this. Should the confederates of Phelps wait? They did not dare. To wait longer might be to sacrifice him, if indeed they had not taken a long chance already. Besides, you yourself had your suspicions and had written the insurance company hinting at murder.'

Dana nodded, involuntarily confessing.

'You were watching them, as well as the insurance investigator, Mr Andrews. It was an awful dilemma. What was to be done? He must be resuscitated at any risk.

'Ah—an idea! Rifle the grave—that was the way to solve it. That would still leave it possible to collect the insurance, too. The blackmail letter about the five thousand dollars was only a blind, to lay on the mythical Black Hand the blame for the desecration. Brought into light, humidity, and warmth, the body would recover consciousness and the life-functions resume their normal state after the anabiotic coma into which Phelps had drugged himself.

'But the very first night the supposed ghouls were discovered. Dana Phelps, already suspicious regarding the death of his brother, wondering at the lack of sentiment which Mrs Phelps showed, since she felt that her husband was not really dead—Dana was there. His suspicions were confirmed, he thought. Montague had been, in reality, murdered, and his murderers were now making away with the evidence. He fought with the ghouls, yet apparently, in the darkness, he did not discover their identity. The struggle was bitter, but they were two to one. Dana was bitten by one of them. Here are the marks of teeth—teeth—of a woman.'

Anginette Phelps was sobbing convulsively. She had risen and was facing Doctor Forden with outstretched hands.

'Tell them!' she cried wildly.

Forden seemed to have maintained his composure only by a superhuman effort.

'The—body is—at my office,' he said, as we faced him with deathlike stillness. 'Phelps had told us to get him within ten days. We did get him, finally. Gentlemen, you, who were seeking murderers, are, in effect, murderers. You kept us away two days too long. It was too late. We could not revive him. Phelps is really dead!'

'The deuce!' exclaimed Andrews, 'the policy is incontestible!'

As he turned to us in disgust, his eyes fell on Anginette Phelps, sobered down by the terrible tragedy and nearly a physical wreck from real grief.

'Still,' he added hastily, 'we'll pay without a protest.'

She did not even hear him. It seemed that the butterfly in her was crushed, as Dr Forden and Miss Tracy gently led her away.

They had all left, and the laboratory was again in its normal state of silence, except for the occasional step of Kennedy as he stowed away the apparatus he had used.

'I must say that I was one of the most surprised in the room at the outcome of that case,' I confessed at length. 'I fully expected an arrest.'

He said nothing, but went on methodically restoring his apparatus to its proper place.

'What a peculiar life you lead, Craig,' I pursued reflectively. 'One day it is a case that ends with such a bright spot in our lives as the recollection of the Shirleys; the next goes to the other extreme of gruesomeness and one can hardly think about it without a shudder. And then, through it all, you go with the high speed power of a racing motor.'

'That last case appealed to me, like many others,' he ruminated, 'just because it was so unusual, so gruesome, as you call it.'

He reached into the pocket of his coat, hung over the back of a chair.

'Now, here's another most unusual case, apparently. It begins, really, at the other end, so to speak, with the conviction, begins at the very place where we detectives send a man as the last act of our little dramas.'

'What?' I gasped, 'another case before even this one is fairly cleaned up? Craig—you are impossible. You get worse instead of better.'

'Read it,' he said, simply. Kennedy handed me a letter in the angular hand affected by many women. It was dated at Sing Sing, or rather Ossining. Craig seemed to appreciate the surprise which my face must have betrayed at the curious combination of circumstances.

'Nearly always there is the wife or mother of a condemned man who lives in the shadow of the prison,' he remarked quietly, adding, 'where she can look down at the grim walls, hoping and fearing.'

I said nothing, for the letter spoke for itself.

I have read of your success as a scientific detective and hope that you will pardon me for writing to you, but it is a matter of life or death for one who is dearer to me than all the world.

Perhaps you recall reading of the trial and conviction of my husband, Sanford Godwin, at East Point. The case did not attract much attention in New York papers, although he was defended by an able lawyer from the city.

Since the trial, I have taken up my residence here in Ossining in order to be near him. As I write I can see the cold, gray walls of the state prison that holds all that is dear to me. Day after day, I have watched and waited, hoped against hope. The courts are so slow, and lawyers are so technical. There have been executions since I came here, too and I shudder at them. Will this appeal be denied, also?

My husband was accused of murdering by poison—hemlock, they alleged—his adoptive parent, the retired merchant, Parker Godwin, whose family name he took when he was a boy. After the death of the old man, a later will was discovered in which my husband's inheritance was reduced to a small annuity. The other heirs, the Elmores, asserted, and the state made out its case on the assumption, that the new will furnished a motive for killing old Mr Godwin, and that only by accident had it been discovered.

Sanford is innocent. He could not have done it. It is not in him to do such a thing. I am only a woman, but about some things I know more than all the lawyers and scientists, and I KNOW that he is innocent.

I cannot write all. My heart is too full. Cannot you come and advise me? Even if you cannot take up the case to which I have devoted my life, tell me what to do. I am enclosing a cheque for expenses, all I can spare at present.

Sincerely yours,
NELLA GODWIN

'Are you going?' I asked, watching Kennedy as he tapped the check thoughtfully on the desk.

'I can hardly resist an appeal like that,' he replied, absently replacing the cheque in the envelope with the letter.

37

THE MAN WITH THE TWISTED LIP

Arthur Conan Doyle

...A broad wheal from an old scar ran right across it from eye to chin, and by its contraction had turned up one side of the upper lip...

Isa Whitney, brother of the late Elias Whitney, D.D., Principal of the Theological College of St. George's, was much addicted to opium. The habit grew upon him, as I understand, from some foolish freak when he was at college; for having read De Quincey's description of his dreams and sensations, he had drenched his tobacco with laudanum in an attempt to produce the same effects. He found, as so many more have done, that the practice is easier to attain than to get rid of, and for many years he continued to be a slave to the drug, an object of mingled horror and pity to his friends and relatives. I can see him now, with yellow, pasty face, drooping lids, and pin-point pupils, all huddled in a chair, the wreck and ruin of a noble man.

One night—it was in June, '89—there came a ring to my bell, about the hour when a man gives his first yawn and glances at the clock. I sat up in my chair, and my wife laid her needle-work down in her lap and made a little face of disappointment.

'A patient!' said she. 'You'll have to go out.'

I groaned, for I was newly come back from a weary day.

We heard the door open, a few hurried words, and then quick steps upon the linoleum. Our own door flew open, and a lady, clad in some dark-coloured stuff, with a black veil, entered the room.

'You will excuse my calling so late,' she began, and then, suddenly losing her self-control, she ran forward, threw her arms about my wife's neck, and sobbed upon her shoulder. 'Oh, I'm in such trouble!' she cried; 'I do so want a little help.'

'Why,' said my wife, pulling up her veil, 'it is Kate Whitney. How you startled me, Kate! I had not an idea who you were when you came in.'

'I didn't know what to do, so I came straight to you.' That was always the way. Folk who were in grief came to my wife like birds to a light-house.

'It was very sweet of you to come. Now, you must have some wine and water, and sit here comfortably and tell us all about it. Or should you rather that I sent James off to bed?'

'Oh, no, no! I want the doctor's advice and help, too. It's about Isa. He has not been home for two days. I am so frightened about him!'

It was not the first time that she had spoken to us of her husband's trouble, to me as a doctor, to my wife as an old friend and school companion. We soothed and comforted her by such words as we could find. Did she know where her husband was? Was it possible that we could bring him back to her?

It seems that it was. She had the surest information that of late he had, when the fit was on him, made use of an opium den in the farthest east of the City. Hitherto his orgies had always been confined to one day, and he had come back, twitching and shattered, in the evening. But now the spell had been upon him eight-and-forty hours, and he lay there, doubtless among the dregs of the docks, breathing in the poison or sleeping off the effects. There he was to be found, she was sure of it, at the Bar of Gold, in Upper Swandam Lane. But what was she to do? How could she, a young and timid woman, make her way into such a place and pluck her husband out from among the ruffians who surrounded him?

There was the case, and of course there was but one way out of it. Might I not escort her to this place? And then, as a second thought, why should she come at all? I was Isa Whitney's medical adviser, and as such I had influence over him. I could manage it better if I were alone. I promised her on my word that I would send him home in a cab within two hours if he were indeed at the address which she had given me. And so in ten minutes I had left my armchair and cheery sitting-room behind me, and was speeding eastward in a hansom on a strange errand, as it seemed to me at the time, though the future only could show how strange it was to be.

But there was no great difficulty in the first stage of my adventure. Upper Swandam Lane is a vile alley lurking behind the high wharves which line the north side of the river to the east of London Bridge. Between a slop-shop and a gin-shop, approached by a steep flight of steps leading down to a black gap like the mouth of a cave, I found the den of which I was in search. Ordering my cab to wait, I passed down the steps, worn hollow in the centre by the ceaseless tread of drunken feet; and by the light of a flickering oil-lamp above the door I found the latch and made my way into a long, low room, thick and heavy with the brown opium smoke, and terraced with wooden berths, like the forecastle of an emigrant ship.

Through the gloom one could dimly catch a glimpse of bodies lying in strange fantastic poses, bowed shoulders, bent knees, heads thrown back, and chins pointing upward, with here and there a dark, lack-lustre eye turned upon the newcomer. Out of the black shadows there glimmered little red circles of light, now bright, now faint, as the burning poison waxed or waned in the bowls of the metal pipes. The most lay silent, but some muttered to themselves, and others talked together in a strange, low, monotonous voice, their conversation coming in gushes, and then suddenly tailing off into silence, each mumbling out his own thoughts and paying little heed to the words of his neighbour. At the farther end was a small brazier of burning charcoal, beside which on a three-legged wooden stool there sat a tall, thin old man, with his jaw resting upon his two fists, and his elbows upon his knees, staring into the fire.

As I entered, a sallow Malay attendant had hurried up with a pipe for me and a supply of the drug, beckoning me to an empty berth.

'Thank you. I have not come to stay,' said I. 'There is a friend of mine here, Mr Isa Whitney, and I wish to speak with him.'

There was a movement and an exclamation from my right, and peering through the gloom I saw Whitney, pale, haggard, and unkempt, staring out at me.

'My God! It's Watson,' said he. He was in a pitiable state of reaction, with every nerve in a twitter. 'I say, Watson, what o'clock is it?'

'Nearly eleven.'

'Of what day?'

'Of Friday, June 19th.'

'Good heavens! I thought it was Wednesday. It is Wednesday. What d'you want to frighten the chap for?' He sank his face onto his arms and began to sob in a high treble key.

'I tell you that it is Friday, man. Your wife has been waiting this two days for you. You should be ashamed of yourself!'

'So I am. But you've got mixed, Watson, for I have only been here a few hours, three pipes, four pipes—I forget how many. But I'll go home with you. I wouldn't frighten Kate—poor little Kate. Give me your hand! Have you a cab?'

'Yes, I have one waiting.'

'Then I shall go in it. But I must owe something. Find what I owe, Watson. I am all off colour. I can do nothing for myself.'

I walked down the narrow passage between the double row of sleepers, holding my breath to keep out the vile, stupefying fumes of the drug, and looking about for the manager. As I passed the tall man who sat by the brazier I felt a sudden pluck at my skirt, and a low voice whispered, 'Walk past me, and then look back at me.' The words fell quite distinctly upon my ear. I glanced down. They could only have come from the old man at my side, and yet he sat now as absorbed as ever, very thin, very wrinkled, bent with age, an opium pipe dangling down from between his knees, as though it had dropped in sheer lassitude from his fingers. I took two steps forward and looked back. It took all my self-control to prevent me from breaking out into a cry of astonishment. He had turned his back so that none could see him but I. His form had filled out, his wrinkles were gone, the dull eyes had regained their fire, and there, sitting by the fire and grinning at my surprise, was none other than Sherlock Holmes. He made a slight motion to me to approach him, and instantly, as he turned his face half round to the company once more, subsided into a doddering, loose-lipped senility.

'Holmes!' I whispered, 'what on earth are you doing in this den?'

'As low as you can,' he answered; 'I have excellent ears. If you would have the great kindness to get rid of that sottish friend of yours I should be exceedingly glad to have a little talk with you.'

'I have a cab outside.'

'Then pray send him home in it. You may safely trust him, for he appears to be too limp to get into any mischief. I should recommend you also to send a note by the cabman to your wife to say that you have thrown in your lot with me. If you will wait outside, I shall be with you in five minutes.'

It was difficult to refuse any of Sherlock Holmes's requests, for they were always so exceedingly definite, and put forward with such a quiet air of mastery. I felt, however, that when Whitney was once confined in the cab my mission was practically accomplished; and for the rest, I could not wish anything better than to be associated with my friend in one of those singular adventures which were the normal condition of his existence. In a few minutes I had written my note, paid Whitney's bill, led him out to the cab, and seen him driven through the darkness. In a very short time a decrepit figure had emerged from the opium den, and I was walking down the street with Sherlock Holmes. For two streets he shuffled along with a bent back and an uncertain foot. Then, glancing quickly round, he straightened himself out and burst into a hearty fit of laughter.

'I suppose, Watson,' said he, 'that you imagine that I have added opium-smoking to cocaine injections, and all the other little weaknesses on which you have favoured me with your medical views.'

'I was certainly surprised to find you there.'

'But not more so than I to find you.'

'I came to find a friend.'

'And I to find an enemy.'

'An enemy?'

'Yes; one of my natural enemies, or, shall I say, my natural prey. Briefly, Watson, I am in the midst of a very remarkable inquiry, and I have hoped to find a clue in the incoherent ramblings of these sots, as I have done before now. Had I been recognized in that den my life would not have been worth an hour's purchase; for I have used it before now for my own purposes, and the rascally Lascar who runs it has sworn to have vengeance upon me. There is a trap-door at the back of that building, near the corner of Paul's Wharf, which could tell some strange tales of what has passed through it upon the moonless nights.'

'What! You do not mean bodies?'

'Ay, bodies, Watson. We should be rich men if we had 1000 pounds for every poor devil who has been done to death in that den. It is the vilest murder-trap on the whole riverside, and I fear that Neville St. Clair has entered it never to leave it more. But our trap should be here.' He put his two forefingers between his teeth and whistled shrilly—a signal which was answered by a similar whistle from the distance, followed shortly by the rattle of wheels and the clink of horses' hoofs.

'Now, Watson,' said Holmes, as a tall dog-cart dashed up through the gloom, throwing out two golden tunnels of yellow light from its side lanterns. 'You'll come with me, won't you?'

'If I can be of use.'

'Oh, a trusty comrade is always of use; and a chronicler still more so. My room at The Cedars is a double-bedded one.'

'The Cedars?'

'Yes; that is Mr St. Clair's house. I am staying there while I conduct the inquiry.'

'Where is it, then?'

'Near Lee, in Kent. We have a seven-mile drive before us.'

'But I am all in the dark.'

'Of course you are. You'll know all about it presently. Jump up here. All right, John; we shall not need you. Here's half a crown. Look out for me tomorrow, about eleven. Give her her head. So long, then!'

He flicked the horse with his whip, and we dashed away through the endless succession of sombre and deserted streets, which widened gradually, until we were flying across a broad balustraded bridge, with the murky river flowing sluggishly beneath us. Beyond lay another dull wilderness of bricks and mortar, its silence broken only by the heavy, regular footfall of the policeman, or the songs and shouts of some belated party of revellers. A dull wrack was drifting slowly across the sky, and a star or two twinkled dimly here and there through the rifts of the clouds. Holmes drove in silence, with his head sunk upon his breast, and the air of a man who is lost in thought, while I sat beside him, curious to learn what this new quest might be which seemed to tax his powers so sorely, and yet afraid to break in upon the current of his thoughts. We had driven several miles, and were beginning to get to the fringe of the belt of suburban villas, when he shook himself, shrugged his shoulders, and lit up his pipe with the air of a man who has satisfied himself that he is acting for the best.

'You have a grand gift of silence, Watson,' said he. 'It makes you quite invaluable as a companion. 'Pon my word, it is a great thing for me to have someone to talk to, for my own thoughts are not over-pleasant. I was wondering what I should say to this dear little woman tonight when she meets me at the door.'

'You forget that I know nothing about it.'

'I shall just have time to tell you the facts of the case before we get to Lee. It seems absurdly simple, and yet, somehow I can get nothing to go upon. There's plenty of thread, no doubt, but I can't get the end of it into my hand. Now, I'll state the case clearly and concisely to you, Watson, and maybe you can see a spark where all is dark to me.'

'Proceed, then.'

'Some years ago—to be definite, in May, 1884—there came to Lee a gentleman, Neville St. Clair by name, who appeared to have plenty of money. He took a large villa, laid out the grounds very nicely, and lived generally in good style. By degrees he made friends in the neighbourhood, and in 1887 he married the daughter of a local brewer, by whom he now has two children. He had no occupation, but was interested in several companies and went into town as a rule in the morning, returning by the 5:14 from Cannon Street every night. Mr St. Clair is now thirty-seven years of age, is a man of temperate habits, a good husband, a very affectionate father, and a man who is popular with all who know him. I may add that his whole debts at the present moment, as far as we have been able to ascertain amount to 88 pounds 10s., while he has 220 pounds standing to his credit in the Capital and Counties Bank. There is no reason, therefore, to think that money troubles have been weighing upon his mind.

'Last Monday Mr Neville St. Clair went into town rather earlier than usual, remarking before he started that he had two important commissions to perform, and that he would bring his little boy home a box of bricks. Now, by the merest chance, his wife received a telegram upon this same Monday, very shortly after his departure, to the effect that a small parcel of considerable value which she had been expecting was waiting for her at the offices of the Aberdeen Shipping Company. Now, if you are well up in your London, you will know that the office of the company is in Fresno Street, which branches out of Upper Swandam Lane, where you found me tonight. Mrs St. Clair had her lunch, started for the City, did some shopping, proceeded to the company's office, got her packet, and found herself at exactly 4:35 walking through Swandam Lane on her way back to the station. Have you followed me so far?'

'It is very clear.'

'If you remember, Monday was an exceedingly hot day, and Mrs St. Clair walked slowly, glancing about in the hope of seeing a cab, as she did not like the neighbourhood in which she found herself. While she was walking in this way down Swandam Lane, she suddenly heard an ejaculation or cry, and was struck cold to see her husband looking down at her and, as it seemed to her, beckoning to her from a second-floor window. The window was open, and she distinctly saw his face, which she describes as being terribly agitated. He waved his hands frantically to her, and then vanished from the window so suddenly that it seemed to her that he had been plucked back by some irresistible force from behind. One singular point which struck her quick feminine eye was that although he wore some dark coat, such as he had started to town in, he had on neither collar nor necktie.

'Convinced that something was amiss with him, she rushed down the steps—for the house was none other than the opium den in which you found me tonight—and running through the front room she attempted to ascend the stairs which led to the first floor. At the foot of the stairs, however, she met this Lascar scoundrel of whom I have spoken, who thrust her back and, aided by a Dane, who acts as assistant there, pushed her out into the street. Filled with the most maddening doubts and fears, she rushed down the lane and, by rare good-fortune, met in Fresno Street a number of constables with an inspector, all on their way to their beat. The inspector and two men accompanied her back, and in spite of the continued resistance of the proprietor, they made their way to the room in which Mr St. Clair had last been seen. There was no sign of him there. In fact, in the whole of that floor there was no one to be found save a crippled wretch of hideous aspect, who, it seems, made his home there. Both he and the Lascar stoutly swore that no one else had been in the front room during the afternoon. So determined was their denial that the inspector was staggered, and had almost come to believe that Mrs St. Clair had been deluded when, with a cry, she sprang at a small deal box which lay upon the table and tore the lid from it. Out there fell a cascade of children's bricks. It was the toy which he had promised to bring home.

'This discovery, and the evident confusion which the cripple showed, made the inspector realize that the matter was serious. The rooms were carefully examined, and results all pointed to an abominable crime. The front room was plainly furnished as a sitting-room and led into a small bedroom, which looked out upon the back of one of the wharves. Between the wharf and the bedroom window is a narrow strip, which is dry at low tide but is covered at high tide with at least four and a half feet of water. The bedroom window was a broad one and opened from below. On examination traces of blood were to be seen upon the windowsill, and several scattered drops were visible upon the wooden floor of the bedroom. Thrust away behind a curtain in the front room were all the clothes of Mr Neville St. Clair, with the exception of his coat. His boots, his socks, his hat, and his watch—all were there. There were no signs of violence upon any of these garments, and there were no other traces of Mr Neville St. Clair. Out of the window he must apparently have gone for no other exit could be discovered, and the ominous bloodstains upon the sill gave little promise that he could save himself by swimming, for the tide was at its very highest at the moment of the tragedy.

'And now as to the villains who seemed to be immediately implicated in the matter. The Lascar was known to be a man of the vilest antecedents, but as, by Mrs St. Clair's story, he was known to have been at the foot of the stair within a very few seconds of her husband's appearance at the window, he could hardly have been more than an accessory to the crime. His defense was one of absolute ignorance, and he protested that he had no knowledge as to the doings of Hugh Boone, his lodger, and that he could not account in any way for the presence of the missing gentleman's clothes.

'So much for the Lascar manager. Now for the sinister cripple who lives upon the second floor of the opium den, and who was certainly the last human being whose eyes rested upon Neville St. Clair. His name is Hugh Boone, and his hideous face is one which is familiar to every man who goes much to the City. He is a professional beggar, though in order to avoid the police regulations he pretends to a small trade in wax vestas. Some little distance down Threadneedle Street, upon the left-hand side, there is, as you may have remarked, a small angle in the wall. Here it is that this creature takes his daily seat, cross-legged with his tiny stock of matches on his lap, and as he is a piteous spectacle a small rain of charity descends into the greasy leather cap which lies upon the pavement beside him. I have watched the fellow more than once before ever I thought of making his professional acquaintance, and I have been surprised at the harvest which he has reaped in a short time. His appearance, you see, is so remarkable that no one can pass him without observing him. A shock of orange hair, a pale face disfigured by a horrible scar, which, by its contraction, has turned up the outer edge of his upper lip, a bulldog chin, and a pair of very penetrating dark eyes, which present a singular contrast to the colour of his hair, all mark him out from amid the common crowd of mendicants and so, too, does his wit, for he is ever ready with a reply to any piece of chaff which may be thrown at him by the passers-by. This is the man whom we now learn to have been the lodger at the opium den, and to have been the last man to see the gentleman of whom we are in quest.'

'But a cripple!' said I. 'What could he have done single-handed against a man in the prime of life?'

'He is a cripple in the sense that he walks with a limp; but in other respects he appears to be a powerful and well-nurtured man. Surely your medical experience would tell you, Watson, that weakness in one limb is often compensated for by exceptional strength in the others.'

'Pray continue your narrative.'

'Mrs St. Clair had fainted at the sight of the blood upon the window, and she was escorted home in a cab by the police, as her presence could be of no help to them in their investigations. Inspector Barton, who had charge of the case, made a very careful examination of the premises, but without finding anything which threw any light upon the matter. One mistake had been made in not arresting Boone instantly, as he was allowed some few minutes during which he might have communicated with his friend the Lascar, but this fault was soon remedied, and he was seized and searched, without anything being found which could incriminate him. There were, it is true, some blood-stains upon his right shirt-sleeve, but he pointed to his ring-finger, which had been cut near the nail, and explained that the bleeding came from there, adding that he had been to the window not long before, and that the stains which had been observed there came doubtless from the same source. He denied strenuously having ever seen Mr Neville St. Clair and swore that the presence of the clothes in his room was as much a mystery to him as to the police. As to Mrs St. Clair's assertion that she had actually seen her husband at the window, he declared that she must have been either mad or dreaming. He was removed, loudly protesting, to the police-station, while the inspector remained upon the premises in the hope that the ebbing tide might afford some fresh clew.

'And it did, though they hardly found upon the mud-bank what they had feared to find. It was Neville St. Clair's coat, and not Neville St. Clair, which lay uncovered as the tide receded. And what do you think they found in the pockets?'

'I cannot imagine.'

'No, I don't think you would guess. Every pocket stuffed with pennies and half-pennies—421 pennies and 270 half-pennies. It was no wonder that it had not been swept away by the tide. But a human body is a different matter. There is a fierce eddy between the wharf and the house. It seemed likely enough that the weighted coat had remained when the stripped body had been sucked away into the river.'

'But I understand that all the other clothes were found in the room. Would the body be dressed in a coat alone?'

'No, sir, but the facts might be met speciously enough. Suppose that this man Boone had thrust Neville St. Clair through the window, there is no human eye which could have seen the deed. What would he do then? It would of course instantly strike him that he must get rid of the tell-tale garments. He would seize the coat, then, and be in the act of throwing it out, when it would occur to him that it would swim and not sink. He has little time, for he has heard the scuffle downstairs when the wife tried to force her way up, and perhaps he has already heard from his Lascar confederate that the police are hurrying up the street. There is not an instant to be lost. He rushes to some secret hoard, where he has accumulated the fruits of his beggary, and he stuffs all the coins upon which he can lay his hands into the pockets to make sure of the coat's sinking. He throws it out, and would have done the same with the other garments had not he heard the rush of steps below, and only just had time to close the window when the police appeared.'

'It certainly sounds feasible.'

'Well, we will take it as a working hypothesis for want of a better. Boone, as I have told you, was arrested and taken to the station, but it could not be shown that there had ever before been anything against him. He had for years been known as a professional beggar, but his life appeared to have been a very quiet and innocent one. There the matter stands at present, and the questions which have to be solved—what Neville St. Clair was doing in the opium den, what happened to him when there, where is he now, and what Hugh Boone had to do with his disappearance—are all as far from a solution as ever. I confess that I cannot recall any case within my experience which looked at the first glance so simple and yet which presented such difficulties.'

While Sherlock Holmes had been detailing this singular series of events, we had been whirling through the outskirts of the great town until the last straggling houses had been left behind, and we rattled along with a country hedge upon either side of us. Just as he finished, however, we drove through two scattered villages, where a few lights still glimmered in the windows.

'We are on the outskirts of Lee,' said my companion. 'We have touched on three English counties in our short drive, starting in Middlesex, passing over an angle of Surrey, and ending in Kent. See that light among the trees? That is The Cedars, and beside that lamp sits a woman whose anxious ears have already, I have little doubt, caught the clink of our horse's feet.'

'But why are you not conducting the case from Baker Street?' I asked.

'Because there are many inquiries which must be made out here. Mrs St. Clair has most kindly put two rooms at my disposal, and you may rest assured that she will have nothing but a welcome for my friend and colleague. I hate to meet her, Watson, when I have no news of her husband. Here we are. Whoa, there, whoa!'

We had pulled up in front of a large villa which stood within its own grounds. A stable-boy had run out to the horse's head, and springing down, I followed Holmes up the small, winding gravel-drive which led to the house. As we approached, the door flew open, and a little blonde woman stood in the opening, clad in some sort of light mousseline de soie, with a touch of fluffy pink chiffon at her neck and wrists. She stood with her figure outlined against the flood of light, one hand upon the door, one half-raised in her eagerness, her body slightly bent, her head and face protruded, with eager eyes and parted lips, a standing question.

'Well?' she cried, 'well?' And then, seeing that there were two of us, she gave a cry of hope which sank into a groan as she saw that my companion shook his head and shrugged his shoulders.

'No good news?'

'None.'

'No bad?'

'No.'

'Thank God for that. But come in. You must be weary, for you have had a long day.'

'This is my friend, Dr Watson. He has been of most vital use to me in several of my cases, and a lucky chance has made it possible for me to bring him out and associate him with this investigation.'

'I am delighted to see you,' said she, pressing my hand warmly. 'You will, I am sure, forgive anything that may be wanting in our arrangements, when you consider the blow which has come so suddenly upon us.'

'My dear madam,' said I, 'I am an old campaigner, and if I were not I can very well see that no apology is needed. If I can be of any assistance, either to you or to my friend here, I shall be indeed happy.'

'Now, Mr Sherlock Holmes,' said the lady as we entered a well-lit dining-room, upon the table of which a cold supper had been laid out, 'I should very much like to ask you one or two plain questions, to which I beg that you will give a plain answer.'

'Certainly, madam.'

'Do not trouble about my feelings. I am not hysterical, nor given to fainting. I simply wish to hear your real, real opinion.'

'Upon what point?'

'In your heart of hearts, do you think that Neville is alive?'

Sherlock Holmes seemed to be embarrassed by the question. 'Frankly, now!' she repeated, standing upon the rug and looking keenly down at him as he leaned back in a basket-chair.

'Frankly, then, madam, I do not.'

'You think that he is dead?'

'I do.'

'Murdered?'

'I don't say that. Perhaps.'

'And on what day did he meet his death?'

'On Monday.'

'Then perhaps, Mr Holmes, you will be good enough to explain how it is that I have received a letter from him today.'

Sherlock Holmes sprang out of his chair as if he had been galvanized.

'What!' he roared.

'Yes, today.' She stood smiling, holding up a little slip of paper in the air.

'May I see it?'

'Certainly.'

He snatched it from her in his eagerness, and smoothing it out upon the table he drew over the lamp and examined it intently. I had left my chair and was gazing at it over his shoulder. The envelope was a very coarse one and was stamped with the Gravesend postmark and with the date of that very day, or rather of the day before, for it was considerably after midnight.

'Coarse writing,' murmured Holmes. 'Surely this is not your husband's writing, madam.'

'No, but the enclosure is.'

'I perceive also that whoever addressed the envelope had to go and inquire as to the address.'

'How can you tell that?'

'The name, you see, is in perfectly black ink, which has dried itself. The rest is of the grayish colour, which shows that blotting-paper has been used. If it had been written straight off, and then blotted, none would be of a deep black shade. This man has written the name, and there has then been a pause before he wrote the address, which can only mean that he was not familiar with it. It is, of course, a trifle, but there is nothing so important as trifles. Let us now see the letter. Ha! there has been an enclosure here!'

'Yes, there was a ring. His signet-ring.'

'And you are sure that this is your husband's hand?'

'One of his hands.'

'One?'

'His hand when he wrote hurriedly. It is very unlike his usual writing, and yet I know it well.'

'"Dearest do not be frightened. All will come well. There is a huge error which it may take some little time to rectify. Wait in patience.—NEVILLE." Written in pencil upon the fly-leaf of a book, octavo size, no water-mark. Hum! Posted today in Gravesend by a man with a dirty thumb. Ha! And the flap has been gummed, if I am not very much in error, by a person who had been chewing tobacco. And you have no doubt that it is your husband's hand, madam?'

'None. Neville wrote those words.'

'And they were posted today at Gravesend. Well, Mrs St. Clair, the clouds lighten, though I should not venture to say that the danger is over.'

'But he must be alive, Mr Holmes.'

'Unless this is a clever forgery to put us on the wrong scent. The ring, after all, proves nothing. It may have been taken from him. '

'No, no; it is, it is his very own writing!'

'Very well. It may, however, have been written on Monday and only posted today.'

'That is possible.'

'If so, much may have happened between.'

'Oh, you must not discourage me, Mr Holmes. I know that all is well with him. There is so keen a sympathy between us that I should know if evil came upon him. On the very day that I saw him last he cut himself in the bedroom, and yet I in the dining-room rushed upstairs instantly with the utmost certainty that something had happened. Do you think that I would respond to such a trifle and yet be ignorant of his death?'

'I have seen too much not to know that the impression of a woman may be more valuable than the conclusion of an analytical reasoner. And in this letter you certainly have a very strong piece of evidence to corroborate your view. But if your husband is alive and able to write letters, why should he remain away from you?'

'I cannot imagine. It is unthinkable.'

'And on Monday he made no remarks before leaving you?'

'No.'

'And you were surprised to see him in Swandam Lane?'

'Very much so.'

'Was the window open?'

'Yes.'

'Then he might have called to you?'

'He might.'

'He only, as I understand, gave an inarticulate cry?'

'Yes.'

'A call for help, you thought?'

'Yes. He waved his hands.'

'But it might have been a cry of surprise. Astonishment at the unexpected sight of you might cause him to throw up his hands?'

'It is possible.'

'And you thought he was pulled back?'

'He disappeared so suddenly.'

'He might have leaped back. You did not see anyone else in the room?'

'No, but this horrible man confessed to having been there, and the Lascar was at the foot of the stairs.'

'Quite so. Your husband, as far as you could see, had his ordinary clothes on?'

'But without his collar or tie. I distinctly saw his bare throat.'

'Had he ever spoken of Swandam Lane?'

'Never.'

'Had he ever showed any signs of having taken opium?'

'Never.'

'Thank you, Mrs St. Clair. Those are the principal points about which I wished to be absolutely clear. We shall now have a little supper and then retire, for we may have a very busy day tomorrow.'

A large and comfortable double-bedded room had been placed at our disposal, and I was quickly between the sheets, for I was weary after my night of adventure. Sherlock Holmes was a man, however, who, when he had an unsolved problem upon his mind, would go for days, and even for a week, without rest, turning it over, rearranging his facts, looking at it from every point of view until he had either fathomed it or convinced himself that his data were insufficient. It was soon evident to me that he was now preparing for an all-night sitting.

He took off his coat and waistcoat, put on a large blue dressing-gown, and then wandered about the room collecting pillows from his bed and cushions from the sofa and armchairs. With these he constructed a sort of Eastern divan, upon which he perched himself cross-legged, with an ounce of shag tobacco and a box of matches laid out in front of him. In the dim light of the lamp I saw him sitting there, an old briar pipe between his lips, his eyes fixed vacantly upon the corner of the ceiling, the blue smoke curling up from him, silent, motionless, with the light shining upon his strong-set aquiline features. So he sat as I dropped off to sleep, and so he sat when a sudden ejaculation caused me to wake up, and I found the summer sun shining into the apartment. The pipe was still between his lips, the smoke still curled upward, and the room was full of a dense tobacco haze, but nothing remained of the heap of shag which I had seen upon the previous night.

'Awake, Watson?' he asked.

'Yes.'

'Game for a morning drive?'

'Certainly.'

'Then dress. No one is stirring yet, but I know where the stable-boy sleeps, and we shall soon have the trap out.' He chuckled to himself as he spoke, his eyes twinkled, and he seemed a different man to the sombre thinker of the previous night.

As I dressed I glanced at my watch. It was no wonder that no one was stirring. It was twenty-five minutes past four. I had hardly finished when Holmes returned with the news that the boy was putting in the horse.

'I want to test a little theory of mine,' said he, pulling on his boots. 'I think, Watson, that you are now standing in the presence of one of the most absolute fools in Europe. I deserve to be kicked from here to Charing Cross. But I think I have the key of the affair now.'

'And where is it?' I asked, smiling.

'In the bathroom,' he answered. 'Oh, yes, I am not joking,' he continued, seeing my look of incredulity. 'I have just been there, and I have taken it out, and I have got it in this Gladstone bag. Come on, my boy, and we shall see whether it will not fit the lock.'

We made our way downstairs as quietly as possible, and out into the bright morning sunshine. In the road stood our horse and trap, with the half-clad stable-boy waiting at the head. We both sprang in, and away we dashed down the London Road. A few country carts were stirring, bearing in vegetables to the metropolis, but the lines of villas on either side were as silent and lifeless as some city in a dream.

'It has been in some points a singular case,' said Holmes, flicking the horse on into a gallop. 'I confess that I have been as blind as a mole, but it is better to learn wisdom late than never to learn it at all.'

In town the earliest risers were just beginning to look sleepily from their windows as we drove through the streets of the Surrey side. Passing down the Waterloo Bridge Road we crossed over the river, and dashing up Wellington Street wheeled sharply to the right and found ourselves in Bow Street. Sherlock Holmes was well known to the force, and the two constables at the door saluted him. One of them held the horse's head while the other led us in.

'Who is on duty?' asked Holmes.

'Inspector Bradstreet, sir.'

'Ah, Bradstreet, how are you?' A tall, stout official had come down the stone-flagged passage, in a peaked cap and frogged jacket. 'I wish to have a quiet word with you, Bradstreet.' 'Certainly, Mr Holmes. Step into my room here.' It was a small, office-like room, with a huge ledger upon the table, and a telephone projecting from the wall. The inspector sat down at his desk.

'What can I do for you, Mr Holmes?'

'I called about that beggarman, Boone—the one who was charged with being concerned in the disappearance of Mr Neville St. Clair, of Lee.'

'Yes. He was brought up and remanded for further inquiries.'

'So I heard. You have him here?'

'In the cells.'

'Is he quiet?'

'Oh, he gives no trouble. But he is a dirty scoundrel.'

'Dirty?'

'Yes, it is all we can do to make him wash his hands, and his face is as black as a tinker's. Well, when once his case has been settled, he will have a regular prison bath; and I think, if you saw him, you would agree with me that he needed it.'

'I should like to see him very much.'

'Would you? That is easily done. Come this way. You can leave your bag.'

'No, I think that I'll take it.'

'Very good. Come this way, if you please.' He led us down a passage, opened a barred door, passed down a winding stair, and brought us to a whitewashed corridor with a line of doors on each side.

'The third on the right is his,' said the inspector. 'Here it is!' He quietly shot back a panel in the upper part of the door and glanced through.

'He is asleep,' said he. 'You can see him very well.'

We both put our eyes to the grating. The prisoner lay with his face towards us, in a very deep sleep, breathing slowly and heavily. He was a middle-sized man, coarsely clad as became his calling, with a coloured shirt protruding through the rent in his tattered coat. He was, as the inspector had said, extremely dirty, but the grime which covered his face could not conceal its repulsive ugliness. A broad wheal from an old scar ran right across it from eye to chin, and by its contraction had turned up one side of the upper lip, so that three teeth were exposed in a perpetual snarl. A shock of very bright red hair grew low over his eyes and forehead.

'He's a beauty, isn't he?' said the inspector.

'He certainly needs a wash,' remarked Holmes. 'I had an idea that he might, and I took the liberty of bringing the tools with me.' He opened the Gladstone bag as he spoke, and took out, to my astonishment, a very large bath-sponge.

'He! he! You are a funny one,' chuckled the inspector.

'Now, if you will have the great goodness to open that door very quietly, we will soon make him cut a much more respectable figure.'

'Well, I don't know why not,' said the inspector. 'He doesn't look a credit to the Bow Street cells, does he?' He slipped his key into the lock, and we all very quietly entered the cell. The sleeper half turned, and then settled down once more into a deep slumber. Holmes stooped to the waterjug, moistened his sponge, and then rubbed it twice vigorously across and down the prisoner's face.

'Let me introduce you,' he shouted, 'to Mr Neville St. Clair, of Lee, in the county of Kent.'

Never in my life have I seen such a sight. The man's face peeled off under the sponge like the bark from a tree. Gone was the coarse brown tint! Gone, too, was the horrid scar which had seamed it across, and the twisted lip which had given the repulsive sneer to the face! A twitch brought away the tangled red hair, and there, sitting up in his bed, was a pale, sad-faced, refined-looking man, black-haired and smooth-skinned, rubbing his eyes and staring about him with sleepy bewilderment. Then suddenly realizing the exposure, he broke into a scream and threw himself down with his face to the pillow.

'Great heavens!' cried the inspector, 'it is, indeed, the missing man. I know him from the photograph.'

The prisoner turned with the reckless air of a man who abandons himself to his destiny. 'Be it so,' said he. 'And pray what am I charged with?'

'With making away with Mr Neville St.-Oh, come, you can't be charged with that unless they make a case of attempted suicide of it,' said the inspector with a grin. 'Well, I have been twenty-seven years in the force, but this really takes the cake.'

'If I am Mr Neville St. Clair, then it is obvious that no crime has been committed, and that, therefore, I am illegally detained.'

'No crime, but a very great error has been committed,' said Holmes. 'You would have done better to have trusted you wife.'

'It was not the wife; it was the children,' groaned the prisoner. 'God help me, I would not have them ashamed of their father. My God! What an exposure! What can I do?'

Sherlock Holmes sat down beside him on the couch and patted him kindly on the shoulder.

'If you leave it to a court of law to clear the matter up,' said he, 'of course you can hardly avoid publicity. On the other hand, if you convince the police authorities that there is no possible case against you, I do not know that there is any reason that the details should find their way into the papers. Inspector Bradstreet would, I am sure, make notes upon anything which you might tell us and submit it to the proper authorities. The case would then never go into court at all.'

'God bless you!' cried the prisoner passionately. 'I would have endured imprisonment, ay, even execution, rather than have left my miserable secret as a family blot to my children.

'You are the first who have ever heard my story. My father was a school-master in Chesterfield, where I received an excellent education. I travelled in my youth, took to the stage, and finally became a reporter on an evening paper in London. One day my editor wished to have a series of articles upon begging in the metropolis, and I volunteered to supply them. There was the point from which all my adventures started. It was only by trying begging as an amateur that I could get the facts upon which to base my articles. When an actor I had, of course, learned all the secrets of making up, and had been famous in the greenroom for my skill. I took advantage now of my attainments. I painted my face, and to make myself as pitiable as possible I made a good scar and fixed one side of my lip in a twist by the aid of a small slip of flesh-coloured plaster. Then with a red head of hair, and an appropriate dress, I took my station in the business part of the city, ostensibly as a match-seller but really as a beggar. For seven hours I plied my trade, and when I returned home in the evening I found to my surprise that I had received no less than 26s. 4d.

'I wrote my articles and thought little more of the matter until, some time later, I backed a bill for a friend and had a writ served upon me for 25 pounds. I was at my wit's end where to get the money, but a sudden idea came to me. I begged a fortnight's grace from the creditor, asked for a holiday from my employers, and spent the time in begging in the City under my disguise. In ten days I had the money and had paid the debt.

'Well, you can imagine how hard it was to settle down to arduous work at 2 pounds a week when I knew that I could earn as much in a day by smearing my face with a little paint, laying my cap on the ground, and sitting still. It was a long fight between my pride and the money, but the dollars won at last, and I threw up reporting and sat day after day in the corner which I had first chosen, inspiring pity by my ghastly face and filling my pockets with coppers. Only one man knew my secret. He was the keeper of a low den in which I used to lodge in Swandam Lane, where I could every morning emerge as a squalid beggar and in the evenings transform myself into a well-dressed man about town. This fellow, a Lascar, was well paid by me for his rooms, so that I knew that my secret was safe in his possession.

'Well, very soon I found that I was saving considerable sums of money. I do not mean that any beggar in the streets of London could earn 700 pounds a year—which is less than my average takings—but I had exceptional advantages in my power of making up, and also in a facility of repartee, which improved by practice and made me quite a recognized character in the City. All day a stream of pennies, varied by silver, poured in upon me, and it was a very bad day in which I failed to take 2 pounds.

'As I grew richer I grew more ambitious, took a house in the country, and eventually married, without anyone having a suspicion as to my real occupation. My dear wife knew that I had business in the City. She little knew what.

'Last Monday I had finished for the day and was dressing in my room above the opium den when I looked out of my window and saw, to my horror and astonishment, that my wife was standing in the street, with her eyes fixed full upon me. I gave a cry of surprise, threw up my arms to cover my face, and, rushing to my confidant, the Lascar, entreated him to prevent anyone from coming up to me. I heard her voice downstairs, but I knew that she could not ascend. Swiftly I threw off my clothes, pulled on those of a beggar, and put on my pigments and wig. Even a wife's eyes could not pierce so complete a disguise. But then it occurred to me that there might be a search in the room, and that the clothes might betray me. I threw open the window, reopening by my violence a small cut which I had inflicted upon myself in the bedroom that morning. Then I seized my coat, which was weighted by the coppers which I had just transferred to it from the leather bag in which I carried my takings. I hurled it out of the window, and it disappeared into the Thames. The other clothes would have followed, but at that moment there was a rush of constables up the stair, and a few minutes after I found, rather, I confess, to my relief, that instead of being identified as Mr Neville St. Clair, I was arrested as his murderer.

'I do not know that there is anything else for me to explain. I was determined to preserve my disguise as long as possible, and hence my preference for a dirty face. Knowing that my wife would be terribly anxious, I slipped off my ring and confided it to the Lascar at a moment when no constable was watching me, together with a hurried scrawl, telling her that she had no cause to fear.'

'That note only reached her yesterday,' said Holmes.

'Good God! What a week she must have spent!'

'The police have watched this Lascar,' said Inspector Bradstreet, 'and I can quite understand that he might find it difficult to post a letter unobserved. Probably he handed it to some sailor customer of his, who forgot all about it for some days.'

'That was it,' said Holmes, nodding approvingly; 'I have no doubt of it. But have you never been prosecuted for begging?'

'Many times; but what was a fine to me?'

'It must stop here, however,' said Bradstreet. 'If the police are to hush this thing up, there must be no more of Hugh Boone.'

'I have sworn it by the most solemn oaths which a man can take.'

'In that case I think that it is probable that no further steps may be taken. But if you are found again, then all must come out. I am sure, Mr Holmes, that we are very much indebted to you for having cleared the matter up. I wish I knew how you reach your results.'

'I reached this one,' said my friend, 'by sitting upon five pillows and consuming an ounce of shag. I think, Watson, that if we drive to Baker Street we shall just be in time for breakfast.'

38

THE CABALLERO'S WAY
O. Henry

...He killed for the love of it—because he was quick-tempered...

The Cisco Kid had killed six men in more or less fair scrimmages, had murdered twice as many (mostly Mexicans), and had winged a larger number whom he modestly forbore to count. Therefore a woman loved him.

The Kid was twenty-five, looked twenty; and a careful insurance company would have estimated the probable time of his demise at, say, twenty-six. His habitat was anywhere between the Frio and the Rio Grande. He killed for the love of it—because he was quick-tempered—to avoid arrest—for his own amusement—any reason that came to his mind would suffice. He had escaped capture because he could shoot five-sixths of a second sooner than any sheriff or ranger in the service, and because he rode a speckled roan horse that knew every cow-path in the mesquite and pear thickets from San Antonio to Matamoras.

Tonia Perez, the girl who loved the Cisco Kid, was half Carmen, half Madonna, and the rest—oh, yes, a woman who is half Carmen and half Madonna can always be something more—the rest, let us say, was humming-bird. She lived in a grass-roofed jacal near a little Mexican settlement at the Lone Wolf Crossing of the Frio. With her lived a father or grandfather, a lineal Aztec, somewhat less than a thousand years old, who herded a hundred goats and lived in a continuous drunken dream from drinking mescal. Back of the jacal a tremendous forest of bristling pear, twenty feet high at its worst, crowded almost to its door. It was along the bewildering maze of this spinous thicket that the speckled roan would bring the Kid to see his girl. And once, clinging like a lizard to the ridge-pole, high up under the peaked grass roof, he had heard Tonia, with her Madonna face and Carmen beauty and humming-bird soul, parley with the sheriff's posse, denying knowledge of her man in her soft melange of Spanish and English.

One day the adjutant-general of the State, who is, ex offico, commander of the ranger forces, wrote some sarcastic lines to Captain Duval of Company X, stationed at Laredo, relative to the serene and undisturbed existence led by murderers and desperadoes in the said captain's territory.

The captain turned the colour of brick dust under his tan, and forwarded the letter, after adding a few comments, per ranger Private Bill Adamson, to ranger Lieutenant Sandridge, camped at a water hole on the Nueces with a squad of five men in preservation of law and order.

Lieutenant Sandridge turned a beautiful couleur de rose through his ordinary strawberry complexion, tucked the letter in his hip pocket, and chewed off the ends of his gamboge moustache.

The next morning he saddled his horse and rode alone to the Mexican settlement at the Lone Wolf Crossing of the Frio, twenty miles away.

Six feet two, blond as a Viking, quiet as a deacon, dangerous as a machine gun, Sandridge moved among the Jacales, patiently seeking news of the Cisco Kid.

Far more than the law, the Mexicans dreaded the cold and certain vengeance of the lone rider that the ranger sought. It had been one of the Kid's pastimes to shoot Mexicans 'to see them kick': if he demanded from them moribund Terpsichorean feats, simply that he might be entertained, what terrible and extreme penalties would be certain to follow should they anger him! One and all they lounged with upturned palms and shrugging shoulders, filling the air with 'quien sabes' and denials of the Kid's acquaintance.

But there was a man named Fink who kept a store at the Crossing—a man of many nationalities, tongues, interests, and ways of thinking.

'No use to ask them Mexicans,' he said to Sandridge. 'They're afraid to tell. This hombre they call the Kid—Goodall is his name, ain't it?—he's been in my store once or twice. I have an idea you might run across him at—but I guess I don't keer to say, myself. I'm two seconds later in pulling a gun than I used to be, and the difference is worth thinking about. But this Kid's got a half-Mexican girl at the Crossing that he comes to see. She lives in that jacal a hundred yards down the arroyo at the edge of the pear. Maybe she—no, I don't suppose she would, but that jacal would be a good place to watch, anyway.'

Sandridge rode down to the jacal of Perez. The sun was low, and the broad shade of the great pear thicket already covered the grass-thatched hut. The goats were enclosed for the night in a brush corral near by. A few kids walked the top of it, nibbling the chaparral leaves. The old Mexican lay upon a blanket on the grass, already in a stupor from his mescal, and dreaming, perhaps, of the nights when he and Pizarro touched glasses to their New World fortunes—so old his wrinkled face seemed to proclaim him to be. And in the door of the jacal stood Tonia. And Lieutenant Sandridge sat in his saddle staring at her like a gannet agape at a sailorman.

The Cisco Kid was a vain person, as all eminent and successful assassins are, and his bosom would have been ruffled had he known that at a simple exchange of glances two persons, in whose minds he had been looming large, suddenly abandoned (at least for the time) all thought of him.

Never before had Tonia seen such a man as this. He seemed to be made of sunshine and blood-red tissue and clear weather. He seemed to illuminate the shadow of the pear when he smiled, as though the sun were rising again. The men she had known had been small and dark. Even the Kid, in spite of his achievements, was a stripling no larger than herself, with black, straight hair and a cold, marble face that chilled the noonday.

As for Tonia, though she sends description to the poorhouse, let her make a millionaire of your fancy. Her blue-black hair, smoothly divided in the middle and bound close to her head, and her large eyes full of the Latin melancholy, gave her the Madonna touch. Her motions and air spoke of the concealed fire and the desire to charm that she had inherited from the gitanas of the Basque province. As for the humming-bird part of her, that dwelt in her heart; you could not perceive it unless her bright red skirt and dark blue blouse gave you a symbolic hint of the vagarious bird.

The newly lighted sun-god asked for a drink of water. Tonia brought it from the red jar hanging under the brush shelter. Sandridge considered it necessary to dismount so as to lessen the trouble of her ministrations.

I play no spy; nor do I assume to master the thoughts of any human heart; but I assert, by the chronicler's right, that before a quarter of an hour had sped, Sandridge was teaching her how to plaint a six-strand rawhide stake-rope, and Tonia had explained to him that were it not for her little English book that the peripatetic padre had given her and the little crippled chivo, that she fed from a bottle, she would be very, very lonely indeed.

Which leads to a suspicion that the Kid's fences needed repairing, and that the adjutant-general's sarcasm had fallen upon unproductive soil.

In his camp by the water hole Lieutenant Sandridge announced and reiterated his intention of either causing the Cisco Kid to nibble the black loam of the Frio country prairies or of haling him before a judge and jury. That sounded business-like. Twice a week he rode over to the Lone Wolf Crossing of the Frio, and directed Tonia's slim, slightly lemon-tinted fingers among the intricacies of the slowly growing lariata. A six-strand plait is hard to learn and easy to teach.

The ranger knew that he might find the Kid there at any visit. He kept his armament ready, and had a frequent eye for the pear thicket at the rear of the jacal. Thus he might bring down the kite and the humming-bird with one stone.

While the sunny-haired ornithologist was pursuing his studies the Cisco Kid was also attending to his professional duties. He moodily shot up a saloon in a small cow village on Quintana Creek, killed the town marshal (plugging him neatly in the centre of his tin badge), and then rode away, morose and unsatisfied. No true artist is uplifted by shooting an aged man carrying an old-style .38 bulldog.

On his way the Kid suddenly experienced the yearning that all men feel when wrong-doing loses its keen edge of delight. He yearned for the woman he loved to reassure him that she was his in spite of it. He wanted her to call his bloodthirstiness bravery and his cruelty devotion. He wanted Tonia to bring him water from the red jar under the brush shelter, and tell him how the chivo was thriving on the bottle.

The Kid turned the speckled roan's head up the ten-mile pear flat that stretches along the Arroyo Hondo until it ends at the Lone Wolf Crossing of the Frio. The roan whickered; for he had a sense of locality and direction equal to that of a belt-line street-car horse; and he knew he would soon be nibbling the rich mesquite grass at the end of a forty-foot stake-rope while Ulysses rested his head in Circe's straw-roofed hut.

More weird and lonesome than the journey of an Amazonian explorer is the ride of one through a Texas pear flat. With dismal monotony and startling variety the uncanny and multiform shapes of the cacti lift their twisted trunks, and fat, bristly hands to encumber the way. The demon plant, appearing to live without soil or rain, seems to taunt the parched traveller with its lush gray greenness. It warps itself a thousand times about what look to be open and inviting paths, only to lure the rider into blind and impassable spine-defended 'bottoms of the bag,' leaving him to retreat, if he can, with the points of the compass whirling in his head.

To be lost in the pear is to die almost the death of the thief on the cross, pierced by nails and with grotesque shapes of all the fiends hovering about.

But it was not so with the Kid and his mount. Winding, twisting, circling, tracing the most fantastic and bewildering trail ever picked out, the good roan lessened the distance to the Lone Wolf Crossing with every coil and turn that he made.

While they fared the Kid sang. He knew but one tune and sang it, as he knew but one code and lived it, and but one girl and loved her. He was a single-minded man of conventional ideas. He had a voice like a coyote with bronchitis, but whenever he chose to sing his song he sang it. It was a conventional song of the camps and trail, running at its beginning as near as may be to these words:

Don't you monkey with my Lulu girl Or I'll tell you what I'll do—and so on. The roan was inured to it, and did not mind.

But even the poorest singer will, after a certain time, gain his own consent to refrain from contributing to the world's noises. So the Kid, by the time he was within a mile or two of Tonia's jacal, had reluctantly allowed his song to die away—not because his vocal performance had become less charming to his own ears, but because his laryngeal muscles were aweary.

As though he were in a circus ring the speckled roan wheeled and danced through the labyrinth of pear until at length his rider knew by certain landmarks that the Lone Wolf Crossing was close at hand. Then, where the pear was thinner, he caught sight of the grass roof of the jacal and the hackberry tree on the edge of the arroyo. A few yards farther the Kid stopped the roan and gazed intently through the prickly openings. Then he dismounted, dropped the roan's reins, and proceeded on foot, stooping and silent, like an Indian. The roan, knowing his part, stood still, making no sound.

The Kid crept noiselessly to the very edge of the pear thicket and reconnoitred between the leaves of a clump of cactus.

Ten yards from his hiding-place, in the shade of the jacal, sat his Tonia calmly plaiting a rawhide lariat. So far she might surely escape condemnation; women have been known, from time to time, to engage in more mischievous occupations. But if all must be told, there is to be added that her head reposed against the broad and comfortable chest of a tall red-and-yellow man, and that his arm was about her, guiding her nimble fingers that required so many lessons at the intricate six-strand plait.

Sandridge glanced quickly at the dark mass of pear when he heard a slight squeaking sound that was not altogether unfamiliar. A gun-scabbard will make that sound when one grasps the handle of a six-shooter suddenly. But the sound was not repeated; and Tonia's fingers needed close attention.

And then, in the shadow of death, they began to talk of their love; and in the still July afternoon every word they uttered reached the ears of the Kid.

'Remember, then,' said Tonia, 'you must not come again until I send for you. Soon he will be here. A vaquero at the tienda said today he saw him on the Guadalupe three days ago. When he is that near he always comes. If he comes and finds you here he will kill you. So, for my sake, you must come no more until I send you the word.'

'All right,' said the stranger. 'And then what?'

'And then,' said the girl, 'you must bring your men here and kill him. If not, he will kill you.'

'He ain't a man to surrender, that's sure,' said Sandridge. 'It's kill or be killed for the officer that goes up against Mr Cisco Kid.'

'He must die,' said the girl. 'Otherwise there will not be any peace in the world for thee and me. He has killed many. Let him so die. Bring your men, and give him no chance to escape.'

'You used to think right much of him,' said Sandridge.

Tonia dropped the lariat, twisted herself around, and curved a lemon-tinted arm over the ranger's shoulder.

'But then,' she murmured in liquid Spanish, 'I had not beheld thee, thou great, red mountain of a man! And thou art kind and good, as well as strong. Could one choose him, knowing thee? Let him die; for then I will not be filled with fear by day and night lest he hurt thee or me.'

'How can I know when he comes?' asked Sandridge.

'When he comes,' said Tonia, 'he remains two days, sometimes three. Gregorio, the small son of old Luisa, the lavendera, has a swift pony. I will write a letter to thee and send it by him, saying how it will be best to come upon him. By Gregorio will the letter come. And bring many men with thee, and have much care, oh, dear red one, for the rattlesnake is not quicker to strike than is "El Chivato" as they call him, to send a ball from his pistola.'

'The Kid's handy with his gun, sure enough,' admitted Sandridge, 'but when I come for him I shall come alone. I'll get him by myself or not at all. The Cap wrote one or two things to me that make me want to do the trick without any help. You let me know when Mr

Kid arrives, and I'll do the rest.'

'I will send you the message by the boy Gregorio,' said the girl. 'I knew you were braver than that small slayer of men who never smiles. How could I ever have thought I cared for him?'

It was time for the ranger to ride back to his camp on the water hole. Before he mounted his horse he raised the slight form of Tonia with one arm high from the earth for a parting salute. The drowsy stillness of the torpid summer air still lay thick upon the dreaming afternoon. The smoke from the fire in the jacal, where the frijoles blubbered in the iron pot, rose straight as a plumb-line above the clay-daubed chimney. No sound or movement disturbed the serenity of the dense pear thicket ten yards away.

When the form of Sandridge had disappeared, loping his big dun down the steep banks of the Frio crossing, the Kid crept back to his own horse, mounted him, and rode back along the tortuous trail he had come.

But not far. He stopped and waited in the silent depths of the pear until half an hour had passed. And then Tonia heard the high, untrue notes of his unmusical singing coming nearer and nearer; and she ran to the edge of the pear to meet him.

The Kid seldom smiled; but he smiled and waved his hat when he saw her. He dismounted, and his girl sprang into his arms. The Kid looked at her fondly. His thick, black hair clung to his head like a wrinkled mat. The meeting brought a slight ripple of some undercurrent of feeling to his smooth, dark face that was usually as motionless as a clay mask.

'How's my girl?' he asked, holding her close.

'Sick of waiting so long for you, dear one,' she answered. 'My eyes are dim with always gazing into that devil's pincushion through which you come. And I can see into it such a little way, too. But you are here, beloved one, and I will not scold. Que mal muchacho! not to come to see your alma more often. Go in and rest, and let me water your horse and stake him with the long rope. There is cool water in the jar for you.'

The Kid kissed her affectionately.

'Not if the court knows itself do I let a lady stake my horse for me,' said he. 'But if you'll run in, chica, and throw a pot of coffee together while I attend to the caballo, I'll be a good deal obliged.'

Besides his marksmanship the Kid had another attribute for which he admired himself greatly. He was muy caballero, as the Mexicans express it, where the ladies were concerned. For them he had always gentle words and consideration. He could not have spoken a harsh word to a woman. He might ruthlessly slay their husbands and brothers, but he could not have laid the weight of a finger in anger upon a woman. Wherefore many of that interesting division of humanity who had come under the spell of his politeness declared their disbelief in the stories circulated about Mr Kid. One shouldn't believe everything one heard, they said. When confronted by their indignant men folk with proof of the caballero's deeds of infamy, they said maybe he had been driven to it, and that he knew how to treat a lady, anyhow.

Considering this extremely courteous idiosyncrasy of the Kid and the pride he took in it, one can perceive that the solution of the problem that was presented to him by what he saw and heard from his hiding place in the pear that afternoon (at least as to one of the actors) must have been obscured by difficulties. And yet one could not think of the Kid overlooking little matters of that kind.

At the end of the short twilight they gathered around a supper of frijoles, goat steaks, canned peaches, and coffee, by the light of a lantern in the jacal. Afterward, the ancestor, his flock corralled, smoked a cigarette and became a mummy in a gray blanket. Tonia washed the few dishes while the Kid dried them with the flour-sacking towel. Her eyes shone; she chatted volubly of the inconsequent happenings of her small world since the Kid's last visit; it was as all his other home-comings had been.

Then outside Tonia swung in a grass hammock with her guitar and sang sad canciones de amor.

'Do you love me just the same, old girl?' asked the Kid, hunting for his cigarette papers.

'Always the same, little one,' said Tonia, her dark eyes lingering upon him.

'I must go over to Fink's,' said the Kid, rising, 'for some tobacco. I thought I had another sack in my coat. I'll be back in a quarter of an hour.'

'Hasten,' said Tonia, 'and tell me—how long shall I call you my own this time? Will you be gone again tomorrow, leaving me to grieve, or will you be longer with your Tonia?'

'Oh, I might stay two or three days this trip,' said the Kid, yawning. 'I've been on the dodge for a month, and I'd like to rest up.'

He was gone half an hour for his tobacco. When he returned Tonia was still lying in the hammock.

'It's funny,' said the Kid, 'how I feel. I feel like there was somebody lying behind every bush and tree waiting to shoot me. I never had mullygrubs like them before. Maybe it's one of them presumptions. I've got half a notion to light out in the morning before day. The Guadalupe country is burning up about that old Dutchman I plugged down there.'

'You are not afraid—no one could make my brave little one fear.'

'Well, I haven't been usually regarded as a jack-rabbit when it comes to scrapping; but I don't want a posse smoking me out when I'm in your jacal. Somebody might get hurt that oughtn't to.'

'Remain with your Tonia; no one will find you here.'

The Kid looked keenly into the shadows up and down the arroyo and toward the dim lights of the Mexican village.

'I'll see how it looks later on,' was his decision.

◆

At midnight a horseman rode into the rangers' camp, blazing his way by noisy 'halloes' to indicate a pacific mission. Sandridge and one or two others turned out to investigate the row. The rider announced himself to be Domingo Sales, from the Lone Wolf Crossing. he bore a letter for Senor Sandridge. Old Luisa, the lavendera, had persuaded him to bring it, he said, her son Gregorio being too ill of a fever to ride.

Sandridge lighted the camp lantern and read the letter. These were its words:

Dear One: He has come. Hardly had you ridden away when he came out of the pear. When he first talked he said he would stay three days or more. Then as it grew later he was like a wolf or a fox, and walked about without rest, looking and listening. Soon he said he must leave before daylight when it is dark and stillest. And then he seemed to suspect that I be not true to him. He looked at me so strange that I am frightened. I swear to him that I love him, his own Tonia. Last of all he said I must prove to him I am true. He thinks that even now men are waiting to kill him as he rides from my house. To escape he says he will dress in my clothes, my red skirt and the blue waist I wear and the brown mantilla over the head, and thus ride away. But before that he says that I must put on his clothes, his pantalones and camisa and hat, and ride away on his horse from the jacal as far as the big road beyond the crossing and back again. This before he goes, so he can tell if I am true and if men are hidden to shoot him. It is a terrible thing. An hour before daybreak this is to be. Come, my dear one, and kill this man and take me for your Tonia. Do not try to take hold of him alive, but kill him quickly. Knowing all, you should do that. You must come long before the time and hide yourself in the little shed near the jacal where the wagon and saddles are kept. It is dark in there. He will wear my red skirt and blue waist and brown mantilla. I send you a hundred kisses. Come surely and shoot quickly and straight.

Thine Own Tonia

Sandridge quickly explained to his men the official part of the missive. The rangers protested against his going alone.

'I'll get him easy enough,' said the lieutenant. 'The girl's got him trapped. And don't even think he'll get the drop on me.'

Sandridge saddled his horse and rode to the Lone Wolf Crossing. He tied his big dun in a clump of brush on the arroyo, took his Winchester from its scabbard, and carefully approached the Perez jacal. There was only the half of a high moon drifted over by ragged, milk-white gulf clouds.

The wagon-shed was an excellent place for ambush; and the ranger got inside it safely. In the black shadow of the brush shelter in front of the jacal he could see a horse tied and hear him impatiently pawing the hard-trodden earth.

He waited almost an hour before two figures came out of the jacal. One, in man's clothes, quickly mounted the horse and galloped past the wagon-shed toward the crossing and village. And then the other figure, in skirt, waist, and mantilla over its head, stepped out into the faint moonlight, gazing after the rider. Sandridge thought he would take his chance then before Tonia rode back. He fancied she might not care to see it.

'Throw up your hands,' he ordered loudly, stepping out of the wagon shed with his Winchester at his shoulder.

There was a quick turn of the figure, but no movement to obey, so the ranger pumped in the bullets—one—two—three—and then twice more; for you never could be too sure of bringing down the Cisco Kid. There was no danger of missing at ten paces, even in that half moonlight.

The old ancestor, asleep on his blanket, was awakened by the shots. Listening further, he heard a great cry from some man in mortal distress or anguish, and rose up grumbling at the disturbing ways of moderns.

The tall, red ghost of a man burst into the jacal, reaching one hand, shaking like a tule reed, for the lantern hanging on its nail. The other spread a letter on the table.

'Look at this letter, Perez,' cried the man. 'Who wrote it?'

'Ah, Dios! it is Senor Sandridge,' mumbled the old man, approaching. 'Pues, senor, that letter was written by "El Chivato" as he is called—by the man of Tonia. They say he is a bad man; I do not know. While Tonia slept he wrote the letter and sent it by this old hand of mine to Domingo Sales to be brought to you. Is there anything wrong in the letter? I am very old; and I did not know. Valgame Dios! it is a very foolish world; and there is nothing in the house to drink—nothing to drink.'

Just then all that Sandridge could think of to do was to go outside and throw himself face downward in the dust by the side of his humming-bird, of whom not a feather fluttered. He was not a caballero by instinct, and he could not understand the niceties of revenge.

A mile away the rider who had ridden past the wagon-shed struck up a harsh, untuneful song, the words of which began:

"Don't you monkey with my Lulu girl Or I'll tell you what I'll do—"

39

THE EMPTY HOUSE

Algernon Blackwood

...A dead silence followed for the space of half a minute, and then was heard a rushing sound through the air...

Certain houses, like certain persons, manage somehow to proclaim at once their character for evil. In the case of the latter, no particular feature need betray them; they may boast an open countenance and an ingenuous smile; and yet a little of their company leaves the unalterable conviction that there is something radically amiss with their being: that they are evil. Willy nilly, they seem to communicate an atmosphere of secret and wicked thoughts which makes those in their immediate neighbourhood shrink from them as from a thing diseased.

And, perhaps, with houses the same principle is operative, and it is the aroma of evil deeds committed under a particular roof, long after the actual doers have passed away, that makes the gooseflesh come and the hair rise. Something of the original passion of the evil-doer, and of the horror felt by his victim, enters the heart of the innocent watcher, and he becomes suddenly conscious of tingling nerves, creeping skin, and a chilling of the blood. He is terror-stricken without apparent cause.

There was manifestly nothing in the external appearance of this particular house to bear out the tales of the horror that was said to reign within. It was neither lonely nor unkempt. It stood, crowded into a corner of the square, and looked exactly like the houses on either side of it. It had the same number of windows as its neighbours; the same balcony overlooking the gardens; the same white steps leading up to the heavy black front door; and, in the rear, there was the same narrow strip of green, with neat box borders, running up to the wall that divided it from the backs of the adjoining houses. Apparently, too, the number of chimney pots on the roof was the same; the breadth and angle of the eaves; and even the height of the dirty area railings.

And yet this house in the square, that seemed precisely similar to its fifty ugly neighbours, was as a matter of fact entirely different—horribly different.

Wherein lay this marked, invisible difference is impossible to say. It cannot be ascribed wholly to the imagination, because persons who had spent some time in the house, knowing nothing of the facts, had declared positively that certain rooms were so disagreeable they would rather die than enter them again, and that the atmosphere of the whole house produced in them symptoms of a genuine terror; while the series of innocent tenants who had tried to live in it and been forced to decamp at the shortest possible notice, was indeed little less than a scandal in the town.

When Shorthouse arrived to pay a 'week-end' visit to his Aunt Julia in her little house on the sea-front at the other end of the town, he found her charged to the brim with mystery and excitement. He had only received her telegram that morning, and he had come anticipating boredom; but the moment he touched her hand and kissed her apple-skin wrinkled cheek, he caught the first wave of her electrical condition. The impression deepened when he learned that there were to be no other visitors, and that he had been telegraphed for with a very special object.

Something was in the wind, and the 'something' would doubtless bear fruit; for this elderly spinster aunt, with a mania for psychical research, had brains as well as will power, and by hook or by crook she usually managed to accomplish her ends. The revelation was made soon after tea, when she sidled close up to him as they paced slowly along the sea-front in the dusk.

'I've got the keys,' she announced in a delighted, yet half awesome voice. 'Got them till Monday!'

'The keys of the bathing-machine, or—?' he asked innocently, looking from the sea to the town. Nothing brought her so quickly to the point as feigning stupidity.

'Neither,' she whispered. 'I've got the keys of the haunted house in the square—and I'm going there tonight.'

Shorthouse was conscious of the slightest possible tremor down his back. He dropped his teasing tone. Something in her voice and manner thrilled him. She was in earnest.

'But you can't go alone=' he began.

'That's why I wired for you,' she said with decision.

He turned to look at her. The ugly, lined, enigmatical face was alive with excitement. There was the glow of genuine enthusiasm round it like a halo. The eyes shone. He caught another wave of her excitement, and a second tremor, more marked than the first, accompanied it.

'Thanks, Aunt Julia,' he said politely; 'thanks awfully.'

'I should not dare to go quite alone,' she went on, raising her voice; 'but with you I should enjoy it immensely. You're afraid of nothing, I know.'

'Thanks *so* much,' he said again. 'Er—is anything likely to happen?'

'A great deal *has* happened,' she whispered, 'though it's been most cleverly hushed up. Three tenants have come and gone in the last few months, and the house is said to be empty for good now.'

In spite of himself Shorthouse became interested. His aunt was so very much in earnest.

'The house is very old indeed,' she went on, 'and the story—an unpleasant one—dates a long way back. It has to do with a murder committed by a jealous stableman who had some affair with a servant in the house. One night he managed to secrete himself in the cellar, and when everyone was asleep, he crept upstairs to the servants' quarters, chased the girl down to the next landing, and before anyone could come to the rescue threw her bodily over the banisters into the hall below.'

'And the stableman=?'

'Was caught, I believe, and hanged for murder; but it all happened a century ago, and I've not been able to get more details of the story.'

Shorthouse now felt his interest thoroughly aroused; but, though he was not particularly nervous for himself, he hesitated a little on his aunt's account.

'On one condition,' he said at length.

'Nothing will prevent my going,' she said firmly; 'but I may as well hear your condition.'

'That you guarantee your power of self-control if anything really horrible happens. I mean—that you are sure you won't get too frightened.'

'Jim,' she said scornfully, 'I'm not young, I know, nor are my nerves; but *with you* I should be afraid of nothing in the world!'

This, of course, settled it, for Shorthouse had no pretensions to being other than a very ordinary young man, and an appeal to his vanity was irresistible. He agreed to go.

Instinctively, by a sort of sub-conscious preparation, he kept himself and his forces well in hand the whole evening, compelling an accumulative reserve of control by that nameless inward process of gradually putting all the emotions away and turning the key upon them—a process difficult to describe, but wonderfully effective, as all men who have lived through severe trials of the inner man well understand. Later, it stood him in good stead.

But it was not until half-past ten, when they stood in the hall, well in the glare of friendly lamps and still surrounded by comforting human influences, that he had to make the first call upon this store of collected strength. For, once the door was closed, and he saw the deserted silent street stretching away white in the moonlight before them, it came to him clearly that the real test that night would be in dealing with *two fears* instead of one. He would have to carry his aunt's fear as well as his own. And, as he glanced down at her sphinx-like countenance and realised that it might assume no pleasant aspect in a rush of real terror, he felt satisfied with only one thing in the whole adventure—that he had confidence in his own will and power to stand against any shock that might come.

Slowly they walked along the empty streets of the town; a bright autumn moon silvered the roofs, casting deep shadows; there was no breath of wind; and the trees in the formal gardens by the sea-front watched them silently as they passed along. To his aunt's occasional remarks Shorthouse made no reply, realising that she was simply surrounding herself with mental buffers—saying ordinary things to prevent herself thinking of extra-ordinary things. Few windows showed lights, and from scarcely a single chimney came smoke or sparks. Shorthouse had already begun to notice everything, even the smallest details. Presently they stopped at the street corner and looked up at the name on the side of the house full in the moonlight, and with one accord, but without remark, turned into the square and crossed over to the side of it that lay in shadow.

'The number of the house is thirteen,' whispered a voice at his side; and neither of them made the obvious reference, but passed across the broad sheet of moonlight and began to march up the pavement in silence.

It was about half-way up the square that Shorthouse felt an arm slipped quietly but significantly into his own, and knew then that their adventure had begun in earnest, and that his companion was already yielding imperceptibly to the influences against them. She needed support.

A few minutes later they stopped before a tall, narrow house that rose before them into the night, ugly in shape and painted a dingy white. Shutterless windows, without blinds, stared down upon them, shining here and there in the moonlight. There were weather streaks in the wall and cracks in the paint, and the balcony bulged out from the first floor a little unnaturally. But, beyond this generally forlorn appearance of an unoccupied house, there was nothing at first sight to single out this particular mansion for the evil character it had most certainly acquired.

Taking a look over their shoulders to make sure they had not been followed, they went boldly up the steps and stood against the huge black door that fronted them forbiddingly. But the first wave of nervousness was now upon them, and Shorthouse fumbled a long time with the key before he could fit it into the lock at all. For a moment, if truth were told, they both hoped it would not open, for they were a prey to various unpleasant emotions as they stood there on the threshold of their ghostly adventure. Shorthouse, shuffling with the key and hampered by the steady weight on his arm, certainly felt the solemnity of the moment. It was as if the whole world—for all experience seemed at that instant concentrated in his own consciousness—were listening to the grating noise of that key. A stray puff of wind wandering down the empty street woke a momentary rustling in the trees behind them, but otherwise this rattling of the key was the only sound audible; and at last it turned in the lock and the heavy door swung open and revealed a yawning gulf of darkness beyond.

With a last glance at the moonlit square, they passed quickly in, and the door slammed behind them with a roar that echoed prodigiously through empty halls and passages. But, instantly, with the echoes, another sound made itself heard, and Aunt Julia leaned suddenly so heavily upon him that he had to take a step backwards to save himself from falling.

A man had coughed close beside them—so close that it seemed they must have been actually by his side in the darkness.

With the possibility of practical jokes in his mind, Shorthouse at once swung his heavy stick in the direction of the sound; but it met nothing more solid than air. He heard his aunt give a little gasp beside him.

'There's someone here,' she whispered; 'I heard him.'

'Be quiet!' he said sternly. 'It was nothing but the noise of the front door.'

'Oh! Get a light—quick!' she added, as her nephew, fumbling with a box of matches, opened it upside down and let them all fall with a rattle on to the stone floor.

The sound, however, was not repeated; and there was no evidence of retreating footsteps. In another minute they had a candle burning, using an empty end of a cigar case as a holder; and when the first flare had died down he held the impromptu lamp aloft and surveyed the scene. And it was dreary enough in all conscience, for there is nothing more desolate in all the abodes of men than an unfurnished house dimly lit, silent, and forsaken, and yet tenanted by rumour with the memories of evil and violent histories.

They were standing in a wide hall-way; on their left was the open door of a spacious dining-room, and in front the hall ran, ever narrowing, into a long, dark passage that led apparently to the top of the kitchen stairs. The broad uncarpeted staircase rose in a sweep before them, everywhere draped in shadows, except for a single spot about half-way up where the moonlight came in through the window and fell on a bright patch on the boards. This shaft of light shed a faint radiance above and below it, lending to the objects within its reach a misty outline that was infinitely more suggestive and ghostly than complete darkness. Filtered moonlight always seems to paint faces on the surrounding gloom, and as Shorthouse peered up into the well of darkness and thought of the countless empty rooms and passages in the upper part of the old house, he caught himself longing again for the safety of the moonlit square, or the cosy, bright drawing-room they had left an hour before. Then realising that these thoughts were dangerous, he thrust them away again and summoned all his energy for concentration on the present.

'Aunt Julia,' he said aloud, severely, 'we must now go through the house from top to bottom and make a thorough search.'

The echoes of his voice died away slowly all over the building, and in the intense silence that followed he turned to look at her. In the candle-light he saw that her face was already ghastly pale; but she dropped his arm for a moment and said in a whisper, stepping close in front of him—

'I agree. We must be sure there's no one hiding. That's the first thing.'

She spoke with evident effort, and he looked at her with admiration.

'You feel quite sure of yourself? It's not too late═'

'I think so,' she whispered, her eyes shifting nervously toward the shadows behind. 'Quite sure, only one thing═'

'What's that?'

'You must never leave me alone for an instant.'

'As long as you understand that any sound or appearance must be investigated at once, for to hesitate means to admit fear. That is fatal.'

'Agreed,' she said, a little shakily, after a moment's hesitation. 'I'll try═'

Arm in arm, Shorthouse holding the dripping candle and the

stick, while his aunt carried the cloak over her shoulders, figures of utter comedy to all but themselves, they began a systematic search.

Stealthily, walking on tip-toe and shading the candle lest it should betray their presence through the shutterless windows, they went first into the big dining-room. There was not a stick of furniture to be seen. Bare walls, ugly mantel-pieces and empty grates stared at them. Everything, they felt, resented their intrusion, watching them, as it were, with veiled eyes; whispers followed them; shadows flitted noiselessly to right and left; something seemed ever at their back, watching, waiting an opportunity to do them injury. There was the inevitable sense that operations which went on when the room was empty had been temporarily suspended till they were well out of the way again. The whole dark interior of the old building seemed to become a malignant Presence that rose up, warning them to desist and mind their own business; every moment the strain on the nerves increased.

Out of the gloomy dining-room they passed through large folding doors into a sort of library or smoking-room, wrapt equally in silence, darkness, and dust; and from this they regained the hall near the top of the back stairs.

Here a pitch-black tunnel opened before them into the lower regions, and—it must be confessed—they hesitated. But only for a minute. With the worst of the night still to come it was essential to turn from nothing. Aunt Julia stumbled at the top step of the dark descent, ill lit by the flickering candle, and even Shorthouse felt at least half the decision go out of his legs.

'Come on!' he said peremptorily, and his voice ran on and lost itself in the dark, empty spaces below.

'I'm coming,' she faltered, catching his arm with unnecessary violence.

They went a little unsteadily down the stone steps, a cold, damp air meeting them in the face, close and mal-odorous. The kitchen, into which the stairs led along a narrow passage, was large, with a lofty ceiling. Several doors opened out of it—some into cupboards with empty jars still standing on the shelves, and others into horrible little ghostly back offices, each colder and less inviting than the last. Black beetles scurried over the floor, and once, when they knocked against a deal table standing in a corner, something about the size of a cat jumped down with a rush and fled, scampering across the stone floor into the darkness. Everywhere there was a sense of recent occupation, an impression of sadness and gloom.

Leaving the main kitchen, they next went towards the scullery. The door was standing ajar, and as they pushed it open to its full extent Aunt Julia uttered a piercing scream, which she instantly tried to stifle by placing her hand over her mouth. For a second Shorthouse stood stock-still, catching his breath. He felt as if his spine had suddenly become hollow and someone had filled it with particles of ice.

Facing them, directly in their way between the doorposts, stood the figure of a woman. She had dishevelled hair and wildly staring eyes, and her face was terrified and white as death.

She stood there motionless for the space of a single second. Then the candle flickered and she was gone—gone utterly—and the door framed nothing but empty darkness.

'Only the beastly jumping candle-light,' he said quickly, in a voice that sounded like someone else's and was only half under control. 'Come on, aunt. There's nothing there.'

He dragged her forward. With a clattering of feet and a great appearance of boldness they went on, but over his body the skin moved as if crawling ants covered it, and he knew by the weight on his arm that he was supplying the force of locomotion for two. The scullery was cold, bare, and empty; more like a large prison cell than anything else. They went round it, tried the door into the yard, and the windows, but found them all fastened securely. His aunt moved beside him like a person in a dream. Her eyes were tightly shut, and she seemed merely to follow the pressure of his arm. Her courage filled him with amazement. At the same time he noticed that a certain odd change had come over her face, a change which somehow evaded his power of analysis.

'There's nothing here, aunty,' he repeated aloud quickly. 'Let's go upstairs and see the rest of the house. Then we'll choose a room to wait up in.'

She followed him obediently, keeping close to his side, and they locked the kitchen door behind them. It was a relief to get up again. In the hall there was more light than before, for the moon had travelled a little further down the stairs. Cautiously they began to go up into the dark vault of the upper house, the boards creaking under their weight.

On the first floor they found the large double drawing-rooms, a search of which revealed nothing. Here also was no sign of furniture or recent occupancy; nothing but dust and neglect and shadows. They opened the big folding doors between front and back drawing-rooms and then came out again to the landing and went on upstairs.

They had not gone up more than a dozen steps when they both simultaneously stopped to listen, looking into each other's eyes with a new apprehension across the flickering candle flame. From the room they had left hardly ten seconds before came the sound of doors quietly closing. It was beyond all question; they heard the booming noise that accompanies the shutting of heavy doors, followed by the sharp catching of the latch.

'We must go back and see,' said Shorthouse briefly, in a low tone, and turning to go downstairs again.

Somehow she managed to drag after him, her feet catching in her dress, her face livid.

When they entered the front drawing-room it was plain that the folding doors had been closed—half a minute before. Without hesitation Shorthouse opened them. He almost expected to see someone facing him in the back room; but only darkness and cold air met him. They went through both rooms, finding nothing unusual. They tried in every way to make the doors close of themselves, but there was not wind enough even to set the candle flame flickering. The doors would not move without strong pressure. All was silent as the grave. Undeniably the rooms were utterly empty, and the house utterly still.

'It's beginning,' whispered a voice at his elbow which he hardly recognised as his aunt's.

He nodded acquiescence, taking out his watch to note the time. It was fifteen minutes before midnight; he made the entry of exactly what had occurred in his notebook, setting the candle in its case upon the floor in order to do so. It took a moment or two to balance it safely against the wall.

Aunt Julia always declared that at this moment she was not actually watching him, but had turned her head towards the inner room, where she fancied she heard something moving; but, at any rate, both positively agreed that there came a sound of rushing feet, heavy and very swift—and the next instant the candle was out!

But to Shorthouse himself had come more than this, and he has always thanked his fortunate stars that it came to him alone and not to his aunt too. For, as he rose from the stooping position of balancing the candle, and before it was actually extinguished, a face thrust itself forward so close to his own that he could almost have touched it with his lips. It was a face working with passion; a man's face, dark, with thick features, and angry, savage eyes. It belonged to a common man, and it was evil in its ordinary normal expression, no doubt, but as he saw it, alive with intense, aggressive emotion, it was a malignant and terrible human countenance.

There was no movement of the air; nothing but the sound of rushing feet—stockinged or muffled feet; the apparition of the face; and the almost simultaneous extinguishing of the candle.

In spite of himself, Shorthouse uttered a little cry, nearly losing his balance as his aunt clung to him with her whole weight in one moment of real, uncontrollable terror. She made no sound, but simply seized him bodily. Fortunately, however, she had seen nothing, but had only heard the rushing feet, for her control returned almost at once, and he was able to disentangle himself and strike a match.

The shadows ran away on all sides before the glare, and his aunt stooped down and groped for the cigar case with the precious candle. Then they discovered that the candle had not been blown out at all; it had been crushed out. The wick was pressed down into the wax, which was flattened as if by some smooth, heavy instrument.

How his companion so quickly overcame her terror, Shorthouse never properly understood; but his admiration for her self-control increased tenfold, and at the same time served to feed his own dying flame—for which he was undeniably grateful. Equally inexplicable to him was the evidence of physical force they had just witnessed. He at once suppressed the memory of stories he had heard of 'physical mediums' and their dangerous phenomena; for if these were true, and either his aunt or himself was unwittingly a physical medium, it meant that they were simply aiding to focus the forces of a haunted house already charged to the brim. It was like walking with unprotected lamps among uncovered stores of gunpowder.

So, with as little reflection as possible, he simply relit the candle and went up to the next floor. The arm in his trembled, it is true, and his own tread was often uncertain, but they went on with thoroughness, and after a search revealing nothing they climbed the last flight of stairs to the top floor of all.

Here they found a perfect nest of small servants' rooms, with broken pieces of furniture, dirty cane-bottomed chairs, chests of drawers, cracked mirrors, and decrepit bedsteads. The rooms had low sloping ceilings already hung here and there with cobwebs, small windows, and badly plastered walls—a depressing and dismal region which they were glad to leave behind.

It was on the stroke of midnight when they entered a small room on the third floor, close to the top of the stairs, and arranged to make themselves comfortable for the remainder of their adventure. It was absolutely bare, and was said to be the room—then used as a clothes closet—into which the infuriated groom had chased his victim and finally caught her. Outside, across the narrow landing, began the stairs leading up to the floor above, and the servants' quarters where they had just searched.

In spite of the chilliness of the night there was something in the air of this room that cried for an open window. But there was more than this. Shorthouse could only describe it by saying that he felt less master of himself here than in any other part of the house. There was something that acted directly on the nerves, tiring the resolution, enfeebling the will. He was conscious of this result before he had been in the room five minutes, and it was in the short time they stayed there that he suffered {he wholesale depletion of his vital forces, which was, for himself, the chief horror of the whole experience.

They put the candle on the floor of the cupboard, leaving the door a few inches ajar, so that there was no glare to confuse the eyes, and no shadow to shift about on walls and ceiling. Then they spread the cloak on the floor and sat down to wait, with their backs against the wall.

Shorthouse was within two feet of the door on to the landing; his position commanded a good view of the main staircase leading down into the darkness, and also of the beginning of the servants' stairs going to the floor above; the heavy stick lay beside him within easy reach.

The moon was now high above the house. Through the open window they could see the comforting stars like friendly eyes watching in the sky. One by one the clocks of the town struck midnight, and when the sounds died away the deep silence of a windless night fell again over everything. Only the boom of the sea, far away and lugubrious, filled the air with hollow murmurs.

Inside the house the silence became awful; awful, he thought, because any minute now it might be broken by sounds portending terror. The strain of waiting told more and more severely on the nerves; they talked in whispers when they talked at all, for their voices aloud sounded queer and unnatural. A chilliness, not altogether due to the night air, invaded the room, and made them cold. The influences against them, whatever these might be, were slowly robbing them of self-confidence, and the power of decisive action; their forces were on the wane, and the possibility of real fear took on a new and terrible meaning. He began to tremble for the elderly woman by his side, whose pluck could hardly save her beyond a certain extent.

He heard the blood singing in his veins. It sometimes seemed so loud that he fancied it prevented his hearing properly certain other sounds that were beginning very faintly to make themselves audible in the depths of the house. Every time he fastened his attention on these sounds, they instantly ceased. They certainly came no nearer. Yet he could not rid himself of the idea that movement was going on somewhere in the lower regions of the house. The drawing-room floor, where the doors had been so strangely closed, seemed too near; the sounds were further off than that. He thought of the great kitchen, with the scurrying black-beetles, and of the dismal little scullery; but, somehow or other, they did not seem to come from there either. Surely they were not *outside* the house!

Then, suddenly, the truth flashed into his mind, and for the space of a minute he felt as if his blood had stopped flowing and turned to ice.

The sounds were not downstairs at all; they were *upstairs*—upstairs, somewhere among those horrid gloomy little servants' rooms with their bits of broken furniture, low ceilings, and cramped windows—upstairs where the victim had first been disturbed and stalked to her death.

And the moment he discovered where the sounds were, he began to hear them more clearly. It was the sound of feet, moving stealthily along the passage overhead, in and out among the rooms, and past the furniture.

He turned quickly to steal a glance at the motionless figure seated beside him, to note whether she had shared his discovery. The faint candle-light coming through the crack in the cupboard door, threw her strongly-marked face into vivid relief against the white of the wall. But it was something else that made him catch his breath and stare again. An extraordinary something had come into her face and seemed to spread over her features like a mask; it smoothed out the deep lines and drew the skin everywhere a little tighter so that the wrinkles disappeared; it brought into the face—with the sole exception of the old eyes—an appearance of youth and almost of childhood.

He stared in speechless amazement—amazement that was dangerously near to horror. It was his aunt's face indeed, but it was her face of forty years ago, the vacant innocent face of a girl. He had heard stories of that strange effect of terror which could wipe a human countenance clean of other emotions, obliterating all previous expressions; but he had never realised that it could be literally true, or could mean anything so simply horrible as what he now saw. For the dreadful signature of overmastering fear was written plainly in that utter vacancy of the girlish face beside him; and when, feeling his intense gaze, she turned to look at him, he instinctively closed his eyes tightly to shut out the sight.

Yet, when he turned a minute later, his feelings well in hand, he saw to his intense relief another expression; his aunt was smiling, and though the face was deathly white, the awful veil had lifted and the normal look was returning.

'Anything wrong?' was all he could think of to say at the moment. And the answer was eloquent, coming from such a woman.

'I feel cold—and a little frightened,' she whispered.

He offered to close the window, but she seized hold of him and begged him not to leave her side even for an instant.

'It's upstairs, I know,' she whispered, with an odd half laugh; 'but I can't possibly go up.'

But Shorthouse thought otherwise, knowing that in action lay their best hope of self-control.

He took the brandy flask and poured out a glass of neat spirit, stiff enough to help anybody over anything. She swallowed it with a little shiver. His only idea now was to get out of the house before her collapse became inevitable; but this could not safely be done by turning tail and running from the enemy. Inaction was no longer possible; every minute he was growing less master of himself, and desperate, aggressive measures were imperative without further delay. Moreover, the action must be taken *towards* the enemy, not away from it; the climax, if necessary and unavoidable, would have to be faced boldly. He could do it now; but in ten minutes he might not have the force left to act for himself, much less for both!

Upstairs, the sounds were meanwhile becoming louder and closer, accompanied by occasional creaking of the boards. Someone was moving stealthily about, stumbling now and then awkwardly against the furniture.

Waiting a few moments to allow the tremendous dose of spirits to produce its effect, and knowing this would last but a short time under the circumstances, Shorthouse then quietly got on his feet, saying in a determined voice—

'Now, Aunt Julia, we'll go upstairs and find out what all this noise is about. You must come too. It's what we agreed.'

He picked up his stick and went to the cupboard for the candle. A limp form rose shakily beside him breathing hard, and he heard a voice say very faintly something about being 'ready to come.' The woman's courage amazed him; it was so much greater than his own; and, as they advanced, holding aloft the dripping candle, some subtle force exhaled from this trembling, white-faced old woman at his side that was the true source of his inspiration. It held something really great that shamed him and gave him the support without which he would have proved far less equal to the occasion.

They crossed the dark landing, avoiding with their eyes the deep black space over the banisters. Then they began to mount the narrow staircase to meet the sounds which, minute by minute, grew louder and nearer. About half-way up the stairs Aunt Julia stumbled and Shorthouse turned to catch her by the arm, and just at that moment there came a terrific crash in the servants' corridor overhead. It was instantly followed by a shrill, agonised scream that was a cry of terror and a cry for help melted into one.

Before they could move aside, or go down a single step, someone came rushing along the passage overhead, blundering horribly, racing madly, at full speed, three steps at a time, down the very staircase where they stood. The steps were light and uncertain; but close behind them sounded the heavier tread of another person, and the staircase seemed to shake.

Shorthouse and his companion just had time to flatten themselves against the wall when the jumble of flying steps was upon them, and two persons, with the slightest possible interval between them, dashed past at full speed. It was a perfect whirlwind of sound breaking in upon the midnight silence of the empty building.

The two runners, pursuer and pursued, had passed clean through them where they stood, and already with a thud the boards below had received first one, then the other. Yet they had seen absolutely nothing—not a hand, or arm, or face, or even a shred of flying clothing.

There came a second's pause. Then the first one, the lighter of the two, obviously the pursued one, ran with uncertain footsteps into the little room which Shorthouse and his aunt had just left. The heavier one followed. There was a sound of scuffling, gasping, and smothered screaming; and then out on to the landing came the step—of a single person *treading weightily*.

A dead silence followed for the space of half a minute, and then was heard a rushing sound through the air. It was followed by a dull, crashing thud in the depths of the house below—on the stone floor of the hall.

Utter silence reigned after. Nothing moved. The flame of the candle was steady. It had been steady the whole time, and the air had been undisturbed by any movement whatsoever. Palsied with terror, Aunt Julia, without waiting for her companion, began fumbling her way downstairs; she was crying gently to herself, and when Shorthouse put his arm round her and half carried her he felt that she was trembling like a leaf. He went into the little room and picked up the cloak from the floor, and, arm in arm, walking very slowly, without speaking a word or looking once behind them, they marched down the three flights into the hall.

In the hall they saw nothing, but the whole way down the stairs they were conscious that someone followed them; step by step; when they went faster IT was left behind, and when they went more slowly IT caught them up. But never once did they look behind to see; and at each turning of the staircase they lowered their eyes for fear of the following horror they might see upon the stairs above.

With trembling hands Shorthouse opened the front door, and they walked out into the moonlight and drew a deep breath of the cool night air blowing in from the sea.

40

THE LEOPARD MAN'S STORY
Jack London

... he was really as anxious to give me a story as I was to get it...

He had a dreamy, far-away look in his eyes, and his sad, insistent voice, gentle-spoken as a maid's, seemed the placid embodiment of some deep-seated melancholy. He was the Leopard Man, but he did not look it. His business in life, whereby he lived, was to appear in a cage of performing leopards before vast audiences, and to thrill those audiences by certain exhibitions of nerve for which his employers rewarded him on a scale commensurate with the thrills he produced.

As I say, he did not look it. He was narrow-hipped, narrow-shouldered, and anaemic, while he seemed not so much oppressed by gloom as by a sweet and gentle sadness, the weight of which was as sweetly and gently borne. For an hour I had been trying to get a story out of him, but he appeared to lack imagination. To him there was no romance in his gorgeous career, no deeds of daring, no thrills—nothing but a gray sameness and infinite boredom.

Lions? Oh, yes he had fought with them. It was nothing. All you had to do was to stay sober. Anybody could whip a lion to a standstill with an ordinary stick. He had fought one for half an hour once. Just hit him on the nose every time he rushed, and when he got artful and rushed with his head down, why, the thing to do was to stick out your leg. When he grabbed at the leg you drew it back and hit him on the nose again. That was all.

With the far-away look in his eyes and his soft flow of words he showed me his scars. There were many of them, and one recent one where a tigress had reached for his shoulder and gone clown to the bone. I could see the neatly mended rents in the coat he had on. His right arm, from the elbow down, looked as though it had gone through a threshing machine, what of the ravage wrought by claws and fangs. But it was nothing, he said, only the old wounds bothered him somewhat when rainy weather came on.

Suddenly his face brightened with a recollection, for he was really as anxious to give me a story as I was to get it.

'I suppose you've heard of the lion-tamer who was hated by another man?' he asked.

He paused and looked pensively at a sick lion in the cage opposite.

'Got the toothache,' he explained. 'Well, the lion-tamer's big play to the audience was putting his head in a lion's mouth. The man who hated him attended every performance in the hope sometime of seeing that lion crunch down. He followed the show about all over the country. The years went by and he grew old, and the lion-tamer grew old, and the lion grew old. And at last one day, sitting in a front seat, he saw what he had waited for. The lion crunched down, and there wasn't any need to call a doctor.'

The Leopard Man glanced casually over his finger nails in a manner which would have been critical had it not been so sad.

'Now, that's what I call patience,' he continued, 'and it's my style. But it was not the style of a fellow I knew. He was a little, thin, sawed-off, sword-swallowing and juggling Frenchman. De Ville, he called himself, and he had a nice wife. She did trapeze work and used to dive from under the roof into a net, turning over once on the way as nice as you please.

'De Ville had a quick temper, as quick as his hand, and his hand was as quick as the paw of a tiger. One day, because the ring-master called him a frog-eater, or something like that and maybe a little worse, he shoved him against the soft pine background he used in his knife-throwing act, so quick the ringmaster didn't have time to think, and there, before the audience, De Ville kept the air on fire with his knives, sinking them into the wood all round the ring-master so close that they passed through his clothes and most of them bit into his skin.

'The clowns had to pull the knives out to get him loose, for he was pinned fast. So the ward went around to watch out for De Ville, and no one dared be more than barely civil to his wife. And she was a sly bit of baggage, too, only all hands were afraid of De Ville.

'But there was one man, Wallace; who was afraid of nothing. He was the lion-tamer, and he had the self-same trick of putting his head into the lion's mouth. He'd put it into the mouths of any of them, though he preferred Augustus, a big, good-natured beast who could always be depended upon.

'As I was saying; Wallace—"King" Wallace we called him—was afraid of nothing alive or dead. He was a king and no mistake. I've seen him drunk, and on a wager go into the cage of a Lion that'd turned nasty, and without a stick beat him to a finish. Just did it with his fist on the nose.

'Madame de Ville—

At an uproar behind us the Leopard Man turned quietly around. It was a divided cage, and a monkey, poking through the bars and around the partition, had had its paw seized by a big gray wolf who was trying to pull it off by main strength. The arm seemed stretching out longer and longer like a thick elastic, and the unfortunate monkey's mates were raising a terrible din. No keeper was at hand, so the Leopard Man stepped over a couple of paces, dealt the wolf a sharp blow on the nose with the light cane he carried, and returned with a sadly apologetic smile to take up his unfinished sentence as though there had been no interruption.

'—looked at King Wallace and King Wallace looked at her, while De Ville looked black. We warned Wallace, but it was no use. He laughed at us, as he laughed at De Ville one day when he shoved De Ville's head into a bucket of paste because he wanted to fight.

'De Ville was in a pretty mess—I helped to scrape him off; but he was cool as a cucumber and made no threats at all. But I saw a glitter in his eyes which I had seen often in the eyes of wild beasts, and I went out of my way to give Wallace a final warning. He laughed, but he did not look so much in Madame de Ville's direction after that.

'Several months passed by. Nothing had happened and I was beginning to think it all a scare over nothing. We were West by that time, showing in 'Frisco. It was during the afternoon performance, and the big tent was filled with woman and children, when I went looking for Red Denny, the head canvas-man, who had walked off with my pocket-knife.

'Passing by one of the dressing tents I glanced in through a hole in the canvas to see if I could locate him. He wasn't there, but directly in front of me was King Wallace, in tights, waiting for his turn to go on with his cage of performing lions. He was watching with much amusement a quarrel between a couple of trapeze artists. All the rest of the people in the dressing tent were watching the same thing, with the exception of De Ville, whom I noticed staring at Wallace with undisguised hatred. Wallace and the rest were all too busy following the quarrel to notice this or what followed.

'But I saw it through the hole in the canvas. De Ville drew his handkerchief from his pocket, made as though to mop the sweat from his face with it (it was a hot day), and at the same time walked past Wallace's back. The look troubled me at the time, for not only did I see hatred in it, but I saw triumph as well.

'"De Ville will bear watching," I said to myself, and I really breathed easier when I saw him go out the entrance to the circus grounds and board an electric car for down town. A few minutes later I was in the big tent, where I had overhauled Red Denny. King Wallace was doing his turn and holding the audience spellbound. He was in a particularly vicious mood, and he kept the lions stirred up till they were all snarling, that is, all of them except old Augustus, and he was just too fat and lazy and old to get stirred up over anything.

'Finally Wallace cracked the old lion's knees with his whip and got him into position. Old Augustus, blinking good-naturedly, opened his mouth and in popped Wallace's head. Then the jaws came together, CRUNCH, just like that.'

The Leopard Man smiled in a sweetly wistful fashion, and the far-away look came into his eyes.

'And that was the end of King Wallace,' he went on in his sad, low voice. 'After the excitement cooled down I watched my chance and bent over and smelled Wallace's head. Then I sneezed.'

'It... it was..?' I queried with halting eagerness.

'Snuff—that De Ville dropped on his hair in the dressing tent. Old Augustus never meant to do it. He only sneezed.'

41

THE SILENT BULLET

Arthur B. Reeve

...it's impossible, just as it is impossible for the regular detectives to antagonize the newspapers...

'Detectives in fiction nearly always make a great mistake,' said Kennedy one evening after our first conversation on crime and science. 'They almost invariably antagonize the regular detective force. Now in real life that's impossible—it's fatal.'

'Yes,' I agreed, looking up from reading an account of the failure of a large Wall Street brokerage house, Kerr Parker & Co., and the peculiar suicide of Kerr Parker. 'Yes, it's impossible, just as it is impossible for the regular detectives to antagonize the newspapers. Scotland Yard found that out in the Crippen case.'

'My idea of the thing, Jameson,' continued Kennedy, 'is that the professor of criminal science ought to work with, not against, the regular detectives. They're all right. They're indispensable, of course. Half the secret of success nowadays is organisation. The professor of criminal science should be merely what the professor in a technical school often is—a sort of consulting engineer. For instance, I believe that organisation plus science would go far toward clearing up that Wall Street case I see you are reading.'

I expressed some doubt as to whether the regular police were enlightened enough to take that view of it.

'Some of them are,' he replied. 'Yesterday the chief of police in a Western city sent a man East to see me about the Price murder: you know the case?'

Indeed I did. A wealthy banker of the town had been murdered on the road to the golf club, no one knew why or by whom. Every clue had proved fruitless, and the list of suspects was itself so long and so impossible as to seem most discouraging.

'He sent me a piece of a torn handkerchief with a deep bloodstain on it,' pursued Kennedy. 'He said it clearly didn't belong to the murdered man, that it indicated that the murderer had himself been wounded in the tussle, but as yet it had proved utterly valueless as a clue. Would I see what I could make of it?

'After his man had told me the story I had a feeling that the murder was committed by either a Sicilian labourer on the links or a negro waiter at the club. Well, to make a short story shorter, I decided to test the blood-stain. Probably you didn't know it, but the Carnegie Institution has just published a minute, careful, and dry study of the blood of human beings and of animals.

'In fact, they have been able to reclassify the whole animal kingdom on this basis, and have made some most surprising additions to our knowledge of evolution. Now I don't propose to bore you with the details of the tests, but one of the things they showed was that the blood of a certain branch of the human race gives a reaction much like the blood of a certain group of monkeys, the chimpanzees, while the blood of another branch gives a reaction like that of the gorilla. Of course there's lots more to it, but this is all that need concern us now.

'I tried the tests. The blood on the handkerchief conformed strictly to the latter test. Now the gorilla was, of course, out of the question—this was no Rue Morgue murder. Therefore it was the negro waiter.'

'But,' I interrupted, 'the negro offered a perfect alibi at the start, and—'

'No buts, Walter. Here's a telegram I received at dinner: "Congratulations. Confronted Jackson your evidence as wired. Confessed."'

'Well, Craig, I take off my hat to you,' I exclaimed. 'Next you'll be solving this Kerr Parker case for sure.'

'I would take a hand in it if they'd let me,' said he simply.

That night, without saying anything, I sauntered down to the imposing new police building amid the squalor of Center Street. They were very busy at headquarters, but, having once had that assignment for the Star, I had no trouble in getting in. Inspector Barney O'Connor of the Central Office carefully shifted a cigar from corner to corner of his mouth as I poured forth my suggestion to him.

'Well, Jameson,' he said at length, 'do you think this professor fellow is the goods?'

I didn't mince matters in my opinion of Kennedy. I told him of the Price case and showed him a copy of the telegram. That settled it.

'Can you bring him down here tonight?' he asked quickly.

I reached for the telephone, found Craig in his laboratory finally, and in less than an hour he was in the office.

'This is a most bating case, Professor Kennedy, this case of Kerr Parker,' said the inspector, launching at once into his subject. 'Here is a broker heavily interested in Mexican rubber. It looks like a good thing—plantations right in the same territory as those of the Rubber Trust. Now in addition to that he is branching out into coastwise steamship lines; another man associated with him is heavily engaged in a railway scheme from the United States down into Mexico. Altogether the steamships and railroads are tapping rubber, oil, copper, and I don't know what other regions. Here in New York they have been pyramiding stocks, borrowing money from two trust companies which they control. It's a lovely scheme—you've read about it, I suppose. Also you've read that it comes into competition with a certain group of capitalists whom we will call 'the System.'

'Well, this depression in the market comes along. At once rumours are spread about the weakness of the trust companies; runs start on both of them. The System—you know them—make a great show of supporting the market. Yet the runs continue. God knows whether they will spread or the trust companies stand up under it tomorrow after what happened today. It was a good thing the market was closed when it happened.

'Kerr Parker was surrounded by a group of people who were in his schemes with him. They are holding a council of war in the directors' room. Suddenly Parker rises, staggers toward the window, falls, and is dead before a doctor can get to him. Every effort is made to keep the thing quiet. It is given out that he committed suicide. The papers don't seem to accept the suicide theory, however. Neither do we. The coroner, who is working with us, has kept his mouth shut so far, and will say nothing till the inquest. For, Professor Kennedy, my first man on the spot found that—Kerr Parker—was—murdered.

'Now here comes the amazing part of the story. The doors to the offices on both sides were open at the time. There were lots of people in each office. There was the usual click of typewriters, and the buzz of the ticker, and the hum of conversation. We have any number of witnesses of the whole affair, but as far as any of them knows no shot was fired, no smoke was seen, no noise was heard, nor was any weapon found. Yet here on my desk is a thirty-two-calibre bullet. The coroner's physician probed it out of Parker's neck this afternoon and turned it over to us.'

Kennedy reached for the bullet, and turned it thoughtfully in his fingers for a moment. One side of it had apparently struck a bone in the neck of the murdered man, and was flattened. The other side was still perfectly smooth. With his inevitable magnifying-glass he scrutinised the bullet on every side. I watched his face anxiously, and I could see that he was very intent and very excited.

'Extraordinary, most extraordinary,' he said to himself as he turned it over and over. 'Where did you say this bullet struck?'

'In the fleshy part of the neck, quite a little back of and below his ear and just above his collar. There wasn't much bleeding. I think it must have struck the base of his brain.' 'It didn't strike his collar or hair?'

'No,' replied the inspector.

'Inspector, I think we shall be able to put our hands on the murderer—I think we can get a conviction, sir, on the evidence that I shall get from this bullet in my laboratory.'

'That's pretty much like a story-book,' drawled the inspector incredulously, shaking his head.

'Perhaps,' smiled Kennedy. 'But there will still be plenty of work for the police to do, too. I've only got a clue to the murderer. It will take the whole organisation to follow it up, believe me. Now, Inspector, can you spare the time to go down to Parker's office and take me over the ground? No doubt we can develop something else there.'

'Sure,' answered O'Connor, and within five minutes we were hurrying down town in one of the department automobiles.

We found the office under guard of one of the Central Office men, while in the outside office Parker's confidential clerk and a few assistants were still at work in a subdued and awed manner. Men were working in many other Wall Street offices that night during the panic, but in none was there more reason for it than here. Later I learned that it was the quiet tenacity of this confidential clerk that saved even as much of Parker's estate as was saved for his widow—little enough it was, too. What he saved for the clients of the firm no one will ever know. Somehow or other I liked John Downey, the clerk, from the moment I was introduced to him. He seemed to me, at least, to be the typical confidential clerk who would carry a secret worth millions and keep it.

The officer in charge touched his hat to the inspector, and Downey hastened to put himself at our service. It was plain that the murder had completely mystified him, and that he was as anxious as we were to get at the bottom of it.

'Mr Downey,' began Kennedy, 'I understand you were present when this sad event took place.'

'Yes, sir, sitting right here at the directors' table,' he replied, taking a chair, 'like this.'

'Now can you recollect just how Mr Parker acted when he was shot? Could you—er—could you take his place and show us just how it happened?'

'Yes, sir,' said Downey. 'He was sitting here at the head of the table. Mr Bruce, who is the 'CO.' of the firm, had been sitting here at his right; I was at the left. The inspector has a list of all the others present. That door to the right was open, and Mrs Parker and some other ladies were in the room—'

'Mrs Parker?' broke in Kennedy.

'Yes: Like a good many brokerage firms we have a ladies' room. Many ladies are among our clients. We make a point of catering to them. At that time I recollect the door was open—all the doors were open. It was not a secret meeting. Mr Bruce had just gone into the ladies' department; I think to ask some of them to stand by the firm—he was an artist at smoothing over the fears of customers, particularly women. Just before he went in I had seen the ladies go in a group toward the far end of the room—to look down at the line of depositors on the street, which reached around the corner from one of the trust companies, I thought. I was making a note of an order to send into the outside office there on the left, and had just pushed this button here under the table to call a boy to carry it. Mr Parker had just received a letter by special delivery, and seemed considerably puzzled over it. No, I don't know what it was about. Of a sudden I saw him start in his chair, rise up unsteadily, clap his hand on the back of his head, stagger across the floor—like this—and fall here.'

'Then what happened?'

'Why, I rushed to pick him up. Everything was confusion. I recall someone behind me saying, 'Here, boy, take all these papers off the table and carry them into my office before they get lost in the excitement.' I think it was Bruce's voice. The next moment I heard someone say, 'Stand back, Mrs Parker has fainted.' But I didn't pay much attention, for I was calling to someone not to get a doctor over the telephone, but to go down to the fifth floor where one has an office. I made Mr Parker as comfortable as I could. There wasn't much I could do. He seemed to want to say something to me, but he couldn't talk. He was paralysed, at least his throat was. But I did manage to make out finally what sounded to me like, 'Tell her I don't believe the scandal, I don't believe it.' But before he could say whom to tell he had again become unconscious, and by the time the doctor arrived he was dead. I guess you know everything else as well as I do.'

'You didn't hear the shot fired from any particular direction?' asked Kennedy.

'No, sir.'

'Well, where do you think it came from?'

'That's what puzzles me, sir. The only thing I can figure out is that it was fired from the outside office—perhaps by some customer who had lost money and sought revenge. But no one out there heard it either, any more than they did in the directors' room or the ladies' department.'

'About that message,' asked Kennedy, ignoring what to me seemed to be the most important feature of the case, the mystery of the silent bullet. 'Didn't you see it after all was over?'

'No, sir; in fact I had forgotten about it till this moment when you asked me to reconstruct the circumstances exactly. No, sir, I don't know a thing about it. I can't say it impressed itself on my mind at the time, either.'

'What did Mrs Parker do when she came to?'

'Oh, she cried as I have never seen a woman cry before. He was dead by that time, of course.'

'Bruce and I saw her down in the elevator to her car. In fact, the doctor, who had arrived; said that the sooner she was taken home the better she would be. She was quite hysterical.'

'Did she say anything that you remember?'

Downey hesitated.

'Out with it Downey,' said the inspector. 'What did she say as she was going down in the elevator?'

'Nothing.'

'Tell us. I'll arrest you if you don't.'

'Nothing about the murder, on my honour,' protested Downey.

Kennedy leaned over suddenly and shot a remark at him, 'Then it was about the note.'

Downey was surprised, but not quickly enough. Still he seemed to be considering something, and in a moment he said:

'I don't know what it was about, but I feel it is my duty, after all, to tell you. I heard her say, 'I wonder if he knew.'

'Nothing else?'

'Nothing else.'

'What happened after you came back?'

'We entered the ladies' department. No one was there. A woman's automobile-coat was thrown over a chair in a heap. Mr Bruce picked it up. 'It's Mrs Parker's,' he said. He wrapped it up hastily, and rang for a messenger.'

'Where did he send it?'

'To Mrs Parker, I suppose. I didn't hear the address.'

We next went over the whole suite of offices, conducted by Mr Downey. I noted how carefully Kennedy looked into the directors' room through the open door from the ladies' department. He stood at such an angle that had he been the assassin he could scarcely have been seen except by those sitting immediately next Mr Parker at the directors' table. The street windows were directly in front of him, and back of him was the chair on which the motorcoat had been found.

In Parker's own office we spent some time, as well as in Bruce's. Kennedy made a search for the note, but finding nothing in either office, turned out the contents of Bruce's scrap-basket. There didn't seem to be anything in it to interest him, however, even after he had pieced several torn bits of scraps together with much difficulty, and he was about to turn the papers back again, when he noticed something sticking to the side of the basket. It looked like a mass of wet paper, and that was precisely what it was.

'That's queer,' said Kennedy, picking it loose. Then he wrapped it up carefully and put it in his pocket. 'Inspector, can you lend me one of your men for a couple of days?' he asked, as we were preparing to leave. 'I shall want to send him out of town tonight, and shall probably need his services when he gets back.'

'Very well. Riley will be just the fellow. We'll go back to headquarters, and I'll put him under your orders.'

It was not until late in the following day that I saw Kennedy again. It had been a busy day at the Star. We had gone to work that morning expecting to see the very financial heavens fall. But just about five minutes to ten, before the Stock Exchange opened, the news came in over the wire from our financial man on Broad Street: '"The System" has forced James Bruce, partner of Kerr Parker, the dead banker; to sell his railroad, steamship, and rubber holdings to it. On this condition it promises unlimited support to the market.'

'Forced!' muttered the managing editor, as he waited on the office phone to get the composing-room, so as to hurry up the few lines in red ink on the first page and beat our rivals on the streets with the first extras. 'Why, he's been working to bring that about for the past two weeks. What that System doesn't control isn't worth having—it edits the news before our men get it, and as for grist for the divorce courts, and tragedies, well—Hello, Jenkins, yes, a special extra. Change the big heads—copy is on the way up—rush it.'

'So you think this Parker case is a mess?' I asked.

'I know it. That's a pretty swift bunch of females that have been speculating at Kerr Parker & Co.'s. I understand there's one Titian-haired young lady—who, by the way, has at least one husband who hasn't yet been divorced—who is a sort of ringleader, though she rarely goes personally to her brokers' offices. She's one of those uptown plungers, and the story is that she has a whole string of scalps of alleged Sunday-school superintendents at her belt. She can make Bruce do pretty nearly anything, they say. He's the latest conquest. I got the story on pretty good authority, but until I verified the names, dates, and places, of course I wouldn't dare print a line of it. The story goes that her husband is a hanger-on of the System, and that she's been working in their interest, too. That was why he was so complacent over the whole affair. They put her up to capturing Bruce, and after she had acquired an influence over him they worked it so that she made him make love to Mrs Parker. It's a long story, but that isn't all of it. The point was, you see, that by this devious route they hoped to worm out of Mrs Parker some inside information about Parker's rubber schemes, which he hadn't divulged even to his partners in business. It was a deep and carefully planned plot, and some of the conspirators were pretty deeply in the mire, I guess. I wish I'd had all the facts about who this red-haired female Machiavelli was—what a piece of muckraking it would have made! Oh, here comes the rest of the news story over the wire. By Jove, it is said on good authority that Bruce will be taken in as one of the board of directors. What do you think of that?'

So that was how the wind lay—Bruce making love to Mrs Parker and she presumably betraying her husband's secrets. I thought I saw it all: the note from somebody exposing the scheme, Parker's incredulity, Bruce sitting by him and catching sight of the note, his hurrying out into the ladies' department, and then the shot. But who fired it? After all, I had only picked up another clue.

Kennedy was not at the apartment at dinner, and an inquiry at the laboratory was fruitless also. So I sat down to fidget for a while. Pretty soon the buzzer on the door sounded, and I opened it to find a messenger-boy with a large brown paper parcel.

'Is Mr Bruce here?' he asked.

'Why, no, he doesn't—' then I checked myself and added 'He will be here presently. You can leave the bundle.'

'Well, this is the parcel he telephoned for. His valet told me to tell him that they had a hard time to find it, but he guesses it's all right. The charges are forty cents. Sign here.'

I signed the book, feeling like a thief, and the boy departed. What it all meant I could not guess.

Just then I heard a key in the lock, and Kennedy came in.

'Is your name Bruce?' I asked.

'Why?' he replied eagerly. 'Has anything come?'

I pointed to the package. Kennedy made a dive for it and unwrapped it. It was a woman's pongee automobile-coat. He held it up to the light. The pocket on the right-hand side was scorched and burned, and a hole was torn clean through it. I gasped when the full significance of it dawned on me.

'How did you get it?' I exclaimed at last in surprise.

'That's where organisation comes in,' said Kennedy. 'The police at my request went over every messenger call from Parker's office that afternoon, and traced every one of them up. At last they found one that led to Bruce's apartment. None of them led to Mrs Parker's home. The rest were all business calls and satisfactorily accounted for. I reasoned that this was the one that involved the disappearance of the automobile-coat. It was a chance worth taking, so I got Downey to call up Bruce's valet. The valet of course recognised Downey's voice and suspected nothing. Downey assumed to know all about the coat in the package received yesterday. He asked to have it sent up here. I see the scheme worked.'

'But, Kennedy, do you think she—' I stopped, speechless, looking at the scorched coat.

'Nothing to say—yet,' he replied laconically. 'But if you could tell me anything about that note Parker received I'd thank you.'

I related what our managing editor had said that morning. Kennedy only raised his eyebrows a fraction of an inch.

'I had guessed something of that sort,' he said merely. 'I'm glad to find it confirmed even by hearsay evidence. This red-haired young lady interests me. Not a very definite description, but better than nothing at all. I wonder who she is. Ah, well, what do you say to a stroll down the White Way before I go to my laboratory? I'd like a breath of air to relax my mind.'

We had got no further than the first theatre when Kennedy slapped me on the back. 'By George, Jameson, she's an actress, of course.'

'Who is? What's the matter with you, Kennedy? Are you crazy?'

'The red-haired person—she must be an actress. Don't you remember the auburn-haired leading lady in the "Follies"—the girl who sings that song about "Mary, Mary, quite contrary"? Her stage name, you know, is Phoebe La Neige. Well, if it's she who is concerned in this case I don't think she'll be playing tonight. Let's inquire at the box-office.'

She wasn't playing, but just what it had to do with anything in particular I couldn't see, and I said as much.

'Why, Walter, you'd never do as a detective. You lack intuition. Sometimes I think I haven't quite enough of it, either. Why didn't I think of that sooner? Don't you know she is the wife of Adolphus Hesse, the most inveterate gambler in stocks in the System? Why, I had only to put two and two together and the whole thing flashed on me in an instant. Isn't it a good hypothesis that she is the red-haired woman in the case, the tool of the System in which her husband is so heavily involved? I'll have to add her to my list of suspects.'

'Why, you don't think she did the shooting?' I asked, half hoping, I must admit, for an assenting nod from him.

'Well,' he answered dryly, 'one shouldn't let any preconceived hypothesis stand between him and the truth. I've made a guess at the whole thing already. It may or it may not be right. Anyhow she will fit into it. And if it's not right, I've got to be prepared to make a new guess, that's all.'

When we reached the laboratory on our return, the inspector's man Riley was there, waiting impatiently for Kennedy.

'What luck?' asked Kennedy.

'I've got a list of purchasers of that kind of revolver,' he said. 'We have been to every sporting-goods and arms-store in the city which bought them from the factory, and I could lay my hands on pretty nearly every one of those weapons in twenty-four hours—provided, of course, they haven't been secreted or destroyed.'

'Pretty nearly all isn't good enough,' said Kennedy. 'It will have to be all, unless—'

'That name is in the list,' whispered Riley hoarsely.

'Oh, then it's all right,' answered Kennedy, brightening up. 'Riley, I will say that you're a wonder at using the organisation in ferreting out such things. There's just one more thing I want you to do. I want a sample of the notepaper in the private desks of every one of these people.' He handed the policeman a list of his 9 'suspects,' as he called them. It included nearly every one mentioned in the case.

Riley studied it dubiously and scratched his chin thoughtfully. 'That's a hard one, Mr Kennedy, sir. You see, it means getting into so many different houses and apartments. Now you don't want to do it by means of a warrant, do you, sir? Of course not. Well, then, how can we get in?'

'You're a pretty good-looking chap yourself, Riley,' said Kennedy. 'I should think you could jolly a housemaid, if necessary. Anyhow, you can get the fellow on the beat to do it—if he isn't already to be found in the kitchen. Why, I see a dozen ways of getting the notepaper.'

'Oh, it's me that's the lady-killer, sir,' grinned Riley. 'I'm a regular Blarney stone when I'm out on a job of that sort. Sure, I'll have some of them for you in the morning.'

'Bring me what you get, the first thing in the morning, even if you've landed only a few samples,' said Kennedy, as Riley departed, straightening his tie and brushing his hat on his sleeve.

'And now, Walter, you too must excuse me tonight,' said Craig. 'I've got a lot to do, and sha'n't be up to our apartment till very late—or early. But I feel sure I've got a strangle-hold on this mystery. If I get those papers from Riley in good time tomorrow I shall invite you and several others to a grand demonstration here tomorrow night. Don't forget. Keep the whole evening free. It will be a big story.'

Kennedy's laboratory was brightly lighted when I arrived early the next evening. One by one his 'guests' dropped in. It was evident that they had little liking for the visit, but the coroner had sent out the 'invitations,' and they had nothing to do but accept. Each one was politely welcomed by the professor and assigned a seat, much as he would have done with a group of students. The inspector and the coroner sat back a little. Mrs Parker, Mr Downey, Mr Bruce, myself, and Miss La Neige sat in that order in the very narrow and uncomfortable little armchairs used by the students during lectures.

At last Kennedy was ready to begin. He took his position behind the long, flat-topped table which he used for his demonstrations before his classes. 'I realise, ladies and gentlemen,' he began formally, 'that I am about to do a very unusual thing; but, as you all know, the police and the coroner have been completely baffled by this terrible mystery and have requested me to attempt to clear up at least certain points in it. I will begin what I have to say by remarking that the tracing out of a crime like this differs in nothing, except as regards the subject-matter, from the search for a scientific truth. The forcing of man's secrets is like the forcing of nature's secrets. Both are pieces of detective work. The methods employed in the detection of crime are, or rather should be, like the methods employed in the process of discovering scientific truth. In a crime of this sort, two kinds of evidence need to be secured. Circumstantial evidence must first be marshalled, and then a motive must be found. I have been gathering facts. But to omit motives and rest contented with mere facts would be inconclusive. It would never convince anybody or convict anybody. In other words, circumstantial evidence must first lead to a suspect, and then this suspect must prove equal to accounting for the facts. It is my hope that each of you may contribute something that will be of service in arriving at the truth of this unfortunate incident.'

The tension was not relieved even when Kennedy stopped speaking and began to fuss with a little upright target which he set up at one end of his table. We seemed to be seated over a powder magazine which threatened to explode at any moment. I, at least, felt the tension so greatly that it was only after he had started speaking again, that I noticed that the target was composed of a thick layer of some putty-like material.

Holding a thirty-two-calibre pistol in his right hand and aiming it at the target, Kennedy picked up a large piece of coarse homespun from the table and held it loosely over the muzzle of the gun. Then he fired. The bullet tore through the cloth, sped through the air, and buried itself in the target. With a knife he pried it out.

'I doubt if even the inspector himself could have told us that when an ordinary leaden bullet is shot through a woven fabric the weave of that fabric is in the majority of cases impressed on the bullet, sometimes clearly, sometimes faintly.'

Here Kennedy took up a piece of fine batiste and fired another bullet through it.

'Every leaden bullet, as I have said, which has struck such a fabric bears an impression of the threads which is recognisable even when the bullet has penetrated deeply into the body. It is only obliterated partially or entirely when the bullet has been flattened by striking a bone or other hard object. Even then, as in this case, if only a part of the bullet is flattened the remainder may still show the marks of the fabric. A heavy warp, say of cotton velvet or, as I have here, homespun, will be imprinted well on the bullet, but even a fine batiste, containing one hundred threads to the inch, will show marks. Even layers of goods such as a coat, shirt, and undershirt may each leave their marks, but that does not concern us in this case. Now I have here a piece of pongee silk, cut from a woman's automobile-coat. I discharge the bullet through it—so. I compare the bullet now with the others and with the one probed from the neck of Mr Parker. I find that the marks on that fatal bullet correspond precisely with those on the bullet fired through the pongee coat.'

Startling as was this revelation, Kennedy paused only an instant before the next.

'Now I have another demonstration. A certain note figures in this case. Mr Parker was reading it, or perhaps re-reading it, at the time he was shot. I have not been able to obtain that note—at least not in a form such as I could use in discovering what were its contents. But in a certain wastebasket I found a mass of wet and pulp-like paper. It had been cut up, macerated, perhaps chewed; perhaps it had been also soaked with water. There was a washbasin with running water in this room. The ink had run, and of course was illegible. The thing was so unusual that I at once assumed that this was the remains of the note in question. Under ordinary circumstances it would be utterly valueless as a clue to anything. But today science is not ready to let anything pass as valueless.

'I found on microscopic examination that it was an uncommon linen bond paper, and I have taken a large number of microphotographs of the fibres in it. They are all similar. I have here also about a hundred microphotographs of the fibres in other kinds of paper, many of them bonds. These I have accumulated from time to time in my study of the subject. None of them, as you can see, shows fibres resembling this one in question, so we may conclude that it is of uncommon quality. Through an agent of the police I have secured samples of the notepaper of every one who could be concerned, as far as I could see, with this case. Here are the photographs of the fibres of these various notepapers, and among them all is just one that corresponds to the fibres in the wet mass of paper I discovered in the scrap-basket. Now lest anyone should question the accuracy of this method I might cite a case where a man had been arrested in Germany charged with stealing a government bond. He was not searched till later. There was no evidence save that after the arrest a large number of spitballs were found around the courtyard under his cell window. This method of comparing the fibres with those of the regular government paper was used, and by it the man was convicted of stealing the bond. I think it is almost unnecessary to add that in the present case we know precisely who—'

At this point the tension was so great that it snapped. Miss La Neige, who was sitting beside me, had been leaning forward involuntarily.

Almost as if the words were wrung from her she whispered hoarsely: 'They put me up to doing it; I didn't want to. But the affair had gone too far. I couldn't see him lost before my very eyes. I didn't want her to get him. The quickest way out was to tell the whole story to Mr Parker and stop it. It was the only way I could think of to stop this thing between another man's wife and the man I loved better than my own husband. God knows, Professor Kennedy, that was all—'

'Calm yourself, madame,' interrupted Kennedy soothingly. 'Calm yourself. What's done is done. The truth must come out. Be calm. Now,' he continued, after the first storm of remorse had spent itself and we were all outwardly composed again, 'we have said nothing whatever of the most mysterious feature of the case, the firing of the shot. The murderer could have thrust the weapon into the pocket or the folds of this coat'—here he drew forth the automobile coat and held it aloft, displaying the bullet hole—'and he or she (I will not say which) could have discharged the pistol unseen. By removing and secreting the weapon afterward one very important piece of evidence would be suppressed. This person could have used such a cartridge as I have here, made with smokeless powder, and the coat would have concealed the flash of the shot very effectively. There would have been no smoke. But neither this coat nor even a heavy blanket would have deadened the report of the shot.

'What are we to think of that? Only one thing. I have often wondered why the thing wasn't done before. In fact I have been waiting for it to occur. There is an invention that makes it almost possible to strike a man down with impunity in broad daylight in any place where there is sufficient noise to cover up a click, a slight 'Pouf!' and the whir of the bullet in the air.

'I refer to this little device of a Hartford inventor. I place it over the muzzle of the thirty-two-calibre revolver I have so far been using—so. Now, Mr Jameson, if you will sit at that typewriter over there and write—anything so long as you keep the keys clicking. The inspector will start that imitation stock-ticker in the corner. Now we are ready. I cover the pistol with a cloth. I defy anyone in this room to tell me the exact moment when I discharged the pistol. I could have shot any of you, and an outsider not in the secret would never have thought that I was the culprit. To a certain extent I have reproduced the conditions under which this shooting occurred.

'At once on being sure of this feature of the case I despatched a man to Hartford to see this inventor. The man obtained from him a complete list of all the dealers in New York to whom such devices had been sold. The man also traced every sale of those dealers. He did not actually obtain the weapon, but if he is working on schedule-time according to agreement he is at this moment armed with a search-warrant and is ransacking every possible place where the person suspected of this crime could have concealed his weapon. For, one of the persons intimately connected with this case purchased not long ago a silencer for a thirty-two-calibre revolver, and I presume that that person carried the gun and the silencer at the time of the murder of Kerr Parker.'

Kennedy concluded in triumph, his voice high pitched, his eyes flashing. Yet to all outward appearance not a heart-beat was quickened. Someone in that room had an amazing store of self-possession. The fear flitted across my mind that even at the last Kennedy was baffled.

'I had anticipated some such anti-climax,' he continued after a moment. 'I am prepared for it.'

He touched a bell, and the door to the next room opened. One of Kennedy's graduate students stepped in.

'You have the records, Whiting' he asked.

'Yes, Professor.'

'I may say,' said Kennedy, 'that each of your chairs is wired under the arm in such a way as to betray on an appropriate indicator in the next room every sudden and undue emotion. Though it may be concealed from the eye, even of one like me who stands facing you, such emotion is nevertheless expressed by physical pressure on the arms of the chair. It is a test that is used frequently with students to demonstrate various points of psychology. You needn't raise your arms from the chairs, ladies and gentlemen. The tests are all over now. What did they show, Whiting?'

The student read what he had been noting in the next room. At the production of the coat during the demonstration of the markings of the bullet, Mrs Parker had betrayed great emotion, Mr Bruce had done likewise, and nothing more than ordinary emotion had been noted for the rest of us. Miss La Neige's automatic record during the tracing out of the sending of the note to Parker had been especially unfavourable to her; Mr Bruce showed almost as much excitement; Mrs Parker very little and Downey very little. It was all set forth in curves drawn by self-recording pens on regular ruled paper. The student had merely noted what took place in the lecture-room as corresponding to these curves.

'At the mention of the noiseless gun,' said Kennedy, bending over the record, while the student pointed it out to him and we leaned forward to catch his words, 'I find that the curves of Miss La Neige, Mrs Parker, and Mr Downey are only so far from normal as would be natural. All of them were witnessing a thing for the first time with only curiosity and no fear. The curve made by Mr Bruce shows great agitation and—'

I heard a metallic click at my side and turned hastily. It was Inspector Barney O'Connor, who had stepped out of the shadow with a pair of hand-cuffs.

'James Bruce, you are under arrest,' he said.

There flashed on my mind, and I think on the minds of some of the others, a picture of another electrically wired chair.

42

INDIAN MAGIC
Edgar Wallace

…love is responsible for more crime than drink…

When love comes barging into a man's business there's generally trouble for everybody. That is the opinion of people with knowledge and education.

There was a schoolmaster—and a real gentleman—who used to work next to me in the shoe-making shop at Dartmoor, who told me that love is responsible for more crime than drink. He gave me the figures, and with a bit of chalk he drew what he called a 'grarf' on the sole of Wigman's boots—Wigman, that shot the policeman in the Harrow Road. A very nice fellow—Wigman, I mean. I never met the policeman.

There used to be a warder at Dartmoor whose wife ran away with a soldier. You ought to hear him talk about women!

There's another thing I despise—foreigners. It stands to reason that foreigners are different to us Christians. There's no sense of, what I might term, honour amongst them. They keep things back like Dhobi, the Indian, kept things from young Sam Baring. Love and foreigners was Sam's ruin, and deny it who can.

Sam is as smart a fellow as you would find between here and… well, anywhere. Quite the gentleman, and well educated. He can read and write, and you can't ask him anything about geography that he couldn't tell you.

He is always well dressed—why, I've seen him mixing with the swells at Ascot like one of themselves. High collar, spotted tie, long-tailed coat, and a handsome brown bowler with a Beatty tilt—he was my idea of what a lord should look like.

Sam and me and an American, named Bisher, made a lot of money out of the electric racing saddle. You put it on a horse and touched a button—and he moves! I've seen experienced trainers watching the effect of the saddle with their mouths wide open. There was a coil inside and a small battery. 'When you touched the button, the horse got a shock, and naturally went a bit faster. It cost about £150 to make, and we took orders for ninety at £50 apiece. I needn't tell you that when we didn't deliver the goods, some unpleasant letters came to the office, but, as Sam said, they were out to defraud the Jockey Club by artificial stimulants, and he was doing a good turn to the sport by besting them. Anyway, they couldn't squeal, and that was something.

Sam had high notions about racing, and we'd hardly packed our parcel before he saw an advertisement of a farm for sale, and he got the idea of training a horse or two. He bought a couple out of selling races at Gatwick and Lingfield: Early Worm was one, and the other was called String of Beans. Sam got a license to train without much trouble. He had never been before the Stewards, and he hadn't tried to sell electric saddles to the swell trainers at Newmarket, so, as the song says, the breath of scandal ne'er sullied his fair name. And he hadn't been in the hands of the police either.

Luck is a funny thing. Both those horses he bought were pretty good. We used to run 'em down the course for a bit. They wouldn't be trying a yard. Then, when the money was down, we let loose the head of String of Beans, and the way he won was both exciting and cheerful.

We might have gone on, and packed enough money to live like princes, if it hadn't been for this girl I've been referring to.

Her name was Virginia, the same as the country in America, but she was English. Personally, I never saw anything in her, and when one day I heard her say to her father, 'Who is that funny little man with the big red nose?' referring to me, she passed out of my life, and I lost all respect for her. Her father's name was Major Rice, and he had a stable near ours. He trained a few horses, mostly his own, but he had a couple belonging to a young gentleman named Tarbot,

Captain Harold Tarbot.

Sam got quite friendly with them, and used to go over to late dinner all dressed up in evening clothing, which was swank.

Well, to cut a long story short, he fell in love with this girl, and meeting her out one day on the Downs, he up and told her that she was the only girl in the world, and that all he had, including the house and furniture, Early Worm, and String of Beans, was hers, which wasn't right, because me and Bisher had a share in the horses, and all the chairs in the dining-room I bought with my own money.

I don't exactly know what happened, but Sam came home with bits of Sussex sticking to his clothes and a black eye. Sam was wrong, but he was always a bit rough with women, and I gather that this captain happened to be handy.

'This comes of lowering yourself to the level of common people,' said Sam, when he told us all about it. 'I thought I was doing her a favour, which, considering her father is in debt, and this captain hasn't got two shillings to rub together, I certainly was. I'll give him Blue Rat!'

'I shouldn't give him anything if I were you, Sam,' I said, and Bisher agreed with me. 'If the young woman won't let you walk out with her, she's got bad taste. As to a blue rat—well, I've never heard of it, but I've seen pink ones in my time, especially in the United States, where good alcohol and lives are cheap.'

'Blue Rat is his horse,' said Sam, who was putting a bit of sticking-plaster on his cheek in front of the looking-glass. 'He has been saving it all the year to win a selling plate at Newmarket. And to think,' he said bitterly, 'that I have been giving him advice and helping, so to speak, to get the horse together!'

Knowing how he felt, I was a bit astonished the next day when he went over to Major Rice's, saw the young lady and the captain, and apologized. He didn't tell us what his object was, and my own opinion then was that it was sheer gentlemanliness, for Sam Baring is as polite a fellow as ever drew the breath of life.

Anyway, everything must have been all right, for Major Rice came over to look at String of Beans. It was the first time he had ever been in our house, and Sam made a great fuss of him. The young lady didn't come, but I saw her, that same week, strolling across the Downs with the captain, and I must say that they looked on affectionate terms, so far as it is possible for a man of the world to judge.

One night Sam came in to where me and Bisher were playing a quiet game of bezique and he said:

'I have entered String of Beans for a mile selling plate at Newmarket. It is the same race that Blue Rat is entered for, and I want to warn you fellows that if the major asks you if String of Beans is any good, you've got to say no. I am going to give that captain the shock of his life.'

We had a couple of lads that Sam had picked up, to look after the horses, and he gave these boys instructions that String of Beans was only to be exercised at full strength when Major Rice wasn't on the Downs. Therefore, it was more remarkable still when Sam told us one day at lunch that Major Rice was bringing Blue Rat across the following morning, to give him a trial spin with String of Beans.

'Oh, boy!' said Bisher, who, being an American, used strange expressions.

'There's going to be nothing funny about it,' said Sam seriously. 'I am putting a bit of extra weight on String of Beans, my idea being to know just how I stand with this Blue Rat. I've told the lad to ride him out.'

The next morning the trial came off, and, to Sam's astonishment. Blue Rat made rings round String of Beans. Led him all the way, and won the trial in a hack canter; and the time was good, as I know, because I had my watch on the spin from start to finish.

Sam looked down his nose when he came back to the house.

'That Blue Rat horse is going to win,' he said.

'What about the weight you gave String of Beans?'

Sam shook his head.

'It doesn't matter,' he said; if String of Beans had a stone less, he couldn't have won that trial. This is horrible, Nosey.' (I might remark that that was the name by which my intimate friends called me.)

Anyhow, Sam wasn't quite satisfied, and he persuaded the major to give the horses another trial, and this time they carried the weights they were set to carry in the race, and Blue Rat did just what he liked with String of Beans—waited on him to the distance, and then came away and won his race, dancing.

'All my best laid plans are dissolving in smoke,' groaned Sam, who was a very high-class talker when he liked to give his mind to literary conversation. 'I have been kidding Rice all along that his horse was the best, and quite unexpectedly I have been telling the truth.'

'If you don't want Blue Rat to win, why not get at the other horse!' said Bisher. 'It is dead easy to give him a pill a couple of days before the race.'

'Not so easy,' said Sam. 'You don't suppose,' he asked contemptuous, 'that I have been going in and out of that house without knowing the lay of the stables? Besides, if you gave him poison he wouldn't run, and if he wouldn't run, that way the captain wouldn't lose his money, would he?' which is common sense and logic, as we all agreed.

It was a week before the race when we met Mr Dhobi. He was an Indian person—I will not call him a gentleman—a little fellow, very thin, with a high forehead and gold spectacles. Sam had met him somewhere in town, where he used to run a fortune-telling business, in a little turning off Regent Street.

I never saw a man wear a frock-coat and a top-hat on a hot day so elegantly.

Nobody expected him.

'The fact is, gentlemen,' he said in his foreign way, 'I happened to know that Mr Baring was down at Luscombe, and as Mr Baring has been a very good friend of mine, I couldn't very well avoid giving him a chance of securing the golden harvest, which the brave and the fortunate alike deserve.'

I've got a good memory for words, even if I don't know the meaning of them, and that was what he said.

'I am glad to see you, Dhobi; how is the crystal fake going?'

Dhobi shook his head.

'The constabulary of London have interfered, tyrannously and arbitrarily,' he said. 'Because I am a stranger to your land, being an Indian, as you will notice by the pigmentation of my countenance, I have been victimized by a trick of brutality. But knowing that Mr Baring was in the racecourse business, I have brought to him the discovery of a fellow-countryman of mine, hoping that a suitable honorarium will reward me for trouble taken and traveling expenses incurred.'

And then he told us the most wonderful story. Personally, I didn't believe it, being by nature suspicious, and by profession a teller of the tale. But this Dhobi had a drug which was called Indian Magic. He brought out a big packet and showed us. It looked like dried tea leaves, but it was the dried leaf of a certain Indian bush which only grew on the high mountains, and it had the effect of increasing the stamina of any human being or horse that ate it. Whether or not there are high mountains in India, I don't know. Sam said there were certain hills called the Emma Layers or Hindoo Push, and geography was his passion.

Naturally, being experienced tale-pitchers, and having behind us a record of ninety electric saddles sold and paid for, we didn't exactly fall upon his neck.

'It sounds all right, Dhobi,' said Sam.

'The proof of the pudding is in the eating,' said Dhobi, highly enthusiastic. 'I do not ask you to buy a pig in a poke, or make a leap in the dark. Give one handful to any horse you have before he goes out to exercise, and then tell me if I am indulging in fairy stories or fantastic exaggerations.'

That seemed fair.

We put Dhobi up for the night and brought him into a game of Solo with the idea of testing his intelligence. He was more intelligent by three pounds ten and sixpence than Sam and me when we got up to go to bed.

'We will try it on String of Beans,' said Sam. 'He has always struck me as being a horse liable to take kindly to intoxication.'

So, before the sun was up, we all went to String of Beans's stall, and Dhobi mixed with the horse's corn a handful of the Indian Magic.

String of Beans ate off all right. He'd eat anything. He had a special partiality for mutton bones and cabbage stalks, which is strange, considering that most of his ancestors were vegetarians.

The only thing we had to try him with was Early Worm, who wasn't a bad horse by any means; moreover, he had been in the trial spin with Blue Rat, and he had been up sides with String of Beans all the way, and had only been beaten a neck.

So we went out to the Downs, and String of Beans was the liveliest member of the party. The way he tiptoed and pranced and walked sideways and backways was both alarming and instructive. I've never seen a horse get jovial before, but String of Beans was all that; he did everything except laugh. I don't know whether people will believe what I'm going to tell them.

String of Beans jumped off at the start, made all the running, and beat Early Worm by the length of the street. There was nothing wrong about the gallop, because three of us put the clock on him and he did the mile in one-forty dead.

Sam drew a long sigh, and his eyes shone with a soft light.

'Thank you, Dhobi,' he said, 'you are indeed a welcome guest.'

But he wasn't parting with any money until we had seen how String of Beans got over his jag. The wonderful thing about Indian Magic was that it showed no sign on the horse's coat. He didn't break out in a sweat or go mad, and when the race was over he was just as lively as he was before it started. In fact, Indian Magic had no effect at all upon him, except when we galloped him a few days after the trial he didn't go any faster than Early Worm. To make absolutely sure, we tried a handful of Indian Magic on Early Worm, and then put the two horses together in a fast mile spin. Early Worm went ahead and stayed there, and when it was over, and we clicked down our watches, Sam said:

'Boys, this Captain What's-his-name is going to get a jar.'

He had quite recovered his position with the Rices: he used to go over there regular, and the captain couldn't do enough for him. Especially when Sam gave him advice about Blue Rat. I heard him one day when we were up on the Downs exercising our two animals. The captain and the young lady rode up to us just before we left.

'Are you running yours at Newmarket, Mr Baring?' says the captain.

'Yes, I shall run him,' says Sam, shaking his head mournfully. 'But what's the use? Your Blue Rat is going to put it all over us.'

'I wonder whether I shall get a good price?' says the captain thoughtfully.

'If you don't advertise it, and nobody knows anything about the trial, you'll get six to one for your money,' says Sam. 'I shall back mine,' he went on, 'for old association's sake. String of Beans has been a good friend of mine, and I don't think he'd like to know that I let him run without having fifty on him. In fact,' he says, 'I shouldn't be surprised if my horse wasn't favourite, but don't you take any notice of that, Captain. The public always dash in and back the wrong horse.'

'I have been looking at the entries,' says the captain, pulling a paper out of his pocket. 'Do you see anything there that is likely to beat mine, Mr Baring?'

He handed down the paper and Sam took it.

'No,' he says, 'there is nothing there to beat yours. String of Beans will head most of them; but, of course, the poor old String won't see the way your horse is going.'

'I hope not,' says Miss Virginia, in an absent-minded kind of way, and she looks at the captain with a kind of scared look. 'It is an awful lot of money to risk on a selling plater, Harold,' she says. 'Daddy doesn't like the idea at all.'

'Believe me,' says Sam, very earnest, 'and I speak as a sportsman of experience and a man of the world, backing Blue Rat is like picking up money. It is like taking pennies from a child,' he says. 'If I wasn't an honest man—which, thank God, I am,' says Sam, 'and not a word has ever been spoken against my character, and no stain of dishonour has blotted my coat-of-arms, which is a lamb crouching before a lion ramping, if I wasn't—well, anyway, I'm not going to back your horse, not for a penny,' he says. 'I wouldn't spoil your market. It would be almost caddish,' he says.

'Do you think the trial was right?' says the captain.

'Right?' says Sam scoffingly, 'why, of course it was right; you took the time, the clock cannot lie. No, poor old String of Beans can't win, and if you would rather I didn't run him—'

'Not at all,' says the captain hastily, 'especially if he is likely to become a public favourite. That will make the price of Blue Rat a better one.'

Walking home to the farm, Sam was a bit remorseless.

'When that dud goes broke, I am going along to the sale of his goods to buy some of his heirlooms,' he says. 'I won't half tell him what I think of him, either! As to the girl, I wouldn't marry her if she threw herself at me. I'm finished with women. Nosey. They are just vampires and bloodsuckers. Besides,' he says, 'what's beauty I If I was the Prime Minister I would have a law passed stopping women from showing their faces. It would give the plain ones a chance. The only difference between the plainest woman in the world and the ugliest woman, is her face. Has that ever struck you. Nosey?'

I told him it had. It was curious how Sam was able to put into words thoughts that had been in your mind for years without your being able to express them.

'I don't suppose I shall ever be Prime Minister,' said Sam. 'Politics I have never understood, and never shall.'

'You won't miss much,' says I.

'I don't suppose I shall,' says Sam, 'but it must be rather wonderful being a Prime Minister and having all the swells tell you when their horses are going to win, and when they're not trying.'

He got String of Beans to Newmarket, or rather at a little place between Royston and Newmarket, and on the day of the race we walked him over to the course.

Sam had made his plans. He was going into Tattersalls' ring, wait for the market to be formed, and then sail in and back String of Beans with all the money we had. Bisher was going to look after the horse in the paddock and give him his feed, whilst the previous race was being run and nobody was about; and I was going into the 'silver ring' to put on as much money as I could bet before the price came tumbling down.

We were walking across the Heath when we overtook the captain and Miss Virginia; I thought she was looking very worried. Sam took off his hat like a gentleman.

'Good morning, Mr Baring,' she said; 'perhaps you will help me to try and persuade Captain Tarbot—'

The captain was a bit annoyed, I think, but she went on.

'Captain Tarbot is going to put a thousand pounds on his horse; I think that is madness, don't you, Mr Baring?'

'Not at all,' said Sam, very firm. 'If he had two thousand pounds he ought to put it on that horse; it is one of the finest horses that I have ever seen in a selling plate. The only danger is, that he may not be able to afford to bid up at the auction to buy it in. That horse,' he says, 'will fetch at least a thousand pounds—'

'If it wins,' says the girl. 'But suppose it doesn't win—'

Sam sort of smiled.

'It is humanly impossible for that horse not to win, Miss Virginia,' he says. 'I speak as a sportsman and a man of the world, and I tell you that though funny things happen in racing, I never expect to see anything so comic as that horse not winning. I have been looking up his pedigree, and I say that it is a sin and a shame that a horse of that class and character should be running in a selling plate. But be that as it may, miss,' he says, 'you couldn't stop him winning unless you built a wall across the course, and even then he'd jump it.'

'You hear, my dear?' says the captain. 'Mr Baring understands these things.'

'So does father,' she says obstinately, 'and he says that Blue Rat is only a moderate horse, and if there is anything in the race that can gallop, your horse will be beaten.'

'With all due respect to the major,' says Sam, 'and a nicer man and more perfect gentleman I have never met, and highly educated too—he is not up to date if he says that this horse, Blue Rat, isn't the best performer he has ever trained. I'll tell you what I'll do—I'll give you a thousand pounds for that horse as he stands, if you will let me run him and give me the market for myself.'

It was very handsome of Sam, but he knew that the captain wouldn't accept. Even the young lady was impressed.

'Very well,' she says; 'I suppose you know best,' and that was the end of the conversation, for soon after we left them.

At the last minute Sam changed his plans and sent Bisher into the ring to back the horse, whilst he went into the paddock to give String of Beans his final preparation. I was in the 'silver ring' when String of Beans went down to the post. He went down, first on his hind legs, then on his front legs, then all his legs together, and I could see by the way he was doing circles in the middle of the course that the Indian Magic was worth all the fifty pounds that Sam had given to Mr Dhobi.

String of Beans was a good favourite; by the time I had finished backing him, he was at five to two; I had the curiosity to inquire the price of Blue Rat before I went into Tattersalls and joined Bisher and Sam. Blue Rat was at six to one, and was still six to one when I climbed the stand to where Sam and Bisher were standing.

'How did he go down?' says Sam.

'Fine,' I says. 'Look at him, he's still waltzing.'

'I gave him a double dose,' says Sam in a low voice. 'We can't afford to take any risks.'

'He certainly went down like a high-spirited thoroughbred,' says Bisher.

'Have you got the money on?' I asked.

Sam nodded.

'This is money from home, Nosey,' he says. 'You have never in your life had a chance of collecting wealth so easily. 'When I look down at those bookmakers,' he says, 'I have a sort of feeling of sorrow for them. Little do they know as they stand there, howling their blinking heads off, that in a few minutes their vast and capacious pockets will be emptied into my hat. I think we'll go to London tonight to celebrate,' he says. 'There's a new show on at the Palladium, and I have engaged the Royal box.'

It was a very long time before the race started. String of Beans, being slightly the worse for Indian Magic, thought the winning-post was in the other direction, and wouldn't turn his head to the tape. And when he did, he started teaching the other horses a new classy step he'd learnt, and they began imitating him. Then he tried to walk about on his hind legs, like one of those horses you see in the British Museum, but at last they got his head right and up went the tape.

You could see Sam's blue-and-pink jacket very plainly, for the sun was shining, and before the field had gone a furlong. String of Beans was lobbing along in front, about ten lengths ahead of anything.

'There ought to be a statue put up to the man who found this Indian Magic,' says Sam, and we both agreed with him.

Before they got to Bushes Hill, String of Beans was twenty lengths in front, with Blue Rat about five lengths in front of anything else.

I looked round the stand, not expecting to find the captain, because he, being a swell, should have been in the members' enclosure; but there he was, and the young lady, and her face was the colour of chalk.

Coming down Bushes Hill, String of Beans, striding out like a lion, was a half a furlong in front, and even if he dropped dead, the speed he was going would have carried him past the winning-post. But he didn't drop dead. He sailed past the winning-post at forty miles an hour, and the smile on Sam's face was a pleasure to see.

We waited, and we had to wait a long time, for the second, which was Blue Rat, to get past the judge's box, and then Sam says:

'Come on, boys, let's lead him in.'

'Wait a minute,' says Bisher; 'he hasn't stopped yet.'

String of Beans ought to have turned off to the left and gone into the paddock, and we could see the jockey pulling his head off, but the reins weren't made that could hold String of Beans that day. He went over the heath, and we watched him on the skyline as he suddenly swerved to the right, and went galloping across the heath in the direction of Cambridge. Then he swerved again, and came back toward Newmarket town. After that we didn't see him. By all accounts he went through Newmarket town, turned down a side street, dashed through a kitchen garden on to a tennis lawn, taking the net like a steeple-chaser, through a field, back to the Royston Road, and about half an hour later was stopped by two policemen in Cambridge.

I must say the Stewards were very decent. They waited twenty minutes for String of Beans to come back, and it was only after somebody had telephoned that he had been seen racing a Ford car on the Cambridge Road, that they disqualified him and gave the race to Blue Rat.

It was the double handful of Indian Magic that had done it. 'We reckoned afterwards that with one handful the jockey would have pulled him up within a mile of Newmarket, and he'd have got back in time for the jockey to have weighed in.

Dhobi promised to meet Sam after the race, but he didn't turn up. Sam spent all the evening looking for him.

43

VIOLET'S OWN

Anna Katherine Green

...Where had it vanished, and through whose agency had this misadventure occurred?...

'It has been too much for you?'
'I am afraid so.'

It was Roger Upjohn who had asked the question; it was Violet who answered. They had withdrawn from a crowd of dancers to a balcony, half-shaded, half open to the moon—a balcony made, it would seem, for just such stolen interviews between waltzes.

Now, as it happened, Roger's face was in the shadow, but Violet's in the full light. Very sweet it looked, very ethereal, but also a little wan. He noticed this and impetuously cried:

'You are pale; and your hand! see, how it trembles!'

Slowly withdrawing it from the rail where it had rested, she sent one quick glance his way and, in a low voice, said:

'I have not slept since that night.'

'Four days!' he murmured. Then, after a moment of silence, 'You bore yourself so bravely at the time, I thought, or rather, I hoped, that success had made you forget the horror. I could not have slept myself, if I had known—'

'It is part of the price I pay,' she broke in gently. 'All good things have to be paid for. But I see—I realize that you do not consider what I am doing good. Though it helps other people—has helped you—you wonder why, with all the advantages I possess, I should meddle with matters so repugnant to a woman's natural instincts.'

Yes, he wondered. That was evident from his silence. Seeing her as she stood there, so quaintly pretty, so feminine in look and manner—in short, such a flower—it was but natural that he should marvel at the incongruity she had mentioned.

'It has a strange, odd look,' she admitted, after a moment of troubled hesitation. 'The most considerate person cannot but regard it as a display of egotism or of a most mercenary spirit. The cheque you sent me for what I was enabled to do for you in Massachusetts (the only one I have ever received which I have been tempted to refuse) shows to what extent you rated my help and my—my expectations. Had I been a poor girl struggling for subsistence, this generosity would have warmed my heart as a token of your desire to cut that struggle short. But taken with your knowledge of my home and its luxuries, it has often made me wonder what you thought.'

'Shall I tell you?'

He had stepped forward at this question and his countenance, hitherto concealed, became visible in the moonlight. She no longer recognized it. Transformed by feeling, it shone down upon her, instinct with all that is finest and best in masculine nature. Was she ready for this revelation of what she had nevertheless dreamed of for many more nights than four? She did not know, and instinctively drew herself back till it was she who now stood in the semi-obscurity made by the drooping vines. From this retreat, she faltered forth a very tremulous No, which in another moment was disavowed by a Yes so faint it was little more than a murmur, followed by a still fainter, Tell me.

But he did not seem in any haste to obey, sweetly as her low-toned injunction must have sounded in his ears. On the contrary, he hesitated to speak, growing paler every minute as he sought to catch a glimpse of her downcast face so tantalizingly hidden from him. Did she recognize the nature of the feelings which held him back, or was she simply gathering up sufficient courage to plead her own cause? Whatever her reason, it was she, not he, who presently spoke saying as if no time had elapsed:

'But first, I feel obliged to admit that it was money I wanted, that I had to have. Not for myself. I lack nothing and could have more if I wished. Father has never limited his generosity in any matter affecting myself, but—' She drew a deep breath and, coming out of the shadow, lifted a face to him so changed from its usual expression as to make him start. 'I have a cause at heart—one which should appeal to my father and does not; and for that purpose I have sacrificed myself, in many ways, though—though I have not disliked my work up to this last attempt. Not really. I want to be honest and so must admit that much. I have even gloried (quietly and all by myself, of course) over the solution of a mystery which no one else seemed able to penetrate. I am made that way. I have known it ever since—but that is a story all by itself. Some day I may tell it to you, but not now.'

'No, not now.' The emphasis sent the colour into her cheek but did not relieve his pallor. 'Miss Strange, I have always felt, even in my worst days, that the man who for selfish ends brought a woman under the shadow of his own unhappy reputation was a man to be despised. And I think so still, and yet—and yet—nothing in the world but your own word or look can hold me back now from telling you that I love you—love you notwithstanding my unworthy past, my scarring memories, my all but blasted hopes. I do not expect any response; you are young; you are beautiful; you are gifted with every grace; but to speak—to say over and over again, 'I love you, I love you!' eases my heart and makes my future more endurable. Oh, do not look at me like that unless—unless—'

But the bright head did not fall, nor the tender gaze falter; and driven out of himself, Roger Upjohn was about to step passionately forward, when, seized by fresh compunction, he hoarsely cried:

'It is not right. The balance dips too much my way. You bring me everything. I can give you nothing but what you already possess abundance—love, and money. Besides, your father—'

She interrupted him with a glance at once arch and earnest.

'I had a talk with Father this morning. He came to my room, and—and it was very near being serious. Someone had told him I was doing things on the sly which he had better look into; and of course he asked questions and—and I answered them. He wasn't pleased— in fact he was very displeased—I don't think we can blame him for that—but we had no open break for I love him dearly, for all my opposing ways, and he saw that, and it helped, though he did say after I had given my promise to stop where I was and never to take up such work again, that—' here she stole a shy look at the face bent so eagerly towards her—'that I had lost my social status and need never hope now for the attentions of—of—well, of such men as he admires and puts faith in. So you see,' her dimples all showing, 'that I am not such a very good match for an Upjohn of Massachusetts, even if he has a reputation to recover and an honourable name to achieve. The scale hangs more evenly than you think.'

'Violet!'

A mutual look, a moment of perfect silence, then a low whisper, airy as the breath of flowers rising from the garden below: 'I have never known what happiness was till this moment. If you will take me with my story untold—'

'Take you! take you!' The man's whole yearning heart, the loss and bitterness of years, the hope and promise of the future, all spoke in that low, half-smothered exclamation. Violet's blushes faded under its fervency, and only her spirit spoke, as leaning towards him, she laid her two hands in his, and said with all a woman's earnestness:

'I do not forget little Roger, or the father who I hope may have many more days before him in which to bid good-night to the sea. Such union as ours must be hallowed, because we have so many persons to make happy besides ourselves.'

The evening before their marriage, Violet put a dozen folded sheets of closely written paper in his hand. They contained her story; let us read it with him.

DEAR ROGER—

I could not have been more than seven years old, when one night I woke up shivering, at the sound of angry voices. A conversation which no child should ever have heard, was going on in the room where I lay. My father was talking to my sister—perhaps, you do not know that I have a sister; few of my personal friends do—and the terror she evinced I could well understand but not his words nor the real cause of his displeasure.

There are times even yet when the picture, forced upon my infantile consciousness at that moment of first awakening, comes back to me with all its original vividness. There was no light in the room save such as the moon made; but that was enough to reveal the passion burningly alive in either face, as, bending towards each other, she in supplication and he in a tempest of wrath which knew no bounds, he uttered and she listened to what I now know to have been a terrible arraignment.

I may have an interesting countenance; you have told me so sometimes; but she—she was beautiful. My elder by ten years, she had stood in my mother's stead to me for almost as long as I could remember, and as I saw her lovely features contorted with pain and her hands extended in a desperate plea to one who had never shown me anything but love, my throat closed sharply and I could not cry out though I wanted to, nor move head or foot though I longed with all my heart to bury myself in the pillows.

For the words I heard were terrifying, little as I comprehended their full purport. He had surprised her talking from her window to someone down below, and after saying cruel things about that, he shouted out: 'You have disgraced me, you have disgraced yourself, you have disgraced your brother and your little sister. Was it not enough that you should refuse to marry the good man I had picked out for you, that you should stoop to this low-down scoundrel—this—' I did not hear what else he called him, I was wondering so to whom she had been stooping; I had never seen her stoop except to tie my little shoes.

But when she cried out as she did after an interval, 'I love him! I love him!' then I listened again, for she spoke as though she were in dreadful pain, and I did not know that loving made one ill and unhappy. 'And I am going to marry him,' I heard her add, standing up, as she said it, very straight and tall.

Marry! I knew what that meant. A long aisle in a church; women in white and big music in the air behind. I had been flower-girl at a wedding once and had not forgotten. We had had ice cream and cake and—

But my childish thoughts stopped short at the answer she received and all the words which followed—words which burned their way into my infantile brain and left scorched places in my memory which will never be eradicated. He spoke them—spoke them all; she never answered again after that once, and when he was gone did not move for a long time and when she did it was to lie down, stiff and straight, just as she had stood, on her bed alongside mine.

I was frightened; so frightened, my little brass bed rattled under me. I wonder she did not hear it. But she heard nothing; and after awhile she was so still I fell asleep. But I woke again. Something hot had fallen on my cheek. I put up my hand to brush it away and did not know even when I felt my fingers wet that it was a tear from my sister-mother's eye.

For she was kneeling then; kneeling close beside me and her arm was over my small body; and the bed was shaking again but not this time with my tremors only. And I was sorry and cried too until I dropped off to sleep again with her arm still passionately embracing me.

In the morning, she was gone.

It must have been that very afternoon that Father came in where Arthur and I were trying to play—trying, but not quite succeeding, for I had been telling Arthur, for whom I had a great respect in those days, what had happened the night before, and we had been wondering in our childish way if there would be a wedding after all, and a church full of people, and flowers, and kissing, and lots of good things to eat, and Arthur had said No, it was too expensive; that that was why Father was so angry; and comforted by the assertion, I was taking up my doll again, when the door opened and Father stepped in.

It was a great event—any visit from him to the nursery—and we both dropped our toys and stood staring, not knowing whether he was going to be nice and kind as he sometimes was, or scold us as I had heard him scold our beautiful sister.

Arthur showed at once what he thought, for without the least hesitation he took the one step which placed him in front of me, where he stood waiting with his two little fists hanging straight at his sides but manfully clenched in full readiness for attack. That this display of pigmy chivalry was not quite without its warrant is evident to me now, for Father did not look like himself or act like himself any more than he had the night before.

However, we had no cause for fear. Having no suspicion of my having been awake during his terrible interview with Theresa, he saw only two lonely and forsaken children, interrupted in their play.

Can I remember what he said to us? Not exactly, though Arthur and I often went over it choked whispers in some secret nook of the dreary old house; but his meaning—that we took in well enough. Theresa had left us. She would never come back. We were not to look out of the window for her, or run to the door when the bell rang. Our mother had left us too, a long time ago, and she lay in the cemetery where we sometimes carried flowers. Theresa was not in the cemetery, but we must think of her as there; though not as if she had any need of flowers. Having said this, he looked at us quietly for a minute. Arthur was trying very hard not to cry, but I was sobbing like the lost child I was, with my cheek against the floor where I had thrown myself when he said that awful thing about the cemetery. She there! my sister-mother there! I think he felt a little sorry for me; for he half stooped as if to lift me up. But he straightened again and said very sternly:

'Now, children, listen to me. When God takes people to heaven and leaves us only their cold, dead bodies we carry flowers to their graves and talk about them some if not very much. But when people die because they love dark ways better than light, then we do not remember them with gifts and we do not talk about them. Your sister's name has been spoken for the last time in this house. You, Arthur, are old enough to know what I mean when I say that I will never listen to another word about her from either you or Violet as long as you and I live. She is gone and nothing that is mine shall she ever touch again.

'You hear me, Arthur; you hear me, Violet. Heed me, or you go too.'

His aspect was terrible, so was his purpose; much more terrible than we realized at the time with our limited understanding and experience. Later, we came to know the full meaning of this black drop which had been infused into our lives. When we saw every picture of her destroyed which had been in the house; her name cut out from the leaves of books; the little tokens she had given us surreptitiously taken away, till not a vestige of her once beloved presence remained, we began to realize that we had indeed lost her.

But children as young as we were then do not long retain the poignancy of their first griefs. Gradually my memories of that awful night ceased to disturb my dreams and I was sixteen before they were again recalled to me with any vividness, and then it was by accident. I had been strolling through a picture gallery and had stopped short to study more particularly one which had especially taken my fancy. There were two ladies sitting on a bench behind me and one of them was evidently very deaf, for their talk was loud, though I am sure they did not mean for me to hear, for they were discussing my family. That is, one of them had said:

'That's Violet Strange. She will never be the beauty her sister was; but perhaps that's not to be deplored. Theresa made a great mess of it.'

'That's true. I hear that she and the Signor have been seen lately here in town. In poverty, of course. He hadn't even as much go in him as the ordinary singing-master.'

I suppose I should have hurried away, and left this barbed arrow to rankle where it fell. But I could not. I had never learned a word of Theresa's fate and that word poverty, proving that she was alive and suffering, held me to my place to hear what more they might say of her who for years had been for me an indistinct figure bathed in cruel moonlight.

'I have never approved of Peter Strange's conduct at that time,' one of the voices now went on. 'He didn't handle her right. She had a lovely disposition and would have listened to him had he been more gentle with her. But it isn't in him. I hope this one—'

I didn't hear the end of that. I had no interest in anything they might say about myself. It was of her I wanted to hear, of her. Weren't they going to say anything more about my poor sister? Yes; it was a topic which interested both and presently I heard:

'He'll never do anything for her, no matter what happens; I've heard him say so. And Laura has vowed the same.' (Laura is our aunt.)

'Besides, Theresa has a pride of her own quite equal to her father's. She wouldn't take anything from him now. She'd rather struggle on. I'm told—I don't know how true it is—that she's working in a department store; one of the Sixth Avenue ones. Oh, there's Mrs Vandegraff! Don't you want to speak to her?'

They moved off, leaving me still gazing with unseeing eyes at the picture before which I stood planted, and saying over and over in monotonous iteration, 'One of the department stores in Sixth Avenue! One of the department stores in Sixth Avenue!'

Which department store?

I meant to find out.

I do not know whether up till then I had had the least consciousness of possessing what is called the detective instinct. But, at the prospect of this quest, so much like that of the proverbial needle in a haystack, as I did not even know my sister's married name and something within me forbade my asking it, I experienced an odd sense of elation followed by a certainty of success which in five minutes changed me from an irresponsible girl to a woman with a deliberate purpose in life.

I am not going to write down here all the details of that search. Some day I may relate them to you, but not now. I looked first for a beautiful woman, for the straight, slim, and exquisite creature I remembered. I did not find her. Then I tried another course. Her figure might have changed in the ten years which had elapsed; so might her expression. I would look for a woman with beautiful dark eyes; time could not have altered them. I had forgotten the effect of constant weeping. And I saw many eyes, but not hers; not the ones I had seen smiling upon me as I lay in my crib before the days I was lifted to the dignity of the little brass bed. So I gave that up too and listened to the inner voice which said, 'You must wait for her to recognize you. You can never hope to recognize her.' And it was by following this plan that I found her. I had arranged to have my name spoken aloud at every counter where I bargained; and oh, the bargains I sought, and the garments I had tried on! But I made little progress until one day, after my name had been uttered a little louder than usual I saw a woman turn from rearranging gowns on a hanger, and give me one look.

I uttered a low cry and sprang impetuously, forward. Instantly she turned her back and went on hanging, or trying to hang up, gowns on the rack before her. Had I been mistaken? She was not the sister of my dreams, but there was something fine in her outline; something distinguished in the way she carried her head which—

Next minute my last doubt fled! She had fallen her length on the floor and lay with her face buried in her hands in a dead faint.

Oh, Roger, Roger, Roger! I had that dear head on my breast in a moment. I talked to her, I whispered prayers in her unconscious ear. I did everything I should not have done till they all thought me demented. When she came to, as she did under other ministrations than mine, I was for carrying her off in my limousine. But she shook her head with a gesture of such disapproval, that I realized I could not do that. The limousine was my father's, and nothing of his was ever to be used for her again. I would call a cab; but she told me that she had not the money to pay for it and she would not take mine. Carfare she had; five cents would take her home. I need not worry.

She smiled as she said this and for an instant I saw my dream-sister again in this weary half-disheartened woman. But the smile was a fleeting one, for this was to be her last day in the store; she had no talent as a saleswoman and was merely working out her week.

I felt my heart sink heavily at this, for the evidences of poverty were plainly to be seen in her clothes and the thinness of her face and figure. How could I help? What could I do? I took her to a restaurant for food and talk, and before she would order, she looked into her purse, with the result that we had only a little toast and tea. It was all she could afford and I, with a hundred dollars in bills at that moment in my bag, could not offer her anything more though she was needing nourishment and dishes piled with savoury meats were going by us every moment.

I think, if she had let me, I would have dared my father's displeasure and been disobedient to his wishes by giving her one wholesome meal. But she was as resolute of mind as he, and, as she said afterwards, had chosen her course in life and must abide by it. My love she would accept. It took nothing from Father and gave her what her heart was pining for—had pined for for years. But nothing more—not another thing more. She would not even let me go home with her; and I knew why when her eyes fell at the searching look I gave her. Something would turn up, and when her husband's health was better and she had found another position she would send me her address and then I could come and see her. As we walked out of the restaurant we ran against a gentleman I knew. He stopped me for a passing word and in that minute she disappeared. I did not try to follow her. I could get her street and number from the store where she had worked.

But when I had done this and embraced the first opportunity which offered to visit her, I found that she had moved away in the interim, leaving everything behind in payment of her rent, except such small things as she and her husband could carry. This was discouraging as it left me without any clue by which to follow them. But I was determined not to yield to her desire for concealment in the difficult and disheartening task I now saw before me.

Seeking advice from the man who has since become my employer, I entered upon this second search with a quiet resolution which admitted of no defeat. It took me six months, but I finally found her, and satisfied with knowing where she was, desisted from rushing in upon her, till I had caught one glimpse of her husband whom, in the last six months, I had heard described but had never seen. To understand her, it was perhaps necessary to understand him, and if I could not hope to do this offhand, I could not fail to get some idea of the man from even the most casual look.

He was, as I soon learned, the fetcher and carrier of the small ménage; and the day came when I met him face to face in the street where they lived. Did he disappoint me; or did I see something in his appearance to justify her desertion of her father's home and her present life of poverty? If I say 'Yes' to the first question, I must also say it to the last. If handsome once, he was not handsome now; but with a personality such as his, this did not matter. He had that better thing—that greatest gift of the gods—charm. It was in his bearing, his movement, the regard of his weary eye; more than that it was in his very nature or it would have vanished long ago under disappointment and privation.

But that was all there was to the man—a golden net in which my sister's youthful fancy had been caught and no doubt held meshed to this very day. I felt less like blaming her for her folly, after that instant's view of him as we passed each other in the street. But, as I took time to think, I found myself growing sorrier and sorrier for her and yet, in a way, gladder and gladder, for the man was a physical wreck and would soon pass out of her life leaving her to my love and possibly to our father's forgiveness.

But I did not know Theresa. After her husband's death, which occurred very soon, she let me come to her and we had a long talk. Shall I ever forget it or the sight of her beauty in that sordid room? For, account for it as you will, the loveliness which had fled under her sense of complete isolation had slowly regained its own with the recognition that she still had a place in the heart of her little sister. Not even the sorrow she felt for the loss of her suffering husband—and she did mourn him; this I am glad to say—could more than temporarily stay this. Six months of ease and wholesome food would make her—I hardly dared to think what. For I knew, without asking her, or she telling me, that she would accept neither; that she was as determined now, as ever that nothing which came directly or indirectly from Father should go to the rebuilding of her life. That she intended to start anew and work her way up to a place where I should be glad to see her she did say. But nothing more. She was still the sister-mother, loving, but sufficient to herself, though she had but ten dollars left in the world, as she showed me with a smile that made her beautiful as an angel.

I can see that shabby little purse yet with its one poor greasy bill—a sum to her but to me the price of a luncheon or a gift of flowers. How I longed, as I looked at it to tear every jewel from my poor, bedecked body and fling them one and all into her lap. I had worn them in profusion, though carefully hidden under my coat, in the hope that she would accept one of them at least, But she refused all, even such as had been gifts of friends and schoolmates, only humouring me this far, that she let me hang them for a few minutes about her neck and in her hair and then pull them all off again. But this one vision of her in the splendour she was born to comforted me. Henceforth in wearing them it would be of her and not of myself I should think.

Well, I had to leave her and go home to my French and Italian lessons, my music-masters and all the luxuries of our father's house. Should I ever see her again? I did not know; she had not promised. I could not go often into the quarter where she lived, without rousing suspicion; and she had bidden me not to come again for a month. So I waited, half fearing she would flit again before the month was up. But she did not. She was still there when—

But I am going too fast. The meeting I was about to mention was a very memorable one to me, and I must describe it from the beginning. I had ridden in my own car as near as I dared to the street where she lived; the rest of the way I went on foot with one of the servants—a new one—following close behind me. I was not exactly afraid, but the actions of some of the people I had encountered at my former visit warned me to be a little careful for my father's sake if not for my own. Her room—she had but one—was high up in a triangular court it was no pleasure to enter. But love and loyalty heed nothing but the object sought, and I was hunting about for the dark doorway which opened upon the staircase leading to her room when—and this was the great moment of my life—a sudden stream of melody floated down into that noisome court, which from its clearness, its accuracy, its richness, and its feeling startled me as I had never before been startled even by the first notes of the world's greatest singers. What a voice for a place like this! What a voice for any place! Whose could it be? With a start, I stopped short, in the middle of that court, heedless of the crowd of pushing, shouting children who at once gathered about me. I had been struck by an old recollection. My sister used to sing. I remembered where her piano had stood in the great drawing-room. It had been carted away during those dreadful weeks and her music all burned; but the vision of her graceful figure bending over the keyboard was one not to be forgotten even by a thoughtless child. Could it be—oh, heaven! if this voice were hers! Her future was certain; she had but to sing.

In a transport of hope I rushed for the dim entrance the children had pointed out and flew up to her room. As I reached it, I heard a trill as perfect as Tetrazzini's. The singer was Theresa; there could be no more doubt. Theresa! exercising a grand voice as only a great artist would or could.

The joy of it made me almost faint. I leaned against her door and sobbed. Then when I thought I could speak quite calmly, I went in.

Roger, you must understand me now—my desire for money and the means I have taken to obtain it. My sister had the makings of a prima-donna. Her husband, of whose ability I had formed so low an estimate, had trained her with consummate skill and judgment. All she needed was a year with some great maestro in the foreign atmosphere of art. But this meant money—not hundreds but thousands, and the one sure source to which we might rightfully look for any such amount was effectually closed to us. It is true we had relatives—an aunt on our mother's side, and I mentioned her to Theresa. But she would not listen to the suggestion. She would take nothing from any one whom she would find it hard to face in case of failure. Love must go with an advance involving so much risk; love deep enough and strong enough to feel no loss save that of a defeated hope. In short, to be acceptable, the money must come from me, and as this was manifestly impossible, she considered the matter closed and began to talk of a position she had been offered in some choir. I let her talk, listening and not listening; for the idea had come to me that if in some way I could earn money, she might be induced to take it. Finally, I asked her. She laughed, letting her kisses answer me. But I did not laugh. If she had capabilities in one way, I had them in another.

I went home to think.

Two weeks later, I began, in a very quiet way to do certain work for the man who had helped me in my second search for Theresa. The money I have earned has been immense; since it was troubles of the rich I was given to settle, and I was almost always successful. Every cent has gone to her. She has been in Europe for a year and last week she made her debut. You read about it in the papers, but neither you nor any one else in this country but myself knew that under the name she chosen to assume, Theresa Strange, the long-forgotten beauty, has recovered that place in the world, to which her love and genius entitle her.

This is my story and hers. From now on, you are the third in the secret. Some day, my father will be the fourth. I think then, a new dawn of love will arise for us all, which will stay the whitening of his dear head—for I believe in him after all. Yesterday when he passed the wall where her picture once hung—no other has ever hung there—I saw him stop and look up, and, Roger, when he passed me a minute later, there was a tear in his hard eye.

44

THE MAN WHO KNEW HOW

Dorothy Sayers

...all these murderers are so incompetent—they bore me....

For perhaps the twentieth time since the train had left Carlisle, Pender glanced up from *Murder at the Manse* and caught the eye of the man opposite.

He frowned a little. It was irritating to be watched so closely, and always with that faint, sardonic smile. It was still more irritating to allow oneself to be so much disturbed by the smile and the scrutiny. Pender wrenched himself back to his book with a determination to concentrate upon the problem of the minister murdered in the library. But the story was of the academic kind that crowds all its exciting incidents into the first chapter, and proceeds thereafter by a long series of deductions to a scientific solution in the last. The thin thread of interest, spun precariously upon the wheel of Pender's reasoning brain, had been snapped. Twice he had to turn back to verify points that he had missed in reading. Then he became aware that his eyes had followed three closely argued pages without conveying anything whatever to his intelligence. He was not thinking about the murdered minister at all—he was becoming more and more actively conscious of the other man's face. A queer face, Pender thought.

There was nothing especially remarkable about the features in themselves; it was their expression that daunted Pender. It was a secret face, the face of one who knew a great deal to other people's disadvantage. The mouth was a little crooked and tightly tucked in at the corners, as though savouring a hidden amusement. The eyes, behind a pair of rimless pince-nez, glittered curiously; but that was possibly due to the light reflected in the glasses. Pender wondered what the man's profession might be. He was dressed in a dark lounge suit, a raincoat and a shabby soft hat; his age was perhaps about forty.

Pender coughed unnecessarily and settled back into his corner, raising the detective story high before his face, barrier-fashion. This was worse than useless. He gained the impression that the man saw through the manoeuvre and was secretly entertained by it. He wanted to fidget, but felt obscurely that his doing so would in some way constitute a victory for the other man. In his self-consciousness he held himself so rigid that attention to his book became a sheer physical impossibility.

There was no stop now before Rugby, and it was unlikely that any passenger would enter from the corridor to break up this disagreeable *solitude à deux*. But something must be done. The silence had lasted so long that any remark, however trivial, would—so Pender felt—burst upon the tense atmosphere with the unnatural clatter of an alarm clock. One could, of course, go out into the corridor and not return, but that would be an acknowledgment of defeat. Pender lowered *Murder at the Manse* and caught the man's eye again.

'Getting tired of it?' asked the man.

'Night journeys are always a bit tedious,' replied Pender, half relieved and half reluctant. 'Would you like a book?'

He took *The Paper-Clip Clue* from his attaché-case and held it out hopefully. The other man glanced at the title and shook his head.

'Thanks very much,' he said, 'but I never read detective stories. They're so—inadequate, don't you think so?'

'They are rather lacking in characterisation and human interest, certainly,' said Pender, 'but on a railway journey——'

'I don't mean that,' said the other man. 'I am not concerned with humanity. But all these murderers are so incompetent—they bore me.'

'Oh, I don't know,' replied Pender. 'At any rate they are usually a good deal more imaginative and ingenious than murderers in real life.'

'Than the murderers who are found out in real life, yes,' admitted the other man.

'Even some of those did pretty well before they got pinched,' objected Pender. 'Crippen, for instance; he need never have been caught if he hadn't lost his head and run off to America. George Joseph Smith did away with at least two brides quite successfully before fate and the *News of the World* intervened.'

'Yes,' said the other man, 'but look at the clumsiness of it all; the elaboration, the lies, the paraphernalia. Absolutely unnecessary.'

'Oh, come!' said Pender. 'You can't expect committing a murder and getting away with it to be as simple as shelling peas.'

'Ah!' said the other man. 'You think that, do you?'

Pender waited for him to elaborate this remark, but nothing came of it. The man leaned back and smiled in his secret way at the roof of the carriage; he appeared to think the conversation not worth going on with. Pender, taking up his book again, found himself attracted by his companion's hands. They were white and surprisingly long in the fingers. He watched them gently tapping upon their owner's knee—then resolutely turned a page—then put the book down once more and said:

'Well, if it's so easy, how would *you* set about committing a murder?'

'I?' repeated the man. The light on his glasses made his eyes quite blank to Pender, but his voice sounded gently amused. 'That's different; *I* should not have to think twice about it.'

'Why not?'

'Because I happen to know how to do it.'

'Do you indeed?' muttered Pender, rebelliously.

'Oh, yes; there's nothing in it.'

'How can you be sure? You haven't tried, I suppose?'

'It isn't a case of trying,' said the man. 'There's nothing tentative about my method. That's just the beauty of it.'

'It's easy to say that,' retorted Pender, 'but what *is* this wonderful method?'

'You can't expect me to tell you that, can you?' said the other man, bringing his eyes back to rest on Pender's. 'It might not be safe. You look harmless enough, but who could look more harmless than Crippen? Nobody is fit to be trusted with *absolute* control over other people's lives.'

'Bosh!' exclaimed Pender. 'I shouldn't think of murdering anybody.'

'Oh, yes, you would,' said the other man, 'if you really believed it was safe. So would anybody. Why are all these tremendous artificial barriers built up around murder by the Church and the law? Just because it's everybody's crime, and just as natural as breathing.'

'But that's ridiculous!' cried Pender, warmly.

'You think so, do you? That's what most people would say. But I wouldn't trust 'em. Not with sulphate of thanatol to be bought for twopence at any chemist's.'

'Sulphate of what?' asked Pender sharply.

'Ah! you think I'm giving something away. Well, it's a mixture of that and one or two other things—all equally ordinary and cheap. For ninepence you could make up enough to poison the entire Cabinet—and even you would hardly call that a crime, would you? But of course one wouldn't polish the whole lot off at once; it might look funny if they all died simultaneously in their baths.'

'Why in their baths?'

'That's the way it would take them. It's the action of the hot water that brings on the effect of the stuff, you see. Any time from a few hours to a few days after administration. It's quite a simple chemical reaction and it couldn't possibly be detected by analysis. It would just look like heart failure.'

Pender eyed him uneasily. He did not like the smile; it was not only derisive, it was smug, it was almost—gloating—triumphant! He could not quite put a name to it.

'You know,' pursued the man, thoughtfully pulling a pipe from his pocket and beginning to fill it, 'it is very odd how often one seems to read of people being found dead in their baths. It must be a very common accident. Quite temptingly so. After all, there is a fascination about murder. The thing grows upon one—that is, I imagine it would, you know.'

'Very likely,' said Pender.

'Look at Palmer. Look at Gesina Gottfried. Look at Armstrong. No, I wouldn't trust anybody with that formula—not even a virtuous young man like yourself.'

The long white fingers tamped the tobacco firmly into the bowl and struck a match.

'But how about you?' said Pender, irritated. (Nobody cares to be called a virtuous young man.) 'If nobody is fit to be trusted——'

'I'm not, eh?' replied the man. 'Well, that's true, but it's past praying for now, isn't it? I know the thing and I can't unknow it again. It's unfortunate, but there it is. At any rate you have the comfort of knowing that nothing disagreeable is likely to happen to *me*. Dear me! Rugby already. I get out here. I have a little bit of business to do at Rugby.'

He rose and shook himself, buttoned his raincoat about him and pulled the shabby hat more firmly down above his enigmatic glasses. The train slowed down and stopped. With a brief good-night and a crooked smile the man stepped on to the platform. Pender watched him stride quickly away into the drizzle beyond the radius of the gas-light.

'Dotty or something,' said Pender, oddly relieved. 'Thank goodness, I seem to be going to have the carriage to myself.'

He returned to *Murder at the Manse*, but his attention still kept wandering.

'What was the name of that stuff the fellow talked about?'

For the life of him he could not remember.

It was on the following afternoon that Pender saw the news-item. He had bought the *Standard* to read at lunch, and the word 'Bath' caught his eye; otherwise he would probably have missed the paragraph altogether, for it was only a short one.

'WEALTHY MANUFACTURER DIES IN BATH
'WIFE'S TRAGIC DISCOVERY

'A distressing discovery was made early this morning by Mrs John Brittlesea, wife of the well-known head of Brittlesea's Engineering Works at Rugby. Finding that her husband, whom she had seen alive and well less than an hour previously, did not come down in time for his breakfast, she searched for him in the bathroom, where, on the door being broken down, the engineer was found lying dead in his bath, life having been extinct, according to the medical men, for half an hour. The cause of the death is pronounced to be heart failure. The deceased manufacturer ...'

'That's an odd coincidence,' said Pender. 'At Rugby. I should think my unknown friend would be interested—if he is still there, doing his bit of business. I wonder what his business is, by the way.'

It is a very curious thing how, when once your attention is attracted to any particular set of circumstances, that set of circumstances seems to haunt you. You get appendicitis: immediately the newspapers are filled with paragraphs about statesmen suffering from appendicitis and victims dying of it; you learn that all your acquaintances have had it, or know friends who have had it, and either died of it, or recovered from it with more surprising and spectacular rapidity than yourself; you cannot open a popular magazine without seeing its cure mentioned as one of the triumphs of modern surgery, or dip into a scientific treatise without coming across a comparison of the vermiform appendix in men and monkeys. Probably these references to appendicitis are equally frequent at all times, but you only notice them when your mind is attuned to the subject. At any rate, it was in this way that Pender accounted to himself for the extraordinary frequency with which people seemed to die in their baths at this period.

The thing pursued him at every turn. Always the same sequence of events: the hot bath, the discovery of the corpse, the inquest; always the same medical opinion: heart failure following immersion in too-hot water. It began to seem to Pender that it was scarcely safe to enter a hot bath at all. He took to making his own bath cooler and cooler every day, until it almost ceased to be enjoyable.

He skimmed his paper each morning for headlines about baths before settling down to read the news; and was at once relieved and vaguely disappointed if a week passed without a hot-bath tragedy.

One of the sudden deaths that occurred in this way was that of a young and beautiful woman whose husband, an analytical chemist, had tried without success to divorce her a few months previously. The coroner displayed a tendency to suspect foul play, and put the husband through a severe cross-examination. There seemed, however, to be no getting behind the doctor's evidence. Pender, brooding fancifully over the improbable possible, wished, as he did every day of the week, that he could remember the name of that drug the man in the train had mentioned.

Then came the excitement in Pender's own neighbourhood. An old Mr Skimmings, who lived alone with a housekeeper in a street just round the corner, was found dead in his bathroom. His heart had never been strong. The housekeeper told the milkman that she had always expected something of the sort to happen, for the old gentleman would always take his bath so hot. Pender went to the inquest.

The housekeeper gave her evidence. Mr Skimmings had been the kindest of employers, and she was heartbroken at losing him. No, she had not been aware that Mr Skimmings had left her a large sum of money, but it was just like his goodness of heart. The verdict was Death by Misadventure.

Pender, that evening, went out for his usual stroll with the dog. Some feeling of curiosity moved him to go round past the late Mr Skimmings's house. As he loitered by, glancing up at the blank windows, the garden-gate opened and a man came out. In the light of a street lamp, Pender recognised him at once.

'Hullo!' he said.

'Oh, it's you, is it?' said the man. 'Viewing the site of the tragedy, eh? What do *you* think about it all?'

'Oh, nothing very much,' said Pender. 'I didn't know him. Odd, our meeting again like this.'

'Yes, isn't it? You live near here, I suppose.'

'Yes,' said Pender; and then wished he hadn't. 'Do you live in these parts too?'

'Me?' said the man. 'Oh, no. I was only here on a little matter of business.'

'Last time we met,' said Pender, 'you had business at Rugby.' They had fallen into step together, and were walking slowly down to the turning Pender had to take in order to reach his house.

'So I had,' agreed the other man. 'My business takes me all over the country. I never know where I may be wanted next.'

'It was while you were at Rugby that old Brittlesea was found dead in his bath, wasn't it?' remarked Pender carelessly.

'Yes. Funny thing, coincidence.' The man glanced up at him sideways through his glittering glasses. 'Left all his money to his wife, didn't he? She's a rich woman now. Good-looking girl—a lot younger than he was.'

They were passing Pender's gate. 'Come in and have a drink,' said Pender, and again immediately regretted the impulse.

The man accepted, and they went into Pender's bachelor study.

'Remarkable lot of these bath-deaths there have been lately, haven't there?' observed Pender carelessly, as he splashed soda into the tumblers.

'You think it's remarkable?' said the man, with his usual irritating trick of querying everything that was said to him. 'Well, I don't know. Perhaps it is. But it's always a fairly common accident.'

'I suppose I've been taking more notice on account of that conversation we had in the train.' Pender laughed, a little self-consciously. 'It just makes me wonder—you know how one does—whether anybody else had happened to hit on that drug you mentioned—what was its name?'

The man ignored the question.

'Oh, I shouldn't think so,' he said. 'I fancy I'm the only person who knows about that. I only stumbled on the thing by accident myself when I was looking for something else. I don't imagine it could have been discovered simultaneously in so many parts of the country. But all these verdicts just show, don't they, what a safe way it would be of getting rid of a person.'

'You're a chemist, then?' asked Pender, catching at the one phrase which seemed to promise information.

'Oh, I'm a bit of everything. Sort of general utility-man. I do a good bit of studying on my own, too. You've got one or two interesting books here, I see.'

Pender was flattered. For a man in his position—he had been in a bank until he came into that little bit of money—he felt that he had improved his mind to some purpose, and he knew that his collection of modern first editions would be worth money some day.

He went over to the glass-fronted bookcase and pulled out a volume or two to show his visitor.

The man displayed intelligence, and presently joined him in front of the shelves.

'These, I take it, represent your personal tastes?' He took down a volume of Henry James and glanced at the fly-leaf. 'That your name? E. Pender?'

Pender admitted that it was. 'You have the advantage of me,' he added.

'Oh! I am one of the great Smith clan,' said the other with a laugh, 'and work for my bread. You seem to be very nicely fixed here.'

Pender explained about the clerkship and the legacy.

'Very nice, isn't it?' said Smith. 'Not married? No. You're one of the lucky ones. Not likely to be needing any sulphate of ... any useful drugs in the near future. And you never will, if you stick to what you've got and keep off women and speculation.'

He smiled up sideways at Pender. Now that his hat was off, Pender saw that he had a quantity of closely curled grey hair, which made him look older than he had appeared in the railway carriage.

'No, I shan't be coming to you for assistance yet awhile,' said Pender, laughing. 'Besides, how should I find you if I wanted you?'

'You wouldn't have to,' said Smith. '*I* should find *you*. There's never any difficulty about that.' He grinned, oddly. 'Well, I'd better be getting on. Thank you for your hospitality. I don't expect we shall meet again—but we may, of course. Things work out so queerly, don't they?'

When he had gone, Pender returned to his own arm-chair. He took up his glass of whisky, which stood there nearly full.

'Funny!' he said to himself. 'I don't remember pouring that out. I suppose I got interested and did it mechanically.' He emptied his glass slowly, thinking about Smith.

What in the world was Smith doing at Skimmings's house?

An odd business altogether. If Skimmings's housekeeper had known about that money ... But she had not known, and if she had, how could she have found out about Smith and his sulphate of ... the word had been on the tip of his tongue then.

'You would not need to find me. *I* should find *you*.' What had the man meant by that? But this was ridiculous. Smith was not the devil, presumably. But if he really had this secret—if he liked to put a price upon it—nonsense.

'Business at Rugby—a little bit of business at Skimmings's house.' Oh, absurd!

'Nobody is fit to be trusted. *Absolute* power over another man's life … it grows on you.'

Lunacy! And, if there was anything in it, the man was mad to tell Pender about it. If Pender chose to speak he could get the fellow hanged. The very existence of Pender would be dangerous.

That whisky!

More and more, thinking it over, Pender became persuaded that he had never poured it out. Smith must have done it while his back was turned. Why that sudden display of interest in the bookshelves? It had had no connection with anything that had gone before. Now Pender came to think of it, it had been a very stiff whisky. Was it imagination, or had there been something about the flavour of it?

A cold sweat broke out on Pender's forehead.

A quarter of an hour later, after a powerful dose of mustard and water, Pender was downstairs again, very cold and shivering, huddling over the fire. He had had a narrow escape—if he had escaped. He did not know how the stuff worked, but he would not take a hot bath again for some days. One never knew.

Whether the mustard and water had done the trick in time, or whether the hot bath was an essential part of the treatment, Pender's life was saved for the time being. But he was still uneasy. He kept the front door on the chain and warned his servant to let no strangers into the house.

He ordered two more morning papers and the *News of the World* on Sundays, and kept a careful watch upon their columns. Deaths in baths became an obsession with him. He neglected his first editions and took to attending inquests.

Three weeks later he found himself at Lincoln. A man had died of heart failure in a Turkish bath—a fat man, of sedentary habits. The jury added a rider to their verdict of Misadventure, to the effect that the management should exercise a stricter supervision over the bathers and should never permit them to be left unattended in the hot room.

As Pender emerged from the hall he saw ahead of him a shabby hat that seemed familiar. He plunged after it, and caught Mr Smith about to step into a taxi.

'Smith,' he cried, gasping a little. He clutched him fiercely by the shoulder.

'What, you again?' said Smith. 'Taking notes of the case, eh? *Can I do anything for you?*'

'You devil!' said Pender. 'You're mixed up in this! You tried to kill me the other day.'

'Did I? Why should I do that?'

'You'll swing for this,' shouted Pender menacingly.

A policeman pushed his way through the gathering crowd.

'Here!' said he, 'what's all this about?'

Smith touched his forehead significantly.

'It's all right, officer,' said he. 'The gentleman seems to think I'm here for no good. Here's my card. The coroner knows me. But he attacked me. You'd better keep an eye on him.'

'That's right,' said a bystander.

'This man tried to kill me,' said Pender.

The policeman nodded.

'Don't you worry about that, sir,' he said. 'You think better of it. The 'eat in there has upset you a bit. All right, *all* right.'

'But I want to charge him,' said Pender.

'I wouldn't do that if I was you,' said the policeman.

'I tell you,' said Pender, 'that this man Smith has been trying to poison me. He's a murderer. He's poisoned scores of people.'

The policeman winked at Smith.

'Best be off, sir,' he said. 'I'll settle this. Now, my lad'—he held Pender firmly by the arms—'just you keep cool and take it quiet. That gentleman's name ain't Smith nor nothing like it. You've got a bit mixed up like.'

'Well, what is his name?' demanded Pender.

'Never you mind,' replied the constable. 'You leave him alone, or you'll be getting yourself into trouble.'

The taxi had driven away. Pender glanced round at the circle of amused faces and gave in.

'All right, officer,' he said. 'I won't give you any trouble. I'll come round with you to the police-station and tell you about it.'

'What do you think o' that one?' asked the inspector of the sergeant when Pender had stumbled out of the station.

'Up the pole an' 'alf-way round the flag, if you ask me,' replied his subordinate. 'Got one o' them ideez fix what they talk about.'

'H'm!' replied the inspector. 'Well, we've got his name and address. Better make a note of 'em. He might turn up again. Poisoning people so as they die in their baths, eh? That's a pretty good 'un. Wonderful how these barmy ones thinks it all out, isn't it?'

The spring that year was a bad one—cold and foggy. It was March when Pender went down to an inquest at Deptford, but a thick blanket of mist was hanging over the river as though it were November. The cold ate into your bones. As he sat in the dingy little court, peering through the yellow twilight of gas and fog, he could scarcely see the witnesses as they came to the table. Everybody in the place seemed to be coughing. Pender was coughing too. His bones ached, and he felt as though he were about due for a bout of influenza.

Straining his eyes, he thought he recognised a face on the other side of the room, but the smarting fog which penetrated every crack stung and blinded him. He felt in his overcoat pocket, and his hand closed comfortably on something thick and heavy. Ever since that day in Lincoln he had gone about armed for protection. Not a revolver— he was no hand with firearms. A sandbag was much better. He had bought one from an old man wheeling a barrow. It was meant for keeping out draughts from the door—a good, old-fashioned affair.

The inevitable verdict was returned. The spectators began to push their way out. Pender had to hurry now, not to lose sight of his man. He elbowed his way along, muttering apologies. At the door he almost touched the man, but a stout woman intervened. He plunged past her, and she gave a little squeak of indignation. The man in front turned his head, and the light over the door glinted on his glasses.

Pender pulled his hat over his eyes and followed. His shoes had crêpe rubber soles and made no sound on the sticking pavement. The man went on, jogging quietly up one street and down another, and never looking back. The fog was so thick that Pender was forced to keep within a few yards of him. Where was he going? Into the lighted streets? Home by 'bus or tram? No. He turned off to the left, down a narrow street.

The fog was thicker here. Pender could no longer see his quarry, but he heard the footsteps going on before him at the same even pace. It seemed to him that they were two alone in the world—pursued and pursuer, slayer and avenger. The street began to slope more rapidly. They must be coming out somewhere near the river.

Suddenly the dim shapes of the houses fell away on either side. There was an open space, with a lamp vaguely visible in the middle. The footsteps paused. Pender, silently hurrying after, saw the man standing close beneath the lamp, apparently consulting something in a notebook.

Four steps, and Pender was upon him. He drew the sandbag from his pocket. The man looked up.

'I've got you this time,' said Pender, and struck with all his force.

Pender had been quite right. He did get influenza. It was a week before he was out and about again. The weather had changed, and the air was fresh and sweet. In spite of the weakness left by the malady he felt as though a heavy weight had been lifted from his shoulders. He tottered down to a favourite bookshop of his in the Strand, and picked up a D.H. Lawrence 'first' at a price which he knew to be a bargain. Encouraged by this, he turned into a small chop-house, chiefly frequented by Fleet Street men, and ordered a grilled cutlet and a half-tankard of bitter.

Two journalists were seated at the next table.

'Going to poor old Buckley's funeral?' asked one

'Yes,' said the other. 'Poor devil! Fancy his getting sloshed on the head like that. He must have been on his way down to interview the widow of that fellow who died in a bath. It's a rough district. Probably one of Jimmy the Card's crowd had it in for him. He was a great crime-reporter—they won't get another like Bill Buckley in a hurry.'

'He was a decent sort, too. Great old sport. No end of a leg-puller. Remember his great stunt about sulphate of thanatol?'

Pender started. *That* was the word that had eluded him for so many months. A curious dizziness came over him and he took a pull at the tankard to steady himself.

'... looking at you as sober as a judge,' the journalist was saying. 'He used to work off that wheeze on poor boobs in railway carriages to see how they'd take it. Would you believe that one chap actually offered him—'

'Hullo!' interrupted his friend. 'That bloke over there has fainted. I thought he was looking a bit white.'

45

THE POISONED DOW '08

Dorothy Sayers

'Ah!' said the inspector. 'Take a seat, will you, Mr—ha, hum—Egg. Perhaps you can give us a little light on this affair...

'Good morning, miss,' said Mr Montague Egg, removing his smart trilby with something of a flourish as the front door opened. 'Here I am again, you see. Not forgotten me, have you? That's right, because I couldn't forget a young lady like you, not in a hundred years. How's his lordship to-day? Think he'd be willing to see me for a minute or two?'

He smiled pleasantly, bearing in mind Maxim Number Ten of the *Salesman's Handbook*, 'The goodwill of the maid is nine-tenths of the trade.'

The parlourmaid, however, seemed nervous and embarrassed.

'I don't—oh, yes—come in, please. His lordship—that is to say—I'm afraid——'

Mr Egg stepped in promptly, sample case in hand, and, to his great surprise, found himself confronted by a policeman, who, in somewhat gruff tones, demanded his name and business.

'Travelling representative of Plummet & Rose, Wines and Spirits, Piccadilly,' said Mr Egg, with the air of one who has nothing to conceal. 'Here's my card. What's up, sergeant?'

'Plummet & Rose?' said the policeman. 'Ah, well, just sit down a moment, will you? The inspector'll want to have a word with you, I shouldn't wonder.'

More and more astonished, Mr Egg obediently took a seat, and in a few minutes' time found himself ushered into a small sitting-room which was occupied by a uniformed police inspector and another policeman with a note-book.

'Ah!' said the inspector. 'Take a seat, will you, Mr—ha, hum—Egg. Perhaps you can give us a little light on this affair. Do you know anything about a case of port wine that was sold to Lord Borrodale last spring?'

'Certainly I do,' replied Mr Egg, 'if you mean the Dow '08. I made the sale myself. Six dozen at 192*s*. a dozen. Ordered from me, personally, March 3rd. Dispatched from our head office March 8th. Receipt acknowledged March 10th, with cheque in settlement. All in order our end. Nothing wrong with it, I hope? We've had no complaint. In fact, I've just called to ask his lordship how he liked it and to ask if he'd care to place a further order.'

'I see,' said the inspector. 'You just happened to call to-day in the course of your usual round? No special reason?'

Mr Egg, now convinced that something was very wrong indeed, replied by placing his order-book and road schedule at the inspector's disposal.

'Yes,' said the inspector, when he had glanced through them. 'That seems to be all right. Well, now, Mr Egg, I'm sorry to say that Lord Borrodale was found dead in his study this morning under circumstances strongly suggestive of his having taken poison. And what's more, it looks very much as if the poison had been administered to him in a glass of this port wine of yours.'

'You don't say!' said Mr Egg incredulously. 'I'm very sorry to hear that. It won't do us any good, either. Not but what the wine was wholesome enough when we sent it out. Naturally, it wouldn't pay us to go putting anything funny into our wines; I needn't tell you that. But it's not the sort of publicity we care for. What makes you think it was the port, anyway?'

For answer, the inspector pushed over to him a glass decanter which stood upon the table.

'See what you think yourself. It's all right—we've tested it for fingerprints already. Here's a glass if you want one, but I shouldn't advise you to swallow anything—not unless you're fed up with life.'

Mr Egg took a cautious sniff at the decanter and frowned. He poured out a thimbleful of the wine, sniffed and frowned again. Then he took an experimental drop upon his tongue, and immediately expectorated, with the utmost possible delicacy, into a convenient flower-pot.

'Oh, dear, oh, dear,' said Mr Montague Egg. His rosy face was puckered with distress. 'Tastes to me as though the old gentleman had been dropping his cigar-ends into it.'

The inspector exchanged a glance with the policeman.

'You're not far out,' he said. 'The doctor hasn't quite finished his post-mortem, but he says it looks to him like nicotine poisoning. Now, here's the problem. Lord Borrodale was accustomed to drink a couple of glasses of port in his study every night after dinner. Last night the wine was taken in to him as usual at 9 o'clock. It was a new bottle, and Craven—that's the butler—brought it straight up from the cellar in a basket arrangement——'

'A cradle,' interjected Mr Egg.

'—a cradle, if that's what you call it. James the footman followed him, carrying the decanter and a wineglass on a tray. Lord Borrodale inspected the bottle, which still bore the original seal, and then Craven drew the cork and decanted the wine in full view of Lord Borrodale and the footman. Then both servants left the room and retired to the kitchen quarters, and as they went, they heard Lord Borrodale lock the study door after them.'

'What did he do that for?'

'It seems he usually did. He was writing his memoirs—he was a famous judge, you know—and as some of the papers he was using were highly confidential, he preferred to make himself safe against sudden intruders. At 11 o'clock, when the household went to bed, James noticed that the light was still on in the study. In the morning it was discovered that Lord Borrodale had not been to bed. The study door was still locked and, when it was broken open, they found him lying dead on the floor. It looked as though he had been taken ill, had tried to reach the bell, and had collapsed on the way. The doctor says he must have died at about 10 o'clock.'

'Suicide?' suggested Mr Egg.

'Well, there are difficulties about that. The position of the body, for one thing. Also, we've carefully searched the room and found no traces of any bottle or anything that he could have kept the poison in. Besides, he seems to have enjoyed his life. He had no financial or domestic worries, and in spite of his advanced age his health was excellent. Why should he commit suicide?'

'But if he didn't,' objected Mr Egg, 'how was it he didn't notice the bad taste and smell of the wine?'

'Well, he seems to have been smoking a pretty powerful cigar at the time,' said the inspector (Mr Egg shook a reproachful head), 'and I'm told he was suffering from a slight cold, so that his taste and smell may not have been in full working order. There are no fingerprints on the decanter or the glass except his own and those of the butler and the footman—though, of course, that wouldn't prevent anybody dropping poison into either of them, if only the door hadn't been locked. The windows were both fastened on the inside, too, with burglar-proof catches.'

'How about the decanter?' asked Mr Egg, jealous for the reputation of his firm. 'Was it clean when it came in?'

'Yes, it was. James washed it out immediately before it went into the study; the cook swears she saw him do it. He used water from the tap and then swilled it round with a drop of brandy.'

'Quite right,' said Mr Egg approvingly.

'And there's nothing wrong with the brandy, either, for Craven took a glass of it himself afterwards—to settle his palpitations, so he says.' The inspector sniffed meaningly. 'The glass was wiped out by James when he put it on the tray, and then the whole thing was carried along to the study. Nothing was put down or left for a moment between leaving the pantry and entering the study, but Craven recollects that as he was crossing the hall Miss Waynfleet stopped him and spoke to him for a moment about some arrangements for the following day.'

'Miss Waynfleet? That's the niece, isn't it? I saw her on my last visit. A very charming young lady.'

'Lord Borrodale's heiress,' remarked the inspector meaningly.

'A very *nice* young lady,' said Mr Egg, with emphasis. 'And I understand you to say that Craven was carrying only the cradle, not the decanter or the glass.'

'That's so.'

'Well, then, I don't see that she could have put anything into what James was carrying.' Mr Egg paused. 'The seal on the cork, now—you say Lord Borrodale saw it?'

'Yes, and so did Craven and James. You can see it for yourself, if you like—what's left of it.'

The inspector produced an ash-tray, which held a few fragments of dark blue sealing-wax, together with a small quantity of cigar-ash. Mr Egg inspected them carefully.

'That's our wax and our seal, all right,' he pronounced. 'The top of the cork has been sliced off cleanly with a sharp knife and the mark's intact. 'Plummet & Rose. Dow 1908.' Nothing wrong with that. How about the strainer?'

'Washed out that same afternoon in boiling water by the kitchenmaid. Wiped immediately before using by James, who brought it in on the tray with the decanter and the glass. Taken out with the bottle and washed again at once, unfortunately—otherwise, of course, it might have told us something about when the nicotine got into the port wine.'

'Well,' said Mr Egg obstinately, 'it didn't get in at our place, that's a certainty. What's more, I don't believe it ever was in the bottle at all. How could it be? Where *is* the bottle, by the way?'

'It's just been packed up to go to the analyst, I think,' said the inspector, 'but as you're here, you'd better have a look at it. Podgers, let's have that bottle again. There are no fingerprints on it except Craven's, by the way, so it doesn't look as if it had been tampered with.'

The policeman produced a brown paper parcel, from which he extracted a port-bottle, its mouth plugged with a clean cork. Some of the original dust of the cellar still clung to it, mingled with fingerprint powder. Mr Egg removed the cork and took a long, strong sniff at the contents. Then his face changed.

'Where did you get this bottle from?' he demanded sharply.

'From Craven. Naturally, it was one of the first things we asked to see. He took us along to the cellar and pointed it out.'

'Was it standing by itself or with a lot of other bottles?'

'It was standing on the cellar floor at the end of a row of empties, all belonging to the same bin; he explained that he put them on the floor in the order in which they were used, till the time came for them to be collected and taken away.'

Mr Egg thoughtfully tilted the bottle; a few drops of thick red liquid, turbid with disturbed crust, escaped into his wineglass. He smelt them again and tasted them. His snub nose looked pugnacious.

'Well?' asked the inspector.

'No nicotine there, at all events,' said Mr Egg, 'unless my nose deceives me, which, you will understand, inspector, isn't likely, my nose being my livelihood, so to speak. No. You'll have to send it to be analysed of course; I quite understand that, but I'd be ready to bet quite a little bit of money you'll find that bottle innocent. And that, I needn't tell you, will be a great relief to our minds. And I'm sure, speaking for myself, I very much appreciate the kind way you've put the matter before me.'

'That's all right; your expert knowledge is of value. We can probably now exclude the bottle straight away and concentrate on the decanter.'

'Just so,' replied Mr Egg. 'Ye-es. Do you happen to know how many of the six dozen bottles had been used?'

'No, but Craven can tell us, if you really want to know.'

'Just for my own satisfaction,' said Mr Egg. 'Just to be sure that this *is* the right bottle, you know. I shouldn't like to feel I might have misled you in any way.'

The inspector rang the bell, and the butler promptly appeared—an elderly man of intensely respectable appearance.

'Craven,' said the inspector, 'this is Mr Egg of Plummet & Rose's.'

'I am already acquainted with Mr Egg.'

'Quite. He is naturally interested in the history of the port wine. He would like to know—what is it, exactly, Mr Egg?'

'This bottle,' said Monty, rapping it lightly with his finger-nail, 'it's the one you opened last night?'

'Yes, sir.'

'Sure of that?'

'Yes, sir.'

'How many dozen have you got left?'

'I couldn't say off-hand, sir, without the cellar-book.'

'And that's in the cellar, eh? I'd like to have a look at your cellars—I'm told they're very fine. All in apple-pie order, I'm sure. Right temperature and all that?'

'Undoubtedly, sir.'

'We'll all go and look at the cellar,' suggested the inspector, who in spite of his expressed confidence seemed to have doubts about leaving Mr Egg alone with the butler.

Craven bowed and led the way, pausing only to fetch the keys from his pantry.

'This nicotine, now,' prattled Mr Egg, as they proceeded down a long corridor, 'is it very deadly? I mean, would you require a great quantity of it to poison a person?'

'I understand from the doctor,' replied the inspector, 'that a few drops of the pure extract, or whatever they call it, would produce death in anything from twenty minutes to seven or eight hours.'

'Dear, dear!' said Mr Egg. 'And how much of the port had the poor old gentleman taken? The full two glasses?'

'Yes, sir; to judge by the decanter, he had. Lord Borrodale had the habit of drinking his port straight off. He did not sip it, sir.'

Mr Egg was distressed.

'Not the right thing at all,' he said mournfully. 'No, no. Smell, sip and savour to bring out the flavour—that's the rule for wine, you know. Is there such a thing as a pond or stream in the garden, Mr Craven?'

'No, sir,' said the butler, a little surprised.

'Ah! I was just wondering. Somebody must have brought the nicotine along in something or other, you know. What would they do afterwards with the little bottle or whatever it was?'

'Easy enough to throw it in among the bushes or bury it, surely,' said Craven. 'There's six acres of garden, not counting the meadow or the courtyard. Or there are the water-butts, of course, and the well.'

'How stupid of me,' confessed Mr Egg. 'I never thought of that. Ah! this is the cellar, is it? Splendid—a real slap-up outfit, I call this. Nice, even temperature, too. Same summer and winter, eh? Well away from the house-furnace?'

'Oh, yes, indeed, sir. That's the other side of the house. Be careful of the last step, gentlemen; it's a little broken away. Here is where the Dow '08 stood, sir. No. 17 bin—one, two, three and a half dozen remaining, sir.'

Mr Egg nodded and, holding his electric torch close to the protruding necks of the bottles, made a careful examination of the seals.

'Yes,' he said, 'here they are. Three and a half dozen, as you say. Sad to think that the throat they should have gone down lies, as you might say, closed up by Death. I often think, as I make my rounds, what a pity it is we don't all grow mellower and softer in our old age, same as this wine. A fine old gentleman, Lord Borrodale, or so I'm told, but something of a tough nut, if that's not disrespectful.'

'He was hard, sir,' agreed the butler, 'but just. A very just master.'

'Quite,' said Mr Egg. 'And these, I take it, are the empties. Twelve, twenty-four, twenty-nine—and one is thirty—and three and a half dozen is forty-two—seventy-two—six dozen—that's O.K. by me.' He lifted the empty bottles one by one. 'They say dead men tell no tales, but they talk to little Monty Egg all right. This one, for instance. If this ever held Plummet & Rose's Dow '08 you can take Monty Egg and scramble him. Wrong smell, wrong crust, and that splash of white-wash was never put on by our cellar-man. Very easy to mix up one empty bottle with another. Twelve, twenty-four, twenty-eight and one is twenty-nine. I wonder what's become of the thirtieth bottle.'

'I'm sure I never took one away,' said the butler.

'The pantry keys—on a nail inside the door—very accessible,' said Monty.

'Just a moment,' interrupted the inspector. 'Do you say that that bottle doesn't belong to the same bunch of port wine?'

'No, it doesn't—but no doubt Lord Borrodale sometimes went in for a change of vintage.' Mr Egg inverted the bottle and shook it sharply. 'Quite dry. Curious. Had a dead spider at the bottom of it. You'd be surprised how long a spider can exist without food. Curious that this empty bottle, which comes in the middle of the row, should be drier than the one at the beginning of the row, and should contain a dead spider. We see a deal of curious things in our calling, inspector—we're encouraged to notice things, as you might say. 'The salesman with the open eye sees commissions mount up high.' You might call this bottle a curious thing. And here's another. That other bottle, the one you said was opened last night, Craven—how did you come to make a mistake like that? If my nose is to be trusted, not to mention my palate, that bottle's been open a week at least.'

'Has it indeed, sir? I'm sure it's the one as I put here at the end of this row. Somebody must have been and changed it.'

'But—' said the inspector. He stopped in mid-speech, as though struck by a sudden thought. 'I think you'd better let me have those cellar keys of yours, Craven, and we'll get this cellar properly examined. That'll do for the moment. If you'll just step upstairs with me, Mr Egg, I'd like a word with you.'

'Always happy to oblige,' said Monty agreeably. They returned to the upper air.

'I don't know if you realise, Mr Egg,' observed the inspector, 'the bearing, or, as I might say, the inference of what you said just now. Supposing you're right about this bottle not being the right one, somebody's changed it on purpose, and the right one's missing. And, what's more, the person that changed the bottle left no fingerprints behind him—or her.'

'I see what you mean,' said Mr Egg, who had indeed drawn this inference some time ago, 'and what's more, it looks as if the poison had been in the bottle after all, doesn't it? And that—you're going to say—is a serious look-out for Plummet & Rose, seeing there's no doubt our seal was on the bottle when it was brought into Lord Borrodale's room. I don't deny it, inspector. It's useless to bluster and say 'No, no,' when it's perfectly clear that the facts are so. That's a very useful motto for a man that wants to get on in our line of business.'

'Well, Mr Egg,' said the inspector, laughing, 'what will you say to the next inference? Since nobody but you had any interest in changing that bottle over, it looks as though I ought to clap the handcuffs on you.'

'Now, that's a disagreeable sort of an inference,' protested Mr Egg, 'and I hope you won't follow it up. I shouldn't like anything of that sort to happen, and my employers wouldn't fancy it either. Don't you think that, before we do anything we might have cause to regret, it would be a good idea to have a look in the furnace-room?'

'Why the furnace-room?'

'Because,' said Mr Egg, 'it's the place that Craven particularly didn't mention when we were asking him where anybody might have put a thing he wanted to get rid of.'

The inspector appeared to be struck by this line of reasoning. He enlisted the aid of a couple of constables, and very soon the ashes of the furnace that supplied the central heating were being assiduously raked over. The first find was a thick mass of semi-molten glass, which looked as though it might once have been part of a wine bottle.

'Looks as though you might be right,' said the inspector, 'but I don't see how we're to prove anything. We're not likely to get any nicotine out of this.'

'I suppose not,' agreed Mr Egg sadly. 'But'—his face brightened—'how about this?'

From the sieve in which the constable was sifting the ashes he picked out a thin piece of warped and twisted metal, to which a lump of charred bone still clung.

'What on earth's that?'

'It doesn't look like much, but I think it might once have been a corkscrew,' suggested Mr Egg mildly. 'There's something homely and familiar about it. And, if you'll look here, I think you'll see that the metal part of it is hollow. And I shouldn't be surprised if the thick bone handle was hollow, too. It's very badly charred, of course, but if you were to split it open, and if you were to find a hollow inside it, and possibly a little melted rubber—well, that might explain a lot.'

The inspector smacked his thigh.

'By Jove, Mr Egg!' he exclaimed, 'I believe I see what you're getting at. You mean that if this corkscrew had been made hollow, and contained a rubber reservoir, inside, like a fountain-pen, filled with poison, the poison might be made to flow down the hollow shaft by pressure on some sort of plunger arrangement.'

'That's it,' said Mr Egg. 'It would have to be screwed into the cork very carefully, of course, so as not to damage the tube, and it would have to be made long enough to project beyond the bottom of the cork, but still, it might be done. What's more, it has been done, or why should there be this little hole in the metal, about a quarter of an inch from the tip? Ordinary corkscrews never have holes in them—not in my experience, and I've been, as you might say, brought up on corkscrews.'

'But who, in that case——?'

'Well, the man who drew the cork, don't you think? The man whose fingerprints were on the bottle.'

'Craven? But where's his motive?'

'I don't know,' said Mr Egg, 'but Lord Borrodale was a judge, and a hard judge too. If you were to have Craven's fingerprints sent up to Scotland Yard, they might recognise them. I don't know. It's possible, isn't it? Or maybe Miss Waynfleet might know something about him. Or he might just possibly be mentioned in Lord Borrodale's memoirs that he was writing.'

The inspector lost no time in following up this suggestion. Neither Scotland Yard nor Miss Waynfleet had anything to say against the butler, who had been two years in his situation and had always been quite satisfactory, but a reference to the records of Lord Borrodale's judicial career showed that, a good many years before, he had inflicted a savage sentence of penal servitude on a young man called Craven, who was by trade a skilled metal-worker and had apparently been involved in a fraud upon his employer. A little further investigation showed that this young man had been released from prison six months previously.

'Craven's son, of course,' said the inspector. 'And he had the manual skill to make the corkscrew in exact imitation of the one ordinarily used in the household. Wonder where they got the nicotine from? Well, we shall soon be able to check that up. I believe it's not difficult to obtain it for use in the garden. I'm very much obliged to you for your expert assistance, Mr Egg. It would have taken us a long time to get to the rights and wrongs of those bottles. I suppose, when you found that Craven had given you the wrong one, you began to suspect him?'

'Oh, no,' said Mr Egg, with modest pride, 'I knew it was Craven the minute he came into the room.'

'No, did you? You're a regular Sherlock, aren't you? But why?'

'He called me "sir",' explained Mr Egg, coughing delicately. 'Last time I called he addressed me as "young fellow" and told me that tradesmen must go round to the back door. A bad error of policy. "Whether you're wrong or whether you're right, it's always better to be polite," as it says in the *Salesman's Handbook*.'

46

THE STOLEN CIGAR-CASE
Bret Harte

...You would say that even if you had embraced some young person in a sealskin sacque what had that to do with the robbery....

I found Hemlock Jones in the old Brook Street lodgings, musing before the fire. With the freedom of an old friend I at once threw myself in my old familiar attitude at his feet, and gently caressed his boot. I was induced to do this for two reasons; one that it enabled me to get a good look at his bent, concentrated face, and' the other that it, seemed to indicate my reverence for his superhuman insight. So absorbed was he even then, in tracking some mysterious clue, that he did not seem to notice me. But therein I was wrong—as I always was in my attempt to understand that powerful intellect.

'It is raining,' he said, without lifting his 'head.

You have been out then?' I said quickly.

'No. But see that your umbrella is wet, arid that your overcoat, which you threw off on entering, has, drops of water on it.'

I sat aghast 'at his penetration. After a pause he said carelessly, as if dismissing, the subject: 'Besides, I hear the rain on the window. Listen.'

I listened. I could scarcely credit my ears, but there was the soft pattering of drops on the pane. It was evident, there' was no deceiving this man!

'Have you been busy lately?' I asked, changing the' subject. 'What new problem—given up by Scotland Yard as inscrutable—has occupied that gigantic intellect?'

He drew back his foot slightly, and seemed to hesitate ere he re-turned it to its original position. Then he answered wearily: 'Mere trifles—nothing to speak of. The Prince Kopoli has been here to get my advice regarding the disappearance of certain rubies from the Kremlin, the Rajah of Pootibad, after vainly beheading his entire bodyguard, has been obliged to seek my assistance to recover a jewelled sword. The Grand Duchess of Pretzel-Brauntswig is desirous of discovering where her husband was on the night of the 14th of February, and last night'—he lowered his voice slightly—'a lodger in this very house, meeting me on the stairs, wanted to know "Why they don't answer his bell."'

I could not help smiling—until I saw a frown gathering on his inscrutable forehead.

'Pray to remember,' he said coldly, 'that it was through such an apparently trivial question that I found out, 'Why Paul Ferroll killed his wife,' and 'What happened to Jones!'

I became dumb at once. He paused for a moment, and then suddenly changing back to his usual pitiless, analytical style, he said: 'When I say these are trifles-they are so in comparison to an affair that is now before me. A crime has been committed, and, singularly enough, against myself. You start,' he said; 'you wonder who would have dared to attempt it! So did I; nevertheless, it has been done. I have been robbed.'

'You robbed—you, Hemlock Jones, the Terror of Peculators!' I gasped in amazement, rising and gripping the table as I faced him.

'Yes; listen. I would confess it to no other. But you who have followed 'my career, who know my methods, yea, for whom I have partly lifted the veil that conceals my plans from ordinary humanity; you, who have for years rapturously accepted my confidences, passionately admired my inductions and inferences, placed yourself at my beck and call, become my slave, grovelled at my feet, given up your practice except those few unremunerative and rapidly-decreasing patients to whom, in moments of abstraction over my problems, you have administered strychnine for quinine and arsenic for Epsom salts; you, who have sacrificed everything and everybody to me—you I make my confidant!'

I rose and embraced him warmly, yet he was already so engrossed in thought that at the same moment he mechanically placed his hand upon his watch chain as if to consult the time. 'Sit down,' he said, 'have a cigar?'

'I have given up cigar smoking,' I said.

'Why?' he asked.

I hesitated, and perhaps coloured. I had really given it up because, with my diminished practice, it was too expensive. I could only afford a pipe. 'I prefer a pipe,' I said laughingly. 'But tell me of this robbery. What have you lost?'

He rose, and planting himself before the fire with his hands under his coat tails, looked down upon me reflectively for a moment. 'Do you remember the cigar-case presented to me by the Turkish Ambassador for discovering the missing favourite of the Grand Vizier in the fifth chorus girl at the Hilarity Theatre? It was that one. It was incrusted with diamonds. I mean the cigar-case.'

'And the largest one had been supplanted by paste,' I said.

'Ah,' he said with a reflective smile, 'you know that?'

'You told me yourself. I remember considering it a proof of your extraordinary perception. But, by Jove, you don't mean to say you have lost it.'

He was silent for a moment. 'No; it has been stolen, it is true, but I shall still find it. And by myself alone! In your profession, my dear fellow, when a member is severely ill he does not prescribe for himself, but calls in a brother doctor. Therein we differ. I shall take this matter in my own hands.'

'And where could you find better?' I said enthusiastically. 'I should say the cigar-case is as good as recovered already.'

'I shall remind you of that again,' he said lightly. 'And now, to show you my confidence in your judgment, in spite of my determination to pursue this alone, I am willing to listen to any suggestions from you.'

He drew a memorandum book from his pocket, and, with a grave smile, took up his pencil.

I could scarcely believe my reason. He, the great Hemlock Jones accepting suggestions from a humble individual like myself! I kissed his hand reverently, and began in a joyous tone:

'First I should advertise, offering a reward; I should give the same intimation in handbills, distributed at the 'pubs' and the pastry-cooks. I should next visit the different pawnbrokers; I should give notice at the police station. I should examine the servants. I should thoroughly search the house and my own pockets. I speak relatively,' I added with a laugh, 'of course, I mean your own.'

He gravely made an entry of these details.

'Perhaps,' I added, 'you have already done this?'

'Perhaps,' he returned enigmatically. 'Now, my dear friend,' he continued, putting the note-book in his pocket, and rising—'would you excuse me for a few moments? Make yourself perfectly at home until I return there may be some things,' he added with a sweep of his hand towards his heterogeneously filled shelves, 'that may interest you, and while away the time. There are pipes and tobacco in that corner and whiskey on the table.' And nodding to me with the same inscrutable face, he left the room. I was too well accustomed to his methods to think much of his unceremonious withdrawal, and made no doubt he was off to investigate some clue which had suddenly occurred to his active intelligence.

Left to myself, I cast a cursory glance over his shelves. There were a number of small glass jars, containing earthy substances labelled 'Pavement and road sweepings', from the principal thoroughfares and suburbs of London, with the sub-directions 'For identifying foot tracks.' There were several other jars labelled 'Fluff from omnibus and road-car seats,' 'Cocoanut fibre and rope strands from mattings in public places,' 'Cigarette stumps and match ends from floor of Palace Theatre, Row A, 1 to 50.' Everywhere were evidences of this wonderful man's system and perspicacity.

I was thus engaged when I heard the slight creaking of a door, and I looked up as a stranger entered. He was a rough-looking man, with a shabby overcoat, a still more disreputable muffler round his throat, and a cap on his head. Considerably annoyed at his intrusion I turned upon him rather sharply, when, with a mumbled, growling apology for mistaking the room, he shuffled out again and closed the door. I followed him quickly to the landing and saw that he disappeared down the stairs.

With my mind full of the robbery, the incident made a singular impression on me. I knew my friend's habits of hasty absences from his room in his moments of deep inspiration; it was only too probable that with his powerful intellect and magnificent perceptive genius concentrated on one subject, he should be careless of his own belongings, and, no doubt, even forget to take the ordinary precaution of locking up his drawers. I tried one or two and found that I was right—although for some reason I was unable to open one to its fullest extent. The handles were sticky, as if someone had opened them with dirty fingers. Knowing Hemlock's fastidious cleanliness, I resolved to inform him of this circumstance, but I forgot it, alas! Until—but I am anticipating my story.

His absence was strangely prolonged. I at last seated myself by the fire, and lulled by warmth and the patter of the rain on the win do I fell asleep. I may have dreamt, for during my sleep I had a vague semi consciousness as of hands being softly pressed on my pockets—no doubt induced by the story of the robbery. When I came fully to my senses, I found Hemlock Jones sitting on the other side of the hearth, his deeply concentrated gaze fixed on the fire.

'I found you so comfortably asleep that I could not bear to waken you,' he said with a smile.

I rubbed my eyes. 'And what news?' I asked. 'How have you succeeded?'

'Better than I expected,' he said, 'and I think,' he added, tapping his note-book—'I owe much to you.'

Deeply gratified, I awaited more. But in vain. I ought to have remembered that in his moods Hemlock Jones was reticence itself. I told him simply of the strange intrusion, but he only laughed.

Later, when I rose to go, he looked at me playfully: 'If you were a married man,' he said, 'I would advise you not to go home until you had brushed your sleeve. There are a few short, brown seal .skin hairs on the inner side of the fore-arm—just where they would have adhered if your arm had encircled a seal-skin sacque with some pressure!'

'For once you are at fault,' I said triumphantly, 'the hair is my own as you will perceive, I have just had it cut at the hair-dressers, and no doubt this arm projected beyond the apron.'

He frowned slightly, yet nevertheless, on my turning to go he embraced me warmly—a rare exhibition in that man of ice. He even helped me on with my Overcoat and pulled out and smoothed down the flaps of my pockets. He was particular; too, in fitting my arm in my overcoat sleeve, shaking the sleeve down from the armhole to the cuff with his deft fingers. 'Come again soon!' he said, clapping me on the back.

'At any and all times,' I said enthusiastically. 'I only ask ten minutes twice a day to eat a crust at my office and four hours' sleep at night, and the rest of my time is devoted to you always—as you know.'

'It is, indeed,' he said, with his impenetrable smile.

Nevertheless I did not find him at home when I next called. One afternoon, when nearing my own home I met him in one of his favourite disguises—a long, blue, swallow-tailed coat, striped cotton trousers, large turn-over collar, blacked face, and white hat, carrying a tambourine. Of course to others the disguise was perfect, although it was known to myself, and I passed him—according to an old understanding between us—without the slightest recognition, trusting to a later explanation. At another time, as I was making a professional visit to the wife of a publican at the East End, I saw him in the disguise of a broken-down artisan looking into the window of an adjacent pawn shop. I was delighted to see that he was evidently following my suggestions, and in my joy I ventured to tip him a wink it was abstractedly returned.

Two days later I received a note appointing a meeting at his lodgings that night. That meeting, alas! was the one memorable occurrence of my life, and the last meeting I ever had with Hemlock Jones! I will try to set it down calmly, though my pulses still throb with the recollection of it.

I found him standing before the fire with that look upon his face which I had seen only once or twice in our acquaintance—a look which I may call an absolute concatenation of inductive and deductive ratiocination—from which all that was human, tender, or sympathetic, was absolutely discharged. He was simply an icy, algebraic symbol! Indeed his whole being was concentrated to that extent that his clothes fitted loosely, and his head was absolutely so much reduced in size by his mental compression that his hat tipped back from his forehead and literally hung on his massive ears.

After I had entered, he locked the doors, fastened the windows, and even placed a chair before the chimney. As I watched those significant precautions with absorbing interest, he suddenly drew a revolver and presenting it to my temple, said in low, icy tones:

'Hand over that cigar-case!'

Even in my bewilderment, my reply was truthful, spontaneous, and involuntary. 'I haven't got it,' I said.

He smiled bitterly, and threw down his revolver. 'I expected that reply! Then let me now confront you with something more awful, more deadly, more relentless and convincing than that mere lethal weapon—the damning inductive and deductive proofs of your guilt!' He drew from his pocket a roll of paper and a note-book.

'But surely,' I gasped, 'you are joking! You could not for a moment believe—'

'Silence!' he roared. 'Sit down!'

I obeyed.

'You have condemned yourself,' he went on pitilessly. 'Condemned yourself on my processes—processes familiar to you, applauded by you, accepted by you for years! We will go back to the time when you first saw the cigar-case. Your expressions,' he said in cold, deliberate tones, consulting his paper, 'were: "How beautiful! I wish it were mine." This was your first step in crime—and my first indication. From "I wish it were mine" to "I will have it mine," and the mere detail, "How can I make it mine," tic advance was obvious. Silence! But as in my methods, it was necessary that there should be an overwhelming inducement to the crime, that unholy admiration of yours for the mere trinket itself was not enough. You are a smoker of cigars.'

'But,' I burst out passionately, 'I told you I had given up smoking cigars.'

'Fool!' he said coldly, 'that is the second time you have committed yourself. Of course, you told me! what more natural than for you to blazon forth that prepared and unsolicited statement to prevent accusation. Yet, as I said before, even that wretched attempt to cover up your tracks was not enough. I still had to find that overwhelming, impelling motive necessary to affect a man like you. That motive I found in passion, the strongest of all impulses—love, I suppose you would call it,' he added bitterly; 'that night you called! You had brought the damning proofs of it in your sleeve.'

'But,' I almost screamed.

'Silence,' he thundered. 'I know what you would say. You would say that even if you had embraced some young person in a sealskin sacque what had that to do with the robbery. Let me tell you then, that that sealskin sacque represented the quality and character of your fatal entanglement! If you are at all conversant with light sporting literature you would know that a sealskin sacque indicates a love induced by sordid mercenary interests. You bartered your honour for it—that stolen cigar-case was the purchaser of the sealskin sacque! Without money, with a decreasing practice, it was the only way you could insure your passion being returned by that young person, whom, for your sake, I have not even pursued. Silence! Having thoroughly established your motive, I now proceed to the commission of the crime itself. Ordinary people would have begun with that—with an attempt to discover the whereabouts of the missing object. These are not my methods.'

So overpowering was his penetration, that although I knew myself innocent, I licked my lips with avidity to hear the further details of this lucid exposition of my crime.

'You committed that theft the night I showed you the cigar-case and after I had carelessly thrown it in that drawer. You were sitting in that chair, and I had risen to take something from that shelf. In that instant you secured your booty without rising. Silence! Do you remember when I helped you on with your overcoat the other night? I was particular about fitting your arm in. While doing so I measured your arm with a spring tape measure from the shoulder to the cuff. A later visit to your tailor confirmed that measurement. It proved to be the exact distance between your chair and that drawer.'

I sat stunned.

'The rest are mere corroborative details! You were again tampering with the drawer when I discovered you doing so. Do not start! The stranger that blundered into the room with the muffler on—was myself. More, I had placed a little soap on the drawer handles purposely left you alone. The soap was on your hand when I shook it at parting. I softly felt your pockets when you were asleep for further developments. I embraced you when you left—that I might feel if you had the cigar-case, or any other articles, hidden on your body. This confirmed me in the belief that you had already disposed of it in the manner and for the purpose I have shown you. As I still believed you capable of remorse and confession, I allowed you to see I was on your track twice, once in the garb of an itinerant negro minstrel, and the second time as a workman looking in the window of the pawnshop where you pledged your booty.'

'But,' I burst out, 'if you had asked the pawnbroker you would have seen how unjust—'

'Fool!' he hissed; 'that was one of your suggestions search the pawnshops. Do you suppose I followed any of your suggestions—the suggestions of the thief? On the contrary, they told me what to avoid.'

'And I suppose,' I said bitterly, 'you have not even searched—your drawer.'

'No,' he said calmly.

I was for the first time really vexed. I. went to the nearest drawer and pulled it out sharply. It stuck as it had before, leaving a part of the drawer unopened. By working it, however, I discovered that it was impeded by some obstacle that had slipped to the upper part of the drawer, and held it firmly fast. Inserting my hand, I pulled out the impeding object. It was the missing cigar-case. I turned to him with a cry of joy.

But I was appalled at his expression. A look of contempt was now added to his acute, penetrating gaze. 'I have been mistaken,' he said slowly. 'I had not allowed for your weakness and cowardice. I thought too highly of you even in your guilt; but I see now why you tampered with that drawer the other night. By some incredible means-possibly another theft—you took the cigar-case out of palm and like a whipped hound restored it to me in this feeble, clumsy fashion. You thought to deceive me, Hemlock Jones: more, you thought to destroy my infallibility. Go! I give you your liberty. I shall not summon the three policemen who wait in the adjoining room—but out of my sight for ever.'

As I stood once more dazed and petrified, he took me firmly by the ear and led me into the hall, closing the door behind him. This reopened presently wide enough to permit him to thrust out my hat, overcoat, umbrella and overshoes, and, then closed against me for ever!

I never saw him again. I am bound to say, however, that thereafter my business increased, I recovered' much of my old practice—and a few of my patients recovered also. I became rich. I had a brougham and a house in the West End. But I often wondered, pondering on that wonderful man's penetration and insight, if, in some lapse of consciousness, I had not really stolen his cigar-case!

47

THE TRAILOR MURDER MYSTERY
Abraham Lincoln

...At this disclosure, all lingering credulity was broken down, and excitement rose to an almost inconceivable height...

In the year 1841, there resided, at different points in the State of Illinois, three brothers by the name of Trailor. Their Christian names were William, Henry and Archibald. Archibald resided at Springfield, then as now the seat of Government of the State He was a sober, retiring, and industrious man, of about thirty years of age; a carpenter by trade, and a bachelor, boarding with his partner in business—a Mr Myers. Henry, a year or two older, was a man of like retiring and industrious habits; had a family, and resided with it on a farm, at Clary's Grove, about twenty miles distant from Springfield in a northwesterly direction. —William, still older, and with similar habits, resided on a farm in Warren county, distant from Springfield something more than a hundred miles in the same North-westerly direction. He was a widower, with several children.

In the neighbourhood of William's residence, there was, and had been for several years, a man by the name of Fisher, who was somewhat above the age of fifty; had no family, and no settled home; but who boarded and lodged a while here and a while there, with persons for whom he did little jobs of work. His habits were remarkably economical, so that an impression got about that he had accumulated a considerable amount of money

In the latter part of May, in the year mentioned, William formed the purpose of visiting his brothers at Clary's Grove and Springfield; and Fisher, at the time having his temporary residence at his house, resolved to accompany him. They set out together in a buggy with a single horse. On Sunday evening they reached Henry's residence, and stayed overnight. On Monday morning, being the first Monday of June, they started on to Springfield, Henry accompanying them on horseback. They reached town about noon, met Archibald, went with him to his boarding house, and there took up their lodgings for the time they should remain.

After dinner, the three Trailors and Fisher left the boarding house in company, for the avowed purpose of spending the evening together in looking about the town. At supper, the Trailors had all returned, but Fisher was missing, and some inquiry was made about him. After supper, the Trailors went out professedly in search of him. One by one they returned, the last coming in after late tea time, and each stating that he had been unable to discover anything of Fisher.

The next day, both before and after breakfast, they went professedly in search again, and returned at noon, still unsuccessful. Dinner again being had, William and Henry expressed a determination to give up the search, and start for their homes. This was remonstrated against by some of the boarders about the house, on the ground that Fisher was somewhere in the vicinity, and would be left without any conveyance, as he and William had come in the same buggy. The remonstrance was disregarded, and they departed for their homes respectively.

Up to this time, the knowledge of Fisher's mysterious disappearance had spread very little beyond the few boarders at Myers', and excited no considerable interest. After the lapse of three or four days Henry returned to Springfield, for the ostensible purpose of making further search for Fisher. Procuring some of the boarders, he, tighter with them and Archibald, spent another day in ineffectual search, when it was again abandoned, and he returned home.

No general interest was yet excited.

On the Friday, week after Fisher's disappearance, the Postmaster Springfield received a letter from the Postmaster nearest William's residence, in Warren county, stating that William had returned home without Fisher, and was saying, rather boastfully, that Fisher was dead, and had willed him his money, and that he had got about fifteen hundred dollars by it. The letter further stated that William's story and conduct seemed strange, and desired the Postmaster at Springfield to ascertain and write what was the truth in the matter.

The Postmaster at Springfield made the letter public, and at once, excitement became universal and intense. Springfield, at that time, had a population of about 3,500, with a city organization. The Attorney General of the State resided there. A purpose was forthwith formed to ferret out the mystery, in putting which into execution, the Mayor of the city and the Attorney General took the lead. To make search for, and, if possible, find the body of the man supposed to be murdered, was resolved on as the first step.

In pursuance of this, men were formed into large parties, and marched abreast, in all directions, so as to let no inch of ground in the vicinity remain unsearched. Examinations were made of cellars, wells, and pits of all descriptions, where it was thought possible the body might be concealed. All the fresh, or tolerably fresh graves in the graveyard, were pried into, and dead horses and dead dogs were disintered, where, in some instances, they had been buried by their partial masters.

This search, as has appeared, commenced on Friday. It continued until Saturday afternoon without success, when it was determined to despatch officers to arrest William and Henry, at their residences, respectively. The officers started on Sunday morning, meanwhile, the search for the body was continued, and rumours got afloat of the Trailors having passed, at different times and places, several gold pieces, which were readily supposed to have belonged to Fisher.

On Monday, the officers sent for Henry, having arrested him, arrived with him. The Mayor and Attorney Gen'l took charge of him, and set their wits to work to elicit a discovery from him. He denied, and denied, and persisted in denying. They still plied him in every conceivable way, till Wednesday, when, protesting his own innocence, he stated that his brothers, William and Archibald, had murdered Fisher; that they had killed him, without his (Henry's) knowledge at the time, and made a temporary concealment of his body that, immediately preceding his and William's departure from Spring field for home, on Tuesday, the day after Fisher's disappearance, William and Archibald communicated the fact to him, and engaged his assistance in making a permanent concealment of the body; that, at the time he and William left professedly for home, they did not take the road directly, but, meandering their way through the streets, entered the woods at the North West. of the city, two or three hundred yards to the right of where the road they should have travelled, entered them; that, penetrating the woods some few hundred yards, they halted and Archibald came a somewhat different route, on foot, and joined them; that William and Archibald then stationed him (Henry) on an old and disused road that ran near by, as a sentinel, to give warning of the approach of any intruder; that William and Archibald then removed the buggy to the edge of a dense brush thicket, about forty yards distant from his (Henry's) position, where, leaving the buggy, they entered the thicket, and in a few minutes returned with. the body, and placed it in the buggy; that from his station he could and did distinctly see that the object placed in the buggy was a dead man, of the general appearance and size of Fisher; that William and Archibald then moved off with the buggy in the direction of Hickox's mill pond, and after an absence of half an hour, returned, saying they had put him in a safe place that Archibald then left for town, and he and William found their way to the road, and made for their homes.

At this disclosure, all lingering credulity was broken down, and excitement rose to an almost inconceivable height. Up to this time, the well-known character of Archibald had repelled and put down all suspicions as to him. Till then, those who were ready to swear that a murder had been committed, were almost as confident that Archibald had had no part in it. But now, he was seized and thrown into jail; and indeed, his personal security rendered it by no means objectionable to him.

And now came the search for the brush thicket, and the search of the mill pond. The thicket was found, and the buggy tracks at the point indicated. At a point within the thicket, the signs of a struggle were discovered, and a trail from thence to the buggy track was traced. In attempting to follow the track of the buggy from the thicket, it was found to proceed in the direction of the mill pond, but could not be traced all the way. At the pond, however, it was found that a buggy had been backed down to, and partially into the water's edge.

Search was now to be made in the pond; and it was made in every imaginable way. Hundreds and hundreds were engaged in raking, fishing, and draining. After much fruitless effort in this way, on Thursday morning the mill dam was cut down, and the water of the pond partially drawn off, and the same processes of search-again gone through with.

About noon of this day, the officer sent for William, returned having him in custody, and a man calling himself Dr Gilmore, came in company with them. It seems that the officer arrested William at his own house, early in the day on Tuesday, and started to Springfield with him, that after dark awhile, they reached Lewiston, in Fulton county, where they stopped for the night that late in the night this Dr Gilmore arrived, stating that Fisher was alive, at his house, and that he had followed on to give the information, so that William might be released without further trouble; that the officer, distrusting Dr Gilmore, refused to release William, but brought him on to Springfield, and the Dr accompanied them.

On reaching Springfield, the Dr. re-asserted that Fisher was alive, and at his house. At this the multitude for a time, were utterly confounded. Gilmore's story was communicated to Henry Trailor, who, without faltering, reaffirmed his own story about Fisher's murder. Henry's adherence to his own story was communicated to the crowd, and at once the idea started, and became nearly, if not quite universal that Gilmore was a confederate of the Trailors, and had invented the tale he was telling, to secure their release and escape. Excitement was again at its zenith.

About three o'clock the same evening, Myers, Archibald's partner, started with a two-horse carriage, for the purpose of ascertaining whether Fisher was alive as stated by Gilmore, and if so of bringing him back to Springfield with him.

On Friday a legal examination was gone into before two Justices, on the charge of murder against William and Archibald. Henry was introduced as a witness by the prosecution, and on oath re-affirmed his statements, as heretofore detailed and at the end of which he bore a thorough and rigid cross-examination without faltering or exposure. The prosecution also proved, by a respectable lady, that on the Monday evening of Fisher's disappearance, she saw Archibald, whom she well knew, and another man whom she -did not then know, but 'whom she believed at the time of testifying to be William, (then present) and still another, answering the description of Fisher, all enter the timber at the North West of town, (the point—indicated by Henry) and after one or two hours, saw William and Archibald return without Fisher.

Several other witnesses testified, that on Tuesday, at the time William and Henry professedly gave up the-search for Fisher's body, and started for home, they did not take the road directly, but did go into the woods, as stated by Henry. By others, also, it was proved, that since Fisher's disappearance, William and Archibald had passed rather an unusual number of gold pieces. The statements heretofore made about the thicket, the signs of a struggle, the buggy tracks, &c., were fully proven by numerous witnesses.

At this the prosecution rested.

Dr Gilmore was then introduced by the defendants. He stated that he resided in Warren county, about seven miles distant from William's residence; that on the morning of William's arrest, he was out from home, and heard of the arrest, and of its being on a charge of the murder of Fisher; that on returning to his own house, he found Fisher there; that Fisher was in very feeble health, and could give no rational account as to where he had been during his absence; that he (Gilmore) then started in pursuit of the officer, as before stated; and that he should have taken Fisher with him, only that the state of his health did not permit. Gilmore also stated that he had known Fisher for several years, and that he had understood he was subject to temporary derangement of mind, owing to an injury about his head received in early life.

There was about Dr Gilmore so much of the air and manner of truth, that his statement prevailed in the minds of the audience and of the court, and the Trailors were discharged, although they attempted no explanation of the circumstances proven by the other witnesses.

On the next Monday, Myers arrived in Springfield, bringing with him the now famed Fisher, in full life and proper person.

Thus ended this strange affair and while it is readily conceived that a writer of novels could bring a story to a more perfect climax, it may well be doubted whether a stranger affair ever really occurred. Much of the matter remains in mystery to this day. The going into the woods with Fisher, and returning without him, by the Trailors; their going into the woods at the same place the next day, after they professed to have given up the search; the signs of a struggle in the thicket, the buggy tracks at the edge of it; and the location of the thicket, and the signs about it, corresponding precisely with Henry's story, are circumstances that have never been explained. William and Archibald have both died since—William in less than a year, and Archibald in about two years after the supposed murder. Henry is still living, but never speaks of the subject.

It is not the object of the writer of this to enter into the many curious speculations that might be indulged upon the facts of this narrative; yet he can scarcely forbear a remark upon what would, almost certainly, have been the fate of William and Archibald, had Fisher not been found alive. It seems he had wandered away in mental derangement, and, had he died in this condition, and his body been found in the vicinity, it is difficult to conceive what could have saved the Trailors from the consequence of having murdered him. Or, if he had died, and his body never found, the case against them would have been quite as bad, for, although it is a principle of law that a conviction for murder shall not be had, unless the body of the deceased be discovered, it is to be remembered, that Henry testified that he saw Fisher's dead body.

48

THE CHOPHAM AFFAIR

Edgar Wallace

… At eight o'clock on Christmas morning Superintendent Oakington was called from his warm bed by telephone…

There was a man who had a way with women. His name was Alphonse de Riebiera, and he described himself as a Spaniard, though his passport was issued by a South American republic. Sometimes he presented visiting cards which were inscribed 'Le Marquis de Riebiera', but that was only on very special occasions.

He was young, with an olive complexion, faultless features, and showed his two rows of dazzling white teeth when he smiled. He found it convenient to change his appearance. For example: when he was a hired dancer attached to the personnel of an Egyptian hotel he wore little side whiskers, which, oddly enough, exaggerated his youthfulness; in the Casino at Enghien, where by some means he secured the position of croupier, he was decorated with a little black moustache. Staid, sober and unimaginative spectators of his many adventures were irritably amazed that women said anything to him, but then it is notoriously difficult for any man, even an unimaginative man, to discover attractive qualities in successful lovers.

And yet the most unlikely women came under his spell and had to regret it. There arrived a time when he became a patron of the gambling establishments where he had been the most humble and the least trusted of servants, when he lived royally in hotels, where he once was hired at so many *piastre* per dance. Diamonds came to his spotless shirt front, pretty manicurists tended his nails and received fees larger than his one-time dancing partners had slipped shyly into his hand.

There were certain gross men who played interminable dominoes in the cheaper cafés that abound on the unfashionable side of the Seine, who are amazing news centres. They know how the oddest people live and they were very plain spoken when they discussed Alphonse. They could tell you, though heaven knows how the information came to them, of fat registered letters that came to him in his flat in the Boulevard Haussman, Registered letters stuffed with money, and despairing letters that said in effect (and in various languages) 'I can send you no more—this is the last.' But they did send more.

Alphonse had developed a well organised business. He would leave for London, or Rome, or Amsterdam, or Vienna, or even Athens, arriving at his destination by sleeping-car, drove to the best hotel, hired a luxurious suite—and telephoned. Usually the unhappy lady met him by appointment, tearful, hysterically furious, bitter, insulting, but always remunerative.

For when Alphonse read extracts from the letters they had sent to him in the day of the Great Glamour and told them what their husbands' income was almost to a pound, lira, franc or guilder, they reconsidered their decision to tell their husbands everything and Alphonse went back to Paris with his allowance.

This was his method with the bigger game; sometimes he announced his coming visit with a letter discreetly worded, which made personal application unnecessary. He was not very much afraid of husbands or brothers; the philosophy which had germinated from his experience made him contemptuous of human nature. He believed that most people were cowards and lived in fear of their lives, and greater fear of their regulations. He carried two silver-plated revolvers, one in each hip pocket. They had prettily damascened barrels and ivory handles carved in the likeness of nymphs. He bought them in Cairo from a man who smuggled cocaine from Vienna.

Alphonse had some twenty 'clients' on his books and added to them as opportunity arose. Of the twenty, five were gold mines (he thought of them as such) the remainder were silver mines.

There was a silver mine living in England, a very lovely, rather sad-looking girl, who was happily married except when she thought of Alphonse. She loved her husband and hated herself and hated Alphonse intensely and impotently. Having a fortune of her own she could pay—therefore she paid. Then in a fit of desperate revolt she wrote saying: 'This is the last, etc.' Alphonse was amused. He waited until September when the next allowance was due, and it did not come. Nor in October, nor November. In December he wrote to her; he did not wish to go to England in December, for England is very gloomy and foggy, and it was so much nicer in Egypt; but business was business.

His letter reached its address when the woman to whom it was addressed was on a visit to her aunt in Long Island. She had been born an American. Alphonse had not written in answer to her letter; she had sailed for New York feeling safe.

Her husband, whose initial was the same as his wife's, opened the letter by accident and read it through very carefully. He was no fool. He did not regard the wife he wooed as an outcast; what happened before his marriage was her business—what happened now was his.

And he understood these wild dreams of hers, and her wild uncontrollable weeping for no reason at all, and he knew what the future held for her.

He went to Paris and made inquiries: he sought the company of the gross men who play dominoes and heard much that was interesting.

Alphonse arrived in London and telephoned from a call box. Madam was not at home. A typewritten letter came to him, making an appointment for the Wednesday. It was the usual rendezvous, the hour specified, an injunction to secrecy. The affair ran normally.

He passed his time pleasantly in the days of waiting. Bought a new Spanza car of the latest model, arranged for its transportation to Paris and in the meantime amused himself by driving it.

At the appointed hour he arrived, knocked at the door of the house and was admitted...

Riebiera, green of face, shaking at the knees, surrendered his two ornamented pistols without a fight...

At eight o'clock on Christmas morning Superintendent Oakington was called from his warm bed by telephone and was told the news.

A milkman, driving across Chobham Common, had seen a car standing a little off the road. It was apparently a new car and must have been standing in its position all night. There were three inches of snow on its roof, beneath the body of the car the bracken was green.

An arresting sight even for a milkman, who at seven o'clock on a wintry morning had no other thought than to supply the needs of his customers as quickly as possible and return at the earliest moment to his own home and the festivities and feastings proper to the day.

He got out of the Ford he was driving and stamped through the snow. He saw a man lying, face downwards, and in his grey hand a silver-barrelled revolver. He was dead. And then the startled milkman saw the second man. His face was invisible; it lay under a thick mask of snow that made his pinched features grotesque and hideous.

The milkman ran back to his car and drove towards a Police station.

Mr Oakington was on the spot within an hour of being called. There were a dozen policemen grouped around the car and the shapes in the snow; the reporters, thank God, had not arrived.

Late in the afternoon the superintendent put a call through to one man who might help in a moment of profound bewilderment.

Archibald Lenton was the most promising of Treasury Juniors that the Bar had known for years. The Common Law Bar lifts its delicate nose at lawyers who are interested in criminal cases to the exclusion of other practice. But Archie Lenton survived the unspoken disapproval of his brethren and concentrating on this unsavoury aspect of jurisprudence was both a successful advocate and an authority on certain types of crime, for he had written a text hook which was accepted as authoritative.

An hour later he was in the superintendent's room at Scotland Yard, listening to the story.

'We've identified both men. One is a foreigner, a man from the Argentine, so far as I can discover from his passport, named Alphonse or Alphonso Riebiera. He lives in Paris and has been in this country for about a week.'

'Well off?'

'Very, I should say. We found about two hundred pounds in his pocket. He was staying at the Nederland Hotel and bought a car for twelve hundred pounds only last Friday, paying cash. That is the car we found near the body. I've been on the 'phone to Paris, and he is suspected there of being a blackmailer. The police have searched and sealed his flat, but found no documents of any kind. He is evidently the sort of man who keeps his business under his hat.'

'He was shot you say? How many times?'

'Once, through the head. The other man was killed in exactly the same way. There was a trace of blood in the car, but nothing else.'

Mr Lenton jotted down a note on a pad of paper.

'Who was the other man?' he asked.

'That's the queerest thing of all—an old acquaintance of yours.'

'Mine? Who on earth—?'

'Do you remember a fellow you defended on a murder charge—Joe Stackett?'

'At Exeter, good Lord, yes! Was that the man?'

'We've identified him from his finger prints. As a matter of fact, we were after Joe—he's an expert car thief who only came out of prison last week; he got away with a car yesterday morning, but abandoned it after a chase and slipped through the fingers of the Flying Squad. Last night he pinched an old car from a second-hand dealer and was spotted and chased. We found the car abandoned in Tooting. He was never seen again until he was picked up on the Chobham Common.'

Archie Lenton leant back in his chair and stared thoughtfully at the ceiling.

'He stole the Spanza—the owner jumped on the running board and there was a fight—' he began, but the superintendent shook his head.

'Where did he get his gun? English criminals do not carry guns. And they weren't ordinary revolvers. Silver-plated, ivory butts carved with girls' figures—both identical, There was fifty pounds in Joe's pocket; they are consecutive numbers to those found in Riebiera's pocket book. If he'd stolen them he'd have taken the lot. Joe wouldn't stop at murder, you know that, Mr Lenton. He killed that old woman in Exeter although he was acquitted. Riebiera must have given him the fifty—'

A telephone bell rang; the superintendent drew the instrument towards him and listened. After ten minutes of a conversation which was confined so far as Oakington was concerned to a dozen brief questions, he put down the receiver.

'One of my officers has traced the movements of the car, it was seen standing outside "Greenlawns", a house in Tooting. It was there at 9.45 and was seen by a postman. If you feel like spending Christmas night doing a little bit of detective work, we'll go down and see the place.'

They arrived half an hour later at a house in a very respectable neighbourhood. The two detectives who waited their coming had obtained the keys but had not gone inside. The house was for sale and was standing empty. It was the property of two old maiden ladies who had placed the premises in an agent's hands when they had moved into the country.

The appearance of the car before an empty house had aroused the interest of the postman. He had seen no lights in the windows and decided that the machine was owned by one of the guests at the next door house.

Oakington opened the door and switched on the light. Strangely enough, the old ladies had not had the current disconnected, though they were notoriously mean. The passage was bare, except for a pair of bead curtains which hung from an arched support to the ceiling.

The front room drew blank. It was in one of the back rooms on the ground floor that they found evidence of the crime. There was blood on the bare planks of the floor and in the grate a litter of ashes.

'Somebody has burnt papers—I smelt it when I came into the room,' said Lenton.

He knelt before the grate and lifted a handful of fire ashes carefully.

'And these have been stirred up until there isn't an ash big enough to hold a word,' he said.

He examined the blood prints and made a careful scrutiny of the walls. The window was covered with a shutter.

'That kept the light from getting in,' he said, 'and the sound of the shot getting out. There is nothing else here.'

The detective sergeant who was inspecting the other rooms returned with the news that a kitchen window had been forced. There was one muddy print on the kitchen table which was under the window and a rough attempt had been made to obliterate this. Behind the house was a large garden and behind that an allotment. It would be easy to reach and enter the house without exciting attention.

'But if Stackett was being chased by the police why should he come here?' he asked.

'His car was found abandoned not more than two hundred yards from here,' explained Oakington, 'He may have entered the house in the hope of finding something valuable and have been surprised by Riebiera.'

Archie Lenton laughed softly.

'I can give you a better theory than that,' he said, and for the greater part of the night he wrote carefully and convincingly, reconstructing the crime, giving the most minute details.

That account is still preserved at Scotland Yard, and there are many highly placed officials who swear by it.

And yet, something altogether different happened on the night of that 24th of December...

The streets were greasy. The car lines abominably so. Stackett's mean little car slithered and skidded alarmingly. He had been in a bad temper when he started out on his hungry quest; he grew sour and savage with the evening passing on with nothing to show for his discomfort. The suburban high street was crowded too; street cars moved at a crawl, their bells clanging pathetically; street vendors had their stalls jammed end to end on either side of the thoroughfare; stalls green and red with holly wreaths and untidy bunches of mistletoe; there were butcher stalls, raucous auctioneers holding masses of raw beef and roaring their offers; vegetable stalls; stalls piled high with plates and cups and saucers and gaudy dishes and glassware, shining in the rays of the powerful acetylene lamps...The car skidded. There was a crash and a scream. Breaking crockery has an alarming sound...A yell from the stall owner; Stackett straightened his machine and darted between a tramcar and a trolley...

'Hi, you!'

He twisted his wheel, almost knocked down the policeman who came to intercept him and swung into a dark side street, his foot clamped on the accelerator. He turned to the right and the left, to the right again. Here was a long suburban road; houses monotonously alike on either side, terribly dreary brick blocks where men and women and children lived, were born, paid rent and died. A mile further on he passed the gateway of the cemetery where they found the rest which was their supreme reward for living at all. The police whistle had followed him for less than a quarter of a mile. He had passed a policeman running towards the sound—anyway, flatties never worried Stackett. Some of his ill-humour passed in the amusement which the sight of the running copper brought.

Bringing the noisy little car to a standstill by the side of the road, he got down and, relighting the cigarette he had so carefully extinguished, he gazed glumly at the stained and battered mudguard which was shivering and shaking under the pulsations of the engine.

Through that same greasy street came a motor-cyclist, muffled to the chin, his goggles dangling about his neck. He pulled up his shining wheel near the policeman on point duty and, supporting his balance with one foot in the muddy road, asked questions.

'Yes, sergeant,' said the policeman. 'I saw him. He went down there. As a matter of fact, I was going to pinch him for driving to the common danger, but he hopped it.'

'That's Joe Stackett,' nodded Sergeant Kenton of the C.I.D. 'A thin-faced man with a pointed nose?'

The point duty policeman had not seen the face behind the windscreen, hut he had area the car, and that he described accurately.

'Stolen from Elmer's garage. At least, Elmer will say so, but he probably provided it. Dumped stuff. Which way did you say?'

The policeman indicated, and the sergeant kicked his engine to life and went chug-chugging down the dark street. He missed Mr Stackett by a piece of bad luck, bad luck for everybody, including Mr Stackett, who was at the beginning of his amazing adventure.

Switching off the engine, he had continued on foot. About fifty yards away was the wide opening of a road superior in class to any he had traversed. Even the dreariest suburb has its West End, and here were villas standing on their own acres; very sedate villas, with porches and porch lamps in wrought-iron and oddly coloured glass and shaven lawns, and rose gardens swathed in matting, and no two villas were alike. At the far end he saw a red light, and his heart leapt with joy: Christmas—it was to be Christmas after all, with good food and lashings of drink and other manifestations of happiness and comfort peculiarly attractive to Joe Stackett. It looked like a car worth knocking off, even in the darkness. He saw somebody near the machine and stopped. It was difficult to tell in the gloom whether the person near the car had got in or had come out. He listened. There came to him neither the slam of the driver's door nor the whine of the self-starter. He came a little closer, walked boldly on, his restless eyes moving left and right for danger. All the houses were occupied. Bright lights illuminated the casement cloth which covered the windows. He heard the sound of respectable revelry and two gramophones playing dance tunes. But his eyes always came back to the polished limousine at the door of the end house. There was no light there. It was completely dark, from the gabled attic to the ground floor.

He quickened his pace. It was a Spanza. His heart leapt at the recognition. For a Spanza is a car for which there is a ready sale. You can get as much as a hundred pounds for a new one. They are popular amongst Eurasians and wealthy Hindus. Binky Jones, who was the best car fence in London, would pay him cash, not less than sixty. In a week's time that car would be crated and on its way to India, there to be resold at a handsome profit.

The driver's door was wide open. He heard the soft purr of the engine. He slid into the driver's seat, closed the door noiselessly and almost without as much as a whine the Spanza moved on.

It was a new one, brand new...A hundred at least. Gathering speed, he passed to the end of the road, came to a wide common and skirted it. Presently he was in another shopping street, but he knew too much to turn back towards London. He would take the open country for it, work round through Esher and come into London by the Portsmouth Road. The art of car stealing is to move as quickly as possible from the police division where the machine is stolen and may be instantly reported to a 'foreign' division, which will not knew of the theft until hours after.

There might be all sorts of extra pickings. There was a big luggage trunk behind, and possibly a few knick-knacks in the body of the car itself. At a suitable moment he would make a leisurely search. At the moment he headed for Epsom, turning back to hit the Kingston By-pass. Sleet fell—snow and rain together. He set the screen-wiper working and began to hum a little tune. The Kingston By-pass was deserted. It was too unpleasant a night for much traffic. Mr Stackett was debating what would be the best place to make his search when he felt an unpleasant draught behind him. He had noticed there was a sliding window separating the interior of the car from the driver's seat, which had possibly worked loose. He put up his hand to push it close.

'Drive on, don't turn round or I'll blow your head off!'

Involuntarily he half-turned to see the gaping muzzle of an automatic and in his agitation put his foot on the brake. The car skidded from one side of the road to the other, half turned and recovered.

'Drive on, I am telling you,' said a metallic voice. 'When you reach the Portsmouth Road turn and bear towards Weybridge. If you attempt to stop I will shoot you. Is that clear?'

Joe Stackett's teeth were chattering. He could not articulate the 'yes'. All that he could do was to nod. He went on nodding for half a mile before he realised what he was doing.

No further word came from the interior of the car until they passed the racecourse; then unexpectedly the voice gave a new direction:

'Turn left towards Leatherhead.'

The driver obeyed.

They came to a stretch of common. Stackett, who knew the country well, realised the complete isolation of the spot.

'Slow down, pull into the left...There is no dip there. You can switch on your lights.'

The car slid and bumped over the uneven ground, the wheels

crunched through beds of bracken...

'Stop.'

The door behind him opened. The man got out. He jerked open the driver's door.

'Step down,' he said. 'Turn out your lights first. Have you got a gun?'

'Gun? Why the hell should I have a gun?' stammered the car thief.

He was focused all the time in a ring of light from a very bright electric torch which the passenger had turned upon him.

'You are an act of Providence.'

Stackett could not see the face of the speaker. He saw only the gun in the hand, for the stranger kept this well in the light.

'Look inside the car.'

Stackett looked and almost collapsed: there was a figure huddled in one corner of the seat—the figure of a man. He saw something else—a bicycle jammed into the car, one wheel touching the roof, the other on the floor. He saw the man's white face...Dead! A slim, rather short man, with dark hair and a dark moustache, a foreigner. There was a little red hole in his temple.

'Pull him out,' commanded the voice sharply.

Stackett shrank back, but a powerful hand pushed him towards the car.

'Pull him out!'

With his face moist with cold perspiration, the car thief obeyed; put his hands under the armpits of the inanimate figure, dragged him out and laid him on the bracken.

'He's dead,' he whimpered.

'Completely,' said the other.

Suddenly he switched off his electric torch. Far away came a gleam of light on the road, coming swiftly towards them. It was a car moving towards Esher. It passed.

'I saw you coming just after I had got the body into the car. There wasn't time to get back to the house. I'd hoped you were just an ordinary pedestrian. What is your name?'

'Joseph Stackett.'

'Stackett?' The light flashed on his face again. 'How wonderful! Do you remember the Exeter Assizes? The woman you killed with a hammer? I defended you!'

Joe's eyes were wide open. He stared past the light at the dim grey thing that was a face.

'Mr Lenton?' he said hoarsely. 'Good God, sir!'

'You murdered her in cold blood for a few paltry shillings and you would have been dead now, Stackett, if I hadn't found a flaw in the evidence. You expected to die, didn't you? You remember how we used to talk in Exeter Gaol about the trap that would not work when they tried to hang a murderer and the ghoulish satisfaction you had that you would stand on the same trap?'

Joe Stackett grinned uncomfortably.

'And I meant it, sir,' he said, 'but you can't try a man twice—'

Then his eyes dropped to the figure at his feet, the dapper little man with a black moustache, with a red hole in his temple.

Lenton leant over the dead man, took out a pocket case from the inside of the jacket and at his leisure detached ten notes.

'Put these in your pocket.'

He obeyed, wondering what service would be required of him, wondered more why the pocket book with its precious notes was returned to the dead man's pocket.

Lenton looked back along the road. Snow was falling now, real snow. It came down in small particles falling so thickly that it seemed that a fog lay on the land.

'You fit into this perfectly... a man unfit to live. There is fate in this meeting.'

'I don't know what you mean by fate.'

Joe Stackett grew bold: he had to deal with a lawyer and a gentleman who, in a criminal sense was his inferior. The money obviously had been given to him to keep his mouth shut.

'What have you been doing, Mr Lenton? That's bad, ain't it? This fellow's dead, and—'

He must have seen the pencil of flame that came from the other's hand. He could have felt nothing, for he was dead before he sprawled over the body on the ground.

Mr Archibald Lenton examined the revolver by the light of his lamp, opened the breech and closed it again. Stooping, he laid it near the hand of the little man with the black moustache and, lifting the body of Joe Stackett, he dragged it towards the car and let it drop. Bending down, he clasped the still warm hands about the butt of another pistol. Then, at his leisure, he took the bicycle from the interior of the car and carried it back to the road. It was already white and fine snow was falling in sheets.

Mr Lenton went on and reached his home two hours later, when the bells of the local Anglo-Catholic church were ringing musically.

There was a cable waiting for him from his wife:

'A HAPPY CHRISTMAS TO YOU, DARLING.'

He was ridiculously pleased that she had remembered to send the wire—he was very fond of his wife.

49

THE SNIPER

Liam O'Flaherty

...There was no pain—just a deadened sensation, as if the arm had been cut off...

The long June twilight faded into night. Dublin lay enveloped in darkness but for the dim light of the moon that shone through fleecy clouds, casting a pale light as of approaching dawn over the streets and the dark waters of the Liffey. Around the beleaguered Four Courts the heavy guns roared. Here and there through the city, machine guns and rifles broke the silence of the night, spasmodically, like dogs barking on lone farms. Republicans and Free Staters were waging civil war.

On a rooftop near O'Connell Bridge, a Republican sniper lay watching. Beside him lay his rifle and over his shoulders was slung a pair of field glasses. His face was the face of a student, thin and ascetic, but his eyes had the cold gleam of the fanatic. They were deep and thoughtful, the eyes of a man who is used to looking at death.

He was eating a sandwich hungrily. He had eaten nothing since morning. He had been too excited to eat. He finished the sandwich, and, taking a flask of whiskey from his pocket, he took a short drought. Then he returned the flask to his pocket. He paused for a moment, considering whether he should risk a smoke. It was dangerous. The flash might be seen in the darkness, and there were enemies watching. He decided to take the risk.

Placing a cigarette between his lips, he struck a match, inhaled the smoke hurriedly and put out the light. Almost immediately, a bullet flattened itself against the parapet of the roof. The sniper took another whiff and put out the cigarette. Then he swore softly and crawled away to the left.

Cautiously he raised himself and peered over the parapet. There was a flash and a bullet whizzed over his head. He dropped immediately. He had seen the flash. It came from the opposite side of the street.

He rolled over the roof to a chimney stack in the rear, and slowly drew himself up behind it, until his eyes were level with the top of the parapet. There was nothing to be seen—just the dim outline of the opposite housetop against the blue sky. His enemy was under cover.

Just then an armored car came across the bridge and advanced slowly up the street. It stopped on the opposite side of the street, fifty yards ahead. The sniper could hear the dull panting of the motor. His heart beat faster. It was an enemy car. He wanted to fire, but he knew it was useless. His bullets would never pierce the steel that covered the gray monster.

Then round the corner of a side street came an old woman, her head covered by a tattered shawl. She began to talk to the man in the turret of the car. She was pointing to the roof where the sniper lay. An informer.

The turret opened. A man's head and shoulders appeared, looking toward the sniper. The sniper raised his rifle and fired. The head fell heavily on the turret wall. The woman darted toward the side street. The sniper fired again. The woman whirled round and fell with a shriek into the gutter.

Suddenly from the opposite roof a shot rang out and the sniper dropped his rifle with a curse. The rifle clattered to the roof. The sniper thought the noise would wake the dead. He stooped to pick the rifle up. He couldn't lift it. His forearm was dead. 'I'm hit,' he muttered.

Dropping flat onto the roof, he crawled back to the parapet. With his left hand he felt the injured right forearm. The blood was oozing through the sleeve of his coat. There was no pain—just a deadened sensation, as if the arm had been cut off.

Quickly he drew his knife from his pocket, opened it on the breastwork of the parapet, and ripped open the sleeve. There was a small hole where the bullet had entered. On the other side there was no hole. The bullet had lodged in the bone. It must have fractured it. He bent the arm below the wound. the arm bent back easily. He ground his teeth to overcome the pain.

Then taking out his field dressing, he ripped open the packet with his knife. He broke the neck of the iodine bottle and let the bitter fluid drip into the wound. A paroxysm of pain swept through him. He placed the cotton wadding over the wound and wrapped the dressing over it. He tied the ends with his teeth.

Then he lay still against the parapet, and, closing his eyes, he made an effort of will to overcome the pain.

In the street beneath all was still. The armored car had retired speedily over the bridge, with the machine gunner's head hanging lifeless over the turret. The woman's corpse lay still in the gutter.

The sniper lay still for a long time nursing his wounded arm and planning escape. Morning must not find him wounded on the roof. The enemy on the opposite roof covered his escape. He must kill that enemy and he could not use his rifle. He had only a revolver to do it. Then he thought of a plan.

Taking off his cap, he placed it over the muzzle of his rifle. Then he pushed the rifle slowly upward over the parapet, until the cap was visible from the opposite side of the street. Almost immediately there was a report, and a bullet pierced the center of the cap. The sniper slanted the rifle forward. The cap clipped down into the street. Then catching the rifle in the middle, the sniper dropped his left hand over the roof and let it hang, lifelessly. After a few moments he let the rifle drop to the street. Then he sank to the roof, dragging his hand with him.

Crawling quickly to his feet, he peered up at the corner of the roof. His ruse had succeeded. The other sniper, seeing the cap and rifle fall, thought that he had killed his man. He was now standing before a row of chimney pots, looking across, with his head clearly silhouetted against the western sky.

The Republican sniper smiled and lifted his revolver above the edge of the parapet. The distance was about fifty yards—a hard shot in the dim light, and his right arm was paining him like a thousand devils.

He took a steady aim. His hand trembled with eagerness. Pressing his lips together, he took a deep breath through his nostrils and fired. He was almost deafened with the report and his arm shook with the recoil.

Then when the smoke cleared, he peered across and uttered a cry of joy. His enemy had been hit. He was reeling over the parapet in his death agony. He struggled to keep his feet, but he was slowly falling forward as if in a dream. The rifle fell from his grasp, hit the parapet, fell over, bounded off the pole of a barber's shop beneath and then clattered on the pavement.

Then the dying man on the roof crumpled up and fell forward. The body turned over and over in space and hit the ground with a dull thud. Then it lay still.

The sniper looked at his enemy falling and he shuddered. The lust of battle died in him. He became bitten by remorse. The sweat stood out in beads on his forehead. Weakened by his wound and the long summer day of fasting and watching on the roof, he revolted from the sight of the shattered mass of his dead enemy. His teeth chattered, he began to gibber to himself, cursing the war, cursing himself, cursing everybody.

He looked at the smoking revolver in his hand, and with an oath he hurled it to the roof at his feet. The revolver went off with a concussion and the bullet whizzed past the sniper's head. He was frightened back to his senses by the shock. His nerves steadied. The cloud of fear scattered from his mind and he laughed.

Taking the whiskey flask from his pocket, he emptied it a drought. He felt reckless under the influence of the spirit. He decided to leave the roof now and look for his company commander, to report. Everywhere around was quiet. There was not much danger in going through the streets. He picked up his revolver and put it in his pocket. Then he crawled down through the skylight to the house underneath.

When the sniper reached the laneway on the street level, he felt a sudden curiosity as to the identity of the enemy sniper whom he had killed. He decided that he was a good shot, whoever he was. He wondered did he know him. Perhaps he had been in his own company before the split in the army. He decided to risk going over to have a look at him. He peered around the corner into O'Connell Street. In the upper part of the street there was heavy firing, but around here all was quiet.

The sniper darted across the street. A machine gun tore up the ground around him with a hail of bullets, but he escaped. He threw himself face downward beside the corpse. The machine gun stopped.

Then the sniper turned over the dead body and looked into his brother's face.

50

MARKHEIM

Robert Louis Stevenson

... he should not have used a knife; he should have been more cautious, and only bound and gagged the dealer, and not killed him...'

'Yes,' said the dealer, 'our windfalls are of various kinds. Some customers are ignorant, and then I touch a dividend on my superior knowledge. Some are dishonest,' and here he held up the candle, so that the light fell strongly on his visitor, 'and in that case,' he continued, 'I profit by my virtue.'

Markheim had but just entered from the daylight streets, and his eyes had not yet grown familiar with the mingled shine and darkness in the shop. At these pointed words, and before the near presence of the flame, he blinked painfully and looked aside.

The dealer chuckled. 'You come to me on Christmas Day,' he resumed, 'when you know that I am alone in my house, put up my shutters, and make a point of refusing business. Well, you will have to pay for that; you will have to pay for my loss of time, when I should be balancing my books; you will have to pay, besides, for a kind of manner that I remark in you to-day very strongly. I am the essence of discretion, and ask no awkward questions; but when a customer cannot look me in the eye, he has to pay for it.' The dealer once more chuckled; and then, changing to his usual business voice, though still with a note of irony, 'You can give, as usual, a clear account of how you came into the possession of the object?' he continued. 'Still your uncle's cabinet? A remarkable collector, sir!'

And the little pale, round-shouldered dealer stood almost on tiptoe, looking over the top of his gold spectacles, and nodding his head with every mark of disbelief. Markheim returned his gaze with one of infinite pity, and a touch of horror.

'This time,' said he, 'you are in error. I have not come to sell, but to buy. I have no curios to dispose of; my uncle's cabinet is bare to the wainscot; even were it still intact, I have done well on the Stock Exchange, and should more likely add to it than otherwise, and my errand to-day is simplicity itself. I seek a Christmas present for a lady,' he continued, waxing more fluent as he struck into the speech he had prepared; 'and certainly I owe you every excuse for thus disturbing you upon so small a matter. But the thing was neglected yesterday; I must produce my little compliment at dinner; and, as you very well know, a rich marriage is not a thing to be neglected.'

There followed a pause, during which the dealer seemed to weigh this statement incredulously. The ticking of many clocks among the curious lumber of the shop, and the faint rushing of the cabs in a near thoroughfare, filled up the interval of silence.

'Well, sir,' said the dealer, 'be it so. You are an old customer after all; and if, as you say, you have the chance of a good marriage, far be it from me to be an obstacle. Here is a nice thing for a lady now,' he went on, 'this hand glass—fifteenth century, warranted; comes from a good collection, too; but I reserve the name, in the interests of my customer, who was just like yourself, my dear sir, the nephew and sole heir of a remarkable collector.'

The dealer, while he thus ran on in his dry and biting voice, had stooped to take the object from its place; and, as he had done so, a shock had passed through Markheim, a start both of hand and foot, a sudden leap of many tumultuous passions to the face. It passed as swiftly as it came, and left no trace beyond a certain trembling of the hand that now received the glass.

'A glass,' he said hoarsely, and then paused, and repeated it more clearly. 'A glass? For Christmas? Surely not?'

'And why not?' cried the dealer. 'Why not a glass?'

Markheim was looking upon him with an indefinable expression. 'You ask me why not?' he said. 'Why, look here—look in it—look at yourself! Do you like to see it? No! nor I—nor any man.'

The little man had jumped back when Markheim had so suddenly confronted him with the mirror; but now, perceiving there was nothing worse on hand, he chuckled. 'Your future lady, sir, must be pretty hard favoured,' said he.

'I ask you,' said Markheim, 'for a Christmas present, and you give me this—this damned reminder of years, and sins and follies—this hand-conscience! Did you mean it? Had you a thought in your mind? Tell me. It will be better for you if you do. Come, tell me about yourself. I hazard a guess now, that you are in secret a very charitable man?'

The dealer looked closely at his companion. It was very odd, Markheim did not appear to be laughing; there was something in his face like an eager sparkle of hope, but nothing of mirth.

'What are you driving at?' the dealer asked.

'Not charitable?' returned the other, gloomily. 'Not charitable; not pious; not scrupulous; unloving, unbeloved; a hand to get money, a safe to keep it. Is that all? Dear God, man, is that all?'

'I will tell you what it is,' began the dealer, with some sharpness, and then broke off again into a chuckle. 'But I see this is a love match of yours, and you have been drinking the lady's health.'

'Ah!' cried Markheim, with a strange curiosity. 'Ah, have you been in love? Tell me about that.'

'I,' cried the dealer. 'I in love! I never had the time, nor have I the time to-day for all this nonsense. Will you take the glass?'

'Where is the hurry?' returned Markheim. 'It is very pleasant to stand here talking; and life is so short and insecure that I would not hurry away from any pleasure—no, not even from so mild a one as this. We should rather cling, cling to what little we can get, like a man at a cliff's edge. Every second is a cliff, if you think upon it—a cliff a mile high—high enough, if we fall, to dash us out of every feature of humanity. Hence it is best to talk pleasantly. Let us talk of each other: why should we wear this mask? Let us be confidential. Who knows, we might become friends?'

'I have just one word to say to you,' said the dealer. 'Either make your purchase, or walk out of my shop!'

'True true,' said Markheim. 'Enough, fooling. To business. Show me something else.'

The dealer stooped once more, this time to replace the glass upon the shelf, his thin blond hair falling over his eyes as he did so. Markheim moved a little nearer, with one hand in the pocket of his greatcoat; he drew himself up and filled his lungs; at the same time many different emotions were depicted together on his face—terror, horror, and resolve, fascination and a physical repulsion; and through a haggard lift of his upper lip, his teeth looked out.

'This, perhaps, may suit,' observed the dealer: and then, as he began to re-arise, Markheim bounded from behind upon his victim. The long, skewerlike dagger flashed and fell. The dealer struggled like a hen, striking his temple on the shelf, and then tumbled on the floor in a heap.

Time had some score of small voices in that shop, some stately and slow as was becoming to their great age; others garrulous and hurried. All these told out the seconds in an intricate, chorus of tickings. Then the passage of a lad's feet, heavily running on the pavement, broke in upon these smaller voices and startled Markheim into the consciousness of his surroundings. He looked about him awfully. The candle stood on the counter, its flame solemnly wagging in a draught; and by that inconsiderable movement, the whole room was filled with noiseless bustle and kept heaving like a sea: the tall shadows nodding, the gross blots of darkness swelling and dwindling as with respiration, the faces of the portraits and the china gods changing and wavering like images in water. The inner door stood ajar, and peered into that leaguer of shadows with a long slit of daylight like a pointing finger.

From these fear-stricken rovings, Markheim's eyes returned to the body of his victim, where it lay both humped and sprawling, incredibly small and strangely meaner than in life. In these poor, miserly clothes, in that ungainly attitude, the dealer lay like so much sawdust. Markheim had feared to see it, and, lo! it was nothing. And yet, as he gazed, this bundle of old clothes and pool of blood began to find eloquent voices. There it must lie; there was none to work the cunning hinges or direct the miracle of locomotion—there it must lie till it was found. Found!

ay, and then? Then would this dead flesh lift up a cry that would ring over England, and fill the world with the echoes of pursuit. Ay, dead or not, this was still the enemy. 'Time was that when the brains were out,' he thought; and the first word struck into his mind. Time, now that the deed was accomplished—time, which had closed for the victim, had become instant and momentous for the slayer.

The thought was yet in his mind, when, first one and then another, with every variety of pace and voice—one deep as the bell from a cathedral turret, another ringing on its treble notes the prelude of a waltz-the clocks began to strike the hour of three in the afternoon.

The sudden outbreak of so many tongues in that dumb chamber staggered him. He began to bestir himself, going to and fro with the candle, beleaguered by moving shadows, and startled to the soul by chance reflections. In many rich mirrors, some of home design, some from Venice or Amsterdam, he saw his face repeated and repeated, as it were an army of spies; his own eyes met and detected him; and the sound of his own steps, lightly as they fell, vexed the surrounding quiet. And still, as he continued to fill his pockets, his mind accused him with a sickening iteration, of the thousand faults of his design. He should have chosen a more quiet hour; he should have prepared an alibi; he should not have used a knife; he should have been more cautious, and only bound and gagged the dealer, and not killed him; he should have been more bold, and killed the servant also; he should have done all things otherwise: poignant regrets, weary, incessant toiling of the mind to change what was unchangeable, to plan what was now useless, to be the architect of the irrevocable past. Meanwhile, and behind all this activity, brute terrors, like the scurrying of rats in a deserted attic, filled the more remote chambers of his brain with riot; the hand of the constable would fall heavy on his shoulder, and his nerves would jerk like a hooked fish; or he beheld, in galloping defile, the dock, the prison, the gallows, and the black coffin.

Terror of the people in the street sat down before his mind like a besieging army. It was impossible, he thought, but that some rumour of the struggle must have reached their ears and set on edge their curiosity; and now, in all the neighbouring houses, he divined them sitting motionless and with uplifted ear—solitary people, condemned to spend Christmas dwelling alone on memories of the past, and now startingly recalled from that tender exercise; happy family parties struck into silence round the table, the mother still with raised finger: every degree and age and humour, but all, by their own hearths, prying and hearkening and weaving the rope that was to hang him. Sometimes it seemed to him he could not move too softly; the clink of the tall Bohemian goblets rang out loudly like a bell; and alarmed by the bigness of the ticking, he was tempted to stop the clocks. And then, again, with a swift transition of his terrors, the very silence of the place appeared a source of peril, and a thing to strike and freeze the passer-by; and he would step more boldly, and bustle aloud among the contents of the shop, and imitate, with elaborate bravado, the movements of a busy man at ease in his own house.

But he was now so pulled about by different alarms that, while one portion of his mind was still alert and cunning, another trembled on the brink of lunacy. One hallucination in particular took a strong hold on his credulity. The neighbour hearkening with white face beside his window, the passer-by arrested by a horrible surmise on the pavement— these could at worst suspect, they could not know; through the brick walls and shuttered windows only sounds could penetrate. But here, within the house, was he alone? He knew he was; he had watched the servant set forth sweet-hearting, in her poor best, 'out for the day' written in every ribbon and smile. Yes, he was alone, of course; and yet, in the bulk of empty house above him, he could surely hear a stir of delicate footing—he was surely conscious, inexplicably conscious of some presence. Ay, surely; to every room and corner of the house his imagination followed it; and now it was a faceless thing, and yet had eyes to see with; and again it was a shadow of himself; and yet again behold the image of the dead dealer, reinspired with cunning and hatred.

At times, with a strong effort, he would glance at the open door which still seemed to repel his eyes. The house was tall, the skylight small and dirty, the day blind with fog; and the light that filtered down to the ground story was exceedingly faint, and showed dimly on the threshold of the shop. And yet, in that strip of doubtful brightness, did there not hang wavering a shadow?

Suddenly, from the street outside, a very jovial gentleman began to beat with a staff on the shop-door, accompanying his blows with shouts and railleries in which the dealer was continually called upon by name. Markheim, smitten into ice, glanced at the dead man. But no! he lay quite still; he was fled away far beyond earshot of these blows and shoutings; he was sunk beneath seas of silence; and his name, which would once have caught his notice above the howling of a storm, had become an empty sound. And presently the jovial gentleman desisted from his knocking, and departed.

Here was a broad hint to hurry what remained to be done, to get forth from this accusing neighbourhood, to plunge into a bath of London multitudes, and to reach, on the other side of day, that haven of safety and apparent innocence—his bed. One visitor had come: at any moment another might follow and be more obstinate. To have done the deed, and yet not to reap the profit, would be too abhorrent a failure. The money, that was now Markheim's concern; and as a means to that, the keys.

He glanced over his shoulder at the open door, where the shadow was still lingering and shivering; and with no conscious repugnance of the mind, yet with a tremor of the belly, he drew near the body of his victim. The human character had quite departed. Like a suit half-stuffed with bran, the limbs lay scattered, the trunk doubled, on the floor; and yet the thing repelled him. Although so dingy and inconsiderable to the eye, he feared it might have more significance to the touch. He took the body by the shoulders, and turned it on its back. It was strangely light and supple, and the limbs, as if they had been broken, fell into the oddest postures. The face was robbed of all expression; but it was as pale as wax, and shockingly smeared with blood about one temple. That was, for Markheim, the one displeasing circumstance. It carried him back, upon the instant, to a certain fair-day in a fishers' village: a gray day, a piping wind, a crowd upon the street, the blare of brasses, the booming of drums, the nasal voice of a ballad singer; and a boy going to and fro, buried over head in the crowd and divided between interest and fear, until, coming out upon the chief place of concourse, he beheld a booth and a great screen with pictures, dismally designed, garishly coloured: Brown-rigg with her apprentice; the Mannings with their murdered guest; We are in the death-grip of Thurtell; and a score besides of famous crimes. The thing was as clear as an illusion; he was once again that little boy; he was looking once again, and with the same sense of physical revolt, at these vile pictures; he was still stunned by the thumping of the drums. A bar of that day's music returned upon his memory; and at that, for the first time, a qualm came over him, a breath of nausea, a sudden weakness of the joints, which he must instantly resist and conquer.

He judged it more prudent to confront than to flee from these considerations; looking the more hardily in the dead face, bending his mind to realise the nature and greatness of his crime. So little a while ago that face had moved with every change of sentiment, that pale mouth had spoken, that body had been all on fire with governable energies; and now, and by his act, that piece of life had been arrested, as the horologist, with interjected finger, arrests the beating of the clock. So he reasoned in vain; he could rise to no more remorseful consciousness; the same heart which had shuddered before the painted effigies of crime, looked on its reality unmoved. At best, he felt a gleam of pity for one who had been endowed in vain with all those faculties that can make the world a garden of enchantment, one who had never lived and who was now dead. But of penitence, no, not a tremor.

With that, shaking himself clear of these considerations, he found the keys and advanced towards the open door of the shop. Outside, it had begun to rain smartly; and the sound of the shower upon the roof had banished silence. Like some dripping cavern, the chambers of the house were haunted by an incessant echoing, which filled the ear and mingled with the ticking of the clocks. And, as Markheim approached the door, he seemed to hear, in answer to his own cautious tread, the steps of another foot withdrawing up the stair. The shadow still palpitated loosely on the threshold. He threw a ton's weight of resolve upon his muscles, and drew back the door.

The faint, foggy daylight glimmered dimly on the bare floor and stairs; on the bright suit of armour posted, halbert in hand, upon the landing; and on the dark wood-carvings, and framed pictures that hung against the yellow panels of the wainscot. So loud was the beating of the rain through all the house that, in Markheim's ears, it began to be distinguished into many different sounds. Footsteps and sighs, the tread of regiments marching in the distance, the chink of money in the counting, and the creaking of doors held stealthily ajar, appeared to mingle with the patter of the drops upon the cupola and the gushing of the water in the pipes. The sense that he was not alone grew upon him to the verge of madness. On every side he was haunted and begirt by presences. He heard them moving in the upper chambers; from the shop, he heard the dead man getting to his legs; and as he began with a great effort to mount the stairs, feet fled quietly before him and followed stealthily behind. If he were but deaf, he thought, how tranquilly he would possess his soul! And then again, and hearkening with ever fresh attention, he blessed himself for that unresting sense which held the outposts and stood a trusty sentinel upon his life. His head turned continually on his neck; his eyes, which seemed starting from their orbits, scouted on every side, and on every side were half-rewarded as with the tail of something nameless vanishing. The four-and-twenty steps to the first floor were four-and-twenty agonies.

On that first storey, the doors stood ajar, three of them like three ambushes, shaking his nerves like the throats of cannon. He could never again, he felt, be sufficiently immured and fortified from men's observing eyes, he longed to be home, girt in by walls, buried among bedclothes, and invisible to all but God. And at that thought he wondered a little, recollecting tales of other murderers and the fear they were said to entertain of heavenly avengers. It was not so, at least, with him. He feared the laws of nature, lest, in their callous and immutable procedure, they should preserve some damning evidence of his crime. He feared tenfold more, with a slavish, superstitions terror, some scission in the continuity of man's experience, some wilful illegality of nature. He played a game of skill, depending on the rules, calculating consequence from cause; and what if nature, as the defeated tyrant overthrew the chess-board, should break the mould of their succession? The like had befallen Napoleon (so writers said) when the winter changed the time of its appearance. The like might befall Markheim: the solid walls might become transparent and reveal his doings like those of bees in a glass hive; the stout planks might yield under his foot like quicksands and detain him in their clutch; ay, and there were soberer accidents that might destroy him: if, for instance, the house should fall and imprison him beside the body of his victim; or the house next door should fly on fire, and the firemen invade him from all sides. These things he feared; and, in a sense, these things might be called the hands of God reached forth against sin. But about God himself he was at ease; his act was doubtless exceptional, but so were his excuses, which God knew; it was there, and not among men, that he felt sure of justice.

When he had got safe into the drawing-room, and shut the door behind him, he was aware of a respite from alarms. The room was quite dismantled, uncarpeted besides, and strewn with packing cases and incongruous furniture; several great pier-glasses, in which he beheld himself at various angles, like an actor on a stage; many pictures, framed and unframed, standing, with their faces to the wall; a fine Sheraton sideboard, a cabinet of marquetry, and a great old bed, with tapestry hangings. The windows opened to the floor; but by great good fortune the lower part of the shutters had been closed, and this concealed him from the neighbours. Here, then, Markheim drew in a packing case before the cabinet, and began to search among the keys. It was a long business, for there were many; and it was irksome, besides; for, after all, there might be nothing in the cabinet, and time was on the wing. But the closeness of the occupation sobered him. With the tail of his eye he saw the door—even glanced at it from time to time directly, like a besieged commander pleased to verify the good estate of his defences. But in truth he was at peace. The rain falling in the street sounded natural and pleasant. Presently, on the other side, the notes of a piano were wakened to the music of a hymn, and the voices of many children took up the air and words. How stately, how comfortable was the melody! How fresh the youthful voices! Markheim gave ear to it smilingly, as he sorted out the keys; and his mind was thronged with answerable ideas and images; church-going children and the pealing of the high organ; children afield, bathers by the brookside, ramblers on the brambly common, kite-flyers in the windy and cloud-navigated sky; and then, at another cadence of the hymn, back again to church, and the somnolence of summer Sundays, and the high genteel voice of the parson (which he smiled a little to recall) and the painted Jacobean tombs, and the dim lettering of the Ten Commandments in the chancel.

And as he sat thus, at once busy and absent, he was startled to his feet. A flash of ice, a flash of fire, a bursting gush of blood, went over him, and then he stood transfixed and thrilling. A step mounted the stair slowly and steadily, and presently a hand was laid upon the knob, and the lock clicked, and the door opened.

Fear held Markheim in a vice. What to expect he knew not, whether the dead man walking, or the official ministers of human justice, or some chance witness blindly stumbling in to consign him to the gallows. But when a face was thrust into the aperture, glanced round the room, looked at him, nodded and smiled as if in friendly recognition, and then withdrew again, and the door closed behind it, his fear broke loose from his control in a hoarse cry. At the sound of this the visitant returned.

'Did you call me?' he asked, pleasantly, and with that he entered the room and closed the door behind him.

Markheim stood and gazed at him with all his eyes. Perhaps there was a film upon his sight, but the outlines of the new comer seemed to change and waver like those of the idols in the wavering candle-light of the shop; and at times he thought he knew him; and at times he thought he bore a likeness to himself; and always, like a lump of living terror, there lay in his bosom the conviction that this thing was not of the earth and not of God.

And yet the creature had a strange air of the commonplace, as he stood looking on Markheim with a smile; and when he added: 'You are looking for the money, I believe?' it was in the tones of everyday politeness.

Markheim made no answer.

'I should warn you,' resumed the other, 'that the maid has left her sweetheart earlier than usual and will soon be here. If Mr Markheim be found in this house, I need not describe to him the consequences.'

'You know me?' cried the murderer.

The visitor smiled. 'You have long been a favourite of mine,' he said; 'and I have long observed and often sought to help you.'

'What are you?' cried Markheim: 'the devil?'

'What I may be,' returned the other, 'cannot affect the service I propose to render you.'

'It can,' cried Markheim; 'it does! Be helped by you? No, never; not by you! You do not know me yet; thank God, you do not know me!'

'I know you,' replied the visitant, with a sort of kind severity or rather firmness. 'I know you to the soul.'

'Know me!' cried Markheim. 'Who can do so? My life is but a travesty and slander on myself. I have lived to belie my nature. All men do; all men are better than this disguise that grows about and stifles them.

You see each dragged away by life, like one whom bravos have seized and muffled in a cloak. If they had their own control—if you could see their faces, they would be altogether different, they would shine out for heroes and saints! I am worse than most; myself is more overlaid; my excuse is known to me and God. But, had I the time, I could disclose myself.'

'To me?' inquired the visitant.

'To you before all,' returned the murderer. 'I supposed you were intelligent. I thought—since you exist—you would prove a reader of the heart. And yet you would propose to judge me by my acts! Think of it; my acts! I was born and I have lived in a land of giants; giants have dragged me by the wrists since I was born out of my mother—the giants of circumstance. And you would judge me by my acts! But can you not look within? Can you not understand that evil is hateful to me? Can you not see within me the clear writing of conscience, never blurred by any wilful sophistry, although too often disregarded? Can you not read me for a thing that surely must be common as humanity—the unwilling sinner?'

'All this is very feelingly expressed,' was the reply, 'but it regards me not. These points of consistency are beyond my province, and I care not in the least by what compulsion you may have been dragged away, so as you are but carried in the right direction. But time flies; the servant delays, looking in the faces of the crowd and at the pictures on the hoardings, but still she keeps moving nearer; and remember, it is as if the gallows itself was striding towards you through the Christmas streets! Shall I help you; I, who know all? Shall I tell you where to find the money?'

'For what price?' asked Markheim.

'I offer you the service for a Christmas gift,' returned the other.

Markheim could not refrain from smiling with a kind of bitter triumph.

'No,' said he, 'I will take nothing at your hands; if I were dying of thirst, and it was your hand that put the pitcher to my lips, I should find the courage to refuse. It may be credulous, but I will do nothing to commit myself to evil.'

'I have no objection to a death-bed repentance,' observed the visitor.

'Because you disbelieve their efficacy!' Markheim cried.

'I do not say so,' returned the other; 'but I look on these things from a different side, and when the life is done my interest falls. The man has lived to serve me, to spread black looks under colour of religion, or to sow tares in the wheat-field, as you do, in a course of weak compliance with desire. Now that he draws so near to his deliverance, he can add but one act of service—to repent, to die smiling, and thus to build up in confidence and hope the more timorous of my surviving followers. I am not so hard a master. Try me. Accept my help. Please yourself in life as you have done hitherto; please yourself more amply, spread your elbows at the board; and when the night begins to fall and the curtains to be drawn, I tell you, for your greater comfort, that you will find it even easy to compound your quarrel with your conscience, and to make a truckling peace with

God. I came but now from such a deathbed, and the room was full of sincere mourners, listening to the man's last words: and when I looked into that face, which had been set as a flint against mercy, I found it smiling with hope.'

'And do you, then, suppose me such a creature?' asked Markheim. 'Do you think I have no more generous aspirations than to sin, and sin, and sin, and, at the last, sneak into heaven? My heart rises at the thought. Is this, then, your experience of mankind? Or is it because you find me with red hands that you presume such baseness? And is this crime of murder indeed so impious as to dry up the very springs of good?'

'Murder is to me no special category,' replied the other. 'All sins are murder, even as all life is war. I behold your race, like starving mariners on a raft, plucking crusts out of the hands of famine and feeding on each other's lives. I follow sins beyond the moment of their acting; I find in all that the last consequence is death; and to my eyes, the pretty maid who thwarts her mother with such taking graces on a question of a ball, drips no less visibly with human gore than such a murderer as yourself. Do I say that I follow sins? I follow virtues also; they differ not by the thickness of a nail, they are both scythes for the reaping angel of Death. Evil, for which I live, consists not in action but in character. The bad man is dear to me; not the bad act, whose fruits, if we could follow them far enough down the hurtling cataract of the ages, might yet be found more blessed than those of the rarest virtues. And it is not because you have killed a dealer, but because you are Markheim, that I offer to forward your escape.'

'I will lay my heart open to you,' answered Markheim. 'This crime on which you find me is my last. On my way to it I have learned many lessons; itself is a lesson, a momentous lesson. Hitherto I have been driven with revolt to what I would not; I was a bond-slave to poverty, driven and scourged. There are robust virtues that can stand in these temptations; mine was not so: I had a thirst of pleasure. But to-day, and out of this deed, I pluck both warning and riches—both the power and a fresh resolve to be myself. I become in all things a free actor in the world; I begin to see myself all changed, these hands the agents of good, this heart at peace. Something comes over me out of the past; something of what I have dreamed on Sabbath evenings to the sound of the church organ, of what I forecast when I shed tears over noble books, or talked, an innocent child, with my mother. There lies my life; I have wandered a few years, but now I see once more my city of destination.'

'You are to use this money on the Stock Exchange, I think?' remarked the visitor; 'and there, if I mistake not, you have already lost some thousands?'

'Ah,' said Markheim, 'but this time I have a sure thing.'

'This time, again, you will lose,' replied the visitor quietly.

'Ah, but I keep back the half!' cried Markheim.

'That also you will lose,' said the other.

The sweat started upon Markheim's brow. 'Well, then, what matter?' he exclaimed. 'Say it be lost, say I am plunged again in poverty, shall one part of me, and that the worse, continue until the end to override the better? Evil and good run strong in me, haling me both ways. I do not love the one thing, I love all. I can conceive great deeds, renunciations, martyrdoms; and though I be fallen to such a crime as murder, pity is no stranger to my thoughts. I pity the poor; who knows their trials better than myself? I pity and help them; I prize love, I love honest laughter; there is no good thing nor true thing on earth but I love it from my heart. And are my vices only to direct my life, and my virtues to lie without effect, like some passive lumber of the mind? Not so; good, also, is a spring of acts.'

But the visitant raised his finger. 'For six-and-thirty years that you have been in this world,' said be, 'through many changes of fortune and varieties of humour, I have watched you steadily fall. Fifteen years ago you would have started at a theft. Three years back you would have blenched at the name of murder. Is there any crime, is there any cruelty or meanness, from which you still recoil?—five years from now I shall detect you in the fact! Downward, downward, lies your way; nor can anything but death avail to stop you.'

'It is true,' Markheim said huskily, 'I have in some degree complied with evil. But it is so with all: the very saints, in the mere exercise of living, grow less dainty, and take on the tone of their surroundings.'

'I will propound to you one simple question,' said the other; 'and as you answer, I shall read to you your moral horoscope. You have grown in many things more lax; possibly you do right to be so—and at any account, it is the same with all men. But granting that, are you in any one particular, however trifling, more difficult to please with your own conduct, or do you go in all things with a looser rein?'

'In any one?' repeated Markheim, with an anguish of consideration. 'No,' he added, with despair, 'in none! I have gone down in all.'

'Then,' said the visitor, 'content yourself with what you are, for you will never change; and the words of your part on this stage are irrevocably written down.'

Markheim stood for a long while silent, and indeed it was the visitor who first broke the silence. 'That being so,' he said, 'shall I show you the money?'

'And grace?' cried Markheim.

'Have you not tried it?' returned the other. 'Two or three years ago, did I not see you on the platform of revival meetings, and was not your voice the loudest in the hymn?'

'It is true,' said Markheim; 'and I see clearly what remains for me by way of duty. I thank you for these lessons from my soul; my eyes are opened, and I behold myself at last for what I am.'

At this moment, the sharp note of the door-bell rang through the house; and the visitant, as though this were some concerted signal for which he had been waiting, changed at once in his demeanour.

'The maid!' he cried. 'She has returned, as I forewarned you, and there is now before you one more difficult passage. Her master, you must say, is ill; you must let her in, with an assured but rather serious countenance—no smiles, no overacting, and I promise you success! Once the girl within, and the door closed, the same dexterity that has already rid you of the dealer will relieve you of this last danger in your path. Thenceforward you have the whole evening—the whole night, if needful—to ransack the treasures of the house and to make good your safety. This is help that comes to you with the mask of danger. Up!' he cried; 'up, friend; your life hangs trembling in the scales: up, and act!'

Markheim steadily regarded his counsellor. 'If I be condemned to evil acts,' he said, 'there is still one door of freedom open—I can cease from action. If my life be an ill thing, I can lay it down. Though I be, as you say truly, at the beck of every small temptation, I can yet, by one decisive gesture, place myself beyond the reach of all. My love of good is damned to barrenness; it may, and let it be! But I have still my hatred of evil; and from that, to your galling disappointment, you shall see that I can draw both energy and courage.'

The features of the visitor began to undergo a wonderful and lovely change: they brightened and softened with a tender triumph, and, even as they brightened, faded and dislimned. But Markheim did not pause to watch or understand the transformation. He opened the door and went downstairs very slowly, thinking to himself. His past went soberly before him; he beheld it as it was, ugly and strenuous like a dream, random as chance-medley—a scene of defeat. Life, as he thus reviewed it, tempted him no longer; but on the further side he perceived a quiet haven for his bark. He paused in the passage, and looked into the shop, where the candle still burned by the dead body. It was strangely silent. Thoughts of the dealer swarmed into his mind, as he stood gazing. And then the bell once more broke out into impatient clamour.

He confronted the maid upon the threshold with something like a smile.

'You had better go for the police,' said he: 'I have killed your master.'